文
景

Horizon

攻 玉 集

镜子和七巧板

The Mirror and the Jigsaw

杨周翰 著

上海人民出版社

出版说明

　　杨周翰先生（1915—1989）是中国杰出的外国文学和比较文学学者，卓尔不群的西方文学翻译家，学贯中西，博通古今。杨先生提出的"研究外国文学的中国人，尤其要有一个中国人的灵魂"，深深影响了后辈几代外国文学和比较文学研究者。在东西方文明越来越多地注重彼此交流、互相借鉴的当下，杨周翰先生前瞻性的眼光和恢宏的视野，其价值愈发凸显。

　　《杨周翰作品集》（全六卷）是杨先生一生学术研究的重要结晶，共收入著作4种，译作8种。卷目如下：

　　第一卷 《埃涅阿斯纪　特洛亚妇女》

　　第二卷 《变形记　诗艺》

　　第三卷 《蓝登传》

　　第四卷 《亨利八世　情敌　我的国家》

　　第五卷 《十七世纪英国文学》

　　第六卷 《攻玉集　镜子和七巧板　The Mirror and the Jigsaw》

　　杨先生精通英、法、拉丁等多种语言，第一至四卷收录的是他从拉丁文、英文译出的经典译作，优雅流畅的译笔，纯粹古典的文学趣味，几十年来哺育了一代又一代年轻人的灵魂；第五、六两卷是他在英国文学与比较文学领域的重要论述，从中国学者的独特视角出发提出诸多鲜明创见，奠定了中国当代比较文学、英国文学和莎士比亚研究的坚实基础。杨周翰先生不畏艰辛的学术热情、究本求源的治学态度，令后辈学人感佩。

杨先生的作品译作、著作兼有，中文、外文错杂，题材广泛，写作和出版时间跨度大，编辑体例亦不统一，我们此次整理，以依循底本、尊重原作为基本原则重新编排，对明显的排印错误予以改正，并对格式、标点、数字用法等做了技术性的统一。

目 录

镜子和七巧板

The Mirror and the Jigsaw

攻玉集

据北京大学出版社 1983 年 3 月初版《攻玉集》整理

前　言

　　研究外国文学的目的，我想最主要的恐怕还是为了吸取别人的经验，繁荣我们自己的文艺，帮助读者理解、评价作家和作品，开阔视野，也就是洋为中用。这里收集的十二篇文章都是在这个指导思想下写的，因此取名为《攻玉集》。至于写得好或坏，对与不对，那要由读者来评定，从作者来说，只是野人献曝的意思。

　　这些文章在集成付印前作了一些局部的修改，仍然难免有错误，也希望读者指正。

　　这本小册子是在北京大学出版社鼓励下编成出版的，国外文学编辑部陆嘉玉和冯国忠两同志给了大力帮助，一并在此向他们表示感谢。

杨周翰 1982.7

关于提高外国文学史编写质量的几个问题

解放以来，我们在外国文学史编写方面（当然也包括外国文学研究）取得了很大的成绩。这主要表现在我们力图用马列主义的立场、观点、方法来阐述外国文学发展的规律，对作家进行阶级分析，注意作家作品在当时当地阶级斗争形势中所起的作用。我们根据反映论，强调文学反映现实，肯定了现实主义创作方法。本文不想全面总结解放后我们在编写外国文学史中的经验，只想就当前我们工作中个人所看到的几个问题，提出来探讨研究，因为我感到这些问题的解决关系到本门学科水平的提高，关系到更好地适应新形势，适应新时期教学和指导青年阅读的需要。

这些问题的产生，有主观原因，也有客观原因。解放后我们编写外国文学史是从学习苏联开始的。苏联是第一个用马列主义系统地研究西方文学的国家，苏联学者在这方面起了开创的作用。但苏联学者编写的外国文学史在方法上存在不少问题，而我们亦步亦趋，也出现了不少问题。"四人帮"在古为今用、洋为中用、批判地继承优秀文化遗产、百家争鸣等重大问题上，又混淆是非，造成极大的思想混乱。他们对外国作家，包括在历史上起过进步作用的作家，一律扣上封、资、修的帽子，一棍子打死。在许多理论问题上，如人道主义、典型性等，都以"左"的姿态和形而上学的方法予以否定和歪曲。

随着揭批"四人帮"，拨正他们在文艺领域中颠倒了的是非，回顾我们编写的外国文学史，我们感到必须从种种错误思想中解放出来，提高我们马克思主义的思想水平，发扬学术民主，我们的外国文学史编写工作才能有所进展。当然，我们的马列主义水平的提高有一个过程，今之视昔一定亦犹后之视今，而认识过程总难免有曲折以至错误。以下仅就五个方面，约略提出个人的看法，不当之处请读者指正。

（一）进一步贯彻唯物辩证法，贯彻实事求是、一分为二的精神

我想一部文学史首先要求能做到一个"信"字。我国历史学的传统也历来强调"信史"、"实录"，不仅要求"其事核"，而且要求"不虚美，不隐恶"。"信"就要求符合事实，而要符合事实，就不能有片面性，也就是必须一分为二。不能只讲好的不讲坏的，也不能好的都好，坏的都坏。在选择材料问题上，要从客观实际出发，要从作家在历史上的影响出发，不能凭主观好恶而决定取舍。

反观我们编写的外国文学史，常常给人这样的印象，即客观存在的文学现象（流派、作家、作品）往往同文学史的表述之间存在矛盾。这种情况表现在把历史上进步的作家说得比原来更进步，把一些不那么进步的作家宁可说成反动。这种倾向在苏联某些文学史里已见端倪，如阿尼克斯特编的《英国文学史纲》把英国第一部史诗《贝奥武甫》中的主人公说成是"人民之父"，这样就掩盖了此

诗的贵族性质，而诗中其实并未有过这样的提法，相反，在绝大多数场合都称他为"王"、"君主"。这种喜欢拔高的倾向，比比皆是。

对待莎士比亚，这种倾向也是占主导地位，从西方浪漫派评论开始，通过苏联到解放后我国的文学史和评论，对莎士比亚很少有贬词。伏尔泰和托尔斯泰对莎士比亚的批评，固然是出于时代风尚不同或文学主张不同，未必全对，有时是误解，但是他们不迷信莎士比亚。

对当代资本主义世界一些文学流派的评价则反映了另一种倾向，尽量贬低，以至把它们看成一无是处。

过去我们写英国二十年代小说家乔依斯是这样写的：他的主要作品《攸利希斯》以几十万字写了广告经纪人布鲁姆及其妻和青年斯蒂芬一天的生活，写他们精神苦闷，思想肮脏腐朽，没有希望。由于阶级斗争的进一步尖锐化，中小资产阶级惶恐失望、厌世，以至仇视人类。前一时期虚伪的唯美主义和享乐主义被更为反动的对"潜意识"活动的追求所代替……

这部小说确实反映了资产阶级的没落彷徨的情绪，但是否因此就对它采取完全否定的态度呢？我觉得正是因为它反映了这种精神状态，因而有极高的认识价值。这类作家之所以能深刻地反映这种精神状态，则是因为他们对资本主义社会生活和精神生活有极深的感受，同时在表达方式上刻意寻求他们认为最好的方式（当然也有形式主义成分）。

极力贬低的倾向往往出于好意，怕对青年产生不良影响。鲁迅在《中国小说的历史的变迁》中有一段话，说得极好。他说：

> 至于说到《红楼梦》的价值，可是在中国底小说中实在是不可多得的。其要点在敢于如实描写，并无讳饰，和从前的小说叙好人完全是好，坏人完全是坏的，大不相同，所以其中所

叙的人物，都是真的人物。……但是反对者却很多，以为将给青年以不好的影响。这就因为中国人看小说，不能用赏鉴的态度去欣赏它，却自己钻入书中，硬去充一个其中的脚色。所以青年看《红楼梦》，便以宝玉，黛玉自居；而年老人看去，又多占据了贾政管束宝玉的身分，满心是利害的打算，别的什么也看不见了。[1]

青年主要要靠正面理想的教育，把立足点站稳，用分析批判的眼光，放眼古今中外，一切可以拿来为我所用，丰富自己的知识和智慧，毒草尚且可以肥田。消极抵挡，"封闭疗法"，自己搞得被动，得不到积极的效果。

文学史（也包括文学评论）还有一种倾向，就是对作家提出过高的要求。如对西方四十年代后期迄六十年代的存在主义文学、荒诞派戏剧、黑色幽默小说，评论者认为这些流派纵然反映了资本主义社会的荒谬、丑恶、阴暗面，但事实是资本主义社会的腐烂和丑闻已无法掩饰，以至政客们也利用彼此的荒谬丑恶互相攻讦。评论者认为这些流派的作者做些不痛不痒的嘲讽，不能损害垄断资产阶级半根毫毛，不触及本质；评论者并指责这些作家不反映劳动人民的悲惨处境和英勇斗争，却宣扬荒谬是永恒的，人类只有毁灭，因而这些都是反动流派。对历史上的批判现实主义作家也有类似的评价，说他们并不是要从根本上推翻资本主义社会，实际上却是为了维护和巩固资产阶级统治服务的。

我们评论一个作家只能就他所提供的材料来判断。据此，恩格斯称赞巴尔扎克的作品说，从中学到的东西比从经济学家和统计学

---

[1]《鲁迅全集》1957 年版第 8 卷第 350 页。

家的全部著作中加起来所学到的还要多。要求一个资产阶级作家具有无产阶级先进的世界观是过高的要求。政治上的反动应当同资产阶级世界观区别开来。

我个人感到象六十年代黑色幽默小说如美国海勒的《军规二十二条》总的倾向是揭露性的，应当肯定。尤其是作者的《出了毛病》，态度是严肃的。这部小说距前一部相隔十二年，出来以后评论界大失所望，可能因为里面很少噱头，但这正说明作者思想的深化，这部小说没有什么奇特惊险的情节，平淡地叙述主人公的职业关系、家庭关系以及和其他一些他接触到的人之间的关系，而他总是处理不好这些关系。我们从中可以看出美国社会和资本主义制度"出了毛病"，尽管作者得不出答案来。同样，象荒诞派尤内斯科和贝克特的戏剧，尤其是后者影响空前的《等待戈多》，如果作者仅仅是玩世不恭，就不可能对资本主义社会精神危机有深刻的感受，如果在艺术实践上没有探索精神，也写不出这样在资本主义世界引起广泛共鸣、产生长远影响的作品的。这类作品就其性质来讲当然是悲观的，但是对我们有极高的认识价值，值得研究，也不能全盘否定。

我们有时把文学上的不同作家不同流派，写得壁垒森严，泾渭分明，俨然是两个阶级，而事实上并不如此。如所谓消极浪漫主义反映了贵族阶级对法国资产阶级革命和启蒙思想的敌视，鼓吹忍耐驯服，妄图开历史倒车；积极浪漫主义则反映了资产阶级民主倾向，往往同民主民族解放运动相结合，有不同程度的革命要求。这样粗线条的概括不够真实。其实两派无论从阶级地位和思想意识以及文化艺术背景讲都有共同处。像英国的华兹华斯一方面要一分为二，他固然害怕雅各宾专政，脱离了斗争，但拿破仑的侵略战争，也是使他失望的一个原因。另一方面即如所谓的"积极"浪漫主义诗人之间也很不相同，有的文学史就说拜伦的动力是傲慢，雪莱的动力是爱，也许正因如此，才有传说的马克思的论断：雪莱可能发展成为革命者，而拜伦可能会成为一个反动的资产者。两派虽有不同，但我们往往把这不同绝对化，而各派成员既有对立又有相同的一面。具体事物应该具体分析。

我们写文学史当然要站在无产阶级立场，文学也直接间接与政治发生关系，但我们往往见到有时执笔人惟恐没有"突出政治"，不能从文学的客观实际出发，因而不能得出正确的结论。例如我们在分析莎士比亚的《李尔王》时，把主题思想说成是描写一个专制独裁的暴君，由于刚愎自用，经过一场痛苦的经历，翻然悔悟。这部悲剧揭露了原始积累时期的利己主义，批判了对权势和财富的贪欲。它还反映了圈地运动所引起的广大农民流离失所的英国现实。莎士比亚通过李尔的口表达了他对农民的同情。这样的表述同剧本一对照（且不论李尔转变这一复杂问题），就会发现这里把全剧中的一个"部件"扩大为"主体结构"，考其原因就是这段台词是能够同当时现实政治挂得上钩的。接着，就从这一点出发，进行批判，说这种同情正暴露了作者的资产阶级人性论、人道主义观点；这种求助于剥削阶级发善心以解决社会矛盾的想法，是一种调和阶级矛盾、维护专制帝王统治的改良主义。

差以毫厘，失之千里。这种分析同剧本所客观反映的情况，可以说风马牛不相及了。莎士比亚同情农民的话，起了一个说明权威与社会正义对立的作用。这出戏不是写怎样把农民从圈地运动的灾难中解救出来；莎士比亚也有不少地方丑化农民群众。至于维护专制帝王统治，作为"专制帝王"的李尔既然悔悟了，也就是被否定了，又如何谈得上"维护"呢？事实上，莎士比亚一贯鼓吹改造封建君主，以便打破封建割据，促进民族国家的形成，有进步意义。

至于十九世纪工人运动中的改良主义，安在莎士比亚头上，也是文不对题。

这里，资产阶级一些评论家的看法值得我们参考。从十九世纪以来，一般公认《李尔王》具有高度概括性和哲学意义。我们在这里无法详论，简单说来，此剧写了权威与爱或人道的对立，权威与真理的对立，权威与社会正义的对立，提出"新"与"旧"的矛盾，而处处贯穿着作者对自然与人性善恶的观点。诗言志。"作为观念形态的文艺作品，都是一定的社会生活在人类头脑中的反映的产物。"这"头脑"二字十分重要。培根在《学术的推进》一书中也说过："人的头脑远非一面光洁正确的镜子，真实地反映事物，而是一面魔镜。"现实生活经过莎士比亚的头脑——即按照他的世界观，进行分析、综合、概括，反映出来。我们倘要批判莎士比亚，应批判他那唯心主义哲学概括本身。上述那种急于"突出政治"其实没有达到预期的效果，反而引起连锁式的不良学风。

顺便谈一下现实主义问题。翻开一部英国文学史，可能除了弥尔顿、雪莱等少数作家以外，几乎所有重要作家如乔叟，他是当然的现实主义作家；莎士比亚的戏剧"是文艺复兴时期社会生活的最充分的艺术上的反映"；王政复辟时期的喜剧是"生活的真实描写"；十八世纪从笛福以下一大批小说家更是当然的现实主义作家，至少是先驱；浪漫派诗人如拜伦的《别波》是他转向现实主义的初次卓越表现，而现实主义的《唐·璜》则是他最优秀的作品；十九世纪的小说家那就更不必说了。似乎现实主义是衡量一个作家的惟一标准，分析抒情诗也要把作者作为一个人物——抒情主人公，来加以分析，象小说一样。

说某个作家是现实主义作家，如果仅仅说他的作品反映现实，那是毫无意义的，因为一切文艺作品都是现实生活的反映。从英美文学史上看，"现实主义"作为文艺批评术语最早（1856）是出现在罗斯金的《当代画家》，"现实主义作家"这个词则首先是批评家莱斯利·斯梯芬用来称呼菲尔丁的，指的是细节准确生动，而这些细节都是令人不快的、丑恶的，也就是所谓"批判的现实主义"吧。[1] 从这个词的发生，再看恩格斯的定义（1888）："除细节的真实外，还要真实地再现典型环境中的典型性格"，更容易看出恩格斯在这个问题上发展了当时一般理解的内涵。

最广泛的意义下的现实主义等于没有说。作为一种创作态度或倾向，在历史上，无例外地指的是揭露、批判社会罪恶。因此这个词也被用在十九世纪中期以前的作家身上。作为一个小说流派则主要指十九世纪。作为创作方法，首先要求如实地反映现实社会生活，包括细节的真实。恩格斯的定义又把现实主义严格地同自然主义区别开来了。从我们的文学史的叙述看来，不管怎样，现实主义创作方法似乎是独一无二的方法，作家的成就也以现实主义为衡量的标准。我觉得这是对反映论的狭隘理解。

首先是对现实的理解。人的社会活动是客观现实、社会生活作用于人，使人产生某种感情、希望、或某种精神状态，我以为这些也是客观现实的组成部分，而这些就不是现实主义创作方法所能反映出来的，于是产生了抒情诗、乌托邦小说、"心理现实主义"或"意识流"小说等等。其次是反映现实的方法。即使以严格的现实社会生活为描写对象，在古代就有神话、寓言；莎士比亚就用古代的、异国的情节；在近代则有象征主义、表现主义、印象主义等等流派。把现实主义视为评价的惟一标准，不能概括文学发展的客观实际。现实主义可能是主要方法，但不应有排他性，对其他方法也

---

[1] 美国小说家豪威尔斯（1837—1920）在十九世纪八九十年代提出的现实主义，则强调平凡的日常生活一面。

要进行分析和借鉴，或创制新方法，这对繁荣社会主义文艺有莫大好处。文学史在这方面应当总结一些经验。

造成文学史中以上这些现象的原因，可能是因为过去在批判客观主义、超阶级观点的倾向的同时，掩盖了另一种倾向，即忽视了科学的客观态度，甚至在文学史中造成"虚说传而不绝，实事没而不见"的现象，不能作到"文非泛论，按实而书"，或多或少陷入实用主义，而且不从实际出发，不一分为二，陷入形而上学。这些恐怕是影响文学史水平提高的根本障碍。

（二）历史连续性问题

我们过去写的外国文学史有这样一种现象，详希腊而略罗马，详文艺复兴而略中世纪，详十九世纪而略以前各时期。理由是罗马文学、中世纪文学成就不高；其次是要厚今薄古，甚至有这样的担心，现在是两千多年的文学史，再过两千年，古的都要讲怎么得了。

历史的对象本来就是过去的事，历史不讲古，古代的事由哪门学科来管？不要说文学史两千年，地质学、古生物学都以一亿年为单位。而所谓厚今薄古，不是不要古。研究古，仍是为了今。不过，这里有个用什么、如何用的问题。过去，我们的外国文学史只讲作家作品，以为这些可以借鉴，这固然是对的，但这并没有充分发挥文学史的作用。罗马文学、中世纪文学相对来说，其成就当然不及希腊、文艺复兴，但从历史角度看，把它们忽略过去，就总结不出什么规律性的东西来。

文学史，就其使用来说，不外两种，一种供查检，一种供通读。外国文学史只写作家作品，就变成了供查检的作家辞典，尽管略有脉络贯串，但十分单薄。供通读的文学史以脉络为主，味道应象读故事小说，但更重要的是记录文学发展，总结出规律，这样的用处要比个别作家的评价大些。这样，作为通读读物，就更具备"可读性"。

马克思主义经典作家一向告诫我们不要割断历史。恩格斯在《反杜林论》中批判杜林的政治第一性、经济第二性和政治暴力是社会发展动力的论点时，谈到奴隶制的进步意义，指出：

> 只有奴隶制才使农业和工业之间的更大规模的分工成为可能，从而为古代文化的繁荣，即为希腊文化创造了条件。没有奴隶制，就没有希腊国家，就没有希腊的艺术和科学；没有奴隶制，就没有罗马帝国。没有希腊文化和罗马帝国所奠定的基础，也就没有现代的欧洲。我们永远不应该忘记，我们的全部经济、政治和智慧的发展，是以奴隶制既为人所公认，同样又为人所必需这种状况为前提的。在这个意义上，我们有理由说：没有古代的奴隶制，就没有现代的社会主义。

> 用一般性的词句痛骂奴隶制和其他类似的现象，对这些可耻的现象发泄高尚的义愤，这是最容易不过的做法。可惜，这样做仅仅说出了一件人所周知的事情，这就是：这种古代的制度已经不再适合我们目前的情况和由这种情况所决定的我们的感情。但是，这种制度是怎么产生的，它为什么存在，它在历史上起了什么作用，关于这些问题，我们并没有因此而得到任何的说明。[1]

---

[1] 恩格斯：《反杜林论》，《马克思恩格斯选集》第3卷第220页。

恩格斯把古代奴隶制一直联系到现代的欧洲，一直联系到现代的社会主义。我们的研究方法比较孤立，满足于仅仅说明希腊文学是在什么社会环境中产生的，有些什么成就，但作为具有相对独立性的文学这一上层建筑一旦产生对后来文学发展，包括现代西方文学有什么继承关系，则注意不够；特别对于同样是奴隶制产物的罗马文学注意不够。其实文艺复兴时期的作家受罗马文学影响比希腊文学可能更大些。从文艺复兴时期产生的史诗、喜剧、悲剧、抒情诗中处处可以看到罗马作家的影响。但丁为什么要维吉尔作他的向导呢？到十七世纪古典主义，甚至十八世纪诗歌、小说，都是如此。只有到浪漫主义以后，罗马文学在欧洲文学发展上，其影响才逐渐减弱。即使在中世纪，一些罗马作家的作品仍为教会中人所传抄阅读。

　　对中世纪，我们也同样忽略。但恩格斯在《路德维希·费尔巴哈和德国古典哲学的终结》中批判机械唯物论有两段话值得我们再学习：

　　　　它（引者按：指机械唯物论）不能把世界理解为一个过程，理解为一种处在不断的历史发展中的物质。这是同当时的自然科学状况以及与此相联系的形而上学的即反辩证法的哲学思维方法相适应的。[1]

恩格斯接着又说：

　　　　这种非历史的观点也表现在历史领域中。在这里，反对中

---

[1]《马克思恩格斯选集》第4卷第224页。

世纪残余的斗争限制了人们的视野。中世纪被看做是由千年来普遍野蛮状态所引起的历史的简单中断：中世纪的巨大进步——欧洲文化领域的扩大，在那里一个挨着一个形成的富有生命力的大民族，以及十四和十五世纪的巨大的技术进步，这一切都没有被人看到。这样一来，对伟大历史联系的合理看法就不可能产生，而历史至多不过是一部供哲学家使用的例证和插图的汇集罢了。[1]

恩格斯在这里不仅批判了割断历史的机械唯物论和实用主义，而且肯定了中世纪的成就。现在西方许多事物都发轫于中世纪。恩格斯指出，欧洲同阿拉伯和东方的交通给欧洲带来了科技的进步，欧洲现代的民族国家，都在中世纪初具雏形，这些都是荦荦大端。以文化艺术而论，就有所谓"十二世纪文艺复兴"。欧洲建筑艺术的杰作——大教堂的兴建；欧洲著名大学如巴黎、波罗涅、牛津和剑桥大学的成立；哲学上唯名、唯实（唯物、唯心）的斗争，思想界十分活跃；文坛上出现了行吟诗人，恩格斯对他们有很高的评价。欧洲文学中三大主题——爱情、冒险、宗教在骑士文学中得到集中表现，也可以说是欧洲近代文学的"滥觞"吧。中世纪不仅是文艺复兴的对立面，文艺复兴也是中世纪的继续。但丁对中世纪就既有批判，也有继承。中世纪的影响一直延续到十九世纪以至当代。可以说，不了解中世纪，也不容易充分了解当代。比如说宗教。我们对欧洲的宗教很少研究。我们抽象地认识宗教是麻醉人民的鸦片，但是它到底影响有多大，没有感性认识。举一个例子。三十年代英国发现一部英国最早的传记（自传），作者是玛吉瑞·肯

---

[1]《马克思恩格斯选集》第4卷第225页。

普，生于1364年，是林市市长的女儿，嫁给当地一个富有的市民。她可以算是被宗教鸦片麻醉的牺牲品。她的自传记载她经常同上帝对话，上帝对她说"我是上帝，藏在你心里"；为了上帝，她受人责骂也快乐；她老感到魔鬼在迫害她；她从不自称为"我"，而自称为"这个东西"（即上帝的创造物）；她可以冒险去罗马、西班牙朝圣。她虽然生了十四个孩子，但不愿丈夫接近她。她变成了一个失去"人格"的精神病患者。最近在圭亚那发生的所谓"人民圣殿教"集体自杀事件，说明在资本主义制度下有一部分人精神生活空虚，宗教就乘虚而入；一方面是科学昌明，一方面是中世纪的愚昧。当代美国小说家厄普代克，黑人作家鲍尔德温等人的作品充斥着过时的神学观点和宗教情绪。

又比如说中世纪文学三大主题中的冒险主题。在中世纪，冒险、抢劫本是骑士的职业，在传奇中加以美化。到了文艺复兴时期，塞万提斯既讽刺了骑士冒险的荒唐，又惋惜骑士道的没落。而与此同时，市民阶层接过这个主题，创立了所谓"流浪汉小说"，歌颂市民的机智，讽刺封建阶级的愚蠢。高尔基说得对，资产阶级小说的主人公都是骗子。"流浪汉小说"从此象一把钥匙开动了西方小说这部机器，生产出十八、十九世纪大批的以个人奋斗、揭发社会黑暗为内容的作品，到了当代，资产阶级提不出理想人物了，就出现所谓"反英雄"的小说和五十年代的"探索身份"的大批文学作品。个人在社会中迷失了方向，提出了"我是谁？"的问题。我们的文学史如能研究一下这类问题的发展，我想才算尽到历史的责任，真实地再现了文学的历史，对研究文学现象，包括当代文学现象，将有帮助。（附带提一下，我们对当代外国文学发生兴趣，很可理解，也是应当的，但不能孤立地研究，要历史地看问题，包括结合前此的发展过程和当前的社会背景——当前也是历史的一部分。这样的历史，对创作家，也可以起到开拓思路，有所借鉴和有所助益的作用。此外，文学类型、文学主题、文学题材、流派以及象普列汉诺夫所提到的美学心理和审美趣味等的发展线索，也应当研究。）

西方作家是在西方文化传统的影响下创作的。我们要了解并正确评价他们，对全部西方文明不能不研究、了解。其实，学西方语言也是如此，语言本身的规律要掌握，但语言是毛，必须附在皮上，没有无内容的语言。西方作家包括科学家，他们所受的教育是西方文化传统的教育，包括从古希腊、罗马直到当代资本主义、帝国主义时代的文化知识。举两个极端的例子。乔依斯的《攸利希斯》，我们从思想内容上批判是比较容易的，但要评论他的艺术技巧和匠心，就不那么容易。这部小说的结构，事件严格控制在一天之内，十八个情节严格符合荷马史诗中十八个情节。他套用荷马史诗，并不能简单地扣上一顶形式主义的帽子了事，也是与他的思想内容有机结合的。因此，要对乔依斯此书作出有说服力的评论，离不开对荷马的研究。

又如艾略特的《荒原》，作者有意识地汲取西方文化各种因素为其主题思想服务，这里有古希腊罗马文学、基督教经典著作、人类学、中古传奇文学、但丁、英国文艺复兴时期诗歌和戏剧、印度宗教哲学、十八世纪文学、世纪末颓废派诗歌等等。要对这首诗作出详尽而令人信服的评论，也必须了解他所汲取的思想素材。

这些都是极端的例子，但是可以说，没有一部作品能脱离一定的文化传统和文学传统。塞万提斯反对骑士传奇，但《堂·吉诃德》就是骑士传奇。菲尔丁在小说尚未被上流社会所接受的时候，把他的作品称为"散文体的滑稽史诗"，把旧的文学形式改头换面。希腊悲剧之于哈代，西部口头文学传统之于马克·吐温，也说明传统的重要。即使惠特曼的自由诗也是以格律诗为其对立面而存在的。你不了解格律诗，也不可能欣赏评价他的自由体。

对历史连续性重视不够，原因很多。对厚今薄古的不恰当的理解是其一。其次是对如何古为今用、洋为中用的问题理解不一。作家作品的研究是有用的，但从大处总结一些经验，真实地再现文学的历史，在某种意义上说，借鉴作用更大。作为大学课程，过去也是讲作家作品多，讲历史发展少。主要原因是研究跟不上，因此应当大力展开研究。在这方面，我们的课题是很多的，如文学类型、主题、题材、典型、创作方法的发展，都值得我们进行系统的研究。

（三）提倡比较法

我们的文学史即使仅仅是论作家作品也往往平铺直叙，孤立叙述，不利于加深对作家作品的理解，也不利于阐明历史的发展。没有比较就没有鉴别。马克思说，有意思的是把《农夫彼尔斯》的作者朗格兰同高雅的《坎特伯雷故事集》作者乔叟比较一下。他比较了莎士比亚和席勒，据说还比较了雪莱和拜伦。普列汉诺夫提出"对立的原理"，并据此比较了十七世纪复辟王朝英国的文学审美趣味同文艺复兴时期的差异，指出其"社会原因"，从而使两个不同时代的特点更加鲜明，给读者深刻的印象，至今读来，仍有清新的感觉。

事实上，比较是表述文学发展、评论作家作品不可避免的方法，我们在评论作家、叙述历史时，总是有意无意进行比较，我们应当提倡有意识的、系统的、科学的比较。

精辟的评论往往是从比较得来的。例如十九世纪英国批评家柯尔律治评莎士比亚有这样一段话：

> 麦辛哲（英国剧作家，1553—1640）像佛兰芒（荷兰）画家，他所描绘的对象同现实界一样，很有力，很真实，在观者心中产生同现实界对象同样的效果。但莎士比亚超乎此，他在考虑一事之时，总是用比喻和形象把过去的经验和可能的经验概括起来，使之具有普遍意义。

经过这一比较，即使我们没有看过麦辛哲的剧作，我们对莎士比亚创作的高度概括力和形象性，也有了一个鲜明而深刻的印象。而平铺直叙就很难产生这样的效果。

这里不妨约略谈谈比较文学。这门学科在欧洲十九世纪末已有开端，至二十世纪二十年代大大发展。苏联反对比较文学，因为比较文学不作阶级分析，即不探讨普列汉诺夫说的"社会原因"，主张打破民族文学的界限，表现了"世界主义倾向"。我国解放前在这方面有些成就，解放后在国内根本没有人提。

比较文学不联系社会生活当然是违反历史唯物主义的。但作为一种方法，可以研究。这一学科尽管有不同流派，各国也有所不同，但有些共同的基本主张。他们都认为一个民族的文学与其他民族的文学比较，才能显出其特点来；主张对文学的主题、文学类型、文学潮流、批评和审美标准或诗学进行比较研究，研究相互影响；把文学与其他文艺领域进行比较，研究其关系，在相互比较之中发现一些文学发展的共同规律。

就在从事比较文学研究的学者中也有人看到这门学科过分注意某一文学现象的渊源和影响，而忽略作家的主观取舍、作家的用意和目的、作品的客观效果的片面性，并承认比较文学只是一种辅助学科。但他们也认为如果使用得当，可以帮助我们了解作家的创作过程，扩大文学史的知识，也有助于评价；比较可以避免把文学现象看成孤立现象，他们把这种研究称为"综合"。我觉得，我们有辩证唯物主义的指导，就文学史中某些问题如文学主题、文学题材、劳动人民形象、妇女问题，在不同民族不同社会的文学中的反映作一比较，应能得出有意义的成果。

这里想着重谈谈观点的比较。我觉得我们应当在马克思主义基本原理指导下，参看国外的评论，集思广益，开拓思路，一定能够提高我们评论的水平，丰富马克思主义的基本原理。我们过去的缺点是满足于贴标签，生硬联系实际，没有能够很好地批判地继承大批优秀的评论遗产。"四人帮"更变本加厉，三个斯基都一棍子打死。所谓兼听则明，这个道理也是很简单的。

再举莎士比亚研究为例。我们的研究很少把他和他同时代剧作家作比较。当时英国剧坛可以说是群星灿烂，莎士比亚是其中最明亮的一颗，如果作一些比较研究，更能显出其光辉。这是一方面。另一方面，我们对他的评论，只限于指出他的人文主义思想的进步性和阶级局限性，他反映社会现实的广度和深度，人物的典型性，情节的生动性，语言的形象性等。这几乎成了一个框框，怎样突破这框框再前进一步呢？

二十世纪以来，莎学家不满于十九世纪浪漫派评论，都想另辟蹊径，从不同角度考察，有的虽然继承浪漫派评论，但也是别开生面。一小部分，特别是所谓心理学派把哈姆雷特解释为恋母情结，病理学派把麦克白解释为幻想狂，把泰门解释为自大狂，把奥塞罗解释为患虚弱症，还有的评论把《李尔王》看成是荒诞派，把《仲夏夜之梦》看成是兽性的解放等等，都很成问题。大多数不那么偏激的评论，往往有一两点的合理见解，可以为我们吸收。我们吸收了其中合理的成分，并不是修改马克思主义，而是充实它。我们从西方评论家对英国戏剧传统的研究中，可以看出莎士比亚是如何继承和创新的；从他们对舞台演出的研究中，我们可以对人物和情节得到进一步的理解；他们对政治、社会、历史事件的研究，虽然忽略阶级分析，流于影射，但解决了不少具体问题；对诗歌形象的分析，有助于我们对主题的理解；对当时哲学思想、社会思潮的研究，对我们分析概括作者的思想极有帮助，从中可以看出作者的积极方面和消极方面。

比较法要起到帮助我们正确反映文学的客观现实，作出正确的评价，必须在坚持辩证唯物论的原则下，从实际出发，不是从主观出发，尊重事物本身的矛盾——一分为二，这样，比较法才能产生积极效果。

（四）关于作家的介绍

读者接触一部作品，实际也是读者同作者发生思想感情的接触（有意识地或无意识地同意、同感、不同意、反感，部分地同感、同意）。司马迁说："余读孔氏书，想见其为人。"这是很自然的要求。要正确理解并评价一个西方作家和他的作品，对他的生活知之不多，也是办不到的。有的作品的作者不可考，或材料不多，那也没办法。有的材料很丰富，怎样对待材料就成为主要问题。

我们现在编写文学史的做法是交代时代背景，关于作者则交代他的阶级出身、政治性的活动、作品清单。这是一种写简历、做政治鉴定的办法。其用意是好的，因为要说明作者在历史上有无进步意义以及对人民的态度。但这样做，有许多不足之处。一部文学史所有的作家都冠以资产阶级或小资产阶级的头衔，作家们面目相同。这只能说明其共性，而共性只能通过个性表现出来。其次，容易产生简单化和片面性，或则美化或则丑化。其结果反而不能正确说明他在历史中的作用和对人民的态度。

我们再举拜伦为例。

我们介绍拜伦的生平，大致是这样：介绍他的出身，受的贵族教育，接受了法国启蒙思想，1809 年大学毕业，入上议院，但他在贵族社会中处处受到歧视，因而感到孤独，同年就离开英国到大陆旅游。1812 年发表了《查尔德·哈洛德游记》，支持"勒德运动"，在上议院发表演说反对"压制破坏机器法案"。反动统治阶级以他离婚事件为借口，迫使他永远离开英国，他在意大利参加了烧炭党，又到希腊参加民族独立斗争，病死于希腊。这中间穿插着先后发表的作品，和一些评语，如：他不理解工人运动，一度陷入思想矛盾因而孤独、绝望、悲观，一直有个人主义等等。

试比较资产阶级著者编写的文学史关于拜伦的介绍。有一部文学史教科书大致是这样写的：

拜伦生于法国革命前一年。我们评判他，不要过苛，因为他的血统有污点。父亲生活荒唐、道德败坏到不可名状的地步。母亲是苏格兰富家女，继承了大笔遗产，性格偏狭，易激动。其父把妻子财产挥霍精光，把她遗弃。拜伦的母亲对拜伦"一会儿溺爱，一会儿虐待"。拜伦十一岁，伯祖父弃世，他继承了子爵爵位。拜伦丰神俊美，他的跛足更引人怜爱。这一切，加上他的社会地位，他的"假英雄主义"的诗歌和放荡的生活（他故意又罩上一层浪漫、神秘的幕纱），吸引了许多没头脑的青年男女对他的倾慕，这样就使他更轻易、更快地走上了符合他天性的下坡路。加以他天性慷慨，很容易受爱慕他的人所左右。因此，总的说来，他是他自己的弱点和不幸的环境的牺牲品。他的《哈洛德游记》一、二章出版后，一举成名。他自己说："我一天早上醒来，发现已经成名了。"拜伦当时最大的缺点是不诚恳，故作英雄姿态。他的名声远扬欧洲，连歌德都被他瞒过了。

他在英国的名气维持了几年，他和富家女密尔班克结婚，不久突然离异，女方当然保持缄默，但社会舆论不难猜出个中缘由，看穿了神秘幕纱后面的厚脸皮的偶象，因而反对他。1816年他永远离开了英国。在国外拜伦慷慨援助意大利和希腊的革命运动。但拜伦是否也有想扮演英雄的念头呢？他也看到希腊反抗土耳其压迫的革命群众的许多缺点。

还有的文学史把拜伦看做是"世纪病"在英国的代表，这种世纪病是他的痛苦的精神状态的根源，是他傲慢态度的原动力，是他给欧洲各国的影响。这种病态因素是他内心生活的核心；这就可能导致他人格的崩溃，因而在他的动机和行动中找不到什么规律，表现为时而有真心诚意的诚恳态度，时而只是表面诚恳。

还有的文学史根据他少年时代的生活断定在他心灵中产生了一种自卑感，这种自卑感表现为傲慢、睥睨一切、鄙视一切。又有的说他开始登上历史舞台的形象是一个藐视一切的纨绔子弟、一个浅尝辄止的游戏文学的人。

以上这些文学史编者，对拜伦生平的材料的取舍，以及从这些材料引出的判断和结论同我们的判断和结论出入很大。拜伦是个复杂人物，所以历来文学史对他毁誉参半，他的作品本身具有两重性。从苏联编的文学史开始，对拜伦都有隐恶溢美的倾向。拜伦的作品总的说来应该说是进步的，但我们对他参加到进步潮流的动机研究不够。从资产阶级著者编写的文学史对他的介绍，我们可以看到一些信息，使我们能更好地理解为什么马克思说他发展下去可以变成反动。

资产阶级著者编写的文学史不进行阶级分析，对拜伦的社会活动不感兴趣，这当然不对。但他们对作家的心理精神状态，对个人与个人之间的关系最感兴趣。我觉得这一点不应忽视。作者的思想感情和心理状态，也就是毛主席说的"作家的头脑"是同作品直接发生关系的。资产阶级文学史家掌握了比较全面的材料，看到了一些现象，这些都值得我们参考，我们如果也看到了，就不能视而不见，不予考虑。他们进一步分析这些现象时，不说完全错误吧，究竟没有分析到根本上，但恐怕也不能一概否定。

社会生活→作家→作品这样一个文学的生产公式，我们对作家这个环节研究不够，对作家不全面研究，对作品的分析就难免生硬，不能贴切，我们过去不甚提倡传记文学，偶然翻译一些作家传，也比较枯燥；近来传记多起来了，这是可喜的现象。作家的研究不仅是为了使文学史写得生动，有血有肉，增加其"可读性"，而且对正确评价作家、作品，如实反映文学发展历程，总结一些规律性的东西，也是必不可少的一环。

（五）直接进入研究对象，充分掌握材料，接触不同的观点

翻译外国文学作品是普及文化必不可少的手段；翻译文学对推动我国新文学的发展起过积极作用，这是人所共知的。但依靠翻译进行研究工作就有其天然的局限性；研究工作必须直接进入研究对象（原作）；翻译再好，不能代替原作。以朱生豪译的莎士比亚剧本为例。朱译总的说来是行文流畅，词语丰富，通俗易懂，基本上正确，后来又经校订，读者对莎剧的故事情节、人物性格、甚至语

言风格特点，可以知其梗概。但根据朱译或任何其他译本来评论莎剧，至少是不够的。例如《李尔王》一剧，"自然"（也就是"人性"）一词，连同它的反义词、同义词，在剧中出现不下四五十次。读原著，这个词贯串全剧始终，几十次地出现，使读者不得不注意到它。在译本中，我约略统计了一下，作为正义词，有这样一些译法："天地"、"生性"、"天性"、"本性"、"大自然"、"造化"、"上天"、"人"、"任何人"、"天伦"、"伦常纲纪"、"身体"、"生命"、"天然"、"精神"、"人情"、"仁慈"、"慈悲"、"孝道"、"身心"、"天道人伦"、"孝心"、"孝顺"；有时不译。作为反义词，有："罪大恶极"、"违反自然"、"超乎寻常"、"什么东西"、"恶魔"、"冷酷无情"、"不孝"、"没有心肝"、"畜生"、"乖离"、"冷淡"、"怠慢"、"亏待"、"没有良心"、"荒谬"、"无理"、"不近人情"、"下贱"；有时也不译。在原作中，这些都是"自然"一词和它的形容词和明显的同义词和反义词，是《李尔王》主题思想的主要组成部分，内容是两个哲学范畴："自然"和"人性"，是我们理解莎士比亚的世界观的关键概念（在其他剧本中同样出现这个词）。从译本中，这两个范畴既然被掩盖了（至少大部分被掩盖了），我们就无法在理解和评论中着重考虑这问题，成了无的放矢。

至于语言风格，则更微妙，往往挂一漏万，甚至走样。例如"我总是愿意贡献我的一得之愚的。殿下和夫人光临蓬筚，欢迎得很。"原文并没有这样典雅。李尔临终时对科底丽亚说："你虐待我还有几分理由"，她连连回答两个"没有理由，没有理由"，表现出她绝对不能同意老父的意见，急于和解，并安慰他，拯救他。而译文只作"谁都没有这理由"。我们对外国文学的评论以小说、戏剧为多，很少涉及诗歌。这是一个很大的漏洞。文学同哲学、政治经济学、法学等社会科学不同，十分复杂，很难翻译，诗歌尤其如此，这方面还有很多问题，这里不是议论的场合，我只想说明直接进入研究对象的重要性。

当然，我并非非难翻译，翻译有它自己的困难，如果把上述有关"自然"的词，一律译成"自然"，根本是不可能的。译文有译文的服务对象。英国学者霍克思翻译《石头记》，在第一卷《引论》结尾时说："我自始至终遵守一个原则，每个字都译，包括双关语。这部小说虽然是'未完成的'小说，但是一位伟大的艺术家用他一生心血写成的。因此我认为这里面每字每句都有用意，不能忽略。我不敢说我已处处成功地做到这一点，但如果我能把我读这部小说时感到的乐趣，哪怕一小部分，传达给读者，我这一生就算没有白白度过。"翻译不可能是"再现"，只可能是"再创造"。

还有个充分掌握资料问题。马克思、恩格斯早在《共产党宣言》中就指出了"世界市场"的科学论断，自从资本主义产生，自给自足、闭关自守的物质生产已被互相往来、互相依赖的物质生产所代替。精神生产也是如此。我们是世界的一部分，世界各国的文学，包括我国的文学，世界各国的意见，包括我国的意见，都是互相影响的。我们研究本国文学，需要了解外国对我国文学的研究、评论；我们研究外国文学更需要了解国外的"行情"。不仅一般地了解"行情"，更根本的是要充分掌握资料。死的资料，活的舆论，通过翻译可以解决一部分问题，但不能彻底解决问题。仅仅利用译的资料，包括作品、有关作家的资料、有关社会历史、思潮、艺术技巧的材料和评论，势必使自己处在十分被动、受局限、不自由的地位。而且把这些资料翻译出来，要占用大量人力和时间，影响研究本身的进展。要推进我们对外国文学的研究工作，提高质量，使马克思主义的外国文学研究工作能进一步发展，相互交流，参加到世界舆论中去，在国际评论界取得发言权，掌握外文这一工具就刻不容缓地提到日程上来了。我认为有条件的，应学一点外文，特别是在培养中的青年研究工作者应把外文作为必修课程。

以上五个问题只是个人所见，水平有限，很肤浅，也不全面。不过我觉得实事求是、一分为二，是个很重要的问题，也是以上五个问题中最根本的问题。掌握外文也是为了更好地从实际出发。实事求是、一分为二不仅是个方法问题，也是个学风问题，学风不正，不仅不能推动研究工作，引出正确结论，总结经验，贯彻批判继承的方针，而且会影响到下一代，下两代，应当引起严重注意。

（1978 年 11 月在广州全国外国文学研究工作规划会议
上的发言。原载《外国文学研究集刊》第 2 辑，1980 年；
1982 年 12 月修改）

莎士比亚的诗作

　　莎士比亚的作品包括戏剧和诗歌，他的戏剧也是用诗体写的，戏剧中还常常穿插一些可以歌咏的独立短诗。所谓莎士比亚的诗歌，是指戏剧创作以外的诗作。

　　这些诗作都在诗人生前出版，绝大部分是诗人的作品，只有少数几首短诗大概不是出自诗人之笔。出版最早的是《维纳斯与阿都尼》（1593）和《鲁克丽丝》（1594），这两首长诗可能经过诗人审阅定稿。稍后出版的是《爱情的礼赞》（1599），共二十一首短诗，其中只有五首肯定是莎士比亚的作品（第一、二首即《十四行诗集》的一三八、一四四首，第三、五、十七首摘自《爱的徒劳》一剧）。大约是出版商鉴于莎士比亚的诗很受欢迎（《维纳斯与阿都尼》到1599年已出第五、第六版，《鲁克丽丝》在1598年也又再版，十四行诗至少有一部分以手抄本形式在文艺爱好者中间广为流传），因此拼凑一集，冠以莎士比亚之名，刊印牟利。从这一诗集的第十六首起，出版商又插进了一个新的标题《乐曲杂咏》。接着《爱情的礼赞》而出版的是《凤凰和斑鸠》（1601）。当时诗人罗勃特·切斯特为了歌颂他的贵族恩主夫妇的爱情，写了《凤凰和斑鸠》一诗，出版商又请其他诗人写了十四首咏同一诗题的诗作，合成一集，以《凤凰和斑鸠》为全书名称出版，其中第五首据称是莎士比亚所作，所以也收进了莎士比亚诗集。《十四行诗集》出版最晚（1609），集后附有《情女怨》。这一诗集显然是由出版商搜集了手抄流传的莎士比亚的十四行诗，未经诗人自己审订而出版的。

这些诗歌的写作年代大致和出版先后的顺序符合。《维纳斯与阿都尼》大半写成于1592—1593年间，即作者二十八九岁时；《鲁克丽丝》大半写成于1593—1594年；《爱情的礼赞》中有三首采自《爱的徒劳》，这出喜剧则是1594年左右写成的；《十四行诗集》显然不是一个短时期内写成的，一般认为是在1592—1598这几年之间陆续写成，也就是莎士比亚二十八岁到三十四岁之间的作品。《凤凰和斑鸠》大半是最晚的诗作，可能写成于1600年。

莎士比亚诗歌的基本内容是赞美美好的事物，歌颂友谊，抒写爱情，总括说来，是表达他的理想的。这些主题在他的戏剧里也都接触到，只是在诗歌里，作者以抒情诗、叙事诗和说理诗的形式，表现得更加集中。因此，这些诗歌可以和他的戏剧相互参照，而要给他在诗歌中所表达的理想作出正确的评价，也必须联系到他的整个世界观和他在十六世纪英国社会斗争中所处的地位。

莎士比亚的最高社会理想，如果用一句话概括，那就是要求人与人之间的和谐，以发展人的天赋和才能。这一思想反映了英国新兴资产阶级的要求，贯串着他的戏剧和诗歌，成为它们最基本的主题思想。他常用许多琴弦同时合奏的音乐来象征这种"和谐"：

> 凡是灵魂里没有音乐的人，
> 不能被美妙音乐的和声打动的人，
> 必然会干背叛、暴动、掠夺等等勾当；
> 他的精神活动象黑夜一样的迟钝，

他的情感就象地府一样的阴暗：

千万不可信任这种人。

     ——《威尼斯商人》第五幕，第一场，83—87行

在第八首十四行诗中，他把一张琴上不同的琴弦比作夫妇、父母、子女，琴弦发出的和谐的音乐，象征了他们之间的和谐关系。在个人生活方面，他反对兄弟手足的阋墙之斗；在社会和国家生活方面，他既反对上欺下，也反对下"犯"上，也反对上层之间的矛盾冲突。

一个国家，虽然可以区分高等、低等、更低等的人，

但要靠大家协力同心，才能保持，

才能具有完满而自然的节奏，象音乐一样。

     ——《亨利五世》第一幕，第二场，180—182行

争取人与人之间的和谐关系的目的是发展"人"的天赋和才能。哈姆雷特说："如果人的至高无上的享受和事业无非是吃吃睡睡，那还算人吗？那就是畜生了！上帝造我们，给我们这么多智慧，使我们能瞻前顾后，决不是要我们把这种智能，把这种神明的理性，任其霉烂而不用。"在《特洛依勒斯和克丽西达》一剧中（第一幕，第三场），攸利西斯的话把莎士比亚的想思表达得更为具体。他认为自然界有秩序，人类社会也应有秩序，一个紊乱的社会对于"人"的"上进心"、"事业心"的发展是不利的。在一个充满封建内战、农民起义、贫民暴乱或受到外国威胁的国家里，刚刚登上历史舞台的资产阶级无法实现它的"雄心壮志"。实现"雄心壮志"在当时的历史条件下，又意味着发展"城市与城市之间的协

作，海外的和平贸易"。

十六世纪英国资产阶级处于新兴阶段，无论在政治上或经济上，它和封建势力的力量对比还很悬殊，它要求一个和平环境来发展自己，莎士比亚的作品正是反映了这种要求。这时，资产阶级既有反对封建特权的一面，又因力量还微弱而有和封建贵族妥协的一面。[1] 在政治上，它希望在封建政权的体系之内，进行改造，拥护君主，打击诸侯。因此，攸利西斯把君主比作太阳，统帅群星，使它们能按轨道运行。这里不须要叙述莎士比亚的全部政治观点，只须指明莎士比亚不是彻底反对封建贵族的。这一点，把他和密尔顿的言论比较一下，便更明显了。十七世纪中叶，在农民反封建运动蓬勃发展的形势下，资产阶级对封建贵族的反抗性就表现得比较激烈，以至敢于杀掉国王的头。而莎士比亚对君主以及贵族中某些人物还是寄予希望的。

莎士比亚认为，如果社会上层（比如贵族）某些个别人物能变得好，通过他们使社会秩序得到整顿，人的聪明才智便能获得发展。也就是说，他想通过培养一种"新人"，来达到改造社会的目的，并且相信这种"新人"是能够通过道德改善的途径培养出来的。他的这种信心是以人性论为其依据。他认为人性中存在着善和恶的因素，一般说来，就连最坏的，象理查三世、克劳迪斯、甚至牙戈都有一星一点的"良心"，都有自惭形秽的顷刻（《奥塞罗》第五幕，第一场，十九行）。莎士比亚看到恶的存在，"任何事不可能十全十美，总受到某种不纯的东西的玷污"《鲁克丽丝》848—849行），他以为恶归根结底是放纵情欲的结果。情欲必须受理性的调节，哈姆雷特对他的学友霍拉旭说："血性（情欲）和判断（理性）

---

[1] 英国历史证明，即使在资产阶级强大以后，在劳动人民的革命要求面前，它仍会和封建贵族妥协。

高度调和的人是最有福的人，命运女神就不会把他们当一管笛子，随意吹出她所愿吹的调子"（第三幕，第二场，70行以下）。情欲和理性任何一者走向极端必然导致灾难，最少也是可笑的，如福尔斯塔夫或《爱的徒劳》中的庇隆。调节理性和情欲就能获得善，完成人的道德改善过程。身受恶的灾害的人应当采取谅解与和解的态度；作恶的人应当悔悟。

下面分别谈一谈莎士比亚的几部主要诗作。

《维纳斯与阿都尼》和《鲁克丽丝》都是献给骚散普顿伯爵的，许多研究者认为《十四行诗集》中的青年也是骚散普顿。他是新贵族的代表，他的祖父是第一代伯爵，是十六世纪前半新封的贵族，四十年代当过宰相。骚散普顿本人在莎士比亚献诗的时候，不过二十岁。他八岁继承爵位，青年时代就参加政治生活，从军，接近具有新思想的文人学者。这种人物和父亲未死以前的哈姆雷特相仿佛，是莎士比亚作为一个新兴资产阶级人文主义作家心目中的偶象。莎士比亚无疑赞赏他们的仪表、才华、教养。莎士比亚把作品献给骚散普顿，不仅因为当时文人尚未职业化，必须投靠"恩主"，通过投靠争取更高的社会地位或获得职务；而更多是因为他把骚散普顿看作是"世界未来的希望"（见《献词》），向他表示爱戴。

《维纳斯与阿都尼》的题材来源于罗马诗人奥维德的《变形记》，写爱情女神维纳斯追求青年阿都尼，但阿都尼不爱她，只爱打猎，在一次行猎中为野猪所伤致死，引起维纳斯的悲恸。在阿都尼死去的地方，血泊里生出一种花，名为白头翁，维纳斯把它带回自己的塞浦路斯岛。长诗的故事到此为止。根据神话，地下神感于维纳斯的悲痛，准许阿都尼每年还阳六个月，和维纳斯相聚。这一神话发源于腓尼基一带，是这一带早期人类发展了农业以后，对大自然植物界冬灭春生的规律的形象解释。在腓尼基、埃及、希腊等地每年举行阿都尼节日。莎士比亚这首长诗的主题并不是时序的代谢，而是在于说明爱情是不可抗拒的，是自然的法则；其次，从原来神话中青春再生的思想，引申出美好的事物应当永存的思想。

莎士比亚为什么把具有这样思想的诗献给骚散普顿？这思想和"世界未来的希望"又有什么关系呢？这首诗以古典文学为题材，投合骚散普顿这类有贵族教养的读者的趣味，但这不是献诗的主要原因。阿都尼象征美，他不仅外表俊美，而且有一种降龙伏虎的力量，能够给世界带来光明、秩序、和谐，是抗拒或改变黑暗、丑恶、意外、不幸、疾病的力量（参看1093—1110行）。这一形象在神话人物的外衣下体现了莎士比亚理想中的贵族、"新人"、"美"、"未来的希望"。既然是"未来的希望"，因此必须使之长存不朽，不可成为一现的昙花。"美"只有通过和爱情的结合，才能使青春永驻。这一思想在十四行诗中有更集中的表现，在《维纳斯与阿都尼》中，诗人突出地强调了爱情的力量，其原因也正在此。在莎士比亚看来，爱情本身就是和谐关系的象征，世界上如果没有爱情，一切都要倾倒，小则人与人之间将产生不忠不信，大则引起战争和灾难（参看1135—1164行）。因此，阿都尼拒绝爱情必然导致死亡。

莎士比亚利用神话传说把维纳斯写成为不可抗拒的爱情的象征，也还有反对禁欲主义的一面。这是资产阶级早期在思想意识领域里反封建斗争的一个主要方面。他反对"爱情伤身论"（409行以下），反对贞操观念（751行以下），反对清教徒或教会的爱情观（787行以下）。他用马作为比喻（259—288行一段），说明爱情是合乎自然规律的。这些反对禁欲主义的论证，使这首诗具有反对清教徒禁欲主义的一面，也在很大程度上具有说理诗的性质。

强调爱情，必然对爱情的心理活动感到兴趣。英国文艺复兴时期抒情诗歌继承了彼特拉克的传统而有所发扬，对人的心理活动的描写更丰富了。心理描写不仅成为资产阶级抒情诗歌，而且成为以后小说的一个基本特征。在《维纳斯与阿都尼》里（以及《鲁克丽丝》里），大段的对话或独白也无非是要表现当事人的内心感情和思想。这种思想感情的"丰富性"常常表现为展示恋爱的当事人内心的两类截然相反的感情、状态、处境，例如信任和不信任、希望和失望、幸福和痛苦、热和冷等等，这些相反的状态交织在一起，在人的内心里相互交战。这种爱情心理的描写在十四行诗里也是很普遍的。

《维纳斯与阿都尼》主要写理想，而《鲁克丽丝》则更多反映了现实。《鲁克丽丝》的故事可以追溯到奥维德的《岁时记》，在文艺复兴时期这个故事已由意大利、法国传到英国。故事发生在罗马历史早期，叙述王政时期最后一个国王塔昆纽斯的儿子塞克斯图斯·塔昆纽斯从战场奔回，奸污了同族科拉丁努斯的美丽的妻子鲁克丽丝，鲁克丽丝召回了出征的丈夫，嘱咐他报仇雪耻之后自杀而死。莎士比亚的长诗到此基本结束，最后简单交代了故事的收场：王朝被推翻，建立了贵族共和国。

这首诗具有一定的反暴、民主的人文主义思想。作者从恶必然存在这一观念出发，恶由于"机缘"而表现为行动和事实。恶在这首诗里的基本内容是私欲、妒羡、对荣誉和友谊的损害、缺乏同情怜悯、损人不利己的行为等。诗人尤其反对损害荣誉这一端。可以看出莎士比亚写这首诗的目的，是给贵族提供殷鉴，希望贵族中某些"优秀"人物如骚散普顿在道德自我完善的过程中知道应当警戒什么。因此在诗中，莎士比亚着力描写塞克斯图斯如何不顾贵族荣誉，为了满足私欲，背叛了友谊，在内心里产生了强烈矛盾（190行以下），而鲁克丽丝则长篇大论地向同情、怜悯和人道呼吁，向贵族荣誉呼吁，并向塞克斯图斯作为统治的王朝的成员申述君道。

在封建主义向资本主义过渡时期，欧洲许多国家如意大利、英国的统治集团中，用暴力和恐怖手段来满足私欲的情况极为普遍，因此鲁克丽丝的悲剧是带有时代特征的。这种情况在莎士比亚和其他剧作家的作品中都有所反映，不乏塞克斯图斯这类罪恶的化身。莎士比亚同情被侮辱、被蹂躏的一方；他认为女子是软弱的，所以尤其同情被蹂躏的女性。他反对暴力，但从他的"和谐"说出发，他既反对塞克斯图斯式的暴力，也反对广大人民的暴力（722—723行），只主张用同情为武器来和暴力斗争（561—562，584—588，594—595行）。也许正因为如此，在布鲁图斯领导下推翻塔昆纽斯王朝的事迹就一笔带过了。

荣誉问题在文艺复兴时期新兴资产阶级思想家的著作中特别受到重视。[1] 圭恰底尼认为荣誉给人以动力，使人不怕困难、危险、耗费，换言之即资产阶级的"事业心"。莎士比亚所推崇的荣誉既不是封建骑士或军人的以勇武为内容的荣誉（这在《亨利四世》中福尔斯塔夫身上被否定了），也还不是"事业心"或"进取心"，而是不破坏友谊、不破坏作为社会基础的家庭幸福（27—28行）、不利用别人的坦率和信赖（33—35，85—88行）这样一种道德准则。荣誉问题经常出现在莎士比亚的戏剧中（如《维洛那二绅士》、《奥塞罗》），反映了在资本主义因素发展起来的历史时期，资产阶级为了维持正常发展，必须标榜信用。在《威尼斯商人》中，安东尼奥宁肯牺牲生命，也不肯破坏契约的规定。另一方面，为了维护家庭幸福也必须保卫荣誉。这可以说就是莎士比亚在这首诗里向理想的贵族青年提出来的要求。

这两首长诗在风格上也表现了贵族趣味。旨在打动感官的描

[1] 参看 Jacob Burckhardt: *The Civilization of the Renaissance in Italy*（布克哈特：《意大利文艺复兴时期的文明》（英文本），伦敦，1945 年版。

写，古典题材的选择，都说明这一点，上文已经指出。此外，贵族的牧歌传奇文学的影响也很显著，如打猎场面的描写。更突出的是文字的华丽雕琢，文字游戏、诡辩式的概念游戏，这显然是受了当时流行的贵族文学"攸弗伊斯"文体的影响。有时莎士比亚为了追求比喻，还暴露了许多败笔（如《维纳斯与阿都尼》955 行以下三段，1037 行以下三段，1063 行一段，《鲁克丽丝》50 行以下四段等）。

关于莎士比亚的十四行诗，历来聚讼纷纭，归纳起来，不外以下五类问题。一、创作时期问题，是八十年代？九十年代？甚至十七世纪初年？二、次序安排问题，包括如何分段问题，是莎士比亚自己安排的次序还是出版商安排的？应分为六段呢还是更多的段落？三、出版商的献词中的 Mr. W. H. 是谁？诗中的青年是谁？争宠的诗人是谁？黑妇人是谁？"告密人"是谁？对象是男子还是女子？四、意图和内容，是自传性的抒情呢？还是戏剧式的、故事式的描写别人？是寓意呢？还是写实？还是只代表一时的诗歌风尚？五、是莎士比亚写的呢？还是罗利或培根写的？等等。我们根据思想内容和某些可以肯定的事实，可以断定十四行诗大半成于九十年代一段时期里；诗有一定的连续性，但既然不是一气呵成，思想上的中断不足为奇；诗中的人物未能确凿考证出来是谁并不妨碍得出这样的结论，即诗中前半的"你"是一个贵族青年，诗人通过自己和诗中人物的关系，抒发自己的理想和不同情况下的感受；至于作者问题，反对的理由是很难成立的。

莎士比亚的十四行诗是他的诗歌中，也是文艺复兴时期英国大量的十四行诗集中最好的作品。十四行诗从四十年代起从意大利输入英国，成为抒情诗人最欢迎的一种诗歌形式，在莎士比亚以前就出版了锡德尼、但尼尔、康斯特布尔、斯宾塞等人的十四行诗集，成为一时风尚。以十四行为一单位（一首），长度比较适合于描写一种心情，也可以串联若干首，对一种心情进行各方面的对比、类比、引伸、烘托，也可以中断而换写另一思想情感。英国诗人在意大利诗歌的基础上把这形式发展得更为完美，把原来的四四三三的分法改为四四四二，更好地发挥了一首诗中起承转合的章法，到莎士比亚手中，最后两行具有画龙点睛的作用，把全诗的思想集中到或扭转到一对押韵的警句上。[1]

莎士比亚的一五四首十四行诗，大致说来，从第一到一二六首是致一个青年的，从一二七到一五二首是致一女子的，最后两首虽然符合莎士比亚诗歌的思想，但实际上是希腊诗歌的仿作，附赘于全诗之尾的。

《十四行诗集》按内容可以分为三类：歌颂美的诗，以友谊为题的诗，以爱情为题的诗。

莎士比亚是把美作为一种抵抗丑恶现实的理想来写的，这一点在《维纳斯与阿都尼》中已提到。这一主题在十四行诗里表现得更为集中。

> 但如今黑既成为美的继承人，
> 于是美便招来了侮辱和诽谤。
> 因为自从每只手都修饰自然，
> 用艺术的假面貌去美化丑恶，
> 温馨的美便失掉声价和圣殿，
> 纵不忍辱偷生，也遭了亵渎。[2]（一二七首）

---

[1] 莎士比亚十四行诗押韵的安排一般是 ABAB CDCD EFEF GG，每行十个音，而彼特拉克则采用 ABBA ABBA CDE CDE，或 ABBA ABBA CDC CDC。

[2] 这里及以下所引的诗，均用人民文学出版社出版的《莎士比亚全集》中的译文。

这几行诗概括了莎士比亚的出发点。现实是丑的，所以他歌颂美；现实充满虚伪和恶，所以他提出美必须和真、善结合：

> "美、善和真"，就是我全部的题材，
> "美、善和真"，用不同的词句表现；
> 我的创造就在这变化上演才，
> 三题一体，它的境界可真无限。（一〇五首）

美、真、善三者，归根结底，最重要的是善。不美不要紧，不善最糟（一三一首，13—14行）。灵魂的善，必然表现为外表的美，待人接物的真；相反，灵魂的恶也必然表现为外表的丑，待人接物的虚伪。善就是心灵的美，它的基本内容则是仁慈。大致说来，这就是莎士比亚关于美的总的看法。

莎士比亚把美的理想寄托在某个个别贵族人物身上。他在十四行诗中对那青年说："你是这世界的鲜艳的装饰"（第一首9行），"人人都注视着你的可爱的目光"（第五首2行）。可以联系《哈姆雷特》中莪菲丽亚赞美王子的话来看："美好国家的期望和花朵，高雅风尚的镜子，优美的典范，举世瞩目的中心。"这里莎士比亚都是在指上层社会某些"优秀"的贵族分子，这都是不言而喻的了。因此，这个美的理想的化身必然是个男子，而不是女性。既然他是诗人希望之所寄托，因此是个青年，而不是老人。诗人多方歌颂他的美，希望这种美好的人能抗住时间的侵蚀而不朽。"时间"本来也可作"时代"解，诗人希望这一理想的青年能够抵抗住社会灾难的侵袭。这一切不是表示诗人对某种抽象的美好事物的渴望，而是表示对某一类型的人——即资产阶级心目中的"新人"的殷切期望。他希望这种"新人"不要断绝，能把他的"美"传之后代，因此敦促他结婚；同时，诗人一再宣称要用诗歌把他的"美"永远记录下来，使它的不朽得到双重保证。诗人对文学艺术的功能的推崇是所有人文主义者的共同特点。

　　莎士比亚所歌颂的青年贵族的美，不仅是形体的俊美，他更着重"精神的美"、"灵魂的美"（六九首5—10行）。要保持心灵的美，绝对不可和俗人同流合污。有了灵魂的美，即善，就不怕诽谤（七〇首）。莎士比亚警戒贵族青年不要让他的美丽的身躯被罪恶所占据：

> 哦，那些罪过找到了多大的华厦，
> 当它们把你挑选来作安乐窝，
> 在那儿美为污点披上了轻纱，
> 在那儿触目的一切都变清和！
> 　　警惕呵，心肝，为你这特权警惕；
> 　　最快的刀被滥用也失去锋利！（九五首）

愈是俊美，愈应当有善的灵魂。由此可见，所谓"灵魂的美"、"善"等等实际上就是贵族在社会中，尤其是在上层社会、朝廷中的待人接物之道，通过它来取得"和谐"。通过什么样的"善"来取得和谐呢？莎士比亚一贯认为只有仁慈。真正美的人也必然仁慈：

> 难道憎比温婉的爱反得处优？
> 你那么貌美，愿你也一样心慈……（十首）

这和《暴风雨》中所说："恶不可能居住在这样一个美好的庙宇（身体）内"（第一幕，第二场，454行）的思想是一致的。莎士比亚在这里把人文主义的理想寄托在俊美的贵族青年身上。

关于"真"的问题更多牵涉到友谊和爱情。

"友谊"在人文主义者看来是个人与个人，尤其是从事社会活动的男子与男子之间的和谐关系的表现。文艺复兴时期的诗人、哲学家特别关心这问题。他们认为友谊应当真诚，不背叛友谊即是保持了荣誉。塞克斯图斯之所以受到谴责，其原因之一正是他破坏了友谊。友谊实质上反映了新兴资产阶级要求在彼此交往之时所恪守的一条信用准则，上文已经论及。此外，培根还提出一点：互助[1]。达也是符合资产阶级在发展自身和在反对封建的斗争时的需要的。但莎士比亚所宣扬的友谊则更强调"平等"一面。他自己是一个演员、文人，对方是贵族，两人的社会地位悬殊。他自己很意识到这一点（三六首9—12行，三七首5—8行）。因此从社会地位上来说，他们之间不可能存在平等的友谊，他只能在精神上向贵族讨平等，这就是为什么莎士比亚特别强调他和贵族青年尽管年龄、地位都有差异，而精神是结合的（一一六首），而且强调只有这种友谊是持久的，即使两人身处两地，还能在精神上不分离，因为"我的心存在于你的胸中"（二二首6—7行），正是所谓"心心相印"。

莎士比亚的友谊观念的特点是他所处的地位所决定的。资产阶级当它处在新兴阶段还不可能把"平等"作为一种鲜明的政治口号提出来，它的知识分子——人文主义者从古代伦理学中借来友谊的概念作为反对等级制度、争取社会地位的思想武器，这时的平等观念也还只限于个人与个人的关系，还多少带一些希望贵族恩赐的想法。培根在他的文章里说得很清楚，他说友谊就是"交心"，"你可

---

[1] 见培根：《论说文集》中《论友谊》一篇。

以向朋友倾吐悲哀、欢乐、畏惧、希望、疑虑、劝告以及一切压在你心上的东西”，但帝王们由于他们和臣民距离很大，就不可能获得这种好处，因此他们只能把臣民中“某些人提升上来，成为类似侣伴一样的人，成为几乎和他们平等的人”。

莎士比亚所歌颂的真诚友谊一方面反映了资产阶级向贵族争取平等的要求，希望贵族阶级能够“礼贤下士”，另一方面他希望这种友谊只存在于社会上层之间，而不及于社会下层，社会下层只是同情怜悯的对象。这一观点具体体现在他的戏剧中，而培根则给予了理论的阐述。他认为“只有野兽或上帝才喜欢孤独”，人的天性要求友谊，但是“一群人不等于侣伴”。

《十四行诗集》的前一二六首，除少数诗外，可以肯定都是致青年男子的。但是莎士比亚在歌颂友谊的时候，用的完全是爱情的词汇。有人认为这是因为莎士比亚找不到歌颂友谊的诗歌先例，只能借用男女爱情的词汇。这也有一定的道理。此外，莎士比亚所理解的友谊，是心的结合，和爱情没有什么区别，只不过存在于同性之间，因此用爱情的词汇也很自然。事实上，有些诗也未始不可理解为爱情诗。作为爱情诗，莎士比亚再次表现了爱情就是个人幸福的思想（二十五、二十九首），其中占有观念极为强烈（二十一、八十七、九十二首），因而在许多诗中他也突出地描写了自己的患得患失的心理活动（四十八、六十四、七十五首），以至消极绝望（七十三首）。

一二七首以后，除少数诗外，大部分是致一女子的，即所谓“黑妇人”（一个黑睛、黑发、深色皮肤的有夫之妇）。这一组诗和传统的爱情诗在思想风格上都迥乎不同，不论是否系莎士比亚个人的抒情诗，总之反映了当时社会生活中的一种风貌：对待恋爱的一种玩世不恭的态度。他所歌颂过的“真诚”的爱情过去似乎被理想化了，在这里遭到了否定（一三八、一三九首），同情、怜悯这些"高贵"品质也打动不了变了心的人（一四二、一四三首）。这一组诗里的批判性显著增强了。现实世界颠倒了黑白、美丑，现实世界中的爱情，如在《鲁克丽丝》中所描写的，无非是"赌假咒、嗜血、好杀、满身是罪恶、凶残、粗野、不可靠、走极端"的情欲。

莎士比亚的十四行诗虽然总的说来是抒发他的理想的，但他的理想是以现实为其对立面的，因此最优秀的诗往往能用简炼的语言概括当时的现实，成为他的十四行诗的一个显著特色。这种现实主义在十四行诗中，象在他的戏剧里一样，常表现为一种时代感：

> 当着残暴的战争把铜像推翻，
> 或内讧把城池荡成一片废墟，
> 无论战神的剑或战争的烈焰
> 都毁不掉你的遗芳的活历史。（五五首）

> 当我眼见前代的富丽和豪华
> 被时光的手毫不留情地磨灭；
> 当巍巍的塔我眼见沦为碎瓦，
> 连不朽的铜也不免一场浩劫……（六四首）

这里可以看出封建主的城堡，巍峨的教堂和寺院，这些封建制度的象征，在封建内战和历史潮流的冲击下已经倾圮坍塌。同样，当时宫廷和社会的现实也在他笔下得到反映：宦海的争宠、失宠和祸福无常（二五、一二四、一二五首），社会的动荡不安（一〇七首），整个社会的不正义（六六首）。在一一五首里，他指出时代变幻莫测，它能使誓言和君主的法令失效，抹黑神圣的美，磨平人的锐气，使意志刚强的人随从流浴。他用现实中的丑恶来衬托出美好事物和友情之可贵。有时他只用一句话就既概括了现实，又表达了自己的主观愿望：

看见这样珍宝，忠诚也变扒手（四八首）

现实和理想的矛盾也体现在诗人自己的态度上。他歌颂平等、忠诚，但他自己也不免阿谀（八八、八九首）。他所赞美的贵族青年，不仅眷顾另一诗人，而且夺去了诗人自己的情妇，在这种情况下，诗人的态度却是怨而不怒，称他为"高贵的贼"、"优雅的登徒子"（四〇首），大力歌颂谅解（三三、三四、三五、一一九、一二〇首）。

现实的描写在十四行诗中往往和大自然和诗人自己的情绪揉合在一起，有形象，有情感，也有说理的因素，使每首诗浑然一体。这类技巧纯熟的诗可以六四、六五、七三首为代表，诗人以强烈对照的方法，以极大的说服力，使读者受到感染。

既然铜、石、或大地、或无边的海，
没有不屈服于那阴惨的无常，
美，她的活力比一朵花还柔脆，
怎能和他那肃杀的威严抵抗？（六五首）

在我身上你或许会看见秋天，
当黄叶，或尽脱，或只三三两两
挂在瑟缩的枯枝上索索抖颤——
荒废的教堂，那里百鸟曾合唱。（七三首）

有些诗则是纯粹抒情的，如二九、三〇首，直接表达诗人自己在现实中的感受；或则通过自己的活动，如到外省巡回演出归来，抒发自己的感受：

> 唉，我的确曾经常东奔西跑，
> 扮作斑衣的小丑供众人赏玩，
> 违背我的意志，把至宝贱卖掉，
> 为了新交不惜把旧知交冒犯……（一一〇首）

有些则是纯粹说理的，如九四首。莎士比亚就在这些方面，以及在起承转合的章法，生动的形象和含蓄的语言上，超过了同时代大批的十四行诗人。但是他也染上了当时流行的贵族人文主义诗歌的习气。象在他许多早期喜剧和上面论及的两首长诗里那样，十四行诗里也常有概念游戏（如一三三首等）、为比喻而比喻（如二四、三四首等）、文字游戏（如一三五、一三六首等），有时思维方式也接近于诡辩（如二二首等）。

　　莎士比亚十四行诗另一风格特点是生动的比喻。诗中大量引用大自然中的景象和事物，如时序、日月星辰、阴晴昼晦、风雨霜露、花鸟虫兽等。此外，他还从社会生活中大量汲取形象，如贫富、战和、封建宫廷、贵族生活、城镇、法庭、行旅、疫疠、科学活动、舞台、文艺创作等等方面，增加了诗歌的时代气息。尤其值得注意的是从资本主义贸易经营活动中采取了大量的比喻：遗产、所有权、囤积、税收、利润、利息、租金、租期、契约、抵押、债务、帐目、破产、交易、供应等等。这使人想到现代派诗歌用大都会生活中的形象入诗，许多人不能接受，而三百多年前莎士比亚已经作了大胆的突破。

莎士比亚的十四行诗有少数并非十四行，有一首（九九）是十五行，有一首（一二六）仅有十二行，两行一押韵，有一首（一四六）残缺，还有一首（一四五）虽然是十四行，但每行只有八个音。这些不完整的情况可能是因为作者并未最后定稿，或流传讹抄。

最后谈一谈《凤凰和斑鸠》。凤凰象征爱情，斑鸠象征忠贞。这首诗历来认为含义晦涩，其实这首诗的主题很明确：

> 爱情和忠贞已经死亡；
> 凤和鸠化作一团火光
> 一同飞升，离开了尘世。

并且强调了建立在精神结合的基础上的爱情：

> 它们是那样彼此相爱，
> 仿佛两者已合为一体，
> 分明是二，却又浑然为一：
> 是一是二，谁也难猜

这里对爱情和理想的悲观失望情绪在十四行诗中已有所表现，这是符合人文主义作家的倾向的，因为人文主义者所抱的理想——美好的人、纯洁的爱情、幸福等等——尽管在当时起了反封建的作用，但同时也都被资本主义本身带来的现实所否定，人文主义诗人如果不是盲目乐观，不可避免地要陷入不能解决的矛盾，而发出忧郁痛苦的呼声：

厌了这一切，我向安息的死疾呼，（六六首）

厌了这一切，我要离开人寰。（六六首）

莎士比亚的诗歌，和他的戏剧一样，既体现了新兴资产阶级作家的理想，也体现了他们的理想和资本主义本身的矛盾。

（原载《文学评论》第 2 期，1964 年）

莎士比亚如是说

诗言志。大凡一个作家写一部作品总是要表明他自己对事物的看法，并希望按照他的世界观改造世界。为写作而写作的作家是不存在的。莎士比亚写作的动机，在我们今天来看，可以说是为资产阶级登上历史舞台作舆论准备，尽管他自己未必意识到这一点。文艺复兴本来是资产阶级第一次启蒙运动，是在思想意识领域里的反封建运动。作为文艺复兴时期的一个巨人，莎士比亚通过他的诗歌和三十几部剧作提出了什么样的见解呢？我觉得可以用两句话概括。第一句话就是罗马诗人维吉尔在《牧歌》第十首中那句话 Omnia vincit Amor: et nos cedamus Amori——爱征服一切，让我们屈服于爱吧。这个消息二百年前的乔叟已经透露了，他刻画的女修道院长胸前挂着一串念珠，上面挂着一根别针，别针上刻着一个"A"字，下面附了 Amor vincit omnia 一句话。这正是新兴资产阶级企图改变封建社会人与人的关系而提出的口号。

第二句话就是罗马作家西塞罗《论神性》一文中的一句话：ad harmoniam canere mundum——宇宙和谐地歌唱。这句话点出了宇宙和大自然是一个和谐的整体，它把个人之间的爱扩而大之，包括了全宇宙，体现了把纷乱的人类社会建成一个有秩序的社会的理想（res in ordinem redigere），按当时具体的历史情况说，就是反对封建割据、封建战争。这个思想在《特洛伊罗斯与克瑞西达》一剧俄底修斯一段话中表达得再清楚不过。在一次军事会议上，希腊将领研究为什么十年来不能覆灭特洛亚，俄底修斯认为不是因为特洛亚强大，而是因为希腊一方软弱，软弱的原因是大将阿奇琉斯出于个人恩怨，不服从调度，闹独立性，不肯出战。俄底修斯这篇精采的演说，其主旨就是一个词："等级"。他说，无论自然界或人类社会都必须遵守等级。天上的星辰不按轨道运行，就是越轨（non sufficit orbis），就会引起瘟疫、地震、风暴；人间的越轨则表现为秩序的破坏、城市中的不和、破坏国与国之间的和平、颠倒长幼之序。"只消把次序取消。让这根琴弦走了调，听吧！多少刺耳的噪音就会发出来；一切事物都将互相抵牾"。和谐的社会关系，按其实质来讲，仍以爱为出发点。所以上面两句话中，第一句话是核心，也就是莎士比亚的人文主义的中心内容。

莎士比亚的诗歌和喜剧固然歌颂爱，他的悲剧也以爱为出发点，这一点下面还要谈到。即以他的以英国历史为内容的历史剧而论，他探讨的是君权问题，表明他反对封建内讧，希望在一个开明君主的统治下建成一个统一民族国家。如果我们分析一下他所塑造的反面君主形象，大都由于处理不好君主同贵族的关系，以私利为重，在不同程度上违反了和谐和仁爱的原则。这些君主中最突出的莫过于理查三世，他那种凶残阴险，不择手段的性格和行为完全同仁爱原则背道而驰。再拿他的以罗马历史为题材的剧本来看。科利奥兰纳斯那种傲慢和仇恨心理，完全谈不上仁爱。在《凯撒》中，正直的布鲁图斯之所以伙同一批政客刺杀凯撒，不是出于任何个人恩怨，而是因为"一旦给凯撒戴上王冠，就可能改变他的天性"，"就等于在他尾巴上安上了毒刺"，"有了权势，就忘了怜悯。"《安东尼与克莉奥佩特拉》批判了渥大维的阴险,歌颂了宽宏慷慨、天生情种的安东尼。虽然安东尼那种越轨的豪放,他的那种纵情态度——"让罗马融化在台伯河的流水里吧!这儿是我的生存的空间。生命的光荣存在于一双心心相印的情侣的及时互爱和热烈拥抱之中"受到批判,但安东尼的钟情还是为莎士比亚所赞许,而把他写成一个高贵的正面人物。纵情胜于无情。

纲举目张。只有正确理解莎士比亚的创作动机,了解他要写的是什么,才能给他的作品以正确的评价,正确地分析主题思想、人物性格、戏剧情节和语言技巧。时代背景、作者生平、创作发展、主题分析、人物的典型性、情节、艺术特点都要介绍,但倘若抓不准对象,尽管面面俱到,往往隔靴搔痒,甚至起副作用,反而不如不求面面俱到,但能确实掌握对象,作鞭辟入里的分析,更有好处。

例如对《威尼斯商人》的分析,说它反映了新旧法律的矛盾,夏洛克代表封建旧法律,鲍西娅代表资产阶级新法律,因而夏洛克败诉。又说莎士比亚也批判了新法律,认为它也不公平,对夏洛克惩罚太重,因而揭穿了资产阶级的法律面前人人平等的谎言。

我以为莎士比亚可能但未必把法律分为新旧,而是用法律这一总体概念来象征反人道精神。他不止一次表明这种观点,如《哈姆雷特》里,他提到"被鄙弃的爱情所感受的苦楚,法律的拖延"。法律同仁爱是两个对立物。鲍西娅叫夏洛克割肉,要他请一位外科医生来治伤,不要让安东尼奥死了。夏洛克回答说,契约上没有写明这一款。鲍西娅说:"契约上是没有说明,但那又怎么样呢?为了仁慈,你应当作这么一件好事嘛。"最后,按律科罚了夏洛克,很严,安东尼奥出来说情,保留了夏洛克一部分财产,责成他死后传给女儿、女婿,并要求他皈依基督教,而基督正是仁慈的化身。

又如对夏洛克这个人物的分析。我们往往只谈莎士比亚批判他的一面，还引用了马克思的话来证明莎士比亚刻画这个人物的成功。我们说夏洛克不仅象莫利哀笔下的阿巴公是一个守财奴，而他还有报仇心重和刻毒的特点。但我们往往避免或少谈莎士比亚同情夏洛克的一面，而夏洛克为自己辩护的那一段话："难道犹太人没有眼睛吗？……你们用刀剑刺我们，我们不是也会出血的吗？……要是你们欺侮了我们，我们难道不会复仇吗？……"真是振振有词，是剧中一段绝妙的文字。我们有时把这段文字解释为莎士比亚对受歧视的少数民族的同情。我想同情是对的。但不一定是因为夏洛克是少数民族。莎士比亚站在当时还处在被压迫的资产阶级的立场上，同情被压迫的人，不管什么民族，所以与其说他同情受歧视的少数民族，毋宁说他的同情更为广泛。就《威尼斯商人》全剧来说，莎士比亚鼓吹的就是仁爱原则。

夏洛克性格的矛盾牵涉到所谓的典型性问题。既然他是个反面人物，为什么作者又对他表示同情？这岂不有损于典型性？这个问题值得讨论，我只想指出一点，即莎士比亚剧本中这类矛盾的性格比比皆是。拿一个著名的例子福尔斯塔夫来说，早在十八世纪末，摩尔根就发现，用理性来衡量，福尔斯塔夫当然是个懦夫，是个可鄙的反面人物，是个流氓；但从感觉、感情或印象出发，则发现他很可爱、很机智幽默、兴高采烈、存心也不坏。摩尔根认为这是莎士比亚的手法。摩尔根看出了人物的矛盾，但未作出正确的答复。其实，矛盾是现象，实质是统一的，都统一于莎士比亚的思想或世界观。福尔斯塔夫有典型的一面，也有不典型的一面。用高度严格的典型性要求莎士比亚笔下的人物恐怕是办不到的。

还是回到开始的命题：诗言志。马克思给拉萨尔的信批评席勒式的人物是"时代精神的单纯的传声筒"。马克思在这里并未反对人物应当是时代的传声筒，只是反对他变成"单纯的"传声筒。思想性要加上艺术性。莎士比亚的人物是否可以说是他的思想的传声筒呢？我以为是的，只不过是艺术性较高罢了。莎士比亚的人物从根本上说就是他的思想的传声筒。

在西方从浪漫主义批评家开始集中注意评论莎士比亚的人物，到二十世纪初的布拉德雷而登峰造极。布拉德雷之后开始了反作用，这一反作用表现为多种形式。例如所谓历史学派，其中有的研究从中世纪以还的戏剧传统这个角度看莎士比亚剧作的地位；有的从十六世纪英国舞台结构的特点、当时观众的趣味和要求对剧作家的影响，来看莎士比亚剧作的特点；有的研究莎剧同当时政治、社会重大事件的关系，带有影射派的色彩；有的干脆认为莎士比亚反映了维护封建君主制和封建等级制的观点。又如有不少从诗歌文字角度研究莎剧的评论流派，其中以所谓"意象派"或"语义派"最为突出，他们研究莎剧中的主导意象，或诗歌文字所提示的形象，来证明莎剧的主导思想，例如从《哈姆雷特》中，根据文字统计可以得出结论说这部悲剧的主导"意象"是疾病，而《罗密欧与朱丽叶》中的主导意象则是光明，《麦克白斯》中的主导意象之一是一个矮小卑贱的人物被不合身的大衣服压垮，如此等等。

这些评论流派有的当然荒诞不经，连在西方评论界也吃不开，以致只成为一现的昙花，难以为继。例如用弗洛依德心理学"恋母情结"来解释哈姆雷特，说他所以仇恨叔父，是因为他的杀父娶母的这种潜意识被他叔父实现了。除了这种牵强附会的观点之外，不少见解尽管片面，对我们全面理解莎士比亚的思想仍有参考价值。例如英国三十年代评论家奈茨写过一篇文章，标题是《麦克白斯夫人生了多少子女？》。这标题本身就是讽刺布拉德雷人物分析派把人物从莎士比亚规定的情节范围，莎士比亚剧本所表达的主题思想中游离出来，孤立地分析人物，必然会引起这样的疑问，即麦克白斯夫人怎么会这么狠毒，竟表示不惜摔死自己喂奶的婴儿，以至追问她到底生过儿女没有这种离题万里的问题。根据奈茨从剧本文字分析，他得出结论断定《麦克白斯》有三个主题：价值观念的颠倒，"美的就是丑的，丑的就是美的"；违反自然的、无秩序的紊乱："等待混乱的局面澄清；等待战斗判出输赢"；以及怀疑犹豫的情绪，"我们何时再会？""我们何处再会？"他还引了十九世纪浪漫派批评家科勒律治一段话："[莎士比亚同时代剧作家]麦辛哲就象荷兰派画家，他所描绘的对象同现实界一样，很有力，很真实，在观者心中产生同现实界对象同样的效果。但莎士比亚超乎此，他在考虑一事之时，总是用比喻和形象把过去的经验和可能的经验概括起来，使之具有普遍的意义。"

这些评论家都是从历史唯心主义观点出发研究莎士比亚，但有一定的合理内核，例如抓住作者的思想和创作意图，找到生动的形象背后的哲学概括，这一点值得我们参照，有时他抓得很准。有时我们由于急于联系政治，反而打偏了。例如我们过去分析李尔王，倾向于简单地把这出戏说成是一个刚愎自用的封建暴君，一意孤行，受到代表利己主义的两个女儿的挫折，接触到一些同样的不幸者，最后悔悟，转变成新人，而这些不幸者如乞丐则是圈地运动的产物。我们说，莎士比亚批判暴君和利己主义，同情破产的农民，李尔个人的悲剧同人民的悲剧、广大群众的悲剧结合在一起了，如此等等。这里突出的是封建暴君、原始积累的牺牲品、资产阶级的利己主义，这些含有直接政治内涵的概念。

这样联系政治未免太直接了些。如果我们客观地从剧本出发来看，这个剧本确实是写李尔王的转变。根据奈茨的看法，转变的契机有三。一是李尔受到长女次女的挫折，李尔认为她们这样对待他是违反人性，违反自然的。他诅咒大女儿说："大自然女神啊，要是你想使这畜生生男育女，请你改变你的意旨吧！"当次女也拒绝他的时候，他骂她是"违反天性的母夜叉"。二是李尔遇到衣服褴褛假扮疯人的埃德加，埃德加实际上是李尔的一面镜子，李尔说："倘若他没有违反天性的女儿，不可能使他自己的天性沦落到这个地步。"三是黑夜里无情的暴风雨的原野，大自然本身在全剧占了中心地位，用来烘托人间的不仁。

大自然同人性本来是一个概念，大自然的残暴无情同人性的残暴无情是一致的。埃德加说："大自然女神啊，你是我的女神。"李尔王也高呼："暴风雨啊，打碎大自然的模型，把培育出忘恩负义的人类的种子统统泼掉。"

可见莎士比亚从唯心的自然观和人性观出发，认为无论大自然或人性都有恶的一面，当然也有善的一面。李尔的转变是对恶与善的认识过程，他最终认识了代表爱和善的科底丽娅。没有爱或善，大自然就出现风暴、混乱，人类社会也就出现自私、残酷。国王的权威无力惩恶，李尔说："我只得忍耐。"只能用爱的原则克服恶。可见《李尔王》一剧包含一个高度的哲学概括。若说它有政治意义，其根本的政治意义在于它伸张了资产阶级所鼓吹的人道主义。它反映的圈地运动在剧本中是次要的。

那么，莎士比亚能不能说是一个现实主义作家呢？如果从他是否直接反映了十六世纪英国社会生活来说，或是否直接取材于当时生活来说，那么莎士比亚不能算是现实主义作家，而他的同时代剧作家本·琼生、戴克等倒能算是现实主义作家。西方评论家很少给莎士比亚戴上现实主义作家的帽子。他的人物、情节都是取材于历史或外国或传说，他用的都是现成的故事，有时竟大段抄录他所依据的素材，或略加修改。这些人物或情节尽管都不是英国当代的产物，但在一些外国名称的外衣下仍然反映的是英国当代的现实生活，在这意义上他当然是现实主义作家。

不过，我们不必把现实主义作为衡量一个作家的惟一标准，虽然现实主义是创作方法中的主要方法；而现实的含义也往往超过一些具体的人和具体的环境。比如说，本世纪初"现代派"小说家乔依斯的《攸利希斯》反映了现实没有呢？荒诞派的戏剧反映了现实没有呢？浪漫派的诗歌反映了现实没有呢？我觉得人们的思想、情绪、心理活动等等都是客观现实的一部分。浪漫派诗歌，意识流的小说，荒诞派的戏剧，对于我们了解资本主义不同发展阶段人们的思想情绪有很高的认识价值。大凡有影响的作家或流派必然满足两个条件才能产生影响，一是生活体验深刻，深入思考问题，内容深刻；二是表现方法上必然有所创新。上述那些流派或作家，都不是现实主义的，但都符合这两个条件。我们用现实主义的尺子衡量作家作品，往往会把自己用一个框框限制起来，束缚思路，阻碍我们从客观实际出发去观察评定。

莎士比亚之所以伟大，比他同时代人伟大，正是因为他在他那时代的作家中思想和感受是属于最深刻的一流，而在艺术方法上有很大的创新，达也包括他对语言的创造性的运用。我们研究莎士比亚最好能直接进入对象，这对正确理解他的思想和他所要传递的信息起决定性的作用。例如上引《李尔王》中，李尔诅咒长女次女"你们这些违反自然的母夜叉"，而现有的译文作："你们这两个不孝的妖妇"。又如李尔对埃德加说："倘若他没有违反天性的女儿，不可能使他自己的天性沦落到这个地步。"而现有的译文作："他没有不孝的女儿，怎么会流落到这等不堪的地步？"又如李尔呼号："听呀，大自然女神，听呀！"接着他吁请自然女神停止他的女儿生男育女的机能，因为她干的是违反天性的坏事。这里译文作"造化的女神"。

莎士比亚的大自然即人性的哲学思想，被译文的"不孝"这一封建伦理思想掩盖了。而"造化"无疑是很好的翻译，但终究从中仍看不出莎士比亚的哲学思想。译文常常阻碍我们准确全面地理解莎士比亚，而莎士比亚同十九世纪小说家不一样，他写的是诗，诗歌的语言比散文容纳思想感情的能力要高得多。最好是能直接进入对象。身入虎穴，方得虎子。正确理解，才能正确评说。

莎士比亚的人物性格往往是矛盾的，情节往往不可信，有时勉强，他的语言功夫，在早期喜剧和历史剧中或嫌造作，但后期作品，则运用自如，多所发明，进入了自由王国。他的语言随人物不同而变化，随人物情绪不同而变化。例如哈姆雷特说话喜欢重复，他对霍拉旭说真心话，语气诚挚；对罗森格兰兹二人先说真心话，迨发现他们是侦探，语调大变。他对波洛涅斯、国王、王后各不相同，有时嬉笑嘲弄，有时旁敲侧击，有时如怒目金刚。他对演员则和蔼亲切，单独一人则沉思痛苦。莎士比亚的许多文字脍炙人口，古人说："言之不文，行之不远。"例如《安东尼和克莉奥佩特拉》一剧中伊诺巴勃斯随安东尼回到罗马之后向好奇的罗马官员描述克莉奥佩特拉乘船游尼罗河的情景，彩色缤纷，香风四溢，把埃及皇后的豪华、逸乐、放荡，刻画得淋漓尽致。又如《麦克白斯》开始时，邓肯王同班柯到达麦克白斯的城堡，两人的一段很短的对话，描写了城堡的外观，其作用不过是代替布景，但莎士比亚突出了邓肯王的善良和毫无戒备，"一阵阵和风轻轻地吹拂着我的安详的五官"，而班柯在描写城堡上的燕巢时，把燕子称为"夏天的客人"，邓肯也是麦克白斯的客人，按照古老的传统，客人是应当受到主人的保护的。班柯还把燕巢称为"它所钟爱的府邸"，"天上的和风象求爱一般散发出芬芳"，"在这摇篮似的巢窠，它生息繁殖"，如此等等，莫不是一片生机和乐，安知城堡内却埋伏着杀机和死亡、凶残和罪恶。莎士比亚用暗含的对比烘托出"戏剧讽刺"。

以上不过是一两个例子。莎士比亚的语言艺术值得专门研究，这是他值得我们学习借鉴的一个重要方面。《文心雕龙》里有两句话，借来形容莎士比亚的语言颇为恰当："秘响旁通，伏采潜发"，"深文隐蔚，余味曲包"，而据刘勰分析，这里面的道理是："根盛而颖峻"，这是说得很对的。

（根据一次讲稿改写。原载《文艺论丛》第 8 辑，1979 年）

十九世纪以前西方莎评

——《莎士比亚评论汇编（上）》引言

　　莎士比亚评论是一门很有趣味的学问。我们从历代莎评不仅可以看到时代的变迁，各时代、各阶级、各种流派的批评标准，从而看出其文学趣味、文学风尚，更重要的是这些评家从不同时代、不同阶级、不同观点论述莎士比亚，或褒或贬，给我们今天提供了许多有意思的意见。莎士比亚处于一个特殊有利的地位，因为他是世界文学中被人们评论得最多的作家之一，从十七世纪一直到今天，三百多年没有间断。十九世纪以前的英、德、法、俄，古典主义者、浪漫派、现实主义者，纷然杂陈；进入二十世纪后，各种资产阶级批评流派更是五花八门，也可算是百家争鸣吧。十月革命前后，出现了试图用马克思主义观点重新估价莎士比亚的评论著作。以上种种评家，他们的观点我们不一定同意，但他们各抒所见，往往有精到之处，有合理的部分，可以供我们参考。这不仅对我们对莎士比亚作出比较全面的评价很有帮助，而且一般地说，对发展马克思主义文学评论，也应有所裨益。有些评论是颇为荒谬的，但这也可以从反面推动我们思考问题。不论是好的、比较好的、甚至不那么好的评论，都能开拓我们的眼界，启发我们的思考，作到兼听则明。

在莎士比亚还活着的时候，他的成就已经被他的同行所承认。本·琼生就称他为"时代的灵魂"，说他"不属于一个时代而属于所有的世纪"。即使象罗勃特·格林这样的剧作家，在他临死时虽警告同行要警惕那只"暴发户式的乌鸦，用我们的羽毛装扮他自己，在演员的皮下包藏着虎狼之心"，也从反面说明莎士比亚的成就，说明他是善于吸收并改进他人的长处的。由于时代太近，当时的评论不可能是深入细致的分析，但却也在大处指出了他的作品在当时所起的作用。

德莱登是十七世纪最重要的莎评家。莎士比亚死后二十六年，清教徒封闭剧院，同时开始了资产阶级革命。在此前后，莎评可以说是空白。弥尔顿在革命前也只写了一首纪念诗，只是泛泛赞美莎士比亚的诗句流畅感人；在《欢乐》一诗中称他为"最最温柔的莎士比亚"，富于幻想，他的诗是天籁。资产阶级掌权没有多久，封建复辟，宫廷中带来了法国文学趣味。德莱登的评论，所谓新古典主义（以区别于罗马奥古斯都时代的古典文学）评论，就是迎合从法国来的宫廷的趣味的。这一潮流支配了十七世纪末和十八世纪英国文学评论。德莱登是第一个严肃地系统地阐述新古典主义文学创作原则和批评标准的作者。他以希腊、罗马和法国戏剧同莎士比亚相比较，既承认莎士比亚伟大，又感到他的方法不令人满意；既表现了民族自豪感，又不想违反时髦的法国风尚；他认为莎士比亚的语言不规范，不合贵族的典雅的趣味。但是他肯定，莎士比亚悲剧的情节尽管破坏了三一律，却引起良好的效果。他特别肯定在塑造人物方面，尤其在描绘各种感情（他称为"激情"）方面，莎士比亚是个能手。如把德莱登同新古典主义狂热分子莱莫比较，则德莱登不仅开明，而且有见地。（莱莫称《奥瑟罗》为一出"手帕的悲剧"，做妻子的应从中得到教训，不可随意遗失衣物；是一出流血闹剧，毫无味道，云云。）

新古典主义莎评大致有这样两派：极端派和开明派。德莱登应属开明派。新古典主义第二位大师约翰孙也是属于这派，但理论内容有所不同。约翰孙提出理性和常识为批评标准，作品优劣要由时间来考验，在方法上他也强调比较。他比德莱登在更大程度上从新古典主义下解放出来。他认为莎士比亚是"自然的诗人"，他的作品是生活的镜子，他写的人物既有"共同人性"，"普遍人性"，又有个性。伏尔泰说莎士比亚把克劳迪斯国王写成酗酒之徒是不成体统，约翰孙反驳说，伏尔泰没有抓着克劳迪斯性格中的"普遍人性"。他认为莎剧中悲喜交错虽不合法则，但合乎生活，用常识、历史本身的发展，来为莎士比亚破坏三一律辩护。他批评莎士比亚的严重缺点在于缺少道德目的，不评是非。他这种思想是同稍前和当时流行的伸张市民道德的市民悲剧相一致的。这也是他不完全理解莎士比亚的地方。他又批评莎氏情节松散，使人不生快感，语言俚俗或华丽夸张，也说明他未能摆脱古典趣味。不过他强调莎氏善于观察、学习，是有说服力的。他指出莎剧的感染力来自它能引起观众的同情，这种从主观感受评定莎剧已肇浪漫派之端。

英国十八世纪后期出现了三个对人物性格专门进行分析的评论家。托马斯·惠特利（Thomas Whately，卒于 1772 年）在 1770 年前写了《关于莎士比亚某些人物的意见》；威廉·理查生（William Richardson，1743—1841）写了《对莎士比亚某些卓绝人物的哲学分析和说明》（1774）；莫尔根写了《论约翰·福斯塔夫爵士的戏剧性格》（1774）。惠特利是国会议员，他的文章没有写完，他明确指出批评的对象应是剧中的人物。他比较了麦克白与理查三世，指出这两个人物表面的结局尽管相同，但性格迥异，他的分析很有启发性。理查生则是格拉斯哥大学拉丁文教授，他的文章分析了麦克白、哈姆莱特、杰奎斯、伊摩琴，后来他又撰文分析了理查三世、李尔、泰门和福斯塔夫，他赞美莎士比亚擅长描绘各种激情，塑造各种各样的人物。莫尔根则是三人中最重要的一个，他之所以重要在于他提出了一个理论：对作品的正确评论来源于印象和感受，而不靠理性的分析。其次，他突出人物，把人物独立于剧情之外，开一代的风气。这种强调人物分析，探索人物的内心世界，强调观众或读者的主观感受，已具有浪漫主义的特征了。他们对加深对人物的理解起了推进作用。

浪漫派莎评在英国有三个主要代表：柯尔律治、赫士列特和兰姆。从浪漫派开始，英国莎评就失去了古典主义的平衡，形成了莎氏崇拜，不一分为二，直到二十世纪（艾略特可能是一个例外）。他们一味钩隐剔奥，诠释欣赏。其次，浪漫派一切从主观出发，强调感受。兰姆说，我们就是李尔王；赫士列特说，我们就是哈姆莱特；柯尔律治也说，我身上也有点哈姆莱特的味道，如果我可以这样说的话。他们强调要探索人物的内心世界。他们强调莎士比亚是诗人，兰姆由于不满于十八世纪以还舞台上对莎剧的歪曲，甚至认为莎剧不能上演，这种看法很普遍，歌德也有此见。

不过浪漫派也作出了极大的贡献。他们对人物性格和情感的分析鞭辟入里。赫士列特论莎剧人物的专著指出莎士比亚由于观察入微，想象力高，他的人物是真实的，在行动中有变化，特点多，可以称为"戏剧人物"。如果莎士比亚有缺点的话，那是才太高，情思太奔放的过失。

柯尔律治的莎评集中在两点：莎士比亚作为伟大的艺术家所创造的人物；莎士比亚作为诗人所创造的诗。他反驳古典主义者所说的莎剧不合规范和莎士比亚没有判断力（理性）的论点。柯尔律治说莎士比亚有他自己的规则，他的剧是天然形成的，是由内部必然性而形成的；他说古典主义的规则不等于有机的形式，作品的形式是由内因决定的。因此，柯尔律治从理论上肯定了莎剧的形式。他对莎剧的人物，除了认为他们合乎自然以外，还指出情节是为人物服务的，而故事又是为情节服务的，因而把莎剧中的纷纭现象集中到一点——人物上。他进而指出莎士比亚塑造人物性格，不是直接告诉读者，而是要读者自己去体会，往往是通过人物与人物的关系烘托出来。他也认为莎氏所创造的人物无比丰富，具有各种不同的性格、激情、行为、表现。

人们说浪漫派的莎评是英国最伟大的批评，它提高我们对莎剧的认识，刺激我们对莎剧的兴趣，帮助人们发现莎剧令人惊奇之处。它的缺点是主观、片面，突出一点，不及其余；是过火，道出莎氏原来不曾有的意思（二十世纪新批评派，也可叫语义派，往往陷入牵强附会，实导源于柯尔律治）。

德国对莎士比亚的注意是同狂飙突进运动分不开的。在反封建斗争中，德国作家、批评家发现莎氏是一个有力的同盟军。莱辛在写《汉堡剧评》的时候，他的目的是要建立一个德国民族戏剧，要从德国封建统治阶级所培植的法国古典趣味中解放出来，他转向古希腊和英国，发现莎士比亚可以作为德国戏剧作家的榜样。他认为莎剧真实地反映人生，合乎自然，因此违反古典主义规则没有关系。莱辛大力提倡现实主义，他的现实主义不在表面真实，而在"本质"上的真实，用以启蒙，教育人民。很有趣的是，莱辛不仅推崇莎士比亚，也推崇被英国浪漫派所否定的李娄，并模仿李娄的"市民悲剧"写了《莎拉·辛普森小姐》。（席勒的《阴谋与爱情》也属此类。）

赫尔德对莎评的贡献在于分析莎士比亚创造戏剧的历史环境，这种环境同希腊人的环境不同，因而不能强求莎士比亚写出希腊悲剧，但莎氏的悲剧却完全符合亚理士多德的要求。

歌德对莎士比亚没有系统的论述。他也要求戏剧从三一律的束缚中解放出来，而在莎剧中得到了启发。他惊异于莎士比亚把政治历史大事搬上舞台；他认为莎剧反映了自然，创造了活生生的人物，就象普罗米修斯创造人类一样，进而对莎剧人物进行了分析。有一点特别值得注意，歌德认为哈姆莱特实际上是作者自抒理想，正因为莎士比亚自己对生活有丰富而深切的感受，才能说出人物内心的多方面的感受，这样就指出了客观现实同作家头脑之间的联系，不是把人物看成孤立的客观存在，或是客观现实的直接反映，而是看成客观现实在作家头脑中的反映的产物。歌德进而指出莎剧之所以真实还在于他写出了生活中的矛盾，因此富于戏剧性。作为诗人，他的语言功夫极高，比在舞台上通过感官所见所闻，更能打动人的内心。

史雷格尔同柯尔律治有异曲同工之妙。作为德国浪漫派的代表，他也强调人物内心活动。他认为莎士比亚的悲剧都有内部联系，形成整体。以哈姆莱特为例，他的内心就是各种矛盾的集结点，他代表了"人类心灵"和命运的矛盾，在恶的世界中，理智走向了绝望。因而史雷格尔给莎氏悲剧起了一个名字——"哲理悲剧"。他对英国浪漫派批评影响极大。

法国是欧洲古典主义的故乡。古典主义莎评的代表人物当然是伏尔泰，他成了浪漫派一致攻击的靶子。其实，伏尔泰也很冤枉，他无非从古典主义高雅趣味批评了莎剧的方法不合规范。伏尔泰用的词有些过火（"粗俗野蛮"，"烂醉的野蛮人"等等），但他也有欣赏莎氏的一面，认为莎剧中有新东西，他从启蒙者的立场肯定了莎剧的思想内容，他自己还翻译介绍了莎剧的片段。

斯达尔夫人和夏多布里昂从不同立场反映了法国浪漫派的一些

侧面。斯达尔夫人认为法国文学要从古典主义中解放出来，必须以北方人即英国人和德国人为师，具体说，就是莎士比亚和席勒。她欣赏莎剧中的各种激情的描写，不受程式的限制，自由表现，故而真实。夏多布里昂也欣赏莎剧中激情和思绪的描写，但从反动政治立场，认为莎剧所描写的恐怖正是雅各宾专政下的恐怖。他一方面认为莎氏语言造作，创作没有法则，缺乏"趣味"，但又赞赏莎氏擅长悲喜对比，相互交错。

斯汤达的贡献在于他提出了舞台假象说。他说舞台剧需要观众善于想象，剧情所占时间与演出所占时间是不可能相同的，需要观众去想象。莎剧最富于完美的假象。这样就把三一律的时间整一律否定掉了。斯汤达区别史诗的快感和戏剧的快感，前者来自诗句的华丽，后者来自动作。如果只注意莎剧的诗句，就妨碍假象。这一点同浪漫派正好针锋相对，而斯汤达所说的浪漫主义其实是现实主义。

十九世纪俄国莎评正是突出莎士比亚的现实主义，这是同革命民主主义者反沙皇专制的斗争分不开的。最早的普希金提到莎士比亚的悲剧写了人民的命运。

俄国评论家分析莎剧往往十分深刻。别林斯基把莎士比亚看作是他提倡现实主义的得力助手和同盟。莎氏的现实主义首先体现在人物塑造上。别林斯基认为莎氏同席勒不一样，莎氏的人物是活生生的形象，不是抽象思维的产物，但这并不是说莎氏没有理想，相反他认为莎士比亚比席勒更有理想。他认为莎氏能从个别中看到普遍，从形象中体现思想，达到内容与形式的完全一致。

别林斯基不仅提出莎士比亚善于把正剧、喜剧、悲剧、神话剧溶为一体，他在分析莎氏的悲剧时提出了悲剧只能建在必然性上，不能建在偶然性上这一重要观点。莎氏的悲剧如苔丝狄蒙娜之死正是如此。他提出悲剧的一般特点是写人的欲望与道德责任或障碍之间的矛盾，而矛盾体现在主要人物身上，如哈姆莱特。他对喜剧的分析也极精辟，他认为喜剧有两种，一种写欢笑，一种写嘲讽，两者都是生活现象与生活实质之间的矛盾所引起的。

赫尔岑虽无专论莎剧的著作，但也提出一些值得参考的看法。俄国评论家的一个好传统就是联系社会来考察文学。赫尔岑对莎氏悲剧的产生就联系到当时的时代缺乏信仰（是否正确可以商讨），诗人没有安身立命的支柱，因而绝望、诅咒，因而莎氏写内心的痛苦极为擅长。

车尔尼雪夫斯基也主张悲剧是人物与命运的矛盾，他接受亚理士多德的说法，悲剧人物之结局是由于他那方面的过失或弱点。他也认为悲剧的基础是必然性，如果矛盾可以避免，也就无所谓悲剧。不过他进而指出悲剧之崇高在于它表现了人物的坚强性格，在顽强斗争之后必然失败，正反映了黑暗势力之强大，而莎剧的特点正在此，他举了苔丝狄蒙娜、奥菲利娅为例。

车尔尼雪夫斯基善于分析矛盾。他在论《裘力斯·凯撒》时，不是机械地把双方看成是简单的矛盾冲突，而是各有是非，因而矛盾会发生变化。他的分析极为生动，富于辩证思想。

杜勃罗留波夫赞赏莎士比亚作为艺术家比哲学家所揭示的真理还多，发现了人的心灵，道出了人们所仅仅意识到的东西，除此之外，他对李尔王的具体分析颇能一语中的——李尔的权力地位使他失去自知之明，使他自我崇拜。可惜他分析下去，就陷入了人性论。

屠格涅夫并不理解莎士比亚，他说哈姆莱特是自我中心的利己主义者，是对群众无用之人，并不爱奥菲利娅，而是个好色之徒，他同靡菲斯特一样代表"否定精神"等等。他也提出哈姆莱特有狡诈残酷的一面。他的错误在于主观地把哈姆莱特联系到俄国当时现实中的"多余人"，把他们的特点硬套到哈姆莱特的身上。

不正确地联系现实，不正确地理解现实主义所导致的荒谬结果，伟大的托尔斯泰体现得最突出。托尔斯泰也可说是不理解莎士比亚的，他认为莎剧中的矛盾不是出于人物性格和事件的自然进程，而是作者任意安排的，唤不起观众同情。他根据现实生活判断李尔王没有理由退位，没有理由认不出肯特，艾德伽领着父亲去跳崖使人不能相信；李尔王生于公元前八百年，而登场人物则是中世纪的，既不真实，也唤不起人们的兴趣。《奥瑟罗》一剧也是如此，而使人们盲目崇拜到催眠状态的哈姆莱特是个没有性格的人，说的全是莎士比亚安排他说的话。凡是莎氏的改作统统不及原作。他的结论是莎士比亚不会塑造人物，不是艺术家。这正是狭隘地理解现实主义可能产生的结论。

不过从托尔斯泰的反对言论中，也可以看出莎氏的一些缺点。托尔斯泰说得对，莎氏的人物是他的传声筒；有些人物如伊阿古，他说写得太坏，因而不真实，也是有道理的。这对我们如何理解典型性很有启发，坏人就单纯是坏，好人就单纯是好，写过了头，是否还真实？很值得研究。

二十世纪莎评

——《莎士比亚评论汇编（下）》引言

　　二十世纪的西方莎评可以说是当代西方文学批评的一张缩影。传统的批评方法继续被用来研究莎作，而且日益深入；各种新的方法也无不以莎氏为试金石来证明自己的成效。不论传统的方法或新的方法流派都有足资借鉴的地方。

　　二十世纪西方莎评从莎评史本身来看是十九世纪的展发，而十九世纪又是十七、十八世纪的展发。十七、十八世纪的评论家出于古典主义趣味，对莎氏不无微辞。但到了十九世纪，莎氏一变而成为偶象。偶象有两个方面：一方面是人们盲目崇拜他；另一方面也是人们发现了莎氏之伟大，对莎氏的思想、艺术，不仅有进一步的认识，而且有很深刻的认识。二十世纪，在十八、十九世纪的基础上大大发展，出现了百花齐放、百家争鸣的局面，评论数量之多，范围之广，实为空前。

　　早在十九世纪就成立了专门学会，如"莎士比亚协会"（Shakespeare Society），"新莎士比亚协会"（New Shakespeare Society）。到了二十世纪，英、德、美和其他国家都成立了专门学会；各种专门图书馆也在英、美各国建立；而专门刊物，英、美、德各国都办了起来，有的国家不止一种。至于专著，直是汗牛充栋，而散出的论文更是浩如烟海。这些著作和文章对莎氏的生平、文化教养、哲学思想、时代背景、时代思潮、艺术师承、舞台、语言各方面的研究，恐怕很少有哪个作家有这样多的人来进行这样多方面的研究的。甚至莎评本身的发展史也成为研究对象。至于舞台演出，可谓无日不有。

二十世纪莎评已经成了一种"企业"。其所以兴盛，一个重要原因是一些学科、学说、方法如心理学、人类学、社会学、语言学、美学、比较文学的空前发展，这些提供了许多新的角度。试图用马克思主义评价莎作的著作也在二三十年代初露头角。此外，有些流行一时的资产阶级哲学思潮如存在主义对莎评也发生过分散的、不同程度的影响。

不过在没有谈论莎评本身之前，应先谈谈二十世纪西方学者在"基础研究"方面所进行的大量工作。

校订学是一切评论的基础。十八世纪的校勘虽也有精当之处，但往往以臆测代替考证，把校订者自己的揣测强加给作者。十九世纪校雠家吸收了十八世纪的成果，更趋于严谨、"科学"，如《新刊各家集注莎氏剧》（The New Variorum）、《寰球本莎氏全集》（The Globe edition）。到了二十世纪，精采的版本更多，其中重要的有《耶鲁本》（Yale）、《新阿登本》（New Arden）、《新剑桥本》（New Cambridge）以及一卷本《河畔本》（Riverside）等等。校订家研究十六、十七世纪流行的各种四开本以及各对开本的依据，判断它们是从作者手稿，还是从传抄本，还是从演员台词本而排印的；研究现存各种版本之间的关系；研究当时排印操作过程等，以求得到最接近莎氏原作的一个版本。有时研究者争论不休，不能作出定论；已有定论的，又受到怀疑。哈姆莱特的第一个独白"但愿这一太太坚实的肉体会溶解、消散，化成一堆露水"，原文"坚实的"solid，已为一般校订家所接受，但迄今也还有人宁愿选择"玷污的"sullied，并举出许多理由。即使校勘没有争论，早先的注解又被推翻，如哈姆莱特骂波洛涅斯为"鱼贩子"，一向被理解为"老鸨"，但近人考证应作"不老实的人"来理解。以上两例虽然都是一字之差，但都关系到对人物心理状态和性格的理解，足见考证、注释决非雕虫末技。

对莎士比亚时代的社会政治生活方面的研究，西方学者作了大量的、系统的工作，使研究者对那个时代有一个很具体、生动、细致、全面的认识。这里功劳最大的应属哈里森（G. B. Harrison）。哈里森把有关莎士比亚时代英国政治社会生活各方面的原始材料从 1591 迄 1603 年尽可能逐日集成《伊丽莎白朝日志》三巨册（*Elizabethan Journals*, 1628—1933）；又从 1603 迄 1610 年集成《詹姆斯朝日志》两册（*Jacobean Journals*，1941—1958）。罗利（W. Raleigh）在哈里森之前也编了《莎士比亚的英国——生活与风俗记述》（*Shakespeare's England: An Account of the Life and Manners of his Age*，1916，1926）。这类著作还有很多，它们虽然只注重具体的历史、政治、社会事件、琐碎的日常生活和风俗习惯，但通过它们研究者可以获得不少感性认识，如身临其境，有助于对莎剧的理解。

二十世纪对作家生平的研究也有很大的进展，除一般的评传之外，钱伯斯（E. K. Chambers）的《威廉·莎士比亚——事实与问题的研究》（*William Shakespeare: A Study of Facts and Problems*，1930）两卷，把有关莎氏生平和著作、舞台、同时代人对他的看法以及后代的传说等材料搜罗详备，成为一部权威性的不可缺少的参考书。此外如舍恩包姆的《简明文献传记》（S. Schoenbaum: *A Compact Documentary Life*，1977），本特利的《传记手册》（G. E. Bentley：*Shakespeare：A Biographical Handbook*，1961），都作了重要的补充。

此外，关于当时舞台、舞台的传统、剧团的组织、演出、设施等方面的研究（如钱伯斯的《伊丽莎白朝舞台》*The Elizabethan Stage*，1923，四卷）；有关莎作中故事的渊源的研究；有关作品中某些具体方面如法律、宗教信仰、莎氏的文化教育、医学知识、对农村生活的体验，以至关于鸟兽虫鱼的知识等方面的研究，都为研究者提供了不少背景知识，促进了研究的兴趣。

　　以上著作都可以称之为基础研究，很少涉及评论本身。当然，莎氏传记则不得不对莎氏作品有所评述。事实上，关于莎氏生平的资料本来不多，传记作者只能把大部分篇幅根据自己主观见解用在评论作品上，仁者见仁，智者见智。历史学家劳斯（A. L. Rowse）1963年写的《威廉·莎士比亚》就从历史学者的角度写莎氏的生平和创作。不过这些传记中的评论仍属于所谓"传统的莎评"范围，并没有标新立异。

　　所谓"传统的"批评方法，包括从版本、文字训诂角度研究莎作，从历史或作者生活经历来解释作品，或从思想内容来论述莎剧。

　　传统的莎评在二十世纪仍有长足进展，而且在数量上也是领先的。本世纪初，布拉德雷（A. C. Bradley）的《莎士比亚悲剧》（*Shakespearean Tragedy*，1904）标志着从柯尔津治以来"浪漫派"莎评的顶峰。在这一系列演讲中，他在黑格尔客观唯心主义影响下（以克罗齐为代表）着力于深入分析人物和矛盾斗争，二十世纪西方莎评莫不受他影响。不过，他的人物分析往往脱离作者主观意图和作品的中心思想，尤其脱离历史现实，为分析人物而分析人物，引起评论界的异议，因而从二十年代开始出现了所谓"历史—现实派"的莎评。[1]

---

[1] 这一派既反对把莎士比亚"浪漫"化，也反对把他"维多利亚"化，后者如道顿（E. Dowden）用维多利亚时代的温情主义理解莎剧，如把其中的女主人公说成是温柔、纯洁的象征等。

"历史—现实派"仍然属于"传统莎评"的范畴。它的主要出发点是：把莎剧同莎氏生活联系起来看，把莎剧放到当时的历史现实环境中考察，放到当时的戏剧传统、舞台结构、演员的特点、演出技巧、观众的结构、当时的风俗习惯以及各种流行的思想，一句话，放在"客观现实"之中来考察。在研究莎氏其人时，多根据有限的资料，推论其为人，设想他的生活和工作条件、家庭关系、交游、阅历、学识以至宗教信仰，如哈里森的《莎士比亚在工作》（*Shakespeare at Work*，1922），勃朗（Ivor Brown）的《莎士比亚一天中的经历》（*How Shakespeare Spent His Day*，1963）。至于莎剧是培根所作之说，是很难成立的。

这一派的评论包括的方面极广，一直是莎评的主力，颇能加深读者和观众对莎剧的理解。这派评家虽然总的倾向是一致的，但侧重不一。这派主要代表人物，德国人许金（L. L. Schücking）和美国人斯托尔（E. E. Stoll）都从舞台和戏剧传统出发来分析莎剧，所不同者，许金侧重舞台和传统对人物的影响，而斯托尔侧重舞台和传统对全剧的效果。许金认为当时舞台传统中的独白技巧使人物可以向观众自我表白，这样来表现人物性格，例如通过这种技巧就能显示出哈姆莱特性格中自我谴责的内向特点。他又从观众的接受能力来解释人物的塑造，例如他说《凯撒》中的勃鲁托斯，哈姆莱特父亲的亡魂，在自我刻划时都近于自我夸耀，就是怕观众对"人物的主要轮廓发生误解"。他也强调要抓住作者意图，但他主要注意的是客观条件对舞台人物形象的影响。他认为用"现实主义"[1] 的标准衡量莎剧人物往往走不通。

---

[1] 布拉德雷继承了十九世纪浪漫派的衣钵，用客观唯心主义，脱离时空来分析矛盾和性格，故称为"浪漫派"。但他具体分析人物情节时，又脱离舞台传统和技巧，把人物情节按现实生活的似与不似来衡量，即许金这派所谓的"现实主义"。

同样，斯托尔也反对象布拉德雷那样把莎剧当作真人真事的重现。例如，他认为对喜剧应当了解当时人的喜剧概念，人们必须承认一些假设，如误认、伪装，才能进入喜剧世界，引起喜剧效果。"我们如果同浪漫主义批评家一样，考虑到福斯塔夫少年时如何充满希望，老年时又如何落魄失望，或把他的缺德行为看作是假装的，他就不成其为可笑的人物了。"

这一派的一个重要评论家是格兰威尔-巴克（H. Granville-Barker）。他本人是演员、导演、剧作家，有丰富的实际舞台经验。他为一系列莎剧写了《序》，这些《序》既有助于演出，也是文学批评。巴克从反对浪漫派兰姆和布拉德雷开始。后二者都把莎剧看成是"诗"（书斋读物），而巴克的大前提则是莎氏是为演出而写作的。演员有好有坏，不能因为演得不好而否定演出。象斯丹尼斯拉夫斯基一样，巴克主张演员要进入角色，忘掉自己，进入"诗"的境界。莎氏作为有经验的剧作家，十分注意戏剧效果。这就牵涉到舞台的物质条件、演技和观众的接受能力。这些"技术"问题不解决，其他问题的探讨（如思想内容）就会迷失方向。

巴克阐明了莎氏如何利用没有布景的空台，自由地运用时间和地点；利用传统的独白刻划人物（莎剧中哈姆莱特的独白最多）；如何利用传统的舞台技巧来安排情节的进展。巴克就是这样从外在条件和戏剧效果的角度来考察莎氏的创作过程，分析人物及其行动，人物的发展，人物之间的关系，以至剧本的思想内容。巴克的评论是行家的评论，无怪多佛·威尔逊称他的评论是划时代的（巴克本人又自称受益于威尔逊）。巴克提供了理解莎剧的一个新的角度，缺点和布拉德雷一样是不联系历史实际。

巴克从舞台实践分析莎氏创作过程，另一类分析莎氏创作过程的研究则侧重莎氏如何改造旧素材，用以说明作者意图和人物情节。例如，罗伯逊（J. M. Robertson）认为莎剧有许多不可理解的特点，如哈姆莱特的一再拖延，其答案应从莎氏创作时所依据的、失传的老本《哈姆莱特》里去找。莎氏要把一个原来粗野的故事套在一个高度敏感的哈姆莱特身上，自然会引起性格上的不协调。

多佛·威尔逊是"历史—现实派"的大师。他既从事版本考订，也从事时代背景的研究和作者生平的研究以及舞台研究。作为评论家，他也是从不同意布拉德雷开始，结合戏剧传统，来分析莎剧的人物情节。在他的名著《福斯塔夫的命运》一书中，他认为《亨利四世》是中古道德剧的发展，福斯塔夫不是象布拉德雷所肯定的那样，而是个中世纪道德剧中代表放荡骚乱的反派角色的后裔。对这个人物应当回到古典主义评论家约翰逊的"不偏不倚"的评论。

"历史—现实派"另一支派以哈里森为代表。哈里森除搜集了十六、十七世纪之际的历史社会材料之外，在评论中也是把莎剧同当时的具体的历史政治事件联系起来。例如他认为在《约翰王》里就反映出西班牙无敌舰队的威胁；1595年又是女王七九六十三岁，当时迷信，人生七年一个关口，六十三正是第九个关口；英法关系恶化。又如艾塞克斯党人在叛乱前夕上演《理查二世》，女王大怒，对人说："你不知道么，理查二世就是我。"这类对莎剧的诠释，恐怕不能简单地称为"影射"。"影射"似乎削弱了作品的"现实主义典型意义"，其实这类诠释并不妨碍作品的"典型性"，相反，它有助于深入理解作品。不能设想象莎士比亚这样的有思考的作家，对当时的重大政治事件置若罔闻，相反，恐怕连身边最微细的琐事也没有逃出他的注意。一个作家怎样感受时代的脉搏？还不是通过无数的大大小小的具体事件？在这感性的基础上，他形成意见、概念，找出规律。因此莎氏剧中有当时人物和事件的痕迹是很可能的，也是必然的。

用传统方法评论莎剧的另一流派着重探索莎氏的世界观和哲学思想，作出了很大贡献，代表人物有蒂里亚德和丹比，前者的《伊丽莎白朝的世界图象》，后者的《莎士比亚的自然观》，公认是标准著作。

　　蒂里亚德（E. M. W. Tillyard）从研究莎氏历史剧开始，发现莎氏剧中所描写的政治上的紊乱是以理想中的政治上的"秩序"为对照的，而政治上的"秩序"又是整个宇宙秩序的一个组成部分。他根据丰富的材料——天文学的、医学的、哲学的——得出结论，这种宇宙秩序的观念则是从中世纪继承下来的，并以莎剧和当时其他作家的作品相互印证。蒂里亚德的优点在于使人们认识到莎氏世界观、历史观中的继承的一面，而这一面常是我们所忽略的。

　　丹比（J. F. Danby）的论点形成于他对《李尔王》的研究过程中。他认为《李尔王》的形式是道德剧，通过剧中人物表达两种自然观，亦即人性观。他联系到当时哲学思想的代表人物，探索莎氏思想的渊源，例如当时流行的书籍和思潮，莎氏接触的人物，认为《李尔王》中两种不同的自然观，一种以培根、胡克为代表，是旧的、中世纪的自然观，自然代表善；一种以霍布斯为代表，是新的、资产阶级的自然观，自然代表恶，这后者反映在人性上就是极端利己主义。丹比认为莎氏是同情旧的，基本上反对新的，但也看中新哲学中所提出的平等要求。如果把莎士比亚的思想比做一只上锁的柜子，蒂里亚德和丹比不啻为我们提供了两把钥匙。

　　二十世纪西方莎学学者有一个很普遍的特点，就是把莎氏同旧传统联系起来，很少把莎氏当做一个新时代的代表，这当然是片面的。但若只看莎氏新的一面，忽视继承的一面，也同样是片面的，因为莎氏生活在一个新旧交替的时代，有人文主义新思潮，但旧思想的势力更加强大。同时，我们也不能忽视，新旧思想也并非泾渭分明，截然对立的。

考格希尔（Nevill Coghill）评论莎氏喜剧也是倾向于联系中世纪。他认为莎氏喜剧的特点与琼生不同，琼生的喜剧是从希腊罗马引进的新喜剧，其性质是讽刺的，而莎氏喜剧的特点是浪漫的，是中古传奇的继续，但比之中古传奇、莎氏的人物、情节、语言大大超过前人。在考格希尔之前，恰尔登（H. B. Charlton）也持这一观点，他也认为"浪漫"喜剧是从中古传奇脱胎而来，它歌颂爱情，富于幻想，为当时观众所喜爱。

在莎学学者中还有一种思想存在，即不可知论。例如斯图厄特（J. I. M. Stewart），他在总结了六十年代以前各批评流派的得失的基础上，提出莎氏在剧中并没有提出正面的道德观，似乎莎氏没有是非观念，认为剧中人物的言论不能代表莎氏的思想，莎士比亚仅仅是客观地、如实地反映人们的道德面貌。他认为读者或观众对人物的评价可以仁者见仁，各取所需，采取折衷主义态度。这种机械的"反映论"忽略作者的主观意图，显然也是片面的。

用比较文学的方法研究莎剧也是很普遍的。[1] 大批评家艾略特（T. S. Eliot）研究莎士比亚悲剧中的影响，指出他采用了塞内加悲剧中表现的"坚忍"态度，为人物刻划和戏剧效果服务，指出塞内加对莎氏的影响不在思想内容而在创作技巧。这种看法颇为别致。

西方莎评所谓方法上的流派区分并不严格，只是各有其主导的一面，特别进入六十年代，更是相互吸收，参杂运用，特别是各种"传统派"莎评，有些基本观点竟是相同的。例如后起的有影响的

---

[1] 比较方法的一个突出的侧面是研究莎士比亚所受的影响，如哲学思想方面受法国蒙田（Montaigne）的影响，技巧方面受罗马塞内加悲剧的影响等，往往能说明问题。二十世纪最早的著作有罗伯逊（J. M. Robertson）的《蒙田与莎士比亚》（1909，第一版1897）。

评家奈茨（L. C. Knights）早在 1946 年就反对布拉德雷的人物性格分析法，写了《麦克白夫人有多少孩子？》的论文；他也反对"历史学派"从戏剧传统的观点或从时事政治角度分析莎剧；也反对探讨莎剧的哲学思想。他主张要研究莎剧的"诗"，探讨莎氏如何通过语言技巧在读者意识中产生复杂的感情反应、疑问、深思。实际上，他仍然不免要分析思想，未脱浪漫派和历史派的窠臼，不过他不称为"思想"而称为"主题"（关于"主题派"见下）。如他认为《麦克白》一剧是"恶的陈述"，主题是"价值的颠倒"，"违反自然而引起的混乱"。他综合了六十年来莎评的一些论点，对《李尔王》作了全面分析，并无标新立异之处，仍是通过人物分析阐明剧本的思想。他主张分析"诗"，实际上是受了"语义派"（见下）的影响。

三十年代作为对布拉德雷和历史现实派的一个反作用，出现了所谓"意象—象征—语义"派莎评，形成了"传统派"批评方法以外的新的批评流派。在心理学的影响下，人们对人的意识发生兴趣，文学使用的语言如何作用于人的意识成为人们研究的问题。理查兹（I. A. Richards）1924 年出版《文学批评原理》，1929 年出版《实用批评》便是**信号**。这派批评完全从形式入手，从艺术表现入手，完全不顾作者和作品产生的历史社会生活。他们不是不知道产生作品的时代背景，而是反对那种不谈作品本身、大谈文学以外种种事物的倾向。他们要把读者的注意力引到作品上来，强调作品是文学。只是他们有些矫枉过正，而且他们的方法被一些人滥用。这一派的"缺点"正是它的优点，因为没有形式，谈不上内容，内容只能通过形式掌握。脱离形式空谈内容必然陷入公式化或主观主义。这派方法如在唯物主义观点指导下运用，应当能获得更令人满意的成果。

诗人布伦顿（Edmund Blunden）首先从语言文字入手，分析莎剧的深层涵义。例如他发现李尔王表面上语无伦次的疯话背后有一条连贯的线索，这条线索反映了李尔的一个牢固的思想，从这思想可以看出李尔的性格。

不过，意象派的开山鼻祖、影响最大的莎评家要算斯珀津（Caroline Spurgeon）。可能在象征派诗歌的影响下，她研究了莎剧语言中的意象，作成卡片，分类，发现莎剧，尤其悲剧，每部都有一个或一个以上的主导意象。她认为这种意象的出现绝非偶然，而是同作者创作剧本时的主导思想密切联系着的。例如她指出在《罗密欧与朱丽叶》中一个反复出现的主导意象是光，表现为太阳、月亮、繁星、电、火药爆炸时的闪光，"构成了一幅一瞬间光采夺目的鲜明图画和气氛，有力地影响着读者的想象。"爱情是光明的，但也是瞬息的光明，因此是悲剧。

斯珀津的方法可以使人窥见莎氏创作过程，窥见莎氏的形象思维的方式，使莎剧的主题思想同艺术形式，有机地、令人信服地结合起来。此后的莎评都或多或少受到她的启示，接受她的方法，并有所发展。

莎评的"语义分析"派在大西洋两岸到四五十年代达到了高峰。美国"新批评派"的布鲁克斯（Cleanth Brooks），英国的里维斯（F. R. Leavis）可以代表。他们都在斯珀津的启示下，取得了进一步的发展。他们分析字义、比喻、联想、典故、象征、意象，来阐明人物的内心活动、全剧的思想意义以及作者的写作技巧。布鲁克斯分析了《麦克白》中赤裸的婴儿和雄伟的外衣这两个意象，分析它们的象征意义，细致入微。他认为这两个突兀的意象是同"全剧结构"发生关系的，同人物的伪装善良的形象，他的恐惧和他的失败的命运，密切相关的。

里维斯则认为用写实的观点或用"情理"的观点去解释莎剧，往往解释不通，看不出每出莎剧的完整性，但"主题借助意象和象征而发展，而意象和象征又影响我们理解剧中人物性格、情节和结构"，"我们不能擅自假定莎剧的组织如何"。里维斯举《冬天的故事》为例，指出评论家多认为里昂提斯的嫉妒毫无理由，不真实，但里维斯认为莎氏的目的不在刻划性格，而是通过意象、象征、节奏、插曲，表现"生—老—死—生"这一主题的。这种用"主题"分析文学作品是同人类学的发展联系着的。

人类学同心理学一样，都对人的行为动机发生兴趣。心理学从生物学角度主要研究个人行为（见下），而人类学则研究集团，如民族的行为，并把行为同这个集团的文化和宗教联系考察。个人的潜意识以梦的形式表现，一个民族的希望、恐惧或价值观念则用神话的形象得到象征性的表现。例如日、火、天，在西方和东方许多民族都象征创造力、父道、智慧，落日象征死亡，黑色象征混沌、恶，圆象征完整、统一等等。围绕这些象征产生了许多神话或"主题"，例如为了安抚神怒，就必须作一次或作定期的祭献（我国也有河伯娶妇的传说），文学中就产生"牺牲"主题。这种观点和方法当然也应用到莎评上，把莎剧同宗教和原始神话进行比较研究。例如神话中有"生—死—再生"循环不已的主题。这是正常的发展过程。这个正常过程有时遭到破坏，如疾病、瘟疫破坏了它，就必须补救纠正，必须献出牺牲。《哈姆莱特》正反映这过程。丹麦有了病（克劳狄斯杀死兄王），哈姆莱特作为原始神话中拯救氏族的英雄，生活在疾病的环境中，受到影响，不愿担任这个角色，但最后仍不得不牺牲自己，丹麦才得到再生。

威尔逊·奈特（G. Wilson Knight）可以算这一派的代表，不过他分析《哈姆莱特》的角度与上述例子有所不同。他也反对按故事发展、情节来源、作者意图、人物性格这种传统的方法分析莎剧。他也主张从静止、平面、"空间"角度分析,即从"主题"或"象征"出发,即亚理士多德的"思想的一律",来分析作品。他指出莎氏悲剧一般都有三个主要人物,分别代表崇高的人类、善和恶,三者都是具有普遍意义的象征。这些象征代表一些哲学原则和生活态度,如爱、恨世。上述三个原则有着错综复杂的关系,相互冲突,相互转化。哈姆莱特之所以使人迷惑不解,使人永远对他发生兴趣,就是因为他既是爱的原则,又是恨的原则,"既是正面人物,又是反面人物","又是崇高的人类",他反映了莎氏"整个的心灵"。

奈特还用暴风雨和音乐这两个带有普遍意义的象征分析《威尼斯商人》。暴风雨象征冲突、恨,音乐象征和谐、爱。奈特特别强调象征的多种涵义和联想,例如海既象征灾难也象征财富。他认为象征象一条红线贯串莎作的全部,使全部作品呵成一气。

奈特这派评论虽然有形式主义之病,抽象,显得神秘,但它并不排除人物的个性化,不排斥作品的心理和伦理因素,却勾出象征来,从中看出作品的思想构图或图案,对作品的理解,不无帮助。

同样在人类学的影响下,奈特把莎剧,特别是悲剧,同宗教类比,认为其中的祭献、牺牲观念突出,因此在演出时应带有宗教仪式或程式化的风格。希腊文学教授基托(H. D. F. Kitto)在批评了历史派、心理派以及多佛·威尔逊的不可知论之后,也提出莎氏悲剧如《哈姆莱特》是一出宗教剧。基托不谈象征,而把《哈姆莱特》同希腊悲剧类比,指出其中天意或命运操纵一切,并进而探讨罪恶观念。但在这问题上,《哈姆莱特》同希腊悲剧有所不同,希腊悲剧只处理个别罪恶及报应,而《哈姆莱特》则强调罪恶的性质和影响。

传统派莎评方法很少涉及形式、艺术性、语言；意象派和神话象征派几乎不涉及历史社会和作家个人经历；心理派实际上也不涉及历史社会客观环境，可以说是意象派和神话派的补充。事实上这些方法也常被评论家混合使用。

弗洛依德心理学的核心是"里比多"（Libido，欲，主要指性欲），里比多受到自我（意识）和超自我（社会伦理道德、舆论、法律等）的压抑，成为"潜意识"，"潜意识"表现为各种变态心理或"情结"（Complex），如犯罪心理、自卑心理、俄底浦斯情结。弗洛依德原是依据这一理论来医疗精神病患者，是一种尝试。但他本人和以后的文学评论家把这理论应用到文学评论，其结果总的说来至少是说服力不够，往往牵强，以至悖谬。

这类莎评最著名的例子是琼斯（Ernest Jones）。琼斯 1910 年发表《用俄底浦斯情结解释哈姆莱特之谜》，认为哈姆莱特之所以仇恨克劳狄斯是因为后者所作所为——杀死哈姆莱特的父亲，娶了他的母亲——正是哈姆莱特自己潜意识里所想做的，但他又无力去反对对手克劳狄斯，因为他受着"犯罪心理"的限制，同时，杀死克劳狄斯就等于自杀，因为克劳狄斯代表他所希望作到的一切。俄底浦斯情结还促使哈姆莱特憎恨其他女性（奥菲利娅），如此等等。

这派在分析《威尼斯商人》时，指出安东尼奥在开场时表现的忧郁是同性爱的反映，因为巴萨尼奥要结婚了。

从以上两例可以见出心理分析可以发展到荒谬的地步，即在西方也遭到不同程度的否定。不过心理学派之所以失败是由于在一切心理状态中只突出变态心理，但我们不能因此而否定对作品中人物的一般心理的分析。

从二三十年代起，国外的马克思主义莎评渐次开始。苏联在这方面进行的工作最多，开创了马克思主义莎评，英、美、东欧次之。这类莎评虽都企图用马克思主义的观点和方法分析，但侧重不同，情况复杂。苏联莎评家以莫洛佐夫（Морозов）、斯米尔诺夫（А. А. Смирнов）、阿尼克斯特（А. Аникст）、克缅诺夫（В. Кеменов）等为代表，他们的观点是我们所熟悉的。其主要特点是：1）力图贯彻唯物主义观点，把莎作放到历史发展和阶级斗争中去考察；2）强调莎作的历史进步意义，反对把他同中世纪意识形态和艺术方法联系起来看；3）强调莎氏之人民性；4）与以上诸特点相联系，强调莎氏的乐观主义；5）强调莎氏的现实主义。以上的方向应当说基本上是正确的，但往往缺乏辩证观点。强调革新，忽视继承，不承认莎氏无论在"道"或"文"上与中世纪有继承关系。在人民性的模糊观念下，为莎氏文过饰非，莎氏虽有赞美个别劳动者的地方，但明明也有藐视、害怕劳动者和劳动群众的地方，但苏联学者多避而不谈，相反，他们有不适当地拔高莎氏的思想意识的倾向。帝王将相的品德在他们笔下也说成是非帝王将相所独有。莎氏在写悲剧时明明已堕入悲观的深渊，他们必定要说并不悲观。这种一味肯定，同传统的浪漫派莎评如出一辙。他们强调现实主义也有片面或表面性，突出人物形象的"典型意义"，忽略人物是莎氏思想的传声筒，忽视莎氏的主观意图的一面。而且分析的公式化，使读者很难看到评者的主观感受和个人的看法。

英、美诸国的马克思主义莎评也开创了一个新的方向，打破了二三百年资产阶级莎评的垄断局面，但成就也是不平衡的，并或多或少受到非马克思主义评论的影响。最早的英国马克思主义评论家之一，柯德维尔（C. Caudwell）虽没有专门研究莎氏的著作，但在他的《幻想与现实》一书中，从经济基础（资本原始积累）和相应的政治斗争形势出发，来分析莎剧，这无疑是正确的，也能使读者正确理解莎剧人物的社会本质，但联系比较直接。（柯氏的全部理论掺杂了不少心理学、人类学、宗教概念，显得驳杂，不够成熟。）

英美各国用马克思主义观点系统地研究莎氏创作的著作不多见。在莎氏诞生四百周年纪念时出版了两部莎士比亚评论文集，其一是拉卜金（Norman Rabkin）编的《通向莎士比亚的途径》（*Approaches to Shakespeare*），其二是凯特尔（A. Kettle），编的《莎士比亚在变化中的世界里》（*Shakespeare in a Changing World*），都是从不同方面分析莎氏。美国人安奈特·鲁宾斯坦（Annette Rubinstein）在《英国文学中的伟大传统》（*The Great Tradition in English Literature*）中比较系统地分析了莎氏的创作。她指出研究莎氏应联系莎氏生活的新旧交替时代的社会政治斗争，联系莎氏反对封建内战、主张民族统一的立场，联系莎氏对君主的职责和继承问题、个人野心与政治的关系、对宗教与政治的关系等一系列莎氏的政治社会哲学。但她分析作品时往往失之片面，如过分突出《罗密欧与朱丽叶》中反映的封建内讧和经济问题（卖药人面有菜色），哈姆莱特由于性格软弱，不符合一个君主的要求而导致悲剧，《威尼斯商人》和《奥瑟罗》似乎主要只表明莎氏没有种族歧视观念，而《暴风雨》是写殖民过程，凯列班是受剥削的、慷慨的土著，他最后也未能获得自由，这是莎氏的现实主义所在。过分强调一面，说服力不大。这类方法上的片面性也表现在零散的评论里，如马修斯（G. M. Matthews）的《奥瑟罗和人的尊严》一文承认此剧是"社会剧"，但更是一出写种族歧视的剧。

马克思主义莎评总是把作品同历史现实生活和人民性联系考察，例如波茨坦师范学院教授魏曼（Robert Weimann）就说："莎士比亚之所以能驾驭他的素材当然是因为他对现实有无比深刻的感受，因为他的人道精神；但他之所以能一直牢固地做到这一点，则是因为有一个活生生的群众文化传统。"

卢卡契（Georg Lukács）虽然没有专门论述莎氏的著作，但他在谈到莎氏时，强调莎氏在今天的现实意义。在他的《论历史小说》（Der Historische Roman）中他从现实主义出发指出莎氏的历史剧并不是在细节方面忠实于历史，而在于能抓住历史中的矛盾冲突，这种矛盾冲突体现在典型人物身上。

有的马克思主义评家则侧重用辩证法分析莎剧，如布莱希特（Bertolt Brecht），他也没有关于莎剧的专著，但在论及莎剧时，他也用这方法，从而提供了一个新的角度。例如，在《安东尼与克莉奥佩特拉》中爱情与政治的辩证关系，在《科里奥兰纳斯》中平民与贵族、外患与内乱、分裂与团结等的辩证关系都能使我们进一步发掘莎剧的内在涵义。

存在主义思潮出现以后，影响所及，在莎评中也有反响。出生于波兰的扬·柯特（Jan Kott）就是代表人物。他把莎氏《李尔王》悲剧比作荒诞剧，因为他认为人物逃不出命运的捉弄，因为人物要在已定的命运之内作出选择，他认为《李尔王》是一出抽象的、有象征意义的道德剧，它象《旧约》中的约伯，写的是人类受损害受苦难变成赤裸裸的人（异化）的过程；剧中人物都是命运捉弄的丑角，一句话，是荒诞的。他认为《李尔王》所宣扬的是：生活是最后一局棋，是绝望。因此，演出也须用哑剧的方式，不能用现实主义、自然主义的方法，才能突出其荒诞性。这种评论实际上是借莎剧来阐明当代某些人的哲学政治观点，移花接木，并非都是莎氏自己的观点。也就是勒文（Harry Levin）所说的把莎士比亚"现代化"（updating）。

英国进步批评家威斯特（Alick West）与柯特基本上持相反意见，他批评柯特的历史观是消极的，他反对柯特把人类说成是"在冲突面前软弱无力"。威斯特认为人类可以改造社会，理想的价值观念是可以实现的，《李尔王》是有积极意义的。

从我国目前莎评界（以至整个外国文学评论界）来看，方向是明确的，莎士比亚研究很兴旺，发表的文章数量很多，作出了一定成绩，但如何进一步发展，这个问题似乎没有解决。在这样的时刻，介绍一些国外的评论流派和方法可能有些好处。西方莎评五花八门，尽管同我们在根本出发点上有所不同，但他们的探索精神，接触问题的角度，某些结论，对我们还是有启发的。苏联以外的、试图以马克思主义为指导的莎评，对我们来说也比较陌生，他山之石，可以为错，对我们的前进也应有裨益。至于所有流派中的错误观点，也可以从反面当作鉴戒。

百尺竿头，十方世界

——漫谈莎士比亚研究

莎士比亚在西方作家中，如果不是被人们研究得最多的，也是最多的当中的一个。我们研究莎氏的文章著作数量也不少，对普及莎作，帮助读者理解和作出评价，取得了一定的成绩。现在我们面临一个如何百尺竿头更进一步的问题。本文拟就平时想到的有关莎士比亚研究的一些问题，提一点看法，很不全面，提出来供讨论，错误的地方，请读者指正。

先谈谈人物情节分析。这是我们最熟悉的方法。人物情节要不要分析？当然要分析。一出戏总是有人物、有故事。安东尼奥是新兴商业资本家，夏洛克是旧式高利贷者，主要情节就是围绕他们之间的矛盾展开的；此外，剧中还有一两条平行情节线索。

莎剧的人物情节两百多年来吸引了许多评论家。十八世纪英国诗人蒲伯（Alexander Pope）编订莎集，他在序里曾说："莎剧中每个人物都具有个性，和在生活里一样，要找到两个完全一样的人物是不可能的，有些人物看来关系密切，极相近似，几乎象孪生子女，但仔细一比较，就发现他们很不相同……假如把他们的台词印出来，不附姓名，我相信我们可以很有把握地指出哪句话是谁说的。"这是 1725 年写的。人物个性化，人物符合生活真实。

本世纪初英国莎学家布拉德雷（A. C. Bradley）在分析莎氏悲剧时，有两个出发点：1）"首先，从外部开始，这样一部悲剧[按：指莎氏悲剧] 给我们提供了相当多的人物（比一出希腊悲剧中的人物多得多，如果不算合唱队的成员的话），但是它主要是一个人物，即'主人公'的故事，或至多两个人物，即'男主人公'和'女主人公'的故事。"其次，2）就是情节结构：显示矛盾冲突、决定性的转折、悲剧结局；起、伏、张、弛。布拉德雷的分析仍然集中在人物，加上故事情节。那是 1904 年。

但是一种方法，象一种文学形式一样，本身有疲劳枯竭的时候。当然，人物是莎剧很重要的一面，对人物性格也还可以有不同的理解，可以引起争论，还可以从不同角度加深对人物的理解与评价。但是人物并非莎剧全部内容，除人物外还有许多可以研究的课题，可以导向对莎剧更充分的理解。人物分析是重要的基础工作，但这个方法很难再发现新问题，限制了对莎剧这一丰富矿藏的深入发掘。所以布拉德雷以后，评家都纷纷另辟蹊径。社会在前进，新的一代在成长，旧的方法本身不完美，这些情况都要求改变。

为了更进一步，就有必要扩大眼界，扩大研究范围，也就是要看看十方世界。我觉得有下面几个方面值得考虑。

（一）多读莎评，尤其现、当代莎评。西方评论家多喜不断探索，不断求新。他们不尽成功，有的为新而新，说服力不大，但多数是认真的，有一定真知灼见，反映出某些隐藏的特点。

西方莎评的特点之一是概念丰富。概念就是客观事物在评论家头脑中的反映。他们的概念有些很模糊，有些是新瓶旧酒，但凡是概念而能言之成理者，必然反映客观存在在莎作中的某一方面或某些方面的特点。试看下面这段文章：

喜剧中的"言过其实"（Comic Overstatement）目的在产生荒诞的效果，不产生这种效果，它也就平淡无奇。悲剧中的"言过其实"，相反，目的在使人相信，如不能或多或少使人信以为真，这种手法只会停留在装腔作势的水平。[1]

这段文章的作者不满于布拉德雷对莎氏悲剧的结构的分析，想作一些"小小的补充"（a modest supplement）。他说"自从1904年以来，已经有大量的流水从批评的桥下流逝了"，布拉德雷曾认为是莎氏结构上的缺点和失误，今天看来却正是莎氏成功之处。莎氏悲剧除了外部结构以外，还有个内部结构。[2] 这内部结构最主要的构件是"主人公"，而主人公总是"言过其实"的人（overstater）。主人公又总有一个"衬托者"（foil），这衬托者的话就比较平庸冲淡，如哈姆雷特之与霍莱休。这就是所谓内部结构。这段引文的作者看到这一点，形成概念，造出名词，给读者提供了一个理解莎剧的角度。

再看这一段分析《威尼斯商人》的结构的文章：

《威尼斯商人》正如剧名所示，表现的是文明财富所能做到的善行，无偿的给予，以仁慈为怀来使用财富，以便能在一个人与人关系和谐的集团里生活。这出戏，通过夏洛克这个角色，写的是金钱引起的忧虑，金钱有力量使人与人发生矛盾。在我们这个以经济准则衡量一切的时代，我们把财富主要看成是个实际问题，抽象地热中于工作，而不把它看成是能实际感

---

[1] Maynard Mack: The Jacobean Shakespeare. 见 *Modern Shakespearean Criticism*, ed. Alvin B. Kernan, N. Y. 1970.
[2] 作者显然受了乔姆斯基（Chomsky）语言学理论的启发。

受到的节日欢乐。但在文艺复兴时期，对新兴的商业文明来说，财富表现为［可见、可感到的］闪闪发光的黄金，光采夺目的丝绸，十里飘香的香料[1]。

这段文章的作者认为莎氏喜剧多半为节日而写，有其特殊结构：诗意与嘲弄，罗曼斯与讥讽，成为对称的结构，《威尼斯商人》里的对称的结构就是对财富的两种不同态度。这种分析可能更接近莎氏的思想水平和原意。类似这样一步是达到阶级分析前所必不可少的。

每个人的思想都有很大的局限，须要和别人的思想砥砺切磋，以便形成或修正自己已形成的意见。有时会发现自己的意见，别人已先我而有之，那别人的意见就可以作为佐证。

阅读莎评和阅读莎作有相同的地方，我们也要考虑写评论的人所处的时代。每个时期的莎评不仅反映莎作某些特点，也反映评者本人和他的时代。任何时期的莎评只能是相对的真理，每个时代、每个评者都按自己的需要立论。演出也是一种评论，是导演对剧本的理解。例如去年法国阿维农艺术节上演的《李尔王》把李尔对女儿的爱演成乱伦的关系[2]，这种极端的例子只能说明导演（评者），不能说明莎氏。

（二）要读莎氏全部作品，要读莎氏同时代其他剧作家、诗人、小说家、哲学家等的作品，还要读莎氏读过的书。

我们的评介工作习惯于只介绍几个作家，一个作家只介绍几部作品，名曰有重点，名曰考虑读者需要和接受能力。作为普及工

---

[1] C. L. Barber: *The Mechant and the Jew of Venice: Wealth's Communion and an Intruder.* 见前引书。
[2] 《人民戏剧》，1981 年 12 期，54 页。

作的原则，本应这样，也只需要这样，但也产生一个问题，即给读者一个错误印象，似乎莎士比亚是一花独秀，或他的精华尽于此矣。另外，即便介绍一个作家、一部作品，没有广泛的研究基础，也往往只能就事论事，没有比较，甚至认为这样就是研究莎士比亚了。莎氏创作前后历时二十多年，有一个发展过程；这一段历史有变化，变化得很厉害，莎氏作为一个诗人、剧作家也在变，思想在变，艺术手法在变，语言风格、诗歌格律在变，人物也在变。假定我们研究哈姆莱特，而不知道他是一系列人物的深化衍变的结果，我们就只能就事论事，很难加深理解。同样，我们不读当时流行的复仇剧，就不可能作第一手的比较，而看出《哈姆莱特》哪些地方不同于它们，哪些地方超越过它们，哪些地方和它们一致。莎氏的创作和同时代或稍前稍后的戏剧（和其他类型的文学）的关系是十分密切的，他受前人和同代人的影响，但又超越过他们。《哈姆莱特》戏中戏的台词就是一种戏拟，哈姆莱特对演员的指示就是他对当时演出的评论。而且当时戏剧确实繁荣，出了许多优秀作家，他们的作品本身成就很高，值得研究。

莎士比亚研究还有一个特殊的问题，即他的题材都是现成的，这些原始材料至少应当浏览涉猎。但还不止此，一个作家的世界观的形成固然主要由于生活遭际，但他的思想的素材或材料往往是从他接受的前人遗产或当代人的言论著作中来，因此除了涉猎莎剧的原始材料之外，还应广泛阅读他可能阅读过的书籍。英国第一部诗史的作者沃登（Thomas Warton）在他的《论斯宾塞的"仙后"》（1754）一书中可能是第一次对一个评家或研究者提出这一要求，他说：

可以说，在评论弥尔顿、约翰逊、斯宾塞或我国其他早期诗人时，不仅需要对古代古典学问有足够的知识，而且应当涉猎某些书籍，这些书籍，现在已经被人忘记了或散佚了，但在作家生前却是人人皆知的，而且作家也很可能读过的。[1]

他身体力行，研究斯宾塞，就读斯宾塞读过的书。史密斯评论道：他就象一个探险家，航海探险，使我们感染到他所感到的兴奋。从此，沃登成了一位"坚定的研究工作者"（a confirmed researcher）。

这也就是我们通常所说的"充分掌握材料"。举个熟悉的例子。如《暴风雨》二幕一场，冈扎罗的理想国的描写，或哈姆莱特所表现的怀疑主义，都说明莎氏受蒙田的影响。《暴风雨》写于弗洛里欧（Florio）蒙田英译本出版（1603）之后，《哈姆莱特》写于其前。但莎氏和弗洛里欧两人都曾是骚桑普顿伯爵座上客，所以有人认为莎氏读过译稿。不管怎样，蒙田的思想在当时是流行的。我们常谈作家世界观的问题，世界观不是抽象的。说莎士比亚的世界观是人文主义，不具体。它总是由种种具体的思想构成的，这些具体的思想往往直接间接从书本中来。研究一个作家应读他读过的书，一个原因就在此。

（三）莎士比亚的比较研究。这方面我们做过一些零散工作，如莎士比亚与汤显祖的比较，莎剧和京剧的比较。这也只是初步。比较的方法本来是根本的方法，前面提到把莎氏和同时代作家比，把某一莎剧与其他莎剧比，都是比较。但国与国比，就进入了比

---

[1] David Nichol Smith: *Warton's History of English poetry*（*Warton Lectures on English poetry, British Academy*），OUP, 1929. 伊丽莎白一世幼年时的老师希腊文教授阿斯克姆主张学童写拉丁文散文要想写得象西塞罗，不能直接模仿西塞罗，而要模仿西塞罗的模特儿。探本穷源，同一道理。

较文学领域。比较文学范围广大，可以研究相互影响。在莎氏这位具体作家身上恐怕谈不上中国对他的影响，而莎氏对中国的影响则是个很有兴趣的问题。影响常是通过翻译产生的，因此研究莎剧的翻译也是一个重要课题，比较莎士比亚的诗剧和中国古典戏曲，例如主题、悲剧喜剧的概念、结构、人物等等方面，既可发现各自特点，也可找出共同规律，这种研究将会很富于成果。对不同时期，不同国家莎剧演出进行比较研究，一定也很有趣味。

（四）研究莎氏的语言文字功夫。莎士比亚是个诗人，他用诗体写剧本，他的"诗"是他的艺术很重要的一个组成部分。英国有个批评家说得好，把莎氏只看成是一个伟大的"人物创造者"，"诗只是外加的装饰"，那就大错了。[1] 研究这方面通过翻译只能发掘出他巨大成就中的很小一部分。吴兴华译的《亨利四世》，这是一个比较好的译本，在上篇二幕四场里，福斯塔夫假装国王训斥太子。在开始时他有这样几句台词："文武大臣，两厢站好"，"别哭了，王后；因为流泪是徒然的"，"贤卿们，护送我悲哀的王后回宫，/因为泪已经堵住她双眸的水门。"（原文是："Stand aside, nobility"，"Weep not, sweet queen, for trickling tears are vain,"，"For Goa's sake, Lords, convey my tristful queen, /For tears do stop the flood-gates of her eyes,"）莎士比亚这里是在模仿并嘲笑 1569 年出版的一个剧本《堪拜西王》，或其他流行剧。父王要训儿子了，王后哭了，父王要人把她送回宫去，造成一个训子的环境。这是一个"噱头"的开始，情景是机伶的福斯塔夫脑子里想象出来的，未免有些荒诞。既然荒诞，用二三流的诗句最恰当不过。莎氏对诗的语言十分敏感，独具慧眼，普列斯顿（Preston）的《堪拜西王》或其

---

[1] L. C. Knights: How Many Children Had Lady Macbeth？见前引书。

他流行剧的诗句正好是现成材料。福斯塔夫的台词一直是散文，这里突然出现两句诗，特别显得突出。（其实，福斯塔夫以下几段散文，亦庄亦谐，亦假亦真，非常精采。）莎士比亚确实是运用语言的里手，译文再好也很难传达。

　　当然，莎氏对语言的运用也有一个过程。他开始时也常常华而不实，后来逐渐达到炉火纯青。研究他的语言，要培养语感。英语在十六世纪后半到十七世纪初正是进入"早期现代英语"阶段，本身变化很大。莎氏当时的观众生活在语言急剧变化的时代，对语言极敏感；有教养的观众由于当时修辞学、诗学的发达，对古代文学的兴趣甚浓，对莎氏的语言功夫是能够充分欣赏的[1]。但是过了三四百年，现在英语国家的读者和观众是否能同样充分享受这种乐趣，便成了疑问。尽管如此，莎士比亚语言运用的经验和成就是很值得研究的。

　　莎士比亚写的是诗剧，诗剧也很值得研究。诗剧本来是西方的传统，希腊、罗马戏剧，中世纪戏剧都是诗剧，正如中国元明杂剧。看戏的人也是在这传统中成长的，和旧时听京戏或昆曲的听众一样。因此，作家有条件充分利用诗剧的特点。既然是诗，就是形象的语言，富于想象。柯尔律治（Coleridge）给"想象"下的定义是一种能把普遍的和具体的、把思想和形象结合在一起的能力。诗的特点就是通过形象表达思想感情。莎士比亚可以说是一个诗的语言的魔术师，有的评论家甚至提出这样的警告：莎氏的文字使我们眼花缭乱，以致迷失全剧的意义，说他的语言是座"陷井"[2]。这种例子俯拾皆是。波洛纽斯派人去刺探他儿子在巴黎的情况，要用

---

[1] 即使一般市民对语言也能欣赏，他们是剧场观众的大多数；有名的传道牧师往往是大文章家，市民空巷来听，如醉如痴，说明他们能欣赏优美语言。

[2] John Russell Brown: Shakespeare's Plays in Performance，见前引书。

假话勾出他的真相来，他说 Your bait of falsehood takes this carp of truth "用你假话的鱼钩钓出他真实情况的鲤鱼"。用转弯抹角的办法找出他走的路子：with assays of biasa / By indirections find directions out "像灌铅的木球，弯投正中"。克利奥帕特拉乘坐游艇在尼罗河上冶游，一派豪华气象，至于她本人，那更是无法形容：For her own person, / It beggared all description，"任何形容词都会寒伧得像叫化子一样"。他写麦克白斯犯罪后的悔罪这种抽象感情：Will all great Neptune's ocean wash this blood/Clean of my hand? No, this my hand will rather / The multitudinous seas incarnadine, / Making the green one red. "伟大的海神的全部海洋能洗净我手上的血迹吗？不行，相反，我这只手倒会把波涛万千的海洋染赤，使碧绿变成一色红"。先是自问自答，表示疑虑不安，略带悔恨，但意识到他犯的罪实在太大了，用了两个极大的字眼。"Multitudinous"，莎士比亚是第一个用这个词的作家，而且是用来形容海之大和海上无际的波涛，以后才被其他作家用来形容人群。"in carnadine" 一词也是不久前才从法国引进的新词，是形容词，莎士比亚把它用作动词。这两个拉丁词占据差不多一行，音节多，前面一行基本是英语单音词，后面一行也是，它们夹在当中，它们也很陌生，使人听了产生一种沉重可怕的感觉。最后一行起了解释前面陌生字眼的作用，使形象简单鲜明，把不可思议的罪一下变成真实无误明明白白的罪行。

　　从上面几个例子可以看出莎士比亚形象的语言能适应各种情绪，从滑稽到狡猾、艳羡以至复杂的心理状态。他充分利用诗剧提供的可能性，利用诗的节奏、音乐性、烘托出气氛和思想感情，达到他要求的戏剧效果。因此，他的剧不仅要用眼睛看，而且要用耳朵听。

　　前面谈到莎氏语言有个从不成熟到成熟的过程。早期，他常常以辞害意，为语言而语言，到后期就像 1623 年《全集》的两位编者在《致读者》中所说，作到了"得心应手"。我们可以比较一下罗密欧之死和奥赛罗之死。[1]

罗密欧临死前看到朱丽叶，他把死亡夺走的生命比作蜜；他见她面容和生前一样美丽，就把嘴唇和面色的红润比作一面红色的美的旗帜，而死亡的旗帜是白色的，用了一个军事比喻；死神成了情种，死亡成了"黑夜的宫殿"；腐蚀尸体的蛆虫是"宫娥"；把最后一吻比作订立契约的印记；把毒酒比作去死亡路上的向导、领港人，把自己比作一条船。比喻和修辞未免太丰富了一些，真挚的感情被华丽的外衣所遮没。这是早期。

奥赛罗临死前的心理状况是很复杂的：他坦荡、平静，也有悔恨、醒悟，也有爱，有正确的自我估计和赴死的决心，但文字干净，虽也用了一个典故（印度人或犹太人抛珠）以表示悔恨，一个比喻（阿拉伯胶树）用以形容眼泪一滴一滴的流下（朱生豪译"泛滥"不妥），而且象一付能医病的药（朱译遗漏），但这些和人物在特定条件下的心情一致，而不是像早期文字那样，仅仅是多余的点缀品。

不论早期还是后期，莎氏一直是位"形象思维"的能手。有的评论家说，"他用整个身体思想"。

莎氏作为语言大师值得研究的地方还很多，以上不过是我想到的几点，怎样把莎氏这方面的经验介绍给我国读者和作家，是一项值得从事的工作。

---

[1] 参看 George Rylands: Shakespeare the Poet, 见 *A Companion to Shakespeare Studies*, ed. Granville-Barker and Harrison, CUP, 1946.

弥尔顿《失乐园》中的加帆车

——十七世纪英国作家与知识的涉猎

弥尔顿《失乐园》（1665）第二章写撒旦听说上帝创造了世界，决定去一探虚实。第三章，他来到了地球，有这样三行诗。诗人把撒旦比作一只雕，从喜马拉雅山飞下，想飞向印度去猎取食物，但

> 途中，它降落在塞利卡那，那是
> 一片荒原，那里的中国人推着
> 轻便的竹车，靠帆和风力前进。

（437—439）

塞利卡那意即丝绸之国，中国。中国文物制度出现在西方作家作品中，近代以来，在文学史里已是常见的事。弥尔顿诗中和十七世纪其他作家著作中援引中国文物制度也屡见不鲜。这里，我想先谈谈加帆车这一事物，它本身有一个很有趣的经历。

李约瑟在《中国科学技术史》这部巨著中（IV. 2. p. 274ff）详尽地追溯了加帆车在西方的报导、传播以至仿造的历史。据他考证，欧洲人最早的记载是西班牙人冈扎雷斯·德·门多萨（Gonzales de Mendoza）的《中华大帝国风物史》（1585 年出版）。很快，

三年后，英国人罗勃特·帕克（Robert Parke）受地理学家哈克路特（Hakluyt，1552—1616）之托，将此书译成英文。其中有一段这样写道：

> 中国人最善于发明，他们有各种张帆而行的车辆。制作精巧，使用轻便。许多人都见到过此物，相信不是假的。此外，还有许多印度群岛人和葡萄牙人也见到从中国进口的布匹和陶器上，绘着这种车，足见这种图象是有实际根据的。

十几年后，荷兰航海家林硕吞（Jan Huyghen van Linschoten，1563—1611）的《东西印度群岛游记》（1596，英译本 1598）里也有这样一段记载：

> 中国多能工巧匠，从中国来的制品可以证明。他们制造并使用带帆的车辆（象船一样），也有车轮，制作十分巧妙，在田野里行走时，靠风力推动，好像在水上飘行一样。

李约瑟还引了英国人科克斯（R. Cocks）1614 年给东印度公司打的报告，其中谈到高丽"发明一种大车，扁轮，张帆，象船一样，用来载货"，又说日本天皇曾想用这种车运兵进攻中国，但为高丽某贵族所阻。意大利哲学家坎帕内拉（Campanella）写的《太阳城》（1623）把加帆车说成是产在锡兰，并增加了想象成分："车上插帆，即使逆风也能前进，因为车轮里套着车轮，制作奇妙。"

可见这样一件事物和其他东方和欧洲以外的事物一样，在十六、十七世纪之交深深抓住了欧洲人的想象，这种兴趣往前可以推到中世纪，往后一直延续到弥尔顿时代以后，直到十九世纪。

关于加帆车不仅有文字记载，而且十六七世纪西欧舆地学家在绘制地图时多在中国境内绘上加帆车，如出生在荷兰的德国舆地学家沃尔提留斯（Ortelius）所制的《舆地图》（1570）[1]，麦卡托[2]（Mercator）的《舆地图》（1613）都有图形。英国人斯比德（J. Speed）的《中华帝国》（1626）一书中也有加帆车的插图。[3]

加帆车在欧洲不仅见诸记载和舆图，而且有人仿造。在弥尔顿之前最轰动一时的是佛兰芒（比利时）数学家、工程师斯特文（Simon Stevin）。李约瑟（IV.1. pp. 227—228；IV.2. pp. 279—280）详细报导了这次试验。斯特文约在1600年左右在荷兰舍文宁根海滨，在奥兰治的摩理斯亲王的资助下，制造了大小两架加帆车，试验结果从舍文宁根行驶到普登，五十四英里的距离，用了不到两小时，而步行则要十四小时。李约瑟为此加了按语说："这种运输工具的速度对欧洲文化的冲击是不容低估的。这种从中国来的刺激，至少是不容忽视的，事实是它产生了了不起的后果。"斯特文的陆地舟据说在欧洲一再为人所仿造，历二百年不衰。[4]

可见就这件具体的东西说，在欧洲即使不是家喻户晓，也是广为人知的。而且传播之快，也是惊人的，事实上，弥尔顿并非在英国文学中把加帆车用在诗里的第一个诗人。李约瑟在谈到整个十七世纪欧洲人是如何钦佩中国的技术发明时，提到了弥尔顿在他不朽的诗篇中引用了加帆车这一形象。但在弥尔顿之前，本·琼生写的假面剧《新大陆新闻》（1620）也已经提到了。这出讽刺新兴的新

---

[1] 利玛窦（Matteo Ricci）1583年到中国就携带了沃氏的《舆地图》。
[2] 麦卡托（Mercator），佛兰芒舆地学家，荷兰文作 Kremer, 1512—1594。
[3] 范存忠教授来函指出斯威夫特也曾提及，见 Prose Works, ed. Temple. Scott, 1907, I. 87。
[4] 明末，我国大发明家王征（1571—1644）几乎同时也受到《帝王世纪》的启发，制作随风而行的飞车。

闻事业的喜剧有这样一段关于在月球上发现了新大陆这条"新闻"的对话：

> 信使甲（"外勤记者"）那里的车辆很象贵妇人的脾气——随风转。
> 记录员（"主笔"）：妙，就象中国的手推车一样。

足见这一事物在十七世纪初，至少在英国知识界确已颇为人所熟知了。更有趣的是斯特文的试验也出现在琼生的作品中。他的喜剧《新客栈》1629年上演，其中有这样一段对话。无业游民弗莱、军官提普托和店主在谈论击剑。店主说，欧几理德和阿基米德都是击剑师，前一个礼拜还在乐园里比赛。这明明是胡说，在追问之下，店主继续扯谎说，三天之前从乐园来人谈到了此事，弗莱也作证道：

> 弗莱：是的，是那人告诉我们的。
> 他是从奥兰治亲王击剑师那儿听来的。
> 提普托：是斯特文吗？
> 弗莱：是的，他曾抬出三十件武器向欧几理德
> 挑战，阿基米德都没有见过这许多武器，
> 还有各种机械，多半是他自己发明的。

斯特文（1548—1620）和琼生（1572—1637）生活在同一时代而略早，他在奥兰治亲王摩理斯宫廷任职，设计过一套水闸，作为军事防御工事。看来这位发明家在当时已成为一个传奇式人物了。

这种车在中国的记载最早是《博物志》和《帝王世纪》，郭璞

注《山海经》可能就根据《博物志》。《博物志》[1] 说："奇肱民善为栻杠，以杀百禽。能为飞车，从风远行。汤时西风至，吹其车至豫州，汤破其车，不以视民。十年东风至，乃复作车遣返。其国去玉门关四万里。"这显然是一种传说，但也抓住了中国文人的想象。据李约瑟调查，两晋以后，沈约《竹书纪年》注、梁元帝《金楼子》、任昉《述异记》都有记载，宋以前广为人知。但这种飞车属于神话传说，并非实物。这种传说中的飞车最早的图形在中国著作中见诸《异域图志》(1489)，后来陆续有王崇庆 (1597)、吴任臣 (1786)、郝懿行 (1809)、汪绂 (1895) 等所制，都是《山海经》的插图。作为实物，中国文献记载极少，不知始于何时。实物图形在李约瑟著作中提到麟庆《鸿雪因缘图记》(1849) 最早，以后又有刘仙洲《中国机械工程史料》(1935)。这些图形就是李约瑟所说"现在山东河南还能看到的"加帆车的近代写实图形。马可·孛罗时期中国有没有加帆车，不能肯定，他的游记里没有提到。但他也没有提到长城，不能就此说长城不存在。至少可能在明末是有这种东西的。据李约瑟，斯特文仿制加帆车是受到朱载堉 (1536—1611) 的启发。当时正是西方商人航海冒险家和传教士涌向东方的时候，接触到中国社会和中国学者，中国的文物制度直接间接得以传播到欧洲。弥尔顿得知中国有加帆车是并不奇怪的。但具体是从哪本书或哪本地图上得来的，很难考证。美国学者汤姆逊 (E. N. S. Thompson) 1919 年曾发表文章《弥尔顿的地理知识》可能有所考证。我怀疑弥尔顿很可能是从当时流行的黑林 (Peter Heylyn，1599—1662) 著《小宇宙志》(*Microcosmus；a Little Description of the Great World*，1621；后来扩大为《宇宙志》*Cosmography*，1652)

[1] 《艺文类聚》作《括地图》。

里得来。这部描写世界各国概况的书讲到中国时，有这样一段话：
"中国地势平坦，货车和车乘张帆而行。"弥尔顿诗中的一些地名
多采用黑林的拼法。此外当时通行的舆地图，弥尔顿也很可能有所
涉猎。

加帆车这段小小故事说明一个问题。十五六世纪随着西欧各国
国内资本主义的兴起而出现了海外探险的热潮，带回来许多关于
外部世界闻所未闻的消息，引起了人们无限的好奇心。另一方面，
人们对封建现实不满，向古代和远方寻求理想，如饥似渴地追求
着。仅仅理想国的设计，几乎每个作家都或多或少画了一个蓝图，
从《乌托邦》、《太阳城》、培根的《新大西国》、锡德尼的《阿刻底
亚》、莎士比亚的《暴风雨》到不大被人注意的勃吞的《忧郁症的
解剖》中的《致读者》一章。这种追求古今西东知识的渴望是时代
的需要，作家们追求知识为的是要解决他们最关心的问题。加帆车
不过是这一持久的浪潮中的一滴水珠而已。

当然，文艺复兴时期人们所获得的知识真假混杂。关于中国的
文物制度，他们倾向于把它理想化。[1]一些具体的事物也往往以讹
传讹，如大学者斯卡立哲（Scaliger，1540—1609）就说中国瓷器能
免毒，能取火，勃朗（Sir Thomas Browne，1605—1682）在《常见
的谬误》一书中予以纠正，但这种讹说当时是很流行的，英国诗人
马伏尔（Andrew Marvell，1621—1678）《给画家的最后指示》一诗
中仍保持这讹说。不过另一方面，对东方的知识也是日益丰富的，
中国的文物出现在文学作品里也渐渐多起来。中国的丝绸不必说
了，中国药材、酒、瓷器、鹅、桔，都见于十七世纪英国著作和文

---

[1] 另一种倾向是贬抑，如《第十二夜》(2.3.77)，《温莎风流娘儿们》(2.1，147)，理想
化和贬抑都是讹误。

学作品中。[1]

正是在这样一个追求知识的热潮中，涌现出一大批饱学之士，其中许多在文学史上占着很重要的地位。在弥尔顿同时代人当中有一个很奇特的作家——即上面提到的罗勃特·勃吞（Robert Burton，1577—1640）。他可以算做是个"皓首穷经"的书生，他在牛津大学做了三十年学问，可以说学贯古今西东。他自况为"一条闲游的狗，看见鸟儿就要向它汪汪叫"。他把这些学问用于解决时代病。他和哈姆雷特一样，认为人是自然的杰作，但目前处境可悲——从神的地位降到了兽的水平。他概括地称此病为"忧郁症"[2]。他研究人类罹疾的种种表现和病因。和弥尔顿一样，他认为人类的不幸总根源在亚当抵不住引诱而堕落，从此引出天人两界的灾难。因而他写了《忧郁症的解剖》。这是一部有待介绍的奇书，文字幽默机智，形象生动。

勃吞的书谈到中国的地方有三十多处，主要来源是马可·孛罗游记和利玛窦的出访中国记（Expeditiones apud Sinas）。涉及的内容有宗教、迷信、偶像崇拜、巫术、鬼神；政治制度、经济、法律、科举制度、城市规划、地理、卫生、饮食、医药、心理、幻觉、精神病、嫉妒。贯串这部巨著的总的精神还是人文主义，例如他赞扬中国的科举[3]，因为科举表明重才而不重身世；赞扬规划完善的城市，其中包括元代的大都（出自马可·孛罗）；赞扬中国人民的勤劳和国家的繁荣。其借鉴的目的是很明显的。

---

[1] 莎士比亚《一报还一报》（2.1.90）：庞培："当时我们家里只有两个煮梅子，那是好久以前的事了，放在果盘子里，盘子大概值三便士吧，两位大人一定见过这种盘子，虽说不是中国的瓷盘子，也是不错的盘子。"

[2] 他本人也患忧郁症。

[3] 中国科举制度给西方人的印象极深，直到当代帕金森（C. Northcote Parkinson）的小品集《帕金森定律》（1961），讽刺英国官场，还拿来和英国铨选官吏的制度对比。

我们不妨看看他的广博的知识中有关地理的知识。如前所述，近代西欧人向外扩张，发现了新大陆，地理发现这一新鲜事物引起人们极大兴趣，十七世纪初、中叶作家的作品中，地理知识很显著突出。地理书籍、游记成了当时的畅销书，考虑到当时的印刷条件，转译之速也是惊人的。作家、著作家有的有海外经历，但多数要靠间接知识，即使到海外，象弥尔顿，最远也不过意大利。我们从勃吞接触到的地理书籍也可以了解弥尔顿的地理知识。

勃吞不象徐霞客，他足不出户，在书斋里神游六合。他说："我从不旅行，我只读地图，我读地图时，我的思想自由翱翔，我一向喜欢研究宇宙志。"又说："我觉得任何人面对一幅地图都会很高兴的。'地理提供的知识，品类之多，令人不能置信，在人们心里勾引出无穷乐趣，刺激着人们去追求更多的知识。'[1] 在地舆图、地形图上，似乎可以亲眼看到世界上远方的州、府、县、市，而足迹不必出书斋。在地图上还可以用比例尺和罗盘测量那些地方的范围、距离，考察其位置。"勃吞接着又讲了一个掌故："查理大帝有三张银桌，一张桌子的桌面上刻着君士坦丁堡的地图，一张刻着罗马地图，第三张刻着世界地图，他十分喜爱。"

勃吞的叙述使我们生动地看到当时人们是怎样热中于追求知识以及从中得到的满足。我们不妨再看看他所读过的舆图和游记作家。这些包括沃尔提留斯、麦卡托、洪狄乌斯的舆图、坎姆登（Camden，1551—1623）、马可·孛罗、哈克路特、林硕吞的游记和有关哥伦布和维斯普契（Vespucci，1451—1512）的著作，不下二三十种。弥尔顿的地理知识来源恐怕也不外乎这些。

十七世纪初期英国出了一批大学问家，他们有的研究历史，有

---

[1] 这是勃吞引荷兰人洪狄乌斯（Hondius，即 Abraham d Hondt, c, 1638—1691）为麦卡托的著作写的序里的话。

的从事文学创作，有的是教会人士，如考古学家坎姆登，国教理论家胡克（Hooker，1554—1600），圣经翻译家、理论家安德鲁斯（Andrewes，1555—1626），培根，历史学家塞尔登（Selden，1584—1654），哲学家霍布士，医生勃朗，牧师泰勒（Jeremy Taylor，1613—1667），文学家如邓恩、琼生、弥尔顿。这些著作家、诗人的共同特点是知识面广，古代文史哲、宗教文学、外邦异域的知识以至近代科学，无所不包。他们的文章和诗歌旁征博引。他们的文风和诗风竟然形成了一个独特的流派——"巴罗克"（Baroque）。"巴罗克"从思想上说，代表了一种追求、动荡不安的精神状态，在艺术上则崇尚靡丽雕饰，是文艺复兴前期肯定自然与理性这种精神趋向衰退和精神困惑的表现，到十七世纪后期和十八世纪，理性和信心才又恢复。这批作者喜欢炫耀学问，从表面看，带有装饰性，事实上在许多场合也确是装饰品，但从根本上说，学问知识是起机能作用的，是作者的精神、思想、感情所需要的，是为这些服务的。

以泰勒而论，他是个牧师，散文大家，十八世纪几乎完全被人遗忘了，还是十九世纪初浪漫派批评家重新"发现"了他。他和他同时代人，也包括弥尔顿，一样，考虑的是一些重大的、根本性的问题：上帝与人，天堂与地狱，善与恶，光明与黑暗，健康与疾病，生与死，基督教与古代文化等等之间的矛盾，反映出人们在动荡的历史时期的苦闷和彷徨。他企图调和宗教和理性，来解决矛盾。他阅读范围之广，英国十九世纪初浪漫派诗人、评论家柯尔律治称之为"汪洋无际"（oceanic reading）。他饱读宗教文献、古代文史哲和当代史地，这些正是构成他思想的原料。一切文艺作品都是社会生活在作家头脑中的反映的产物。因此研究作家头脑的构成应是文学评论的一个重要组成部分。头脑里装些什么？头脑怎样工作？这些都是很值得研究的问题。这使人想起艾略特一段话。他在论玄学派诗人时说：

> 当一个诗人的头脑装备完善可以开始工作的时候，他的头脑就不停顿地综合着各种南辕北辙的经验；普通人的经验是杂乱的、无规律的、零碎的。普通人堕入情网或阅读斯宾诺莎，这两种经验互不为车，和打字机的声音或烧菜的味道也联系不起来，但在诗人头脑里，这些经验永远在形成新的整体。

这话似乎给我们打开了一扇通向创作的奥秘过程的门，给一般认为很神秘的创作过程——灵感、神思等等，以科学的解释。只有象孙悟空钻进铁扇公主的肚子，"钻进"作家的头脑里去，评论才能入木三分。

泰勒在地理知识方面，不能和勃吞或弥尔顿相此。但地理知识、天文知识给他提供了一个广阔的时空视野。这是他的思想所要求的，他的思想要求高度概括性和普遍性。这一点他和弥尔顿很相似。他要宣扬宗教，他认为宗教是解决人类根本的、普遍的问题的钥匙。他的目光因之也就放诸四海。他是这样用"巴罗克"风格渲染上帝的仁慈的：

> 就如太阳向南回归线运行的时候，谛视着晒得黎黑的埃塞俄比亚人，但同时又从它的后门放射出光芒，散发出影响；它能一直看到东方的地角，而它却面向着西方，因为它是一团火球，它酷似具体而微的"无极"。上帝的仁慈也正是这样。

许多评论家都指出他在风格上和勃朗、弥尔顿，甚至莎士比亚有相似之处（称他为"圣职人员中的莎士比亚"）。这不仅是风格问题，风格和思想感情是分不开的。王国维曾说："昔人于诗词，有景语、情语之别。不知一切景语皆情语也"，也是同一道理。

在十七世纪前半这一批作家中，弥尔顿当然是最有成就的。他不仅是个革命活动家，同时是个饱学之士。他的兴趣范围很广，除古代文学、宗教、音乐之外，还潜心史地。他写了一系列著名的政论文章，还写了一部《不列颠史》（1646—1670）。他仔细研究了以前的英国史，认为水分太多，不及希腊罗马史家严谨，因此他自己写了一部。他还写过一部《莫斯科公国简史》，写成于 1650 年。英国革命后，革命政府很关心俄国的态度。俄国驱逐了英国商人，英国国务会议曾提出抗议。书中引用的材料有哈克路特的航海记，波切斯（Samuel Purchas, 1575？—1626）《巡礼记》（又名《世界概况及历代宗教》，1613）以及《续哈克路特，英国和各国海陆旅行家的游记中所见世界历史》。弥尔顿还改写过伊利莎白朝一些旅行家的游记，删刈其中迷信猎奇成分，修改了其中华丽词藻或过分朴实的文字，于死后 1682 年出版。这些工作成果都反映在《失乐园》等诗篇中。此外，在语言研究上，弥尔顿也下过一番工夫。本·琼生编过一本英文文法，弥尔顿则编了一部拉丁文法，还着手编纂拉丁字典，但未完成。

我粗略统计了一下《失乐园》第一章约八百行中的地名，取自《圣经》的有三十四个，取自古典文学的有十六个，取自传奇文学的有三个，一般地名三十个，自创地名一个（"万魔国" Pandemonium）。从地域看，极北到挪威（以后各章最远伸展到北极），极南到非洲（以后推到好望角），极东到印度（以后尚有中国），极西到古代世界的极西点赫斯佩利亚（西班牙）、直布罗陀和爱布兰（以后到大西洋、美洲）。从全诗看来，弥尔顿的视野不仅遍及全世界，而且上天入地，包括整个宇宙。

弥尔顿之所以需要这样大的活动空间，决定于他的史诗的性质和主旨。弥尔顿的史诗，所谓"文人史诗"或"第二史诗"和荷马史诗，所谓"原始史诗"不同。欧洲史诗从荷马以后，性质有了改变。荷马史诗通过生动的神话传说，反映英雄主义，风格机智活泼。维吉尔的史诗，所谓"第二代史诗"，虽然还保留了英雄主题，而且在形式上竭力模仿荷马，但故事单薄，而主要是反映他的政治哲学思想，风格庄严凝重，有时迷离哀婉。史诗这形式经过一系列作家运用之后，到了《失乐园》，除了某些技巧特点之外，已经丧失了荷马史诗的英雄主义，也没有哪个"人物"称得上"史诗英雄"。弥尔顿自己称《失乐园》为"一首十二章的诗"。《失乐园》的主题更加接近维吉尔的《伊尼德》和但丁的《神曲》。在某种意义上说，它们都是政治诗、寓言诗，有的牵涉到帝国的命运，有的牵涉到人类的命运，带有普遍意义，在风格上也相似。英国评论家阿诺德（Matthew Arnold，1822—1888）在他的演讲集《论翻译荷马》把弥尔顿和荷马的风格作了一个比较，并指出这种风格上的差异是和思想分不开的："荷马的节奏流畅、迅速，相反，弥尔顿的节奏吃力、故意迟缓。他们各自的节奏和格律是和他们的思想方式相一致的，是由思想方式决定的。弥尔顿的脑子里充满了思想、想象、知识，以致他的诗格都无法包容。……这种饱和的、紧密的、压缩的、含蓄的思想，体现在节奏的运行之中，造成了他的特有风格——崇高但艰深而严峻。"弥尔顿在《失乐园》里怀着沉痛的心情总结了英国革命失败的教训，他赋予了一个民族的命运以全人类的普遍意义，把英国民族如何在政治上得救的问题写成对人类命运的探索。他的意图既然如此，因此从题材的选定到场景的规划都为此服务。主题涉及全人类，故事所需的活动范围顺理成章地应是全宇宙了。因此我们读《失乐园》有一个感受，即空间概念非常突出。

《失乐园》里有一段描写，很有代表性，也曾引起过争议。这一段（第十一章）写上帝因耶稣说情，同意不毁灭人类，但派天使迈克尔把亚当和夏娃驱逐出乐园。迈克尔领他们走上一座高山，指点给他们看人类从那时起，迄洪水止的一段"历史"。就在这样一座山上，后来撒旦又指点给耶稣看人间的荣耀，来引诱耶稣。原诗不妨试译如下：

两人登上这座山（指亚当、夏娃）

去看上帝展示的未来。这座山
是乐园最高处，从山巅可以清晰地
看到半圆的大地伸向目力
所能达到的最最遥远的远方。
这座山同魔鬼在荒野为了另一目的
引诱第二个亚当所在的那座山（指耶稣）
高度不相上下，视野也相同，
魔鬼向他指点了人间帝业和荣耀。
在这里他极目望去，可以看到（"他"指耶稣）
负有盛名的古今都会，最伟大的
帝国的都城，从喀塔伊可汗的都城（喀塔伊，即中国）
汗八里克的坚固的城垣和帖木儿（汗八里克，即北京）
王座所在、俄诺克斯河畔的撒马尔罕，
到西那诸王的北京，从这里再瞩目（西那，即中国）
伟大的莫卧儿的亚格拉和拉合尔，
再沿着黄金的马六甲半岛看下去，
波斯皇帝夏宫所在的埃克巴丹，

以及后来的伊斯法罕，俄国沙皇的

莫斯科，土耳其苏丹所住的拜占庭；

此外，他还可以看到许多地方：

埃塞俄比亚帝国和它极东的港口

厄尔科科，还有海运不甚发达的

王国：蒙巴萨、基洛洼、马林迪，

和一度被误认为俄斐的索法拉，

还有刚果王国，和极南的安哥拉；

从这里，从尼日尔河到阿特拉斯山，

还有阿尔曼索尔、费兹、苏兹、

摩洛哥、阿尔及尔和特累米森诸王国；

从此到欧罗巴，罗马将要统治

全世界：此外，他还通过想象看到（因在地球背面）

莫特祖默皇帝统治的富饶的墨西哥，

还有秘鲁的库斯科，阿塔拨里帕王

在这里治理着更加富饶的国土，还有

未被蹂躏的圭亚那，它的都会

西班牙人称之为黄金城。迈克尔摘除了

亚当的障眼膜，为他展示了更壮丽的远景。

　　这种地名的堆砌断然引不起现代读者的兴趣，可能被认为是《失乐园》的败笔。翻译家遇到这种地方更感绝望，翻起来吃力不讨好。[1] 但是还没有评论家认为弥尔顿的这类描写是节外生枝或充填篇幅。它不仅是史诗这种类型要求有的组成部分（catalogue——

---

[1] 据说塔索的史诗《解放了的耶路撒冷》有三四十节都是地名的堆砌，而且与诗歌情节毫无关系。

检阅式的罗列），而且与主题思想有密切联系。这一点，下面再论。这里想先谈谈大批评家艾略特对这段的批评。

艾略特最不欣赏弥尔顿（后来态度略有改变）。他说："弥尔顿无论哪一时期的诗歌，形象性都不明显"，弥尔顿不善于使人感到"具体的地点、具体的时间。"他反对的是弥尔顿的描写不具体，形象不鲜明。殊不知这正是弥尔顿的长处，也是他意趣所在。英国小说家福斯特（E. M. Forster）在《小说的方方面面》一书中提出一个有趣的论点正好为弥尔顿辩解。福斯特说，多数小说家有地点感，如阿诺德·班内特（Arnold Bennett）的小说《五城》，但很少小说家有空间感，而空间感是托尔斯泰的非凡的才具。他说："主宰《战争与和平》的是空间，不是时间。"此话虽然显得有些偏颇，但很有道理。[1] 有时，印象派批评颇能一语破的。不妨把福斯特的话译出来：

> 在人们读了一会儿《战争与和平》之后，心里感到某种回响，但是不能确定是什么东西起了这回响。不是故事引起的，当然托翁和司各脱一样也关心情节的发展，和班内特一样也是诚恳的小说家。也不是哪些插曲，更不是哪些人物引起的。这回响是由俄国广袤的土地引起的，作者把一些情节和人物撒在了这片土地上，是由多少大小桥梁、冰冻的河川、森林、道路、花园、田野累积起来而产生的，在读者经过了这些桥梁河川等等之后，产生了一种宏伟和洪亮的感受。

这段话说得非常好，用在《失乐园》也是再恰当不过的。除了弥尔

---

[1] 此外，福斯特绝对没有认为人物和故事不重要。

顿语言的洪亮的音乐效果外，它还给人以无限的宏伟的空间感。除了空间感以外，它还给人以宏伟的历史感、时间感。这种境界的造成，不是靠一般的真实的细节，而是靠另一种构成空间感的细节。弥尔顿的地理知识，也包括历史知识，起了决定性的作用。这种知识并不是外来的技术性的枝节，而是他的宇宙观和人生观的一部分，是他对人类历史看法的一部分。

这里有两种见解值得研究。一种是把细节看成是技术性的小节，是附加在作品的"局势气脉"上的。林纾《畏庐论文》有一段话就是这个意思。他说：

> 盖局势气脉者，文之大段也；绮章绘句，原属小技，然亦不可不知。大处既已用心，此等末节，亦不能不垂意及之。[1]

小技末节应是同作家的世界观有机地联系起来的，是由它决定的。

另一种见解是认为作者所以能产生宏伟的气势，是因为他能超脱。英国现代诗人宾宁（Laurence Binyan）论弥尔顿就说："在《失乐园》中，呈现在眼前的一切差不多都是从一定距离以外见到的。"王国维在《人间词话》里也有类似的话："诗人对宇宙人生，须入乎其内，又须出乎其外。入乎其内，故能写之；出乎其外，故能观之。入乎其内，故有生气；出乎其外，故有高致。"这类"距离说"的言论是很多的。一入一出，入比较容易体会，出是什么意思？站远一点？保持一定的距离？怎样保持距离？怎样"观"法？

---

[1] 林纾讲的是写文章时用"拼字法"，他说作文时要善于"用寻常经眼之字，一经拼集，便生异观。""蜂蝶者，常用字也，凄惨二字亦然，一拼为蝶凄蜂惨，则异矣。"他讲的方法很象约翰逊论玄学派诗人，"使不和谐的东西，和谐起来"（discordia concors），"把最最不相干的意念硬套在一起"。

是不是如英国十九世纪浪漫派诗人沃兹沃斯所说的"平静中的回忆"？从弥尔顿的《失乐园》来讲"气脉"也好，"高致"也好，都是他的思想境界的体现。同一现实，作家头脑不同，反映在作品里，有的境界高，有的低。境界的高低是决定作品有无价值的一个重要标准。[1] 弥尔顿的境界高，思想有深度，力图捕捉根本性的问题。也许这就是所谓"出"吧。

回到弥尔顿这一段诗。它引起了争论。争论的另一方，即辩护的一方，基本上能着眼于弥尔顿的用意。例如英国学者蒂理亚德（Tillyard）就这样分析："弥尔顿眼前的目的是要给读者这样一个印象——大地各处广阔的空间，历史的各个伟大的时代。简明扼要地罗列一番对这首诗的体制是很必要的。"他批评艾略特说："每个人名或地名都和历史上某一重大事件紧密联系着的，有些地方或因旅行家的游记而出名。而艾略特先生发这样的议论，俨然马可·孛罗和卡蒙斯[2] 从来没有存在过，从来没有引起人们的好奇心似的。"

蒂理亚德仅仅提到好奇心当然是不够的，但是他很精明地注意到弥尔顿的地名人名都和历史上重大事件有关，可惜没有发挥下去。我们知道弥尔顿在少年青年时代就对生活采取十分严肃的态度，立志有所作为。他诗篇中这些地理名词，历史人名的"堆砌"，正表现了在他那种精神状态的推动下长年积累下来的知识，这些知识又反过来影响他的宇宙观人生观的形成，表现在诗篇里就成其"高致"。知识和"小技"、"末节"一样，不是附加的装饰，而是宇宙观人生观的素材，是同根本有关的东西。

---

[1] 美国当代小说家欧文·肖的《富人，穷人》，生活面很广，反映美国社会很生动，但境界不高，表现在作者所最感兴趣的东西，都十分浅露，以至庸俗。许多所谓"现实主义"的小说，都有此病。

[2] 卡蒙斯（camoëns, Luis de, 1524—1580）葡萄牙诗人，军事冒险家，到过印度果阿和中国澳门。

这段诗的情节很简单，不过是要说迈克尔引着亚当和夏娃到乐园的高山上去向他们展示未来，这座山同后来撒旦引诱耶稣时所登上的山，高低和视野都差不多。但诗人却用了三十几行的篇幅，岂非小题大作？而且这个比喻，即撒旦引诱耶稣的图景，在《复乐园》（Ⅲ. 251ff）又大致重复了一遍，只是规模范围略小，足见在弥尔顿思想里占很重要的地位。魔鬼指点山下图景是"为了另一目的"，即用帝国权势引诱耶稣，那么在这里的目的是什么呢？我以为弥尔顿的目的是要把撒旦引诱耶稣时展示的荣华权势和迈克尔即将展示给亚当看的前景作一比较。这前景就是人类吃了禁果以后充满罪恶和灾难的历程以及最后得救的希望。异教的荣华对耶稣是个考验，人类堕落后的灾难对亚当也是个考验。因此把亚当登上的山和耶稣登上的山类比，并大作文章，自有其内在的联系。为达到此目的，他就征用他的丰富的史地知识。从这些知识里，我们可以看出他对这些知识的态度。作为一个人文主义者，他对这些"世俗"的伟业是崇敬的，只是作为一个宗教信徒，作为一个虔诚的清教徒，他才对它持否定态度。弥尔顿的宇宙观人生观是矛盾的，但他始终不能忘怀于人文主义。通过知识的涉猎（当然这不是惟一的途径）形成了他的人文主义宇宙观人生观，而人文主义的宇宙观人生观又使他无限眷恋这些知识，两者互为依存，并在诗歌里流露出来。

作家知识的涉猎和积累牵涉到文学史上常提到的影响问题。这当然只是作家接受外界影响的一条途径。影响问题很复杂，非三言两语所能说清。这里有两个方面值得研究。

影响有偶然因素，但最终决定于作者的需要。有一般的需要，如满足好奇心，有为达到某一具体需要而去积累知识。有些知识遭到天然扬弃——遗忘，有些被批判否定，但并不见得就排除于记忆之外。但文学史上所谓的影响多半指正面的接受。这里面主观因素很大。作者对对象往往怀着同意、同情、热爱、尊敬以至崇拜的心情。勃吞在设计他的理想国时，以墨西哥和中国为借鉴，他说"耶稣会士利玛窦等人笔下的中国人十分勤劳，土地富庶，国中没有一个乞丐或游手好闲的人，因此他们兴旺发达。我们的条件也一样，我们的人民体魄强健，思想活泼，物产应有尽有，如羊毛、亚麻、铁、锡、铅、木材等，也有优秀的工匠来制造产品，但我们缺少勤奋。我们把最好的商品运往海外，他们能很好利用，满足需要，把我们的货物分别加工，又运回到我国，高价出售，有时用零碎原料制成一些廉价品，反回来卖给我们，价钱比成批原料还贵"，如此等等。勃吞为了满足自己对比的需要，而将对象美化。

有时作家只要能满足需要，不求甚解的情况也是有的。例如上引弥尔顿一段诗里，汗八里克即元大都，即下面的北京；有时称中国，有时称塞利卡那，有时称喀塔伊，有时称西那。这里显然有各种不同来源的混淆。也不排除弥尔顿知道是同物异名。他的目的只是要能烘托气势，制造铿锵的音调，即使不尽准确也没有关系。到底文学上的影响有多少是讹传、歪曲、误解，倒是很有趣味的问题。但是作品中准确的材料来源并不一定能构成杰作，文学史上颇有些例子，如福楼拜的《萨朗波》，英国女小说家乔治·爱略特的《罗慕拉》，两位作者都作了实地调查，积累了大量准确知识，但作品都不成功。特别有趣的是这两部作品一部发表在1862年，一部在1863年，看来都是受了实证主义，注重表面事实的影响吧，因而混淆了历史和文学的界限。[1]

---

[1] 《随园诗话》卷五，"宋严有翼诋东坡诗误以葱为韭，以长桑君为仓公……然七百年来，人知有东坡，不知有严有翼"。布什（Douglas Bush）在《牛津英国文学史》卷二评新译《圣经》说："不管旧译有什么缺点，尽管新译很准确，但新译是否超度了更多的灵魂到天堂，很值得怀疑。"

我们讲扩大知识、接受影响，主要指接受优秀文化遗产，也是从我们主观要求出发，关于接受优秀文化遗产的重要性，经典作家的言论俱在，不必赘言。

其次一个问题，影响从某个意义上讲也可理解为思想的接触、砥砺，引起深入思考，把消极的接受变为积极的"探讨"。仅有实践和生活还不足以产生伟大作品，还必须有一定的高度、深度、崇高的境界（也包括表现方式），才能产生伟大作品。英国评论家阿诺德在这方面有值得参考的见解。阿诺德的文学主张是保守的，他把古典文学、文化，奉为标准和规范。他特别强调批评的作用，他认为批评可以帮助促成人们对优秀文学的正确看法，使当代文学向古典优秀文学看齐，这一点正是他保守所在。但他认为批评可以活跃思想界，这是完全正确的。他断言（《批评在当前时代的功能》）思想不活跃，精神生活没有生气，产生不出伟大作品。这话有一定道理（这当然不是惟一的条件，因为产生伟大作品的条件很多）。社会如此，一个作家也是如此。他的思想不和活着的和死了的人的敏锐思想接触、砥砺、对比、参照，很难达到深度，获得"高致"。弥尔顿卷入革命不可谓不深，倘若他不多所涉猎，在涉猎中找到思想素材，找到培养思想的温床，找到磨炼思想的砥石，找到他认为适当的表达手段，也写不出《失乐园》这样不朽的诗篇。

弥尔顿在《再次为英国人民声辩》这篇政论文中有一段著名的自述。他以光明磊落、满怀激情的语气，答复政敌对他个人的诽谤。他写他怎样"从青年时代起，就致力于研究法律，不问是教会法或世俗法，都把它放在优先于一切的地位，因为我考虑到，不管我能否起作用，都应该随时准备为国家、为教会、为那些为传播福音而出生入死的人们服务"。他写他青年时代如何专心致志苦攻学问，大学毕业后在父亲田庄仍然"倾全力阅读希腊拉丁作家的著作，有时也到城里调剂一下生活，不是去买书，便是去吸取一些数学和音乐上的新知识，这些是我当时最感兴趣的东西"。在意大利一年多的旅行，全是同知识界的交往切磋，"使学识和友谊同时获得交流"，"把搜集到的书装船运回"。回国以后，"非常愉快地继续了中断的读书生活，让那些受人民委托的人、特别是上帝，去处理当前的问题"。（指革命前夕的政治。）他采取了"用之则行，舍之则藏"的态度。在十年资产阶级革命风暴中，他积极投身到政治斗争中去，运用他的丰富的学识，写了一系列铿锵有声的政论文章，取得了辉煌的战果。革命失败后，他痛定思痛，如骨鲠在喉，不吐不快，运用他的丰富的学识，写了三部不朽的诗篇。马克思把他比作春蚕，说"弥尔顿出于同春蚕吐丝一样的必要而创作《失乐园》，那是他的天性的能动表现"（《剩余价值理论》）。天性正是说明他的抱负或革命责任感。他把他的学识当作体现这种责任感和抱负的手段。

从弥尔顿和十七世纪一批作家可以看出，他们追求知识都是为满足各自的需要，也是时代的需要。知识对他们的宇宙观人生观起着一定的影响。但仅仅靠知识丰富并不能造成伟大作家。有的作家的作品堆砌知识，有的作家知识很丰富，但仍没有产生第一流的文学作品。但是反过来，如果弥尔顿没有丰富的学识，他的这三部作品乃至其他一切作品也都是不可想象的。具体的知识学问可以在作品里表现出来，但也不一定。学识从根本上说是提高思想境界的一种手段。弥尔顿的学识表现在他的"高致"，也在作品中有具体的表现。在他的"汪洋无际"的学识中，加帆车只能算沧海一粟而已。

（原载《国外文学》第 4 期，1981 年）

菲尔丁论小说和小说家

——介绍《汤姆·琼斯》各卷首章

　　几年来我们介绍了不少现代派作家，介绍了科幻小说、侦探小说、畅销书。这些使我们开阔了文学视野，也值得我们借鉴，但给人的印象似乎是古典的优秀的作家相形之下介绍得少了。这些作家有的已介绍过，有的则还根本没有介绍过，介绍过的也还有待全面和深入的发掘。下面披露的是英国十八世纪小说家菲尔丁的一组文章，希望能重新引起读者的兴趣。[1]

　　菲尔丁（Henry Fielding，1707—1754）是十八世纪英国四大小说家之一，与理查生、斯末莱特、斯特恩齐名。但作为小说家，理查生和斯特恩的影响并未成为此后小说中的主流，斯末莱特的成就也略逊于菲尔丁。近代英国文学史家斯蒂芬（Leslie Stephen）有这样一段话评价菲尔丁：

　　　　若要对英国十八世纪艺术价值很高的文学作一全面的评论，那就必须把菲尔丁放在中心地位，以他为准绳来衡量其他作家，看他们是远远落后于他，还是比较接近他。(《十八世纪

---

[1]　见《国外文学》1981年第2、3期。

英国思想史》)

而十九世纪英国小说家司各脱则径称菲尔丁为"英国小说之父"。

菲尔丁写过二十几部剧本，四部小说，办过期刊。他的小说以《汤姆·琼斯》最有份量。这部小说共十八卷，每卷首章都是一篇散文，这里刊登的是全部"首章"十八篇。他在稍早的一部小说《约瑟夫·安德鲁斯》中也有两篇议论文性质的"首章"，这些和他在期刊中发表的一些文章，都涉及他对创作，特别是小说和小说家的看法（参看《文艺理论译丛》1，1958），很值得重读一遍。

在小说里打断故事的进程，插进去与故事显然无关的议论，我们已不习惯。不过，在菲尔丁时代，小说尚未定型。正如他自己所说，"新领域既然由我开创，规则也可以由我订立"。其实，菲尔丁也不是无可援的先例。塞万提斯在讲故事以前也有过一篇致读者的开场白，莎士比亚有些剧本也有报幕人在开始或结尾时代表作者向观众致辞。作者向读者直接谈话，可能来源于口头文学，中国小说中的"看官如何如何"，也应属此类。再说，小说也无非是作者通过故事和人物向读者表达他的思想观点，对生活的评价。有的作家在故事进程中，也偶尔现身说法。只是菲尔丁把这种作法独立出来，给以独立于故事以外的形式。菲尔丁这位作家写作时，心里总有读者，这不只表现在他力求使情节结构和人物刻划能引人入胜，也表现在与读者直接见面。他在下面第十八卷第一章里就把作者比作是读者的有趣的旅伴。十九世纪英国女小说家乔治·爱略特（George Eliot）曾说过：

菲尔丁好像是把他的安乐椅挪到前台，用他那美妙的英语，精力充沛而又不慌不忙地和我们闲谈一样。

在菲尔丁以后，托尔斯泰在《战争与和平》里也写过一些"首章"，表达他的历史观和哲学（九卷一章、十一卷一章、十三卷一章、尾章），悲天悯人，不管你同意与否，他那严肃认真的态度是十分深挚感人的。菲尔丁当然同托尔斯泰气质很不一样，但他们有一个共同点，那就是大凡他们最关注的问题，感受最深的问题，形象所不能表达或未充分表达的，都出之于单独的篇章，以补其不足。这两家的文章，在各自规定的范围内，立论精辟，写得十分漂亮雄辩，都是极好的散文。菲尔丁的散文还有一个特点，同他的性格一样，就是讽刺性强，笔之所之，对当时社会上和文学界各方面的陋习偏见都不放过，以幽默的笔调给以嘲弄，使人读来兴味盎然，也使人联想到鲁迅的杂文。因此，问题不在应不应该写这些"首章"，而是在写得好不好。写得好，读者不仅得到教益，也得到享受，丰富了整部作品对读者心理上产生的效应。从这一点说，"首章"不能看作是节外生枝，赘疣，蛇足，破坏了形象。如果读者认为罗唆，他尽可跳过不读。不过，不读确是个损失。

要谈菲尔丁的《汤姆·琼斯》各卷首章，恐怕要从菲尔丁其人谈起。

菲尔丁出生在1688年"光荣革命"之后，英国是个资产阶级和贵族联合统治的局面，贵族还很有力量。菲尔丁的曾祖父是个伯爵，父亲是个将军，他对上流社会是很熟悉的。他在伊顿中学读书，又到荷兰莱登大学学文学。但他本人经济地位不过中等，并无正业，靠写作为生，性挥霍，好杯中物。他经营了"小剧院"，他的时事讽刺剧《1736年历史纪录》导致了1737年议会颁布出版检查法，剧院停业。他一方面改学法律，1740年获律师资格，一方面改写小说。1748年他被任命为伦敦威斯敏斯特区的治安法官。1754年他到葡萄牙养病，同年死于里斯本。

菲尔丁对下层人民十分同情，称他们为"第四等级"见《修道院花园》周报，第47期，1752；参看《文艺理论译丛》1，1958）。他讽刺得最厉害的是贵族。但是他只限于讽刺他们的愚蠢和虚荣，而忽略他们的虚伪与罪恶。他要的是嘲笑而不是憎恶。他揶揄丑恶，希望在一笑之中起到改善道德的作用。他对一切既讪笑，也谅解，因为他觉得"十全十美的好人只存在在墓碑上的铭文里"。这正是他的幽默的根源，成为英国小说传统中的一个突出的特点，或许也是弱点。

菲尔丁的创作就是在这样的思想基础上进行的。

《汤姆·琼斯》各卷首章可以说是他对自己的丰富的戏剧创作和小说创作的经验总结。他把这套总结出来的理论付之创作实践，因此他可以说是一个有意识的小说家。在这一点上，他很象现代派诗人艾略特。他的这些议论可以同他的小说相互印证。他的小说理论总的说来是现实主义的。他对小说的性质、内容、情节结构、人物刻划、对话诸方面都有看法。这在小说理论史上占有重要地位。在菲尔丁之前只有关于作为叙事文学的史诗的理论，还没有关于小说的理论。特别是他对小说家应具备的条件，虽然都是老生常谈，今天读来也还能起到提醒的作用。

菲尔丁的出发点是反对传奇小说。这里需要交代一下。在菲尔丁写小说以前，法国和英国先后出现了一批这类小说。对这类小说最好的描写莫过于1751年问世的一篇文章，题为《论菲尔丁先生奠定的新的写作品种》，极力称赞菲尔丁，而反对传奇。其言曰："在这新的写作品种出现之前，社会上有些书泛滥成灾，它们一般叫作传奇或小说、故事等等，充满了最离奇古怪的东西。所有这些作品中，可能性是不需要的；想法越离奇，读者越觉得其味无穷。什么钻石的宫殿、飞马、青铜堡垒等等都被看作合情合理，合乎高级趣味，一句话，是这类作品中最完美的作品，其实只不过是一团乌烟瘴气，驴唇不对马嘴。这个怪物首先产生在法国，我们从我们这邻邦进口了许多荒唐东西，其中也有它，而且感到很骄傲……这种疾病已变成了流行病，简直没有希望治愈，直到菲尔丁先生出来向人们证明，纯真的'自然'和那些虚无缥缈、不存在的形象相比，同样能提供快感和兴趣。"《汤姆·琼斯》第六卷和第八卷的首章主要讲这个问题。

当然，在菲尔丁写小说之前，已有笛福、斯威夫特、理查生写过小说。前二人无论从人物的刻划或情节的安排讲，都比较粗线条或机械，理查生则视野狭小，小市民说教气味浓厚，为菲尔丁所反对。再往前，艾迪生的人物肖像画更是零散，属于素描性质，没有放在大的社会环境中来写。再往前则有塞万提斯和流浪汉小说，菲尔丁无疑受到他们的影响，但那些小说也是情节结构松散。因此菲尔丁必须制订自己写作的指导方针。他虽无系统的论著，但从本书、《约瑟夫·安德鲁斯》和其他文章中，可以看出他接触到了小说创作的主要问题。在内容问题上，他说他要写的是"人性"，又说他写的是"历史"，也就是以现实生活为其内容。他讲到人物既要有共性，又要有个性，他讲到小说的结构是由作者选择的重点事件决定的，不应事无巨细，平铺直叙，象写传记那样。他讲到刻划人物要用对比的方法。他甚至考虑到读者的反应。所有这些方面的意见，考虑到他所处的时代，不能不说是一个极大的创举。

当然，菲尔丁也得力于古代文艺理论，特别是亚理士多德的模仿说和贺拉斯的合乎自然和善于判断的主张。

菲尔丁把他的小说叫作"用散文写的喜剧性的史诗"，规定了小说的性质、内容与形式。所谓史诗主要是指生活画面的广阔。所谓诗，一方面为小说争取地位，一方面应象十八世纪诗歌那样含有道德内容。所谓散文应是指用诗歌叙述故事的时代（如中世纪传奇诗）已过去了。他在重病在身去里斯本养病途中写的《里斯本航行记》中有这样一段话："历代对荷马的崇高诗篇给予了公正的赞美，但我不得不承认，如果他用卑微的散文写他那时代的真实历史，我将更加尊崇他，热爱他。我读荷马，虽说感到十分钦佩，拍案叫绝，但我读（希腊历史家）希罗多德、修西底德、色诺芬却更觉愉快和满意。"

在所有这些"首章"中，最系统最重要的要数第九卷第一章（第十三卷第一章又扼要重复一遍）。菲尔丁在这里所谈的问题当然又是老生常谈，但不妨将他提出这几点的思想背景谈一谈。

十八世纪是理性时代，一切以"自然"为准。不过"自然"是一条变色龙，浪漫派理解的自然同古典主义者很不一样。在古典主义者看来，合乎"自然"即合乎"理性"和"常识"。那么，什么又是理性和常识，我们已经有许多著作分析过了，这里不重复。文学创作也应遵循自然，模仿自然。菲尔丁正是在这样的思潮下生活和创作的。因此他反对传奇，强调文学的真实性。要获得真实性，就必须在观察现实有判断力，即他所说的要能发现"所观察事物的真正本质"。这种能力，他称为天才，而天才是"自然所赋予的"。归根到底，就是诗人蒲伯所说的："首先要服从自然，按照她的公正的、永不可变的准绳，来形成你的判断。"

自然的准绳，联系到文艺的创作，已经反映在古代希腊、罗马亚理士多德、贺拉斯等人所立下的创作法则里了。因此，作家要有学识，学识是判断的工具。当然，学识也还有文化修养的涵义，也就是读书破万卷的意思。也许，除了某些纯朴的抒情诗、民间故事以外，文学，尤其长篇小说，脱离了深厚的文化传统，没有广博的学识，深刻的哲学思想内容，很难成为伟大的作品。即使抒情诗和民间故事也不可能完全脱离文化传统。西方有些学者喜欢研究一个作家读过哪些书。奥斯丁·多布逊在《十八世纪人物素描》中估计菲尔丁的藏书，同文豪约翰逊和大学教授诗人格雷相埒。他翻检菲尔丁死后拍卖藏书的清单，共计653组，其中包括荷马史诗，柏拉图、亚理士多德的哲学著作，普鲁塔克的传记，希腊喜剧家和悲剧家的作品，希腊讽刺家琉善，塞万提斯，蒙田，以及当代戏剧、传记、科学、哲学、神学、历史和大量法律著作和其他古典文学，以至字典。他去里斯本养病途中还带着柏拉图，可以说是饱学而终生手不释卷。他读书，而且消化，成为自己文化修养的一部分。有人这样评论他："有人拿学问来夸耀自己，而他从小养成读书习惯，十分熟悉其内容，因此他用的时候很方便，毫无学究气，好象完全是与生俱来的一样。"（多布逊引《评论季刊》1855）

值得注意的是他并不是只重学识，也注重了解人生，向生活学习，就是他所说的"交往"。他强调实践和观察生活，以补书本知识之不足。这一点也是从古代作家那里继承来的。贺拉斯的《诗艺》尽管大部分谈技巧问题，但他的前提还是"到生活中，到风俗习惯中，去寻找模型"，甚至"从那里汲取活生生的语言吧"。在这方面，菲尔丁本人的经历提供了例证。他不象格雷一生呆在书斋，也不象约翰逊生活局限于伦敦的俱乐部，而是接触面极广。他出身贵族乡绅，但不得不与贫困打交道，靠一支笔谋生。他为政府办刊物，他自办剧院，与演员作家交往，后来学了法律，当了法官，各地巡回，既接触到地方上绅士大户、教会人物、医生、律师，也接触到社会下层。从这大致轮廓来看，他的生活经历是很丰富的，也使他认识到要创作成功必须有生活知识，有意识地接触各种各类的人。但有意思的是他把生活体验放在学识之下，两次如此。中国古语也是先说读万卷书后说行万里路，可能也有一定道理。先没有思想和广博的知识武装，一头扎进生活，也是看不出问题的，更何论站得高，看得远呢？

在谈到"交往"时，菲尔丁强调面要广，不仅要熟悉上层，也要熟悉下层，因为上下层是相互为依据的，就是他在第五卷首章所说，一切存在于矛盾和对比之中。

最后他提出作者应具备好心肠，感受力要强。他继承了贺拉斯"自己哭才能使读者哭，自己笑才能使读者笑"的原理，强调作者自己必须先有感受，这一原则也是老生常谈，但也是正确的。但从菲尔丁的创作实践看，他使人笑的时候占多数，很少几乎从不使人哭或忿怒。他并不疾恶如仇，而是用幽默宽容的态度对待一切。这竟成了英国批判现实主义传统中的一根支柱。即以这部小说的主人公而论，他既不是史诗般的英雄，也非传奇式的英雄，也非纯粹的流浪汉，而是个仅具中人之才，天真善良又有弱点和缺点的人物。菲尔丁的理论是，把人物写得太理想化，太高大，非常人所能企及，不能达到劝善的效果；人物要合乎"情理"。一部小说使好人变得聪明些，这是比较容易办到的，而要使坏人变好是很难的。菲尔丁可以算作最早的"中间人物论"者。

关于菲尔丁在小说方面的成就（如有人说《汤姆·琼斯》是英国小说中结构最好的一部）和缺点（如人物平板），不属本文范围，从略。从以下文章可以引伸议论的东西也还不少，但比较明白易晓，也一律从略。

（原载《国外文学》第 2 期，1981 年）

斯末莱特和他的《蓝登传》

　　斯末莱特是十八世纪英国优秀的小说家之一。高尔基在《俄国文学史》中曾说："继菲尔丁而起的有斯末莱特，他以绝大的魄力描写出当时英国社会的缺点，而且是第一个把政治倾向性的描写引进小说范围内的人。"斯末莱特的小说描写了十八世纪英国的政治，暴露了殖民战争的残酷，议会的腐败，政府的贪污和官吏的无能。他所描写的十八世纪"英国社会的缺点"有一定的广度；在艺术风格上，虽然说他和同时代的前辈菲尔丁有相似的地方，但是菲尔丁的叙述保持着史诗般的、缓慢的步伐，语言比较含蓄，而斯末莱特的小说则是一个情节接着一个情节，速度比较紧迫，用粗线条勾勒出贵族和资产阶级的肮脏、丑恶、凶狠的面貌。

　　斯末莱特（1721—1771）出生于苏格兰小地主家庭。祖父是当地一个法官，父亲因不是长子，没有继承权。作者生后不久，父亲逝世，自己成了孤儿，从此一生就和贫困打交道。他在少年时代曾到格拉斯哥跟一个医生当学徒，但他爱好文学，在十八岁那年写了一部诗体悲剧《弑君者》，并带了这部作品到伦敦去，希望上演，但没有成功。在二十岁那年，他设法当了一名海军军医助手，参加了 1741 年英、法争夺西班牙在西印度群岛殖民地的战争，战争结束后，他退出海军，在牙买加住下来。1744年他携带妻子回国，从此靠行医和写作维持生活。他在1748、1751、1753年连续发表了三部小说《蓝登传》、《皮克尔传》、《菲迪南伯爵传》。1755年翻译了《唐·吉诃德》。1757年出版了一部《英国史》，从1689写到出书的年份。同时，1756年他还办了一个杂志，名为《评论杂志》，在杂志里他抨击海军将领，因此于1759年被捕入狱。1762年他为托利党（贵族保守党）人办了一个周刊，名为《不列颠人》，托利党原想利用刊物进行宣传，但结果反而树敌更多，就勒令斯末莱特停刊。1763年，由于长期在贫困中紧张写作，健康受损，他到国外休养，并写了《法意游记》（于1766年发表）。1765年他回国后，仍然紧张工作，因为体力不支和肺病的缠磨，又不得不出国。他想求得意大利来亨城领事职位，但没有成功，就在来亨附近继续从事写作，完成了讽刺英国两党政治的小说《原子传》（1769年发表）、诗歌《独立颂》和最后一部优秀小说《克林克传》（1771年发表）。1771年死于意大利。

斯末莱特生活的时代正是英国资本主义发展的时期。资产阶级在政治上的地位已经巩固。残酷的圈地运动已经接近完成，农村已经开始完全资本主义化，同时，进一步对殖民地的掠夺也在进行，农民继续被剥夺土地而成为劳动后备军。资产阶级用残酷的手段在国内外积累资本，给工业革命创造条件。斯末莱特最后一部小说《克林克传》正反映了工业革命开始后的英国现实。在社会上，封建的土地贵族把土地分成小块出租，自己在伦敦或国外过着寄生享乐的生活，他们和大资产阶级——金融资本家、英格兰银行的股东、大公司老板是一鼻孔出气的。自从1689年以后，英国统治阶级内部就是资产阶级和贵族的妥协局面，大贵族也已经资产阶级化。当然，社会上封建残余并未完全肃清，例如还有大贵族以外的中小地主，他们住在田庄上，把土地出租，在乡间佃户中还是作威作福，充当治安推事，以一种封建家长的姿态称霸一方。这些人时常成为菲尔丁、斯末莱特小说中攻击的主要对象。农村中的自耕农和小租佃者，由于资本主义扩张的结果，绝大部分濒于破产。圈地运动把他们驱离自己的土地，公地也被人夺去，不能使用，就连打鱼、打猎、砍柴都不允许，他们无法为生，或成为农业、纺织业的雇工，或被迫入济贫所。大批农民流入城市，"幸运"的成为出卖劳力的雇工或散工，不幸的则沦为乞丐、小偷、流氓，妻女则沦为娼妓。这样，阶级分化就越来越厉害了。

介乎贫富之间的是一大批中小资产阶级，就是独立经营的商人、店主、手工艺人等等。这一阶层的幅度也比较大，其中有殷实的商人、店主，他们受到大公司的排挤，但要争取发财的机会，因而要求"公平交易"。他们继承了清教徒的传统或其他反对国教的教派的传统，来抵抗和大资本家大贵族结合的国教，他们要求在议会中有他们的地位，因而反对辉格党首相沃尔浦尔的政府对议会的控制，反对政府的贪污贿赂，因此也有赞成托利党的。但是他们也主张扩大帝国和殖民主义。他们有可能爬上大资产阶级的地位，也可能下降。狄福即属于这一阶层。在这一阶层的另一端，则是一些手工艺者，他们每天劳动多达十四小时，妻子儿女也参加劳动，生活可以免于饥寒。他们的命运取决于贸易是否繁荣，由于贸易不稳定，他们的生活经常受到威胁。机器的发明、廉价的自由劳动市场的存在，对他们威胁最大，因此他们为了争取生存权利，也组织起来，时常举行反对政府的起义，并且得到贫民的支持。但是贸易情况有起色，粮食落价，生活得到改善，他们的反抗意识也相应减弱。

在这样一个阶级对立的形势之中，斯末莱特所处的是怎样一个地位呢？斯末莱特的祖父虽然是个中小地主，但他自己的经济地位却是属于中小资产阶级的知识分子，因此他具有一般资本主义社会的中小资产阶级知识分子的共同点，也具有十八世纪英国社会中这一阶层的特点。从作者的全部创作中来看，从他的《弑君者》到《独立颂》，他的主要倾向应该就是反对当时大资产阶级和资产化了的贵族的联合统治。他在历史剧《弑君者》中（这是一出以十五世纪初英格兰历史为题材的剧本），通过从英国回来登位的苏格兰王詹姆士一世的口，说道："我发现你们这可怜的国家处在疮痍和绝望之中；城镇在内战中沦落了，田野荒芜了；秩序荡然无存，文艺凋敝；无人劳动，只有一些肮脏的手在祸国殃民；没有法律来保护穷人，钳制罪恶的大人物；丑恶的饥馑和吃人的瘟疫这一双姐妹联合起来，造成一片地狱般的景象。"这是作者十八岁时写的。在他五十岁逝世那一年，他写了一首题名为《独立颂》的诗，歌颂美国争取独立的斗争。诗中谴责了历史上一系列的封建专制暴君，赞美欧洲十六七世纪以来的资产阶级民主革命，一直到他当时的意大利民族解放运动。他在诗中这样歌颂资产阶级的民主自由：

> 他[1] 是我的精神向导，在我青年时代，
> 教导我去鄙视煊赫，把它看成草芥；
> 他鞭笞我，叫我口中只说真理，
> 我心里不这样想，嘴里也决不奉承。

作者的政治见解最明显地表现在《蓝登传》里。他说："每个人天生就有享受自由的权利；国王要人民效忠，他就得保护他们；

---

[1] "他"指"自由"。

如果因为国王暴虐而破坏了这种相互的关系，破坏了君民之间的契约，那么国王就应该负责任，并受法律的处罚；英国人的历次起义……是挽救天赋予人民的自由的壮举。"这是资产阶级革命时期提出的社会契约说和自然权利论的反映。十七世纪英国诗人弥尔顿在《论君权》的政论中就提出这种主张。不过斯末莱特则更接近于"光荣革命"后的洛克的政治见解。洛克反对专制制度，但主张君主立宪。斯末莱特的政治见解基本上属于洛克的范畴。

说明作者的世界观和理解《蓝登传》这部作品的关系尤其直接，因为这部小说可以说是一部自传性的小说，小说主人公的遭遇基本是根据作者自己的遭遇写的。当然这并不意味蓝登就是作者自己，蓝登的结局就是作者自己的结局；相反，小说是经过加工的，某些地方夸大了，某些地方更加集中，某些地方则包含着虚构。这样，蓝登就更加成为当时英国社会的一个典型。

在十八世纪中叶的英国，象蓝登这样的人物比比皆是，他们不是出身于豪门贵族，而是人数众多的破落贵族。这批人由于生活地位的不稳定，对现实处处不满，但他们绝不是革命的，而是想在现存秩序内向上爬，加入统治集团，要求改变现存秩序也只是从这一点出发。这些人充斥了小说中议员克林哲的住宅和海军部的接待室，徘徊在权贵府邸的门外。小说中这种人不只蓝登一个，还有汤姆逊、杰克逊、麦洛波因等等，他们都是一些飘浮在历史潮流上面的人物。蓝登是一个"出身好"，"谦卑而有品德"的青年；他的祖父是个小地主，父亲是少子，在婚姻上违背了祖父的意旨，违反了封建道德，以致弄得妻子惨死，自己也发疯"失踪"。蓝登自幼受堂兄（长孙）和堂姐妹的气，靠当海员的舅父赒济，才上了大学，后来接济中断，又去学外科医生。当时的外科医生的社会地位和理发师差不多，业务上也接近，因此蓝登就听了师父的劝告，到伦敦去谋生活。在路上他遇见老同学、现在当了理发师的斯特拉普，一同到伦敦去冒险，这好比是唐·吉诃德找到了他的桑科·潘札。到伦敦后，他夤缘苏格兰议员克林哲，想求一军医之职，不成，又去投考军医，但考中之后，却无缺可补。房主人推荐他到一个法国人开的药店去当伙计，遇见了和他命运相似的威廉斯。命运好象故意要捉弄他：他想从大门入海军没有成功，却从旁门进去了——他被拉壮丁的拉进了海军，参加了西印度殖民战争，受到无数屈辱与惊险，才回到本国。刚一回到本国国土，就遇到抢劫，经赛治利夫人的介绍，给水仙的姑母当仆人，爱上了水仙，但受到地主提摩太的妒恨和迫害，逃到海滨，又被海盗俘去，挟到法国，走投无路，当了雇佣军，参加了德汀根战役，又遇见斯特拉普，决定利用这位理发师的积蓄，伪装贵族，靠欺骗发财。于是他初试锋芒，出入凡尔赛宫廷，颇有春风得意之感。回到伦敦后，他就过着流氓骗子的生活，和一班贵族骗子厮混，生活不外是骗人、受骗。随后，他尾随一个有钱而残废的女子到了巴斯，在巴斯又遇见水仙，但水仙哥哥和贵族奎佛韦特从中作梗，将水仙劫持而去。蓝登也追到伦敦，以负债入狱，亏得舅父及时把他从监狱中赎出，一同出海贩卖黑奴，在中美遇见父亲，父亲早已致富，于是父子回国，主人公和水仙结成了美满婚姻，衣锦还乡。

从蓝登的一生遭遇可以看出，他和一百五十年或二百年以前的"皮卡罗"（骗子）本质相同，但在表现上已有显著的不同。他们都是飘浮在历史潮流上面的人物，但历史潮流本身已起了变化，所以飘浮在上面的碎木杂草也不同了。文艺复兴时期的"皮卡罗"是封建关系崩溃时被投到社会上的一批叫化子、雇佣武士、冒险家，其典型人物即莎士比亚创造的福尔斯塔夫。他们接近流氓，破坏着一切对自己不利的东西。封建道德已经不能维系，资产阶级道德没有确立，因此他们不遵循任何道德准则。而蓝登的时代则是贵族—资产阶级的统治已经巩固，他完全接受了资产阶级一套道德标准和社会秩序，谋求个人出路。他也反封建，批判资本主义制度，但又肯定封建关系，肯定贩卖黑奴的罪恶制度。一个是盲目破坏，一个是肯定现存制度。蓝登和早一代的鲁滨孙又不同，鲁滨孙是个小商人、小店主的典型，有可能爬上大资产阶级的地位；而蓝登则是乡村小地主的次子的儿子，社会地位在下降，但他有技能，有文化修养，有强烈的"自尊心"，看不起手工业者、小商人。蓝登又不同于当时或稍后的激进民主派的知识分子如霍恩·图克或卡特莱特，因为他不接近人民运动。他和大卫·考柏菲尔有相同的地方，两个作者的意图——引起读者的同情——也是一致的，但蓝登的性格中还没有感伤主义的成分，这和小资产阶级在不同时代所处的不同的地位又是分不开的。在斯末莱特后期作品中，感伤成分开始冒头，但蓝登性格中则有更多的愤懑与不平。他和稍早的吉尔·布拉斯所采取的道德标准和遭遇也有相似之处，但是吉尔·布拉斯的流氓式的乐观主义则是蓝登所没有的，而吉尔·布拉斯的积极参加政治活动，最后成为小贵族，是和法国专制政治有关，不可能发生在蓝登身上。蓝登并不是不愿意替贵族奔走的，他趋奉斯触特威尔，愿意做驻外大使的秘书，但在英国政治舞台上贵族的势力已经是强弩之末了，所以不可能得到吉尔·布拉斯的结局。

蓝登这一典型人物只可能产生在十八世纪中叶英国资本主义社会的环境中。这一类人的出路，作者在小说中点得很充分、很清楚。一条就是投靠统治阶级，为它服务；再一条就是赌博冒险。蓝登有一定的知识，希望以此为本钱和统治阶级达成买卖关系。他早期的努力无非想在海军里求得一官半职，但这条路并不通。蓝登、汤姆逊、杰克逊、包凌、摩根等人的遭遇都说明了这一点。要作个

"自由职业者"的作家，如果不同流合污，出路也只可能是欠债坐牢。这是作者现实主义成功的地方。此外就是赌博冒险这条路子。这是十足的寄生者的道路。蓝登的社会地位虽然"谦卑"，但他自认为是一个"有品德的人"，有知识分子的架子。他对自己没有受到贵族式的教育，总是显得酸溜溜的。斯特拉普和他同学，而且在一定意义上也是同行，但蓝登决不愿意做个手艺人或"下等人"，在外科医生和理发师之间，他根本没有考虑过后一种职业。可以做贵族的家庭教师（如蓝登之父），可以给资本家、大地主管帐（如汤姆逊），但要脱离后来所谓的"白领子"阶层，那是坚决不干的。斯特拉普和他的关系很微妙，既是平等的朋友，又是他的仆人，是仆人又不付工资，反向仆人求赒济，但斯特拉普主要是仆人，是他的桑科·潘札。这样的关系也就说明，在蓝登心目中，做一个自食其力的手艺人是不屑为的，显然这不是什么真正的出路。他自己在水仙家当仆人则是另有目的，处处强调自己有教养，出身好。他在黎姆斯时盘算道："作生意吧，本钱小，海上有风险，有仇人，还有市场上的竞争，这条路不能走。回到苏格兰挂牌行医吧，医生这一行在苏格兰已人满之患。……作官吧，我既不善逢迎拍马，又不肯鬻笔为腐败可耻的政府写文章辩护。"因此只有冒险、赌博。这一点也是作者现实主义成功的地方。作者在小说中给我们描绘了各种不同的冒险赌博的具体方式：娶阔女人、猎取遗产、到殖民地去冒险、做强盗、或竟是名符其实的赌钱。这些道路，蓝登几乎都尝试过。但主人公最后的成功则完全是作者的幻想。

蓝登之所以选择冒险赌博的道路是和他的人生哲学分不开的。他幼年受到封建家庭的迫害，后来在资产阶级统治的社会里到处碰钉子，因此他要求反抗。他说："我们不是那么轻易把仇恨忘掉的。"但是他的反抗手段就是资产阶级教给他的，和他所反抗的对象同样腐朽。他从资本主义社会学到的是："救人先救己"，"世界为我存在，不是我为世界存在"，"贫困犹如可怕的恶魔，必须驱除它"。一句话，就是以利己主义攻利己主义。因此，为了个人利益，他可以牺牲他所推崇的原则，可以逆来顺受，可以朝三暮四。蓝登的反抗完全出于他的屈辱的社会地位。他总爱吹嘘他的才华、出身、教育、知识、勇敢，甚至漂亮的外表，以这些向封建、资产阶级社会来表白自己。他一方面表现为高傲、自尊、热爱"真理"，而另一方面也必然表现为虚伪苟且、没有原则。因此，蓝登从反抗封建家庭的不公正出发，而结果发展到贩卖黑奴起家，婚姻美满，衣锦荣归。这样的思想与行动也正是这一时代的典型产物。

在小说里，蓝登式的人物——他的影子，也还有不少。汤姆逊这青年是蓝登的同乡，也是医生，也是求官不得，而处于山穷水尽的地步。他之所以能入海军，全靠偶然与原来补缺者的姓名相同。他有一定的正义感，但性格不如蓝登"坚强"，在暴力面前无能为力，他解决矛盾的办法是投海自杀。杰克逊也是蓝登一位同乡青年医生，他的遭遇也很典型，与蓝登不同的地方是他有些纨袴习气，喜欢挥霍享乐，结果入了监牢，以至疯癫。斯特拉普则是蓝登这一阶层更"下一等"的人物，他是鞋匠之子，有一定文化，职业是理发师。他为人慷慨善良，但善良得似乎有些愚蠢，而且十分胆怯。他只能作奴仆。但他既然是好心人，就应该得好报。麦洛波因在作者笔下被写成一个学识渊博、才气横溢、道德高尚、为人谦逊的正面人物。他的命运是当时稍微进步一些的职业作家普遍遭受的命运。他的剧本脚本被人丢在厨房当废纸烧了（斯末莱特的《弑君者》也被某贵族丢入厕所）。他最终的命运也只能是负债入狱。威廉斯可以看成是女蓝登或女斯特拉普，她的命运也正是小资产阶级妇女的命运。这些人物在一定意义上是蓝登性格的补充，同时通过他们，作者更广泛地反映了十八世纪这一阶层的青年的命运，拿威廉斯的话来说："瞻望前途，等待我的只是警官和监狱。"因此作者向社会提出控诉，因为这社会认为不幸就是犯罪。此外，象具有海员特点的包凌和摩根，作者都赋予他们以善良的品质和不幸的遭遇。作者对他们都表示同情，但由于他分析不出不幸的原因，所以这些人只能如威廉斯所说："我一定得亲手给自己开辟一条得救的道路"，也就是说，用个人奋斗的办法寻找出路。这种办法也是具有典型意义的。作者给其中一些人以不幸的归宿，另一些人包括主人公在内，以幸福的结局。这正说明了作者思想中的矛盾：他看出在那社会里，这种人是没有出路的，正如他自己潦倒的一生那样，但同时他仍旧幻想在现存秩序范围之内可以找到个人出路。

小说中另外一些人物，如赛治利夫人、水仙姑母、特别是水仙本人，则完全是一些幻想的、抽象的、概念化的人物，缺乏典型意义。女主人公的特点有三：一美貌；二懂道理，也就是顺从；三有教养，也就是"上等人"；而最重要的是四，有钱。女主人公的形象只说明作者思想的局限性，缺乏真实性。

小说中的反面人物塑造得比较成功。通过他们，作者揭露了十八世纪英国社会的黑暗。最突出的反面形象欧克姆，这个军舰舰长蛮横凶残，鞭死一批病兵而无动于衷，同时又是愚蠢无知，胆小怯懦，隐瞒自己天主教的信仰。他死后留下一大笔资财，表明他生前是个贪污克扣军饷的人。他的亲信麦克贤则媚上欺下，草菅人命。新舰长则是另一类型，与欧克姆成一鲜明对照，代表一种完全腐朽的阶级。他把自己打扮得香喷喷的象个女人，把别人都看成肮脏的下等动物，用望远镜了望来访者，生怕访者的"浊气"把他熏昏过去。通过这些生动形象，我们可以清晰地看到当时形形色色的魑魅魍魉的面貌。

值得注意的是大多数反面人物都是贵族地主之流，如上述两个舰长，又如怯懦无能的葛奇，只注意人们衣装服饰的恰特，粗暴的水仙哥哥，凶恶、淫秽的提摩太爵士，以及蓝登的堂兄、祖父，虚伪贪财而又好色的斯触特威尔，甚至比较清醒的班特也是一个玩世不恭的厌世者。作者描绘了这一系列人物，使我们看到十八世纪作为英国统治阶级的贵族的腐朽性，这是符合历史真实的。但是作者常是从个人恩怨出发，从知识分子自诩的才华观点出发，例如对西印度殖民战争的描写，作者只从将帅不和、领导无能等角度来描写战争的失败，揭发欧克姆的凶暴，也难免表面化。

　　但是作者所描绘的画面毕竟还是有一定的广度，而骗子小说的形式也有助于作家拓展他的批判面。主人公从苏格兰出发到了"魔鬼的客厅"——伦敦，从伦敦到牙买加、卡塔吉纳，从中美又回到英国南部色塞克斯郡，又被劫往法国，从布隆港到阿棉城，参加雇佣军到德国德汀根打仗，打过仗又到了黎姆斯和巴黎，从巴黎又回到伦敦，从伦敦到巴斯，又回伦敦，又到色塞克斯郡，又往非洲，到巴拉圭，从这里回到英国，又回到苏格兰。他经历了三大洲，三四个国家，出入于英国贵族的府邸、政府的衙门、议员的客厅、时髦的游憩场所、小商店、军舰、公路、文人荟萃的咖啡馆、赌场、黑店、殖民者的庄园、以至监狱，妓馆。作者揭露批判比较成功的有以下几个方面。封建和资本主义关系；社会的贫困化；殖民战争和海盗行为；统治机器的腐败和黑暗。

　　主人公的父亲就是因为违背了封建道德，以致妻子死去，自己也一度患了精神病。主人公的堂姐希望得到祖父遗产而不住地亲吻垂死的老头子，不嫌恶臭，但是她一听到没有留给她遗产，她就晕厥过去。贵族的腐朽性和寄生性也在作者笔下受到尖锐讽刺，最成功的应算斯触特威尔。他表面象一位长者，温和、坦率、关心青年、慈祥，又有古典文学修养，但骨子里却是个骗子、寄生虫，专靠欺骗过活。他骗去了蓝登的怀表，但这还不是他最坏的品质，他主要的特征还在于他是个荒淫无耻的禽兽。除他以外，"魔鬼的客厅"还充满了大大小小的寄生虫，他们造谣言、赌博，专靠吸吮别人的血来过活。他们凶恶、怯懦又虚伪。在水仙哥哥身上体现了小地主恶霸的本色，他以金钱要挟自己的妹妹屈从他的意旨。在麦洛波因的插曲中也揭露了早期资本主义社会中文坛的商业化。甚至象包凌这样的人都不肯把钱交给自己心爱的外甥，因为钱就是权力，钱不在手，他说话就没有分量，不能控制外甥。整个资本主义社会人与人的关系都充满了欺诈、虚伪。

在这样一个社会里，受苦难的是穷人，在工业革命前夕的英国，社会两极分化是很急遽的。被剥夺了土地的农民，有的去当了兵，即使不成炮灰，也被官长折磨死。贫富的分化使一部分人铤而走险，英国的公路正是英国社会的缩影。作者通过主人公赴伦敦途中的遭遇，被走私人劫持，以及将钱缝在裤腰夹层内等等细节，充分反映了当时英国社会的现实。因此主人公曾说："天地之大，唯有英国这个国家，老实的穷人最难生存。"这还是很有概括意义的。

作者以极大篇幅描写了英国殖民地扩张的肮脏过程，从拉壮丁到在军舰上受虐待，过着非人的生活，到战争中遭到的悲惨结局；从公开宣布海盗的合法性到贩卖黑奴。通过这些描写，读者可以比较具体地认识到资本主义原始积累这一残酷过程中的这一环节。

作者在这部作品中也揭露了英国统治机器的腐败与黑暗，主要是政府的贪污、官吏的无能和对老百姓的欺压。在辉格党人沃尔浦尔执政的漫长年代里，贪污之风、拉裙带关系等泛滥一时，作品中反映的也是真实情况。此外，对于作为统治阶级压迫工具的监狱，作者的描写也是十分真实的。最典型的要算威廉斯在狱中的生活，连寻死的自由也都被剥夺了，因而她说："只有布莱德威尔教养院（按即监狱）最接近于我心目中一向想到的地狱。"

《蓝登传》这部小说从好的方面讲，通过蓝登一生的经历，揭露了十八世纪中叶英国社会的黑暗面，这一点应予充分的肯定。但主人公对一切的愤慨完全从个人出发，得意则喜悦，失意则愤慨，而且同流合污，随俗浮沉。也就是说，作者尽管有民主倾向，还没有能透过社会现象看到社会问题的本质。正如高尔基在《苏联的文学》中所说："叛逆的个人在批判自己的社会的生活的时候，通常是……为了自己的生活的失败以及它的耻辱而图谋复仇的愿望，"很少是"出自对社会经济各种原因的意义的深刻正确的理解"。当然我们不必苛求古人，但是这一点是必须指出的。

作者的优点和弱点也体现在作品的艺术上的成就和不足之处。总的说来，斯末莱特和菲尔丁这一派小说家是介乎文艺复兴和十九世纪批判现实主义之间的小说家。斯末莱特继承了塞万提斯的传统，首先有意识地否定类似骑士传奇这类毫无现实根据的"荒唐的奇谈"，肯定小说应该反映现实。他们在人物性格的塑造上也是介乎这两个时代之间的。斯末莱特在《蓝登传》前言中所说的"寓言"手法可以概括他的特点。他的人物也有夸张，但也企图通过若干特征来刻划出人物的性格，这样的人物也具有一定典型性。文艺复兴时期英国喜剧作家本·琼生的《气质论》主张人物性格按气质划分，这种方法正是十八世纪的起点，但在十八世纪，性格刻划有了更进一步的发展，尤其在菲尔丁的评论中可以看到。菲尔丁虽然从抽象的人性出发来刻划人物，但他已注意到人物的共性与个性的关系，在他的实践和斯末莱特的实践中也体现了这一点。在斯末莱特的小说中的青年，每个人有他一定的个性特点。随着个人与社会矛盾的加深，资产阶级小说中的人物性格也更加复杂，十九世纪批判现实主义作家更以心理描写丰富了人物的塑造。

　　这是从发展关系上看斯末莱特创作的地位。就人物性格塑造本身而论，如上面指出，他们还缺乏深度，这是和作者的思想感情和观察分不开的。斯末莱特刻划人物的特点在于以粗犷见长，而不是象菲尔丁那样细致含蓄。这又和作者的对社会的态度分不开的。在作者给自己限定的范围之内，他也有他独到之处。他的笔触接近于素描或漫画，往往用精炼几笔就勾勒出人物的轮廓。例如拉特林给主人公介绍欧克姆和包凌的争吵，这是在作品中第一次提到欧克姆，作者写道："我们那时正在提伯隆湾抛锚，夜里三班值更，包凌大尉值中班，他守夜总是非常警惕，忽然他发现外海上有三点灯光，连忙跑下大舱请船长发命，船长正在睡觉，他只得把船长叫醒，船长正在好睡，被人叫醒便大发雷霆，对大尉泼口大骂，骂他瘟死的苏格兰崽仔，婊子养的，蠢猪，笨驴等等（我正在掌舵间站岗，故此都听见了）。大尉也就和他回顶起来，你一言我一语，顶了许久，最后船长起来，抓起一根藤鞭便抽大尉，大尉对他说，若不看在他是上司分上，他一定把他操下水去，又说一定要到岸上去和他算帐。"这段短短叙述粗线条地刻划出了两个不同性格：一个是粗暴、野蛮、自私、缺乏责任感，一个是耿直、不屈。等到欧克姆正式登场，那是大副摩根把病号名单呈给他看的时候，他的反应是："妈的！我的船上怎么出了六十一个病号！注意，我决不让我船上有一个病号，告诉你！……连你的名单一块儿给我滚开。我当一天船长，船上就不准有病号。"

　　其他人物的刻划也大多如此。

　　作者自己在小说中提到亚理士多德、贺莱斯的创作理论，他提到人物要对照美妙、突出有力，衬托人物也要好。在小说中，作者大力下了功夫。正面人物和正面人物，反面人物和反面人物，正面和反面人物，都有比较、衬托、补充。一个欧克姆不够，再写一个怕臭味的、纨袴子弟出身的船长；一个蓝登不够，还塑造不少大大小小的蓝登；一个贵族不够，又创造了一批形形色色的贵族。作者用化整为零的办法来描绘整个一个阶级或阶层。

作者在小说中也谈到作品的布局，根据他理解的古典创作方法，他认为起局应该缓慢，引人入胜，转局要奇突，结局应感人。就全部小说来说，作者一般算是满足了自己提出的要求，至于结局是否感人，那要看是什么人。在个别情节上作者的叙述也能做到曲折有致，例如主人公和斯触特威尔一段交道。主人公如约去拜访他，不见，等他明白了必须贿赂门房，才被引进去，但又久久不见主人出来会客，却又来了一个仆人假意捅火，主人公也不解其意，后来才理解也要行贿才能通报，原来这位老爷是不给门房仆役工资的。主人公和斯触特威尔本人的接触也是逐步地、曲折地揭露那贵族的无耻意图的。

作者在刻划人物时很注意人物的语言，如包凌爱用海员的成语，摩根在动感情的时候爱用三个不同的词表达同一意思。这一技巧在作者写《克林克传》时更趋成熟。作者自己的叙述语言中常爱用反语来进行讽刺，例如描写行军时士兵的遭遇。作者写主人公走得两条腿里面因为摩擦以致皮都摩掉了："这件倒楣事情全是因为我身上肉太多了一些……反倒羡慕骨瘦如柴的伙伴，把他们身上的油水都榨出来也不够普通烧一顿饭用，因此就不可能把腿裆里的皮都摩掉。不住的疼痛使我一阵阵发脾气，看到我同伴们那副可怜相，一阵风吹过来就会把他们象麸皮一样吹个七零八落，却轻松愉快地干着行军的苦活……更增加了我的不快。"

作者的创作意图是很明显的。从小说的主题思想到创作方法都是为一个目的服务：表现作者的不平之鸣，要读者"心中燃起人道的激情"。我们知道斯末莱特在青年时代比较接近普通人，在苏格兰常和农民来往，在军队中又和水兵在一起生活，并为他们治病，他小说中的正面人物也多是这样一些被屈辱被损害的小人物，作者也是在代他们呼吁，表现一定的民主倾向和反对统治阶级的政治倾向。同时在斯末莱特的小说里，已经可以看到十九世纪英国批判现实主义的温情主义和软弱性。在作者个人利益和社会发生尖锐矛盾时，作者也作出了尖锐猛烈的、虽然不够深刻的批判。《蓝登传》基本上还是一部优秀的暴露小说，通过这部小说，读者对资本主义社会在十八世纪英国的面貌可以增加不少认识。

1961.9

新批评派的启示

新批评派作为一个批评流派，产生于本世纪三十年代的美国。作为一种方法则在二十年代末已在英国出现，迄今已半个世纪。但这一派的批评方法已被评论界广泛吸收，所产生的影响已不可磨灭。

这一派是在心理学发展的影响下产生的，他们认为文学，尤其诗歌，是一种"美感的传递"[1]，是思想感情的交流，作品的价值在于丰富人的经验[2]。布鲁克斯和瓦伦合著的《理解诗歌》[3]中谈到训练学生读诗的目的是引导他们"不去使用一套陈词滥调，这些陈词滥调可以被鹦鹉学舌似的用在任何诗上，而是去体验诗，从直觉的体验到逐渐深入的体验。换言之，鼓励学生把诗理解成个人经验的继续，也是对个人经验的评比，是个人经验通过想象的扩大，发现自我中所存在的潜力"。

从这点讲，新批评派的渊源可以推溯到十九世纪初的浪漫派批

---

[1] Aesthetic transaction，见 Rene Wellek: The New Criticism. Pro and Contra 1978，转引自 Cleanth Brooks: The New Critic 一文，见 *Sewanee Review*, Fall 1979。

[2] 参看 I. A. Richards: *Principles of Literary Criticism*, 1924。

[3] Cleanth Brooks and R. P. Warren: *Understanding Poetry*, 1938, 1976 四版。

评家柯尔律治[1]。这可以扣上主观唯心主义和脱离社会现实的帽子。但是文学的社会作用不妨说是文学对每个个人的作用的总和，人可以分为阶级、阶层、集团，但归根结底我们还是要研究文学对每个人的作用。现代流行的现象学、接受美学[2]正是这方面的发展。后面这两种学派认为新批评派对具体作品理解入微但缺乏理论概括[3]，是实证主义，它不研究文学的共性，没有表达共性的术语，即使有术语，如"讽刺"，涵义也太松散，不精确，因此一个作品和另一个作品无法进行比较。这是从比较文学的角度发出的批评，但不能也没有否定新批评派对经验的强调。

为什么新批评派强调经验？主要是因为他们反对在西方，尤其在英美流行的历史学派。

所谓历史学派就是指英美传统的批评流派，它强调对文学作品进行历史的研究，包括作者生平、作品考证、文化社会背景、文学传统、文学类型诸方面。这一派无疑主要是在泰纳[4]的影响下形成的，注重研究文学的产生原因。新批评派认为这种评论只接触到文学的外围，就是韦勒克和瓦伦[5]所说的"外在批评"，没有接触到文学的本质和核心，因此要强调"内在批评"。他们当然也遭到历史学派的反对，例如肯纳就反对他们不谈"外围知识"，布鲁克斯对此的答复是："我的意思——允许我重复一遍——不是说一部文学作品是怎样产生的、作者的生平细节、当时的文学趣味以

---

[1] Jonathan Culler；*Structuralist Poetics*，1975，认为新批评派是浪漫主义的个人主义的后裔。

[2] Rezeptionsästhetik，参看 D. W. Fokkema and E. Kunne-Ibsch: *Theories of Literature in the Twentieth Century*，1977。

[3] D. W. Fokkema: New Strategies in the Comparative Study of Literature and their Application to Contemporary Chinese Literature. 《新亚学术集刊》，1978，卷一，香港中文大学。

[4] Hippolyte Taine.

[5] René Wellek and Austin Warren: *Theory of Literature*，1942，1977 重印。

及文学传统、思想意识的发展等等不值得研究。我们只是强调瓦伦和韦勒克在他们的《文学理论》一书中所说的'内在批评'，即对作品文字的解释和评价，而不强调'外在批评'和一般的文学研究。"[1]

历史学派的"外在批评"当然不是我们所习惯理解的历史唯物主义批评，充其量不过是社会学、文化史、文学史的研究。不过，它和我们三十年来外国文学研究有相似之处。我们根据我们所理解的历史唯物主义，强调文学的"外围"，主要表现在文学和阶级斗争的关系上。我们和英美的马克思主义文学批评家还有所不同，他们是把文学同经济基础联系起来（如英国考德威尔[2]），变成经济决定论。我们则把文学同政治联系起来。这是必要的，但仅仅或过分注意这点，就必然导致把文学作品看成是文献而不是文学。文学和政治的关系是个很复杂的问题，牵涉到作家，特别是古典作家，是否意识到自己是在进行阶级斗争的问题，作家主观意图和作品客观效果的问题，这里不想多谈。我只想指出我们对"外围知识"强调过分，而对文学本身的规律特别是艺术性强调不够，而这一点正是新批评派给我们的启示。其实他们并不是没意识到"外围知识"的重要性，即使最纯粹的文字批评家燕卜荪[3]也认为作品和阅读作品都是社会现象，一部作品一旦问世，就变成社会的财产。只是，新批评派把"外围知识"只当作背景或前提，集中注意文学作品本身，往往把作品和社会的关系抛诸脑后，即使联系也不是历史唯物主义的联系法。

---

[1] Hugh Kenner: "The Pedagogue as Critic"，见 Cleanth Brooks: The New Critics, *Sewanee Review*, Fall 1979。

[2] Christopher Caudwell: *Illusion and Reality*, 1937.

[3] 参看 Christopher Norris: William Empson and the Philosophy of Literary Criticism, 1978. 转引自上引 Brooks, *Sewanee Rev.* 中一文。

我们强调"外在批评,"可能和政治标准第一、艺术标准第二这个文艺批评原则有关。由于种种原因,例如对这原则的理解不同,或在实践中运用不当,引出了三个后果。

(一)割裂内容和形式,见诸我们的文学史和评论文章,先分析思想性,然后分析艺术性,内容和形式之间缺乏有机联系。我认为作家创作的程序是内容到形式,而理解、分析、评论一部作品的程序应当相反,从形式到内容。这是符合认识规律的,即由表及里,从现象到本质。而这正是新批评派的方法,当然他们究竟发现了多少本质,那是另一问题。行文的先后只是一个形式问题,关键在执笔者思想里是否把内容和形式有机结合,是否按认识规律观察研究。

(二)突出思想性或称"突出政治",而又非实事求是地、仔细地、科学地从形式出发,必然导致印象派的批评或简单化、公式化的批评,片面地从作品中寻找有关政治和思想性的现象,并由此而作出评价性的结论,与作品的实质可能风马牛不相及。评论者立论的依据往往是片面的,甚至是些假象,而要读者对评论笃信不疑,是很难办到的。凭公式或简单联系作出结论,说服力不大。新批评派主张精读、细读和恰如其分的阅读[1] 应当说是一切正确评价的第一步。

(三)由于突出思想性和政治而否定了文学的独立性,文学成为政策、哲学、伦理的婢女和附庸。评论者评论的不是文学,注意的不是文学本身的特点、特性和它作为"人学"的全部复杂性。这里涉及文学的社会功能问题。文学作为一种社会现象当然或多或少和政治有关,但人的生活要求多种多样,例如对美的要求。文学直

---

[1] close reading, adequate reading. 见布鲁克斯上引文。或译"封闭读法",不妥。

接为政治、哲学服务未尝没有，如西塞罗的演说，密尔顿的政论，卢克莱修的《物性论》，老子的《道德经》，但这些都具有较高的文学特点（特殊风格的散文、形象化的语言、韵律），而不是纯粹说理文章，更不是标语口号。即使如此，他们也只和文学有些表面联系，不是严格的文学。新批评派强调的另一点正是作品本身[1]，而不是作者生平、创作动机、历史文化背景。孤立地看作品当然是新批评派的弱点，但对文学之所以为文学，新批评派对这点表现了足够的重视。

新批评派自称他们的目的是提供一个新的方法。新批评派的创始人之一克莱恩[2]有这样一段话："任何批评原理都不是绝对的信条，也不是基于历史必然的信念，而是研究和分析的工具，因此批评家不必赞成某种信条，他的信念是假设性的。"又说："诗人，区别于其他人的诗人，不是表现自己或自己的时代，不是解决心理或道德问题，不是表达理想世界，不是供人娱乐，不是以这种或那种方式运用文字，如此等等——虽然这些他是会涉及到的——而是通过他的艺术，以语言和经验为材料，把它建筑成各种各样的整体，在我们体验这些整体的时候，我们不仅仅看出它技巧上的价值，主要能看出它的目的所指。"

这段话有三点值得注意：一，强调新批评是一种方法；二，是把文学作品作为一个完整的独立的个体考察；三，是考察它的构成，也就是形式，从形式出发去找内容。

布鲁克斯有一段话讲得更明确具体[3]："我们向人类学家、文

---

[1] The text.

[2] R. S. Crane: *Critics and Criticism: Ancient and Modern. Introduction*. 1952. 转引自 W. K. Wimsatt and Monroe C. Beardsley: *TheVerbal Icon*, 1954.

[3] Cleanth Brooks: *The Well Wrought Urn: Studies in the Structure of Poetry*, 1947, 1975 再版。

化史家，学习得太多了，我认为现在的危险不是不知道各历史时期各种诗歌的区别，而是忘记了它们的共同点——使这些诗之所以成为诗的品质，以及决定何者是好诗、何者是坏诗的品质。好坏不是绝对的，要参照价值标准来定。绝对的标准是不存在的。我们必须尽量客观，尽量'科学'些。在实践中，我们通常只能把诗歌同产生它的文化联系起来看。但把诗歌联系到某一特定的教条或某一主题或某类意象，都告失败。因此我们只能集中注意在诗是怎样构造的，诗在诗人头脑中成长过程中怎样定型的，诗的形式结构、修辞组织、含义的层次、象征手法、意义的矛盾冲突、讽刺、作为一个有机体的诗。我们应当探索的是一种工具，借此可以作出准确的批评，用于所有的诗。"

布鲁克斯在这段话里承认一首诗不是孤立的，而是同文化有联系的，也就是一个大的文化结构的一部分[1]。历史派批评它孤立分析一个作品，不是没有道理，因为，确实有象理查兹[2]那样"不让学生知道诗歌的作者"，"自由评论"，这样极端的例子。但理查兹是在做试验，要看读者对作品的心理反应。布鲁克斯有所不同，他提供有关作者的一些材料，而且设问，启发引导。这可能是因为对一首诗的理解不可能不牵涉到其他文化因素。但是他不肯再进一步同思想性、信仰联系起来，而集中到创作过程和技巧。这后面的主导思想是：不管文学表达的思想是什么，文学之为文学有它自己的特点，文学作品的优劣不在思想内容，而在表达方式，亦即形式。表达的好坏是批评的标准，只有用此衡量才"科学"，此外都是主观的、失败的。

这种态度显然是形式主义的态度。但是对文学的独立性的探索

---

[1] Context.
[2] I. A. Richards: *Practical Criticism: A Study of Literary Judgment*, 1929.

和尝试还是值得肯定的。事实上，新批评派的实践说明，他们也不可能完全把一部作品孤立起来，而是通过形式的分析进入内容。例如布鲁克斯分析十七世纪玄学派诗人邓恩的《册封圣徒》[1] 一诗，从语言上看，这首诗充满矛盾，诗人把一对情侣比作宗教里的圣徒，情侣是入世的，圣徒是出世的，无法类比。但布鲁克斯通过对语调、比喻、形象、含意、戏剧性的组织结构，说明形式上的矛盾同诗人思想上的矛盾的一致性。

也有批评家用新批评派的方法分析小说。例如有一篇文章分析二十年代英国小说家福斯特的《印度之行》[2]。作者从文字分析，看出这部小说是一部关于"空隙"、"裂痕"、"缺乏"、"排斥"的书。她指出小说中有一句话提供了理解它的钥匙："我们非把一些人从我们这集会里排除出去不可，否则我们什么都剩不下了。"该文作者还指出，这部小说中否定句特别多，"不"、"不是"、"从不"、"没有"占突出地位。她说，这既非偶然，也非某个时期某个社会阶层的独特语言习惯。她指出，作品的主题是：人与人之间应建立友好的关系，小说作者用否定的语言处处勾勒出印度和英国两种不同文化之间的鸿沟，不论人们希望是如何美好，但即使两方接触了，鸿沟仍不能填平，人力之外是一片空无。

这种分析方法是我们所不习惯的，我们习惯于人物的典型性的分析，而新批评派的分析法很值得参考。新批评派从形式到内容，而文字是最基本的形式。从文字里同样可以检验出作者的创作意图。小说作者既着力要说明英国和印度两种文化之间的隔阂是无法沟通的，必定要通过人物、人物之间的关系、情节等因素来表达，而这些必然要通过语言手段，是不是可以说形式分析，语言是第一

---

[1]　Brooks: *Well Wrought Urn*, 1947, 1975.
[2]　Gillian Beer: Negation in "A Passage to India", *Essays in Criticism*, April, 1980.

性的呢？文学是语言的艺术，作家是，应当是，语言工具的熟练的运用者，福斯特的主导思想既然如彼，行文之时否定性的语言可以说是思想的自然流露。从语言形式入手，似乎可以更直接地接触到作者的创作意图。这也是为什么新批评派更多的是评论诗歌，而小说的因素复杂得多。

新批评派给我们的一个最重要的启示就是从形式到内容。王蒙同志谈到他创作过程时说，他要把"故国八千里、风云三十年"的内容压缩到较短的篇幅内，就不能用传统的按时间顺序的写作方法。他给他自己规定的任务迫使他改变形式，因此他试验着抓住人物内心所受的考验这一点来写，结果表现在形式上就是时序的错乱、意识流的描写等等。如果我们不知道作者的意图，我们还是能从作品的表现形式出发去探求的。"新"形式由于人们不熟悉，常常不能为人们所接受。我们对王蒙同志的评论只能限于两点：这种形式是否完美地表达了他要表达的内容；对内容本身的评价。在这两点上，新批评派认为批评家的任务是第一点，第二点是政治、伦理学、哲学、历史等等的领域，不是文学本身。这当然是新批评派的偏激之处，是浪漫派以至唯美派的影响。

新批评派既然把作品看成是一个独立体，不与外围任何事物联系，当然很少对作品内容评价，它要评价就评价作品对读者的"经验"有无扩大、修正。它很少评论作品内容是否真实反映客观世界。但当它谈到真实性的时候，它的理解对我们倒是很有启发。

理查兹在《文学批评原理》一书谈到这问题时举《鲁滨逊漂流记》为例说：这部小说的"真实性乃是故事的可接受性"，而不是照抄塞尔柯克的事迹。他说，真实性是"内在必然性"。《李尔王》和《吉诃德》，如写成幸福结局，就违反了"内在必然性"，就不真实，不能为人所接受，因为读者一路读来，已积累了一定的反应，到此必须是悲剧结局才对，才成为一个完整的经验，前后一致的经验，不紊乱的反应。

理查兹又接着说，作品有可接受性才有说服力，但在有人看来，未见得可以接受，如十八世纪批评家托玛斯·莱默对莎士比亚《奥瑟罗》中的人物牙戈的塑造就感到不能接受。理查兹认为莱默是从外在原因出发，莱默说"莎士比亚用一些新奇的、令人吃惊的东西来取悦于观众，而这些东西则是违反常理和自然的，他硬把一个包得很紧、伪装善良的恶棍塞给观众，而不是把他写成一个心胸开阔、坦率、有什么说什么的军人，而这本是几千年来人们赋予一个军人的性格"。"事实是，莎氏脑袋里装满了恶棍式的、违反自然的形象。"

理查兹就此评论道："莱默的依据是亚理士多德的'艺术家必须保存典型，但还要使之崇高化'这一原则。但莱默是按照他的方式理解亚理士多德的，对莱默来说，典型是由传统固定下来的，他接受下来，而并未考虑其内在的必然性，他只是按外在的规定评论。""但是不论我们对典型的概念是否从以上那种荒谬方式得来，还是从，比如说，动物学教科书中得来的，关系不大。对批评来说，最危险是用外在的教规。当莱默提出，在威尼斯共和国从来没有过一个摩尔人当过大将时，他则又用另一种外在标准，即历史事实。但这一错误，危险性小些。"

理查兹与莱默之争实际上是浪漫主义与古典主义之争的延续，这里不谈。但这里有两个问题今天还有意义，这两个问题也是相互联系的，即文学反映历史现实的问题和典型的问题。新批评派认为文学作品是独立的存在，把文学同历史现实联系起来，虽然危险，但还允许。我们习惯于认为文学反映现实是通过典型环境典型性格，即现实主义。我们和新批评派相同的一点是在我们都认为文学作品不是照抄现实，但不同的在于我们认为典型是反映社会本质，只有反映本质才真实，而新批评派则从心理学观点来判断真实性，认为典型的概念是外在的教规。我觉得我们多年来被典型的概念束缚住了，应当从这个概念的束缚下解放出来，常常象莱默那样用一个固定典型概念去套一部作品。我们在有些作品里，如《印度之行》，看不见典型，就不能接受。文学作品反映现实是否一定要通过典型？现实是否一定要看得见、听得到、摸得着的？我觉得人的心理活动本身就是客观存在，它又是看得见、听得到、摸得着的现实的反映。一部作品完全反映这样的现实，恐怕也完全可以。王蒙同志也有同样看法，他说"生活中有抽象的东西，抽象的东西也会激动人心，某些抽象与诗的形象也是一种灵感"。如果这一点得到肯定，那么创作方法也必须突破。接着的问题便是怎样评价这个突破的成功和失败呢？新批评派的答案——内在必然性——是否可以成为一种新的方法、新的标准呢？

其实，这种方法也是"古已有之"的。突破时空，专写感情，不仅意识流作家如此，其实这些作家也是有所本的，如十八世纪英国感伤主义小说家斯泰恩，也打破时空观念，着重写感受，据说，马克思早期写小说还模仿过他[1]。

新批评派兴起的地点可以说是大学的课堂，教师在讲授文学课程的时候发现了学生在理解上的缺陷，诸如错误的理解、似是而非的理解以至于完全不理解，为了探索一种方法（如布鲁克斯）提高学生的接受能力，或根据一种理论，通过课堂试验，总结出一套方法（如理查兹），从而产生出一个新的批评方法的流派，它的影响扩散到大学以外的评论界。它当然也遭到不同观点的反对，就是在

---

[1] 柏拉威尔：《马克思和世界文学》，三联书店，1980。

这一派之内侧重也不尽相同[1]，有的侧重"心理主义"，有的侧重词义学，但这是以后的发展。

理查兹在《实用批评》一书的开头中说："我编写这部书有三个目的。第一，提供一个新的搜集材料的方法给那些对当前文化状况有兴趣的人，他们可能是批评家、哲学家、教师、心理学家或仅仅好奇的人。第二，提供一个新的技巧给那些希望独立发现自己对诗歌（和其他类似性质的东西）的想法和感受以及发现为什么喜欢或不喜欢的理由的人。第三，为一种更有效的教育方法铺平道路，以发展我们对耳闻的或阅读的东西作出分析判断，发展我们的理解能力。

"为达到第一个目的，我引用了大量材料，这些材料是我在剑桥大学任教时和在其他地方收集来的。若干年来我一直在做一个试验，我向听众印发一些诗歌——不同性质的诗歌，从莎士比亚到艾拉·惠勒·韦尔科克斯——要求他们自由评论，写下来。我不让他们知道诗歌的作者，十之八九他们也辨认不出来。一周之后，我收回他们的评论。……再下一周，我上课，小部分时间讲这首诗，大部分时间评论交上来的评论。

"这一过程的结果是，写评论的人和讲课的人都大吃一惊。……我没有理由可以认为，在我们目前的文化状况下能够轻易取得更高水平的批评分析能力。"

我想再用一些篇幅引一段话。布鲁克斯在回顾新批评派的缘起时[2]说：

　　三十年代早期罗伯特·潘·瓦伦和我都在一所很大的州立

---

[1]　参看 W. K. Wimsatt and Monroe C. Beardsley: *The Verbel Icon*.1954。
[2]　见上引文。

大学教"文学型式和类型"课，我们发现学生们虽然很多头脑聪敏，有一定的想象力，有相当的生活经验，但是不知道怎样去阅读故事或剧本，更不知道怎样去读一首诗。有的是因为根本没有人教过他们，有的是因为教法完全不对头。……

他们手里捧着的文学教科书几乎等于毫无用处。教科书的编纂者讲了几句关于诗人生平和某一首诗写作的环境的话。他提到济慈某天夜晚在汉姆斯特德住宅花园里听到夜莺啼叫因而写了《致夜莺》。但是他并没有把读者引入这首诗里去，或一般地说没有引入诗境，这类教材大多如此。编者在结束时往往还写上几句糊里糊涂的印象派的评论，这是肯定不能满足需要的。编者对一首诗的结论是模糊的、华而不实的、仅仅是打动读者感情的。这些话只对已经知道如何读诗和比较熟悉诗歌的人才有意义。

这两位新批评派创始人的两段话里所暴露的缺点，如文学脱离实际，前面已经谈到。而值得注意的是他们把大学的文学教学看成是整个文化活动的一个组成部分，而不是把教育和文化截然分为两个互不相干的部门。文化中存在的问题必须要在大学里反映出来，我想这也就是为什么一个发源于大学的批评流派会产生社会影响的原因所在。大学应当形成文学批评流派或任何学术流派，才能促成百家争鸣的局面。

根据以上两段文章反映的情况，似乎那些大学生的水平也很有限，但是新批评派的这些学者可以说是一些有心人，从大学生提出的"令人吃惊"的问题，进行分析研究，居然提出一套完整的批评方法以至理论，这一点也很有启发。在大学里常听到这样一种论调，似乎教入门的、技术性的课程没有什么值得研究的，我觉得新批评派的经验值得借鉴。问题不是没有可研究的问题，而是我们专业理论武装不够。瑞士儿童心理学家皮亚热研究的对象是学龄前儿童，他的成就也说明这一点。

新批评派的出发点是针对那些华而不实、陈词滥调的评论，企图有所突破，引导学生去独立思考，这一点也是值得肯定的。我们现在不仅在大学里，也在评论界，一些评论概念如幽灵附体，非但摆脱不了，更严重的是我们已意识不到幽灵的存在。文学实践已有所突破，如还用老一套的评论概念去衡量，必然格格不入。这也就是为什么有的新作不能为人接受的原因之一。

新批评派自认为提出了一套非印象派的、不笼统的、理性的、"科学的"分析方法。他们提出的方法不尽科学，前面已经谈到，首先他们就不联系历史现实。但是他们提出了一个重要问题，那就是文学本身的规律是什么。他们的答案并不完善，而对我们来说这个问题也还有待解决。

（原载《国外文学》第 1 期，1981 年）

艾略特与文艺批评

艾略特[1]自称政治上拥护君主制，宗教上属盎格鲁天主教，文学上是古典主义者。但是中国有句古语，"天下有可废之人，无可废之言"。艾略特作为文学评论家有许多观点涉及文学理论中若干重要问题，颇值得我们今天参考。

艾略特的重要评论文章有《传统和个人才能》（1917）、《批评的功能》（1923）、1932—1933在哈佛大学的演讲集《诗歌的用途和批评的用途》，此外还有关于诗剧和个别剧作家和诗人的文章，其中很大一部分是关于文艺复兴时期英国剧作家的。艾略特自己说他没有关于诗歌的一般理论，但他接触到了许多问题，对其中若干重要问题我们今天是会感到兴趣的。这些问题有文学（文化）传统问题、诗歌（文学）的功能问题、作家的创作过程和作家的特殊功能问题、批评的标准问题和批评的方法问题。

下面我把艾略特几篇主要论文的内容简单介绍一下，在叙述过

---

[1] 艾略特（T. S. Eliot, 1888—1965），英国诗人和文学批评家，生于美国，1915年定居英国，1927年加入英国国籍。他的诗歌与文艺批评对二十世纪英美诗歌产生了重大影响，1948年获诺贝尔文学奖金。

程中会分别接触到以上归纳出来的五个问题。

在《传统和个人才能》一文中，艾略特提出了他的一个根本观点，那就是把一个民族的文学看成是一个有机整体，推而广之，把欧洲文学看成是一个有机整体，也就是他称为"传统"的那个东西。每个作家都是传统的一部分。他说："历史感迫使作家在写作时不仅骨髓里有他那个时代，而且感到从荷马以下的整个欧洲文学，其中也包括他本国文学，都同时存在，组成一个同时并在的秩序。"他认为从荷马以来，整个欧洲文学是一个完整的体系，每一部新作品都不能脱离这个传统，必然受它的影响和制约；但一部新作品一旦出现，又使那个整体起了变化，哪怕是极微小的变化。艾略特本人的实践也说明了这一点，英国诗歌在艾略特的《荒原》出现以前是一个有固定形态的传统，《荒原》的出现既是这个传统的产物，也改变了这个传统的面貌，《荒原》以后英国诗歌传统的面貌进一步证实了此点。

由此，艾略特提出：一个作家的价值只能把他同以往的作家比较或对照才能看出来，他认为这是一个批评的原则。在他看来，一个作家既然不能脱离传统，因此不可能是完全个性化的，但他可以使传统起变化。艾略特用了一个比喻，他说作家就象一根铂丝引进一个有氧气和一氧化硫的容器一样，产生了亚硫酸。那么，诗人的个人才能体现在什么地方呢？他说，诗人头脑中贮存着无数的感觉、词句、意象，只待某种感情触发他们，加以组织安排，就形成诗歌。关于这一点，他在《批评的功能》中又加以发挥。

《批评的功能》进一步阐述了他的"总体论"。他说，世界文学、欧洲文学、各国文学不是作家作品的汇集，而都是有机的整体；作家作品只有同这个整体联系起来才有意义。在评论的标准问题上，他同密德尔顿·莫瑞[1]论争，莫瑞以为批评应以自己的"内心呼声"为准（按：这是浪漫派批评的出发点）；而艾略特认为批评应有"外在权威"即传统（按：即古典主义批评原则）。但事实上，艾略特是自相矛盾的，下面再谈。

在作家的才能表现在什么地方这个问题上，艾略特补充了前文，提出作家的个人才能还表现在技巧方面。他说，大部分创作过程是筛选、综合、组织、排除、改动、试验的过程，所以创作过程也是一种判断过程。这种活动愈深入、愈强，成就也就愈大。对一个成熟的作家来说，这种劳动已不落痕迹了，换言之已做到了炉火纯青、得心应手的境界。

作家的创作过程既是这样，批评家本人最好也是创作家才能体会创作的甘苦，但这还不够，"一个批评家还必须具备高度发达的事实感"。主观的"解释"或"洞察"必须有事实的凭证，用事实来检验，因此批评家最好不要"解释"而要把读者不易觉察的事实摆在他的面前。事实，即使是最琐细的，如莎士比亚的洗衣费要花多少钱，好象无用，也切勿立刻作出结论，很可能某个天才批评家可以从中看出意义。批评家的主要工具是比较和分析，要注意比较什么，分析什么，而不是滥用比较分析。

艾略特这个主张，在他的实践里也得到了应用。例如他的《莎士比亚和塞内卡[2]的苦修主义》一文就是把一个人所未见的事实摆在了读者的面前，那就是莎士比亚某些悲剧人物在遭到毁灭前的"自我戏剧化"。他举了几个例子，如奥赛罗在自杀前作了长篇的自我表白，哈姆雷特在临终前同霍莱休的告别辞。奥赛罗的最后一段

---

[1] 密德尔顿·莫瑞（Middleton Murry，1889—1957），英国具有唯美倾向的文学批评家。
[2] 塞内卡（Lucius Annaeus Seneca，？—公元65年），罗马哲学家。译文见《莎士比亚评论汇编》（下）。

台词，在艾略特看来，并非象一般评论家所说是反映了他的高贵天性，而是反映了他天性中的弱点；奥赛罗是在"自我鼓气"，是在逃避现实，他不再想到苔丝德蒙娜，只想到他自己，把自己想得了不起，把自己想成另外一个人，是自欺。艾略特比较了莎士比亚的人物的死同马洛的人物的死，发现后者是冲向毁灭，而莎士比亚的人物在毁灭之前表现了自我意识。艾略特还用比较和分析的方法，比较了斯特莱契[1]、莫瑞和刘易斯[2]三家的看法，斯特莱契把莎士比亚比作一个在印度做过殖民官的退休了的英国人，莫瑞把莎士比亚看成一个宣扬印度神秘哲学的预言家，刘易斯则把他看成是忿怒的复仇者参孙。艾略特批评他们不对，他批评的依据是：文学家不是哲学家。艾略特，不言而喻，认为莎士比亚反映的是人性。

艾略特进一步分辨了塞内卡的影响和塞内卡戏剧的影响之不同，所谓影响往往同施加影响的主体不同或不完全相同。例如玛基维里[3]在文艺复兴时期英国戏剧界的影响，同玛基维里本人是两回事，玛基维里的影响甚至可以说是"反玛基维里主义"。塞内卡戏剧对莎士比亚的影响主要表现为"自我意识"，而自我意识在戏剧中则表现为"自我戏剧化"。艾略特的结论是：莎士比亚利用塞内卡戏剧中的这种"态度"来达到他刻划人物天性的戏剧目的。

莎士比亚之所以受到塞内卡戏剧的影响是根据两个事实：一，莎士比亚读过塞内卡的戏剧，而多半没有读过塞内卡散文伦理哲学著作；二、在伊丽莎白朝，个人面对的是一个冷漠甚至敌对的世界，社会动荡，个人无法抵御，塞内卡的坚韧哲学就成了个人的避

---

[1] 斯特莱契（Lytton Strachey, 1880—1932），英国传记作家、批评家。

[2] 刘易斯（Wyndham Lewis, 1884—1957），英国小说家、文学批评家。

[3] 玛基维里（Niccolò Machiavelli, 1469—1527），意大利政治哲学家，著有《君主论》等著作。

风港，起了一种鼓气的作用。这种处世态度当时很流行，因此即使莎士比亚的思想同这种思想有共同之处，未必就是直接从塞内卡处得来的。他从塞内卡处学到的只是塞内卡悲剧中含有的这种态度，并把它利用到自己的戏剧里，来表现人物的天性。这就是为什么艾略特把作家叫做"匠师"（fabbro）[1]。

在这篇文章中，艾略特还提出思想同感情的差别，他认为诗歌（文学）是通过感情来表达思想的，思想必须同感情融合，而诗歌（文学）首先是感情的产物。在另一处，他说感情只能用"客观对应物"，即事物情景、一连串事件来表达，因此，写诗不是纵情，而是逃情，不是表现人格，而是逃避人格。

关于文学的特殊功能，他在《诗歌的用途和批评的用途》演讲集和其他文章中有进一步的阐发。他说，"为艺术而艺术"这个口号，不过是说说罢了，没有人实行过；不过这口号有它的合理部分，那就是诗人不要做非分的事。诗人有诗人的社会功能，但不要把诗人同神学家、牧师、经济学家、社会学家混同起来。诗人的职责是写诗。关于诗人的职责，有各种说法。最早的诗歌是丛林中野蛮民族的击鼓声，所以诗歌至今还保留节奏，但诗歌不能用它的社会功能来定性。有用来纪念节日或重大事件的诗歌，有举行宗教仪式用的诗歌，有的诗歌改变人们的敏感，改变人们的感受或评价的方式，或重新认识世界——这些都是人所共知的老生常谈。艾略特避免正面提出一个看法，不过从他对具体的诗人的评价中可以见到他的主张。他非常不欣赏雪莱，因为雪莱用诗来表达观念。在上引《塞内卡》一文中他也说文学不是哲学，莎士比亚若写哲学就写

---

[1] 按：艾略特这个观点是直接从十七世纪英国古典主义批评家德莱登承袭而来。德莱登在《黄昏之恋》一剧的序中就说："一般说来，诗人的职责就象精巧的造枪工匠或钟表工匠：铁或银都非他们所有；成品的价值也不在铁或银，全在精巧的制作工夫。"

不出伟大的诗歌；理性化了的人生观同诗歌大有区别；诗人的作品中有什么思想的话，都是掇拾当时流行的思想碎片，嵌进自己的诗中，并无系统的思想。他欣赏雪莱诗歌中形象性强的诗句，但他认为很可惜，这类诗句也受到抽象诗句的影响而减弱了读者的欣赏。他认为拜伦不过是供上流社会娱乐的诗人罢了。他最欣赏济慈的一句话："天才的伟大处在于他象某种稀薄的元素，作用于中性头脑这一质量上——但天才没有任何个性，没有任何确定的性质。"这句话可能就是艾略特自己"铂丝"论的根据。那么，他的"亚硫酸"具体指的是什么呢？

艾略特虽然在许多问题上同理查兹[1]有争议，但据我看，艾略特在诗歌（文学）的功能上和理查兹是有共同之处的。在当时文学受心理学的影响这一历史形势下，理查兹提出诗歌（文学）的功能在于扩大人们的感受、意识、经验。艾略特在《传统》一文中也隐约提到文学记载的是意识，一个新作家出现，继承了过去的意识，也发展了它。他在论但丁时说，诗歌需要有深意，经得起咀嚼，读一首好诗既是一时的经验，也是终身的经验，弥久弥深。他说，一部诗剧，可以提供几层欣赏，一般人可以看故事，深入一些的人看人物以及人物之间的角斗，文人欣赏词句，爱好音乐的人可以欣赏节奏，而敏感和悟性高的人则可以挖掘出深意来。要分析一首好诗为什么能给人享受，评论者本人必须感到这种享受，不能靠理论；谈诗是读诗的伸延，都是经验或感受的一部分，读诗或谈诗的过程是我们组织我们的经验或感受的过程。

以上就是艾略特评论的基本观点。关于艾略特的这个欧洲文学整体论，是否同当时的"世界主义"思潮有关，是一个问题。但欧

---

[1] 理查兹（L. A. Richards，1893—1979），英国著名批评家和语义学家。

洲文学这个概念确实反映了客观实际，欧洲文学与东方文学相比，有相异之处，是一个独立的整体。马克思和恩格斯也谈到，随着资本主义世界市场的形成，也形成了打破民族界限的精神生产，这主要应指资本主义发达的欧洲而言。艾略特在强调民族文学传统的同时，也强调全欧传统（主要指西欧）；民族传统之间可能有隔阂，一个民族的诗人不一定被另一民族所理解，在这个意义上但丁作为一个"全欧"诗人，艾略特认为更容易为人所理解。有机整体论作为一个批评原则很重要，我们评论一个西方作家，不单单要把他同他的社会联系起来，而且要把他放在西方文学传统的背景上来理解，他之不能脱离这一传统或整体正如他之不能脱离社会斗争一样。我们现在讨论文学（意识形态）的相对独立性，艾略特的一个民族或欧洲的文学整体论应当算是相对独立性的一个可以参考的内容。

艾略特强调传统，这显然是一种贵族倾向（élitism），西方评论家也认为他是文学上的保守派。按照他对作家的要求办事，那么工人作家就无法创作了。但这只是问题的一个方面，另一方面任何作家都不能脱离传统进行创作，这也是符合创作规律的，也是文学史证明了的。我想历史上即使劳动人民、民间诗人，在他们创作时，也不可能脱离传统，完全脱离传统，作者同读者之间就没有共同语言，无法沟通。所谓"天籁"，恐怕只有婴儿的啼哭，人一旦有了思想意识，他的思想意识必然在打上阶级烙印的同时也打上文学传统（文化传统）的烙印。没有深厚的文学传统的修养，仅靠"天籁"，就能创造伟大作品，文学史早已否定了这一点。

艾略特的错误在于没有把文学传统和社会生活联系起来，孤立地谈传统问题。我们主张文学，不管作者本人是否意识到，总是同社会发生联系的，直接地或曲折地为政治服务的。有时一部作品既直接服务于某一具体的政治举动又在广义上为政治服务，如莎士比亚的《理查二世》就被艾塞克斯伯爵为他的叛乱造舆论，又是莎士比亚总的反封建斗争的一个小小组成部分。但是我们不应把文学和政治等同起来，忽略了文学的相对独立性。艾略特所提出的传统说，作家和传统的关系，作家的创作过程和作家的功能的论点，很有参考价值。艾略特认为每个新作家的出现既是传统的继承，又是对传统的丰富和改变；新作家发展了文学的表达能力，扩大了人类的感受和经验，这应当算是"历史进步作用"的一个内容吧。

文学究竟怎样对读者起作用这个问题，也很值得研究。单部头的文学作品或群众性的艺术如戏剧、电影，尽管它们同时对大批读者和观众发生影响，但归根结底它是影响着每个个人的。个人如何接受影响，读者或观众的心理状态或意识、经验的变化如何，我们主观上希望作品起什么效果，这些问题很值得研究。艾略特一理查兹的扩大经验说着眼读者的感受，对我们很有启发。作为文学评论的一个方面，评论家似乎也应当指出一个作家是否或在哪些方面提高了读者或观众的感受，使读者的欣赏力有所提高。

艾略特对作家个人才能的看法实际上是一个创作过程问题。他的"铂丝"论似乎给人以这样的印象，即作家是一个不自觉的催化剂。不过这仅仅是一个比喻。他触及到了形象思维和逻辑思维的问题，他说创作过程就是一个判断过程，是个判断活动，包括筛选、综合、组织等方面。同时他又提出诗歌表达情感，必须用"客观对应物"。他对形象思维和逻辑思维的问题基本上是这样解决的，而且在实践中也是这样应用的。他的长诗《荒原》典型地用冷静的头脑，把许多思想、意象、情景、事件、掌故、引语等等，搭配成一幅图案来表现第一次世界大战后社会上存在的一种迷惘的情绪。用文学史上的术语说，他用严格的古典主义方法写一个崭新的、先锋派的内容，使人一望（在没有理解之前）就受到这种情绪的"感染"，在扩大了传统的同时，扩大了读者的经验和感受。（这至少是作者的主观意图。）

艾略特虽然强调以传统为批评的客观标准，但在他的实践中，他同时也强调批评者的"洞察力"，并从感受出发。任何评论总是主观感受和某种客观（或主观）标准相结合的产物。艾略特虽然强调传统这一客观标准，但从他许多文章来看，他总是从某种感受或察觉出发，实际上是浪漫派的批评方法。客观标准是须要的，但不能拿来当做框框去套一部作品，而是从真实感受出发，正如英国文艺复兴时期诗人锡德尼所说："向你的内心探求，再写。"艾略特主张评论"不能靠理论"，这点恐怕很难成立。事实上，他自己也有他自己的理论，不管是自觉的还是不自觉的。但如果把"理论"读作"教条"，他的话完全可以成立。艾略特的评论不从固定框框出发，不面面俱到，每篇都有一定"独到"的见解，因此读来真实、新鲜，导致读者思想的活动。十九世纪浪漫派评论家之所以启发性强也正在于此。

当然所谓"洞察"必须在广博的生活经验和阅读的基础上才能出现，前引艾略特论莎士比亚和塞内卡一文，就引证了当代评论家八人，十八、十九世纪评论家八人，哲学家、思想家、神学家八人，古代、中古、十六七世纪诗人、剧作家十三人，法国十九世纪作家二人，只有在广博的基础上才能进行比较和对照。

艾略特评论的"洞察"还表现在他的文章中的许多"警句"，例如"伟大的诗人在写他自己的时候就是在写他的时代"。这话对我们今天来说也是很有启发的。艾略特谈到他那时代的文学评论界有两大流派：心理学派和社会学派。他表面表示两派都不赞成，但实际上，他倾向心理学派，另一方面他也不是不承认文学同社会和时代的关系。他认为作家既生活于一定的时代也生活在一定的文学传统内。我们也认为一个作家不可能脱离时代社会生活，不可能超阶级超政治，所以一个作家只要写他自己熟悉的生活，即使他自己并不意识到，客观上他是在从他那角度写他那时代和他那个阶级。作家写他熟悉的题材，不仅不会脱离时代，而且会更生动地反映时代。

艾略特又说批评活动就是"用一个新的错误观点驱走一个旧的错误观点"。艾略特所持的是一种不可知论的观点，我们则认为真理是可知的。但在他这似乎错误的话中也有合理的内核：（一）看出错误，推翻它，是一个进步，但对新提出来的看法自己也不应过于自信；（二）人类的认识是无止境的。

艾略特在比较和分析的方法上十分细致。他说在伊丽莎白时代英国戏剧中，塞内卡的"影响"比在塞内卡自己的戏里还明显得多。这里，他指的当然是"自我戏剧化"的技巧。不过经他这样细致的比较和分析，我们对莎士比亚的理解加深了，对莎士比亚和塞内卡的同异一目了然了。

艾略特是一个例子，说明西方文学评论，尤其当代文学评论是一个很丰富的矿藏，等待我们去发掘。既然是矿藏，当然有无用的石头和泥土，但也有值得利用的矿物。

（原载《世界文学》第 1 期，1980 年）

从艾略特的一首诗看现代资产阶级文学

　　读了李文俊同志的文章，[1] 颇有同感。现在只想谈一个问题，怎样看待资本主义没落时期的文学。历史上伟大作家的产生是否取决于经济的繁荣或衰落，政治的稳定或动荡，有待研究。我看也不一定。甚至也不一定取决于他的世界观。黑格尔是个唯心主义者，但不失其伟大。这是一个很复杂的问题。不过，有一点是可以肯定的，那就是伟大的作家必然对生活有深刻的观察、感受和思考。文学史上，无论"太平盛世"（如法国十七世纪、中国十八世纪）或动乱之秋，都产生过伟大作家。事实上，社会矛盾是自始至终存在的，"太平盛世"也不是没有矛盾。因此，资本主义社会即使在没落阶段，只要作家严肃地对待矛盾，认真思考，艺术修养高，技巧上下功夫或有所创新，就能产生伟大的时代纪录。政治态度和世界观当然会影响作品的真实程度，但你要求作家，特别是历史上的或资产阶级的作家，在这两点上十全十美，是不可能的，即使这样来要求社会主义的作家，也是不切实际的。所以评定一个作家主要看他是否在他能力范围之内，全力以赴地认真考虑了他所面临

---

[1]　见《现代美国文学研究》，山东大学，1979.2。

的矛盾，用艺术形式把它反映出来。这样的作品的社会效果必然会很大。资本主义没落阶段的文学也有各种各样，一般"畅销书"纯粹为了牟利或迎合低级趣味，当然是不足取的。但是不少严肃的作品，我们不能因为它们所含的道德价值、政治倾向或艺术手法不是我们所能同意的，而一概抹杀。我们可以，甚至应当，不同意它们的内容，但作为人类意识的纪录，它仍不失为独一无二的、不可磨灭的、很有价值的。

我们试举艾略特为例。他自称政治上拥护君主制，宗教上倾向英国天主教，文学上是古典主义者。但我们不能因人废言。作为评论家，他有许多论点是十分精辟的。我在另一篇文章里已扼要论述。[1] 只举一例吧。他说，每个作家在写他自己的时候，就是在写他那个时代。这话就很有见地。不管是第一流、第二流或末流作家，不管是重大题材或身边琐事甚至刹那间的感受，总是从某一个角度反映了时代，总是反映了社会某个或某些方面。其次，这句话也意味着作家应当写他熟悉的生活。非工农出身的作家，甚至工农出身而长期脱离工农的作家，必须同工农相结合，熟悉他们的生活感情、要求、希望，才能动笔。再次，知识分子作家写他熟悉的生活，同样能反映社会主义时代。这些都是常识范围的事，无须争议。问题只在于怎么写，从什么角度写，用什么技巧写。所谓从什么角度，就意味着作家的观点、视野的广度、思考的深度、感受的深度。我们不妨看看艾略特本人的创作。

艾略特的作品一般公认以他早期的诗歌最有代表性，为英美诗歌开辟了一个新起点。这一评价就决定了他在英美诗歌史上的历史地位。我们且来看看他的一首不算很长的诗《小老头》：

---

[1] 见本书，《艾略特与文艺批评》。

你既无青春也无老年
而只有象饭后的瞌睡，
梦见它们。[1]

看我，干旱月份里的一个老头子
靠孩子念给我听，等待下雨，
我既没有在火热的城门前出现过，
也没有在热雨中战斗过，
也没有在没膝的盐沼里挥舞弯刀，
挨飞蝇的叮咬，战斗过。
我的房子是一所败落的房子，
窗台上蹲着的那个犹太人，是房主，
是安特卫普小馆子里滋生出来的，
在布鲁塞尔挨人臭骂，在伦敦被人家补了又剥。
头上那片地里的那头山羊夜里就咳嗽；
岩石、苔藓、石葱、铁、粪球。
那女人管厨房，准备茶，
她傍晚捅着那别扭的阴沟打嚏喷。
　　　　　　　　　我是个老头子，
风口里一个迟钝的脑瓜。

朕兆如今被人当作奇迹。"显个兆给我们看看！"[2]
小道[3]中的大道，连小道也说不出，

---

[1] 引自莎士比亚《一报还一报》第三幕，第一场，32—34行。
[2] 见《马太福音》十二章，三十八节。
[3] 见《约翰福音》第一句。

裹在黑暗的襁褓之中。在一年的青春期
老虎基督来了

在堕落的五月天，山茱萸和栗子，开花的紫荆，
给人吃掉，给人分掰，给人喝下去
在窃窃私语之中；有希尔维罗先生
用温存的双手，在利莫日城[1]
他整夜价在隔壁房间走呀走；
有博川[2]，对着四周的提相[3]的画幅鞠躬如也；
有德·托恩奎斯特夫人，在黑房间里
搬动着蜡烛；德国小姐冯·库尔普
在过道里转身，一只手搭在门上。空梭子
织着风。我没有魂魄，
在一所到处通风的房子里的一个老头子
上面是个招风的园疙瘩。

有了这样的知识，得到什么宽恕呢？想一想吧，
历史有许多捉弄人的甬道，精心设计的走廊
和出口，用低声细语的野心欺骗着我们，
用虚荣引导着我们。想一想吧。

当我们的注意力被分散，她就给，
而她给的东西，她是用轻快、使人迷惑的方式给的

---

[1] 法国城市。
[2] 日本无此姓，系作者杜撰。
[3] 十六世纪意大利画家。

因而愈给愈感到追求的饥渴。给的是人们
不信仰的东西，而且给得太迟了，即使还信，
也只是回忆中的了，是重新考虑过的激情。
交给了弱者的手中，这又给得太早了，想到的事
可以不管，直到不去管它产生一种恐惧。想一想
恐惧也好，勇气也好都拯救不了我们。违反自然的
　　　　　罪恶
是由我们的英雄主义生养出来的。美德
是我们的无耻的罪行强加给我们的。
这些泪珠是从结着忿怒之果的树上摇下来的。

新年里老虎跳跃。他吃了的是我们。最后想一想，
当我在这租来的房子里挺了尸，
我们还是没有得到结论。最后想一想
我这番表演不是漫无目的的，
也不是受一群落后的魔鬼
所鼓动才做出来的。
在这问题上我愿意老实地同你打交道。
我从前是贴近你的心的，后来被移开了，
在恐惧中失掉了美，在宗教裁判所失掉了恐惧。
我已经失去了我的激情：我何必保存它呢
因为被保存的东西一定会被玷污的？
我已经丧失了目力、嗅觉、听觉、味觉和触觉：
我该怎样用它们来和你贴近呢？

这些，还有成千的琐碎的考虑

延长着它们的冰冷的昏迷带来的好处，

当感官冷却了，它们用刺鼻的汤汁

刺激着膜组织，在汪洋的镜海中

成倍地增殖品种。蜘蛛该做什么呢，

暂停它的作业吗，象鼻虫会

迟迟不来吗？德·拜哈什、弗莱斯卡、卡莫尔太太

旋转着，飞向抖颤的大熊的轨道之外，

变成碎裂的原子。逆风的鸥鸟，在多风的

贝尔岛海峡，或在合恩角上翱翔，

雪中的白色羽毛，被湾流[1]索去，

还有一个老头子被信风驱赶

到一个昏昏欲睡的角落，

       房子里的住户，

干旱季节里干枯的头脑的思考。

  翻译的诗总是要走样的，不过为了说明问题，不得不勉强译出来。《小老头》这首诗可以说是第一次世界大战以后西方一部分知识分子的那种悲观绝望、无能为力，缺乏安全感的绝好纪录，在技巧上有重大的突破，也可以说是划时代的。这两个方面决定了我们不能轻易地把它一笔抹杀。从内容上讲，它是消极的。放在当时整个英国美国文学界的状况中看，它肯定是右的。但它反映了时代的一个侧面，反映的方式是高度集中、新颖、有效。

  开始的引诗既是引子也是主题。在莎士比亚的《一报还一报》里，克洛迪欧被判死刑，希望求得不死，假扮僧侣的公爵对他讲

---

[1] 墨西哥海湾。

了一番话，大意是生不如死，不如准备死。引诗中的"你"指的是
"生命"、"人生"。

艾略特的基本方法是用冷静的头脑——即古典主义的克制，把
思想、意象（形象）、情景、事件、掌故、引语等等搭配成一幅图
案。内容写的是一种情绪、精神状态，但不是象浪漫派那样用个人
抒情方式，而是用十七世纪所谓"玄学派"诗人的方法。也就是思
想必须同感情融合。在《小老头》一诗里，我们看不见作者本人。
作者是个匠师，把零件拼凑成一个有机整体。因此，在二十年代一
般熟悉浪漫派或维多利亚时代的诗歌的人，就不承认它是诗。等到
后来，评论家的调子就变了，即使细节不懂，但整首诗的气氛、情
调是感染人的，而且多读几遍，越能咀嚼出它的涵义。

精神的空虚感主要由"小老头"这个形象来表达。他可能是个
水手或商人，处于穷途末路，他双目失明，正在考虑未来，回想过
去，感到过去一事无成，未来渺茫不测。开始的两行，借用人类学
对原始民族的研究，把雨当成生命的象征，通过六七十行诗，到了
最后四行，又回到原来的主题和形象。当中是由若干片段组成，片
段与片段之间有转折，片段与片段之间有对比，内容是老人的回忆
和老人的想望。三至六行，老人自忖没有这方面的回忆，他过去的
生活是平庸的，他希望有过这样的有意义的生活。接下去是对比当
前的环境，一幅渺小、肮脏、堕落的图景。十四至十五行起着象乐
曲中的叠句的作用。

接着转向宗教。"显个兆给我们看看"是《新约》中《约翰福
音》里法利赛人嘲弄揶揄耶稣的话。在老人的回忆中，青年时期所
有的崇高的宗教感情却被大都会的腐朽堕落所吞没，纯洁的变成了
腐臭的。"我没有魂魄"，在我周围没有值得回忆的东西。关于历史
和信仰这一段独白反映了作者最核心的思想。他受到十九世纪关于

历史和进化论思想的熏陶，承认一切在变，但他认为有价值的东西却在变的过程中中断了，因而要追求一种永恒的东西，要得到变中的不变。这一段独白简单说来就是他对历史的否定，对"变"的感受，用感受来表达思想。一切都变成了碎裂的原子。海鸥这生命的象征，纯洁的象征也被湾流吞蚀了，只剩下被历史的信风吹到一个昏昏欲睡的角落、毫无希望地等待生命的甘雨的小老头。在这一点上《小老头》与《等待戈多》有异曲同工之妙。

以上的解释挂一漏万，不过基本思想有了。在方法上，最突出的就是把部件组织成一个整体，这个整体没有明显的逻辑连贯性，而每个部件的暗示性很强，引起读者的联想。另一方面，每个具体的意象（形象）又极鲜明准确。头上那片地里那头山羊夜里就咳嗽——形象鲜明，又暗示了病态，而山羊历来是淫欲的象征。其他具体形象也莫不如此。

尽管作者反对把自己放进诗里，但事实上是不可能的，我们处处可以看到作者的态度，主要是嘲讽。

艾略特主张传统，他认为整个英国、欧洲的文学以至文化是一个传统，一个新作家一方面是这传统的一部分，另一方面他的出现又改变了这个传统。艾略特的创作可以说体现了他的学说。他的创新的成功处，除其他因素外，在于他高度集中地反映"时代精神"——战后的现实。一个小说家要用几百页的篇幅，他只用了七十几行诗。当然，小说的内容要复杂丰富得多，反映现实要具体得多，这是不言而喻的。但我们不能不对艾略特的成就表示肯定。从思想内容上讲，他仍是继承了文艺复兴时期的人文主义思想，在探索生活的意义，只是他的答案是虚无主义的。

从以上的论述，是否可以得出这样一个结论：资产阶级文学本身是好是坏是问题的一个方面，问题的另一方面是我们读者的态度。再引一次鲁迅的话："中国人看小说，不能用鉴赏的态度去欣赏它，却自己钻入书中，硬去充其中一个脚色。所以青年看《红楼梦》，便以宝玉、黛玉自居；而年老人看去，又占据了贾政管束宝玉的身份，满心是利害的打算，别的什么也看不见了。"好或坏，道德评价、政治评价是一回事，作为一个客观现象，我们去研究它，认识它，甚至从中获得教益又是一回事。

（原载《现代美国文学研究》第 2 期，1979 年）

镜子和七巧板

据中国社会科学出版社 1990 年 2 月初版《镜子和七巧板》整理

序

　　近十年来比较文学在我国正如季羡林先生所说已成为"显学"。对这门"复兴"了的边缘学科感兴趣的大有人在，我也是其中的一个。国内"科班出身"的比较文学专家是有的，过去有、现在有、将来更多，但我不在其中。不过，正如有人说过，研究文学而不比较，那还算什么文学研究？这无疑给了我勇气。但终究是邯郸学步，有类效颦而已。

　　这里收集的十一篇文字，都是近年习作。大部分都是发表过的。有四篇原作是用英文写的，承王宁和黄满生两同志译出，由我略加校订。《国际比较文学研究的动向》一篇，属报导性质。《比较文学：界限、"中国学派"、危机和前途》一篇，则是汇集了零散文章中的一些看法，合成一篇，作为参加讨论的发言吧。其他都是就某些题目或某些作家作的一些探索。

　　这些文字虽或多或少都与比较文学有关，但终觉斑驳，称得上是"杂俎"吧。英国十八世纪小说家菲尔丁在他的巨著《汤姆·琼斯》开头的地方曾说：一个作家发表一部作品就象开饭馆的提供菜饭，而不是贵人请客。贵人请客，客人对菜饭只能说好吃，不能说不好吃。作家是开饭馆的，客人花钱来吃饭，饭菜不好，客人可以

批评，甚至可以……。菲尔丁说得很诙谐，但精神可取。我就用他
这段话结束我这短序吧。

1988.6

比较文学：界限、"中国学派"、危机和前途

　　将近十年来，中国比较文学经历了"复兴"而成为"显学"。成立了全国性的学会，许多省、市也成立了省、市的学会。许多大专院校设置了比较文学的教研组织，开出了课程，招收了研究生。出版了许多比较文学的专著和译著，办了一些专门的刊物，包括英文的刊物。在这些刊物和其他刊物上发表的文章更是为数可观。举办过几次全国性的和国际性的讨论会。无论在专著或文章中，或在讨论会上，都发表过不少很好的意见和不同的意见。为了学科的发展，我也想就几个问题谈谈我的意见，参加讨论。

　　（一）比较文学的界限。在一些讨论会上提出一种意见，认为比较文学不一定要跨国界，可以在一国之内进行不同民族的文学的比较研究，这类研究也应纳入比较文学范围。我很同意这看法。1985年全国比较文学学会成立大会期间我就发表过这样的意见。其理由很简单，因为在西方（欧洲），跨国界和跨民族几乎是一回事。当然，在西方所谓"民族国家"中也有多民族的问题，但从西方比较文学的发展史上看，占主导地位的仍是把一个国家的主要民族的文学和另一个或另一些国家的主要民族的文学进行比较研究。一个国家之内，主要民族的文学和少数民族的文学的比较研究，在他们

那里纵使有，恐怕也居次要地位。但在我们这个多民族的国家里，许多少数民族都有自己的文学，尤其是丰富的口头文学，这些文学或者和汉文学有关，或者和汉文学一起同另一个或另一些外国文学有关系。进行这方面的研究怎能说不是比较文学呢？比较文学的界说里还有一条，那就是"不同的语言"。用不同语言创作的文学肯定是不同民族的文学。我想可以说，凡是不同民族的文学的比较研究都应归入比较文学。

混淆民族和国家的界线曾引起过这样一种误解，即将比较文学仅仅看作是一种方法，用这种方法把本民族文学中各种文体、流别进行比较研究也叫做比较文学。这样一来，比较文学在中国也就"古已有之"了。例如春秋时代，中国有许多封建"国家"，把这些"国家"的诗歌进行比较，算不算是比较文学呢？这些"国家"恐怕不能算做不同的民族吧，虽然他们可能有不同的部落渊源。而且书面语言又是相同的。《诗经》中各国的国风，可能有所不同，但恐怕还是属于同一文化系统。强调民族的不同和语言的不同，归根结蒂还是因为文化传统的不同。只有把文学放在不同文化的背景上来研究，求出其异同，其结果才有更丰富的意义。而在春秋时代，华夏文化已形成了。

也许有人说，比较文学已渐渐发展成为一门开放性的学科，而且它本身也未定型，一国文学内部的比较仍应归入这门学科的研究范围。所谓"开放性"这概念来自跨学科的概念，一国文学内部的比较当然不能算是跨学科。诚然，开放性有一个程度的问题。比较文学从影响研究扩展到平行研究，扩展到文学和艺术、和其他人文科学的比较，文学和社会科学的跨学科比较，而且也有了这方面的实践，如文学和历史，文学和神话，文学和心理学，文学和社会学，文学和宗教等的关系的研究。我记得80年代初奥本尼纽约州立大学举行过文学与航天科学的讨论会。人类各种活动本来是互相有关联的，不过文学和航天科学的关系可能是开放性的比较文学迄今为止达到的极限了。但基本的一条是要跨学科。

此外还有一个比较文学的目的和功能的问题。我想比较文学能起到的作用大致有两个方面。一是对文学史起的作用。一个民族的文学不可能在完全封闭状态中发展，往往要受外国文学的影响。因此，要说清楚本国文学的发展，不可能不涉及外国文学。同时，为了说明本国文学的特点，也须要同外国文学对比，这种对比不一定是明比，而是意识到本国文学和外国文学的不同之处。第二，比较文学的目的还在于通过不同民族文学的比较研究来探讨一些普遍的文学理论问题。这两个目的都是一国文学的内部比较研究所无法达到的。这也就是法国人所说的用比较的结果来充实他们所谓的"总体文学"。[1]

（二）所谓"中国学派"。几年来国内外都有一个呼声，要建立比较文学的中国学派。我认为我们不妨根据需要和可能做一个设想，同时也须通过足够的实践，才能水到渠成。所谓"法国学派"、"美国学派"云云，也是根据实践而被如此命名的，起初并非有意识地要建立什么学派。

我说可以有设想，也有人做过设想，如国外学者就提出东方文学之间的比较研究应当成为所谓"中国学派"的特色或重要内容。许多西方学者认识到，尽管目前研究比较文学的论文可以装满几个图书馆，但关于东方文学，特别是东方的文明古国中国和印度文学

---

[1] 法国人发明的"总体文学"的概念，有人认为含糊，但可以作这样的理解，即"指总的文学潮流、问题和理论，或关系"。参看《中国比较文学》，第1期第9页，浙江文艺出版社，1984年版。

的研究，却还很肤浅。[1] 东方文学的研究，东方文学之间的比较研究，不仅可以打破比较文学这一学科迄今的欧洲中心论，而且也是东方比较学者责无旁贷的义务。这里面一定有许多尖端问题有待于我们去探讨和研究。在东方范围之内，我国国内少数民族的比较文学也理应成为"中国学派"的一个重要组成部分。

至于实践，有待于全面总结，在此我只想就两方面提些看法。

第一方面，有的台湾和海外学者用西方的新理论来研究、阐发中国文学。他们认为"中国学派"应走这条路。我觉得这也未尝不可。例如王国维和吴宓就分别用西方哲学和西方文艺观点研究过《红楼梦》，阐发出一些用传统方法所不能阐明的意义。也许有人说，这不是比较文学，只是用舶来的理论的尺度来衡量中国文学，或用舶来的方法阐释中国文学，而不是不同的文学之间的比较研究。不过我认为从效果看，这种方法和比较文学的方法有一致的地方。因为在甲文学和乙文学的比较中，甲文学在很大程度上也是一种尺度或手段，用以阐发出乙文学的蕴义、特色等等。所不同者，文学和文学的关系里还有相互阐发的问题而已。当然，用外来理论有时会产生生搬硬套的弊端，但这不是这种做法本身的弊端。

第二方面就是要回顾一下我国比较文学的历程。发展一门学科总要在前人止步的地方继续走下去。前人错了，我们可以避免他们的错误；前人有好经验，我们应予发扬。

87年6月我在日本京都日本比较文学学会年会上讲了一次《中国比较文学的今昔》，我分析了中西比较文学起源之不同。西方比较文学发源于学院，而中国比较文学（或萌芽状态的比较文学）则与政治和社会上的改良运动有关，是这运动的一个组成部分。西方

---

[1]《域外文集》，第116页，江西人民出版社，1983年版。

比较文学为什么在学院中兴起当然也有社会原因和其他原因（如哲学），不过直接起因是学院里要解决文学史的问题。而中国比较文学则首先结合政治社会改良，而后进入校园的。

要比较，首先要意识到有外国文学的存在。外国文学引进中国是在清末海禁被打开之后。海禁被打开后，使知识界最先接触到外国文学。作为古文家的林纾惊异地发现西方小说写生活尤其写下层社会的生活写得这样生动。西洋小说中情节的曲折，人物的刻划，对话，都给他留下深刻的印象。这些他认为可以和中国史家如司马迁比美，和古文家比美。不过林纾翻译西洋小说不仅因为他欣赏西洋小说的"文笔"，认为中西有相通之处，他也透露了他翻译西洋小说的另一目的。例如他译《黑奴吁天录》就把黑人的遭遇作为借鉴，以警醒黄人。他虽不是改良派，但他恨国力既弱，今日"黄人受虐或加甚于黑人"。所以他译此书，"使倾心彼族者""吾书足以儆醒之"，有很鲜明的社会意识。

梁启超对西洋和日本小说发生兴趣更是出于政治改良的原因。他在《译印政治小说序》（1898）中说："彼美、英、德、法、奥、意、日本各国之日进，则政治小说为功最高焉。"在《论小说与群治之关系》（1902）中，他认为创造一种新型小说可以振奋国民，革新道德、宗教、政治、风俗、学术，以至人心。这些言论当然算不得是比较文学，但有了这样一种思想以后，进一步做比较时，也必以这思想为出发点。例如他在《饮冰室诗话》里说："中国事事落他人后，惟文学似差可颉颃西域。"但他惋惜中国没有长篇史诗，因此他一旦发现黄公度《锡兰岛卧佛》一诗就大为欣喜，说："中国文学界足以豪矣。"并说："吾欲题为《宗教政治关系说》。"梁启超也做过具体的比较文学研究，如《翻译文学与佛典》，在此他指出佛典与中国小说以至杂剧、传奇、弹词也不无关系。顺便说一句，梁启超治史也主张用当时西方的治史方法来改造中国旧史学，主张不为死人写史，主张客观性，主张探索"来因与去果"（虽然他后来又怀疑因果律）。

鲁迅写《摩罗诗力说》（1907）目的也很明确："意者欲扬宗邦之真大，首在审己，亦必知人，比较既周，爰生自觉。"又说："国民精神之发扬，与世界识见之广博有所属。"《摩罗诗力说》本身虽是欧洲浪漫诗人的介绍和比较，但当鲁迅谈到西方文化和思想时，当他总结浪漫派诗歌时，无不和中国进行对比。他在结束时问道："今索诸中国，为精神界之战士安在？有作至诚之声，致吾人于善美刚健者乎？……"

即使象王国维这样一位"纯"学者也不是脱离实际的。他完全意识到中西文化的差异，以及西方人对中国文化理解的缺陷，因而感到有沟通的必要。他在给日本人西村天囚译的《琵琶记》作的序（1913）中有这样的话："近二百年来，瀛海大通，欧洲之人讲求我国故者亦夥矣，而真知我国文学者盖鲜。"其原因是"道德风俗之悬殊"。因此欧洲人翻译的中国"国故""外不能喻于人，内不能慊诸己"。他举例说象英国人大维斯译的《老生儿》（1817）只译了科白，完全不了解"元剧之曲但以声为主，而不以义为主"。

我国比较文学的发端除了结合政治、社会、文化实际这一潮流以外，还有另一股潮流，那便是用从西洋输入的理论来阐发中国文化和文学。前面提到梁启超治史也属于这一潮流。这是一股不容忽视的潮流，因为它是真正做出成绩来的潮流。王国维就是用西洋的观点（叔本华哲学）研究《红楼梦》，用主客观的观点论词（《人间词话》）。他的《宋元戏曲考》虽不属比较文学，但具有宏观的观点，指出《窦娥冤》、《赵氏孤儿》"即列于世界大悲剧之中，亦无愧色"。茅盾研究中国神话用的是比较人类学的方法，把中国神话整理出了一个头绪。茅盾也做了中国神话和希腊、北欧、印度神话的比较研究。郑振铎主张文学改良，主张新文学，主张重新估价中国文学。他和早期鲁迅一样，服膺进化论，他提倡用进化论的观点研究文学（《研究中国文学的新途径》，1927）。他用可能来自普罗普（Vladimir Propp）在《民间故事的形态学》（1927）里的方法研究中山狼的故事。吴宓在《红楼梦新谈》（1920）里，用西方小说的标准衡量《红楼梦》，他的结论是《红楼梦》不仅满足而且超过了这些标准。可见引进外国方法研究中国文学在我国有这传统，而且做出了成绩。

在过去的比较文学实践中，似乎影响研究多于平行研究和跨学科研究。这可能和我国做学问重考据的传统（所谓"汉学"）有关，甚至创作也要"无一字无来历"。梁启超说："中国于各种学问中，惟史学为最发达"[1]，史书多得"不可得遍读"[2]。汉学做学问的传统，史学的发达，说明我国文化中，我国学者的心态中，历史意识特强，事事都要溯源，养成"考据癖"。这种文化熏陶使人们看到本国文学受外来影响，或外国文学中有中国成分，就自然而然要探个究竟。

我国比较文学的历史很值得深入总结，但就以上粗略的回顾，可以看出我国过去比较文学的实践至少有以下几个特点：

1. 介绍和研究外国文学，中外文学的比较研究，都和社会生活相联系。这个传统能不能继承、应该不应该继承呢？我想回答是肯定的。但怎样使比较文学和现在的社会生活联系起来，则有待于进一步探讨。

2. 我国早期学者多用外来的方法和理论来阐发中国文学，卓有

---

[1]《中国历史研究法》，第10页，上海古籍出版社，1987年版。
[2] 同上书，第30页。

成效。这个途径我觉得应当算做"中国学派"的一个特点，理由前面已经提到。

3. 尽管影响研究做得很多，但有待深入，此外还有许多未开垦的处女地有待开发。平行研究过去做得较少，就现状看，更是有待提高。至于跨学科研究，除了老一辈学者如朱光潜、伍蠡甫、钱锺书等外，展开得更少。

国际上也有学者反对区分派别，当然也不赞成讨论建立中国学派，提出与其区分派别，不如共同研究问题。套用胡适的话就是"少谈些学派，多研究问题"。当然比较文学中有大量的问题，特别是文学理论问题迫切须要讨论研究，但这和学派问题并不矛盾，可能反而有助于理论的探讨。

（三）危机与前途。在国外，首先提出比较文学危机的是韦勒克（1958）。他所谓的危机是指法国学派把这门学科变成了"文学外贸"，只以研究相互关系为满足，而忽略了文学本身。到了70年代，西方比较文学界又感到了危机，这次危机指的是一浪追一浪的"新理论"对比较文学的冲击，好象要使比较文学失去它的存在，取消了它应有的作用。此外，在国际上比较文学似乎也不受重视。例如1987年6月日本东京大学国际比较文学讨论会上，荷兰学者塞格斯就说："大家都认为比较文学遇到了危机。危机是有的。它来自比较文学的外部和内部。内部指的是新的文学理论对比较文学的冲击；外部则指在现代技术统治一切的社会，人文科学和比较文学受到轻视和威胁。目前比较文学也确有不能令人满意之处，很难向前推进。因此，比较文学必须寻求新的模式，走出一条新路。"[1] 出路何在呢？塞格斯引英国历史学家汤因比的话说："创造

---

[1] 参看《中国比较文学通讯》第19—20页，北京大学，1987年第2期。

性的工作如不能取得有价值的社会效益，就是空的。"塞格斯接着说："大家都认为目前的人文科学还不如一台复印机，老是重复别人的话。"

国内的比较文学虽然"复兴"不久，但有识之士也看到了隐伏的危机。一方面，和国外一样，我国知识界、研究界、文艺界对比较文学不甚理解。另一方面，危机指的是热心比较文学并积极实践的作者群虽然做了大量的工作，而且也有成绩，但多数停留在浅层次上，有待更上一层楼。

危机并非坏事，有了危机感，事业才能前进。纵观国外国内所谓的危机，有的已成过去，如韦勒克所提出的危机。塞格斯所提出的危机倒是触及一个根本问题，也就是我们前面谈的早期我国比较文学和社会生活紧密结合的问题。这个问题不仅比较文学有，外国古典文学研究，中国古典文学研究，其他人文科学研究都有。怎样产生社会效益？恐怕不能把研究美国小说家黑利的作品和机场、旅馆、银行的管理联系起来来产生社会效益吧。"《三国演义》和人才学"、"《红楼梦》与经济效益"这类题目恐怕也不是联系实际的正路吧。我想比较文学的研究以及人文科学应当能满足时代的精神需要，而不是如塞格斯所说的复印机，这才是一个"新的模式""一条新路"。

至于新理论的冲击，我在另一篇文章里已介绍了这方面的情况，这可能是一个适应问题。新理论，如解构学说，乍看似乎是语言学和哲学上的认识论的问题，与文学无关，很难应用到实际文学批评上来。但是在国外，用这新理论来阐释文学现象已大有人在，这说明了它的有用性。

至于国内的危机云云，我想不能仅看到眼前的状况或不久的将来的可能的状况，而应看到比较文学作为一门学科的前途。它之所以有前途是因为它能起到积极作用，这在前面谈到它的目的和功能时已有所说明。其次，我觉得我们还有许多事情要做。例如，中外文学、中外文化的关系或相互影响还远非已经穷尽。又如东方文学之间的比较研究还刚刚开始。汉文学与少数民族文学、少数民族文学之间、少数民族与外国文学之间的比较研究，有的只有少数人在从事，有的可能还没有人在做。至于跨学科的比较和用某种外来理论研究中国文学，则在目前还是两个弱点。此外一定还有许多空白。

当然要完成这许多任务，须要创造条件。条件指装备问题，物质装备和精神装备，后者包括知识、语言、理论、心态。最后这点颇值得注意。我曾说过："我们的先辈学者如鲁迅等，他们的血液中都充满了中国的文学与文化，中国文化是其人格的一部分。这样他们一接触到外国文学就必然产生比较，并与中国的社会现实息息相关。"[1] 我们多年受的训练则相反，使我们研究外国文学时象科学家对待原子或昆虫那样，与我们自身毫无关系，也就是隔与不隔的差别。我这样说丝毫不是说要陶醉于固有的文化，做个泥古派，而是说要非常熟悉自己的文学、文化，对它们的优秀传统有自己的感受。对一个比较学者来说，还要求对其他国家的文学、文化有相似的修养。这当然是很高的要求，但要做出有价值的成绩，只能取法乎上。

---

[1]《中国比较文学通讯》第 22 页，1987 年第 2 期。

国际比较文学研究的动向

一

国际比较文学协会（ICLA）第十一届大会由于法国和英国都愿意主办而分为两部分：法国会议于 1985 年 8 月 20 日至 24 日在巴黎第三大学举行；英国会议于 1985 年 8 月 27 日至 28 日在色塞克斯大学举行。这次大会与前两次不同，1979 年的奥地利大会讨论的是接受问题，1982 年在纽约大会讨论的是评价问题。第十一届大会对比较文学研究作了详细的分类；重视了欧洲以外的文学；进行了文学理论的探讨。

巴黎会议共分为十二个专题：（一）比较文学和世界文学；（二）文学理论；（三）叙述学、"互文性"（intertexualité）符号学；（四）文化对话（dialogues des cultures）和欧洲文学中的巴罗克（Baroque）；（五）接受美学；（六）翻译；（七）口头的和书面的（oral et écrit），小说中的口语与叙事文体、口头文学的诗学、美国通俗歌曲与诗歌、民间口头文学与书面文学之比较；（八）文学的移植（acculturation），地域性，第三世界所受的影响；（九）新文学的出现；（十）专题讨论（ateliers），文学批评实践，文学分析中的可变因素和不变因素；（十一）讨论会（symposium）：新教徒的流徙（diaspora protentante）和艺术与文学；（十二）讨论会：雨果逝世一百周年。英国的讨论会只有一个主题：文学与价值。

参加这次大会的有五十多国国家的 500 名代表，共提交了论文 500 篇。20 日上午举行了开幕式，从下午开始用了八个半天进行讨论，24 日下午举行了闭幕式和选举国际比较文学协会会长、副会长、秘书和执行局理事。

二

这次大会讨论内容广泛，论文的内容比较庞杂。在关于"比较文学和世界文学"的专题中比较集中的是就"世界文学"这一概念发表了各自的意见；就现有的概念做出评论；第三世界的文学在比较文学中的地位；就文学的某一方面，如关于悲剧的概念、关于诗学，通过比较，取得统一；电脑在世界文学中的作用，如用电脑统计和分析世界神话和编纂字典等。

六十年代以来，西方新的文学理论对文学研究起了很大的冲击作用。正如艾略特关于创作所说的，一部新作品的出现，如果是强有力的而且言之有物（至少部分言之有物），也必然会改变从亚理士多德到阿诺德的整个西方文学体系。不论赞成或反对，人们或多或少受到冲击波的冲击。西方新的文学理论也必然会冲击比较文学。在国际比较文学学者的行列中，大致有两派：一派试图探讨如何吸收，如何结合新理论、新方法到比较文学研究中去；别一派则怀疑或反对。这个情况在国际比较文学协会本届大会上有强烈的反映。

属于反对派的多是些权威学者。美国著名学者雷·韦勒克（René, Wellek）称新经验为"否认生活的感知一面"，"否认美感经验"，"脱离现实"，使"文学成为文字游戏，毫无意义"，"不做好坏的评价"，"瓦解作品"，"无补于实际批评"，因此是"反美学的象牙之塔"，是"新虚无主义"，言辞十分激烈。纽约大学比较文学系主任巴拉基安（Balakian）批评"读者反应"（接受美学）只研究读者作评价的过程，而不研究其评价本身。他认为"解构"理论贬低或无视作品的文学性。比较文学中的影响研究被"互文性"糟踏作践。文本的分析把作品割裂成碎片。她主张文学研究应当是综合而不是分解，方法应当是归纳而不是演绎。她把新理论称做比较文学的"值得怀疑的同路人"。纽约州立大学宾思顿分校布洛克（Block）教授也主张文学理论必须以文学经验为基础，不应拿文学作为借口或跳板去空谈理论。但他并非绝对否定新理论，而是认为比较文学可以作为新理论的"试验场"。他的言论代表怀疑派。

在英国的讨论会上，四个主旨发言都围绕着价值问题。例如得克萨斯州的勒弗尔（André Lefevere）作的《超出解释》的报告中，提出了一个新的概念，叫"重写"（Re-writing），翻译、批评、改写、模仿都是"重写"。海涅在纳粹时代，在西德和民主德国都被"重写"，文选也是重写，重写使得文学作为一个体系能够前进，使文学体系发生变化和变迁。他主张对前人的作品应通过价值判断，积极地取我所需，在此基础上创新前进。协会会长、荷兰乌特勒支大学佛克玛（D. W. Fok kema）教授以《过去和现在的"经典"的形成》为题做了一个报告。他所谓"经典"（Canon）（或称"正经"，指基督教经典中的真正的经典作品，而非伪品），实际指的是文学作品中的精华。每个时代有自己认为的文学珍品，也就是说有自己的价值标准。他认为评价不能排除道德标准，不能不评善恶、美丑、丰富和贫乏、思想性和艺术性。多伦多的比斯特莱（Bisztrary）教授的题目是《价值中立说》。他认为，（新理论）不谈价值，本身就是一种评价，新理论抨击社会学，说它主观，但阐释学也同样主观，虽然它自认为很客观。他认为我们现在不是不需要评价，而是需要一个评价标准。新理论的"价值中立说"不能成立。美国伊利诺大学教授、前美国比较文学学会会长艾德礼（Aldridge）以《美国新人文主义看巴比特的美学》为题，特别强调文学研究中的道德标准。艾德礼认为，巴比特（Babbitt）反对浪漫主义，要求用严格的道德标准衡量作品是可取的，孔子出生在亚理士多德之前，释迦牟尼出生在耶稣之前。孔子从道德的角度谈文学，亚理士多德用"科学"的方法分析文学。他提出比较文学必须"合乎人情"（humane），应当以文学中的精华作为评价的标准。在方法上，他反对形式主义的分析，反对抽象的推论。他甚至说，在考虑美和善的问题上，善应当先于美。

综观各种反对新文学理论的言论，主要有下列两点：一是新理论不作价值判断；二是空谈理论，无补于实际批评。他们维护的是人文主义原则。艾德礼就说，比较文学必须有人的感情在内。在方法论上，他们是经验主义的，主张用归纳法做具体分析，反对假设和推论。他们的价值问题固然提得对，但也不能象他们那样抽象谈价值。要问是什么价值，对谁有价值。其次，他们无视理论探讨的长远意义，不承认理论探讨对思路的开拓。

但是从大会提交的论文来看，绝大多数学者对新文学理论持肯定态度。这些论文有理论的探讨，有历史的叙述，更多的则是实际的应用。理论的探索都是正面看新理论在比较文学研究中的地位和作用。

在"叙述学"的专题中，不少学者用结构主义的方法研究叙事文学，提出了一批论文，有的从文学史的角度加以总结，如从文艺复兴后期各国巴洛克风格的小说、各国流浪汉小说，或某一时期如十九世纪小说，通过比较，总结出一些叙述文学的规律和"美学"。所谓"互文性"（intertextuatité），指的是一部作品、一首诗（"文本"texte）不是一个独立的机体，而是与其他作品（文本）发生关系，这种关系，有的明显，有的隐晦。明显的用典故、成语，或模仿、戏拟；有的不明显，如两首风格不同的抒情诗，两部内容不同的历史小说，一个并没有明显借用另一个，却有相通之处。实际上，这仍是一个传统和创新的问题，而要见到创新，必须与传统作比较研究。怎样进行比较呢？这次大会也提出了不少论文，如对主题、文学概念、比喻、内心独白、叙述者的立场各方面研究，来发现其异同。"互文性"的理论起源于符号学，从结构主义语言学来看，任何符号都是在和其他符号比较下才产生意义的，任何符号的意义取决于它的功能，因此，每个符号本身的意义是不固定的。用这个原理来进行文学的比较研究，也就是一部作品（文体）作为一个符号，必须与其他作品（文体）进行比较，才能发现它的意义。在接受美学范围内，提出的论文更多，接受美学认为以往的文学研究只注意作家和作品，文学过程不完整。作家是作品的生产者，读者是作品的消费者，没有读者，文学也就等于不存在，因此，接受美学把注意力移到读者，并设想从接受美学的角度，重写文学史。新理论强调作品与读者这一环节，强调读者接受和理解的过程。它认为写成文学的作品作为一种传达信息的方式，同用语言直接交际不同。写成的作品虽然貌似一个固定的实体，其实它的意义不是一下子就很明显的，需要读者使它"归化"，才能理解。例如"白发三千丈"要传达的信息是"愁"，但必须经过一个"归化"的过程，有时是很复杂的过程。所谓"互文性"也就发生在这里。有的理论家声称"每个文本都是'引文'的镶嵌画",很象是"无一字无来历"。这实际是文学传统和文化传统的问题。从读者的角度来说，不了解一定的传统，不与传统作比较，也就无从理解作品。

新理论提供了许多新的角度，对文学传达信息的手段，用语言学原理，作了深入的分析，并非无补于实际批评。不过，这些新理论确如反对派所说，不作评价，这是最大的缺点。在概念里兜圈子，离文学实践越来越远。这些理论家把文学和科学研究的对象等同起来，抽掉了文学中复杂的"人"的因素，他们的出发点是语言和语言学，往往用语言学的构架去套作品，因而显得牵强附会。按照这些新理论，语言是符号，它的意义不在它本身，而在它和其他的符号关系之中。一个语言符号只有潜在的意义，读者须在一张复杂的关系网中去寻求意义。这个理论实际上是为现代派作品而设的，用来解释乔伊斯的《芬尼根的守夜》是最适宜不过的。可以说，新理论和现代派是一根藤上的两个瓜，产生在同一块土壤上的。我们只要认清这一点，才不至于在企图了解它的过程中，糊里糊涂堕入迷宫，步入歧途，而能择善而从，取我所需。

三

从第十一届国际比较文学大会来看，国际比较文学界已经意识到第三世界文学的重要性。但由于种种原因，这次和前次的大会上，第三世界文学的比较研究，尤其是"文学大国"如中国、印度、日本等未能充分体现。这里有历史的原因，百余年来，国际上从事比较文学研究的主要是西方国家，他们的学者虽然意识到第三世界，尤其是中国和印度文学的重要性，但缺乏这方面的训练。其次是东方如中国的比较文学研究，一方面早期进行研究的人数不多；另一方面由于各种原因，中断了一段时间，起步也较迟，而且由于语言的隔阂，未能沟通。在这次大会上提交的论文中，有关非洲文学的（用欧洲语言作为媒介的文学）约23篇，有关阿拉伯国家文学的17篇，有关拉美地区文学的14篇，有关东方各国文学的有27篇，其中日本10篇，中国9篇，印度（包括泰戈尔）8篇，以色列、菲律宾、马来西亚各一篇，笼统谈东方的4篇，总共85篇，占总数500篇的17％。在英国讨论会上共宣读66篇论文，其中有关亚非文学的18篇，占27%。在1976年，国际比较文学协会第八届大会上，佛克玛曾主持过一次会议，讨论亚非文学的比较研究。会上也曾谈到国际比较文学协会编写的《欧洲比较文学史》(*A Comparative History of Literature in European Languages*)，能否包括用法、英、葡语写的非洲文学？还希望未来能包括用英语写的印度小说。

在这次会上，还有广大领域被遗漏了，如非欧洲语的古代文学和现代亚非民族语文学，尤其是亚洲各国文学互相关系的比较研究，中东和北非各国文学关系的比较研究，非洲各国文学的比较研究，东西方文学的比较研究，不仅限于影响的研究，还在于类型、文学形式和主题方面的平行研究。

最值得注意的是，在巴黎会议的最后一天上午，最后一个报告是艾金伯勒（René Étiembte）的《中国比较文学的复兴：1980—1985年中国的比较文学》。在大会所有的500篇报告中，他的这个发言恐怕是少数的、也可能是惟一的听众满堂、座无虚席的一次。艾金伯勒是法国巴黎第三大学的教授，国际比较文学界的著名学者，健在的元老。他动过大手术，一般不轻易作大会报告。他列举了解放前中国的比较文学的成就，更主要的是列举了中国近五年来在比较文学教学、研究、学术团体、出版物等方面的大量事实，热情洋溢地向各国学者介绍了中国比较文学方面的情况，并说，中国有十亿人口，有悠久的文学传统，潜力和前景是无限的。他的报告博得了热烈的反响。也许有些听众是慕名而来，但也从中看到了国际比较文学界对中国比较文学发展的关心。

在会外，我们邀请了港台和一些欧洲学者举行了一次中西比较文学研讨会，交流了情况，谈得十分融洽。我们接触到东方一些国家的代表，他们也很愿意和我国取得联系，如印度文化交流委员会（Indian Council of Cultural Relation）也希望我国能参加他们在新德里举行的以《史诗与世界观》为题的国际会议，尤其就《西游记》或《格萨尔》作为史诗到会上谈谈，或从中国角度谈印度史诗如《罗摩衍那》或《摩诃婆罗多》或中亚的史诗。国际文化交流研究协会（International Association of Intercultural Studies）是以研究阿拉伯世界文化和其他文化关系为宗旨的，该会的副主席尤素福（Magdi Youssef）教授也希望和我国的东方文学学者取得联系。

形势给我们提出了一个问题：怎样使比较文学学科真正能成为一门世界性的学科，克服国际间现在的片面性，特别是用我国的丰富的文学遗产和文学实践去充实世界文学，进行比较，从一个比较完整的总体的世界文学中总结出一些理论和规律？

一是大力提倡中外文学的比较研究，在充分而深入地考察、了解中外两方文学的基础上，运用有效的方法，提高我们的研究质量。加强中外文学和理论的基本功训练，搞外国文学的加强中国文学的学习和研究，搞中国文学的加强外国文学的学习和研究，掌握第一手的材料。要求精通多种语言甚至是一切语言是不可能的，我们的有些研究只能通过翻译，但作为一个比较文学工作者至少要求掌握两种文学的第一手材料，这是最起码的要求。

二是在方法上多下功夫。方法是工具，从某种意义上说，一种工具用久了，用旧了，就不能很好地起作用，要修理工具或更新工具。有时我们用的工具也许就是一把钝刀子、或是代用品。我们应当熟悉新理论、研究和分析这些理论，择优选取。当然，文学不象物质原子，它牵涉到人。运用了以科学为对象的方法，不一定完全适用于文学，甚至也不能完全用研究社会科学的方法。泰纳用自然科学进化论的方法，按照种族、环境、时期来研究文学史，把文学现象只从种族、民族、社会背景来考虑，显然是不够的；另一方面，把文学现象从人和社会中抽出来，孤立的研究，也是不够的。我们要不断地改进方法，以提高研究的水平。

三是加强信息和人员的交流。信息交流包括了解国外比较文学的新情况、新发展，向国外介绍我国的研究成果。在我国学者参加过的两次国际比较文学协会的大会上，提交的论文没有几篇，这种情况要改变。广西大学办的 *Cowrie*（文贝）在国外有很好的反应。艾金伯勒的报告主要是根据《文贝》提供的材料。这也说明，我们要跻身于国际学术之林，必须使国际学术界对我们有所了解。人员交流是一个重要方面，用外文来发表和出版我们的论著，影响就更大。国内的信息交流和人员交流更应该积极进行。应该提倡开展协作研究，在认真研究的基础上，加强讨论和争鸣，促进学术的繁荣。

四是抓好比较文学的教学和研究生的培养。全国已有40多所大学开设了比较文学课，有些院校开始招收研究生，不少大学成立了比较文学研究机构和教研室。北京大学、山东大学、辽宁、上海、江苏等地成立了比较文学研究会，民族院校成立外国文学和比较文学研究会。我们已经有了一支队伍，在抓好普及的基础上，抓紧高水平人才的培养。

1985 年 10 月 29 日中国比较文学会的成立，预示着中国比较文学的发展进入了一个新的阶段，只要我们认真努力去做，发扬光大我们过去和今天的成绩，克服不足之处，勇于探索，就一定能对比较文学这门世界性的学科做出贡献。

1986 年 3 月

（此文根据作者笔记和已发表的部分，由张文定同志整理，特志谢忱。原载《中国比较文学年鉴（1986）》）

镜子和七巧板：
当前中西文学批评观念的主要差异

  本文试图对比并简略概述当前中西流行的两种差异极大的批评方法或倾向：其中一种我想用镜子来标志，另一种则用七巧板来标志。

  当前中国文学批评的基本假说均基于这些理论：文学应当反映社会生活，它不能脱离社会生活，它有政治倾向性和教育目的。作家应当不断深入生活，特别要深入劳动人民的生活。因此，批评家主要关注的是作家是否深入了群众，是否成功地反映了社会生活。因此一些批评术语，诸如"世界观"、"倾向性"、"进步性"、"歌颂或暴露"、"本质"、"冲突与矛盾"、"认识价值"（在论及外国文学和中国古典文学作品时用的术语），就经常出现在评论文章中，而批评家则主要探讨作家的生活态度和作品的思想内容；另一些术语，例如"现实主义"、"性格刻划"、"典型"、"体现"、"栩栩如生"、"细节"、"浪漫主义和理想化"等，则常用来探讨作品的美学形式。[1]

与此同时，我们却在西方现代文学批评中发现了一套与之迥然不同的术语。诚然，西方文学批评远远谈不上统一和相同，但照现在的情形来看，各种批评流派都有着一种相互渗透的趋向，因此就自然有一些共同的特色，在这些特征中，最主要者就是专注于文学作品的形式。诸如"肌质"、"模式"、"范围"、"平面"、"结构"、"构成"这类词已成了不可缺少的东西。这些词往往泄露了批评家对他所探讨作品的态度，犹如一位手拿手术刀的外科医师，时刻准备切开作品的各个部分，以找出一部作品的组成零件，也可以说，如同一个面对着七巧板的整套部件苦思苦想的人。

这两套批评术语的不同表明，中国批评家所专注的是反映在作品中的生活，而西方批评家则观照作品本身，不屑于费心探究作品的"外部因素"。前者大致与韦勒克教授归类的外部研究相近，后者则近似于内部研究。其原因可能有多种多样。也许在此作一简略的历史回顾并不多余。

儒家文学观可以用"诗言志"这公式来概括，这可以引申为"诗歌是思想或情感的表达"。诗在此指的是古代所有诗歌的总体，其中大多数收录在《诗经》里。根据这部诗集来看，"诗"实际上已含有超越个人感情或简单抒情之意，它既有社会意义，又

---

[1] 这种观点的理论基础体现在毛泽东的《在延安文艺座谈会上的讲话》。该文认为，文学艺术的主要源泉是生活，而古典文学则是"流"，即次要的灵感；在评价一部文学作品时，政治标准第一，艺术标准第二；作品的历史进步性以及作者对人民大众的态度是衡量作品的尺度，根据这个尺度来判断一部作品的相对价值；同时也体现在列宁主义的"反映论"和恩格斯对现实主义的定义："除了细节的真实外，再现典型环境中的典型人物。"（恩格斯谈及的是小说，即他所谓的"倾向性小说"，而当前的中国文学批评大多恰恰论及这种体裁。实际上，对现实主义的这种专注也体现在对中国古代文论的重新解释中；《文心雕龙》就被说成是一部论述现实主义的著作。批评家们实际上忘记了这一点，即从本意上说，中国文学在刘勰以前的漫长时期里，占主导地位的文学作品恰恰是抒情作品。）

有政治意义，因为诗在这里起着针砭时弊的"刺"的作用，也是赞美的工具。孔子后来进一步扩大了诗的功用，说："诗可以兴，可以观，可以群，可以怨。"他所说的后三个功用不曾在学者中引起过多少争论，而第一个功用，"兴"，开始是一个技术性名词，意为受外部物体刺激而产生的灵感[1]，渐渐带有了道德和政治意义，指产生道德和政治意义的那种灵感。无论如何，诗作为知识（观）的来源，作为外交（群）的工具，作为社会批判（怨）的工具[2]，已牢牢确定下来了。后来又在《毛诗序》中进一步强调了这一概念："先王以是经夫妇，成孝敬，厚人伦，美教化，移风俗。"此后，把文学看作伦理、社会和政治教义的载体的种种观念都来源于此。最后由周敦颐（1017—1075）集中体现在"文以载道"这个口号中，赋予了文学功用以理论的和哲学的基础。

道家文学理论批评的影响直到公元三世纪才体现出来，而且它随之就成了至少主宰三百年之久的一个思潮。它完全摆脱了传统的伦理和社会偏见，提出了许多新的、重要的文学观念。这种概念的改变同佛教的传播同时出现。[3] 有些观念显然是从儒家用语中沿袭来的，并产生了一些新奇的复杂意义。

例如，"气"这个词早在曹丕（187—226）那里就出现过了，当时他在评论徐幹诗歌的特征时使用了这个词，依他之见，"徐幹时有齐气。"将气的原则应用于文学批评是一个重要的变化，因为

---

[1] 刘殿爵译为"刺激想象"（to stimulate the imagination），见刘译：*Confucius. The Analects*, Penguin Classics, London, 1979。

[2] 郑众：《周礼·大司乐》注"兴者以善物喻善事"。郑玄：《周礼·大师》注"兴见今之美，嫌于媚谀，取善事以喻劝之"。

[3] 批评家一般都认为，佛教，尤其是后来的变体禅宗，是真正的披着袈裟的道家或"玄学"。

它把批评家的注意力从社会考察转移到了纯粹的审美观照。这个词也许直接取自孟子的"我善养吾浩然之气",指的是一种道德自我修身,但曹丕的用法却隐含着诗人的气质,这种气质体现在诗人的风格里。同时,提出这一点也颇有意思:曹丕也象丹纳一样,似乎意识到了诗人的气质可以通过他所出生的环境来形成。曹丕在鉴赏同时代另一些诗人的作品时也使用了这个词。

中国古典文评脱离伦理—社会偏见的另一个新的现象是对"兴"的重新解释。陆机(261—303)在《文赋》中着重论述了作品中来自大自然的灵感。[1]并且形象地描绘了灵感是如何发生效应的:"若夫应感之会,通塞之纪,来不可遏,去不可止,藏若景灭,行犹响起。"

道家批评家也象儒家批评家一样,敏锐地意识到了表达的难度——意义与口头或书面语之间的差异。儒家学派并未提出任何解决方法。[2]但值得一提的是,具有道家倾向的批评家,特别是陆机,从庄子那里吸取了灵感,他们试图在中国文学史上首次提出一种想象的理论,并借此提出一个解决方法。[3]陆机不仅把想象力描绘为打破时空束缚之能力,而且还用比喻的语言,描绘了想象何以发展为表达之实际过程。[4]

刘勰(？465—？520)在庄子和《易经》的基础上,重申并进一步阐述了想象的理论。除了指出想象力具有不受束缚之能力外,刘勰还在下列文字中分析了想象力的效用:

---

[1] 遵四时以叹逝,瞻万物而思纷;悲落叶于劲秋,喜柔条于芳春。
[2] 《论语》"辞达而已矣"。孟子《万章上》:"故说诗者,不以文害辞,不以辞害意;以意逆志,是为得之。"
[3] 《文赋》:"精骛八极,心游万仞……观古今于须臾,抚四海于一瞬。"
[4] 《文赋》:"选意按部,考辞就班,……罄澄心以凝思,眇众虑而为言,笼天地于形内,挫万物于笔端。"

故思理为妙，神与物游。神居胸臆，而志气统其关键；物沿耳目，而辞令管其机枢。机枢方通，则物无隐貌；关键将塞，则神有遁心。[1]

刘勰在谈论想象和表达时所用的语言可能会引起不同的解释，因此这个问题一直弄不清楚。[2] 但是这种探求解决表达方法的尝试却给中国文学批评留下了颇有意思的并且很有成效的影响。最深邃、最微妙的东西恰恰是无法言传的，这又成了道家批评家的信条。我们可以从《道德经》的第一句中找到佐证："道，可道，非常道；名，可名，非常名。"这一观点对中国文学批评产生了深刻的影响。每一位诗人的最高愿望就是要取得文字以外的效果，同时这也是判断诗歌之价值的最高标准。这一美学原则可用简短一句话来概括："意在言外"。崇尚暗示，崇尚含蓄已成了中国古代诗歌的特点，在佛教或禅宗的教义里，这一观点被强调为"顿悟"，离言说相，离文说相。

我们可以说，人们已意识到，研究文学可以从心理学和语义学的角度入手，因此我们不妨设想，假如中国文学批评沿着道家—佛教传统发展下去，它也许会和西方批评走过的道路相汇合。但事实上，儒家的那种心理结构，如清醒的常识，永远着眼于现实，对人伦道德的深刻关注，长久以来一直有着占主导地位的影响。十九世纪末二十世纪初，首先是梁启超，接着是王国维从西方引进了"写实主义"（realism）这一术语，从而给中国漫长的传统以画龙点睛之笔。在某种意义上说来，当前的批评观念可以说正是那个传统的延续。

---

[1] 刘勰：《文心雕龙·神思》。
[2]（美国）邵耀成：《试论刘勰二层次的"创作论"》，见《古代文学理论研究》第五辑，上海古籍出版社，1981年版。

在西方，文学批评走的却是另一条迥然不同的发展路线。对马修·阿诺德的反动一直延续着，来自阿诺德阵营以及三十年代左翼阵营（白璧德、莫尔、福斯特）的几次反击都是短暂的。然而，批评的局面总体上是由"形式主义"（用这个词最宽泛的意义来说）控制的。形式主义批评不屑于考虑文学的社会功能，因而不作道德判断。它是一股与现实主义和教育劝诫相悖的强有力潮流。为了简便起见，我不妨仅从现代莎士比亚评论方面举几个例子，因为莎士比亚有幸受到了几乎所有现代批评流派的考察。[1] 我想挑出"模式"（pattern）这个词作为现代西方文学批评精神的特征，因为这个词有时由于其多重用法很难翻译成相应的中文：

现实世界中含有的模式

强度之后的苍白结尾——许多其他诗歌都有这样的模式。

情节通常都按"如愿以偿"这个模式展开。

新喜剧所展示的是亚里士多德因果律的模式。

那些在喜剧中阻碍主人公取得最后胜利的人物……吝啬鬼，忧郁症患者，伪君子，书呆子，势利者……他们的行为都是按照一种外在的模式安排的，一望而知。

莎士比亚的喜剧遵循着一种深刻的"死亡—再生"这一仪式的模式而展开。

不管这个词在作品中作为主题的复现，或象征的再现，或甚至词语的有规律重复，还是人类行为的习惯性或不正常变化，或是社会或世界的组成方式，它们都被设想为一个由各部分组成的整体，

---

[1] 有关引文均引自阿尔文·B.柯南编：《现代莎士比亚评论》，纽约，1970年版。

这些部分可放在一起，亦可拆开。

梅纳德·麦克（Maynard Mack）教授那篇论证严密、写得极好的文章（《詹姆士一世时代的莎士比亚：略论悲剧的结构》，The Jacobean Shakespeare. Some Observations on the Construction of the Tragedies）可证实我的观点。麦克教授正确地批评了布拉德雷（Bradley）对莎士比亚悲剧结构的分析，布氏将其分析为"暴露、冲突、危机、灾难结局的组织安排；进程和场景的对比；经过多方面调节的起落的总体模式"，这样的分析至今仍是"对莎士比亚悲剧之外形所作的最好描绘"。但这种分析也"能用于粗制滥造之作"。麦克教授显然成功地作出了探讨其"内部结构"的尝试，他还探讨了"莎士比亚的……暗示、激发、隐含的才干"，因而"用间接的方式找出了前进的方向"。例如，他选取了《李尔王》中的弄人这一角色，认为这个弄人是某种"表明李尔王头脑里所想之事的戏剧性速记符号"，因为"他直到李尔王变得象弄人那样行为举止时才以一位有台词的人物之身份进入剧中，而且没等到李尔王清醒就不见了身影"。由此可见，弄人这个例子"向我们展示了戏剧结构的一些手法以及记载内部'行动'进展的方法，尽管传统的批评范畴对之毫无提及，但这些手法和方法毕竟是莎士比亚戏剧创作的基本资源"。

与布拉德雷不同的是，麦克教授试图找出莎士比亚悲剧中的"真正的悲剧缪斯"。但是他也象布拉德雷那样，求助于结构分析的方法，但并未用暴露等措词，而是用"主题之再现"、"镜子的场景"和"心灵变化之循环"这一类措词来分析。

当然，历史学派也同样坚持这些，但它的历史概念与马克思主义的概念却大相径庭。其次，历史学派批评家认为，历史反映在文学中，是由实际发生的事件和真实人物所组成，是由社会甚至政治机构所组成，而马克思主义批评家则认为，历史事件只是"社会发展规律"的表现。因此，在讨论文学作品对现实的反映时，他们就着重强调"本质"，而本质则具体体现在"典型"中。再者，马克思主义将现实作为冲突及其解决过程的概念也同历史学派的静止或进化论观点造成鲜明对比。再进一步说，历史学派也和形式主义学派一样，回避道德判断，仅仅意在达到"客观性"，而马克思主义批评则公开或含蓄地强调文学的教育作用。

还应补充一点，当前的中国文学批评倾向产生于诸多原因，其中五十年代苏联学派的马克思主义文论的影响占主导地位。它播种并植根于一块有利于它生长的土壤里，因为在这块土地上，有着儒家思想占统治地位的文学批评传统，它历来就有政治——说教之取向，它也强调生活，强调现实功利性。这种批评倾向的合理之处在于，它坚持文学是一种社会现象，艺术作品不能脱离社会生活而存在于真空中。因此，它有助于读者把作品放在其社会背景下来理解。但在解释生活与艺术之关系时，它却容易流于简单化，因为它仅从一个单一的角度——尽管这个角度也很重要——认为，艺术只是写实的艺术，而常常忽视了这样一系列因素：创作的复杂过程，作者的文化修养，文化传统和思潮，作者和读者的心理，特别是艺术作品的结构及其语言因素。这样一来，中国文学批评实际上到了一个十字路口，如果要想在此前进一步，就得承认创作工作的复杂性。L. C. 奈茨（L. C. Knights）在批评布拉德雷学派时曾这样说过，"把莎士比亚主要看作一位伟大的创造人物的作家，是最不着边际的看法，却影响极大……他能够把这些人物'逼真地'展现在我们面前……而诗意则是一种附加的优点。"这一评语可以很恰当地适用于当前的中国文学批评。然而，现已有迹象表明，中国批评家已开始意识到了文学的内部研究的重要性。

同样，西方文学批评似乎也到了一个十字路口。它虽能帮助读者更深刻地理解和欣赏作品，尤其是新批评派做到了这一点，但其中的一些不尽令人满意之处却在于，它本身也有其局限，它不愿超越文学作品的形式范围。另一位著名的莎士比亚评论家沃尔夫岗·克莱门（Wolfgang Glemen）在《莎士比亚剧作中的意象发之展》（*Development of Shakespeare's Imagery*）一书中指出：

> 　　我们以为，在将诗歌和历史现象划分和再划分为一个鸽笼般的系统之后，再在每一样东西上贴个标签，这样我们的理解力便达到了最终的目的，这是一个很奇怪的错误。这种刻板图解式的分类系统常常既破坏了有着活力的感受，使我们感受不到诗歌作品的整体性和五色缤纷的丰富性。

　　这恰是对西方文学批评的贴切的描述，尽管他所说的"整体性"和"丰富性"还可以商榷。在我看来，整体性应当是文学作品与生活的统一，丰富性也应当是生活本身的丰富多姿。例如，对于《尤利西斯》及其结构的评论，人们已写下不少文章，但可以说很少谈及社会力量对该书创作所产生的作用。如果这一点不阐明，文学批评就只能是不完整的，因为这样的阐明有助于读者更充分地理解这部作品。批评家有无社会意识，差别是很大的，因为他的观点直接影响着他的艺术分析。

　　我希望从以上的分析可以看出：对涉及文学批评的那些大问题进行的比较研究，与对具体的批评概念的比较研究一样，是颇有必要的，也可以说，对具体批评概念的比较研究应当导向对更重大的问题的研究，即研究批评后面的态度或哲学。由此可见，镜子式的探讨或七巧板式的研究都不尽完备，文学批评所需要的应当是一种综合研究，而非彼此排斥，应当择善而从，而不应偏向一面。

"The Mirror and the Jigsaw: A Major Difference between Current Chinese and Western Critical Affitudes"，原载 *Representations* 4, Fall 1983, University of California, Berkeley。王宁译

附记：此文写于1982年，未能涉及结构主义和后结构主义。这两种新理论虽仍是形式主义的理论，但值得作进一步的比较研究。此外，本文也未涉及所谓的"新历史主义"批评，这一批评流派可以说是对形式主义批评的一种反作用，也值得作比较研究。

历史叙述中的虚构
——作为文学的历史叙述

我们通常所说的"历史"有两个涵义。一是指过去发生的一切，一是指历史著作。为了避免混淆，我将采用"历史叙述"（historical narrative）一词来指历史著作，用"历史"来指过去发生的一切。

人们往往拿历史叙述和文学对比，而得出结论，认为历史著作记录的都是以往发生过的"事实"，历史著作是"实录"，或至少应当是"实录"，而文学则是虚构。中国史学始终在追求"真实"，历史叙述必须是信史。司马迁说："余所谓述故事，整齐其世传，非所谓作也。"刘勰论《史传》也说："文非泛论，按实而书。"又说："文疑则阙，贵信史也。"刘知几写《史通》全为和不真实作斗争。直到梁启超在谈写历史的目的时也说："历史的目的在将过去的真事实予以新意或新价值，以供现代人活动之资鉴。"[1] 即使是小说，也追求真实，如毛宗岗序《三国演义》就说此书"据实指陈，非属臆造"，"实叙帝王之实，真而可考"。甚至在今天，这种

---

[1]《中国历史研究法补篇》第一章，见《中国历史研究法》，上海古籍出版社，第148页。.

追求真实的愿望并未消灭。[1] 可见历史著作所记载的都是或都应是真实的这一概念，至今未变。

但人们从历史叙述的实践也看到任何历史著作不可能全真，只能是部分真实。[2] 但历史叙述中有多少虚构成分，虚构是怎样产生的，怎样形成的，历史叙述的虚构在多大程度上接近文学，倒是值得探讨的问题。本文想就几个中西主要史家和史论家的实践和理论，试给这些问题以某种回答。

我们稍加研究后，就会发现历史叙述中的虚构和文学虚构是同一类的问题。历史作品和文学作品在虚构这点上可以类比。过去，我们谈历史著作的文学性，如《史记》的文学性，只限于把它看成传记文学，而它的艺术特点也只限于人物个性、"典型性"的刻划。如果从虚构这个角度插手进去，也许历史叙述的文学性可以更充分地建立起来。

中外史家和历史理论家对虚构的成因有许多看法。我们先看看中国的史论。

中国史家的出发点，如前所述，一向是为了求真，但从历史叙述的实践，他们又发现真实之不可能，因此就极力去追究其原因。下面我们就王充、刘勰、刘知几的论述来考察一下。

王充崇尚理性，有点象法国的伏尔泰，不过比他早一千七百年。他全用理性来衡量一切史籍。他在《论衡》里分析历史叙述中虚构的成因有以下数端：

（一）因缺乏常识而轻信或迷信。在《书虚篇》中他说："世信

---

[1] 《人民日报》1988 年 4 月 12 日李泽厚与刘再复的文学对话中，李：报告文学的特点应是真实。刘：未来史家可能将报纸当成正史，报告文学为野史。李：不管正史、野史，都应真实，如果虚构就变成小说了。
[2] 钱锺书：《管锥篇》一，第 163 页，The whole truth and nothing but the truth. The truth but not the whole truth.

虚妄之书，以为载于竹帛上者，皆圣贤所传，无不然之事，故信而是之，讽而读之。"即孟子所批评的"尽信书"。他举了许多例子，如吴季札出游，见路有遗金，叫一个采薪的人取来给他。王充说："世以为然，迂虚言也。"因为"季子能让吴位，何嫌贪地遗金？"又举传说颜渊和孔子登泰山，孔子东南望吴阊门外有系白马，问颜渊可曾看到，颜渊用尽目力去看，说看到了。下山之后，"颜渊发白齿落，遂以病死"。王充评论道：人们都把这事解释为颜渊的目力不及孔子，所以视为可信，其实"非颜渊不能见，孔子亦不能见也"。

由于迷信而产生的虚构，如《变虚篇》中说宋景公时，荧惑（火星）守心（心宿，二十八宿之一），景公以为祸当及宋，因为心宿是宋国的分野。子韦劝景公移祸于宰相和臣民，景公不肯，火星果然移位。又如《道虚篇》中他批评儒家和道家的许多虚枉传说，如称淮南王得道，"举家升天，畜产皆仙，犬吠于天上，鸡鸣于云中"。

缺乏常识往往出于儒家的偏见，如《儒增篇》中褒称尧舜之世"一人不刑"，文武之世"刑错不用四十余年"。

（二）由语言引起的夸张和虚构。在《艺增篇》里，他说："世俗所患，患言事增其实；著文垂辞，辞出溢其真；称美过其善，进恶没其罪。何则？俗人好奇。不奇，言不用也。故誉人不增其美，则闻者不快其意，毁人不益其恶，则听者不惬于心。闻一增以为十，见百益以为千。"他在《语增篇》中举一例说："传语曰：'圣人忧世深，思事勤，愁扰精神，感动形体，故称尧若腊（干肉），舜若脯（干鸟肉），桀、纣之君，垂腴（腹下肥肉）尺余。'……"刘知几在《史通·曲笔》篇中，他说："子为父隐，直在其中。"又说："事涉君亲，必言多隐讳，虽直道不足，而名教存焉。"但"诬人之恶，持报己仇"，"受金而始书"，"借米而方传，此又记言之奸赋，载笔之凶人"。在《书事》篇中，他表示史家选材要根据政治和道德目的，他完全同意荀悦的立典五志说，即所谓达道义、彰法式、通古今、著功勋和表贤能。他的《人物》篇也讲写人物的目的在于"诫世"和"示后"。

可见刘知几所持的是传统的看法，即历史著作的目的是为当前政治的借鉴，但同时他也透露历史叙述受政治和道德的左右。政治和道德的考虑产生了虚构。

在历史叙述以借鉴为目的的前提下，叙述又不得不具有文学性。"史之为务，必藉于文"（见《叙事》篇）。这就牵涉到语言问题。他服膺"言之不文，行之不远"的原则，但须"文而不丽，质而非野，使人味共滋旨，怀其德音"，亦即只有这样，才能使人真正得到教益。因此，他对有些史书提出批评，他说："今之所作……其立言也，或虚加练饰，轻事雕彩，或体兼赋颂，词类俳优。文非文，史非史。"可见他认为文采是需要的，但不能轻易增加，为文采而文采，历史叙述和文学在他心目中要加以区别。文可以自由地在语言上玩弄华彩，如辞赋，但历史叙述只能适当地具有文学性，不能损害真实，不能冲淡借鉴的作用。

刘知几作这样的比较，我想是因为历史叙述作为文学在当时既不能和抒情诗比，也没有史诗或小说可比。他所引用过的《拾遗记》、《搜神记》都是志怪的，不足信，因此只和辞赋相比，而得出这结论。但除此以外，历史叙述却完全可以互相比较。他写的《模拟》篇就认为写历史应借鉴前人："若不仰范前哲，何以贻厥后来？"但是模拟往往会产生谬误和不实。这就是他所谓的"貌同心异"。所以他反对泥古派的机械模拟前代史家。他说：这是因为"世异则事异，事异则备异"。因此他主张"貌异心同"，并解释道：所谓心同是"取其道术相会，义理玄同，若斯而已"。这与章学诚的"六经皆史"的意思相同。六经是"器"，史也是"器"，都是"明道"或载道的工具。刘知几在此把古代的成功的历史叙述，而不是文学作品，作为模范（paradigm）加在新史料上。

历史叙述离不开语言，但语言有古今中外之分，不如实记录，滥施文采，也会失真。他在《言语》篇中说："后来作者，通无远识，记其当世口语，罕能从实而书，方复追效昔人，示共稽古。……用使周秦言辞，见于魏晋之代，楚汉应对，行乎宋齐之日。而伪修混沌，失彼天然，今古以之不纯，真伪由其相乱。"他批评魏收的《魏书》和牛弘的《周史》"必讳彼夷音，变成华语……华而失实，过莫大焉"。这虽然讲的是对历史人物所说的话在时代和方域方面要存真，但提出了一个更广泛的问题，就是人物所说的话的内容能否存真而无虚构。从历史叙述实践来看，这是不可能的。

刘知几反对混淆古今和中外语言，但又主张应增加的时候，还应增加。在《浮词》篇中他指出叙述语言有时必须增加一些辅助因素才能取得"余音足句"的效果，使其意义完整。但又不能乱增浮词，他说："近代作者，溺于烦富，则有发言失中，加字不惬，遂令后之览者，难以取信。"

概括言之，刘知几认为历史叙述失真的原因（一）是政治和道德的考虑，亦即外界的压力，而且这种失真是不可避免的，甚至是应该的。（二）历史叙述失真的另一个原因就是不区别历史叙述和文学。他虽然认为历史叙述应当具有文学性，但这仅以能增进而不是妨碍道德目的为限。此外，他所能做的历史叙述和文学的比较，并非是把历史叙述和叙事文学比较，而是把历史叙述和辞赋作比较，因此只牵涉到修辞，而与叙事结构无关。他作出的有趣的贡献是由他首先提出的历史人物的语言问题，转述历史人物的话在历史叙述中占很重要的地位。这问题在希腊史家修昔底德（Thucydides）

的著作里也有所讨论。

我们再来看看西方史家的实践和理论。

希腊史家希罗多德（Herodotus）可以说是一位介乎史诗诗人和历史家之间的一位作者。他写他的《历史》，直接的目的是为了批驳波斯史家对这段历史的不实之辞，表现了一种求实精神，同时要维护雅典的尊严。他虽然说他写历史只是为了保存历史，不致被人遗忘，其实他的真正目的是歌颂希腊人在希波战争中所表现的爱国主义，实际上也是一种政治道德目的。

他的叙述方法则完全是采用民间故事的模式，所以他的叙述不仅有局部的虚构，而且在结构上也完全是按照文学叙事的构架形成的，具体说就是民间故事的结构。例如他写传说中利底亚王克利索斯（Croesus）会见希腊元首索伦（Solon）的场面就完全是一个非常完整的民间故事，包括最后的寓意教训。克利索斯问索伦世界上谁最幸福，索伦回答了三次，第一次举了一个不出名的雅典公民，他的几个儿子都品德高尚，他自己在对敌作战中壮烈捐躯。第二次举了两个希腊青年，都是竞技优胜者，因为没有牛，亲自拉车把母亲拉到节日会场，他们都在安详的睡眠中去世。第三次，索伦的回答是：一生富贵不算幸福，光荣地死去才算幸福。

希罗多德的另一个特点就是着力刻划人物。例如他写波斯王薛西斯（Xerxes）渡赫勒斯滂海峡入侵希腊，听说过海峡搭的桥被风吹断，他大怒，命手下抽海峡三百鞭，把镣铐扔到海里。作者还说"不仅如此，我还听说他还叫人把火把也投进海里。不过，有一点我可以肯定，他叫人边抽边用傲慢不恭的外国话骂道：'你这可恨的海，我们的主上就这样惩罚你，因为你对不起他，可他并没有对不起你的地方。是的，不管你愿意不愿意，薛西斯王决心要从你上面过去，你这条混浊的咸水河，没有人祭你是活该.'就这样，他命人惩罚海峡，又命人把原先搭桥的主管统统杀头。"

这是非常戏剧性的，但恐怕离真实很远，和文学有什么不同？

修昔底德（Thucydides）一般认为是最严谨、最科学、最公正、最可靠的古代历史家。他说他所写的历史事件有的是他亲身经历的，有的是别人报道的，他都予以核实。他说他人的报道往往带有党派偏见或记忆的差误，所以要核实。他也承认自己的记忆也不永远完整。他不写神话，因此他说他的历史著作读来可能没有味道，但可以为后代借鉴。不过关于他书中人物的演说词，他也说是不准确的，只能按演说的场合来推断，但大意是不错的。

修昔底德写历史也有他的政治目的和道德目的，即颂扬雅典的伟大，这从伯里克利（pericles）悼念阵亡将士的演说中可以看出。他歌颂雅典伟大的祖先、当代的民主、平等、公正的立法以及文化活动，为这样一个伟大城邦捐躯是有价值的等等。

这里可以附带说一句，有些评论家[1]认为古代史家往往把历史上各种力量的斗争理解为善与恶的道德问题，或理解为成功和失败的问题，而不能看成是运动。奥厄巴赫举修昔底德为例，说他"叙述了一个个前台事件，考虑的是有关人性或命运这类伦理问题，这种考虑是先验的、静止的"。但这种评论只能说历史叙述应从更加宏观的角度去写，展示历史发展规律，却并不能取消历史叙述的道德内容。

另外有的批评家[2]指出修昔底德的历史叙述完全受当时希腊

---

[1] 参看埃利希·奥尔巴赫：《模仿》，特拉斯克译，普林斯顿大学出版社，1974年版，第38页。
[2] 参看阿诺德·T. 汤因比：《历史研究》，骚莫维尔节本，第1章，第44页，引F. M. 孔福德语。

悲剧程式的支配。我想这话却是很有道理的。试举一例。修昔底德在写雅典人远征西西里的西拉库斯（Syracuse）时，写送行者的心情，这完全合乎合唱队的模式；写出征将士的骄傲，即所谓"胡布利斯"（hubris），是人物性格中的缺点（hamartia）；最后失败，幸存者沦为奴隶，在石矿上劳动，作为结尾。

修昔底德另一个文学特点就是人物的刻划。例如他写科林多（Corinth）代表团去斯巴达（Sparta）说服斯巴达人与雅典联盟作战，用激将法讽刺斯巴达人如何保守，怕多事，做事无恒心，对一切表现得无能为力，而雅典人如何爱冒险，喜变，贪婪务得，好战。这虽是集体画像，但也说明作者对人物集团性格的观察和兴趣，和希罗多德异曲同工。

罗马史家几乎没有一个不是抱着爱国精神或党派精神写历史的。[1] 这必然影响历史叙述的真实性。塔西陀（Tacitus）就明确承认[2] 流传下来有关提比略（Tiberius）等四个皇帝的著述是不可信的。"在他们统治时期，恐惧压制了或歪曲了真实"。

这些史家特别擅长事件的叙述，如罗马大史家李维（Livy）写蛮族高卢人洗劫罗马的情景是一篇极生动的故事，结构完整，一个悬念接着一个悬念，把胜利者写得十分怯懦，把失败的罗马人写得庄严无畏。这主要体现在那些留在城里的元老们身上，他们在罗马陷落之后穿着官服静静地坐在府中等候敌人来杀他们："高卢人怀着敬畏的心情站在他们面前，好象他们是一尊尊神像。据说，有一个高卢人捅了一下一个元老的长胡须，这位罗马元老就用权杖敲了他的头来激怒他，结果这位元老是第一个被杀害的。"

塔西陀写尼禄朝罗马大火也极生动，富有戏剧性。

---

[1] 西方十六七世纪历史著作受罗马史学影响可能比受希腊史学影响更多。
[2] 《编年史》序。

人物的描写多通过事件，也作一些独立的描写。人物有时也通过他们的演说显示出性格。演说本身，正如修昔底德所说，只保留了大意，但却是按照修辞模式构成的。所以与其说是实录，不如说是美文或创造性的散文。塔西陀的人物"不是用自己的语言说话，说的是塔西陀的话"[1]。

　　中世纪的西方历史著作，若以比德（Bede）的《英国教会编年史》为例，目的是宣扬宗教，如他自己所说，是"惩恶扬善"，"取悦上帝"。从内容上讲，主要是一些圣徒的言行，夹杂许多奇迹、梦幻等迷信因素。在某些独立的事件，如圣阿尔班（St. Alban）殉教的故事，选择几件突出的事迹，予以戏剧化，文笔简练，具有文学性，目的当然是显示基督教的优越。不过，从全局结构说，并不完整。有些个别意象则很有诗意，如把人生比作寒冬夜晚飞过温暖光亮厅堂的一只麻雀，却脍炙人口。

　　文艺复兴时期的历史著作同样具有政治和道德目的。据布克哈特[2]，意大利城市为了宣扬本城市的光荣而请人写史。此外当然也有通史、中古史之类的著作，大都以罗马史家为范例。在英国，这时期的历史著作也是很多的，也莫不有政治和说教目的——"历史是用实例来教哲学"。同时，写历史更明显地受到政治环境的制约。罗利（Sir Walter Raleigh）写世界史说："读者也许更希望我写一部我们当代的历史……我的回答是，谁要写一部近代史，必须跟随真实跟得很紧，那么他的牙齿可能被打掉。""在我现在的处境，写最古的时代就够了，因为我也能够通过写古代，却指向今天，通过谴责死人，来谴责今天活着的人们的罪恶。如果他们要责备我，我虽无辜，也没有办法。如果有人对号入座，说我把他们抹黑，那

　[1]《模仿》，第38页。
　[2] 布克哈特：《意大利文艺复兴时期的文明》（英文本），伦敦，1945年版，第147—148页。

他们只能怪他们自己才算公道，却怪不得我。"[1] 可见罗利写史还包含不少个人恩怨。

罗利的历史观很值得一提。在人们愈来愈把人生看作舞台，看作是梦的时代，对历史的概念亦复如是。在历史里，上帝是一切的主宰，他赏善惩恶。当人违反上帝的意旨胡作非为、趾高气扬的时候，演的是一出喜剧。而当他最后得到应得的惩罚时，喜剧就变成了悲剧。而历史主要是悲剧。历史人物就象麦克白所说，不过象个演员，在舞台上跳跳蹦蹦一个小时，便无声无阒了。[2] 罗利在他的《世界史·序》中把理查三世的一切行为说成是"悲剧的必然"。理查三世一方面戴上假面具扮演各种角色，掩盖他的罪恶意图，以便操纵利用别人对他的畏惧心情和别人的野心，使他们成为他的工具；另一方面他和他的同党本身也不自觉地成为上帝编的悲剧中的演员。

这明显地表明从观念上，从认识论上，把历史等同于文学的虚构。比起修昔底德来，这时的史家更加有意识地用文学模式来组织历史叙述。

到了十七八世纪，欧洲进入理性时代。历史著作一般分析渐多，纯叙事渐少，或夹叙夹议。所谓分析就是发现历史事件的因果关系。如写《大叛乱史》的克莱伦顿（Clarendon）就注意发掘事件后面当事人的思想和动机。写《罗马衰亡史》的吉朋（Gibbon）整个一部大书就是在追索罗马衰亡的原因。他把主要罪责归到基督教的兴起。这是实证主义、"科学的"历史的起步。这对后来的史论影响很大。

另一方面，吉朋的历史观仍旧是把历史看成悲剧，而他的情调

[1] 以上均见：《世界史·序》。
[2] 斯蒂芬·格林布莱特：《瓦尔特·雷莱》，耶鲁大学出版社，1973 年版，第 26—28 页。

则是抒情的。他认为罗马文明、罗马的国家制度、文物制度，都渐渐地达到了到当时为止的最高峰，忽然间毁于一旦，使他感到无限惋惜。[1] 他认为（古希腊、罗马）异教文明的精神是人道博大，而基督教则是疯狂、无理性。

他所以选择罗马史，是和罗利一样，因为"我怕写现代英国史，每个人物都成问题，每个读者可以是朋友，也可以是敌人；因为大家都希望一个作家挂起党派的旗帜，用尽全力去诟骂敌对的派系"，"我只能写一个比较安全、更博大的题目"。尽管如此，他的第一卷问世后，他的朋友哲学家休谟（Hume）写信给他："你写这题目必然会引起人们对你的怀疑。"并希望他继续写时要谨慎些。

除了他的悲剧历史观以外，评论家一致称赞他的文笔矫健有力，符合当时所提倡的散文风格。

十九世纪英国最重要的史家应当算是麦考利（Macaulay）。他的历史叙事方法越来越接近当代的有关历史叙述的理论。他可能是第一个把写历史完全看成和写小说一样的史家，而且他还明白地申明这一看法。他在他的《论历史》一文中说：一个完善的史家"应当使真实性具有吸引力，这种吸引力一向被虚构的小说（fiction）所篡夺了"。他的方法之一就是通过对史料"作出有判断的选择、抛弃和安排"。"过去英国史家所抛弃的、他们认为有损他们职业尊严的大批的各色各样的事实"都可采用。

此外，他是一个非常出色的风俗画家，大段描绘各个时期的政治、经济、社会、文化，一切"微不足道而生动的事件，丰富的文化社会背景"[2] 他都着力描写，来衬托"历史上大人物"的事迹。他的基本的历史观也是把历史看作戏剧。他在他的《英国史》第一

---

[1] 参看他《自传》中关于他为什么要写《罗马衰亡史》的动念。
[2] 麦考利的后裔屈维林（G. M. Trevelyan）写《英国社会史》实即继续这一传统。

章在叙述英国最早的历史的时候就说："我打算叙述的〔早期英国史中的〕诸事件，只构成一幕戏，〔整部英国史〕延展到许多时代，形成一出伟大而多事的戏剧，如果早期情节不好好交代，整出戏就不可能完全理解。"在谈到叙述中的轶事时，他说："在这些轶事里无疑混杂了许多无可稽考的故事，但不能因此就认为不值得记录下来，因为不管是真是假，这些都是我们祖先信以为真而热心地传下来的，这是一个无可争辩而重要的事实。"

他的实践也正是如此，例如他写格兰科（Glencoe）的大屠杀就极精采。这故事写苏格兰两大家族的政治斗争，其中有地方背景的描写、会盟、战斗屠杀、阴谋诈骗，有曲折，有对话，有人物的心理分析。

凡此种种都被二十世纪西方史论所继承和发展。但二十世纪西方史论略而不谈政治偏见引起的歪曲失实，或一笔带过，而麦考利则具有鲜明的党派性和道德目的。他歌颂的是维多利亚的"时代精神"，对维多利亚时代弊端，他虽也写，但予以开脱。他说正是因为"老有人表示不满，所以才老有改进；如果对当前已感到满足，那我们就停步不前，不必劳动，不必为将来而节约了"。

二十世纪史学家汤因比（Arnold J. Toynbee）也是把历史叙述的虚构同文学虚构等量齐观的。他在他的巨著《历史研究》中根据亚理士多德，声称："有三种不同的方法可以观察和表述我们思考的对象，其中也包括人类生活现象。"[1] 其一是确定和记录"事实"，这是历史学的方法；其二是把确定了的事实加以比较，阐明其中的普遍规律，这是科学的方法；其三是用"虚构"（按指小说或戏剧）的形式给事实以艺术的再创造，这是写戏剧和小说的方法。在他看

---

[1] 汤因比：《历史研究》，骚莫维尔节本，第43—44页。

来，三者的分野并非绝对的。历史著作除纪录外，也可用虚构，也可体现规律。要写一部"伟大的"历史，而不是一部"干巴巴的"历史，就不能完全抛弃虚构的因素，而必须象戏剧或小说那样对事实进行再创造。虚构不仅是不可避免的，而且是使一部历史著作成为伟大的作品所必须的。汤因比举了希腊史家修昔底德为例。我们知道修昔底德是古代希腊最严谨的史家，但是他"把'虚构的'演说词和对话放进'历史'人物的嘴里，使他们戏剧化"。前面已经提到，有人还指出修昔底德是完全按当时希腊悲剧的程式来写他的历史著作的。

汤因比进而比较了历史叙述和小说、戏剧。一方面，历史叙述中必然掺入虚构，而小说和戏剧虽是虚构，却不可能完全是虚构，否则为什么亚理士多德说"诗比历史更真实、更富哲理"呢？小说和戏剧里面也有事实。"我们把一部文学作品称为虚构，我们不过是说其中的人物并非某个真人，有血有肉、真正在世界上生活过的某个人，其中的事件也非在某处真正发生过的事。我们只是说这部作品有一个虚构的人物的前景，而它的背景却是确凿的社会事实。我们能给一部好作品最高的赞美就是'符合生活真实'"。

汤因比这段话实际上已经把历史叙述和文学里的戏剧和小说的根本的异和同说得很清楚了。我们甚至可以进一步说，似乎是纯粹虚构的科幻小说也是以现有的科学成就为出发点，运用推理和想象而炮制成的。

汤因比是拿文明作为单位来研究世界历史的。很有趣的是在他写"英雄时代"这一卷时，他本人也把某一文明的灭亡比作悲剧。在文明社会与野蛮社会之间存在着一条边界，他把这条边界比作堤坝，蛮族向这堤坝施加压力，他们向文明社会学到越来越多的东西，如作战的武器，压力就越来越大，最后就象洪水一样突然把堤坝冲垮。这个例子说明史家在观察、思考历史的时候，往往是通过文学或修辞学里的"比喻"（trope）。下面我们谈到怀特时还要涉及到。

科林伍德（R. G. Collingwood）认为历史学和自然科学不同，历史的内容是可以体验的。"历史事件并非仅仅是现象或观察的对象，史学必须看透现象并辨析出其中的思想"。但历史学又和心理学不同，心理学研究的是直接经验和感觉，历史学无法做到此点。但他认为历史学如果不能找到历史现象后面的思想，例如一场战争这一现象，如不找到这场战争从头到尾贯穿着的人的思想，这场战争就无法理解。历史家的任务不仅是纪录事实，如凯撒渡卢比冈，而是要揭露事实后面的思想。这样，才能构成一个"言之成理的故事"。因此，他从康德的知识论中采用了"建设性"的概念，而提出所谓的"建设性想象"（constructive imagination）这一概念。他的"想象"比麦考利的想象又大大前进了一步。麦考利说："一个完美的历史学家必须具有足够有力的想象，以便使他的叙述能感人而且有声有色。"他注重的只是历史叙述的装饰性和感情色彩，及在读者身上产生的效果。科林伍德的"建设性想象"则与麦考利不同。他的建设性想象不是指通过想象取得某种效果，而是指通过想象去发现历史人物的内心活动。这类叙述在古代历史中也常有，如李维的《罗马史》中写罗马将领玛尔凯鲁斯在毁灭希拉库斯城之前，谛视全城，往事件件涌上心头，有点内心独白的味道。科林伍德所谓的"建设性想象"，在运用上要求史家在自己心里重演事件后面的思想，设身处地想古人之所想，颇象一个演员进入角色那样。史家不可能是目击者，要获得有关历史的知识只能通过这种间接的方法，也就是逻辑上的推理的方法。历史家是今人，不是古人，通过他们的推断，历史只能是今人眼中的历史。正如克罗齐所说"一切历史都是当代历史"。

科林伍德的"建设性想象"实际上是因果论，即从历史事件的果，去推求其原因。因此，他的"建设性想象"涉及对历史的整体结构的理解。这种方法实际上是前面所说十七八世纪史家所使用的方法，此外，如法国十七世纪史家拉班（René Rapin）、十八世纪英国史家波林布洛克（Bolingbroke）就提出要深入到隐藏在表面行动和政策后面的动机。[1]

到了当代历史理论家海登·怀特（Hayden White），则历史叙述和文学叙述几乎是一回事了。他是从结构主义观点来阐释历史叙述的。

怀特也首先指出历史叙述和科学不同，"历史事件不能用试验或观察来检验"。但他和汤因比和科林伍德不同，他不是从文学虚构的形式看历史叙述，而是从结构语言学的角度使历史叙述和文学认同。他认为"历史叙述非常明白无误的是语言虚构（verbal fictions）"。[2] 所谓"语言虚构"就是从结构主义角度看虚构。这里牵涉到弗莱（Northrop Fry）的原型批评。弗莱说："历史家的规划（scheme）如果达到某种无所不包的程度，在形状上就会变成象'神话'，因而在结构上就接近'诗歌'。"拨开这些术语的迷雾，弗莱的意思很简单，一部历史叙述的总体，必然和某一文学（"诗歌"）类型（"神话"）相似。一部历史叙述或者象传奇（如将历史比拟为寻找上帝城的历程，寻求无阶级社会的历程），或者象喜剧（历史叙述以乐观态度写人类进化、进步或革命的过程），或者象悲剧（如吉朋的《罗马衰亡史》或史本格勒的《西方的衰落》），或象一部讽刺作品（如把历史写成一再重复的过程或充满偶然性的过

---

[1] 《牛津英国文学史》，"十八世纪中叶"，第 192 页。
[2] 《论述的热门课题》，约翰斯·霍普金斯大学出版社，1982 年版，第 82 页。

程）。也就是说，一部历史叙述在总体上必然具备这四种文学结构中的一种。

怀特是同意这观点的。他认为历史叙述必须有连贯性。要取得连贯性，就必须将"事实"剪裁（tailoring）一番，使这些"事实"符合某一故事形式的要求。[1]"历史叙述并不是再现（reproduce）事实，而是告诉我们对这些事件应向哪个方向去思考（in what direction to think）并在我们思想里充入（charge）不同的感情价值。"这岂不是对弗莱的理论的极好的解释么？历史叙述这种功能已经超出了推理式的因果论的功能之上了。换言之，历史叙述有两种功能，一种通过找到因果，找到规律，使历史叙述起到借鉴作用；一种则是起到文学作用。怀特的观点属于后一种。

怀特还从另一角度阐述历史叙述的功能。他说历史家的任务就是把对读者来说是一大堆陌生的事实，无意义的事实，用共同文化中的共同概念或形式组织起来，使读者感到熟悉，感到能理解。因此历史叙述具有解释现象的作用，也具有提供知识的作用。所谓共同文化中的共同概念或形式，实即指弗莱的四种原型。怀特称之为"先类型情节结构"（pregcnerie ploi structure）。历史家的任务就是将事实、事件和这"先类型情节结构"结合起来，使历史的意义显现出来，他称此为"施加情节"（emplotment）。这就侧重历史叙述的文学性了。

但历史家往往不承认他在虚构，不承认在写小说，而事实上他的作品却有小说的效果，也就是说"产生意义"（sense-making），

---

[1] 弗雷德里克·詹明信：《政治无意识》，第 82 页："历史不是文本（text），历史基本上不是叙事性的，不是描述性的……除了通过某种有组织的形式（textual form），我们是无法接触到历史的……只有通过事先组织过的或重新组织过的（prior（re）textualisation）形式，我们才能接近历史。"

也就是说有了意义才能使人理解。而小说家也同样在产生意义，使人看到生活中的意义。

怀特进一步声称历史叙述不同于科学叙述，历史叙述没有固定的术语，只能用借喻、象征语言（figurative discourse），即维科（Vico）所说的四种表述方式：隐喻（metaphor）、换喻（metonymy）、提喻（synecdoche，即以部分代全部或相反）和讽喻（irony，即反喻）。同样是法国革命这一事件，某一史家可以把它写成传奇，另一史家可以把它写成悲剧。同样是雾月十八日事件，雨果、蒲鲁东和马克思的三种叙述就截然不同，代表了三种不同的表述方式。

科林伍德和怀特关于历史叙述的理论在西方产生了很大的影响。例如汉学家德瓦斯金[1]在批评麦尔（Mair）的论点——即唐以前或佛教进入中国以前，中国没有有意识创造的虚构小说，只有历史著作——时，就完全根据科林伍德、弗莱、怀特的理论来加以反驳。他说："自从十九世纪以来，我们已普遍接受这样一种看法，即历史学的灵魂不是按年罗列事实，而是解释。""任何历史著作要取得足够的连贯性，取得'叙事'的称号，都是虚构。"德瓦斯金认为创造性的虚构是唐以前一个主要的，甚至是最主要的叙述方式，而佛教文学的影响是次要的。

好了，说到此我们可以总结一下造成历史虚构中的原因。

一、外部原因。

史料本身的残缺，越是古代，越是如此。史料由于种种原因，

---

[1] 肯尼斯·J. 德沃斯金：《论叙述的变革，中国文学：小品文，论文和评论文章》，1983年7月号。

本身便包含谬误，以至以讹传讹。到了近代，又产生了史料过多的问题，时代越近越是如此，在选择过程中必然掺进主观成分。

但造成虚构的更主要的原因则是从外面来的压力。古今中外的历史叙述都无法避免。这外部压力，一方面是政治压力，另一方面是道德压力。政治压力，主要是指史家不敢如实纪录，"宁顺从以保守"（保护自己）。道德压力则指一种约定俗成甚至明文规定的道德准则或道德规范，限制史家奋笔直书。不过政治和道德的压力往往转化为史家的主观意志，例如史家自己也接受"为君亲讳"的原则。这是从消极方面讲。从积极方面讲，如爱国精神，甚至忠君思想，在政治上是积极的，但造成的结果同样也是歪曲和虚构。这就是所谓的"倾向性"（Tendenz）。文学作品里难道没有么？

二、内部原因。

主观判断引起谬误，如王充所说的轻信"虚妄之书"，或二刘所说的"俗皆爱奇"，也就是说缺乏辨别史料真伪的判断力。这种原因只能产生一些初级的、原始的、肤浅的虚构。

其次是推断。从修昔底德一直到科林伍德都承认历史家必然要用推断[1]。推断的作用，是从效果寻找原因和动机，用因果律来串联事体，使整个叙述能成为一个言之成理的故事。但因果律靠的是推断，而推断难免主观，主观难免没有虚构。我们再用《雾月十八日》为例。按马克思说[2]，雨果把这次事变看作"只是一个人的暴力行为"。蒲鲁东则"想把政变描述成以往历史发展的结果"。而马克思则认为是"法国阶级斗争造成了条件和局势，使一

---

[1] 参看克莱伦顿、吉朋。詹明信在《马克思主义与形式》一书中（第211页）也说，历史人物之动机只能用想象再创造。
[2] 马克思：《路易·波拿巴的雾月十八日》第二版序言（1869），见《马恩选集》一，599页。

个平庸可笑的人物有可能扮演了英雄的角色"。可见推论尽管是合乎逻辑的，但不一定合乎事实，事实要比逻辑复杂得多。

比推断更重要的产生虚构的主观原因是历史观（concept of history），这影响到叙述的全局，而不只是局部。我们在上面谈弗莱时已谈到，不赘述。

接下来我想谈谈刘知几提出的"模拟"。这牵涉到历史家在历史叙述中有意或无意采用的模式问题。刘知几说："述者相效，自古而然。"他指的是后代写历史的人往往参考前人的史著，因为中国古代没有史诗、戏剧文学，所以无法用文学模式做历史叙述的范本，在唐以前有辞赋，以辞赋为范，在刘知几这个喜欢简约的人看来是"文胜质"，因而不足取。因此中国的历史叙述和文学相似的地方不在整体模式，而在外在装饰。

西洋历史叙述实践则不同，它从一开始就是在文学叙事的传统下形成的，如民间故事、戏剧、悲剧，以至小说。到了麦考利，我们所说的"历史背景"，在他笔下都变成了五光十色的风俗画，就象在某些戏剧和小说中所呈现的那样。也就是说，西洋历史叙述的实践和理论，使得历史叙述接近甚至吻合某些文学类型，甚至可以说，象怀特那样，历史家是用某种情节结构或类型结构套在历史叙述上的[1]。可能越到后来，这种模仿意识更自觉、更强。这恐怕是历史叙述中产生虚构的最重要的原因或重要的原因之一。詹明信把这过程叫做"简化"（reduction），"用简单化了的模式代替了现实的四维密度（four-dimensional density）"，结果"必然歪曲现实和经

---

[1] 历史叙述含有联续性的意思。富科（Michel Foucault）一反传统，强调写"有效的历史"（effective history），要写"断裂，冒出的时刻"（eruption, the moment of emergence）（见《尼采，系统，历史》一文，转引自伦特里契亚：《新批评之后》第204页）。这仍是用一种模式，不过是另一种模式，套在历史上。

验"。[1] 我觉得我们可以这样理解，即把一个文学类型模式看作是一种抽象思维方式。由此而引起的"歪曲"或虚构，是纯主观的。

从语言角度来看虚构的成因。王充提出语言的夸张问题，刘知几提出语言的装饰性问题和时间、地域不同的问题，认为这些都是造成虚构的原因。此外，由于政治、道德原因，辞多溢美也造成虚构。但这些多半只是由语言引起的表面的失实，容易鉴别。若从更深处着眼，则首先要考虑历史叙述本身所使用的语言。怀特等人就指出历史学不象自然科学，历史学缺少本身一套科学语言。我们甚至可以进一步说，历史学也没有象经济学、政治学、社会学或其他社会科学那样有一套专门术语。历史家只能用文学语言。章学诚说"六经皆史"，当然他的意思是六经都是载道之器，但我们完全可以据此说，六经中的"诗"当然也是"史"，"诗"和"史"的共通点不仅如章氏所说在"道"，我们可以引申说也在语言，即共同载道的工具。这是一点。另外一点则是历史叙述使用的既然不是科学的语言，就必然，按语言的本性说，是比喻的语言（trope）。[2] 难怪许多历史名著，如吉朋的《罗马衰亡史》，即使形象描述不足，却是极好的散文。

再从历史叙述的结构来讲，历史家既然已把历史看作是戏剧或小说，就都十分注意情节的生动，把历史事件尽量戏剧化。中外历史名著莫不如此。如《史记》中的范雎入秦、荆轲刺秦王、鸿门宴、韩信请为假王，以及西洋史家如希罗多德、修昔底德、李维、

---

[1] 《马克思主义与形式》，第222页。

[2] 根据解构学说，语言产生意义不仅靠它本身的二元对立，更重要的是靠语境（context），而语境是无边的（乔纳森·卡勒：《论解构理论》，康乃尔大学出版社，1982年版，第123页），换言之，语言的意义是开放性的，那么科学用的语言岂不也不准确了？解构学说的回答是"字面与比喻是对立的，字面表达〔按：如科学语言、哲学语言〕也是隐喻（metaphor），只是它的比喻性（figurality）已被忘却了"。（同上书，第148页）

塔西陀等等，都是一些死无对证的事。同时历史家也都十分重视人物刻画的生动性。人物刻画往往不是用直接描绘的方式，而是通过写人物的行动和言谈。这里面虚构的成分是很足的。钱锺书认为我国史籍工于记言者，最早应属《左传》，但《左传》的虚构是不言而喻的。他说："上古既无录音之具，又乏速记之方，驷不及舌，而何其口角亲切，如聆謦欬欤？"他举例说："僖公二十四年介之推与母偕逃前之问答，宣公二年钮麑自杀前之慨叹，皆生无傍证，死无对证者。"[1]

我们还可以说，历史叙述和文学（小说、戏剧）都是"模仿"（mimesis）。历史叙述模仿过去的事迹，这些事迹多半是作者未曾亲历的，但也有是作者亲历的，是第一手材料，如修昔底德亲自参加波罗奔尼撒战争，太史公随汉武帝封禅、"负薪塞宣房"而写封禅、河渠。文学家所"模仿"的多半是自己的亲身经历，但也不排斥用第二手材料，如历史小说、历史剧。不论第一手材料或第二手材料，如前所述，里面都有虚构。就象汤因比所说，历史叙述与文学都不可能是纯粹的模仿。刘知几反对"文非文，史非史"，只是一种理想。

历史叙述和文学既然都是"模仿"，"模仿"的目的如前所述，是指示读者应对事件作何种反应，采取什么看法，换言之，"模仿"有方向性，或称倾向性，都是为了，如怀特所说，看到生活中的意义，或如汤因比所说，"模仿不可能在价值判断上是中立的（value-neutral）"。用中国传统说法，就是"载道"。

所以"模仿"之中事先已包含了作者的态度，即钱锺书所说的"诗心"、"文心"，历史和文学莫不皆然。在"模仿"中，在情节

---

[1]《管锥篇》一，164—165 页。

的安排上，在对话中，作者表达出他的同情、反对，甚至抒情、反讽；表达出他的宗教信仰、党派性。所谓"左丘失明，厥有国语"等等，都说明历史写作完全可以和文学一样成为抒发感情（郁结）的工具。

也许有人会提出反对，说历史著作不仅是纯粹的叙述，其中也有议论，而文学是形象性的（imaginative）。反对作者在小说中直接进入叙述，议论人物和事件，或发表不相干的感想，是西方现代才出现的禁忌。从荷马史诗到十九世纪小说，作者的介入是正常的。所谓"议论"，有直接的和暗含的，小说家在叙述过程中，在人物的描绘中，都在暗中议论。有的小说如十八世纪英国小说家斯特恩（Sterne）的《商第传》，全名就叫《商第的生平和意见》，可以说没有什么故事，都是些古怪的言谈议论，不仅有人物的议论，随处都有作者自己的议论。

在时间和空间里所发生的一切，纷纭复杂，浩瀚无际。要使它能被人理解，必须赋以某种范围，也就是只能从中割出一个片段（a slice of life），或一个方面，或几个方面，如历史学中的政治史、经济史、社会史等等。即使是通史，也不可能包罗万象，一般还只是突出政治、经济、文化等几个方面的重大事件。小说、戏剧也同样只能描写千变万化的生活中的某个或某几个片段。

从社会功能讲，历史著作多半是起教谕的功能，作为今天人们活动的参考。文学当然也是。不过大家公认文学还有娱乐的作用。历史著作又何尝没有娱乐作用呢？当然那些断烂朝报、统计数字等不成其为连贯的叙述的东西，不可能成为欣赏的对象。但连贯性的历史叙述，具备故事的结构以及人物的描写，完全可以成为欣赏的对象。

历史学和文学有差异的一面。历史学努力向科学靠拢，要找出人类活动的某些规律，所谓"究天人之际，通古今之变"，如进化的规律、经济决定的规律、因果律、历史循环论、历史必然论、帝王将相是历史主人、人民群众是历史主人等等。文学当然不是如此。不过历史学的这个特点，和历史叙述是两回事，虽然对叙述有一定影响。

其次一个差异，是历史叙述受材料的限制大于文学，文学家从生活中选择材料有更大的自由。但这不影响两者作为叙述是有共通之处的。

如按后结构主义的理论，结构主义主张的二元对立是不存在的，那么文学和非文学的界限如不复存在了。在后现代主义的文学里，严肃文学和通俗文学的界限日趋模糊，是否可以以此类推，历史和文学也不应该有明确的界限呢？从这角度来探讨历史叙述和文学的关系则有待异日了。

维吉尔和中国诗歌传统

　　中国与西方最早的接触可追溯至公元前五到四世纪，当时，印度的一个民族把丝绸带到了希腊，那个民族被古希腊人称为塞勒斯（Seres）。尽管中国与西方世界的这种接触是间接的，但却是持续不断的。到公元前二世纪末、一世纪初时，汉武帝不断往西方派出使节，有时一直把使节派到亚历山大里亚或拜占廷。亚历山大里亚和罗马之间交通来往也是既通畅又频繁不断。但是罗马人仅对所谓的"塞勒斯人"及其居住地有着模糊的概念，诚如汉朝的人对克什米尔以西的那些国家所作的描绘一样：也是含混不清的。贺拉斯曾告诫麦克那斯（Maecenas）说，不要担心中国人会对罗马发动侵略：

> 您关心国家的安定
> 您还焦虑地担心
> 居鲁士统治下的塞勒斯人和巴克特拉人
> 以及倾轧不和的塔那伊斯人与我们的城市对抗。[1]

---

[1]《颂诗》第8章，第29、25页。

同时维吉尔还认为，丝绸就象棉花一样，也是长在树叶子上的。请看《农事诗》第 2 章的第 120 —121 行：

> 说什么埃塞俄比亚的树上长着白色的绒毛，
> 塞勒斯人如何从树叶上梳整出柔软的羊绒？

老普林尼（Pliny the Elder）在他的《自然史》中不无钦佩地提及了中国制造的铁器。[1] 但很明确，这两大帝国彼此都不了解对方的文学。当然，把维吉尔和中国文学扯在一起似乎是不可思议的，但这二者之间却有着某种共同的人性。直到本世纪三十年代初，罗马文学在中国才多少为人所了解，这确实是历史的捉弄。1930 年和 1931 年间，《小说月报》上开始刊登评介维吉尔及其作品的文章，1933 年王力写的一本罗马文学史也随之问世。但是又过了二十多年才有人将维吉尔的《牧歌》（Eclogues，1957 年中文版）从拉丁文译成中文。《牧歌》成了罗马文学的第一部中译作品，这倒是颇有意味的，对这一点暂且不论。我翻译的奥维德的《变形记》（Metamophoses）出版于 1958 年，《诗艺》（Ars Poetica）出版于 1962 年，《埃涅阿斯纪》（Aeneid）则在 1984 年才问世。此外，我还译过塞内加的《特洛亚妇女》（Trojan Women），作为与欧里庇德斯的同名剧本的参照。近几年来，卢克莱修的作品有了译本，塔西图斯的《阿格里克拉传》（Agricola）以及普鲁塔克的作品也有了译本。但是同希腊文学相比，罗马文学在中译方面还远远不能得到充分的反映。荷马史诗，几大悲剧作家的作品，阿里斯多芬的喜剧，甚至包括米南达的作品，柏拉图和亚里士多德的著作，或许还包括那些历史学家的著作，都全

---

[1] 见范文澜：《中国通史》，第 1 卷，第 88 页。

部或部分地有了译本。

造成这种局面的原因其实并不复杂。主要是因为，在大多数欧洲文学教科书中，罗马文学被片面地描绘为仅仅是希腊文学的模仿，毫无自己的个性。它充当了某种介于古希腊文学和现代文学发展之间的"填空的"或"附属的"角色。在文学课程设置中，讲授罗马文学要么仓促了结，要么干脆略而不提。我并不想对教师们求全责备，因为可以找到的译本并不多。但一个更为重要的原因或许在于，人们往往认为罗马文学不那么吸引人，并且在本质上逊于希腊文学。希腊文学在许多方面（史诗的故事成分、性格刻划以及悲剧的戏剧张力）更富有感染力。而且罗马文学对于其后欧洲文学发展的意义并未得到充分的理解或把握，罗马文学本身的特性未完全显示出来，也未被识别出来。在我主编的两卷本《欧洲文学史》（1964，1979）中，尤其是关于罗马文学那一节，我试图在我可以利用的有限篇幅内给读者一个多少完整的概貌，同时，我也试图指出欧洲的这两种古老文学的差异。至于这一尝试有多少成功之处，我尚不知道。我认为，罗马文学的一个本质特征恰在于拉丁语及其表达方式。人们在开始欣赏这种文学之前，非得至少对拉丁语有些知晓。另一个困难则在于，对蕴含在罗马文学作品中的古罗马的历史、地理、宗教、神学和社会发展史缺乏了解。

但尽管如此，罗马文学对于有一定文化教养的中国读者，仍然具有或应当具有自己的感染力。那么为什么维吉尔的《牧歌》会成为罗马文学中的第一部中译作品呢？其一，这部作品篇幅较短。但这还不足以说明问题。《牧歌》的一个方面就在于展现了乡村生活的理想化色彩，这种生活使人摆脱了焦虑和担忧。这些牧歌尽管涉及罗马的历史文物，又有着牧歌文学的传统（吹笛，欢庆爱情，以及吃坚果、苹果和压得很好看的乳酪，这些都是我们所不熟悉的），但其中仍可见出中国诗歌传统的一些对应特征，有时甚至在用词上也颇有相似之处。例如，在第一首牧歌中，两位牧羊人为可能失去自己的牧场而感到的焦虑衬托出他们害怕失去的那种理想的生活：以草作屋顶的简陋农舍（pauperis et tuguri congestum caespite culmen I，68），黄昏时分笼罩在群山的阴影之下的屋顶冒出炊烟（summa procul villarum culmina fumant, / maioresque cadunt altis de montibus umbrae I，82—83）。这些文字读来颇象中国诗人陶渊明的《归田园居五首》中的著名诗行。

> 暧暧远人村，依依墟里烟。

在这两个例子中，意象都与情感密切对应——享受宁静和摆脱焦虑。两位诗人的实际生活境况也许十分不同。陶渊明是在厌倦了十年官场生涯之后写下那五首诗的，而维吉尔则是在被赶出家园后写下那些牧歌的。但他们所向往的那种理想生活却十分相似。

在对焦虑的表达方面大概没有谁能超过维吉尔的著名的第四首牧歌了，这首牧歌预言，一个将带回黄金盛世的神童将诞生于世，将结束时常萦绕人类的恶梦。这种情形也许会结束，也许未必尽然。但即使到那时也依然会"隐匿着古老罪孽的某些踪迹"（pauca tamen suberunt priscae vestigia fraudis，I. 31）。这同样一种焦虑感也在《家蚊》（Cules）中得到了表达。宁静并非永远有所保障。陶渊明也有这种忧心忡忡的感受：

> 野外罕人事，穷巷寡轮鞅，
> 白日掩荆扉，对酒绝尘想。
> 时复墟里人，披草共来往，

相见无杂言，但道桑麻长。

桑麻日已长，我土日已广，

常恐霜霰至，零落同草莽。

当然，人们可以自由地从字面上或隐喻式地去解释"桑麻"，但这种威胁却是存在的。

维吉尔诗歌的另一个显著特征在于其哀惋的基调，这一点同样也和中国诗歌传统十分吻合。"为不幸而流泪，巨大的悲痛打动心田"（"sunt lacrimae rerum et mentem mortalia tangunt"，《埃涅阿斯纪》，I. 462）——这就是埃涅阿斯在观看狄多正在修建的朱诺神庙上描绘特洛亚城陷落的壁画时发出的哀叹。儒家关于诗歌自我表现的理想是要显示"乐而不淫，哀而不伤"（论语·八佾）。当然，儒家的这一理想是节制。维吉尔的理想也是如此。他也许会抱怨朱诺对埃涅阿斯怀有敌意："忿恨能够如此强烈地渗入神圣的胸怀吗？"（tantaene animis caelestibus irae？）回答自然是肯定的。但是凡人又不得不屈从于命运，屈从于诸神的指令。孔子就曾说过"五十而知天命"。

整个史诗的肌质都是由悲痛感构成的，但是却没有一处象分手离别的场景那样突出。当埃涅阿斯背着父亲，挽着儿子（后边跟着妻子），离开一片焦土城池时，他突然发现妻子克列乌莎失踪了。他发狂似的奔回来，在一片混乱中寻找她，直到最后，她的幽灵出现在他面前，忠告他要服从天意。她说，"为了你所热爱的克列乌莎而擦去眼泪吧"（lacrimas dilectae pelle Creusae，II. 783），最后她又说，"现在永别了，要永远珍爱我们共同的孩子"（iamque vale et nati serva communis amorem，II. 789）。

当埃涅阿斯来到布特罗屯（特洛亚王子赫勒努斯同安德洛玛刻

在此结了婚并定居下来）时，又出现了另一个分离的痛苦场景。当安德洛玛刻向赫克托尔的衣冠冢祭扫时，埃涅阿斯和她相遇了。当见到他时的那种惊奇感消失后，她便向他讲述了特洛亚城陷落后她个人的经历。她提出的第一个问题就是："阿斯卡纽斯（埃涅阿斯的儿子——引者）那孩子怎么样了？他还活着么，还呼吸着人间的空气么？"（"Quid puer Ascanius？superatne et vescitur aura？"，Ⅲ.339）在分别时，"安德洛玛刻在这最后诀别的时刻，哀恸欲绝，而在礼节方面她也不愿落后，她拿出几件金地绣花袍子和一件特洛亚款式的斗篷，把这些衣服作为礼物送给阿斯卡纽斯，并对他说：'拿着这些东西吧，孩子，这是我亲手制的，作个纪念，表示我安德洛玛刻，赫克托尔的妻子，是永远爱你的。把亲人的最后礼物拿着吧，你是这样象我的孩子阿斯提阿那克斯，现在只有你能使我想起他的容貌来。他的眼睛，他的手，他的脸，和你的一模一样，他现在要活着也跟你一样岁数，快成人了。'"

我们看到，安德洛玛刻和埃涅阿斯相遇时，正在为赫克托尔而悲伤，而埃涅阿斯的出现则立即使她想起了他的儿子阿斯卡纽斯（或许那孩子也陪伴着父亲）。阿斯卡纽斯反过来又使她想起了她自己的儿子阿斯提阿那克斯。与阿斯卡纽斯的分别又是一次悲伤体验的重复。再者，不管它是活人之间的分离还是死亡造成的分离，都是最后的分离。安德洛玛刻之所以哀伤，是因为这是最后的分离，而她的礼物也正是她所能给予的最后的礼物。

诗人也着力描写了埃涅阿斯离别后的狄多，舵手帕里努鲁斯和父亲安奇塞斯死亡后埃涅阿斯的失落感，而且这些死别的场景在阴间又都重复了一遍。

这种极少带有重聚之希望或根本毫无指望的分离主题深受中国古代诗人的热爱。中国诗歌之黄金时代——盛唐的一位最伟大的诗人杜甫一生共写下一千多首诗，其中至少有一百二十首是写分离主题的。人们与朋友分别时写一些诗是当时的时尚。但是杜甫等诗人同时还写一些夫妻分别、情人分别和亲人分别的别离诗。实际上，在中国最早的诗集《诗经》中，这类诗也并不少见。这种诗甚至可以划归为一般抒情诗范畴下的一种"亚文类"（sub-genre）。在杜甫的这类诗里，有一组六首描写分离的著名诗篇。

《新安吏》描写了该城镇的居民如何被官吏逼迫去当兵的。他们在"青山犹哭声"中被带走，诗人劝道："莫自使眼枯，收汝泪纵横；眼枯即见骨，天地终无情。"

《石壕吏》则描绘了一个非同寻常的情景。官兵来到一位老翁的农舍前想逼迫老人象他的几个儿子和其他青年人一样去当兵。老翁翻墙逃跑，他的老伴对官吏说，只剩下她一人连同那怀有身孕的儿媳妇了。儿媳妇则未露面，因为她身上衣衫褴褛。老妇自告奋勇去服役，她说她会做饭，于是便走了。诗的结尾写道：

> 天明登前途，独与老翁别。

《新婚别》叙述了新郎被迫服兵役时新娘同他道别的场景，诗的结尾写道；

> 人事多错迕，与君久相望。

《垂老别》和《石壕吏》的情节正相反。老翁眼见着自己的儿子们和儿子的儿子统统死于战事，不禁对生活感到绝望，他扔掉手杖，自愿前去当兵。他向伏在路旁的老妻道了别，老妻哭道，冬天即将来临，他却衣衫单薄（老妻卧路啼，岁暮衣裳单）。诗人评道：

> 孰知是死别，且复伤其寒；此去必不归，还闻劝加餐。

这组诗的最后一首《无家别》展现了一个更为奇怪的情景：一位在战争失败后归来的士兵发现，往日有着一百多户人家的村庄竟然成了荒村。狐和狸四处出没，到处可见到一二个年老的寡妇。他依然留了下来，因为他热爱自己的家乡，同时他也着手开荒种地。官吏得知他回来后便再次逼他从军。在离开故土时，他突然发现自己竟处于一种可笑的境地：竟没有可以与之告别的家人，母亲早在五年前就已死去。诗的结尾写道：

> 人生无家别，何以为蒸黎。

维吉尔的诗和杜甫的这两组离别诗之相似是十分惊人的。离别的场景是在战争和动乱的背景上衬托出来的。这里有着一种深层的家庭联系感和血缘感。不管命令是来自皇帝或来自诸神，都得服从。分离成了人类命运的一部分。诗中表现出来的或隐含的哀惋都表明两位诗人共有的深刻的恻隐之心。

英雄埃涅阿斯能唤起中国读者的同情吗？回答既是肯定的又是否定的。说它是肯定的，原因在于，埃涅阿斯体现了他对诸神、国家和家庭的责任感，这一点肯定能得到中国读者的欣赏。埃涅阿斯是一位有着明确坚定的使命感的人——在意大利重建特洛亚城，这一点也是可以理解的。但是当他成为一个阿喀琉斯式的人物（以疯狂杀人取乐）时，这一转变便破坏了人们的和谐和平衡感。但是这一点通过维吉尔对图纳斯的同情心的转变而得到了补偿。

至于这部史诗的形式特征，诸如广泛地运用隐喻，其中包括神话的、文学的和历史上的掌故，这对中国读者是颇为熟悉的，因为中国古代诗人也常这样用典。但是具体的典故自然是迥然不同的，因而也自然带来了一定的困难。对于一位既不熟悉希腊罗马文化又不熟悉中国古代文学和文化的中国现代读者，维吉尔也象杜甫一样难懂。

最后，再略谈一下翻译问题。译者所面临的第一个难题就是要确定，用诗体还是散文体来译。中国古典作诗法中的五言诗或七言诗难以适应这种雄浑的六韵步诗体。全用五言或七言来译这部一万行组成的诗将是难以令人承受的。此外，也从来没有一首中国古典诗达到过如此之长度，因此，译者没有现成的模式可以依循。再者，中国古典诗歌总是押韵的，而《埃涅阿斯纪》则是不押韵的。不押韵的古体诗是难以令人想象的。再说，当今中国很少有人能写作、甚或轻松自如地阅读古代诗文，更不用说去欣赏它了。所以，将《埃涅阿斯纪》翻译成中国古典诗歌体简直是不可能的。

用白话文写的中国现代诗也同样是有争议的。至于诗行的长度或韵律倒是自由不限的，但是尽管现代诗已有了六七十年的历史，但仍然没有逐步形成一种为人们普遍认可的格律，一首诗的效果在很大程度上取决于内容。我们可以尝试着创造一种接近六韵步诗体的白话文诗体，但是由于拉丁文句法有其缜密性特征，因此有着铺陈冗长之特征的白话文便难以与其媲美，而且诗行还会达到不适当的长度。在我看来，《埃涅阿斯纪》的一种较为成功的英译出自 C. 戴·路易斯（C. Day Lewis，1952）之手，他是在英国广播公司第三套节目中朗诵自己的译文的。他在每一行里置六个重音，音节不等，从十二个到十七个。他在朗诵时还注意到速度的有规则性，以便抓住听众的注意力，引人入胜。这要比英雄史诗双行体或甚至无韵诗体高明。我本人的译文是散文体，我的目的仅在于向既不能用拉丁文又不能用其他外国文字阅读的学生及一般读者提供一点这部史诗的基本内容而已。

"Virgil and Chinese Poetic Tradition"，1987 年 11 月 12 日于美国斯坦福大学讲。王宁译

（原载《北京大学学报》，1988 年第 5 期）

预言式的梦在《埃涅阿斯纪》与《红楼梦》中的作用

    在西方和中国文学里，梦作为一种手法，起着多种作用。本文只拟就梦在史诗《埃涅阿斯纪》和小说《红楼梦》这两部叙事文学作品中所起的预示灾难的作用，探讨一下这种手法和两位作者的世界观的关系，这种手法和他们的伟大成就的关系。

    在《埃涅阿斯纪》（以下简称《埃纪》）里，梦的手法运用了不下五次，四次在前半部（2.268—，3.147—. 4.450—，4.556—），一次在后半部（8.31—）。此外，4.256—麦丘利显现在埃涅阿斯面前，5.722—安奇塞斯显现在他面前，他都未入睡，这两次虽不是严格的梦，但其意义和梦并没有什么差别。在这些梦或觉醒时的幻象里，3.147—（家神托梦），4.265—，5.772—和8.31（第表河神托梦）都是鼓励、安慰、敦促、甚至责备，督促他前进去完成神的使命——立国大业，起的是纯粹的指迷作用，推动故事前进。但其他三次，除了有上述作用以外，诗人似乎还有更多的信息要传达。

    4.556—，麦丘利促埃涅阿斯离开迦太基，摆脱温柔乡的引诱，伪称狄多要施展诡计，加害于他（illa dolos dirumque nefas in pectore versat），并用了一句诟骂妇女的话："女人永远是变化不定的"，意思是水性杨花（varium et mutabile semper femina），似乎是要提醒埃涅阿斯，特洛亚战争的十年灾难是由一个女子海伦引起的。这场梦实际上是在预示一场可能发生的灾难。

4.450—，狄多梦见埃涅阿斯在追赶她，她想念推罗同胞而不可得，孑然一身，无限孤凄。诗人用了一个很独特的比喻，说狄多就象"俄瑞斯特斯逃避手持火把和黑蛇为武器的母亲，而复仇女神正坐在门口等着他那样"，来表现她爱和恨的矛盾心理和走投无路的绝望心情。她的梦是在精神错乱的状态下做的（fatis exterrita Dido mortem orat）。在她做梦以前，诗人有一段情景交融的描写：圣水变黑，醇酒变成腥秽的血，狄多恍惚听到她已故丈夫说话和召唤的声音，屋顶上枭鸟哀号，用以烘托神秘恐怖气氛和狄多的绝望情绪。这场梦的作用也是预示灭亡。

2.268—，赫克托尔给埃涅阿斯托梦；其意义和艺术效果都不同于麦丘利托的梦和狄多的梦。麦丘利预言的是假想的灾难，狄多的梦是绝望者的梦。埃涅阿斯这梦，时机很特殊。他是在他以为和平已经到来，忧心消失的心情下做的梦，它不是起烘托作用，而是起强烈对照作用。特洛亚人处在身心完全松懈的状态，全城静悄悄的，但是表面的平静却隐藏着危机，"希腊人的船舰排成队列离开了泰涅多斯岛，在静默的月亮的友好的掩护下，直向早先登陆的地点驶去"，木马里埋伏着的武士也被奸细西农放了出来。赫克托尔的出现正是在这时刻。

为什么安排赫克托尔托梦，而不安排麦丘利或埃涅阿斯的母亲维那斯？赫克托尔一度是特洛亚的支柱和骄傲，是它光荣伟大的象征和最可靠的希望。但是他在梦中的形象则非常可怕，遍体鳞伤，血肉模糊，变成覆灭的象征。

在梦里，赫克托尔对埃涅阿斯说："唉，女神之子，逃跑吧，逃开这熊熊的烈火吧。敌人已经占领了城郊，特洛亚高耸入云的城堡已经坍塌了。祖国和普利阿姆斯的气数已尽，如若人力能保住特洛亚，我早就保住它了。现在特洛亚把它的一切圣物和它的神祇都托付给你了；把它们带着，和你同命运，再给它们找一个城邦，当你飘洋过海之后，你最终是要建立一个城邦的。"

这段话有指点未来归宿的预言，但也着眼于眼前的危机，突出了命运的不可抗拒。如果结合埃涅阿斯在梦里对赫克托尔说的话，似乎其中还另有一层意义。埃涅阿斯说："我们在盼望你……我们经历了各种灾难，十分疲惫，能看到你真是高兴啊。"似乎埃涅阿斯下意识里战争和灾难还没有结束，但是眼前的赫克托尔已是一个身被重创的战士，似乎对他能否保卫国家有些怀疑。这一切使这场梦具有特殊意义。

我们还应结合全诗结尾埃涅阿斯的对手、意大利鲁图利亚青年国王图尔努斯之死来考虑赫克托尔这形象和他的意义。他们两人之死非常相象。阿奇琉斯为了给副手帕特洛克鲁斯报仇，杀死赫克托尔，埃涅阿斯为了给他的青年战友帕拉斯报仇，杀死图尔努斯；赫克托尔上阵穿的是帕特洛克鲁斯的甲胄，图尔努斯则佩了帕拉斯的腰带；在最危急的时刻，赫克托尔向他的助手代佛布斯（雅典娜女神假扮的）索枪，代佛布斯突然消失，同样，图尔努斯在最紧急的时刻，他的神仙姐姐茹图尔娜（前来助战的）也被天神驱走；赫克托尔和图尔努斯都意识到自己的死是天意。赫克托尔是希腊人取胜的主要障碍，图尔努斯是埃涅阿斯立国的主要障碍。看来赫克托尔不啻是图尔努斯的投影和先兆。维吉尔写图尔努斯之死，带着悲悯的心情，用了一个做梦的比喻："就象在睡眠的时候，夜晚的宁静和倦怠合上了我们的眼睛，我们梦见自己在狂热地奔跑，老想跑得再远些，但是老跑不远，正在我们尽最大的努力的时候，我们懊丧地瘫倒在地上，舌头也不会说话了，身体也不象平时那样气力充沛了，声音也没有了，话也没有了。图尔努斯也和这一样，不管他怎样挣扎用力也找不到一条出路，那凶恶的复仇女神处处让他失败。他心乱如麻，他望见了鲁图利亚人和他的都城，他害怕，他踌躇，死亡临头使他战栗，他不知道往哪里躲，也没有力气去和敌人拼，战车也看不见了，驾车的姐姐也看不见了。"[1]

建国是光荣的事业，但对被排除的障碍又表示同情怜悯，这无疑是对这光荣事业本身的怀疑。维吉尔本来是相信历史循环论的，金、银、铜、铁四个时代循环不息。眼前即使是黄金时代，好景也不会长久。在他那首千百年来引起猜测和争议的《牧歌》第四首里，他预言一个婴儿的诞生和黄金时代的来临，但是就在这麦浪黄熟、野果飘香的黄金时代，"古老的罪恶的少数痕迹仍然隐藏在下面，召唤着人们去驾船冒险，用高墙把城镇围起，大地上又挖起沟堑。第二个驾金羊毛船的舵手又要出现，又有好汉们乘上第二艘金羊毛船；第二次战争也又将发生，又一位伟大的阿奇琉斯将被派往特洛亚。"

可以说，梦中出现的赫克托尔不仅预示灾难，而且隐藏着怜悯和怀疑。

《红楼梦》前八十回中要紧的梦有三场：第一回甄士隐的梦，第五回宝玉梦游太虚幻境，和第十三回王熙凤梦见秦可卿。前两场梦是理解全书的钥匙，第三场梦是理解前两场梦的钥匙和出发点。其他的梦看来仅有局部的意义。

第三场梦和赫克托尔的梦都是预言衰亡，只不过后者预言的亡国已在眼前，而前者预言贾氏败落则是此后几年内的事，但两个做

---

[1] 按这比喻也是因袭荷马《伊利亚纪》22，写赫克托尔与阿奇琉斯单独交战前，感到孤单害怕，望着城里，希望有援兵助战，荷马用了一个比喻，把他比作人们在梦中追逐，四肢瘫软无力。

梦的人都仍浑浑噩噩，心理状态相同。他们都不知道命运的规律："祖国和普利阿姆斯气数已尽"[1]，"荣辱自古周而复始，岂人力能可保常的"。他们的梦都是在毫无心理准备的状态下做的。

凤姐的梦和埃涅阿斯的梦一祥，托梦的人和发生的时刻很有意义。它是发生在贾天祥正照风月鉴这段故事之后，贾琏送黛玉回扬州，凤姐"心中实在无趣"的时候。托梦的人又是"淫丧天香楼"的秦可卿。"盖作者大有深意存焉。"[2] 托梦的人和托梦的时刻指向贾氏由盛而衰的一个主要原因。贾氏之败，"造衅开端实在宁"，"家事消亡首在宁"（五回）。在雪芹看来，贾氏之败，原因很多，如南直召祸，子孙不肖，包揽词讼，等等，但祸端在一"淫"字。《红楼梦》大量写"情"，"情"包括"真情"和"纵欲"两方面。第一梦用寓言方式把石头写或"情痴色鬼"、蠢"物"和"真情"的混合体。"真情"必须通过"净化"过程才能脱出"蠢物"的躯壳而显露，因此才有第二梦，在这梦里，那已被"邪魔招入膏肓"的"浊物"必须"领略此仙闺幻境之风光尚如此"之后，才能净化，情而不淫。[3] 宝玉梦中的秦氏起的是净界的作用。

赫克托尔是毁灭的象征，也包含毁灭的种子——他的"荣誉感"，也就是骄傲。秦可卿也是毁灭的象征，也包含毁灭的种子——淫，这两个形象都具象征意义。

在表面兴旺底下看到衰败的迹象是这两位作者的共同点。罗马经过了几百年的战乱，雅努斯庙门终于关闭了。但诗人似乎觉得罗

---

[1] sat patriae Priamoque datum（2.291）这句话有两种不同理解：一、"你已为祖国和普利阿姆斯尽了力"；二、"祖国和普利阿姆斯所应享的已经满足"，以后一种解释更切近讲话场合和诗人的思想。
[2] 庚辰本第十三回脂批。
[3] 二十五回，宝玉蒙魇，癞头和尚说："他如今被声色货利所迷"，也是此意，并暗示他还须进一步净化。

马要建立真正的"罗马和平",须要许多条件,其中一个主要条件就是放弃黩武。西比尔说:"战争,可怕的战争!"概括了诗人的总的态度。全诗写战争毫无荷马的热情,而是突出其悲惨、不人道、疯狂、荒诞和悲剧性。埃涅阿斯最后面对受伤求饶的图尔努斯,只因为看到他佩着帕拉斯的腰带,瞬息间就变成残忍的阿喀琉斯式的人物,举枪把图尔努斯杀死。批评家早已指出,一首罗马帝国的颂歌以图尔努斯之惨死结束,[1]"盖作者大有深意存焉。"埃涅阿斯可以变成阿喀琉斯,何以见得屋大维就不会变成或复原为阿喀琉斯式的人物呢?[2]维吉尔的怀疑使他成为一个精神上的流放者。在《牧歌》和《农事诗》里所表现的陶渊明式的生活理想才是他的精神故乡。[3]事实上,他的足迹也很少到罗马。但是坎帕尼亚田庄上的和平能保持多久,是否可能有一天又变成曼图亚田庄呢?这种忐忑疑虑很容易使他把现实的和平看成是梦,而把可能的战乱想象成现实。这种心情可能就是埃涅阿斯的梦的基础。

---

[1] C. M. 鲍勒:《从维吉尔到弥尔顿》,1945年版。

[2] 屋大维建立和平、整顿罗马,使诗人感激,但屋大维也有使诗人担心的一面。他野心勃勃,冷酷无情,为了大权独揽,不惜发动两次大战,击败政敌布鲁图斯和安东尼。埃格那鸟斯与他争选执政官失败,屋大维怀疑他要谋害他,把他处死。他和安东尼的弟弟鲁奇乌斯作战,把三百名俘虏杀了祭他的义父凯撒。一个垂死的战士请屋大维把他埋葬,屋大维对他说,野鸟会解决他的问题。这些虽然在某种意义上说都是"正常"现象,但仍不能不引起"万事皆堪落泪"的诗人的疑虑。

[3] 维吉尔和陶渊明都追求一种小康生活,诚实躬耕,远离繁华,希望和平无战乱,又都有些担心。例如陶诗"方宅十余亩,草屋八九间","敝庐何必广,取足蔽床席","衣食当须纪,力耕不吾欺",又如"常恐霜霰至,零落同草莽"。维吉尔也处处有这类想法,如《农事诗》(2.458—):"种田人太幸福了……他们远离战火的冲击,最公正的大地为他们从她的土地上自动地倾出轻易可得的生活资料。即使他们没有广厦崇邸,从它豪华的大门或厅堂在黎明时分涌出如潮的访客;即使他们从未见过玳瑁镶嵌的大门、织金的衣服和哥林多的铜钱;即使他们的素白羊毛没有染上亚述的颜料,他们的清油里也没有掺杂桂花,那又何妨?……他们有林木,可以打猎;从青年时代就劳动,不怕吃苦;老年敬神;在他们中间,正义女神的足迹最后离开。"又如《农事诗》(1·145—146),"不懈的劳动,困苦生活的迫切需要将战胜一切"。《牧歌》和《农事诗》内容十分丰富,不能缕举,值得作专门研究。

贾氏一族也是表面一派兴旺，又是排家宴，又是庆元宵，又是贾元春选进凤藻宫，随着是建造大观园，贾氏变成了皇亲国戚，蒸蒸日上。但是福兮祸所伏，盛中孕衰。贾氏要挽回颓势是不可能的，只能求一个不是彻底的覆灭，保住祖茔，继续享血食，子孙读书务正就是上上了。但有许多条件，其中之一就是戒淫欲。庚辰本脂批就秦可卿托梦又写道："然必写出自可卿之意也，则又有他意寓焉。"又写了一首诗："一步行来错，回头已百年，古今风月鉴，多少泣黄泉。"都提供了足够的暗示。雪芹的对策便是伸张"真情"。但是"真情"不见容于现实界，正如黛玉《葬花诗》里所说，"一年三百六十日，风刀霜剑严相逼。"在现实界雪芹也成了一个精神上的逐客。[1]

一个要和平，一个要真情，但是生活和现实使他们怀疑理想能否实现，暂时实现了能否持久，于是由怀疑而悲观。丁尼生在纪念维吉尔1900年忌辰一诗中有两句：

> 人类未可知的命运使你悲伤，
> 在悲伤中，你显得那么庄严。

而雪芹看到的总是那"渐渐露出"的"下世的光景"。一个是"万事都堪落泪"的诗人，一个要"还泪"，直到"泪尽而逝"。

一个值得注意的现象就是在两部作品里写死亡、诀别、葬礼等

---

[1] 雪芹向往的理想国很难断定，不过十八回贾妃归省，说了一番话，她说："田舍之家，虽齑盐布帛，终能聚天伦之乐；今虽富贵已极，然终无意趣。"前此在十七回里，贾政看了稻香村的风景，也表示大有归田之意。在第二回里，雨村谈了一番天地生人的大道理，以赞美的口吻胪举了一大批高人逸士，如许由、陶潜、阮籍等等，称他们为"清明灵秀之气所秉者"。这些都是历来中国失意士大夫的想法，雪芹怕也难免。

极多。[1] 这恐怕正是一种悲剧的人生观和宿命思想的反映。死往往成为一种解脱。特别是尤三姐之死和狄多之死很相似，都是由于对方背弃信义，都是殉情，都是从尴尬而痛苦的局面中求解脱。晴雯之死和狄多之死又有相似处，晴雯死前有海棠夭死半边之兆，狄多死前，如前所述，听到丈夫说话，枭鸟哀鸣，都反映了一种宿命的观点。[2]

悲剧的人生观和宿命论互为表里。在维吉尔看来，命（fatum）是不能变更的，天神都必须服从它；运（fortuna）是变的，不易捉摸的。雪芹也有"有命无运"，"命运两济"之说，命不可易，运有升沉变化，贾氏之衰是命，可卿之劝是争取运好。

悲观宿命导致把现实看作虚幻，而梦境是真实的，所谓"假作真时真亦假"，甲戌本第一回脂批也说"所谓万境都如梦境看也"。埃涅阿斯从冥界出来经过的是象牙门，是假梦之门。在冥界他遇见亡友、受过苦难的亡灵、受到应得惩罚的亡灵，他遇见狄多，他的父亲指点他前途，这一切都点明是假的了，也就是说，过去和未来都是幻梦。

认为现实是梦幻，这是维吉尔和雪芹的哲学和世界观的一部分，他们很自然会把梦幻作为一种艺术手法应用到作品里去。一般

---

[1] 《红楼梦》在开始十六回就有贾瑞、可卿姊弟之死，还点到其他人物之死，十七回以后热闹文字中又有金钏、贾敬、尤氏姊妹、晴雯和一些次要人物之死。《埃纪》前半，埃涅阿斯丧失了妻子、父亲和舵手，引起狄多之死，至于特洛亚战争中和后半部战争中死的人就不计其数了。还可以提到祭司拉奥孔的可怕的死。死亡之外，还有失散和诀别，如英莲之失，克列乌莎先失散后死去，如埃涅阿斯与安德洛玛刻夫妇之诀别，宝玉与晴雯之诀别。在葬礼上，两部书都大事铺张。这些现象都应当进一步具体分析，但都说明在两位作者的思想里，死亡和分离占有很重要的地位。

[2] 雪芹有关于草木与人通灵的哲学，维吉尔的宗教信仰，均不在此赘述。《埃》在狄多死前写她："想尽快割断这可憎的生命"（4.631），写她面对埃涅阿斯留下的衣物，其中包括一柄宝剑，说道："可爱的遗物啊……把我从痛苦中解脱出来吧！"（4.651）《红楼梦》三十六回，宝玉对袭人讲了一番死的道理，也是指作人痛苦，死是解脱。

预言式的梦兆往往只有局部意义，如莎士比亚《凯撒》里，凯撒遇刺前，他的夫人对他说守夜人看到许多可怕的异象，坟墓开口，放出死鬼，血点落到卡匹托山顶神庙上，大街上灵魂尖叫。又如安娜·卡列尼娜自杀前朦胧看到一个胡须蓬乱的小老头俯身倚在铁栏上，似乎想要害她。即使西赛罗的《西丕奥之梦》也只预示了小西丕奥一个人的未来，都不象维吉尔和更大程度上曹雪芹用这手法好象是在预言一个历史过程。其所以具有这种特殊意义，取得这种特殊效果，可能正是因为他们对现实抱有的幻灭感。这种幻灭感实际是对生活的怀疑，因而他们能在所谓的太平盛世看出破绽，使他们预感到历史未来的发展，也就艾略特所说的历史感[1]。他们所写的梦也竟变成了验梦（veridical dream）。

当然，他们的历史感并非科学的推断而是从生活感受中形成的，在作品里以梦的形式表现出来。尽管如此，有没有历史感却是衡量一个作家是否伟大的标尺之一。

（原载《文艺研究》第 4 期，1983 年）

---

[1]　T. S. Eliot: What is a Classic？ 1945.

《李尔王》变形记

在詹姆斯·乔伊斯写的《青年艺术家画像》一书中，爱尔兰青年斯蒂芬与他所在的学校的教务长，一个英国人，有一段有趣的谈话。教务长发现爱尔兰人把烟囱叫作漏斗觉得好笑。斯蒂芬思忖说："我们用以谈话的语言本来是他们的语言，我是后学的，由他的嘴里说出的'家'、'基督教'、'啤酒'、'师长'与我所说的多么不同啊！"

这段插曲表明，不同民族之间是可以互相理解的，没有这种共性，彼此间的交流是不可能的；但同时也存在着彼此间的差异，而这种差异或许更为重要，因为这涉及更深层的更基本的文化、宗教、政治等问题。

乔伊斯想的还只是以英语作为联系紧密而又不同的两个民族的共同语。如果由讲另一种不同语言的人来阐释，差异只会更大。例如，尽管英语与德语相当接近，但最近一位批评家发现有名的施莱格尔与蒂克的莎士比亚译本在美学上也未能尽如人意。他抱怨说，德译本失之于迎合典雅的趣味，而在某种程度上失去了莎士比亚语言的民间本土的具体鲜明的因素。他例举德文译本把"I'll lug the guts into the neighbour room"（*Hamlet*, III, iv）译成"Ich will den Wanst ins nächste Iimmer Schleppen"，并评论道，德译本缺乏原文的动态，原因是语序、选词、时态不同，而句尾又是阴性。他提出了一个他认为更贴切、更妥善的翻译："Ich Schlepp die Kuddeln in den Nachbarraum"。英语与汉语的差异如此之大，我们不必指望有绝对的忠实，而通常倒是恰恰相反。

相反的情况也是存在的。比如英译的李白诗与原文相距多少？举一个极端的例子，我们可以回忆一下庞德对中国诗歌的翻译，有一次他把"皋陶"二字根本写颠倒了。（canton LIII）

本文意在考察一下莎氏的一部主要作品在朱生豪和孙大雨先生的两个中译本里被翻译和省略的一些重要问题，以揭示翻译可能会有多大程度的误解以及误解的原因，并提供一些实例表明跨越语言与文化界线的交流之困难以及由此而来的理解上的困难。

就题材来说，《李尔王》处理的是亲子关系，而这种关系是建立在全剧的重要观念之一即"自然"（Nature）的基础之上。剧中的"自然"可以从两个层次来理解：一是宇宙秩序，一是人类天性。后者作为伦理范畴来自物性自然并与之相对应。这点从第四场第二幕奥本尼对高纳里尔的非难中可以看出："That nature which contemns its origin / cannot be bordered certain in itself, 〔……〕perforce mustwither"（自然若蔑视自己的根源，本身也决难保全……而必然要枯萎）。此处枯萎这个比喻是从植物世界得来的，反映了人类天性与自然之间的联系。

人类天性亦善亦恶，在这点上，中西伦理哲学毫无龃龉，然而一旦天性作为一种伦理观念涉及亲子关系时，差异即随之而生。在《李尔王》中，本性或亲子关系主要是以知恩或忘恩的方式来表现这种关系的。子女对父亲表示感激，就是顺应天性。甚至在同辈中也要求遵守同样的伦理规范。我们可以引用托马斯·艾略奥特爵士《论宰官》一书中的话："依我看来，最可诅咒的、最违反公道的恶行莫过于忘恩负义，一般称之为不仁不义。""不仁不义"原文为 unkindness，原意就是"违反自然"。子女对父母忘恩负义就是违反自然，比之在同辈中的忘恩负义更坏。因而狂怒的李尔诅咒他的两个长女为"堕落的私生子"，"你们这些不顺应天道的巫婆"。所谓"堕落"（degenerate），所谓"不顺应天道"（unnatural），都含有"违反自然"的意思；他评论装成疯丐的爱伽说："只有他那刻薄寡恩的女儿才能使人沉沦到这个地步。"这里的"人"，原文仍是"自然"。

亲子关系中也存在着亲长一方的权威和子女一方的顺从的因素。这可以追溯到亚里士多德，他认为恰如奴隶是财产一样，儿子也是父亲的财产。父亲可以随心所欲处置儿子而不会被指控为不公道。"如果儿子不好，父亲可以和儿子断绝关系，而儿子却不能和父亲断绝关系，因为他所能报答的远不及他受之于父亲的，尤其就他的生命来说更是如此"。[1]

但是由于基督教的教义主张泛爱（体现于耶稣身上），主张每个人作为罪人都面临着同样的最后审判，地位是平等的，因此亲长的权威概念有所改变。理想的亲子关系应建立在爱的基础上。李尔开初对于爱有一种胡涂观念，直至结尾时才对此有了充分的却又是悲剧性的为时太晚的认识。

在朱生豪的标准的中文译本里，剧中四十多处"自然"及其同源词与同义词都根据上下文分别被译成：天地、造化、本性、生性、人、生命、精神、身体、身心、仁慈或慈悲、人伦或天道人伦，而译得最多的是孝。反义词的译法更是五花八门。

在这些迥然不同的翻译中，令人瞩目的是把"自然"译成

---

[1] 参看伯特兰·拉塞尔：《西方哲学史》，第 174 页，纽约，1972 年版。

"孝"。我们会发现对于亲子关系孔子与亚里士多德的伦理观有惊人的相似之处。恰如亚氏认为儿子是父亲的财产，孔子在与其门徒曾子的谈话中也断言儿子的"身体肤发受之父母，不敢毁伤"。

亚里士多德赋予亲长以优先地位，主张下爱上应该甚于上爱下。妻、儿、臣仆之爱夫、父、君主应该甚于后者之爱他们。而孔子在回答什么是孝的问题时，一语破的地宣称"无违"，就是丝毫也不偏离传统或习俗规定的行为规范。在另一场合，他主张儿子不仅要供养父母而且要尊敬他们，因为父母不是狗与马仅只需要供养的。亚里士多德把伦理学看作政治学的分支，他那"宽大为怀的人"很显然是国王的一种楷模。孔子也把孝作为社会政治中上下关系的标准。"明王以孝治天下"，不过，相似之处也就到此为止了。

孔子的伦理规范制约亲子关系比之于西方要严格得多。子女的顺从与亲长的权威同样都是绝对的。这可能是因为西方封建社会政治体制比中国要松弛得多，神圣罗马帝国本身只是个空架子，而每个封建诸侯国里，当地贵族享有一定的独立权。封臣对于领主的效忠也相当有限，而在中国，中央集权的统治是绝对的，子女的行为以上面提到的孔子的言论为依据。在《孝经》里统摄父子关系的原则显然扩展到了君臣关系，以各种方式鼓励儿女的孝顺。如在中国历代史书里，自后汉以降，则辟有专门章节讲述贞女、孝子和忠臣，传说中这类人物也很多。援引其中两例：曹娥，一个巫师的女儿，其父淹死于河中，她到河边哭了十七天以招父魂，尔后自己投江以觅父尸。稍后的一种说法讲到曹娥最终如何抱起父亲浮出河面。另一个众口皆碑的英雄叫郭巨，他夫妻的收入尚难养活老母，因不愿母亲忍饥挨饿而做出活埋自己三岁的小孩这一可怕决定。然而当他掘坑时，他得到了一罐金子。后面这一故事被鲁迅作为纯然的骗局加以严厉的嘲笑。

尽管自1919年五四运动以来，在民主、平等的名号下，对与奴性同义的"孝"做了有力的批判，但"孝"的观念仍以改头换面的形式继续存在着。公道地说"孝"也有好的一面。为使社会顺利运行，需要某些制约行为的规范，包括对老年人的尊重与关心，而这又往往与古老的"孝"的观念相连。

作为宇宙的自然与人世沧桑是密切相连的，宇宙秩序与人世秩序存在着对应的关系。不谐的宇宙会以预兆和暗示显现自身以警告人类，因为它"在城里引起哗乱，在国中制造不和，在宫廷鼓动反叛，使父子关系断裂"。爱德伽一口气数落爱德蒙是叛逆，"不敬神，不敬兄长与父亲"。在李尔看来，至少在起初考狄利娅的行为有宇宙的意味，这是李尔顿时狂怒的根本原因。后来他在疯狂中抱怨道："我是个人，与其说我对别人犯了罪，不如说别人对我犯了罪。"李尔意识到他的罪过只是出自尊长的过失，而他的忘恩负义的女儿却犯下了违背宇宙大法的罪愆。

中国哲学对于天人相应的观念并不陌生，（如董仲舒就有此说。）但寓含在亲子关系中的宇宙原则在《李尔王》原文中当然不是直接显现，而在翻译中便更是如此。翻译比原文更易忽视这一点。

亲子关系尚有另一个方面，即法律的一面。子女赡养父母曾经是，至今仍然是一个实际的社会问题。当社会风气不好时，为确保年迈的父母得到适当的照顾，就必须有某种法律形式的保障。斯蒂芬·格林布拉特教授在其《焦虑的培育：李尔王及其继承人》中引用了爱伦·麦克法兰（《英国个人主义的起源》）所说的："看来古人已很清楚地认识到，没有法律保障，父母就没有任何权利。"[1] 他还借用了十三世纪的一个案例，一位鳏夫叫昂斯林，他同意将女儿

---

[1] 斯蒂芬·J·格林布拉特：《焦虑的培育：李尔王及其继承人》，第92—114页。

嫁给一个名字叫休的人，规定把自己的一半土地给他们，与这对新人住在同一所房子里。"昂斯林走到屋外，在门边把房子交给他们，并乞求收留他住宿。"从法律上说，这个父亲此时就成了一个"寄居者"。

记住亲子关系中法律的一面，我们就会更好地理解剧中一系列说法原非偶然。李尔请求里根而诅咒高纳里尔时说，"请求她的宽恕吗？你看这样王室尊严就成了什么样子！亲爱的女儿，我承认我已衰弱，年老毫无用处。我跪下来乞求您，请您赐给我衣、住、食。"李尔称他的两个长女为"保护人"和"保管人"。里根听到李尔带着仆人来临的消息时说："如果他们来我家寄住，我将不在。"得知李尔在葛罗斯特的家里时，她再次重复寄住一词，"我请求你，父亲，你已朽弱，至少看来如此。如果你裁减了一半随从，回到妹妹家去寄住，等到一月期满，你再来我家。"在全剧开首，葛罗斯特评论李尔的行为说："肯特就这样被放逐了？法兰西王盛怒而去？国王今晚已经出走？交出了他的权力，只靠津贴过活？"[1]李尔发疯时他对着暴风雨大喊："你没有服从我的义务。"当然分国本身是法律性行为，而考狄利娅的回答，"我爱陛下，根据我的义务，不多也不少"，"义务"原文也指"契约"，这也具有明显的法律色彩。但是这种回答太不幸了。这调子不仅和考狄利娅的性格不协调，也是对整个分国一事的讽刺。莎士比亚对法律总是不信任的（"法律的延宕"、"血腥的法律"、"法律这个老小丑"、"重金收买的法律"、"猜谜游戏，哪个是正义，哪个是盗贼？""镀金的罪恶折断了正义之剑"，夏洛克不人道的契约，"我要求的是法律的公道"，安琪罗的"稻草人法律"等等），我们可以推想，考狄利娅使用法

---

[1] 参看《维洛那二绅士》第一幕第8场，第8幕第1场，本·琼森《沉默的女人》。

律用语是一种戏剧手段，因为那与她的性格不符，她的声音总是"那么柔软、温和与婉转"。从剧情的布局来说，考狄利娅这个角色远不如她的两个姐姐那么重要，只是到了后面才开始变化。连布拉德雷也不得不承认，她"不是创造的杰作"，她开头的任性与天生的温和很难互相协调。

从纯法律的角度说，中文译本未能表达出交易的技术性细节。如"寄居"(sojourn)汉语译成"住"这属于日常用语，或译作"留驻"，这用于帝王出巡中途羁留的情景，突出人物的地位。Exhibition 的翻译莫衷一是，有"依靠某某过活"或译成"支应"，这个词曾出现在《西游记》里意为供饭。To subscrible 翻译成意思模糊的"交出"或"让"，有一种宽容的味道。所有译例都尚未显出交易的法律色彩来。中国的法律只约束犯了罪的子女。在《隋书》的《刑法志》中列出了十大罪律，其中之一便是"不孝"。但在大多数情况下，不孝的行为或品行并不是犯罪，只属于道德的范畴。而且孔子的伦理观对惩罚的效果表示怀疑，他相信适当教育的功效。这位哲人自己就曾主张："道之以政，齐之以刑，民免而无耻；道之以德，齐之以礼，有耻且格。"甚至到了今天，中国人也不会把赡养父母看成是纯粹的法律职责。

充满全剧的 nothing 和 all 两词的种种含义导致剧本带有一种哲理色彩。说来也怪，"all"在现代汉语中可译成"一切"，而 nothing 竟没有一个等义词。于是 nothing 的各种意思只得根据其上下文的意思来翻译。结果是这个词本身完全消失了，既听不到也看不到。

一般说来，在《李尔王》中 all 是个正面肯定词，nothing 则是个否定词。从表面看，"all"表示土地和生计，弄人所说的一段话就是此意。他说："我就是把一切家私都给予她们，我也会留下我的鸡冠帽。"李尔对两个不在场的女儿说过："噢，里根，高纳里尔！你们年老和善的父亲，他那慷慨的心给了你们一切。""一切"在这儿既包括父爱也包括权威。剧中 all 与 nothing 的对照不胜枚举，李尔问爱德伽，"你已把一切都给了你的两个女儿？"稍后，李尔又重说："什么！他的女儿们竟把他弄到这个地步？你不能自己留下一点吗？你把一切都给了她们了吗？"

Nothing 的情况则比较复杂。李尔期待考狄利娅说出比她两个姐姐更动听的表白爱的话，但相反，她回答说："没有。"于是惊诧的李尔立刻反唇回驳："没有只能带来没有。"从字面上看，李尔当然是指，如果考狄利娅什么也不说，她就得不到任何土地。但是这个词的意义太丰富了。李尔理解的考狄利娅的"没有"表示没有爱，而且这也就是不顺从，但考狄利娅和读者却明白，这个词反映了她的坦率和真挚，甚至有点任性。随着情节的发展，这个词的意思也在增加。在第一幕第四场，弄人唱了一曲忠言逆耳的小调，劝人谨慎。肯特评说："傻瓜，这没有什么。"弄人转向李尔："老伯伯，这没有什么对你有用么？"对此李尔答道："当然没有，孩子，没有只能产生没有。[1]"在这儿，第一个"没有"表示谨慎或世故。此外，弄人在高纳里尔出现前最后的评论是："你从两边削去了你的智慧，中间则空空如也；削下的一片来了。"这得与后来弄人针对李尔评高纳里尔的皱眉时所说的俏皮话联系起来："现在你是个没有数目的零蛋了。我现在比你要好：我是个傻瓜，你什么也不是。" Nothing 此处主要是指缺乏智慧。在伊利莎白时代，智慧，即心智或 ratio 是人区别于动物的特有的天赋。在被追捕的爱德伽的独白中，他把自己假扮的疯子与真疯子相比，这时 nothing 这个词又有了无实存的意义，"可怜的疯叫化！可怜的汤姆！这倒还是

---

[1] 威廉·燕卜荪：《复义七型》，第 45—46 页，伦敦，1947 年版。

有所指；我爱德伽什么也不是。"而当葛罗斯特感到李尔在场时喊道："噢！这被毁的自然的杰作！这个伟大的世界，也将会残败得如此一无所有。"这个词获得了宇宙秩序完全湮灭的终极意义。

要把涵义深广的 Nothing 译成汉语，译者只得寻求各种方式。其中之一就是把这个词的含义限制在某个方面，使之符合汉语习惯，使中国读者易于理解。肯特的"This is nothig"被译成"这些话一点意思也没有"。在孙大雨先生的译本中为"你这一车子的话没有说出点什么来。"关于弄人的问话"Can you make use of nothing？"朱译为"你不能从没有意思之间探求出一点意思来吗？"更为贴切的孙译作"没有什么，可有什么用处吗？"，但听起来并不是地道的汉语。对李尔王的回答"Why，no，boy，nothing Can be made of nothing"朱译法令人瞠目结舌，"垃圾里是掏不出金子来的。"这听起来象中文谚语，实则不是。虽然"垃圾"这个意思暗含在弄人对肯特的下一段谈话中："请你告诉他，他的土地已这样四分五裂，他还不肯相信一个傻瓜的话。"这句话被翻译成："他有那么多的土地，而现在就要变成一堆垃圾了。"这句翻译本身就很是随意发挥了。这种偏差的原因只能从译者的癖好中去查寻了。因为汉语习惯要求否定词不能与名词相连。译者要解决这一难题，不得不把"nothing"分成两半。这样弄人的"thou hast... left nothing in the middle，"and "thou are nothing"的汉语相似语是"你简直不是个东西"。后面这种翻译在汉语有一点骂人的味道，而原文毫无这种意思。

"Thou art an O without a figure"的不同译法最有趣，朱译为"你已变成一个孤零零的圆圈儿了"。译文引起的意象与原文毫不相关，完全失去了原文的意义，孙译则相当活泼，与原文的文字游戏刚好吻合，"可是如今你主字少了个王"，意为你仅仅变成了个小点。这种翻译用中国的文学批评用语来说，就是"神似"而不是貌似。尽管这个翻译相当机巧，然而其中心词 nothing 却完全消失了。爱德伽的一个独白朱译为："可怜的疯叫化！可怜的汤姆！倒有几分象，我现在不再是爱德伽了。"而 nothing 一字也消逝了。孙译为"如今还有他，我蔼特加没有了"。在译注中，孙先生声明，他在这儿采用了里特逊（Ritson）的解释。最后，对李尔在开场中考狄利娅定调式的"Nothing will come of nothing"的回驳，孙译试图把它的含义局限在分地这桩实际事务上："没有话说，就没有东西。"朱译则试图传达其普遍意义而译作："没有只能换到没有"。但这句话也不太合乎中文习惯。

显然"Nothing"在某些场合是褒义，但总的说来有贬义色彩。它的同源词"naught"及其衍生词 naughty 则纯粹是贬义的。当弄人劝李尔不要走进暴风雨中去，他说"浸泡在这恶毒天气中"。葛罗斯特称里根为"恶毒的妇人"，而李尔请求里根时说："可爱的里根，你的妹妹真狠毒。"失明的葛罗斯特听到且辨认出李尔的声音后喊道："噢，这毁坏了的自然杰作！这个伟大的世界，也将会残败得如此一无所有。"

"Naughty night"孙译作"尴尬"，译者意识到这种翻译不恰当，在译注中提出一个更为近似的翻译。"太坏的"，朱译则作"危险的夜"。"Naughty lady"朱译为"恶妇"。"thy sister's naught"，孙译为"你大姐真是个坏货"，朱译则为"你妹妹太不孝啦"。翻译"World Wearing to naught"译文是成功的，但无法传达出单音节的断然口吻。朱译为"一堆残迹"，孙大雨先生则译为，"这广大的宇宙竟会这么破碎"。

"Nothing"和"all"的对立统一是全剧的中心。开始时，李尔坚信他就是一切，结尾时才认识到，他并不是一切。"他们曾告诉我，我就是一切；这是个谎言。"转折点出现在他的疯狂中，他宣告："我将是一切忍耐的典范；我什么也不说。"现在李尔与考狄利娅一致了，他重复着考狄利娅说的话。李尔经历了人生的炼狱之后也接受了一切。这一点是通过爱德伽说出来的："人们必须忍受他们的离去，甚至忍受他们的到来：成熟就是一切。"跟哈姆雷特一样（"准备就是一切"），李尔在精神上也成熟了。这最后一个音符使人想起蒙田的一句话："哲学就是学习如何死亡"，也使全剧具有一种哲理色彩。

《李尔王》是一个很好的试验，从中可以得出跨文化与语言界线的翻译的一些原则。孙大雨先生的《黎琊王》译本非常精细，但他还是承认把这部杰作译成汉语有着难以克服的困难。他说，不是奇迹出现，就不可能翻译得完美。他提到了施莱格尔－蒂克的译本，尽管这个译本相当好，可还是不断为其他译本所取代。所以，完美的译本永远只是个愿望。孙大雨先生非常有先见之明，避免了混淆中西伦理观。他的整个译本中，只有两处用了"孝"字。在这个字第二次出现时，他在注解中说明，他虽然找到了一个替代词，由于韵律的缘故，不得不用这个字。一般说，他把"love"译成"爱"而不是"孝"。他说这样至少可以避免在把这个伟大而神圣的悲剧译成汉语时，被人误解为是一部儒家道德说教或是佛教因果报应的作品，从而令人产生儒教在西方也流行的印象。孙先生还进一步区别了"Nature"一词的两大含义，并根据上下文作了不同翻译。尽管如此，似乎也不可避免必得使用"逆伦"、"恩情"、"负恩"等词，这样又使读者立即就会联想到儒家的伦理观。财产分配中的法律方面尚未足以显现出来。

比较《李尔王》的两个中译本，孙大雨先生的译本远比朱生豪的要好，因为他对原文理解深刻。总的来说，译文质量上的区别主要在于对原文的理解。当然也在于掌握汉语程度的优劣。两个译本朱生豪译于二十世纪三十年代晚、四十年代初，孙大雨先生则译于1941年，文字都已嫌老。尽管两个译本的翻译及其风格有区别，但二者之间的类似也令人注目。尽管孙大雨先生充分意识到西方伦理的非儒教的特点，从而成功地避免了使用"孝"字，但他至少在两处还是用了"孝"字，并且也使用了其他有强烈的儒教色彩的词。另一方面，朱生豪似乎根本就没有看到这点，至少是不想对此作出区分。进一步说，两个译者都没有认识到财产分配中法律的一面。由于语言特点方面的原因，对"nothing"和"all"的对立统一也没有作出恰当处理。我们的考察表明，虽然理解有相通之处，但是还是要受历史与文化的制约。两位中文译者有共同的文化和语言传统，其不同在于个性差异，其相似则由于共性与共同的文化。莎士比亚或任何其他文本的翻译，都是双重的、共时的过程的结果：一方面是从产生作品的国土异化出来，另一方面是向所植入的文化的归化。

"King Lear Metamorphosed"，原载 *Comparative Literature*, University of Oregon, Vol.39, NO3（Summer 1987）。黄满生译

（原载《国外文学》第2期，1989年）

《十七世纪英国文学》书后

　　我在拙著《十七世纪英国文学》的《小引》里写了一点我对这一时期英国文学的看法，觉得意犹未尽。《读书》杂志给了我一个机会，我就冒不逊之讥，再罗唆几句。

　　1982 年秋天，我在复旦大学外文系为研究生开了一门十七世纪英国文学的课，第二年春天又为北京大学英语系研究生重复了一遍。两次讲完之后，我想何妨把它写出来，可以作为学生学习这段文学史的参考。这就是它问世的缘由。

　　国内通行的外国文学教科书讲到这一段文学时，非常简略，最多只讲三个作家：弥尔顿、班扬和德莱顿。对于一个学英国文学的学生来说，特别是在研究生阶段，这点内容是远远不够的。英文系的学生当然可以读英文的英国文学史，但对一般不能或目前尚不能阅读英文的学生或文学工作者或爱好者，这一段的文学就将是个空白。我这项工作也许可以起到一些拾遗补阙的作用。我又一向倾向于讲文学史要"说说唱唱"，"说"就是讲历史，"唱"就是读作品。对初学者尤其应以"唱"为主，在"唱"的时候把历史发展简要介绍一下。英国文学十七世纪这一段就是对研究生来说恐怕也比较陌生，所以就收了比较多的引文。

我选这一段文学史并不仅仅因为它对我们的专业学生和一般读者比较陌生，更重要的是因为这段文学史本身的重要性。这一点我在本书的《小引》已作了交代。我觉得这一段历史具有全球性的历史意义，在世界史上是资产阶级革命的第一次尝试和失败。在英国，它牵动着每个人的心，也影响到欧洲，而欧洲当时在世界史进程中是处于先进地位的。

我们读历史总是讲英国资产阶级革命是在宗教外衣下进行的。但是宗教到底起什么作用，它的具体内容和表现是什么，学生知之甚少。我企图用几个作家的具体作品，对当时这件五颜六色的宗教"外衣"作些描述，同时指出其重要性。我曾说："我们说政治斗争是在宗教外衣下进行的，是说宗教论争实质上是政治斗争，但当事人在他们主观意识里，恐怕至少有一半是真心诚意地把这场辩论或战争看成是宗教信仰问题的。"

我在《小引》里还同时指出在进行宗教论辩的同时，科学也在长足前进，奠定了方法论的基础，但同时也受到宗教的抵制。

在这矛盾激化、风云变幻的时代，凡是有思考的人都在提出问题，思考问题，而且思考一些带根本性的问题，如生与死、信仰、精神的疾病和创伤。

我也企图说明为什么在这样一个时代，散文特别发达。

现在想来，以上这种理解还欠完全。我觉得，如果从文艺复兴一直看下来，如果说十七世纪使很大部分英国知识界陷入沉思，那么这沉思阶段还应向上摊个二三十年。人文主义在它极盛的时候，确实具有摧枯拉朽的破坏力，形象地体现在一些作家的作品里，如意大利诗人阿利阿斯托（Ariosto）的《发疯的罗兰》着力描写罗兰因失去了爱情被激疯以后的摧毁一切的狂暴行动：他脱光了衣服，拔起大树，砍杀追捕他的人。诗人称他为"毁灭性的火焰"。爱情的力量可以使人丧失理性，摧毁一切。又象拉伯雷，他笔下的巨人更是表现出一股横扫一切、所向无敌的力量，这是我们所熟悉的。这两位有代表性的作家生活在十六世纪初到四五十年代，很能代表当时的"时代精神"。把他们和文艺复兴早期的作家相比，则早期作家只能算是曙光，他们则是烈日。到了八十年代以后，思想界的气候就变了，人文主义虽然呈现出无限好的夕阳景色，却已变成黄昏落日了。蒙田的怀疑论可以看作是当时思想界的晴雨表。塞万提斯的唐吉诃德只能生活在幻想里，一旦幻想破灭，他的生命也就终止了。莎士比亚为什么在九十年代一登上文坛和剧坛就写鲁克丽丝受暴力的欺凌，就写了一批血腥剧？莎士比亚的全部作品具有多少破坏性？怕很难说。琼生就叫他"温和的（或有教养的）莎士比亚"。马娄笔下的"巨人"不是屈服于宗教，就是自我毁灭。这变化说明什么呢？我想这说明资产阶级的思想武器人文主义到了十六世纪后期遇到了挫折。与文艺复兴同时兴起的宗教改革运动也遇到了天主教强有力的反宗教改革的抵制。人文主义失去了它的破坏力，暴露了它的软弱性。这一方面表现为怀疑、悲观、沉思，另一方面又表现为追求感官刺激，夸张情感，失去理性和平衡（发疯的罗兰最后还是恢复了理性），或则表现为两方面的混合。这种精神状态在艺术和文学里就表现为所谓的"巴罗克"风格。因此要讲十七世纪英国文学，恐怕还应向上推几十年。这是我在《小引》里没有说得完的地方。到了1660年复辟以后，英国文学受法国宫廷影响，确实很明显地跨进了另一个时期。所以真正要写一部十七世纪英国文学史，应从十六世纪末写起，包括莎士比亚和他的同时代作家，因为这是文艺复兴的没落阶段。这样一来，恐怕也不能叫"十七世纪英国文学"了，也许可以叫"文艺复兴衰落时期的文学"。

　　我不敢把我这本小书叫做"史"，因为它没有系统，讲作家也不是每个作家都全面讲，有的只讲他一部分作品，有时还作些中外比较。我本来想把它叫做《拾遗集》，给英国文学的讲授填补些空阙。例如我写大家比较熟悉的弥尔顿，就有意不谈他的主要作品《失乐园》等，而其他比较生疏的作家，就介绍得稍全面些。此外，我们对文学的看法，多年来局限于诗歌、小说、戏剧，这确是"纯文学"，这是西方传来的看法，来源于柏拉图和亚里士多德：抒情诗、史诗、戏剧。我们翻翻《文心雕龙》或《昭明文选》，我们的老祖宗对文学的理解就宽广得多。当然西方学者也把文学概念扩大，我们翻翻他们的一些文学史，就会看到他们也不是仅仅把文学看成是以上三大类，也把散文、传记、书信、日记、历史著作，甚至哲学著作都包括了进去。可见天下好文学不尽在三大类之中。

文学是扩大人类经验的手段。人不可能经历一切经验，尤其不可能经历古代的经验。要体验古代人的思想感情，只有阅读他们的作品。这对于一个人的文化修养是很有好处的。

我老有一种感觉，自从我们推行开放政策以来，我们引进了许多现当代的西方文学。十年锁国，与外界情况隔绝，一旦开放便如饥似渴地想了解外界情况，这很可理解。引进来的作品固然增加了我们的知识，但恐怕很少能激励我们的精神，提高我们的境界。另一方面，外国的优秀文学遗产还有许多有待挖掘。以前或则囿于对文学的狭隘看法，或则由于照顾到某种需要（如教学），我们只强调某类作品，或所谓"重点"作家，或"重点"时期，因此很多好的作家作品就放过了，这是很可惜的。现在已经到了可以扩大，可以深入的时候了。

就以外国文学史而言，通史已经出了不少，似乎可以出一些断代史，或某一文学运动的历史，或某一流派的专史。上面我已交代我这本小书并不是"史"，也就是说不是断代史。要写断代史，材料还得比这多得多，方面还要广得多。不过我是企图用"时代精神"把一批作家串联起，用他们的作品来说明这一时代的精神面貌。

但我没有能够严格按照这个宗旨去写，有一定的随意性，例如我写弥尔顿的悼亡诗，我忽而想到中国文学史上从《诗经》开始，历代都有，几乎成了一个抒情诗的"属类"，也成了一个传统，为什么西方这类诗却如凤毛麟角？我因而做了一些比较。若从全书体例来看，这篇东西放在里面不伦不类，虽然这首诗的情调颇符合当时人们的心理。

造成这种情况是由于我有一个隐隐约约的想法，即能不能从一个比较的角度写一段外国文学史？我们已经有不少文章对中外作家和作品进行比较，而对一组作家，或一派作家，或一个时期的作家进行中外比较，似乎还不多。能不能比较，若能，怎样比较，当然都是问题。不过，象我们一向所做的那样，仅在外国或西方的历史和文学传统范围之内谈论西方作家，虽然是完全必要的，但总似乎是象看戏，我们是旁观者，并未介入。如果同我们的文学作一比较，就可能在我们和异国文学之间建立了一座桥梁。不论是异是同，一经比较，更容易理解。例如林纾就把西洋小说同史记、汉书的叙事笔法等同起来，认为合乎古文文法，使得西洋小说对当时士大夫和知识阶层读者读起来不觉得陌生。当然我们并不是要让外国文学"熟化"、"汉化"或"中国化"，而是做真正的比较。实际上，我们读外国文学作品都在比较，不过一般不是有意识地比较罢了。

这种比较的写法有一定的难度，如果不是不可能的话或不需要的话。在西方是可行的。国际比较文学协会早就执行了一项计划，从比较角度写一套多卷本的"用欧洲语言写的文学的历史"，已经出版了的有《表现主义》、《欧洲文学中的象征主义运动》、《启蒙运动时期》，还将陆续出版《二十世纪先锋派》、《用欧洲语言写的非洲文学》、《文艺复兴第一部分》、《浪漫主义的讽刺》等卷。每一种往往是多卷的。在西方这种比较文学史是写得成的，因为欧洲自成一个文化体系，在这文化体系内各国文学关系密切，相互影响，同中有异，异中有同，一个文学运动往往是全欧性的。但用中西比较方法写一段外国文学史，问题就复杂得多，值得讨论。不过，我们站在中国的立场，不仅仅是抱着洋为中用的态度去处理外国文学，而且从中国文学传统的立场去处理它，分辨其异同，探索其相互影响（在有影响存在的地方）也许还是可行的，有助于对双方的理解。我在这本小书里做了一点尝试，枝枝节节，非常谫陋，希望读者批评指谬。

（原载《读书》第 7 期，1987 年）

莎作内外

一

多年来我们研究莎士比亚似乎沿着一条路走，没有什么突破。具体说，就是以苏联五十年代以前的莎学为模式。其实苏联莎学基本上是德国和英国浪漫派莎学的继续，甚至是重复，不过加上所谓的历史唯物主义。而所谓的历史唯物主义又局限于阶级分析。所谓浪漫派批评则专门着力于人物的分析，如希拉德雷那样，把剧中人物完全当做现实生活中的人来看待，我不是说这种研究没有用处，但不能仅仅局限于此。三四十年代以来，西方出现过意象派批评，心理学派批评，宗教神话学派批评，现代派批评（如将莎士比亚比作"荒诞派"作家）等等。不管他们成就如何（有的流派已留下不可磨灭的影响），他们都是在从不同的方面予以突破。在今天新理论的冲击下，我们是否也应当对这样一位作家作重新的考虑呢？我并不是要我们重蹈别人已尝试过的路子，也不是鼓吹把新理论应用到莎学上（这当然可以尝试）。我在 82 年曾提出推进莎学应：一，多读莎评；二，读其全部作品；三，比较研究；四，研究语言。看来这还不够，我今天想提出两个方面的问题，这两个方面的问题可以使我们对莎作的看法有所改变。第一个问题就是重新考虑一下人文主义，这是莎作的基本内容，即此文标题中的"内"。在这个问题上，我们的概念比较含混。第二个问题就是莎士比亚和文艺复兴前前后后的作家群有什么关系，即此文标题中所称的"外"。换言之，对人文主义这问题不研究清楚，对莎士比亚的理解就不可能确切。此外，过去的研究还有一件令人遗憾的事，那便是孤立地研究莎士比亚，没有做横向和纵向的比较研究。本文想就这两个方面做些初步探索，给莎士比亚一个更明确的地位，可能对理解、阐释他的作品的特点有所助益，对莎作中某些问题可以得到一定的解答。

这两个方面代表两种不同的方法，第一种用传统的说法可以叫做釜底抽薪法，即金圣叹评《水浒》所说"略其形迹，伸其神理"。用结构主义的术语就叫做发掘深层结构。莎士比亚的作品是"言语"（parole），我们要研究"语言"（langue），也就是说莎氏作品后面的历史文化体系或意识形态，亦即人文主义。这个意识形态不是一成不变的，而是流动的。第二个方法，还用传统的说法，可以叫烘云托月法，这也是金圣叹用的，用在评点《西厢记》的时候，相当于今天我们的"显学"——比较文学，是一种比较方法（comparative method）或对比方法（Contrastive method）。烘云托月出自中国传统画法，靠画云，把月亮烘托出来，我们过去研究莎士比亚好比用笔画一个圈，把月亮勾出来。我不打算再画圈，而画云，把云画完了，月亮也就显现出来了，莎士比亚的形象也就露出来了。我的文章虽然标出了莎士比亚，但不打算正面大写他。

人文主义作为意识形态在现在的西方也并未绝迹。若从十四世纪算起，那么六百年来，它在西方的社会功能或所起的作用如何呢？近来美籍华裔学者余英时先生有这样的论断："在西方近代世俗化的历史进程中，所谓由灵返肉、由天国回向人间是一个最重要的环节。文艺复兴的人文主义者首先建立起'人的尊严'的观念。……但是由于西方宗教和科学的两极化，人的尊严似乎始终难以建筑在稳固的基础之上。倾向宗教或形而上学一方面的人往往把人的本质扬举得过高；而倾向无神论、唯物论、或科学一方面的人又把人性贬抑得过低。近来深层心理学流行，有些学者专从人的'非理性'的方面去了解人性，以至使传统'人是理性的动物'的说法都受到普遍的怀疑。所谓'人文主义'在西方思想界一直都占不到很高的地位。"[1] 余先生对人文主义的缺乏稳固基础的论点是可以接受的，但它是否因此就一直不占很高的地位，值得研究。所谓"一直"，当然应当包括开始的时候。但事实恐怕并不如此。我认为人文主义在欧洲的社会功能和所起的作用是曲线形的，而所以形成曲线，一则取决于外部的压力（关于外部的压力，本文不拟涉及），一则（也许更重要）取决于其自身的性质。我的意思是说，人文主义在早期还是具有强大的生命力的。我们从早期文学中可以看出它有三个特点特别突出：一是要求个性解放；二是理想主义；三是从效果看，破坏性大。这三个特点是相互联系的。要求个性解放指的是恋爱的自由、争取确立人的地位和尊严、聪明才智的开发等。所谓理想，极大一部分是指政治理想和生活方式方面的理想。所谓破坏性则指的是用理性作武器对中世纪进行批判所造成的结果。

十四五世纪欧洲正处在进入近代的门槛，也就是开始资本主义化或近代化的时期。人文主义起了一个启蒙作用，但它作为意识形态有没有能力把社会推向资本主义化呢？当然，在开始时它对封建的意识形态确实起了摧枯拉朽的作用，这一点我们以后还要分析，

[1] 《中国思想传统的现代诠释》一书内《从价值系统看中国文化的现代意义》一文，台北联经出版事业公司 1987 年版，第 17—18 页。着重号引者所加。

但它并不能完全代表新的意识形态。这是由于它本质上有弱点。其一，它提出人的尊严、以人为本等观念，这只是一种表态，一种理想。其二，它的社会纲领，如乌托邦，当然是空想，实际上是一个以农业和家庭手工业为基础的理想化的中世纪社会，是一个基本上封闭社会，虽然海外扩张已经开始。它与资本主义的发展相去甚远。其三，早期人文主义者固然是先知先觉的知识分子，但他们与旧文化、旧传统仍是藕断丝连，尤其是和天主教并未割断。托玛斯·摩尔（Thomas More）便是最好的例子。他有改革社会的理想，但又不惜为天主教殉节。莎士比亚据说也是天主教徒。总之，人文主义只是一种美好的愿望，而远非行动的纲领。它部分地反映了资本主义意识形态，但在历史转折关头，是显得无力的。从意识形态、从实践的观点来看（不是从经济角度看），真正推动社会进入资本主义的力量是宗教改革。

宗教改革推动资本主义发展这一点在西方早有人发现，如本世纪初的韦伯（Max Weber），稍后还有托尼（R. H. Tawney）等，已成定论。宗教改革虽由马丁·路德发难，但德国经济、政治落后，宗教改革只引起农民战争，最后失败，未能进入资本主义。欧洲最早资本主义化的是英国，英国宗教改革产生了国教，国教并不彻底。真正的推动力是清教，清教的基本教义则取自加尔文。韦伯指出[1]加尔文教提出所谓"神召"的概念（Berufcalling），这是古代文化和天主教所没有的，上帝要人完成他现世的责任和义务，而不是苦修。人勤劳地从事他的职业就是实现神召，也就是有道德的行为。积累财富是责任，是一种道德，是天职。奢侈浪费，包括浪费时间，是不道德的。（按：清教思想是矛盾的：一方面它认为通过

---

[1]《新教伦理与资本主义精神》（1905）。中译本，三联书店，1987。

劳动积累财富是道德的，另一方面又反对一味追逐财富，怕导致游手好闲、享乐、堕落，形成所谓清教徒的禁欲主义。为了避免这弊病，就提倡致富后奉献上帝，但这是没有保证的。这矛盾可能反映了早期资本积累的特点。）不过，这种新的伦理观念带有鲜明的入世性、积极性、实践性、进取性，也就是说符合资本主义精神，靠这种精神推动资本主义的发展。

托尼也指出，清教徒的道德观可以用一句古代格言概括：laborare est orare，劳动就是祈祷。清教徒用劳动代替天主教的祈祷。祈祷不能使灵魂得救。劳动不仅创造财富，而且是为了灵魂的健康。劳动（work）和某些新教徒或天主教徒所理解的"善行"（good work）还不同。"善行"是一系列孤立的行为，是为了补偿某种罪过，或是为了急欲获得名誉。甚至施舍这一慈善行为也被看作是鼓励懒惰，而懒惰是最大的不道德。路德就认为乞讨就是敲诈。还有人认为施舍是一种自私行为，以便生前沽名钓誉，死后有人为施舍者祈祷。穷人不能靠施舍者改善生活，只能靠勤奋工作。清教主张人要积极生活，反对静思（contemplation），静思是自我纵容。"止水易腐"。上帝命令人类劳动得食，不劳动就不是上帝的好仆人。富人也要为他人服务。贫穷不值得称赞，上帝指出一条致富的路，既合法又不损害灵魂，不听，就不是上帝的好臣仆。

最近美国马克思主义学者詹明信（Fredric Jameson）[1] 也重申了"劳动伦理"（work-ethic）这一概念。他指出欧洲封建主义和天主教密不可分，宗教和政治是结合在一起的。宗教本身就是法律和伦理标准，就是文化，就是文学艺术。因此要推翻封建，必须先动摇天主教，用宗教反宗教，即如马克思所说宗教是绝望者的希望。

---

[1] 《后现代主义与文化理论》（1985 年在北大演讲录的中译本），陕西师大出版社，1986。

新教突出个人的"内心光明"（inner light），摆脱教会的束缚；突出"劳动伦理"，用积极勤奋的工作代替消极等待得救。

不难看出这种新的"资本主义精神"在许多方面是和人文主义相抵触的。它其实已经为十九世纪的资本主义理论，如密勒（J. S. Mill）的功利主义打下基础。它和人文主义最大的区别，第一在于它的"实践性"（praxis）。所谓"世俗的禁欲主义"就是要求用一种伦理规范来自我纪律，自我约束，以获得财富，积累财富。从主观上说，这是原始积累的一个途径。（客观上当然是通过剥削。）因此，新教反对挥霍浪费，甚至反对慈善，而且是打着《圣经》的旗号反对慈善的。这和人文主义之主张仁慈（这和天主教教义有关）正好背道而驰。因为它是入世的，所以新教的教义具有行动性，要求人们"劳动"，实地去做，这样灵魂才能得救，而不是仅仅树立一个理想，而没有达到这个理想的切实可行的措施。这又和人文主义的空想性相龃龉。

新教的另一个特点就是承认权威，最高的权威是上帝。在旧教，最高的权威却是上帝的代理人——教皇。对权威应当绝对服从，这也是自我纪律的一个方面。因为他们相信上帝这个最高权力，最高权威，已经做了最好的安排（定命论 predestination），他们不过是上帝的工具，只要绝对服从，按上帝的旨意去行动，就可以得救。[1] 而且仅仅每个个人这样做还不够，必须人人这样做，使整个社会符合上帝的意图。这就要求信仰相同的人组织起来，这样就形成了各种不同的新教教派。这和人文主义的要求个性解放，要求个人自由，缺乏组织性又是背道而驰的。人文主义者不过是个单枪匹马的、象吉诃德那样的空想家而已。

---

[1] 这也是弥尔顿《失乐园》的宗旨。

新教的第三个特点，大致说来，是它的平民性。当然，新教的领袖们都是知识分子，但他们的群众却都是平民和农民，如闵采尔领导的农民战争，法国的胡格诺战争。人文主义，甚至整个文艺复兴运动，大致说来，则是一个贵族运动。早期的人文主义者一般都不是新教徒，极少背叛天主教信仰。他们的兴趣主要在古代，在恢复希腊和罗马的文化。要靠希腊和罗马的文化而进入近代社会是不可能的，正如我们现在不能靠孔子的学说进入现代化一样。他们活动的范围在宫廷、大学和社会上层。他们对平民的影响远不如宗教改革家。

　　从以上的粗略比较可以看出，使西方真正进入近代社会的是与之相适应的新教文化，在英国就是清教徒文化，只有这种文化才能使英国进入工业化经济，并由此而发展为大工业生产。

　　我这样说，并不是否认社会发展决定于生产力的发展，而是指出除经济决定外，当中还有一个重要而不可缺少的环节，即宗教。这正是我们以往所忽略的。我这样说，也不是否认人文主义的进步作用，而是想指出，在我们的教科书和文章中似乎都暗示以人文主义为核心的文艺复兴是唯一的或主要的推进社会的运动，或过分强调这一点，而忽略了更重要的一面。

　　人文主义所起的作用如前面所说，并非一成不变的，在我们要研究的这一段文学史里，它的作用可以说是象一条曲线或斜线。从微弱的开始到全盛，而衰落。在全盛时期它具有一定的破坏性、冒险性，精神上的破坏性，精神上的冒险性。但随着时间的推移，它的威力每况愈下，以至发展成为怀疑悲观，到了枯竭的地步。当然，作为一种思想意识，人文主义在西方并未绝迹，一直到现在它还以各种形式存在着。人文主义在整个西方文化中的起落升降以及它所起的作用，有待进一步研究。就我们现在研究的这一阶段说，它的进程是走下坡路的一条曲线或斜线。

二

对人文主义有了这样一个理解，下面我想以人文主义为中轴，按时期先后，把一些在整个欧洲有代表性的作品附着其上，具体地看看它的表现，以便从这样一个展望可以看出莎士比亚的地位。

当然，前人也不是没有发现这一时期人文主义所经历的变迁。如英国学者威尔逊[1]就把十六世纪后半到十七世纪初的英国文学分为伊利莎伯一世时期和雅各时期两个阶段（以 1603 年为分界），并指出前一阶段的文学是乐观主义的，后一阶段的文学是悲观主义的。他认为莎作也可分为这两个阶段[2]。其实伊利莎伯一世时期的文学已有悲观主义。因此威尔逊又有所修正，他勉强使用了"巴罗克"（baroque）这个名词以区别于文艺复兴盛期[3]，指出文艺复兴盛期的文学表达的是"自然"，是一个"长驻的实体"（Nature as a perennial reality），而"巴罗克"所捕捉的则是"变幻不定的自然"（ever-changing Nature），"消逝着的顷刻"（elapsing moments），并以九十年代作为"新风格"的起点，也就是把伊利莎伯一世朝腰斩了。显然威尔逊的分期是矛盾的、重叠的。按他前后两种说法，就产生出三个问题：文艺复兴究竟有多长，如何分期；作为全欧现象的巴罗克起于何时；如果在英国是九十年代，则莎氏一开始创作就已是巴罗克时代了。前两个问题不可能，也没有必要，做出精确的

---

[1]　F. P. 威尔逊：《伊利莎伯一世时期和雅各时期》，俄克拉何马大学出版社，1945 年版。
[2]　同上书，第 110 页。
[3]　同上书，第 26 页。

答复。最后一个问题却是值得我们认真研究的，因为它牵涉到对莎士比亚的看法，他的地位，对他的特色的理解。我觉得我们若要在现在对莎作的理解的基础上做进一步的理解，例如问一问它没有哪些特点，为什么？又如有些公认的特点能不能从一个新的角度去解释？那么我们就必须把他放到一个历史坐标图上，把他和文艺复兴前期作家作纵向比较，也和他同时代以及稍后的作家作横向比较，把他放在整个文艺复兴时期欧洲文学体系中来考查。

我觉得文艺复兴若要分前后期，应以十六世纪七十年代为分界，要早于九十年代。我甚至想说，文艺复兴就到七十年代为止，甚至更早些，七十年代以后，欧洲文学就进入了巴罗克时期。（德国巴罗克的起迄一般认为是1575—1725，共150年。）当然也可称文艺复兴的衰落期。

三

我在开始时谈到早期人文主义的三个特征：解放个性；理想主义；破坏性。这三者是互相联系的。早期的文学确实给人一种清新之感。如彼特拉克（1304—1374）。他的抒情诗继承了中古后期所谓的行吟诗人的传统，讴歌爱情，强调感官享受。他的爱国诗篇表达了理想，充满信心。即使但丁（1265—1321）的《神曲》，尽管它是建筑在雄厚牢固的神学基础上，仍然透露出强烈的理性之光（如对维吉尔的敬慕，对天主教腐败和罪恶的批判）。但丁继承了希腊罗马文化中那种追求的精神和冒险的精神，就象尤利西斯和埃涅阿斯。例如在《地狱篇》（二章），但丁不敢登山，维吉尔就责备他胆小：

你的精神被怯懦所压服，L'anima tua èda viltate offesa

怯懦经常阻碍人前进，La qual molte fiate l'uomo ingombra

在光荣的事业面前倒退。Siche d'onrata impressa Io rivolve

于是他上山了，于是在进入地狱大门时（第三章），尽管门上写着：

进来的人们，放下一切希望吧！Lasciate ogni speranza

voich' entrate.

他还是冒险进去了。

在进入天堂的时候，他告诫乘小舟跟在他后面的人们：

回去吧，回到你们的岸上去吧，Tornate a riveder li vostri
liti,

不要进入这汪洋大海，因为也许 Nonvi mettete in pelago；
chè forse

你们望不到我了，就会迷途。perdendo me rimarreste smarriti.

他说，他们会比那些跟随取金羊毛的耶松的人们还要感到迷惘。

这种精神和中世纪占统治地位的近乎停滞的精神状态迥乎不同了。

我们现在来集中谈谈早期人文主义的破坏性。所谓破坏性，就是批判性，指对中世纪意识、中世纪观念、中世纪文化的破坏。后期的作家也有破坏性，但十分微弱而不足道，早期的破坏性都是十分强烈的。批判的武器是理性。不过，批判的表现形式不同。一股力量来自先知先觉的知识分子，另一股也是通过知识分子表达出来的，但是它的根却是社会中下层的城市居民和一批不稳定分子——流氓、无赖，或称流氓无产阶级。前一类破坏的动机，是要求个性解放，实现某种理想。它破坏的是陈旧的道德观、价值观。后一类的破坏动机则纯粹是为了求生存。凡是不合理的，都是阻碍生存的东西。它蔑视一切道德，不择手段地去达到目的。前者带有空想性，后者则没有一点建设性。

我们现在可以选一些有代表性的作家和作品，做一些分析。

在前一类中我们可以举出埃拉斯谟（Erasmus，1469—1536）。他攻击天主教会的腐败，神学家的愚昧，但也反对路德的暴力和极端行动。他是天主教徒，在改革问题上他是个温和派。他主张与其在教义上象经院里那样作烦琐的辩论，不如仿效基督的生活，象基督那样，通过说理和对人类的爱，把人类争取到基督方面来。这就是所谓的"基督教人文主义"，也就是通过理性或说理使腐败的天主教恢复原始的纯洁性（prisca simplilitas），在维持天主教的原则下，用理性来加以改造。

作为早期人文主义代表人物，埃拉斯谟相信理性的力量。现行的一切信仰、教义、仪式是否合乎基督的哲学，都须经理性的裁判。他认为我们应当受理性的指导，不应受感情左右。他在《基督教战士手册》（*Enchiridion Militis Christani*，1503）[1] 一书中，一开始就说生活就是战争，我们不可有虚假的安全感。上帝的敌人在进攻，我们必须反抗，不反抗等于发疯。战而能胜是不容置疑的。战斗的武器就是祈祷和知识。"知识用健全的思想武装我们的头脑，使我们永远能分辨善恶。"这和新教提出的"劳动就是祈祷"区别极大。对于理性必胜，他抱有十足的信心，理性可以暂时受压迫，

---

[1] 引自约翰·多兰：《埃拉斯谟全盛期作品的精要》，纽约，1983 年版。

但最终会恢复，"因为神在理性上铭刻着永恒的法则"。

《愚蠢颂》也是以理性为武器进行批判。这部作品和勃朗特（Sebastian Brandt）的《愚人船》（*Narrenschiff*，1494）是一脉相承的。《愚人船》以一百个愚人乘船到愚人国为线索，对社会上各种恶劣愚蠢行为进行鞭挞。埃拉斯谟所写的愚蠢时而说反话，时而说正面话，时而是真正的愚蠢，时而又是智慧，我们不必为这种自相矛盾的表达感到惶惑，能够嘲笑他人，也能自我嘲笑，正是自信的表现。他要通过笑说出真理（ridendo dicere verum）。笑是理性和健全常识的表现，同时也是酒神精神的表现。"巴库斯永远是年轻的"，青春代表生、繁殖、欢乐。我们不能说埃拉斯谟没有破坏性，但他并没有真正动摇天主教的基础。埃拉斯谟的朋友，摩尔（Sir Thomas More，1478—1535）的《乌托邦》（1516）虽然批判了对农民的掠夺、法律的不公正、战争给人民带来的灾难，并指出一切的根源是私有制，但他的对策是空想的，要回到古代宗法社会。从某种意义上说，这无异是用一种虚假的希望，抵消了现实的残酷。不过，《乌托邦》在当时和后代都有很大影响，如拉伯雷《巨人传》第三部，卷一就造了"乌托邦人"。这里顺便谈一下欧洲的乌托邦文学。这类文学当然可以追溯到柏拉图的理想国，它既是一种理想，也是一种逃避。文艺复兴时期盛行的牧歌文学也属于这类。这类作品如圣那札罗（Jacopo Sannazaro，C.1457—1530）的《阿卡狄亚》（*Arcadia*），这是一部韵文散文合璧作品，追求大自然中淳朴的生活方式，缅怀古代，把古代看成黄金时代。但纯粹的田园生活是不存在的，从维吉尔的《牧歌》到八十年代锡德尼的《阿卡狄亚》里和莎士比亚的喜剧里，"田园风光"都不那么纯粹。战争、各种罪恶都闯了进去，这说明所谓"理想"的脆弱性。

下面谈谈十六世纪前半期两个有显著破坏性的人文主义作家：

十六世纪初期最主要的诗人无疑是阿里奥斯托（Ludovico Ariosto，1474—1533）。他的传奇叙事诗《疯狂的罗兰》（*Orlando Furioso*）是博亚尔多（Boiardo，1441—1494）的《热恋中的罗兰》（*Orlando Innamorato*）的续篇。《热恋中的罗兰》是一部骑士爱情传奇，写契丹（Cathay）王迦拉佛朗（Galafron）的女儿安杰丽嘉（Angelica）和她弟弟来到查理大帝宫廷，要引诱基督教骑士到她父亲的国土去。许多骑士都爱上了她，其中有罗兰（Orlando）、阿斯托尔佛（Astolfo）、利那尔多（Rinaldo）等。安杰丽嘉喝了魔泉水爱上了利那尔多，后者也误喝了魔泉水，却反而厌恶安杰丽嘉。一个逃，一个追，一直来到契丹都城。都城被鞑靼王包围，安杰丽嘉原先已许配给鞑靼王，此时罗兰到来杀死了鞑靼王，罗兰把安杰丽嘉带回法国。其间又穿插着罗兰与摩尔人作战。此时利那尔多喝了魔水，却爱上了安杰丽嘉，引起他和罗兰的恶斗。查理大帝进行调解，并把安杰丽嘉托付给巴伐利亚公爵那摩。故事未完，但到此结束。

阿里奥斯托的作品是《热恋中的罗兰》的续篇。全诗共 46 章，1532 年出版。全诗写非洲的回教徒（Saracens）与基督教的战争。国王阿格拉曼特和西班牙的摩尔人联合包围了巴黎。安杰丽嘉从那摩公爵的监护下逃跑。罗兰为她的美貌所迷惑，忘记了自己的职责去追赶她。安杰丽嘉在逃跑中经历了许多惊险，忽然遇见摩尔青年麦多拉（Medora）。麦多拉在狩猎时受伤，安杰丽嘉给他护理，二人由相爱而结婚，在林中度着蜜月生活。罗兰追到，发现安杰丽嘉已经结婚，就陷入疯狂，而且疯狂得出奇。他赤身在野地里奔跑，见物即毁，最后回到了查理大帝营中，治好了疯病。在最后一次战役中，他杀死了阿格拉曼特。

这是主要情节，此外还穿插着两个爱情故事。

这是一部颇为典型的骑士传奇。结构松散，叙述动作简捷，内容则是战争和爱情。但除此之外："他的人物从天使到英雄，他的场景从契丹到苏格兰海外的赫布利底斯群岛。每节诗中都有些新鲜事物：极其详细的战斗场面，异国的法律、风俗、历史地理，风暴和和煦的阳光，高山、海岛、河流、妖怪，轶事，对话——无穷无尽。作者写人们吃的是什么，描写宫廷的建筑。简直象上帝创造的世界一样丰富多彩，象大自然一样取之不尽，用之不竭。阿里奥斯托若使你厌倦，你一定对世界感到厌倦了。"[1]

博亚尔多的作品赞美骑士的爱情和战绩，故事节奏变化快，反映出一种"狂欢节的欢乐"。[2] 而阿里奥斯托是公认为一位推崇理性的诗人，甚至把他和玛基维里相提并论。[3] 罗兰（即奥尔兰多）因为恋人安杰丽嘉和摩尔王子结了婚，而发疯，疯得很厉害。后来另一位骑士阿斯托尔佛飞往月球，取回装有罗兰理性的瓶子，让罗兰从瓶口吸入理性，罗兰恢复正常。恢复理性以后，他又建功立业。

罗兰虽然由于骑士的荣誉感和理性而放弃了爱情，但没有哪个诗人写人文主义者所歌颂的爱情写得这样具有破坏性的。爱情的力量是伟大的，受了损害的爱情的破坏力也是可怕的。其破坏力之大和可怕，令人吃惊。诗人用极其高妙的比喻描写罗兰变疯的过程，罗兰心中的悲痛就象细口瓶里灌满的水，瓶子颠倒过来，水都想涌出来，却被瓶口障住。一旦疯狂发作，他便拔刀乱砍，树木、岩石、羊群、牧人都不能幸免。他把大树连根拔起，投进溪流，搅起泥沙。他脱去盔甲，衣服，赤身裸体，到处骚扰，完全象个野人。[4]

---

[1] 参看 C. S. 路易斯：《爱的寓言》，俄克拉何马大学出版社，1938 年版，第 301 页。
[2] 同上书，第 300 页。
[3] W. L. 雷恩威克：《埃德蒙·斯宾塞》，伦敦，1933 年版，第 42 页。
[4] 《疯狂的罗兰》，约翰·胡勒译，1783 年版。

诗人感叹道（第24章）："谁失足陷进爱神的陷阱，一定要设法逃跑，不要让自己的翅膀缠在网里。"因为爱情是"毁灭性的火焰"。

罗兰在疯狂中捉住一个牧羊人，把牧羊人的头从肩上拧了下来，"就象一个农家人从树茎上或嫩枝上掐一朵花似的那样轻松"。接着他拎起死人的腿，当棍棒，去打其他的牧羊人。他又打死了两个，躺倒在地，恐怕要等到世界末日才能起来了。其他的人都纷纷逃散。有的躲到屋顶，从远处看他把农田扰得天翻地覆。村民们敲钟把大家集合起来，操起棍棒，成千的人从山上下来，成千的人从山谷里上来，来对付罗兰一个人。罗兰把他们杀退。他饿了，就杀野兽充饥。全诗的标题——《疯狂的罗兰》就说明诗人主旨之一就是要通过写失去爱情而产生的破坏，烘托出爱的力量。一般说，骑士得不到爱情就悲叹伤心，绝不发疯。这种狂热只有在早期文艺复兴才可能。就如拉伯雷，为了解放人的本能，就摧枯拉朽。但到了后期，如《唐吉诃德》（25章），桑丘就嘲笑吉诃德想学罗兰的疯狂，但缺乏理由。吉诃德回答说，发疯的奥妙就在于无缘无故。在《仲夏夜之梦》中公爵特修斯（Theseus）一口气把"疯子、情人和诗人"说在一起，不无嘲讽和可笑之感（虽然这句话给后来的文艺理论家提供了创作的依据）。奥赛罗也有类似罗兰的疯狂，但这里爱情已被扭曲，疯狂也未被理性纠正，正好说明早期和后期的区别，后期对理性已失去信心！

《疯狂的罗兰》还提出一些正面的概念，如文艺复兴时期的荣誉观，人际关系要用信义维系，信义女神（fides）穿的是洁白的衣服，[1] 染上污点立刻显现，不论当众或私下与一个人立约，诺言一出，永远有效。而到了福斯塔夫，荣誉就一钱不值了。

---

[1] 《疯狂的罗兰》，赞美苏格兰骑士泽尔比诺的话，参看贺拉斯诗句：洁白难得的信义衣着褴褛。

我们再看《巨人传》。如果说罗兰的疯狂只是他一生中的一个阶段，它的破坏性也是局部的，那么拉伯雷（Rabelais，1483—1553）的破坏性则可以说是贯彻始终的。

我觉得《巨人传》有最主要的两点：一是"干你爱干的事"。第一部中，国王葛朗古杰（Grandgousier）和他的儿子高干大（Gargantua）在打败毕可肖（Picrochole）国王之后犒赏立过战功的修士约翰，给他建立一座修道院叫德廉美（Thélème）。修道院的院规仅此一条。他象征个人的绝对自由，个性的绝对解放。从这部作品似乎可以看到，这种绝对自由与仁慈宽容观念有联系。在战胜毕可肖之后，高干大有一篇长篇演说，歌颂他那王朝历来对战败的敌人宽大，与天主教君主不同。对自己的部下，他也给以慷慨的犒赏。修士约翰也是在这慷慨的精神鼓舞下要求建立这修道院的。

从绝对自由的要求出发，才对举凡他认为阻碍人性发展的不合理的东西，如教会、法律等等表示极大的不敬，予以鞭挞。

其次一点，我觉得可以称为"生殖崇拜"，画龙点睛地表现在最后神瓶的神谕"喝"这个字。巴汝奇（Parurge）在解释"喝"字时说，以酒神的名义让我们喝吧。所以"喝"并非如一般所说是饮知识之泉，而是象征酒神精神。巴汝奇接着说，喝了之后就能刺激生殖，"使我充满人性"。接下去他就谈他长期不得解决的结婚问题。有的批评家也指出这是对人的旺盛的生命力的歌颂，一反中古对人体的蔑视，歌颂人体。[1]

我觉得就是这个对"生"的崇拜使他的作品如此生机勃勃，朝气蓬勃，而对腐朽的世界能够横扫一空。这是晚期作家所少有的。

---

[1] E. 奥尔巴赫：《模仿》（*Mimesis*），特拉斯克译，普林斯顿大学出版社，1974年版，第276页。

人的形体的巨大，只是这种精神的外化。

有的批评家认为他有村夫气质，也就是他非常贴近泥土，不怕说脏话。但同时他又是个大学者，所以他的作品里充满了百科全书式的知识。嬉笑怒骂，无往不适。

人文主义者崇尚理性，拉伯雷在他的讽刺中也表现了此点，如对经院教育的讽刺。（用手势、表情，代替语言，来进行辩论，以说明经院哲学之晦涩，不可理解。）而把理性或理智推到极端，并应用于政治，加以理论化的应是玛基维里（Nicolo Machiavelli, 1469—1527）。他的头脑冷静到了冷酷的程度。他感兴趣的问题是统治术。为取得统治，可以不择手段，可以不顾宗教教条或伦理准则。他说用罪恶的手段，如杀戮国人同胞，欺骗朋友，不信，不仁，来夺得国柄，固然算不得光荣，但一个篡权的暴君须要冒险，须要很大勇气，须要忍受艰苦，克服困难，要有恢宏的志气。可见他不是一味用感情或道德来谴责或咒骂篡权者，而是在必须夺权的前提下，做冷静的、两方面的分析。他又进一步分析为什么有的篡权者能长治久安，有的则朝不保夕，原因在于他施威（cruelta）是否得当。[1] 再如他论仁政和苛政[2]，也不是认为仁政就是一味的好，苛政就是无条件的坏。战争也无所谓正义或非正义，只要对国家有利。玛基维里这种思想是意大利政治生活的反映和总结。外国势力的入侵，内部教皇与各邦的明争暗夺，他自己卷入进去，险遭不测。在那样一种情况下，要求得安定，在他看来只有靠权术。这种环境甚至影响到他的散文风格，据说他写的每一个字以及字的地位都是经过权衡才选定的。玛基维里的理论非常接近资本主义精神，但人文主义者无法接受，从而把他的某些论点夸大、歪曲，使

---

[1] 《王子，人人》，1928，第8章。
[2] 同上书，第17章。

玛基维里在人们心目中，在文学作品中，成为一个恶棍。

理性或合理性本来是一个伸缩性很大的概念，因人而异，因人的社会地位而异。我们上面谈到的理性都是社会上层人士的理性。我们现在来看看社会下层的理性。

《十日谈》（1348—1353）的作者薄迦丘是个商人家庭出身、出入上层的大学者，与《十日谈》性质相似的《七日谈》（*Heptameron*，1558）的"作者"玛格丽特是法国国王法朗索瓦一世的姐姐。虽然他们都属社会上层，但这两部作品却都带有浓厚的市井情调，其来源是中古民间故事的传说。他们讽刺的对象多半是僧侣、贵族、各式各样的骗子。故事内容多半涉及诈骗、通奸、报复、谋杀、强奸，甚至悲剧，穿插着冒险场景、奇遇、巧合、打诨以至暴力。从气氛来讲，这些故事多半是喜剧性的。也就是从某种"清醒的头脑"来看出某些作为的可笑。它们歌颂的是机智。机智（wit）正是理智的一种运用方式或运行方式。例如《七日谈》里有一个故事讲一个厨子给主人烤了一只鹤，他偷吃了一条腿，主人责问他，他带主人到池边看到寒风中的鹤都是单腿独立的。不少故事都象报纸上的社会新闻。据近人考证，《七日谈》中七十个故事，其中有二十个故事是真事[1]。这些故事讽刺的动机是道德的动机。这一点在《七日谈》中尤为显著。这种讽刺是温和的，娱乐性强，破坏性并不太大。

破坏性比较大的，在早期应算《塞列斯蒂娜》（*Lacelestina*，1499，1502）和后来的《小癞子》（1553）。

《塞列斯蒂娜》的作者罗哈斯（Rojas）生于1465年，犹太人，后来改信天主教。这部作品第一次出版于1499年，十六幕，1502

---

[1] 《七日谈》，企鹅丛书，1984年版，第11页。

年版增成二十一幕。每幕前有简单的情节说明（颇似中国小说每回前的诗词，说明本回情节），每幕都是两三个人物的对话（也象元杂剧，不同者杂剧有曲）。随着一幕幕的进展推动故事。

这部悲喜剧写富家子卡利斯托（Calisto）爱上了一个叫梅利贝娅（Melibea）的女子，经塞列斯蒂娜的撮合，成其好事。塞列斯蒂娜是个所谓"拉皮条"的女人。剧情发展到后来，塞列斯蒂娜的两个仆人向她索取好处，双方争吵，两个仆人把她杀死，仆人自己也被正法。一对情侣在幽会时，卡利斯托听到墙外有人争吵，登梯越墙时摔死，梅利贝娅也堕楼殉情。

这出戏在序中开宗明义引了希腊哲学家赫拉克里特（Heraclitus）的一句话："一切起源于讼。"（Omnia secundum litem fiunt）所谓"讼"（lis）就是对立。（有对立斗争才有运动变化。）序中歌颂强力，强力引起冲突，打破常规。"一旦常规打破，那便是冲突"。大自然、动物界莫不如此。有时小能胜大，如老鼠可以胜大象，小鱼能阻止大船前进。这些话正体现了全书的主旨，即用粗鄙的、甚至下流的、来自社会底层的"爱情观"、人生观来破坏"高尚的"爱情观、人生观；把堕入情网看成是一种病，而把粗鄙看成是健康。虽然有的评论家认为此书作者的善恶观念十分明确[1]，但遮盖不住"恶"的勃勃生气。

这一对立原则体现在情节的强烈对比之中。最主要的对比就是作者把才子佳人、骑士美人的爱情故事降格放在流氓社会里。这当然是对爱情的一种嘲讽，因为爱情竟须要一个女流氓、一个宗教上和道德上的"罪人"来撮成！在剧中除了这一对情人外，还有塞列斯蒂娜的仆人帕尔梅诺（Parmeno）和女子阿列乌莎（Areusa）的

---

[1] 见《模仿》，第358页。

苟合，写得颇为露骨，正好又与"高贵"的爱形成对照。一方面是流氓们的冷酷无情，一方面是一对情人的脉脉含情，而前者在精神上战胜了后者。理想化的爱情被践踏得体无完肤。一方面是神圣的，另一方面是亵渎神圣的；一方面嘴里仁义道德，另一方面行为上又是男盗女娼；嘴里说是为对方好，实际上为自己，并陷害对方。两种不同的标准的对立，传统的道德标准和反传统的道德标准的对立，贯穿全书，而反传统的流氓哲学占了主导地位。因此，在剧中，流氓比"正派人"占更重要的地位。塞列斯蒂娜"毁了五千多个处女，又被她们变回成处女"。对她来说，干坏事是一种乐趣，"就象外科医生见了头破血流的人就高兴一样"。她狡猾，故意吊人胃口，"等待磨人心，到他失望时，什么话都听得进。"她拉皮条，看病，制药。对她来说，"除了欺骗是真的，其他都是假的"。她没有价值观念，不保卫任何价值。她没有任何幻想。有幻想，就表明世界还可改善，无幻想实即虚无主义，砸烂一切制度。这种流氓哲学实际上是一种求生哲学，对社会上一切不合理现象的反抗。破坏、讲求实际利益，就是流氓所信奉的"理"。

剧中的情绪也是大起大落，爱在顷刻间就变成恨，忧伤顷刻间又变成快乐。真和假也形成鲜明对照。梅利贝娅在跳楼前一段告别辞，非常真挚，和全书的粗俚又成对比。这种"强烈度"也表现在语言的气势的十分狂放上，例如塞列斯蒂娜对梅利贝娅诉说老年之苦："小姐，有谁跟您说过老人的苦处吗？什么手脚不灵便、疲乏、操心、生病、冷、热、不顺心、肝火旺、爱伤心、一堆堆的皱纹、头发脱了、血色没了、耳聋、眼花、嘴瘪、牙也掉了、力气没了、走路磕磕绊绊、吃饭慢慢腾腾……"活象拉伯雷，是一种精力旺盛的表现。

此书最后虽然表示有警世规劝之意，那不过是一种搪塞，抵不住全书的肆无忌惮。我们不能不说《塞列斯蒂娜》是人文主义入世思想、追求"合理"的理想主义与下层社会结合的产物。有破坏性，无建设性，最后还得求助于旧的道德规范。

和《塞列斯蒂娜》相比，《小癞子》（1553，这一年拉伯雷逝世）就没有那么泼辣。他虽然是社会的对立面，但最后自己也成为这社会的一员。他虽然受欺侮，但他靠自己的机智不仅生存下来，而且取得成功，情调是乐观的。

五十年代以后，欧洲文坛没有出过重要作家，直到七十年代才出现卡蒙斯（Camões，1524？—1580）和塔索（Tasso，1544—1595）。这两位诗人虽都具有新兴民族意识，但卡蒙斯的《卢苏斯的子孙》一译《卢希塔尼亚人之歌》（Os Lusiadas，1570）是一首歌颂葡萄牙帝国的维吉尔式的史诗，写葡萄牙航海家伽玛受国王埃曼纽尔之命于1497年出发，绕道好望角到达印度卡利库特，1499年回到葡萄牙。象维吉尔的史诗那样，《卢希塔尼亚人之歌》也穿插了天神对这次远征的干预、海上的风暴、战斗等史诗因素。卡蒙斯本人到过印度的戈阿和中国的澳门，前后共十六年。他在戈阿参加过两次军事行动。也在这时期，他写了《卢希塔尼亚人之歌》。葡萄牙人认为这是他们的民族史诗。塔索的《被解放的耶路撒冷》（Gerusalemme Liberata，1576，1581，1593）则很不相同。他虽借十字军的故事也想唤起意大利的民族意识，但这首诗内容上的矛盾，发表后所受到的挫折和他坎坷的一生一样，都说明欧洲文学已进入了另一个历史阶段。

这首叙事诗共20章，主要线索是1095年第一次十字军东征，以戈德弗卢瓦（Godefroi de Bouillon）为统帅的基督教国军队，从回教徒手中夺回耶路撒冷。其中穿插着几个爱情故事。如耶路撒冷城中居住的基督徒索弗洛尼娅（Sophronia）和她的情侣俄林多

（Olindo）的故事。耶路撒冷回王阿拉丁因发现他所掠夺的圣母玛利亚的像被偷，要屠杀全城基督徒，索弗洛尼娅自愿承担责任，俄林多则说是他干的。二人一同被判火刑，但得救。

又如协助回教徒的亚马逊女将科罗林达（Clorinda）和诺曼的基督教骑士坦克列德（Tancred）的爱情。但在一次战斗中坦克列德以为她是一般回教女将，把她杀死，死前给她施了洗礼。但当他发现是科罗林达，悲痛得想要自杀。

又如大马士革王的侄女阿尔米达（Armida）施魔术把基督教骑士引诱到她的魔园。埃斯特（Este）族的王子里那尔多（Rinaldo）救出诸骑士，但自己却爱上了阿尔米达，两人过着甜蜜的生活。后来里那尔多当然被召回参战，在攻克耶路撒冷时起了主要作用。

这部作品问世以后，受到教会的强烈攻击，指责作者把十字军东征这样一件"动机神圣"的事业，用魔幻法术，世俗情欲，加以亵渎。作者被迫作了多次修改。但这诗也受到许多人的称赞和喜爱，不胫而走，盗印版甚多。

从诗人致友人的信中可以看出诗人是热衷于感官享受的。人家批评他的诗写纵欲的场面太多，他认为这些段落是他诗中最美的。他早年热爱但丁和彼特拉克的诗，可见他受过人文主义的熏陶。但是天主教会和耶稣会的强大压力，使他不能发展这方面的倾向，而感到压抑。他的生活道路坎坷不平，他主要依附的恩主埃斯特家族的阿尔芳索到后来也对他厌恶。他爱恩主的妹妹（诗中索弗洛尼娅和俄林多据说就是自传性的），但受到恩主的阻挠。凡此种种促成他的精神不正常，总疑心有人要谋害他，有鬼在追他。一次他竟刺杀了恩主妹妹的仆人。他是时代的产物——在宗教改革和反改革的时代，天主教旧势力加倍抑制人文主义，使他郁郁不伸，成为一个悲剧人物。他的作品可以代表那时的精神危机，表现为一种不安定的感觉。进攻的主帅戈德弗卢瓦怕埃及王来援助耶路撒冷回王阿拉丁，而阿拉丁则既怕当前的外敌，又怕他统治的基督教老百姓。例如全诗第一章就写围攻耶路撒冷的十字军主帅一直担心埃及会派军队来帮助耶城的回王阿拉丁："在戈德弗卢瓦心里有一种预见，使他担心，但他小心翼翼，对谁也不说"，"因为他得到确切的消息，说埃及国王已经出发了"。城里的阿拉丁王："这位名叫阿拉丁的君王，最近通过罪恶的手段，登上了王位，一直是忧心忡忡"，"旧罪之上，又添新的疑虑，他很怕他的臣民，也很怕他的敌人"。

第三章当十字军从海上远远望到巴勒斯坦："一开始那种纯粹的欢乐，使他们精神振奋的欢乐，很快就被一种新的感受、一种深刻的抑郁所代替。"这无疑是给全诗定了基调。这种情调在早期作品里是很难遇到的。其次，此诗着力写价值的混淆，如混淆生与死，爱与恨，欺骗与光荣，冷与热。把现实与幻想混为一谈。这正是修辞学上的"矛盾拼合法"（oxymoron）。例如第二章，索弗洛尼娅和俄林多背对背被缚在柱上准备受火刑时，俄林多说："爱情的火焰和我们的厄运给我们准备的火焰是大不一样的。人们把我们分开得太久了，太久了，现在他们用这残酷的方法，让我们在绝望中结合。但我们应当感到安慰，因为他们用这种奇特的方法判我们去死，却使我能分享你的痛苦，虽然命运注定不能分享你的甜蜜……"

又如同一章写索弗洛尼娅挺身而出，要拯救全城的基督徒时，诗人写道："她既羞涩，又勇敢，既勇敢，又稳重，考虑怎样才能救她的同胞。勇气鼓舞她，女孩儿的惊慌又压制她，使她不往那里去想……"她表面装得镇静，心里发慌。诗人写道："啊，光荣的虚假，美丽的欺骗！真理之光可能比你的美还光彩夺目吗？"此外，它还着力写道德与情欲的矛盾。文学是寓教于乐，但在塔索看来，"乐"是一种"香膏"，一种"镇定药"、"迷魂汤"，"喝了迷魂汤，迷了魂，才能得生"。[1] 他以浓彩着力渲染眼泪、恐怖心理、幻视、幻听。这与阿里奥斯托之突出理性截然相反。这些都是巴罗克风格的特点。

在《疯狂的罗兰》中，安杰丽嘉见麦多拉负伤，诗人只轻轻一点："她倾听他抖抖颤颤地讲他受伤的情景，心里感到一阵奇怪的怜悯"，然后就立刻行动，为他去采药敷伤。类似的情况到了塔索的笔下，就大肆渲染。如第四章大马士革王派侄女阿尔米达去引诱基督教徒，被戈德弗卢瓦所拒绝，她装哭。诗人的夸张描写固然有揭发她虚伪的用意，但他不肯放弃这一机会，来渲染一下哪怕是假意的悲哀："她的泪象暑天的密雨，象太阳的金光斜照下的雨点那样明亮，象颗颗明珠，象银色的水晶，象印度矿脉里挖出来的闪光的宝石。她的脸面，被这活生生的阵雨洒过，（雨点沿着她的衣服流下，停留在裙边上。）显得象雪白而又朱红的花朵，湿润得象沾了五月的露水，当浪漫的春天在绿叶的荫影下低语着，把幽闭的心胸坦露给含情脉脉的春风……""明亮的泪珠象夜空稠密的星，落在她美丽的脸上和喘息着的胸前，产生出火一样的威力，谁看见都会在心里暗暗燃起一团火。"正如布克哈特所说[2]，阿里奥斯托强调行动，不强调人物，他的叙述是从一个行动到另一个行动。塔索则主要描写人物，描写心理。足见事隔半个世纪，人们的思想方式已大不相同。早期重行动，晚期重心理。早期破坏性强，晚期变得哀婉了。

正当塔索发表《耶诗》的时候，蒙田（Montaigne，1533—1592）发表了《论文集》（1580，1588）。蒙田可以说是代表文艺复

---

[1] 《被解放的耶路撒冷》（*Jerusalem Delivered*），J. H. 威芬译，1854，第1章，第3节。

[2] 雅克·布克哈特：《意大利文艺复兴时期的文明》，伦敦，1945年版，第197—199页。

兴后期"时代精神"的哲学家。蒙田虽然没有完全否定人，但他对人做了重新估价。他现身说法，分析自己，也就是对"人"进行分析。他发现人不是英雄，人的智力有限（Qne sais je？"我知道什么？"），人在宇宙中的地位并不是高于一切的。他认为世界是在不断的摆动之中，他要谛视的对象老在流动，模糊不定，就象喝醉了一样。他认为一切都是相对的，"我拿猫当玩物，安知猫不更把我当玩物？"一个教派视为善的，另一教派视为恶。他由怀疑[1]、忧郁、空虚感而至于悲观，把人生看做梦，梦即醒，醒即梦；人一生不断在做的事就是建造死的厅堂；哲学就是学习怎样去死的学问。

进入十七世纪，欧洲文坛形势又进一步起了变化，进入颓废期。意大利诗人玛里诺（Marino，1569—1625）的诗华丽雕琢，意在惊人而不在感人。西班牙的贡戈拉（Gongora，1561—1627）的诗，色彩强烈，讲求悦耳动听，玩弄技巧，以至"工具毁灭了用工具的人"。[2] 在法国诗坛，贵族沙龙的"文雅派"（les précieuses）投合贵族趣味。在英国就出现了所谓"玄学派"诗歌。这种诗歌风格潮流，所谓巴罗克，风靡全欧诗坛。

在戏剧和小说领域，维加（Lope ole Vega，1562—1635）虽可称为平民作家，他的剧作有正面价值观，如维护荣誉、爱情、正义，结局往往皆大欢喜。他为人单纯、爱享乐，但也为宗教问题而苦恼，曾出家以减轻失恋的痛苦，他的《圣诗》（Rimas sacras）就记载他的宗教信仰危机。他虽然和贡戈拉结仇，但他的作品里也有巴罗克风格的苗头。他写了一千七百部剧本（留存 470 部），这本身就是一种疯狂，一种求解脱的办法。

西班牙作家克维多（Quevedo，1580—1645）的小说《骗子传》

---

[1] philosopher cest douter 做哲学思考就是怀疑。
[2] J. M. 拜亨：《西方文学史》，企鹅丛书，1956 年版，第 164 页。

（*La Vida delbuscón*）写于 1604 年，1626 年发表，虽然属于《小癞子》一类，但他对人物的描写并不那样轻松有趣，而是充满了厌恶，既荒诞又带有悲剧性，所用的语言也十分雕琢。他的另一部小说《梦》（*Los Sueños*）写于 1607 年，1627 年发表，写作者梦见末日审判，着力描写人物（如律师、理发师、裁缝、法官、诗人、剧作家、贵妇人等）所受的残酷刑罚，"既残忍又可笑，既狂热又怪诞，出自一个疯狂孤独、看着自己国家衰落而无能为力的人的手笔"，"克维多是一个感情炽烈的人文主义者，但晚生了一个世纪。"[1]

蒂尔索·德·莫利纳（Tirso de Molina，1571—1648）的剧本《塞维尔的恶作剧者》（*Burlador de Sevilla*，1630 年以前作）中主角唐璜，追逐享乐，玩弄女性，是文艺复兴时期理想的贵族青年的蜕化变质和堕落，他知道什么是道德，什么不道德，但觉得总有时间改邪归正[2]。最后被他杀害的一个贵族的石像把他交给了魔鬼。他一方面自私，为所欲为，一方面又抱着宿命论的态度生活。

十七世纪初欧洲最伟大的作品中《唐吉诃德》应算一部。这部作品表面上是批判骑士文学，同时也描绘、揭露了社会风习，但中心人物吉诃德的主要特点是他真假不分，完全生活在幻觉之中，完全失去了理性。罗兰的理性得到恢复而建功立业，吉诃德一旦恢复了理性，生命也就中止。人文主义者是要继承骑士的一些美德的——扶贫济弱、主持正义、勇气、建立理想社会，这些理想已成了嘲笑的对象。我们之所以爱吉诃德，（尽管也认为他不识时务，）就是因为他天真地维护这些理想。但到了文艺复兴末期，仅靠一种过时的热忱要去实现理想已不可能了。

文艺复兴最低的低潮恐怕应由卡尔德隆（Calderón，1600—

---

[1] J. M. 拜亨：《西方文学》，企鹅丛书，第 166—167 页。
[2] 同上书，第 157 页。

1681）的剧作《人生是梦》（*La Vidaes sueño*，1635）来代表了。《人生是梦》写波兰王巴希尔（Basil）生了一个儿子塞吉斯蒙多（Segismodo），[1] 王后生前梦见恶兆，生子后就死了。巴希尔以为这是命运降祸于他，因此把儿子幽禁在荒山山洞里，由老人克罗塔尔多监护教育。巴希尔为了试探他能否做国王，让克罗塔尔多把他麻醉了送进宫来。塞吉斯蒙多醒来，表现粗暴，一怒之下把一个仆人投入海里，又伤了他的老监护人。于是他又被幽禁起来，但最后证明他是位好君主。

　　这出戏提出两个问题。一个是人要违抗命运是不可能的。因为王子高贵的天性中就有做君主的本能，又受到监护老人的启发。所以巴希尔囚禁他是错会天意。

　　二，主要的问题还是人生是梦。作者巧妙地用麻醉术，使王子不辨真假。在他再次被囚禁时说出下面一段话来："在这奇怪的世界里，生活就是做梦。经验告诉我们，每个人都以为他是这样生活着，其实他是在做梦，直到他梦醒。国王梦见他在做国王，在幻觉中生活、统治、耀武扬威。他所得到的一切赞美都是借来的，都写在风中，死亡又把他变成灰尘，悲惨的命运啊！……人生是什么？是疯狂、幻象、影子、昏迷、虚构。最好的事也微不足道，人生不过是一场梦，而梦也不过就是梦。"

　　这出戏当然并非彻底消极。克罗塔尔多曾对王子说："我警告你，即使你在做梦，试着做点好事也不会吃亏的。"可见作者是肯定善的，但这话似乎是说："你就装着做些好事吧，假戏真做吧。"结果还是不相信现实世界能有善。在早些时候，当王子要发怒时，老人又曾说过："你即便当了王，也不应如此残暴，因为这也许仅

---

[1] 意为"虚幻的世界"。

仅是场梦。"这话也是同一意思。

四

我们现在来看看莎士比亚之前和稍后的英国"繁荣"的剧坛的情况和一些有代表性的作家的作品。我们记得英国剧坛的繁荣期，其实已经是文艺复兴的衰落期了。这一点很重要。文艺复兴作为一个文化运动已趋衰落，而戏剧和文学却非常繁荣。这一现象很值得注意。我们先谈谈戏剧的一般情况。我打算分喜剧和悲剧来谈，历史剧严格说不能算一个类型，它涉及题材，不涉及戏剧的本质。历史剧一般说来几乎都是悲剧，小部分是喜剧，或悲剧中带有喜剧成分。

根据艾略特，文艺复兴时期英国的喜剧似乎可以分成四种：李利（Lyly）式的喜剧；莎士比亚、波芒和弗莱彻（Beaumont and Fletcher）式的喜剧；密德尔顿（Middleton）式的喜剧；本·琼生（Bem Jonson）和马辛哲（Massinger）式的喜剧。这个分类，显然是从喜剧的性质着眼，可以参考。

所谓李利式的喜剧，如李利的《亚历山大和坎帕斯庞》（*Alesauder and Campaspe*）写马其顿王把他心爱的女俘让给了画家阿佩列斯（Apelles），即所谓"高尚的喜剧"（high comedy）。莎士比亚式的喜剧可以称为"浪漫喜剧"，富于田园诗歌的色彩。密德尔顿式的喜剧和戴克（Dekker）式的喜剧一样都是写伦敦下层生活，带有风俗画的性质。本·琼生这一类喜剧则具有讽刺性。

这几类喜剧中，大都有两面或两个层次：表面的喜剧人物和情节和后面的没有表现出来的东西。李利式的喜剧歌颂的是宽宏大量和自我克制，背后是对自私的批判。浪漫喜剧后面是各种各样的焦虑。浪漫喜剧就是为医治各种各样的焦虑的。"假意开玩笑可以掩饰引起不安的事。"此话是《西班牙悲剧》中（三幕十场）一个人物说的话，其实道出了喜剧的底蕴。又如 1632 年出的一部传奇《威克菲尔德的护畜人》（存牛津图书馆），有一个很长的标题，其中称这部喜剧性的故事有这样的话："它是一副丸药，在垂头丧气的时代，能清除忧郁。"又如《驯悍记》序幕第二场（131 行以下）说："大人，您的演员听说您康复了，特来为您演一出逗乐的喜剧，您的医生也认为过分忧愁使您的血脉凝固，忧郁会引起疯病，因此他们认为看一出戏，心里快活一番，可以消除千种灾害，延年益寿，对您有好处。"这些都是从心理学角度和社会功能角度，解释喜剧的作用，同时也道出了喜剧的言外之意。从这点讲，喜剧和悲剧不过是一个钱币的两面，因为喜剧的反面是一种焦虑、忧郁、失望等等。

因此浪漫喜剧带有极大的空想性和虚幻性。如果我们再以《驯悍记》为例，此剧的大框架是做梦。酒醉的斯赖被众人弄醒，强叫他把假的看成是真的，使他自己也分辨不清是梦是醒。"我是个老爷吗？我有这样一位太太？我是在做梦，还是刚从梦中醒来？我现在没有睡觉啊，我看得见，我听得见，我在说话，我闻到香味，我摸到柔软的东西。我发誓我真是位老爷呢，不是什么补锅匠，也不是克利斯朵夫·斯赖。"这表明感觉之不可靠，而我们知道，感觉却是认识世界的起点，是认识世界的渠道。

所谓密德尔顿式的喜剧则指描写市民生活的喜剧。密德尔顿不止写过市民喜剧，不过他的市民喜剧有一定代表性。如他和戴克合作写的《嚎叫的姑娘》（*The Roaring Girl*, or *Moll Cut-purse*, 1611）写一个慷慨善良的女小偷，如何帮助一对青年结成良缘。宣扬市民道德。这类喜剧大量描写伦敦下层市民生活，也算是一种现实主义。但是大多美化现实，如戴克的《鞋匠的假日》（*The Shoemaker's Holiday*），虽然生活细节很真实，但主要情节则给人一种虚假感。

所谓琼生式的喜剧则是带有批判性的。他的批判是用一种夸张手法，用塞内加的话说，"一切夸张被扩展之后便可通过谎言达到真理"（引自《剑桥英国文学史》卷4，333页）。因而他给喜剧带来了荒诞的因素。情节荒诞，人物也荒诞，说明早期的崇高理想和英雄主义已荡然无存。由此并形成一种理论——幽默论或称气质论（参看下面论琼生一段）。

马辛哲的喜剧也是批判某些不道德的行为的，但带有阴沉色彩，接近悲剧。如《老债新还法》（*A New Way to Pay Old Debts*）中的主人公贪财贪势又残酷，把侄儿的财产夺到手，就把他赶出他的家门，又强迫自己的女儿嫁给贵族。最后他节节失败，入了疯人院。他有一句名言："我最爱看孤儿寡妇受我欺凌而落泪。"实际上这类人物和马娄笔下的马尔他岛的犹太人不相上下，而成为悲剧人物了。这也说明，虚假的喜剧已经写不下去了。

以上一些特点其实已经是巴罗克风格了。

我们再看看悲剧。从内容来讲，这时期的悲剧写的都是暴力、流血、复仇和背叛。它所反映的情绪从忧郁到无法解脱的悲观，从恐惧到沮丧到疯狂，从对潜在的危险的意识到疑虑，总之是不正常、不健康的情绪。从作者的态度来看，一般都是一种无可奈何的同情与怜悯或绝望的心情；如《西班牙悲剧》中（Iiii）一个人物所说："一个人已躺在地上了，也就不会再沉沦了。"而悲剧的解决办法只有一条——死亡。有时作者把人间的悲剧看作一种幻象，一种不真实，一种梦，真即是假，假即是真，以摆脱无可奈何的心情。再举《西班牙悲剧》中的一个例子，如该剧一开始，在战场上被杀死的安德烈的鬼魂就说复仇女神把他从牛角门领出去。《奥德赛》、

《埃涅阿斯纪》都有这说法。在梦中一个人如梦见自己走出象牙门，则梦不会实现，如走出牛角门，梦就会实现。复仇只能在梦中实现。有时，作者又采取一种夸张、粗鄙、甚至恐怖、诉诸感官的策略，来发泄愤懑。他们在技巧上最爱用修辞学里的"正反拼合法"（oxymoron），不仅表现在辞句上，如把生与死、爱与恨、征服与被征服、说话与不说话等等，都等同起来，生即是死，爱即是恨，征服即是被征服；而且在戏剧结构上亦复如此。我们常常为莎氏悲剧中的喜剧场面做种种解释，我想这正是"正反拼合法"在戏剧结构上的表现。而它的心理基础就是人把握不住现实的真实性。悲剧中的这些现象，又都是巴罗克风格的表现。

另外，悲剧基本上都表现出作者的一种无可奈何的心情。这无可奈何的心情，发展下去有两条归宿，一条就是发疯，另一条就是求解脱，于是就在古代希腊罗马哲学中找到了解脱之途，那便是斯多噶哲学。这一点艾略特早已看出，[1] 莎士比亚的悲剧里有，其他剧作家也有，例如恰普曼。再发展下去就变成冷酷、麻木不仁，以至于用艺术家的眼光看待犯罪行为，杀人成为一种艺术。

我们下面就来看看英国剧坛的具体情况。

六十年代初上演的《戈伯德克》（Goboduc），作者诺顿（Thonias Norton）和萨克维尔（Thomas Sackville）写不列颠王戈伯德克生前将国土分给两个儿子，长子不服，要害死弟弟，弟弟为自卫把哥哥杀死。母亲为长子复仇，杀死了次子。民众反对这种暴行，兴师问罪，杀死了国王和王后。国内的贵族之间又发动了内战，死亡累累，国土长期变成一片废墟。这出戏是演给伊利莎伯一世看的，等于告诫她王位继承问题不解决必然要引起纷争。足见这出戏早在

---

[1] 参看《莎士比亚评论汇编》、《莎士比亚和塞内加的苦修主义》。

六十年代就反映了朝野的一种忧虑心情，这种忧虑心情是持久的，例如斯宾塞的《仙后》绝大部分写成于动荡的爱尔兰，何尝不隐约地反映这种情绪，在第二卷（1590 年出版）第十章写英国历史一段就提到这段从杰弗里的《不列颠王朝史》引来的戈伯德克故事。即便在锡德尼的牧歌传奇《阿卡迪亚》（1590 年出版）里也掺杂着阴谋篡夺内讧的场景。

我们再看诗才不亚于莎士比亚的基德（Thomas Kyd）。他的《西班牙悲剧》（约写于八十年代后期，1589 年首演），故事情节并不重要，只提供个口实。它写西班牙王的侄儿罗伦佐反对妹妹贝尔印皮丽亚嫁给她所爱的西班牙大法官歇洛尼谟的儿子霍拉休，而要她嫁给被俘的葡萄牙总督的儿子巴尔萨札。罗伦佐和巴尔萨札把霍拉休刺死，老歇洛尼谟和贝尔印皮丽亚为了报仇杀死了两个仇人，最后自戕而死。从歇洛尼谟这个人物来看，他起初有些怀疑朝廷赏罚可能不公平（霍拉休和国王的侄儿在战场上俘虏了葡萄牙总督的儿子，首功应属霍拉休），后来在花园里看到自己儿子的尸体吊在树上，他悲恸万分，但在寻找凶手的问题上他很谨慎警惕，在设计报仇上考虑得很周全。后来他的夫人因悲痛而自杀，他才神经失常。在失常的情况下，他排演了戏中戏，完成了报仇计划。最后为了抗议逼供，他咬掉自己的舌头，自杀身死。

这是一出复仇剧，而复仇剧在当时十分流行。为什么要复仇？主要因为世界上没有公平可言。《西班牙悲剧》所描绘的世界充满了奸诈和险恶，一个人要生存必须处处小心，如履薄冰。疯或装疯都是恶势力造成的结果。疯狂和死亡是弱者的下场，根本没有恢复理性的希望。死亡虽然能结束弱者们的痛苦，但"他们的悲剧是无止境的"。

批评家都认为此剧是一出"夸张剧"（melodrama），有时荒诞可笑，但很受"低级"观众的欢迎，风行了十五年，原因是此剧，尤其是歇洛尼谟的"疯癫"能引起观众怜悯和恐惧。如第二幕第五场结束处，歇洛尼谟有一段颇长的拉丁文独白，表明他在发现儿子被害后痛不欲生，立意报仇的心情。多半的观众恐怕是听不懂的，增加神秘可怕的气氛。这出戏与希腊悲剧和近代戏剧比较，也许显得"夸张"、荒诞，例如用夸张的词藻表现悲痛（Ⅲ. iii.）（Ⅲ. Vii），但观众的反应强烈而持久（恐怕不限于"低级"观众），这一事实充分证明当时社会上普遍存在的一种情绪，基德的剧正好满足这种情绪，如疑虑、不安全的感觉的要求。

剧中对立物的混同，如欢乐与悲哀，生与死，爱与恨，征服与被征服，平静与不安，表面上是修辞（oxymoron），实际是现实生活的反映和人物，亦即作者矛盾心理的反映。这种现象在当时文学里非常普遍。莎士比亚的悲剧里处处可以见到基德的痕迹，有时甚至词句都有雷同影附之处。

这出戏还有一个值得注意的地方就是"戏中戏"，有时是哑剧，源出于中古道德剧，用来说明剧情。这里，它变成一种手段，来探测对方的心理反应，所谓"用间接求直接"，说明人物的狡黠。但为什么作者不用调查方法，求得人证、物证，来证明对方犯罪，而诉诸"假象"呢？这恐怕和作者对世界的看法不无关系。世界本来就是个大舞台，人的一切行动都是演戏，用演戏作为手段，"以假求'真'"，也是顺理成章的。

和莎士比亚同年出生的马娄在思想境界上是真正的文艺复兴的"巨人"，强烈追求个性解放，具有可怕的破坏性。但是他出生得晚了几十年，不仅他的作品中的人物，而且他本人也在不到三十岁的时候遭到毁灭。他常给我们一种错觉，他创造了一批叱咤风云，所向披靡的人物，颇有文艺复兴的朝气，但这些人的搏斗显得吃力，而且最终还是被命运或宗教所压倒。帖木儿追求权力，力竭而死；浮士德追求知识，以屈服于魔鬼而告终；马耳他的犹太人殉财；狄多殉情；爱德华二世则因滥用主权，放纵私欲（同性恋），导致毁灭。但当爱德华的毁灭是由一个比他更坏的人（Mortimer）促成的时候，马娄又象莎士比亚对待理查二世那样，对他表示同情！摩提墨毫无克制的政治野心最终未能得逞，他落得和麦克白一样的下场。

另一位"大学才子"，格林（Rohnt greene，1560？—1592），就是那骂莎士比亚为"暴发户乌鸦"，用才子们的"羽毛"打扮他自己的格林，也创造了几个帖木儿式的人物，如《阿拉贡王阿尔芳瑟斯》中的阿尔芳瑟斯（Alphousus），《疯狂的罗兰》（*Orlando Furioso*）中的罗兰，甚至象《伦敦的一面镜子和英格兰》（*A Looking-Glass for London and England*）中的尼尼微王拉斯尼（Rasni），和浮士德式的人物如培根僧士（Friar Bacon and Friar Bungayl），但是格林笔下的这类人物已失去其悲壮、不可一世的气概。阿尔芳瑟斯因为他父亲的王位被人篡夺，为父报仇，臣服各国，把各国国王的首级挂在他的伞角上，最后和他主要敌手土耳其王的女儿结婚，结束全剧，完全是一种"降格"（bathos），所以他自称此剧为"喜剧故事"（Comical History）。把格林的罗兰和阿里奥斯托的罗兰相比，格林笔下的罗兰不仅和安杰丽嘉结了婚，而且他的疯狂带有极大的诙谐打诨的味道。本来是悲怆庄严的情感化为笑料，从心理上讲表现的是一种无可奈何的解嘲。格林笔下的浮士德式人物比之马娄的浮士德实际在全剧中属于配角地位，更接近巫卜（相水晶球）、术师（斗法）。他造了一个铜头，希望它能吐出哲理，以便象马娄的浮士德那样能造一堵铜墙把英国保护起来，也失败了。他哀叹命运不允许凡人具有超凡的力量。谈到保卫国家这种爱国主义情绪，马娄有，格林有，莎士比亚也有（例如《理查二世》中的贡特的约翰），格林为了保卫国家，要么依靠法术，要么显得无能为力，只有感叹的份。

　　格林是个知识分子，受过很好的古典文学教育，他后期的剧作如《詹姆斯四世》技巧也比较成熟，但思想境界不高。他虽然感叹当代无人歌颂英雄，荷马、维吉尔俱往矣，他要写一个阿尔芳瑟斯，但可以说是失败的。他的哲学是小市民哲学，特别体现在他笔下的女性形象上。如《詹姆斯四世》中王后表达的安贫、诚实的生活理想，《阿尔芳瑟斯》中土耳其公主之温顺等。甚至象阿尔芳瑟斯的父亲也说"安静的生活胜于一个帝国"。（这正是喜剧所要表达的思想。）这种消极思想也常常形诸文字，如"逆潮流而进是白费力的"。恐怕这也可以部分地解释为什么在格林剧中（和其他同时代剧作家作品中）那样爱用魔术吧。

　　格林的戏剧不管取材于历史也好或意大利故事也好，骨子里都是市民剧，正如同时代剧作家切特尔（Chettle）所说，"他是国内唯一的喜剧家兼通俗作家（vulgarwriter）"，所谓"通俗"即指平民、市民。他宣扬的是市民道德，要维护正常的家庭关系，安贫、诚实。在厄运面前流露出感伤甚至宿命恨世情绪。他笔下的所谓英雄，华而不实，令人发笑（burlesque），严肃的场面有时变成打情骂俏。结尾往往变成"降格"（bathos）。剥去人物的帝王将相外衣，戏剧的核心是市民喜剧或市民悲剧。这是时代特征。从这角度看，莎士比亚的四大悲剧和其他悲剧，其核心都可以被认为是市民悲剧或家庭悲剧。《哈姆雷特》写的是弟杀兄、母改嫁；《李尔王》写分家产和父女矛盾；《奥赛罗》是妒夫，有所谓的第三者插手；《麦克白》写的是夫妻合谋杀死来家作客的恩主；《安东尼和克利奥帕特拉》写的是"狐狸精"，败坏了一个男子的前程；《特洛伊斯和克丽西达》则是女方另有所欢；《泰门》则写朋友无义。把格林和莎士比亚并列可以看出莎士比亚的市民性一面。但是莎士比亚化腐朽为神奇，我想是因为他的同情，善于设身处地，深入到人物内心世界，从而赋予这些情感以更广泛而深入的意义，使之成为"普遍人性"的表露。

在莎士比亚同时代的剧作家中，恰普曼（George Chādman，1559？—1634？）应算是政治意识最强的一个。他的强烈的激情可以和马娄相比。他的哲学在他的戏剧里也表现得最明显。他以当时的"近当代"欧洲历史和古代罗马历史写了一系列悲剧，其中最有代表性的应算《布西·当布瓦》（写于1598？）、《布西的复仇》（写于1610或1611）、《比隆公爵的阴谋和悲剧》（两出戏，1608年出版）和《凯撒和庞培》（1636出版）。在这五出戏里，他塑造了四个人物。

布西·当布瓦（1549—1579）是个冒险家，被法王亨利三世的御弟引进宫廷。这时是法国历史上最混乱的时期，代表天主教势力的吉斯公爵发动了圣巴托罗缪节日对新教徒的大屠杀（1572）。国王想利用新教的力量加强自己的地位以抵制吉斯对王朝的控制。在剧中，布西入朝以后与朝臣不和，在一次冲突中就杀死了三人。他也与吉斯不和。蒙苏利伯爵夫人塔米拉垂青于他，而御弟也爱这位夫人，御弟向伯爵揭发，伯爵用酷刑逼夫人写信召布西，布西来后被伯爵杀死。

比隆（1562—1602）是法国亨利四世朝的元帅，为人勇敢而凶残贪婪。他怨恨国王赏罚不公，阴谋篡国，事败见杀。在剧中，他两次背叛国王。第一次，他受到宽容；第二次他又搞阴谋，被处死。

布西和比隆都被写成是性格暴烈的英雄式的人物，练达物情，傲慢而凶残。有的批评家认为恰普曼翻译过荷马，荷马两部史诗，一部写英雄的怒，一部写有智慧的人。布西和比隆就是"怒"型的英雄性格。但由于他们不能自我克制，在那充满政治矛盾和道德败坏的环境里，走向了死亡。

在这两出戏之后，恰普曼又写了《复仇》和《凯撒》。《复仇》的主人公是布西的弟弟克莱蒙（Clermont）。布西的阴魂促他报仇，他杀死了蒙苏利伯爵，为哥哥报了仇。在剧中，他依附吉斯公爵，后来吉斯被国王亨利三世处死（1588），他非常同情吉斯，感到吉斯之死只能说明人间充满罪恶，愤而自杀。但剧中的中心思想是鼓吹罗马人的坚韧精神——斯多噶精神。克莱蒙和布西一样，也生活在一个充满矛盾和腐败的环境里，但他能保持冷静，自我克制。这出戏里的复仇占极其次要的地位，五分之四是写人物之间对人生、哲学、政治、道德等问题的讨论。克莱蒙有一段话说，人的主要方向是和宇宙结合，是把一和一切相结合。他说要承认必然，不管倔强也好，自愿也好，都要归顺原始的天道，这才是智慧（见第四幕）。

《凯撒》一剧写凯撒和庞培的斗争。罗马的保民官卡托为了阻止凯撒夺权，以保共和，召庞培带兵来保卫罗马。两雄争着要进驻罗马，元老们不置可否，两雄相持不下。凯撒的部下（被写成一群流氓）叫嚣开战。交战结果，庞培败绩。凯撒通过被俘的庞培将领，要与庞培言和。卡托也主张媾和以免生灵涂炭，但庞培不听，和凯撒重新开战，又大败。凯撒派人去刺他。卡托不愿投降凯撒，自杀毕命。

历史上的卡托本来是遵奉斯多噶哲学的。在剧中他也是认为正义的人是自由的，他的灵魂是自由的，灵魂可以自由处置自己的肉体。他说"诸神已放弃一切，我亦要随诸神离开这世界"，"我要从一切忧虑中解脱，我自由了"。在恰普曼看来，卡托体现了荷马另一部史诗中的"人"，有智慧的人。

斯多噶哲学在罗马共和末期和帝国时期广为流行。哲学家塞内加（Seneca，B. C. 4—A. D. 65）和马库斯·奥雷琉斯（Marcus Anrelius，121—180）皇帝都是著名代表人物。这是一种在专制淫威下的自求解脱的哲学。在十六世纪的英国，斯多噶哲学也大为流行，成为一种思潮和运动。这正好说明当时动荡的政治（包括宗教斗争）形势，以及人们无可奈何的精神状态。莎士比亚的悲剧正代表这种精神。

以上作家都比莎士比亚年事稍长，有的如马娄，则和他同龄。下面我们再看看比莎士比亚年轻的剧作家的情况。前面的作家所表现出来的倾向，到了后面的作家就更为尖锐突出了。

本·琼生（Ben Jonson，1572—1637）是英国文艺复兴后期执文坛牛耳的人物。一般都称他为现实主义作家，因为作为喜剧家，他写的都是当时现实生活。他写喜剧的目的是"嘲弄人类的愚蠢，而不是人类的罪恶"，亦即对人类的愚蠢作"理性"的批判，和埃拉斯谟可以说是一脉相承。所谓人类的愚蠢，是从人文主义者的"人的尊严"这一观点出发来加以识别的，即人类的愚蠢表现在人降格到禽兽的水平，如《狐狸》一剧中的主人公象猪一样贪婪，狐狸一样狡猾，狼一样凶狠。为此，琼生还创造了一种理论——幽默论或"体液说"，或"气质说"。这是人文主义者从古代和中古医学中找到的理论，以解释人性、人的气质和人的行为，也是对一些社会现象的解释。某些体液的结合产生某种性格，有的性格如琼生的喜剧中写嫉妒、虚荣心、愚蠢，这些就成为嘲讽的对象。《皆大欢喜》中的贾奎斯的忧郁，甚至哈姆雷特本人的忧郁，都是体液所形成的。这些现象当时都认为是病，所以勃顿（Robert Burton，1577—1640）在《忧郁的解剖》（1621）里提出了疗法。

琼生的悲剧和莎士比亚的历史剧一样，批判不择手段地满足权欲的野心。人文主义者强调理性，强调到了极端便出现玛基维里主义，这又和人文主义的人道思想矛盾。这说明人文主义本身存在的矛盾，也说明它作为一种思想武器的疲弱，与资本主义精神不合。从本·琼生本人的生活道路来看，他由国教而改信天主教，又改回去信国教；他由平民而成为桂冠诗人、伦敦史官，为宫廷创作了40部音乐歌舞剧，粉饰太平，也可以看出人文主义的衰微。关于音乐歌舞剧，莎士比亚在《暴风雨》（四．一．148…）中演出一场音乐歌舞剧之后，让普波斯彼罗说道："我们这些演员，我已和你们说过，都是些精灵，溶化在空气中去了，溶化在稀薄的空气中去了。这是一场虚构的幻景，随着幻景的消灭，那些高入云端的崇楼，华丽的宫殿，庄严的庙宇，甚至巨大的地球本身以及它所继承的一切，都必将溶化，并象这出虚无缥缈的歌舞剧（insnbstantial pageany）淡没消失一样，一缕烟都不剩。"可见音乐歌舞剧这类作品表面热闹，骨子里是虚无和寂寞。

戴克（Thomas Deker, 1570？—1632）基本上也是位喜剧家。和琼生一样，他也被称为现实主义作家。所谓现实主义指的描写市民生活，如他的名作《鞋匠的假日》（1600），以手工艺人的生活为背景，写贵族青年和市民女儿的爱情，为平民争地位，同情弱小。他是位多产作家，充满活力，但缺少思想的广度和深度。他鼓吹的是安贫乐业，不要作非分之想，如他的喜剧《佛图那图斯老人》（*Old Fortunatus*），就写一个老乞丐的故事。命运女神让他从智慧、健康、美、长寿或一个用不完的钱袋中任选一件（这是一个德国民间故事），他选了钱袋。有了钱袋，他经历了一番神奇的事迹，最后还是象浮士德那样，被命运女神（不是魔鬼）夺去了生命。他的儿子，走他父亲的老路，也遭惨死。戴克有很强的幽默感，体现在人物刻划上，但讽而不刺，讥而不怒。他的人情、人道、仁爱、同情同样反映了人文主义的衰落。

在比莎士比亚稍年轻的作家中，我们注意到一个现象，即悲剧作品大量涌现。这些作品的主题不外是背信弃义（如马斯顿Marston 的《安东尼奥和美利达》*Antonio and Mellida*）、复仇（如特纳 Tourneur 的《复仇者的悲剧》*Revenger's Tragedy*，和《无神论者的悲剧》*The Atheist's Tragedy*，又如波芒与弗莱彻的《少女的悲剧》*The Maid's Trcegedy* 等），而大量的则是情杀和乱伦。

悲剧的场面较之前几年更加血腥残暴、断肢、挖心、用各种方法下毒（如画毒画、画像上施毒）。这类恐怖场面已成为一种戏剧风尚，莎剧中许多场面（如《泰特斯·安德洛尼克斯》中的人肉宴，《李尔王》中的挖眼睛）在这种背景上，也不难理解了。这些场面被称作"怪诞"（grotesque），怪诞得令人发笑；或被称为"夸张剧"（melodrama）。这些术语都不能真实反映这类悲剧的实质。这种场面实际上反映了作者的心态，也反映了社会的心态。就象《黄土地》的原始、荒凉，《老井》的落后，《红高粱》的美化兽性、残酷（一切情节都没有动机 motivatian），既反映了作者的心态，又反映了社会心态（观众发出欣赏的笑声、报刊连篇累牍的赞歌）。这类悲剧企图引起的效果，就是观众的战栗。但其效果还不止此。它使观众在战栗之余产生一种对人类的厌恶感。不象希腊悲剧，使观众通过怜悯和恐惧而得到净化。对净化虽有各种不同的解释，但我们看了希腊悲剧，主人公虽然毁灭（如俄迪浦斯），但他那追求真理的精神是给人鼓舞的，而不是对人失去信心。看了英国文艺复兴后期悲剧，使观众对人类产生厌恶感。这和人文主义者对人类的无限潜力的信心形成鲜明的对比。犯罪有理，例如《白魔鬼》（*The White Devil*）中女主角维多利亚和公爵通奸，公爵派人杀死她的丈夫，她对审判她的红衣主教说："请你算算我有多少过失，你会发现我的过失不过是爱美，爱穿花衣服，爱心情快活，胃口好，爱吃酒席，如此而已。""可怜的仁慈啊！很少在穿红衣裳的人的身上发现你。"甚至乱伦也有理，如《可惜她是妓女》（'*Tis a Pity She's a Whore*，作者福特 Ford）中女主角的奶娘说："不要怕，亲爱的，他是你哥哥又怎样？你哥哥是个男人，我希望；我老说，一个年轻姑娘感到情欲发作，随便找个男的，父亲、哥哥都一样。"人文主义者所倡导的个性解放，已完全堕落到不可救药的地步。

这类悲剧也宣扬一种容忍罪恶、理解罪恶的态度。就如上面福特写的这出戏，女主人公与人通奸并怀孕后，嫁给了一个贵族索朗佐，索朗佐发现后要杀她，索朗佐的仆人劝他："她是你的妻子，她嫁给你以前所犯的一切过失，都不是针对你的。唉，可怜的夫人，她所犯的一切，在同样的情况下，哪个意大利的妇女不会犯呢？老爷，请你听你的理智的话，不要顺着性子发脾气，发脾气就不近人情，就象头野兽了。"在这里，我们可以看出淫乱已是时代的风气。所谓婚前淫乱并非针对此后的丈夫，纯属诡辩。其次，人文主义者所崇拜的仁道和理性已变成为淫乱开脱的遁辞。我们若把索朗佐和阿里奥斯托的罗兰比较，两个人都因爱情的挫折而发怒、疯狂，罗兰恢复了理性，以便了解安杰丽嘉与摩尔青年的真正爱情，而索朗佐的仆人用理性来开脱变态的爱。可见人文主义者所高举的爱和理性已完全破灭，不仅遭到危机而已。

莎士比亚后继者之中在悲剧方面最接近他的恐怕要算韦伯斯特（John Webster）。他除了和别人合作写的戏剧和其他剧作外，最精采的有两出悲剧：《白魔鬼》（*The White Devil*）1608 年上演，和《玛尔菲公爵夫人》（*The Duchess of Malfi*）上演于 1614 年以前。《白魔鬼》写勃拉齐亚诺公爵娶佛罗伦斯公爵之妹伊莎贝拉，久而生厌，爱上一个穷书生卡密罗的妻子维多利亚。维多利亚的哥哥佛拉米尼奥从中撮合，害死了卡密罗和伊莎贝拉。维多利亚以通奸罪被判关进教养院。勃拉齐亚诺公爵把她从教养院中偷劫出去，和她结了婚。佛罗伦斯公爵为妹妹报仇，杀死了勃拉齐亚诺公爵。维多利亚和佛拉米尼奥也被公爵手下人杀死。

这个戏写的是一个通奸的故事，复仇的故事。它的主旨在于描写非理性的情欲带来的灾难。佛拉米尼奥的母亲发现儿子干出拉皮条的勾当，叹道："大地震肆虐之后还留下铁或铅或石头，疯狂的肉欲一切不留，只有毁灭。"或象最后一场佛拉米尼奥来逼妹妹同归于尽，妹妹抗议说："你要我离开这为人而创造的世界，沉沦到为魔鬼创造的永恒的黑暗！"这是一种戏剧讽刺。观众心里明白，这世界已经不适于人的生存了，和地狱已经一般无二了。作者似乎是怀着对世界的恐怖感和悲观态度来写这个戏的。因此戏中着力描写拖长了的痛苦和可怕的场面。例如，勃拉齐亚诺公爵戴上浸了毒的头盔，陷入痛苦和半疯狂的状态，作者把这一段写得很长。又如，写公爵害死他夫人所用的手段——在自己的画像上令人涂上毒药，夫人每晚上床前必先吻画像，中毒而死（夫人之死和卡密罗之死都是用哑剧形式表演的）。人们把杀人当成一门艺术，完全是理智的，<u>丝毫不牵涉情感</u>，如同情怜悯。如佛罗伦斯公爵手下人和他讨论如何害死勃拉齐亚诺，就说可以在祷告书上、念珠上、马鞍上、镜子上、网球拍上施毒，方法不厌其妙，愈妙愈好。所谓理性、人道等人文主义者所向往的一切，都已成泡影。

《玛尔菲公爵夫人》写公爵夫人新寡，爱上了她的管家安东尼奥，并秘密结婚。她的两个兄长，一个是红衣主教，一个是菲迪南公爵，反对她再婚。（他们不知道她已秘密结婚。）菲迪南公爵不准她再婚是想得到她的产业，因此派手下一个叫波索拉的去当夫人的养马官，实际是一名坐探。夫人的婚事被发现后，安东尼奥带一儿逃走，夫人被两兄软禁，受尽折磨，最后同自己另外两个孩子一起被勒死。波索拉有后悔之意，因私怨想杀死红衣主教，但在杀死他之前，误将安东尼奥杀死。菲迪南公爵也有悔恨之意，并因此而发了疯，在发疯中把波索拉杀死。

争取婚姻自主当然是此剧的主旨之一。公爵夫人曾说："人不如鸟，鸟还可以自由选择配偶。"但还有更深一层的意义。公爵夫人在剧中被写成是一个完美无缺的女性，"她使过去的时代显得污秽，她给未来指出光明"，是旧时代所没有，是新时代的曙光。她向安东尼奥吐诉爱情非常主动、无畏、解放，她非常相信能战胜旧势力，代表了早期人文主义者的理想，但终于斗不过旧势力。安东尼奥地位低下，但他是个"完美的人"，他是靠自己的品德和行为而立足于天地之间的。他向夫人吐诉爱情，并立即结婚，自信教会无权干涉，只有承认的份。最后他也同样遭到毁灭。这情况十分形象地反映了人文主义的弱点和危机。其原因在本剧中也有所透露。在一开始，安东尼奥从法国回来，大大赞美法国宫廷如何把一切谄媚阿谀的人都驱逐出去。他说朝廷象泉源，泉源清洁，水流就清洁，泉源有毒，水流就有毒。可见人文主义者寄希望于贵族宫廷体制的健全，也就是它的贵族性质。而事实上，贵族已是无可救药，变成了一切毒害的来源，使人文主义者感到绝望，以至疯狂。菲迪南为了折磨幽禁的妹妹，从疯人院放出一批疯人来骚扰她。她说："理智和静默叫我发疯。"世界上的事无法用理性去深思，无法"理"解，又不能沉默，只有发疯。世界变得怪诞。菲迪南得了一种病叫"狼人病"，以为自己是一只狼，半夜去墓地掘墓，背一条死人腿回来。在他清醒的时候，他折磨妹妹，在黑暗中把一只死人的手伸给她，同她"握手"。正如剧终一个人物所说，这些人都将遗臭万年，真正伟大的人应是"真理的主宰"，他们的一生应是

"完整的一生"。但事实上，人早已背叛真理，人生已被罪恶击碎。假表现和真实质已揉在一起，正如夫人对波索拉所说，"你在毒药丸外面裹上金色和糖衣。""我认为这世界是一座令人厌倦的舞台，我所演的角色是违背我的意愿的。"

我们谈韦伯斯特的悲剧处处可以看到莎士比亚的影响——他的影子和回响。我只从《玛尔菲公爵夫人》一剧中举几个例子。如一开始，韦伯斯特把宫廷比作国家的源头，不正是莎士比亚历史剧的根本思想么？红衣主教低估表示不愿再嫁的妹妹，说，"大多数寡妇都这么说。但这种倾向一般长不过颠倒一次沙漏；丧礼上的演说一结束，这种倾向也结束了"。使人想起哈姆雷特责备他母亲的话。剧中有关巫术（蛇的脂肪、犹太人的唾液、婴儿的大便）、迷信（洒盐、野兔过路、流鼻血、马失前蹄、蟋蟀叫）也和莎剧一致。许多意象、比喻也有共同之处，如菲迪南不接受妹妹的恳求，说"不是你那妓女的奶汁，而是你那妓女的血，才能扑灭我的怒火"，马克白夫人也用奶汁比喻马克白的慈心。又如菲迪南警告妹妹要注意名声，一个人一旦丧失了名誉，就再也找不回它来了，这和《理查二世》中"人生一世最是珍贵的就是无瑕的名誉，一旦丧失了它，人不过是一块镀金的泥土"。菲迪南把妹妹幽禁在暗室里，说"你老生活在这样的地方才好，因为你在阳光里太久了"使人想起哈姆雷特回答他叔父的问题"为什么你混身上下老罩在乌云里"时说"不然，我在太阳光里太多了"。公爵夫人在幽禁中对侍女说："我要能和死人说两天话多好，我一定能从他们那儿了解我在这儿永远了解不到的东西。"这似乎是套用哈姆雷特一次独白中所说的"死是未发现的国土，没有旅客从那里回来过"，都是表示对死亡的疑虑。而她又说："必然的命运使我长期痛苦，习惯使我的痛苦容易忍受些。"也使人想起《李尔王》最后一幕二场埃德加所说："人必须忍受到这儿来一样。成熟就是一切。"又如红衣主教差人去侦察安东尼奥时教他许多方法，似乎又是和《哈姆雷特》中波罗纽斯差人去侦察他的儿子一样。又如红衣主教杀死他的情妇朱丽亚以后，有些良心发现，想祈祷，但是他的心已被魔鬼夺去，对祈祷失去了信心。这和《哈姆雷特》中的克劳迪斯又何其相似。又如波索拉误杀安东尼奥之后，认为这是命运的拨弄，他说"我们都是命运的网球，由它打来打去"，又说"我们追求荣华富贵，就象一心想游戏的玩童，追逐的只是吹出来的肥皂泡"。多象《李尔王》中所说，我们都象玩童手中的蜻蜓，由他杀害取乐。凡此种种恐怕不是一种巧合。当然可以说是韦伯斯特受到莎剧的影响，但恐怕说是思想和感情上的相通或共性也许更恰当一些，而两个作家间的思想和感情上的共性又溶化在整个文化、社会、政治气氛之中，是这种气候的症状。它反映了人文主义的危机。

英国文艺复兴最后一位剧作家（或最后剧作家之一）约翰·福特（John Ford），艾略特称他为二流作家。不过我们可以把他当做一个参照点，以看出戏剧发展的弧线。此外，在他的戏剧里也处处可以看出莎士比亚的影响。

他传世的最著名的作品即前引的《可惜她是个妓女》（'Tis Pity She's a Whore），1633 年发表。此剧写的是兄妹乱伦。乔万尼和他的妹妹安娜贝拉通奸成孕，就把她嫁给向她求婚的索朗佐。索朗佐发现妻子有过奸情，通过仆人瓦奎斯设计，发现了奸夫是谁。索朗佐生日设宴请客，也邀请乔万尼，意欲报仇。乔万尼知道索朗佐设宴的用意，但仍前来赴宴。赴宴前他又去和安娜贝拉相会，把她杀死，拿着挖出来的心前去赴宴。在宴席上他杀死了索朗佐，然后自杀。

正如有的评论家所说，人文主义者所歌颂的爱情——正当的爱情，已不能满足人们的要求，必须得到反常的情欲才快活。男女主人公之间所谓的爱，其炽热程度不亚于罗密欧与朱丽叶，但这种"爱"已充满了罪孽。而作者还进一步为这种行为找理由，表示同情，反映出作者和当时一些人们的病态心理。

在这出戏里也回响着莎士比亚的意象、情景、情感、信仰。如五幕三场乔万尼接到赴宴的邀请，有人劝他不要去。他不听，一定要去与安娜贝拉相会，他说："让那些钻进书堆里的书虫子去梦想什么另一个世界吧，我的世界，我的全部幸福在这儿，未来的世界再好，我也不换，享乐的生活就是天堂。"这和莎士比亚笔下放纵情欲的罗马大将安东尼不是具有同一生活观么？

第五幕二场，索朗佐定计设宴，他在宴会上说："我要叫我的这位夫人穿上结婚长袍，我要吻她，温柔地把她抱在怀里。"这又可能是从《奥赛罗》里得到的启发，台丝德蒙娜命侍女（在她要死的晚上）把结婚时的床单铺上。引起观众的悬念、恐惧。

其他还有许多，不一一列举。

五

以上我们把莎士比亚所信奉的人文主义（当然他自己并未意识到这是人文主义，人文主义者这名词在英语中于十七世纪后半叶才出现——1670，用以称谓研究古希腊罗马学问的学者，而"人文主义"作为文艺复兴时期的思潮则到十九世纪才出现。参看《牛津大字典》）在欧洲文艺复兴时期所起的作用交代了一番，又把莎士比亚前后的欧洲作家的情况介绍了一番。现在我们自己作些比较，莎士比亚的形象、他在欧洲文学发展史上的地位，可以放在这一个比较准确的坐标上了。

不过，历来对莎士比亚的看法，人言甚殊。艾略特 1927 年写的《莎士比亚和塞内加的斯多噶主义》[1]一文就举了当时流行的几种看法。有人把莎士比亚看作是一位退休的英国殖民地官员（大半根据《暴风雨》中普罗斯丕洛的形象）。有人把他比作传播福音、传播新哲学、传播新瑜伽术的人。有人把他比作力士参孙。还有人把他比作保守党新闻记者，或自由党新闻记者，或信奉社会主义的新闻记者。还有什么新教的莎士比亚、怀疑派的莎士比亚、英国天主教的莎士比亚甚至教皇派的莎士比亚。我还可以增加人民的莎士比亚，荒诞派的莎士比亚（如扬·柯特 Jan Kott）。这些都是这个世纪以内批评家们给莎士比亚的头衔，如果再往上推，从"时代的灵魂"到"烂醉的野蛮人"，那就更不一而足。我们对莎士比亚又是怎样看呢？我觉得我们几十年来是一贯的，即追随欧洲浪漫派批评家的观点。即使解放后，我们追随苏联的莎学，而苏联的莎学，至少五十年代以前，接的仍是浪漫派的衣钵（如勃拉德雷），只不过加上所谓的历史唯物主义和反映论。我们如果把本文所陈述的情况作为参照，再看莎士比亚，我们不得不把他看作是文艺复兴终期，衰落的人文主义诗人。他远离文艺复兴早期作家，而更接近于十七世纪文坛和艺坛风靡一时的巴罗克流派。有的批评家直截了当地把他划入巴罗克作家之列。

莎士比亚全部戏剧的发展可以这样来描述：他从血腥气中登场，他走进（或逃避到）浪漫的田园世界，同时他逐渐进入痛苦的沉思，最后求得"解脱"，或再度逃避。在最后这阶段，所谓"向前看"，实际也是一种逃避，逃避过去，逃避现在。

在所有这些阶段我们都可以发现在莎剧中有许多技巧或现象，

---

[1] T. S. 艾略特：《论文集》，译文见《莎士比亚评论汇编》。

这些都在结构上具有重要意义，但它们后面的动机不清楚。例如早期喜剧中的伪装，很重要，因为一旦没有了伪装，没有了把甲错认为乙，也就没有戏了，整个结构就垮了。不仅莎氏喜剧中如此，其他作家的喜剧中也如此。在后期的喜剧中，有些很成问题的因素暗暗地溜进了剧里，如《无事生非》里唐约翰这个人物，《皆大欢喜》里杰奎斯这个人物，都和"纯"喜剧的气氛格格不入。唐约翰的敌意，杰奎斯的忧郁，都没有明白的动因。《威尼斯商人》中一开始安东尼奥的忧郁，连他自己也不知道为什么。"中期"喜剧《终成眷属》一开场人物都穿着黑衣服，给卢希庸伯爵服孝，国王病重，海伦娜的父亲已刚去世，为什么以忧伤暗淡的情调开始喜剧？

这类不太可理解的人物和情节，十八世纪古典主义评论家都很不以为然。后来，人们做了许多解释，如说安东尼奥是为了他在海上的商船担忧而不欢，甚至有人说安东尼奥和巴萨尼奥之间有同性恋，后者要结婚了，故而安东尼奥不欢。至于那些有问题的角色，人们作了最简便的解释，即他们是主角们的陪衬，没有他们，戏剧的动作就没有了。

到了后期的"悲喜剧"，情况变得更不可理解。《一报还一报》和《特洛伊勒斯和克丽希达》一直引起理解上的困难。主人公的性格一百八十度的转变无法解释。

在莎氏的伟大的悲剧作品里，李尔的爱与恨，奥赛罗和《冬天的故事》里的莱昂提斯的怀疑和嫉妒，马克白的野心，哈姆雷特的忧郁，虽然动因可以见到，但为什么莎士比亚把这些情欲如此夸大？这样做的，不止莎氏一人，前面提到的作家也如此。

还有，为什么在喜剧中潜伏着悲剧的因素？为什么在悲剧中又有喜剧插曲？

这些问题历来已有各式各样的解答。但是如果我们把莎氏放在上面勾画出来的坐标上，这些问题也许能得到满意的答案。

我们前面已经在谈许多作家时谈到这个问题，并引了修辞学上的"正反拼合法"（oxymoron）作为解释。我们可以就此作进一步的阐述。我觉得莎士比亚对人生和世界有一个最根本的看法，那就是"世界是舞台"。近来也有评论家[1]指出，"伊利莎伯时代牧师的布道文也好，歌曲集子也好，编年史书和通俗小册子也好，都经常提醒人们，人生往往是在模仿舞台。人们经常把世界比作舞台，在许多地方，这种比拟几乎是'自动的'（automatic），说话时无意识地流露出来的……对伊利莎伯时代的人来说，把世界比作舞台是一个无法避免的口头禅，用来表达时代的本质特征。"

这种现象反映了当时人们的精神状态，也可以说是一种病态的文化现象，因为人们已经没有能力把握现实，更不用说改变现实。人们混淆了现实与幻觉、梦和醒、真和假。在喜剧里，甚至悲剧里，甲扮成乙而不被识破，作者和观众都视为当然。现象与实质、真和假、善和恶都可拼合，都是相对的。所以安哲罗可以变好，克丽希达可以变坏。卡西欧和台丝德蒙娜、波利克希尼斯和赫迈欧妮之间不可能成立的关系，被看成是真的。或则演成悲剧，或则通过"机关里出来的天神"这种突变来解决。

这种精神状态或心理状态——对现实的幻觉感，当时也有人企图予以解释。勃顿在《忧郁的解剖》里把这种病态称为"忧郁"。他解释道："生忧郁病的人，想象力特别活跃，长时间用力地想种种事物，就把事物弄错，就把事物引伸扩大，结果在某些人心中就产生一种真实感（以假为真），从而导致忧郁症或其他病症。虽然

---

[1] S. L. 伯塞尔：《莎士比亚和通俗戏剧的传统》，伦敦，1944年版，见该书第二章。安娜·赖特：《莎士比亚和戏剧的观念》，企鹅丛书，1967年版。转引自斯蒂芬·J. 格林布莱特：《瓦尔特·雷莱》，耶鲁大学出版社，1973年版，第118页。

我们的这种幻觉应是用通常的理性官能来克服，受理性的制约调节，但许多人由于内部或外部条件，或由于器官的毛病，这些器官有缺陷或不畅通或受到感染，因此他们的理性也产生缺陷、不畅通或受损害。"他又说："想象是使激情失控的手段，激情失控就经常产生可怕的后果。"

这番话说明人的精神已是有病，想象起了催化剂的作用，使人产生幻觉。勃顿对他所指的幻觉，或"可怕的后果"，有很形象的说明："有些人就想象自己变成了狼，男人变成了女人，女人又变回男人（这是人们经常信以为真的）。也有人从人变成驴或狗或其他形状，魏鲁斯把这些都归因于想象。"这不是在给莎士比亚剧作解释么？织布匠勃特姆变成驴也是这种想象的结果。马克白夫人梦游，医生说："层出不穷的幻觉在折磨她，使她不得安宁。"马克白也说她"头脑有病"，"头脑受到困扰"，"一种危险的东西压在她心上"。

医生勃朗也有同样的见解，不过他比勃顿稍科学些。他说"一般人的错误观念"是由人"有一种内在的倾向，不看事物的本来面目，并记住了这非本来的面目，这是人们头脑的一种错误倾向"。他解释道："人们看我的外表，只看到我的身分和产业，对我的高度，他们就看错了，因为我站得比阿特拉斯神的肩还高。"他的信条是因为是不可能的，所以是可以肯定的（语出二至三世纪神学家Tertullian）。他在《居鲁斯的花园》中称他那时代为"失去正确判断力的时代"（this ill-judging age）。一切都依赖于偶然。

这就是十六七世纪之交的"时代精神"。反映在文学艺术里就形成所谓的巴罗克风格。我在《巴罗克的涵义、表现和应用》一文中曾归纳巴罗克有五个特点。一忧郁、沮丧；二悲哀、怜悯、同情；三幻觉；四放纵；五神秘主义。这些特点都可以在莎剧中找到。

不过这只是问题的一个方面。另一方面，我们如把早期人文主义文学和七十年代以后的人文主义文学作一比较，则会看出早期作品虽然具有朝气和破坏性，但缺乏深度，而后期的文学不但具有深度而且在艺术上也更成熟："诗穷而后工"，"诗可以怨"，这恐怕可以算作一个创作的规律。当代批评家布鲁姆（Harold Bloom）[1]指出英语中 meaning（意义）一词和 moaning（悲叹、呻吟）在古英语中是同一个字。这岂不正好说明只有在痛苦呻吟之际才能找到"意义"吗？

1988 年 4 月为中央戏剧学院讲

---

[1] 哈罗德·布鲁姆：《形式的破坏》，载《解构与批评》，纽约，1985 年版。

中西悼亡诗

我在这一讲里想讨论一下一种特殊的抒情诗，这种诗频繁地出现于中国文学中，但在西方文学中却极为少见。我这里所指的就是悼亡诗，具体说来就是专为哀悼亡妻而作的诗。实际上，这种诗在中国文学中极为常见，因而我们可以说它已经有了一个传统：有自己的成规和意象，并与其他种类的抒情诗有别。

我们可以将它的开端追溯到中国诗歌的源头，《诗经》。在《诗经》中我们可以发现《绿衣》和《葛生》这样的诗篇，人们一般都认为这些就是纪念诗。第一首诗有这样的诗句：

> 绿兮衣兮，绿衣黄里，心之忧矣，曷维其已。
> 绿兮丝兮，女所治兮，我思古人，俾无訧兮。

第二首有这样的诗句：

> 葛生蒙楚，蔹蔓于野，予美亡此，谁与独处。
> 角枕粲兮，锦衾烂兮，予美亡此，谁与独旦。
> 夏之日，冬之夜，百岁之后，归于其居。

当然，第一首诗也可以理解为"生离"而非"死别"。第二首的意思不甚明确。在这里被哀悼的人显然是丈夫，但也可以被理解为是丈夫哀悼妻子。然而，我们所要注意的却是，这类诗中的突出意象就是与家庭生活密切相关的个人的日常用品。这类古代诗歌表达方式虽然单纯质朴，但感情却是真挚的。第二首诗似乎还描绘了一个进程：去墓地，从墓地返回家中，回家后诗人看到了使他想起自己婚姻生活的种种物件，最后发展到一种想要重新与配偶聚会的愿望。这是一种小规模的叙事。早期的这些无名氏的诗作已成为后来诗歌的范式。

我们在讨论到后来的诗歌时，就会发现，这样的诗经常置于一个梦的框架中。我们可以以元稹的《江陵三梦》[1] 为例。这些诗记载了诗人做过的三个梦，当时他新被贬到江陵。在第一个梦中，妻子十分惦念他们的独养女儿，因为元稹把她留在了京城。除了梦的主题外，还有三点值得注意：第一，这些诗写作的场景——诗人被贬到一个远离京城的地方任职，实际上意味着流放；第二，继承了将大自然的成分引入诗歌的传统，但较之《诗经》，这些自然成分更为复杂，并且更为密切地与诗人的感情相一致。在第一首诗的结尾，诗人写道：

坐见天欲曙，江风吟树枝。

第二首诗的结尾则是这样的：

惊觉满床月，风波江上声。

---

[1] 英译文见：《中国诗歌三千年》，安科出版社，纽约，1975 年版，第 216—218 页。

第三首诗的结尾是：

> 坐看朝日出，众鸟双徘徊。

第三，在分离的结尾表现出的某种绝望之感（"我心长似灰"）大大加剧了。元稹被贬的地方——江陵是长江岸边的一个城市。他在提及这个地方时写道：

> 一水不可越，黄泉况无涯。

也许元稹写下这些诗是为了纪念妻子去世三周年。当我们读到宋朝诗人苏轼为纪念妻子去世十周年而写下的一首感人的词时，我们会发现，诗中令人信服地证实了一种永恒的夫妻之爱。在这首词中，诗人简略地叙述了自己在梦中突然返回四川家乡的情景，当时他正在东部沿海的山东密州任上。他在梦中看到妻子象旧时一样正在小窗前梳妆整饰，两人面面相觑，无言对答。"惟有泪千行"。早先还出现过一段有趣的幻想。诗人说，既然妻子的孤零零的墓地远在千里之遥，因此他根本无处发泄自己那哀伤的孤独感，此时，他写道：

> 纵使相逢应不识，尘满面，鬓如霜。

这可以说是奥维德的《黑海诗简》（I. iv. ）中一首诗里两句的字面翻译：

> nec, si me subito videas,agnoscere

possis,aetatis facta est tonta ruina meae.

> 如果你突然见到我，你是不会认得我的，
> 岁月已把我摧残得不成样子了。

我们下面还要谈到奥维德与中国流亡诗人的相似之处。

作为一个突出的特例，我想提一下十七世纪后半叶一位相当失意潦倒的不甚有名的诗人学者：李必恒。他的悼念亡妻的两首诗[1]由在他后去世的同时代诗人沈德潜收入《国朝诗别裁集》。这两首诗各由二十四行组成：第一首描写他妻子临死前的情景：那天早晨，她起身后"清水自膏沐，再拜辞舅姑"，然后委托小姑照料她幼小的儿子，并且嘱咐小姑，秋天来临时，把她的一些简单的结婚衣服为孩子改做，以抵御秋凉。这首诗的一个明显特征在于，诗人引入了某些超自然的成分，以创造出一种预兆死亡的不祥氛围。诗人一开始就写道，

> 一室何啾啾，人语杂鬼哭。
> 飞来白项鸟，哑哑上我屋。

第二首描写了妻子死后的"空房"和一场梦：

> 空房起昼阴，冷气出枕席；
> 窗多蛛结网，案尽鼠行迹。
> 亦有筐中麻，灯火手自绩；

---

[1] 沈德潜曾惋惜李必恒的诗未有全辑。

　　　　亦有所对镜，花钿恣狼藉。
　　　　徘徊思言笑，仿佛面如觌；
　　　　回头遏欲语，抚心一摽擗。

然后，诗人又描述了自己做过的梦：

　　　　前夜梦见之，色惨体更瘠。
　　　　恍惚絮语间，问儿何所食。
　　　　暂时魂魄聚，觉后泉壤隔。
　　　　忘情愧太上，庄缶犹可击。

　　编者沈德潜介绍道，李必恒是一位穷书生，优秀的诗人。中丞宋荦曾高度赞扬过十五位青年诗人的诗才，在这十五人中，他是唯一未获得官职的，死时只是一个诸生。"且耳聋多病，年止中寿，何其厄也。然诗格之高，才力之大，可久者应让此人。"沈德潜在评论他的这两首悼亡诗时评论道："渔洋悼亡诗，风雅之中，纯乎富贵气象，此则元相所云'贫贱夫妻百事哀'也。越琐屑，越见真至，即他人读之，亦为感伤。"

　　这也许是很少见的一段批评文字，对悼亡诗作了某种理论化的概括。也就是说，这种诗与诗人的生平有着最密切的关联，因此读诗时与诗人的生活联系起来就能得到最佳的鉴赏效果。其次，为了达到其效果，还应当注入家庭生活的细节。

　　在前一个方面，李贽为我们提供了一个极好的例子。[1] 他也许不象李必恒那样是一位优秀的诗人，但他的诗作却向我们相当充分

---

[1]　见《焚书》，卷三，《卓吾论述》。

地描述了他那学者和小官员生涯的浮沉，家庭成员的死亡，他的皈依佛教，以及他本人由于微不足道的罪过遭受监禁，最后在狱中自杀身死。从他的文章、书信、自传特写以及遗嘱中，我们得知，他的妻子也与他共度艰辛，二人互敬互爱，当听到妻子死于故乡时，他每天都梦见她，甚至希望她的灵魂不灭，等着他前去与她结合（《焚书》，卷二，《与庄纯夫》）。他还描述了他们一起交谈、辩论以及分别时的情景。此外，他在遗嘱中还提出自己死后应怎样用布把他的尸体包裹起来（《续焚书》，卷四，《李卓吾先生遗言》）。他对死亡的迷恋不禁使人想起了沃尔顿（Izaak Walton）对邓约翰（John Donne）的描绘。

在悼念妻子的诗中，李贽写道：

反目未曾有，齐眉四十年。[1]

我希望从上面的描述已能见出中国悼亡诗的基本特征。一言以蔽之，这种抒情诗常常是由诗人生涯中的失意挫折而诱发的。它反映了诗人所体验着的沮丧潦倒之情感。通过回忆往日在贫穷逆境中的伴侣之情，回忆起亡人曾成功地维系着的和谐的家庭关系，诗人往往为自己的丧失获得了某种心理上的补偿。既然我们考虑到这些写于被贬谪或自我流放时期（李贽就是如此）的诗歌之诱因，那么这类诗歌就可以称为"流亡诗"，其特征就是往往带有一种死别之感，即一种无法重聚的分离。在西方文学中我们所熟悉的一个例子就是奥维德。尽管他存有万一的希望：自己终有一天会被召回罗马，而且流亡毕竟不象丧妻的丈夫那样；他们常常有可能重返家

---

[1] 《焚书》，卷六，《哭黄宜人》。

园，但是他最后终于意识到，赦放是毫无指望的，因此他为自己写下了墓志铭（《哀歌》，III. iii）。在流放地，诗人常常想到妻子是他的精神支柱，因此失去这一支柱便使他感到深切的苦痛。奥维德在这一诗行中表达了自己的这种感情："我的倾圮全靠你这根柱子支撑"（te mea supposita veluti trabe fulta ruina est），这也是中国诗人所共有的一种情感。

为了对不可弥补的丧失作出补偿，诗人不得不求助于某种哲学，希望象哲学家庄子那样，能够超越生与死，超越凡人之爱，或者皈依诸如佛教之类的宗教。这类诗的结尾常表达出或隐含着某种哲学思想，这虽然不是必须有的，但却常常赋予这种诗以一种爱情抒情诗所缺少的沉思冥想特征。这正是那类鼓吹及时行乐的抒情诗的反面。

这样的诗必然要引起回忆。因此它很自然会采取叙事形式：回顾亡妻一生中的事件或回顾与她曾分享过的生活。诗人不仅在醒时想起那些往事，而且那记忆是如此之深刻，因而常常转变成一场梦。[1] 这样就有了梦的主题。在梦中生者与死者相见是基于这样一种理论：按《左传》昭七疏："附形之灵为魄，附气之神为魂。"意为生者的精神叫魄，死者的精神叫魄。生者与死者相会靠魄与魂在梦中的相遇。梦的主题赋予这类诗歌以一种超自然的特质和一种阴森可怕的不祥气氛，这种气氛使这些诗最富于感染力。同时，大自然也作为一个陪衬物被引入了诗人的感情状态中。

抒情诗的这种文类或亚文类的最突出意象是由衣物、床榻、妇女的装饰、纺车、缝补衣裳、招待客人、照料孩子以及父母或家庭中其他成员所组成。这些客体和活动往往分为三组：一组指夫妻之

---

[1] 作为醒时对某样事情的强烈情感经常持续到梦中的例子，我们可以以苏轼的《东坡志林》为证，在这部随笔里，他记载了自己的十几个梦，其中有不少是关于作诗的，因为作诗是他白昼最热衷的事。

爱，第二组指个人装饰，第三组指妻子的义务。当中国诗人写"纯粹的"爱情抒情诗时，一般都是写给妓女的，几乎很少写给未婚妻或妻子的。除非在小说或传奇故事中才有这种婚前的爱情。爱情常是在婚后的友谊、互相理解和互相同情中产生的。其次，严格的道德规范也制约着所有的人际关系。妻子若遵守这一规范，就自然受到尊重和热爱。婚姻从来就不是一种法律的契约。实际上，法律本身甚至政府都屈从于儒家经典树立的道德权威。表达爱情必须限制在一定范围内，配偶的死亡是丧妻者（或丧夫者）唯一可以自由表达感情的时刻。

西方这类抒情诗极其少见的原因是难以说清的，作出一般的论断也难免武断。但是我们不妨作些推测和思考。西方的爱情观与中国的爱情观（或许与整个东方的爱情观）有所不同。在古代中国，甚至未婚男女青年交朋友都被认为是不适当的，更不用说谈情说爱了，而在西方，正如布克哈特（Burckhardt）所指出的[1]，自从文艺复兴以来，个人就从"仅仅作为种族、民族、政党、家庭或团体成员"的意识中得到了解放。他（她）可以作为一个人去自由地爱。甚至在更早些时候，对骑士爱情的崇拜似乎就成了这种解放的先导。而在中国，男人实际上首先是一个受缚于道德伦理网的家庭的成员。在西方，爱情是一种追求，婚姻才是求爱的高潮，而在中国，婚姻只是可能发展为爱情关系的开始。在西方，一旦达到某种结合，人的心理需要就得到了满足，而在中国，这却是婚后的一个漫长的过程。正如伯克利加州大学的已故教授陈世骧所说，"东方文学中的爱情并不是作为一种对永恒未来的追求而出现的，倒是作为过去的某样东西而出现的，是回味的对象，而不是推想的对

---

[1] 《意大利文艺复兴时期的文明》，第81页。

象。"[1] 在中国，妻子之死只是男人可以公开合法地表达自己对配偶之爱的唯一机会。

中国诗歌的传统主要是抒情的，抒情诗也主要被认为是一种诉"怨"的工具（诗可以怨），所以主题多是分离、渴望、逃避、沉思以及同大自然或个人朋友进行感情交流。这一传统使诗人得以利用妻子之死来写诗，并且以悼亡诗的形式表达自己的爱情。

一旦悼亡诗被确立为一种固定的文类，它便开始为人们自由使用了，并被扩展到用来悼念家庭的其他成员，或者悼念通常属于同辈或晚一辈的家族成员（悼念长辈则是不允许的）。这类诗有时甚至可以引出朋友的和诗，使他们一同加入吊唁的行列，这样便使哀悼成了某种社交酬酢，因此常常是敷衍塞责的陈词滥调。

现在我们再看看西方文学中这类抒情诗的一些稀有的例子。我这里仅限于讨论英国文学中的例子。其中一个使我感到最接近中国悼亡诗的例子便是弥尔顿的一首十四行诗：

> 我仿佛看到了去世不久的圣徒般的妻
> 回到了我身边，象阿尔塞斯蒂斯从坟墓
> 被尤比特伟大的儿子用强力从死亡中救出，
> 苍白而虚弱，交给了她的丈夫，使他欢喜。
> 我的妻，由于古戒律规定的净身礼
> 而得救，洗净了产褥上斑斑的玷污，
> 这样的她，我相信我还能再度
> 在天堂毫无障碍地充分地瞻视，
> 她一身素服，纯洁得和她心灵一样，

---

[1] 见《中国文学的文化本质》，载《文化的相互关系》，巴黎，尤奈斯库，1953 年版，第 64 页。

脸上罩着面纱，但我仿佛看见

爱、温柔、善良在她身上发光，

如此开朗，什么人脸上有这等欢颜。

但是，唉，正当她俯身拥抱我的当儿，

我醒了，她逃逸了，白昼带回了我的黑天。

这是一首感人至深的诗，甚至达到了悲怆哀惋之境地，不禁使人想到，当弥尔顿第二次结婚时，他已经双目失明了。这首十四行诗是放在一个梦的框架之中，有首有尾，是一首微型的叙述诗，恰象中国的某些悼亡诗。诗中意象的轮廓模糊，表现出一种迷离神秘的气氛。当诗人醒来后，诗者得到的印象是梦中一别，怕是再无聚首之日了，甚至能否在天国重聚也可怀疑。至于写作的时间和场景，我们可以相当地肯定，他的第二个妻子卡特琳·伍德科克（Catherine Woodcodk）于1658年2月3日去世后不久，弥尔顿就立即写下了这首诗，[1] 随后他的年幼的女儿也于同年三月夭折，这时正值他写作最后一个小册子《论共和国之破裂》（*On the Ruptures of the Commonwelth*，1659年10月）之前。1658年9月，克伦威尔去世，他的儿子查理继任护国主。这时，新生的共和国正面临着迫在眉睫的危险，弥尔顿本人很快也面临着被捕的威胁。正是在这一深为沮丧的时刻，弥尔顿也象那些中国诗人一样，写下了这首十四行诗。但是相似之处仅到此为止。这首诗的最动人之处在于其深刻的宗教特征。他呼唤他那圣徒般的妻子，她不仅在肉体上是纯洁的，而且精神上也是圣洁的，她正是爱情、甜蜜和善良的人格化身。她被比作阿尔塞斯蒂斯这一自我牺牲的象征，甚至可以说是耶稣基督

---

[1] 这首诗是纪念他第一位夫人的抑或是第二位夫人，一向有争议。我认为是纪念后者，此处不详论。

的非基督教对应物，尽管在一个有限的范围内是如此。这一女性观念也许同中世纪日耳曼的崇敬妇女（Frauendiest）之观念有着一些关系，当然这里面骑士的谦卑是没有的，但却保持了宗教崇拜的成分。对于这一态度埃拉斯谟（Erasmus）在《战斗的基督教徒手册》(*Enchiridion Militia Christiani*, I. 7)[1] 中作了最清晰的表述，他在书中说道，"你说你爱你的妻子，因为她是你的配偶。这里其实根本没有什么品德可言。甚至异教徒也能做到这点，这种爱情只是建立在肉体快感上的。但是另一方面，如果你爱她是因为你在她身上看到了基督的形象，在她身上感觉出了基督的虔敬、谦恭和纯洁，那么你爱她并非是爱她的人，而是爱她身上所体现的基督。你爱她身上的基督。这就是我们所说的精神上的爱。"

同时，夫妻之爱常常也被看作是沟通一个人与上帝之间的桥梁。邓约翰的十九首《神圣的十四行诗》都写于妻子安莫尔去世之后，其中第十七首就可被看作是一首悼亡诗：

> 自从她的灵魂过早地被掳进天国，
> 我的心就全然扑在天上的事物。
> 我那颗敬慕她的心灵在此渴望，
> 寻觅你，上帝；就象找到那百川的源头。

在勃朗宁看来，夫妻关系是灵与肉的关系。在《布劳斯琴的冒险》(Balaustion's Adventure) 中，他借阿德米托斯之口表达了自己的伤感，阿德米托斯对替他去死的阿尔克斯蒂斯[2] 说：

---

[1] 见《埃拉斯谟作品精要》，约翰·P.多兰编，纽约，1987年版，第51页。
[2] 即弥尔顿诗中的"阿尔塞斯蒂斯"。

既然死神把这对夫妻分开，
那我离去吧，你且留下
你之于我恰象灵之于肉。

托马斯·哈代写于1912年和1913年间的一系列短诗也许最接近中国的悼亡诗，当时他虽已年过七十，但依然怀念故去的妻子。在这些诗中，他主要回顾了他们友好相处长达近四十年的一些日常琐事：他们一起外出旅行，一块野餐，共享欢乐；并且回忆了他们曾共住过的那间房子。在《散步》（The Walk）中，他描绘了自己漫步到一座熟悉的小山前的情形：

今天我照先前的路径
信步蹀到那儿；
再度独自
观望四下
那熟悉的四周
有什么不同么？
只是归来后对陋室之情状
有着那无可名状之感。

这种表达的简明性和情感的内在性多么中国化：这也许是因为哈代象中国人一样，内心深处是不信宗教的，他冷静超然，所关心的是宇宙间的事。

我在上面已描绘了中国悼亡诗的基本特征，简略地考察了一下中国古典文学中这种现象之出现的社会文化背景，并且指出了这种悼亡诗与英国诗人的一些具有相似性质的诗的主要差别。现在我们要问，研究中国的悼亡诗能对作为抒情诗之亚种的哀歌有何贡献？若仅仅研究西方悼念亡妻的诗是不能充分地表述西方的哀歌的，因为西方的哀歌还包括献给朋友的那些纪念诗（中国文学中这种诗也十分常见），例如，弥尔顿的《黎锡达斯》（Lcydas），雪莱的《阿多尼斯》（Adonais），丁尼生的《纪念》（In Memoriam）以及现代诗人奥登的《怀念叶芝》（In Memory of W. B. Yeats）；或者还有那些献给除了妻子之外诗人十分敬爱的人的纪念诗，例如彼特拉克的《致死亡》（In Morte）中的诗篇，兰多的纪念《罗丝·埃尔默》（Rose Aylmer）的诗，早先邓约翰的《周年纪念》（Anniversaries），中古英语中那首十分动人的诗篇《珍珠》（The Pearl），以及如同乔叟的《公爵夫人的书》（The Book of Duchess）那样的使人产生同感的诗。但是这样铺开一谈将会超出本文的范围。我们现在所能说的就是，如果不考虑到人性的深处，如果不考虑到中国悼亡诗中亲切的家庭生活，以及诗中的种种意象，作为抒情诗之亚种的哀歌的定义就将是不完整的。这一文类通过扩大了抒情内容，也就扩大了抒情感受的表现力，丰富了读者的文学体验。当家庭制度出现了危机、在缓慢地（也许是迅速地）解体时，这种诗也许具有某种意义吧。

"Dao-wang Shi: The Poet Lamenting the Death of His Wife"，1987 年 6 月在日本东京大学国际比较文学讨论会上宣读。日译文见东京大学《比较文学研究》，1988 年 53 号。王宁译

巴罗克的涵义、表现和应用

《中国大百科全书·外国文学卷》没有收巴罗克的条目（可能收入建筑或艺术类了），我们编的外国文学史和我们写的外国文学研究论文中，如果不是从不出现这个词，至少也很少见。这事实说明巴罗克作为文学术语——代表一种风格，或西方文学某一特定时期的风格，还没有受到注意或不予接受。

巴罗克作为一个文学术语，在西方一个世纪以来，经过提出、反对、反复讨论、应用，已被广泛接受，"有可能扩散得更广。"[1]

最早试图应用这个名词到文学上的是瑞士学者佛尔弗林（Heinrich Wölfflin）。在他的《文艺复兴和巴罗克》（Renaissance und Barock）一文中（1888），他论述了罗马的建筑风格，最后他谈到巴罗克风格也可以应用到文学和音乐上去。[2]

佛尔弗林提出这个论点之后，并未引起巨大反响。直到第一次世界大战以后，才掀起关于巴罗克的讨论和研究的第一次高潮，主要发生在德国，波及欧洲其他国家。这一现象正是战后整个欧洲社

---

[1] 韦勒克：《批评概念》，第88页，1963年版。这部论文集里有一篇专论《文学研究中的巴罗克概念》，可参考。

[2] 韦勒克：上引书71页。

会思潮和精神气候的一个组成部分。这种社会思潮集中地、系统地体现在德国哲学家施本格勒（OsWald Spengler，1880—1936）的巨著《西方的没落》（*Un tergang des Abendlandes*，1918—1922）一书中。我们还注意到这一时期也正是德国表现主义戏剧、西欧现代派诗歌和小说抬头的时期。对巴罗克发生兴趣，不是孤立的现象。

西方对巴罗克的研究自第一次世界大战后开端以来，一直兴趣未减，而到了六七十年代，以韦勒克的《文学研究中的巴罗克概念》（1962）为标志，似乎又掀起一次高潮。[1] 这一发展形势和哲学上的存在主义的再发现，语言学中结构主义的兴起，文学上诸如荒诞派戏剧的兴起，在时间上又是吻合的。西方研究界对巴罗克的兴趣到现在也尚未衰竭。

我们今天研究巴罗克有什么意义呢？

这个概念在我们的外国文学研究里比较生疏，研究一下可以提供一些信息；在西方虽然已是老题目在我们还可算新信息。（其实，外国文学中，尤其是时间上稍远一些的，还有许多领域对我们来说仍是"新"的。）其次，巴罗克概念给我们提供了一个新的角度去看待文艺复兴到十七世纪这一段文学的发展。从文艺复兴直接跳到古典主义，其间缺乏联续性、过渡性。当然，是否可以用巴罗克作为断代名词，还值得讨论，下面还要谈到。不过，巴罗克作为一个全欧性的"运动"已是成立了的事实。

此外，巴罗克研究不仅有助于解释文学史的发展，而且对深入理解一种特殊的文学表现形式是非常必要的。这种表现形式有它的时代性，也有它的普遍性。难怪有的评论家认为这种风格贯串整个欧洲文学，从欧里庇德斯到兰波（Rimbaud）。一种风格代表一种精

---

[1] 参看黄德伟：《欧洲白缛文学研究》，新学术出版社，里乞蒙，美国维吉尼亚州，1978年版。

神状态和意识形态，因而有人甚至把这概念引用到哲学、数学、物理学。[1] 作为文学描述术语和批评术语，巴罗克给我们提供了一个新的、有用的角度。

西方近一百年来对巴罗克的研究积累了大量的成果，发表了许多看法，有的是相互矛盾的。我们研究西方文学有必要掌握这些成果和观点，作出我们的判断。在中西比较文学领域里，国外也有不少学者把巴罗克概念应用到中国诗歌和戏剧的研究上。其可行性到底怎样，值得再探讨。

巴罗克这个概念在西方也不是被人一致接受的。不过，时至今日，即使开始持反对立场的法国学者，保守的英国学者，也都逐渐接受。这个概念已被普遍承认和应用了。

巴罗克作为一种艺术风格的术语最早是指文艺复兴后期意大利的建筑的特点。中世纪建筑最高成就应算哥特式教堂，是为宗教服务的。这种建筑给人以一种神秘的感觉，信徒们一进教堂，视线就被逼迫向前，直到神坛。文艺复兴时期的建筑最有代表性的是意大利佛罗伦萨等城市的私人府邸，是为新兴的富商和贵族霸主服务的，核心思想是享乐，物质的享乐和精神的享乐。按照当时的审美观念，这种建筑是匀称的，宏伟的，它给人以一种明朗而不是晦暗，活泼而不是沉思的感觉。文艺复兴时期，即使是教堂也和哥特式教堂迥乎不同，如罗马的圣彼得大教堂，它的平面图是所谓希腊十字架形，即呈正十字形。教堂给人的感受只能站在教堂的中心点才能领略。[2] 它不是引向神秘，而是使人享受周围的美。所以即使是教堂，人还是占据了美的中心。当时的罗马教皇大都出身贵族，在政治上、宗教上镇压新教，在艺术趣味上又是享乐的。

[1] 韦勒克：《批评概念》，第72页。
[2] 尼克罗斯·柏夫斯奈：《欧洲建筑学概要》，企鹅丛书，1945年版，第95页。

由于科学的发展，绘画里开始用透视法，产生了立体感，一反中世纪的平面呆板。也就是说绘画更加现实主义，更加合理，对象的比例更合乎理性。建筑也复如是，一座建筑，各部分的分割（articulation）十分明晰，总体十分和谐、合理。

但是到了文艺复兴后期，美的享受变成了或者说堕落为感官刺激。巴罗克建筑打破了匀称、平衡、合理的原则，给人一种不规则、不稳定的感觉，看不出部分与整体之间的明朗关系，相反却引起一种视觉幻象和戏剧性的效果。例如，巴罗克建筑特别喜欢用椭圆形，把圆形拉长扭曲，大而至于圣彼得大教堂的广场，小而至于窗户。都不是圆的，而呈椭圆形。圣彼得大教堂前由贝尔尼尼（Gian Lorenzo Bernini）设计的两翼圆柱廊把广场合抱，呈椭圆形，面对大教堂正面，给人一种向上瞻望一座舞台的感觉。梵蒂冈宫入口处的有名的"王家走廊"（Scala Regia），它隐藏在周围建筑物之中，它的出现非常突兀。它本身狭长，到终端变得更窄，整座走廊向上倾斜，加上光线两端明，中间暗，使这座建筑具有强烈的戏剧性。在装饰方面，巴罗克建筑从形式到材料都追求新奇怪诞，椭圆形的窗、螺旋形的柱、尖圆顶、多角形、棕榈叶以及许多无意义的花饰。

巴罗克精神体现在绘画和雕塑里就是感情的夸张，特别是哀伤的感情，形象上则是一种扭曲。早期的雕塑和米开朗吉罗的"皮埃塔"（Pieta，圣母玛利亚抱耶稣尸体像，在罗马圣彼得大教堂）就已见端倪，突出了哀恸之情。一百年后贝尔尼尼雕塑的圣铁烈莎像（在罗马胜利的圣玛利亚教堂）把这位西班牙贵族出身、重建白衣僧团的狂热天主教徒塑造成一个疯狂入迷、形似晕厥的姿态，旁边还塑了一个小天使把一支金箭刺进她的心脏。

巴罗克绘画则往往体现为比例的失调，对照的强烈，如廷托雷托（Tintoretto），而最能说明问题的莫过于出生于希腊克里特岛的西班牙画家埃尔·格莱科（El Greco，"希腊人"），他所画的人物形象都是拉长了的，特别是面部，给观者一种忧郁痛苦的感觉，突出人物受难的表情，形象的比例既失调，色彩的对比又非常刺目。无论是巴罗克雕塑还是巴罗克绘画都是夸张感情到了歪曲的程度，而主要是强烈的痛苦感情，精神上的紧张状态。

最有代表性的巴罗克音乐形式莫过于赋格曲，或称遁走曲（Fugue）。这是一种复音乐曲形式，有一个或两个或更多短小的主题，由一个声部唱出或奏出，然后各声部按对位法不断重复模仿，相互交织，给人以一种流动不定、错综复杂、华丽绚烂的感觉。这种形式是在十七世纪形成的，到了巴赫而登峰造极。

从巴罗克艺术来看，它的特点是华丽、扭曲、刺激，反映着一种不安、不稳定的精神状态。用布克哈特（Burckhardt）的话说，它"标志文艺复兴盛期的衰落"。用到文学上，除了这些基本特点之外，它似乎取得更广泛一些的涵义。

艺术术语用到文学理论和文学评论上是寻常的事，如罗珂珂（rococo），哥特式（Gothic），怪诞（grotesque），镶嵌（mosaic）等等。佛尔弗林把巴罗克引用到文学也可说是顺理成章。

巴罗克一词（baroque）的词源，众说不一。一般认为它是从葡萄牙语巴罗珂（barroco）一词演变而来，原来是珠宝商用来称呼形状不规则的珍珠的术语。最初它是一个带有贬义的词，表示不完美、粗糙以至丑陋怪诞，但也有新颖奇特的一面。钱锺书先生在《通感》一文中把它译为"奇崛"。

我们研究巴罗克，我觉得可以从四个方面着手，这四个方面是相互联系的。一、巴罗克文学的效果；二、达到这种效果的手段；三、构思；四、意图，或创作的出发点。

巴罗克文学，尤其是诗歌，最突出的特点就是使人吃惊，好象这些诗人都立意要"语不惊人死不休"一样。读者无论在感受方面或理性方面都受到不同程度的冲击。

产生这种效果的手段，有的学者用两个形象予以概括：刻尔吉（Circe）和孔雀。[1] 刻尔吉是擅长魔法的女神，她把奥德修的伙伴们都变成了猪，因此她象征变幻、谲变的原则；孔雀则象征炫耀、华丽的原则。所谓变幻，在组织上、形式上即变化多端，不平衡，不规则，例如诗歌里不整齐的格律，戏剧里多层中心人物和松散的结构（不严格遵照亚理斯多德的模式），散文里的拖沓或另一极端的压缩。总之都不符合文艺复兴时期所提倡的整齐和谐的理想。在意象方面则趋于怪谲、华丽、触动人的感官。节奏和情景则富于戏剧性。

这些技巧上的特点来源于特定的思维方式。一个就是所谓辩证、论证、辩论思维（dialectic），也就是柏拉图在对话录中的思维方式，目的是通过问答、反复论辩，要对某一问题追问出一个原委来，表现了一种探索的精神，探求真理的精神。从这里就演变出（虽不能说等而下之）所谓的奇思妙想（意大利文的Concetto，西班牙文的Concepto，英文的Conceit）。这个词在十六七世纪本来就相当于"思想"、"观念"，后来才用于奇思、矛盾的诡词、夸张、奇特的比喻等等概念。

另一个就是修辞。修辞本身也是一种思维方法。亚理斯多德就认为辩证和修辞是人类理性活动的两个分支。从中世纪以来直到近代，修辞作为教育和文化的一个重要组成部分，影响着西方人们的思维方式。从历史上看，修辞也是为论辩服务的。甚至象最新的

---

[1] 韦勒克：《批评概念》，第124页。

"解构主义"（Deconstruction）的倡导者德里达（Derrida）追随尼采之后，声称哲学也要从形式、修辞、比喻的角度去探讨。[1] 足见修辞学在西方思想、文化领域影响之深远。

修辞学的核心或最基本的原则，我以为是二分法。例如各种比喻（明喻、隐喻）就是把两项不同而又类似的事物并列在一起；寓言呈现的是一项，实指的则隐在背后；替代法（metonymy）以一物代替与之关联的另一物；矛盾的拼合（oxymoron）把完全对立的两项拼在一起，一般常举的例子如"残酷的慈悲"。一与多的结合也是修辞学中一种主要手段，例如"组格玛"（zeugma）用同一动词或形容词管辖两个不同性质的名词，如"她向那无家可归的孩子打开她的家门和她的心"，"她在舞会上丢失了她的项链和她的心"；又如双关语，一语两义或多义；有时用两个概念代替一个概念（hendiadys），或用更多的词表述一个概核（pleonasm）或重复；或用部分代表全体（synecdoche）。修辞学里还有一类常用的手法就是颠倒词序（chiasmus）或错位（hypallage），所谓错位一般指的是把形容词放在不该放的名词之前，如"不眠之夜"。再就是夸张（hyperbole）和不足（litotes），所谓"不足"就是婉转，不和盘托出，其实是以守为攻，如"不坏"实际意味"很不好"，与粉饰、迂回的说法（euphemism，meiosis）很近似。修辞学中还有所谓的"突降法"（anticlimax），从严肃突然降到轻浮，从崇高突然降到卑下，与读者期待相反，例如"他爱上帝，爱正义，也爱竞赛汽车"。这些手法都包含一正一反。最后，修辞学还有一种手法，就是设问和呼召，设问往往是一种反问手法，设问和呼召都包括说者与听者两方，尽管听者往往不在场。

---

[1] 雅克·德里达：《论文字学》，斯皮瓦克译，约翰斯·霍普金斯大学出版社，1976年版，第22页。

修辞学经常不为我们所注意，但在西方现代以前却是社会文化一项很重要的内容，在很大程度上影响着、支配着特别是作家的思维。随便举个例子。矛盾的拼合法实际上是客观现实的反映。社会本身就充满了凶残暴虐，它偏要用表面的善良掩饰起来，把善与恶硬套在一起。巴罗克作家所表现出来的特点是和客观世界给他们的感受和引起的思想不可分的。从他们使用的这些修辞手段我们可以推断出在这后面隐藏着的他们的心理状态，推断出他们的意图，从这里又可能反过来检验其表现形式和效果。

那么，巴罗克作为一种情感，一种心态，一种精神状态或一种思想意识又是怎样的呢？有人称之为"欧洲良知之危机"，感情与理性失去平衡，理性不能控制感情，人失去了对理性、对人性的信念，失去了天人的和谐观，世界和宇宙失去了完整性。主要表现为：

一、忧郁、沮丧。十七世纪英国作家勃顿就写过一部巨著《忧郁的解剖》。[1]忧郁到了尽头便会想到死亡。莎士比亚为什么要在《哈姆雷特》里特意写了掘墓一场，让丹麦王子拿着约立克的骷髅大做文章？为什么邓约翰在临死前要人把他裹在包尸布里画像？"死亡的舞蹈"是当时绘画的常见的主题。牧师泰勒写了《圣洁的生》和《圣洁的死》两部书。

二、悲哀、怜悯、同情。《哈姆雷特》里莪菲丽亚之死以及王后对她的哀悼；前面提到的米开朗吉罗的"皮埃塔"雕像，都是这种感情的流露。表现这类感情的作品比比皆是。

三、幻觉。混淆现实与幻象，这是一个很重要的特点。它说明人们把握不住现实，对现实不理解。在文学里，人生如梦、人生如

---

[1] 参看拙作《十七世纪英国文学》。

舞台这类话题（topoi）也是俯拾皆是。西班牙作家卡尔德隆就写过叫做《世界大舞台》和《人生如梦》的剧本。在后一剧本中，西吉斯蒙多王子被囚禁、释放、再囚禁、再释放的经历使他学到人生一切幸福都将象梦一样消逝。现实世界就象天上的云、是多变的幻象，忽而象骆驼，忽而象黄鼠狼，忽而象鲸鱼（《哈姆雷特》）。哈姆雷特可能是装疯，但安东尼是自戕前沉痛而清醒地宣称："有时我们看一朵云很象一条龙，有时云气又象熊或狮子，象带箭楼的碉堡，象一座悬崖，好象在和我们的眼睛开玩笑。"

世界既失去了它的"合理性"，也失去了它的联续性，也就变成支离破碎。有人把巴罗克作家看世界比作印象派画家的画，世界仅仅是由无数不同颜色、不同深浅的点构成的，影影绰绰。[1] 宇宙破碎了，诗人的诗作里布满了宇宙的碎片，埃及女王形容安东尼的光辉形象，说他脸上有一个太阳，一个月亮。安东尼失败了，小宇宙破碎了，与之相应，大宇宙也必然支离破碎。

人生是一幅模糊的画，是舞台，是梦，现实与幻象不分，互相混淆。戏剧中经常使用的乔装改扮、误会、魔法巫术、突变等等现象能仅仅解释为戏剧技巧手法么？无宁说这种手法的一再出现反映了一种观念，或者说一种下意识，为许多人所共有，真即是假，假即是真。人生就是幻觉，生活里没有幻觉，生命也就终止了，象唐吉诃德那样。

四、放纵。文艺复兴时期的理想的人是"健全的体魄，健全的头脑"，这一理想已不复存在。爱情由"真诚心灵的结合"这一理想变成了纵情。莎士比亚的《安东尼与克丽奥帕特拉》即是一例。这剧开宗明义第一句台词就点明了这点："唉，我们主帅的迷恋溢

---

[1] 参看穆格夫人：《巴罗克敏感性的欧洲背景》。

出了尺度了。"一个不惜让罗马消溶在第表河里，另一个不惜让埃及消溶在尼罗河里，只要爱情。埃及女王自称"我们是以爱情为职业的"，莎士比亚这里用了一个多义词 trade，可以解作"走惯恋爱的路"，（她以前和凯撒也生过儿子，）也可以解作"交易"，那么爱的涵义就更加等而下之了。

放纵的表现不仅爱情里有，放纵也表现为一种变态的狂疯，甚至表现为对残酷行为的迷恋，表现为虐待狂和受虐待狂。

五、神秘主义。这主要是爱和神秘主义的结合，特别表现在天主教诗人的作品里。在他们身上人文主义思想和天主教意识的矛盾特别尖锐，灵与肉的斗争特别激烈。这恐怕在一定程度上是天主教在宗教改革的巨大浪潮面前施加压力的结果吧。例如英国诗人克拉肖（Crashaw）劝说丹比伯爵夫人皈依天主教，就把接受天主教比作男女之爱，用了许多暗示性很强的意象，而且仿照"配画寓意诗"（emblem-book）[1]，冠以插图。把爱和宗教意识结合起来，还表现为爱即是死。诗人把爱的欢乐与痛苦和死亡等同起来了。克拉肖的《圣铁烈莎颂》就有这样的诗句："你将常常诉说／那甜蜜而又微妙的疼痛，／那难以忍受的快活，／那死亡，死去的人／会爱他的死，还想再死一遍，／希望永远这样被人杀死。"

再如安东尼在他自戕前说："我要象一个新郎那样死去，象登上恋人的床榻一样奔赴死亡。""奔赴"原文作 run into，包含着更进一步的暗示。埃及女王临死前也说："我心里怀着永恒的渴望"，"渴望"原文作 Longing，表示对爱的缠绵、强烈的欲望，而"永恒"immortal 实际是"死亡"的同义词。

---

[1] 十六七世纪盛行于欧洲的一个文类。每篇作品以一句格言开始，下面是一幅画，再下面是诗。这类作品具有（往往是宗教的）象征意义，诗是画的注释。有人认为巴罗克诗歌渊源于此。

有人说，巴罗克诗人充分意识到他有话要说，却又说不明白。他充分了解把意念表达出来的困难，充分了解语言之不足。也就是说，内心的苦闷和痛苦难以言传，诗人必须和语言搏斗，他的诗往往流于晦涩难明。

巴罗克既代表一种矛盾的、激烈斗争的心态，在风格上也表现为充满了矛盾。形象的错乱，比喻的奇特，似非而是的论辩，以至句法的扭曲，大胆运用修辞手法，这一切都与作者的心态是一致的。

巴罗克代表一种心理状态，一种特殊的精神状态，一种哲学，一种世界观。诚如韦勒克所说，它却不限定于某一宗教派别，有天主教的巴罗克，也有新教的巴罗克；也不限定于某一阶级，有贵族的巴罗克，也有市民和农民的巴罗克；甚至不限定于某一民族，而是一个全欧现象。可以说，它是笼罩全欧的"时代精神"。那么是不是可以用巴罗克来作为文学史断代的标记呢？韦勒克认为可以，因为它能概括文艺复兴和古典主义之间欧洲文学的普遍风格，又能包括各国自己的派别，如意大利的玛利诺派，西班牙的冈果拉派，法国的辞藻派，英国的玄学派。但这里问题很多。第一，无论从思想内容还是从风格来说，巴罗克不可能包括这一时期一切文学，似乎也无人尝试作这样的断代。作为一个"文学运动"，象后来的浪漫主义，它有独立的存在，但同时还有其他文学流派并存，它不能包揽一切。此外还有一个民族感情、民族批评传统的问题。断代也还有一个起讫问题，有人把它定在十六世纪最后十年一直到十八世纪中叶，下限似乎太长了，上限又似乎太短。文学史的发展总是盛中就埋伏着衰，衰中又冒出复兴的迹象。总之，巴罗克作为文学史断代的概念还值得研究。

巴罗克作为一种风格概念能否扩大应用？有人认为它是历史上

屡见不鲜的现象，每当伟大的艺术进入衰落时期就出现巴罗克风格，表现为卖弄辞藻和追求戏剧效果。尼采就持此看法。[1] 这里除了有历史循环论的嫌疑之外，衰落的表现未必都仅仅是辞藻的修饰或对戏剧性效果的追求，或其他什么巴罗克特点，可能表现出很不同于巴罗克的一些特点。此外，能不能把巴罗克从产生它的社会历史环境里抽出来，把它孤立起来，变成一个普遍的批评概念，应用于一切文学呢？这是一个复杂的问题。浪漫派诗歌、哥特式小说、罗珂珂风格、现代派诗歌和戏剧，都可以和巴罗克牵连得上，有的神秘，有的华丽，有的怪诞，不是都合乎巴罗克的特点么？也有人曾尝试过把这种风格应用到中国古典戏剧和诗歌上去，如《中国传统舞台的"巴罗克精神"》，《李商隐：九世纪中国的巴罗克诗人》，《中国巴罗克传统中孟郊的诗》。[2] 我觉得巴罗克是特定历史时期、特定空间范围、特定文化下的产物，它和其他意识形态、其他表现方式有相通之处，是否能普遍而又准确地应用于其他文学，值得进一步研究。

我们说巴罗克的产生有它的社会历史原因，如宗教改革和反宗教改革的斗争，各种性质的频繁的战争，政治上的斗争，社会的动荡。这些都是产生巴罗克文学的基本条件，但是独独产生"这一种"文学，而不是其他种类的文学，则有赖于特定的文化，其中包括思潮、哲学、心理形态、文学传统等等。就巴罗克来说，我觉得修辞学是一个很关键的影响。

修辞学在西方人们的文化修养里，在两千多年间，一直占着很重要的地位，虽然在当代西方文化里它已没有什么地位。"修辞学的意思是'说话的技巧'，因此根据这一基本概念，修辞学教人怎

---

[1] 韦勒克：《批评概念》，第 116 页。
[2] 黄德伟：《欧洲白缪文学研究》。

样艺术地组织谈吐。随着时间的迁移，这一最初的观念演变成一门科学、一种艺术、一种生活理想，事实上成为古代文化的一根支柱。"[1] 雅典的民主生活，罗马的法治，希腊化时期的学术研究，中世纪教会的教育，使修辞一直受到重视。到了文艺复兴时期，修辞学不仅仍在学校里教授，修辞学的书也层出不穷。

前面提到亚理斯多德在《诗学》里声称论辩和修辞是人类理性活动的两大分支。我们现在表达思想感情仍离不开修辞，只是我们没有意识到而已。修辞的目的无非是要提高说理和动情的效力。西方系统化了的修辞学无异是思维方式的系统化。夸张是修辞手段，它就是一种思维方式。思维离不开修辞。与修辞最相适应的思维也许应是富于感情色彩的思维。亚理斯多德认为作为悲剧媒介的语言应当是美化了的、给人以快感的语言，即带有节奏性、音乐性的语言，也就是说修辞的语言；他又说要使情节惊心动魄，主要靠突转与发现，这些显然也是修辞手段。奥维德的诗，塞内加的悲剧最为有意识地运用修辞手段，以期达到或则优雅，或则悲惨，或则机巧的效果。他们在创作时运用修辞是很突出的，只是他们做得过分，反而给人以不真实的感觉。

修辞学不仅和文学创作有着密不可分的关系，以至可以说不了解修辞就不可能完全了解西方文学；它和其他艺术也有紧密关系。十五世纪佛罗伦萨建筑师阿尔贝尔蒂（L. B. Alberti）就敦促画家要熟悉"诗人和修辞学家"，因为他们能刺激画家去发明，赋予他们绘画的主题以形式。[2] 所谓发明（inventio）正是演说术五个要素中的第一要素，指的是"新意"，而不是机械的模仿。可见

---

[1] 库尔提乌斯：《欧洲文学和拉丁中世纪》，原德文，英译本，普林斯顿大学出版社，1973年版，第64页。
[2] 同上书，第77页。

修辞学不仅可以向画家提供如何美化作品的启发，更重要的是教他如何构思，如何安排结构。修辞学和音乐的关系更为密切。早在中世纪，"音乐的教学法就采用修辞学的教学法。有的所谓'发明术'（ars inveniendi；参看巴赫的'创意曲'），有所谓音乐题目等等。"[1]培根在他最后的一部著作《自然史》（*Sylvia Sylvarum*）里说："对答曲和遁走曲是与修辞学的手段，与重复和叠字法吻合的。"[2]

可见任何艺术活动都离不开修辞学，任何自我表现都离不开修辞学。因此有人说"接受古代修辞学是西方中世纪以后很长一段时期艺术上自我表现的决定性因素"。修辞学在西方长期以来是教育的一部分，是一个人的文化修养的组成部分。很象"不学诗，无以言"一样。歌德甚至把修辞看作"人类最高的需要"之一。[3]讲究修辞这种风气甚至感染到社会下层，莎士比亚喜剧中的丑角不是因为咬文嚼字出错而受到嘲笑吗？所以说修辞也是社会文化的一部分。在一定的条件下，它就发挥某种特殊的作用。巴罗克就是危机时期修辞发挥特殊作用的表现。我们从宏观的文化角度去考察巴罗克就能更直接地阐明巴罗克之所以为巴罗克的道理。

（1986 年 7 月为全国高等院校外国文学教学研究会

讲习班讲。原载《国外文学》第 1 期，1987 年）

[1] 库尔提乌斯：《欧洲文学和拉丁中世纪》，原德文，英译本，第 78 页。

[2] 英文《牛津大字典》Fugue 条引文。

[3] 黄德伟：《欧洲白缪文学研究》，第 63 页。

The Mirror and the Jigsaw

A Major Difference between Current Chinese and
Western Critical Attitudes

未刊英文论文集；杨选校订整理，王宁审阅

Preface

Most of the essays in this collection were inspired by the vigorous revival, in the course of the past decade, of Comparative Literature in this country, which had lain dormant for thirty years and more. They are thus tentative efforts and deserve properly the name of "essays".

My modest aim of publishing them is to provide for a readership who knows English but no Chinese a glimpse, though imperfect and inadequate, of what Chinese comparatists have been doing. It is hoped that more and better achievements by Chinese comparatists than mine will appear in English and through their active participation in the international community of comparatists Comparative Literature will eventually become truly international and intercultural.

Two of the essays in the collection have previously appeared in print; a third in a Japanese translation; a fourth a translation from the Chinese original. Many of them have appeared in their Chinese versions.

Finally I wish to take this opportunity to express my special gratitude to the Trustees of the National Humanities Center in North Carolina, U. S. A. for a grant of fellowship for 1988-89, and to the invaluable help rendered me by the Center's staff, without which the last essay in the collection could never have been written.

Yang Zhouhan

Department of English

Peking University, Beijing

November 2, 1989

Virgil and Chinese Poetic Tradition [1]

The first contact between China and the West dated back to the 5-4th centuries B. C. when silk was brought to the Greek world by an Indian people whom the Greeks called Σῆρες (Seres). Such contacts between China and the Western world were indirect but continuous. By the end of the 2nd century and the beginning of the 1st century B. C., the emperor Wu of the Han dynasty sent successive missions to the West reaching as far as Alexandria (or Byzantium). The traffic between Alexandria and Rome was busy as well as easy. But the Romans had only a nebulous idea of the people called Seres and where they lived, just had only as the Hans gave confusing accounts of countries west of Kashmir. Horace (*Ode* III.29, 25ff) advises Maecenas not to worry about a possible invasion on Rome by the Chinese:

> Tu civitatem quis deceat status
> curas et urbi sollicitus times
> quid Seres et regnata Cyro
> Bactra parent Tanaisque discors.

> You care for the state that it
> Should be stable and fear anxiously

---

[1] A talk given at Stanford University, Nov. 12, 1987.

What the Seres and Bactra under Cyrus

And discordant Tanais may prepare against our city.

And Virgil thought that silk, like cotton, grew on the leaves of trees.
(*Georgics* II. 120-121)

Quid nemora Aethiopum molli canentia lana,

uelleraque ut foliis depectant tenuia Seres?

Why tell of the Aenthiopian groves all white with downy wool,

Or how the Seres comb from leaves their fine fleeces?

Pliny the Elder in his *Natural History* mentions in admiration the iron tools made in China (Fan Wenlan: *Zhongguo Tongshi* I. p. 88).

But quite definitely neither empire knew the literature of the other. It must be the caprice of history that Roman literature was little known in China until the early 30s of the present century. Articles on Virgil appeared in the literary magazine the *Xiao-shuo Yue-bao*, 1930 and 1931 and a history of Roman literature by Wang Li（王力）was published in 1933. But it took a quarter of a century to see a translation of a Latin work into Chinese—Virgil's *Eclogues* (1957). That the *Eclogues* should be the first work to be translated is significant. This will be dealt with later. My own translation of Ovid's *Metamorphoses* appeared in 1958, the *Ars Poetica* in 1962 and the *Aeneid* in 1984. I also translated Seneca's *Troyan Women* as a parallel text to Euripides' play. In recent years Lucretius was translated, so was Tacitus' *Agricola*, and Plutarch. But compared with Greek literature, Roman literature is far less fully represented in Chinese translation. Homer, the tragedians, Aristophanes and even Menander,

Plato and Aristotle and perhaps the historians have all been translated wholly or in part.

The reason for this is not far to seek. It is primarily because in most textbooks of European literature, Roman literature is represented as merely an imitation of Greek without its own individuality. It plays a kind of gap-filling or subsidiary role between ancient Greek literature and modern developments. In a literature curriculum, Roman literature is taught either perfunctorily or skipped altogether. I would not blame the teachers because not many translated texts were available. But a more important reason may be that Roman literature is thought to be less attractive and intrinsically inferior to Greek. Greek literature in many respects (story-element in the epics, characterisation, the dramatic tension in the tragedies) is more appealing. And the significance of Roman literature to later developments of European literature is not fully understood or appreciated; the distinctive qualities of Roman literature itself are not fully exposed and recognized. In the two-volume *History of European Literature* (1964, 1979) which I edited and to which I contributed, inter alia, the section on Roman literature, I tried to give the reader in the limited space allowed me a more or less complete picture and at the same time to point out the differences between the two ancient European literatures. But with what success I do not know. One of the intrinsic qualities of Roman literature lies, I believe, in the Latin tongue and its mode of expression. One has to have at least a nodding acquaintance with the language before one can begin to appreciate the literature. Another difficulty is the lack of knowledge of Roman history, geography, religion, mythology, social history which abounds in Roman literature works.

But in spite of all this, Roman literature has or should have its appeal to an educated Chinese reader. Why should Virgil's *Eclogues* be the very first work in Roman literature to be translated into Chinese? For one thing, they are short. But that is no sufficient reason. One aspect of the pastoral is the idealisation of country life which provides an escape from anxiety and fear. In spite of the topical allusions and local pastoral convention (piping, celebration of love, a simple fare of nuts and apples and well-pressed cheese) the *Eclogues* find a parallel strain in Chinese poetic tradition, sometimes with verbal similarities. In the first Eclogue for instance, the anxiety of the two shepherds over the possible loss of their farms sets off the ideal life they are afraid of losing: a humble cottage with a roof of turf (pauperis et tuguri congestum caespite culmen, I. 68) and the housetops towards the evening smoking under the shadow of the mountains (et iam summa procul villarum culmina fumant, maioresque cadunt altis de montibus umbrae, I. 82-83). This reads pretty much like the celebrated lines by the Chinese poet Tao Qian [陶 潜 (365-427)] or Tao Yuanming [陶渊明] in one of his *Five Poems on Returning to My Country House* (归田园居五首):

Vague and shadowy the distant village, 暧暧远人村
Lingeringly arises the cottage smoke. 依依墟里烟

In both instances, the image correspond closely with the emotion—the enjoyment of peace and freedom from anxiety. The actual situations of the two poets' lives may be quite different. Tao wrote his series of five poems after he had got tired of ten years of officialdom, and Virgil wrote his *Eclogues* after he had been driven from his land. But the ideal life they celebrate is very similar.

Nowhere perhaps is there a better expression of anxiety than in the famous Fourth *Eclogue* which foretells of the birth of the mysterious child who would bring back the age of gold to the world, so that it may be rid of the bad dreams that had haunted mankind. It may or it may not. Even then "shall some few traces of olden sins lurk behind" (pauca tamen suberunt priscae vestigia fraudis, IV. 31). The same sense of anxiety is expressed elsewhere, e. g. in the *Culex*. That peace is not always secure is feared also by Tao Yuanming:

> In the country there are few worldly affairs:
> Few wheels and harnesses sound in my lone alley.
> Even at daytime my thorny gate is shut;
> Facing a cup of wine, I rid myself of worldly thoughts.
> Occasionally a fellow villager
> Would come in his straw-cape for a visit.
> When met, we talk of nothing
> But how our mulberry and hemp are growing.
> The mulberry and hemp grow day by day,
> And day by day my land too expands.
> My constant fear is the arrival of frost and sleet,
> Then will they wither and droop like weeds.
>
> 野外罕人事，穷巷寡轮鞅，白日掩荆扉，对酒绝尘想。时复墟里人，披草共来往，相见无杂言，但道桑麻长。桑麻日已长，我土日已广，常恐霜霰至，零落同草莽。

One is free to interpret the mulberry and hemp either literally or metaphorically. But the threat is there.

The other salient quality in Virgil's poetry is the elegiac mood, which tallies also very well with Chinese poetic tradition. "There are tears for misfortune, and mortal sorrows touch the heart" (sunt lacrimae rerum et mentem mortalia tangunt. *Aeneid* I. 462)—such is the sigh of Aeneas when he looks at the mural painting in the temple of Juno that Dido is building, depicting the fall of Troy. The Confucian ideal of poetic self-expression is to show "joy without wantonness and sorrow without causing pain" [乐而不淫，哀而不伤（论语·八佾）]. The Confucian ideal is one of moderation. So is Virgil's. He may complain of Juno's enmity towards Aeneas: "Can resentment so fierce dwell in heavenly breasts?" (tantaene animis caelestibus irae? I. 11) and the answer is "yes". But the mortals have to give way and submit to fate, to the mandate of the gods. Confucius said of himself: "At 15 I was ambitious to be learned, at 30 I was established scholar, at 40 I was no longer perplexed, at 50 I acknowledged the mandate of heaven, at 60 I could discern by listening, at 70 I followed the desires of my heart without overstepping the rule."

The sense of sorrow is woven into the texture of the whole epic but nowhere does it stand out so prominently as at scenes of parting and separation. When Aeneas carrying his father on his back and leading his son by the hand and followed by his wife, was making their way out of the burning city, he suddenly found Creusa missing. In a frenzy (*amens*), he rushed back to look for her amidst the turmoil until finally her ghost appeared to him advising him to obey the will of heaven. "Banish the tears for thy beloved Creusa" (lacrimas dilectae pelle Creusae, II. 784), said she, and ended by saying "And now farewell, and guard thy love for our common child (iamque vale et nati serva communis amorem, II. 789).

Another painful scene of separation occurs when Aeneas arrives at Buthrotum where Helenus has married Andromache and settle down. Aeneas meets with Andromache when she is making offerings to the empty tomb of Hector. When her surprise at seeing him is over, she tells her story since the fall of Troy. And the first question she asks is "What of the boy Ascanius? Lives he yet and feeds he on the air of heaven?" (qui puer Ascanius? superatne et vescitur aura? III. 339) And on parting, "Andromache, too, sad at the last parting, brings robes figured with inwoven gold, and for Ascanius a Phrygian scarf, nor fails she in courtesy, but loads him with gifts from the loom, and thus speaks: 'Take these, too, my child, to be memorials of my handiwork and witnesses of the abiding love of Andromache, Hector's wife. Take these last gifts of thy kin, O thou sole surviving image of my Astyanax! Such was he in eyes, in hands and face; even now would his youth be ripening in equal years with thine!'" (III. 482-492)

We have seen that when Andromache meets Aeneas, she is sorrowing for Hector, and the presence of Aeneas reminds her immediately of his son Ascanius (maybe the boy is accompanying his father). And Ascanius in turn reminds her of her own son Astyanax. The parting with Ascanius is a sad experience repeated. Further, whether it is a separation between living people or separation by death, it is always final. Andromache is sad because it is the last parting (digressu maesta supremo), and her gifts are the last gifts she can give (dona extrema).

I need hardly mention Dido after the departure of Aeneas or Aeneas after the deaths of Plinurus and Anchises. And these separations are repeated in the underworld.

This theme of separation with little or no hope of reunion is very much loved by classical Chinese poets. One of the greatest Chinese poets of the golden age of Chinese poetry, Du Fu (杜甫 Tu Fu 712-770) wrote at least 120 poems on parting out of his entire corpus of a little over 1,000 poems. It was of course customary for poets to compose farewell poems on parting with friends. But Du Fu and other poets too write also on separation between husband and wife, between lovers, between members of the family. In fact, in the very earliest collection of Chinese poetry *The Book of Odes* there is no lack of such poems. Such kind of poetry may even be classified as a sub-genre under the general category of lyric. Among Du Fu's poems of this kind, there is a series of six very celebrated pieces depicting separation.

The Sheriff of Xin'an describes how the men of that township were pressed into military service by that officer. They were sent off "amidst sobs and moans that reverberated among the blue mountains" [青山犹哭声] and were advised "not to let tears dry up the eyes lest the bones be bared, for Heaven and Earth are forever without mercy" [莫自使眼枯，收汝泪纵横；眼枯即见骨，天地终无情].

The Sheriff of Shihao describes a very extraordinary situation. The officer came to the cottage of an old man to force him into service as all his sons, like other young men, had already been recruited and were away. The old man fled over the wall, and his old wife told the officer that there were only herself and her daughter-in-law with an infant remaining. The young woman did not appear because she wore only tatters. The old woman offered herself for service as she said she could cook. And so she went. The poem ends:

> At daybreak I started on my journey,
> Bidding farewell to the old man alone.
> 天明登前途，独与老翁别。

Farewell of the Newly-Weds tells of the bride saying goodbye to the groom who was pressed into service and ends with:

Human affairs are unpredictable,

Let us think of each other always.

人事多错迕，与君久相望。

The old Man's Farewell reverses the theme of the *Sheriff of Shihao*. The old man seeing that all his sons and his sons' sons had died in war, despaired of life itself and, throwing away his walking stick, volunteered for military service. He bade farewell to his old wife who lay by the roadside, crying that he was too thinly clad against the approaching winter [老妻卧路啼，岁暮衣裳单]. The poet comments:

Does she not know that they will meet only in death?

Yet she worries over his suffering from cold.

That he will never come back is beyond doubt,

Still she would advise him to take enough food.

孰知是死别，且复伤其寒；此去必不归，还闻劝加餐。

The last of the series, *Farewell of the Homeless* presents a yet more curious situation. A soldier returning from war after it was lost, found the whole village which used to have over a hundred households, entirely deserted. Foxes and raccoons were roaming about. Here and there he saw one or two ancient widows. Still he stayed on for the love of his native village and engaged in working the land. The sheriff learned of his return and pressed him once-again into the army. On leaving, he found himself in the ironical position of having no-one to say goodbye to, his mother having died five years before. The poem ends:

What a life to have no home to bid farewell to!

Which is the common people's minimum due.

人生无家别，何以为蒸黎。

The similarity between these two sets of poetry of separation the Virgilian and the Chinese is astonishing. Separation is set in relief against the background of war and unrest. There is a deep sense of family ties, ties of blood. Whether the mandate comes from an emperor or from the gods, it must be obeyed. Separation becomes part of human destiny. The pathos expressed or implicit points to the deep humanity which is common to both poets.

Would the hero Aeneas arouse sympathy in a Chinese reader? The answer is yes and no. Yes, because Aeneas as the personification of *pietas* embodies a sense of duty to the gods, country and family, and this can be readily appreciated by Chinese reader. That Aeneas is a man of destiny with a determined sense of mission—to rebuild Troy in Italy, is also understandable. But when he becomes an Achilles-like character, taking delight in wanton killings, this transitions jars on one's sense of harmony and balance. But it is compensated by the shift of Virgil's sympathy for Turnus.

As for the formal features of the epic, the extensive use of allusions, mythical, literary and historical, is familiar to the Chinese reader as it is also the practice of classical Chinese poets. But the specific references are of course different and offer difficulty. But to a modern Chinese reader who is unfamiliar with Greek and Roman culture and Chinese Literary and culture past, Virgil is as difficult as Du Fu（杜甫）.

Lastly, a word about translation. The first problem confronting the translator is to decide whether he should use verse or prose. Classical Chinese prosody with each line of five or seven syllables (each character being one syllable) can hardly accommodate the stately hexameter. A poem of 10,000 such lines would be intolerable. Besides, no classical Chinese poem ever reaches such length, so that the translator has no ready model to follow. Further classical Chinese poetry is always rhymed, while the *Aeneid* is not. Unrhymed poetry in classical Chinese is unimaginable. Again, few people in China today can write or even read classical Chinese with ease, let alone appreciate it. So the translation of the *Aeneid* into classical Chinese verse is out of the question.

Modern Chinese poetry to achieve in the vernacular is also problematic. It is as to the length of the line or rhyme, but in spite of its history of 60 or 70 years, it has not evolved a generally recognized prosody. It depends on other elements than prosody poetic effect.

One can try to create a vernacular verse from approximating the hexameter, but owing to the compactness of Latin syntax, the vernacular which by its very nature is diffuse and prolix can hardly match it and the line will run to an awkward length. One of the more successful English translation of the *Aeneid* is, to my mind, by C. Day Lewis (1952) done for recital on the BBC Third Programme. He put in six stresses to each line with syllables varying from 12 to 17. He took care to regulate the speed while reciting in order to arrest the audience's attention and interest. This is better than the heroic couplet or even the blank verse. My own translation is in prose with the modest aim of providing the barest essentials of the epic for students and general readers who read neither Latin nor any other foreign language.

King Lear Metamorphosed

In *A Portrait of the Artist as a Young Man* there is an interesting conversation between Stephen and the English dean of studies where the latter is amused to find that the Irish call a funnel a tundish.[1] Thereupon Stephen reflects: "The language in which we are speaking is his before it is mine. How different are the words *home, Christ, alc, master* on his lips and on mine!"

This episode show that whereas there is community of understanding without which communication would be impossible, there is divergence at the same time which is perhaps more vital because it often involves much deeper and more fundamental issues, cultural, religious, political.

Joyce is thinking of English as a common language used by two closely related yet different peoples. In the interpretation of discourse in one language by a speaker of English and German languages, a recent critic finds the famous Schlegel-Tieck translation of Shakespeare aesthetically unsatisfactory, complaining that the German translation fails in that it caters to cultivated taste and misses the corporeal and physical element in certain aspects of Shakespeare's language that are native to folk literature.[2] He gives as an instance the rendering of "I'll lug the guts into the neighbor room" (*Hamlet*, III, iv) into "Ich will den Wanst ins nächste

---

[1] James Joyce, *A Portrait of the Artist as a Young Man* (London, 1946), pp. 214-15.
[2] Michael P. Hamburger, "*Gestus* and the Popular Theatre," *Science and Society*, 41 (1977), 36-42; the suggested alternate wordings is given on p.40.

Zimmer Schleppen," and comments that the German translation lacks the *gestus* of the original owing to the reversed syntax, choice of word, tense-form, and feminine ending. And he offers what he thinks to be a closer and better translation: "Ich schlepp die Kuddeln in den Nachbarraum." With language as widely different as English and Chinese, absolute fidelity must not be expected. What one normally finds is its opposite.

The reverse is also true. How lose or how different, for instance, is Li Bo in English to the original Li Bo? As an extreme case, one calls to mind Ezra Pound's rendering of Chinese poetry, and in one instance he literally stands Justice Gao-Yao (皋陶) on his head (Canto LIII).

The present paper is an attempt at investigating some key notions in one of Shakespeare's major plays as they are translated or omitted (by necessity) in two Chinese versions, in order to show how far translation may mislead and the causes thereof, and to provide some specific examples of the difficulty of communication across language and cultural barriers, and the concomitant difficulty of interpretation.

To begin with, *King Lear* has for its subject-matter the parent-child relationship, and this relationship is built round one of the key notions of the play—nature. Nature here is conceived on two levels: as cosmic order and as human nature. The latter as a category of ethics finds correspondence with and is derivative from physical nature, as can be seen from Albany's stricture on Goneril in Act IV, scene ii: "That nature which contemns its origin/ Cannot be bordered certain in itself, /[...] perforce must wither." Of course, *origin* here may refer to Lear, but *wither* as a metaphor drawn from the vegetable world betrays the link between human nature and Nature with a capital N.

Human nature is either good or wicked. In both Western and Chinese moral philosophies there is no disagreement on this division.

But differences arise when the ethical concept of nature is applied to the parent-child relationship. In *King Lear*, nature or the parent-child relationship is revealed chiefly in that aspect of the relationship which finds its expression in gratitude or ingratitude. A child who shows gratitude to the parent does so in accord with mature.[1] Even among equals the same ethical code is expected to be observed. One can cite Sir Thomas Elyot's *Governour*: "The most damnable vice and most against justice, in my opinion, is ingratitude, commonly called unkindness." For a child to be ungrateful to his or her parent is to be "unkind," even more so than among equals. Hence the enraged Lear's damning epithets for his two elder daughters: "degenerate bastard," "you unnatural hags"; and his remark to Edgar: "nothing could have subdued nature/ To such a lowness but his unkind daughters."

There is also in the parent-child relation an element of authority on the part of the parent and obedience on the part of the child. This may be traced back to Aristotle who considers a son as the father's property just as a slave is property. The father can do anything to the son without incurring the censure of being unjust. "A father can repudiate his son if he is wicked, but the son cannot repudiate his father, because he owes him more than he can possible repay, especially existence."[2]

But the parental authority is modified by the Christian doctrine of universal love, as embodied in Christ[3] and by the egalitarian position of

---

[1] Cf. also Sir Thomas Browner, *Christian Morals* (published 1716), Par III, section xvii, where he defines "ingratitude" as "degenerate vice," and calls "gratitude" the "generous course of things." Browne offers, too, an interesting description of the psychological process leading to " ingratitude".

[2] Bertrand Russell. *A History of Western Philosophy* (New York, 1972), p. 174.

[3] Cf. Milton, *Paradise Lost*, III, where "filial obedience" (line 269) is described as a means of the realization of the God the Father's "immortal love/ To mortal men" (line 266 f.).

all men as sinners facing the same Last Judgement. And the ideal parent-child relationship is one based on love. Lear begins with a fallacious notion of love and ends with full but tragically belated realization.

In the 40-odd instances where the word *nature* and its cognate and equivalents occur, it is variously rendered in the standard Chinese translation by Zhu Shenghao according to context: *tian-di* (heaven and earth), *zao-hua* (the Creator), *ben-xing* (inherent character), *sheng-xing* (inborn character), *ren* (man), *sheng-ming* (life), *jing-shen* (spirit), *shen-ti* (body), *shen-xin* (body and mind), *ren-ci* or *ci-bei* (mercy with strong Buddhistic undertone), *ren-lun* (codified human relationship) or *tian-dao ren-lun* (the way of heaven and human relationship) and most importantly *xiao* (usually rendered filial piety). The antonyms are even more varied.

In this heterogeneous conglomeration, what chiefly concerns us here is the rendering of *nature* into *xiao*. One will find some striking similarities between Confucian and Aristotelian ethical ideals concerning the parent-child relationship. Like Aristotle who considers the child as the parent's property, Confucius in a dialogue with his disciple Zeng-zi affirms that a son's "body, skin and hair are received from father and mother, and he dares not harm them or destroy them." While Aristotle claims precedence for the parent by laying down that the inferior should love the superior more than superior loves the inferior, and that wives, children and subjects should have more love for husbands, parents and monarchs than the latter have for them, Confucius in answer to questions on *xiao* declares laconically, "No deviation"; that is, no deviation from what is prescribed by rites or the customary code of conduct. And on another occasion he asserts that a son should not only provide for parents but revere them because parents are not mere dogs and horses. What is more, Aristotle considers ethics as a branch of politics and his "magnanimous man"[1] is quite obviously a pattern of the king. Confucius also sets up *xiao* as the prototype of the socio-political superior-inferior relationship: "A sage king governs the state on the principle of *xiao*." But here the parallelism stops.

The Confucian ethical code governing the parent-child relationship is far more stringent than that in the West. Filial obedience is as absolute as paternal authority. This may be due to the fact that the social and political structure in the feudal West was much more loosely strung together than in China. The Holy Roman Empire itself was but an empty frame, while within each feudal state, local nobilities enjoyed considerable independence, and allegiance of vassal to overlord was conditional. In China, centralized feudal rule was absolute; the power of the superior over the inferior was also absolute. Filial conduct is codified in the Confucian dialogue mentioned above the *Xiao-jing*, where the principle governing the parent-child relationship is manifestly extended to the sovereign-subject relationship. Filial obedience was encouraged in various ways. In China's dynastic histories, for instance, from the late Han downwards, there are special sections devoted to the lives of virtuous women, devoted sons, and loyal ministers. Legendary figures are legion. To cite two of them: Cao E, the daughter of a wizard who was drowned while going out on the river to meet the spirits, cried for seventeen days before she drowned herself in order to recover her father's corpse. A later version tells how eventually her own body surfaced with her father in her embrace. Another celebrated hero is Guo Ju, who decided to bury his three-year-old son because his wages together with his wife's were barely enough to keep his mother alive; rather than to starve his mother, he made the gruesome

---

[1] Russell, *A History of Western philosophy*, p. 176.

decision. But while he was digging he found a pot of gold. This latter story has been subject to scathing ridicule by Lu Xun as a pure hoax.

In spite the powerful exposure of *xiao* as synonymous with subservience in the name of democracy and equality since the May Forth Movement of 1919, the notion of *xiao* persists, though in a modified form. Admittedly there is a good side to it. For society to operate smoothly, there needs to be some sort of code governing behavior, including respect and care for the elderly, which is often associated with the ancient concept of *xiao*.

Nature as cosmos is closely linked with the vicissitudes of human affairs. A correspondence exists between the universal order and sublunary order. A discordant cosmos manifests itself in omens and signs on earth to alert men, because it causes "in cities mutinies; in countries, discord; in palaces, treason; and the bond cracked between son and father." In one breath Edgar charges Edmund as a traitor "false to thy gods, thy brother and thy father." In Lear's view, at any rate at the initial stage, Cordelia's behavior bears cosmic significance. That is at bottom the reason why Lear flies into a rage, and later in his madness he complains: "I am a man/ More sinned against than sinning." Lear realizes that his sin is but that of *superbia* while his ungrateful daughters have sinned against the cosmic principle itself.

The concept of a correspondence between the cosmos and the sublunary world is not alien to Chinese philosophy (e. g., it is proposed by Dong Zhong-shu). The cosmic principle subsumed in the parent-child relationship is of course not immediately apparent in the original text of *King Lear*, and still less so in the translation. But it is more easily noticed in the translation than in the original.

There is yet a second aspect of the parent-child relationship, the legal aspect. The maintenance of aged parents by their children was, and still is, a practical social problem. And to ensure that aged parents were properly looked after when social amenities were scant, some form of legal guarantee had to be provided, as Professor Stephen Greenblatt in his "The Cultivation of Anxiety: King Lear and his Heirs" quote from Alan Macfarlane (*The Origins of English Individualism*): "contemporaries seem to have been well aware that without legal guarantees, parent had no wrights whatsoever."[1] And he further quotes from a thirteenth-century lawsuit in which a widower called Anseline, having agreed to give his daughter in marriage to one Hugh, with half of his land, was to live with the married couple in one house. "And the same Anseline went out of the house and handed over to them the door by the hasp, and at once begged lodging out of charity." The father then became legally a "sojourner."

Bearing in mind this legal aspect of parent-child relationship, one would better understand a series of epithets in the play which are not there accidentally. When Lear pleads with Regan against Goneril, he says "Ask her forgiveness? / Do you but mark how this becomes the house: / 'Dear daughter, I confess that I am old; / Age is unnecessary: on my knees I beg/ That you'll vouchsafe me raiment, bed and food.'" Lear calls his two elder daughters "guardians" and "depositories." Regan, referring to the news that Lear with his retinue is coming, says "if they come to sojourn at my house, /I'll not be there." Again she repeats the word "sojourn" on receiving Lear at Gloucester's house. "I pray you, father, being weak, seem so. /If, till the expiration of your month, /You will return and

---

[1] Stephen J. Greenblatt, "The Cultivation of Anxiety: King Lear and His Heirs," *Raritan*, 2(1982), 92-114; in using this citation on p.110, Greenblatt does not indicate its specific location in Alan Macfarlane, *The Origins of English Individualism: The Family, Property, and Social Transition* (*Oxford*, 1978).

sojourn with my sister, /Dismissing half your train, then come to me."
At the early stage of the play, Gloucester comments on Lear's action:
"Kent banished thus? And France in choler parted? /And the king gone
tonight? Subscribed his power, /Confined to exhibition? /"[1] When Lear
has gone mad, he shouts to the winds "You owe me no subscription." Of
course, the division of the kingdom itself is a legal action, and Cordelia's
answer, "I love your majesty/According to my bond; nor more nor less,"
has a distinct legal ring. But the answer is unfortunate. Apart from being
a jarring note from the mouth of Cordelia, it is a slant on the whole
business of division. Remembering Shakespeare's customary distrust of
the law ("the law's delay," "the bloody book of law," "old father antic,
the law," the law that "wicked prize buys out," "handy-dandy, which is
justice, which is thief?" "gilded sin breaks the strong lance of justice,"
the inhumanity of Shylock's bond, "I crave the law," Angelo's scarecrow
law, etc.), one tends to think that Cordelia's use of the legal term must be
a piece of dramatic strategy, because it does not tally with her character,
her voice being "ever soft, gentle and low." In dramatic terms, Cordelia's
role is much less important than that of her sisters until towards the end
of the play. Even Bradley has to admit that she is "not a masterpiece of
invention," as her initial strong-headedness and innate gentleness can
hardly reconcile with each other.

For the purely legal terms, the Chinese translations do not bear out the

---

[1]　Cf. *Two Gentlemen of Verona*, I, iii, where Antonio, sending his son Proteus to the emperor's
court in the wake of Valentine, tells him: "What maintenance he from his friend receives, /
Like exhibition thou shalt have of me." Or Ben Jonson, *Silent Woman*, III, I, where Mistress Otter
says to her husband: "Is this according to the instrument, when I married you? That I would be
princess, and reign in mine own house; and you would be my subject, and obey me? [...] Who
gives you maintenance, I pray you?" And later on: "Go to, behave yourself distinctly, and with
good morality; or, I protest, I'll take away your exhibition."

technicality of the transaction. Thus for *sojourn*, one finds *zhu* which belongs to everyday speech, or *liu-zhu* which emphasizes the dignity of the personage who is making a temporary stop on a progress. *Exhibition* is variously rendered *yi-kao...guo-huo*, to depend on somebody for a living, or *zhi-ying* a term which occurs in the *Xi You Ji* (*Journey to the West*) where it means a supply of food. To subscribe is translated either as *jiao chu*, an ambivalent word which means to hand over, or rang which means to yield, mostly as a gesture of generosity. In all cases the legality of the transaction is hardly borne out. The law in China was binding on the children only when they committed crimes. Thus in the Penal Law section of the *History of Sui* is a list of ten major crimes, one of which is "unfiliality" (*bu xiao*). But in the majority of case, unfilial deed or behavior which does not constitute crime falls within the domain of morality. Further, Confucian ethics looks askance at the effects of punishment and believes in the efficacy of proper education, as the sage himself asserts: "Guiding the people by means of correction and regulating them by means of punishment may result in their not committing crimes but will not teach them the sense of shame. Guiding them by means of virtue and regulating them with the code of proper conduct will result in their having the sense of shame and winning their allegiance besides." Not until today would a Chinese conceive of the maintenance of parents as a purely legal obligation.

The quibbling over *Nothing and All* which runs all through the play lends it a metaphysical undertone. It is a curious linguistic fact that while "all" is translatable by *yi-qie* in modern Chinese, there is no equivalent for "nothing." Therefore the varying meanings of "nothing" have to be rendered in accordance with the context in which it occurs, with the result that the word itself vanishes completely out of sight, or hearing.

In *King Lear*, "all" on the whole is a positive notion while "nothing" is negative. Superficially "all" means land and means of subsistence, and this is the sence when the Fool says, "If I gave them all my living, I'd keep my coxcomb myself" (I, iv, 120-21). But when Lear addresses his two absent daughters, "O Regan, Goneril! / Your old kind father, whose frank heart gave all" (III, iv, 19-20), "all" will include authority as well as paternal love. Instances of the play on the antitheses of *all* and *nothing* can be multiplied: Lear asking Edgar, "Didst thou give all to thy two daughters?" and a little later, Lear repeating, "What! Have his daughters brought him to this pass? / Couldst thou save nothing? Didst thou give them all?" (III, iv, 64-65).

Nothing is much more complicated. When contrary to Lear's expectation of a more pleasing declaration of love, Cordelia answers, "Nothing", it brings out the surprised Lear's immediate retort: "Nothing will come of nothing." Literally, Lear of course means that if Cordelia refuses to *say* anything, she will get no land. But the word is pregnant with meanings.[1] Cordelia's "nothing" as Lear understands it means no profession of love and therefore disobedience, but on Cordelia's part and as the reader understands it, it reflects her candor and truthfulness even to the extent of being strong-headed. New meanings accrue from it as the action goes on. In Act I, scene iv, the fool sings a ditty conveying a lesson of prudence as a piece of home truth. Kent comments: "This is nothing, fool." And the Fool turns to Lear: "Can you make use of nothing,

---

[1] In his essay "The Quality of Nothing" (reprinted as ch. 8 of *Shakespearean Meanings* [Princeton, 1968], pp. 237-59), Sigurd Burckhardt, while contending that *nothing* is substantive and that there is an ultimate immediacy between word and act, does not elaborate on the various contextual meanings of *nothing*.

nuncle?" to which Lear answers: "Why, no, boy; nothing can be made out of nothing."[1] Here the second *nothing* is equivalent to prudence or worldly wisdom. Further, the Fool's last comment before Goneril appears is: "thou has pared thy wit o'both sides, and left nothing in the middle: there comes one of the parings." This must be associated with a later repartee of the Fool's to Lear's comment on Goneril's frowning: "Now thou art an O without a figure. I am better than thou art now: I am a fool, thou art nothing." *Nothing* here means, among other thing, the absence of wit. Wit in the Elizabethan sense of mental power or *ratio* is the natural endowment peculiar to man as distinguished from the lower orders of being. The word assumes a further meaning of non-entity in the pursued Edgar's soliloquy, when he compares himself as a sham Bedlamite with a real one. "Poor Turlygood! Poor Tom! / That's something yet: Edgar I nothing am." But when Gloucester on sensing the presence of Lear cries, "O ruined piece of nature! This great world / Shall so wear out to naught" (IV, vi, 138-39), the word assumes the ultimate meaning of the total annihilation of the cosmic order.

Now to render the meaning-charged word *nothing* into Chinese, the translator has to resort to a variety of strategies. One of them is to restrict the word to one facet only of its meaning so as to fall in with Chinese idiom and to be made intelligible to the Chinese reader. Kent's "This is nothing" is translated into "These words have not a jot of sense"; and in a different version, "Your cartload of words has not expressed anything." For the Fool's question, "Can you make use of nothing?" One finds "Cannot you find out some sense in the midst of no sense?" A closer

---

[1] Empson in *Seven Types of Ambiguity* (London, 1947), pp.45-46, points out the verbal irony of this speech when read with Cordelia's previous answer in mind.

rendering is "Has 'have not anything' not any use?" which, however, sounds very un-Chinese. One Chinese translation of Lear's answer "Why, no, boy; nothing can be made of nothing," becomes surprisingly, "Gold cannot be panned out from rubbish." It sounds like a Chinese proverb but it is not. Apparently the idea of "rubbish" is suggested by the Fool's next speech (to Kent):"Prithee, tell him, so much the rent of his land comes to: he will not believe a fool." This becomes "he has so much land, and now it becomes a heap of rubbish," which is in itself a very free rendering. The cause of this aberration can be sought only in the translator's idiosyncrasy. As the Chinese idiom requires that the negative be attached to other parts of speech than a noun, the translator has to get around this difficulty by splitting "nothing" into two separate elements. Thus for the Fool's "thou has... left nothing in the middle," and "thou art nothing," the Chinese approximation is "you downright are not a thing." Now this latter rendering smacks incidentally of abuse in Chinese, which the original does not suggest at all.

The different translations of "thou art an O without a figure" are most interesting. One rendering reads "you have become a lone circlet." The image this translation conjures up has nothing to do with the original and is quite meaningless. Another, rather happy translation matches the original in word-play:"you are now the character *zhu* (主)" minus *wang* (王) — i. e., you have become a mere dot, because that is what is left of the subtraction. This may perhaps be called in Chinese critical jargon "similitude in spirit," not in exterior form. Clever as this translation is, the vital notion of "nothingness" disappears entirely. One version of Edgar's soliloquy reads "Poor mad beggar! Poor Tom! Somewhat alike; I now am no longer Edgar", with "nothing" entirely left out. Another version is more enigmatic, for it reads: "Now still is he; I Edgar am no longer." In the note, the translator states that he has adopted Ritson's reading which suggests that Edgar is here convinced that it is all over with him. Finally, for Lear's ominous tone-setting rejoinder to Cordelia in the opening scene, "Nothing will come of nothing," one translator tries to localize the meaning to the practical business at hand of sharing out the land: "If you have no word to say, then you will not have anything." Another translator tries to convey the universal significance by rendering it into "One can exchange 'have not' only with 'have not,'" which again is hardly idiomatic Chinese.

Though *nothing* can in certain contexts have a positive connotation, it represents on the whole the negation of positive qualities, while its cognate form *naught* and the derivative *naughty* are definitely derogatory. No trace of its link with the original *nothing* is detectable in translation. When the Fool advises Lear not to go out into the foul weather, he says, "'tis a naughty night to swim in" (III, iv, 114). Gloucester stamps Regan with this damning epithet "naughty lady" (III, vii, 37). When Lear pleads with Regan, he says "Beloved Regan, / Thy sister's naught" (II, iv, 135-36). The blinded Gloucester hearing and recognizing Lear's voice on the health exclaims, "O ruined piece of nature! This great world / Shall so wear out to naught" (IV, vi, 138-39).

For "naughty night" one translation reads "awkward night"; and, realizing that the rendering is not quite apt, the translator suggests in a note a closer rendering, "too bad a night." Another translation reads "dangerous night." For "naughty lady," one has "vicious woman." For "thy sister's naught," one version reads "a bad one!" and another "your sister is too unfilial." For the world wearing to naught, the translations are competent but fail to convey the finality of the monosyllable. One reads, "a heap of ruins,"[1] and another reads, "so shattered."

The dialectic of *nothing* and *all* is central to the play, Lear begins with believing himself to be all and ends with realizing that he is not all: "They told me that I was everything; 'tis a lie" (IV, vi, 107). The turning point occurs when in the midst of afflictions he declares, "I will be the pattern of all patience; I will say nothing" (III, ii, 37-38). Lear is now identified with Cordelia, echoing the very words Cordelia said. Having gone through life's purgatory, Lear reaches a state of acceptance, which is voiced in Edgar's words: "Men must endure / Their going hence, even ad their coming hither: / Ripeness is all" (V, ii, 9-11). Like Hamlet ("The readiness is all"), Lear is spiritually mature. This final note reminds one of Montaigne's "philosopher, c'est apprendre àmourir," and lends the play its philosophic undertone.

King Lear is a good test-case whereby to settle certain principles of interpretation across cultural and linguistic barriers. Sun Dayu, whose translation of *King Lear* is most meticulously done, acknowledges the insurmountable difficulty of translating this masterpiece into Chinese, saying that nothing short of a miracle could produce a perfect version. He mentions the Schlegel-Tieck translation which, good as it is, is superseded by subsequent translations, concluding that a perfect translation will always remain an ideal. He has the perspicacity to avoid confusing Chinese and Western ethics. Throughout his translation, there are only two instances where he employs the word *xiao* (I, iv, 257; II, iv, 51), because, as he remarks in the note to the second appearance, it becomes inevitable there, though even here he offers an alternative which he abandons on

---

[1] This would be an appropriate rendering of Milton's "and ruin seems / Of ancient pile" (*Paradise Lost*, II, 590 f.).

account of rhyme. As a rule, he translates *loves* into *ai*, not *xiao*, lest, he says, this "great heaven-embracing tragedy, translated into Chinese, be misunderstood for a Confucian moral treatise or a Buddhist book of retribution, and produce the impression that Confucianism prevailed also in the West." Sun further distinguishes two major meanings of the word "nature" and renders it differently according to context. But in spite of all this, it appears inevitable to have to employ words like *ni-lun* (unethical), *en-qing* (loving-kindness), *fu-en* (ingratitude) and the like which in Chinese at once involves the reader in the Confucian ethical network. Nor is the legal aspect of the transference of property made apparent in the translation.

Comparing the two Chinese version of *King Lear*, Sun Dayu's translation is far superior to that by Zhu Shenghao because the former demonstrates a profounder understanding of the play. The difference in quality is due, in large measure, to this understanding but also to the superior command of the Chinese language. (Both are dated; Zhu's translation was done in the late 1930s and early 40s, and Sun's in 1941.) But despite their difference in interpretation and style, it is interesting to note the similarities of the two versions. Though Sun is fully aware of the non-Confucian character of Western ethics and has succeeded in avoiding the employment of *xiao*, he has had to use it on at least two occasions and on others to use words with a strong Confucian moral connotation. On the other hand, Zhu does not seem to be aware of or, in any event, to bother about the difference. Further, both translators seem to be unaware of the legal aspect of transference of property. And owing to linguistic peculiarities, justice is not done to the dialectic of *nothing* and *all*. Our survey seems to prove the validity of the observation that interpretation is historically and culturally constrained, though there is community of interpretation. For both Chinese translators share the same cultural and linguistic heritage. The differences are personal while the similarities belong to the community and to shared culture. Shakespeare, and for that matter any text in translation, is at once the result of a twofold simultaneous process, that of alienation from the native ground and of naturalization in an adopted culture.[1]

---

[1] Lecture delivered at U. C. Berkley, 1986, and reprinted from *Comparative Literature*, Vol. 39, No. 3 (summer, 1987), University of Oregon.

Speculation on a Possible Source of Shakespeare's Dramatic Anomalies

In 1927 T. S. Eliot wrote: "The last few years have witnessed a number of recrudescences of Shakespeare. There is a fatigued Shakespeare, a retired Anglo-Indian, presented by Mr Lytton Strachey; there is the messianic Shakespeare, bring a new philosophy and new system of yoga, presented by Mr Middleton Murry; and there is the ferocious Shakespeare, a furious Samson, pretended by Mr Wyndham Lewis in his interesting book, *The Lion and the Fox*. On the whole, we may all agree that these manifestations are beneficial. In any case so important as that of Shakespeare, it is good that we should from time to time change our minds...About anyone so great as Shakespeare, it is probable that we can never be right; and if we can never be right, it is better that we should from time to time change our way of being wrong." And lately Shakespeare has become Absurdist.

On the other hand, over the centuries Shakespeare has been a myth. It is the birthmark of a myth that it is unalterable, complete in itself but invented. Shakespeare needs some demystification, which will however by no means impair his greatness.

In this essay, I propose to present a diseased Shakespeare, a Shakespeare who suffered from a universal ailment of the time. I do not know if there are any records that show that Shakespeare ever contracted any disease. Apparently he enjoyed good health and died a natural death. But from the way he wrote his play, from the many lacunae and discrepancies, one rather suspects that somewhat he was not always in his right mind. And the many objections which the neoclassicists raised may well be raised again.

We notice in Shakespeare's play many devices and features of great structural importance whose real motivation is not clear, though they have been explained away one way or another. In the early comedies, for instance, there is the naïve trick of disguise or mistaken identity, on which the comic action is built. Once that is removed, the whole structure collapses. In the later comedies, certain problematic elements begin to creep in. In *Much Ado*, for instance, the character Don John (very much disliked), and in *As You Like It*, Jacques (to many, a pet) produce a jarring note on "pure" comedy, playing the part of spoilsport, or a black spot on a radiant surface. Don John's animosity and ill humor and Jacques's melancholy and satirical mood have very little cause in the dramatic context. Antonio in the *Merchant of Venice* confesses, in the opening lines, that he is sad without knowing why. If we include *All's Well* among the plays of the "Middle Period", it begins with characters all in black mourning the recent death of the Count of Rousillon, and with the king hopelessly ill, whose would-be physician Helena has also suffered a new loss in the death of her father.

All these incongruities, glaring in the eyes of the rational neoclassicists, have had their explanations. Antonio's melancholy, for instance, has been said to be due to his anxiety over his argosies, and less plausibly due to the prospective marriage of Bassanio. The problematic characters cited above are created, it has been alleged, as foils to the principal characters or merely as mechanical devices to set the action going. Or else things are just taken for granted.

Things become even more inexplicable in Shakespeare's later plays. Both *Measure for Measure* and *Troilus and Cressida* have all along presented problems of interpretation. The change of stance and change of heart on the part of Angelo and Cressida carry no conviction. In his great plays, the love-hate of Lear, the suspicion and jealousy of Othello and Leontes, Macbeth's ambition and Hamlet's dilatoriness and melancholy have little or quite inadequate cause. And moreover these passions are indulged in to excess.

Like the tragic potentials in comedies, there is the so-called "comic relief" in tragedies.

It seems that for dramatic effect Shakespeare chiefly relies on the confusion of reality with illusion or vice versa, or of dream with the waking world (Antigonus:"for ne'er was dream / So like a waking", *The Winter's Tale* III. iii 16-17). Mistaken identity is the comic manifestation of this confusion. The yoking of opposites in characters like Angelo and Cressida—the merging of what seems and what is, manifests the same confusion. In his later and last plays, it assumes even more serious proportions. The "intimacy" between Cassio and Desdemona, between Polixenes and Hermione, which is more apparent than real, leads to tragic result, though ending on the note of reconciliation. There is death in life and life in death. The peripeteia is contrived and the denouement relies heavily on *deus ex machina*.

About the suspicion of Leontes, critics have proved that it has sufficient ground. One critic points out "that Hermione, at the opening of the second scene, is 'visibly pregnant'. Considering that Polixenes standing beside her refers to nine months and to 'standing in rich place', 'Who can fail to wonder whether the man so amicably addressing this expectant mother may not be the father of her child?'"[1] It may be granted that by

[1] Nevill Coghill, "six points of stage in *The Winter's Tale*", *Shakespeare Survey* II (1958) 33. Quoted in Charles Frey, "Shakespeare's vaste Romance", Univ. of Missouri Press, 1980. p. 43.

a close reading between the lines, one may establish an illicit relationship between hostess and guest, thus supplying a motive for Leontes's jealousy. Can the same thing be said about Cassio and Desdemona? Of course critics may search and discover other details to justify Othello's jealousy. But all efforts will not alter the fact that the antagonists are mixing up illusion and reality. What is the motivation behind this? It can be explained as a dramatic device on the part of the playwright. But why should he resort this kind of device?

If we widen our view to embrace other Elizabethan writers, we shall notice the same confusion. The action in the Arcadia is built on mistaken identity, intermingling reality and phantasy. Pyrocles disguises himself as a woman, and king Basilius falls in love with him, while both the king's young queen Gynecia and one of his beautiful daughters, Philoclea, seeing through Pyrocles's disguise, fall in love with him. The complicated tangle of the plot is finally resolved by the appearance of a stranger, another *deus ex machina*. Amidst the idyllic serenity, with flowery meads, where "shepherd boys pipe as though they would never be old", there lurks treachery, strife and revenge. A utopia is juxtaposed with dire reality.

In the *Faerie Queene*, too, the knights flight against all sort of evil forces; goodness is pitched against evil. If we place the *Faerie Queene* and the *A View of the Present State of Ireland* side by side, we shall immediately concur with de Selincourt: "While he (Spencer) feels its (Ireland's) beauty, he is conscious more than ever before, of the 'heavy hapless curse' that now lies upon the country; and his imagination gains sublimity as it broods over the instability of things on earth. The theme had been recurrent, as a faint undertone, throughout his poetry, in tune to that reflective melancholy which often served to heighten by contrast his keen sense of the joy and the splendor of life; now it became the dominant note of his work."[1]

This is a very good description of the mood of all sensitive people and of the intellectual climate of the time. Further, the *View* reflects a sense of imminent danger and disaster. "All (the Irish) have their ears upright, waiting when the watchword shall come that they shall all rise generally into rebellion, and cast away the English subjection. To which there now little wanteth." In 1598, Spenser narrowly escaped with bare life. Under the outward glamour of the reign of Elizabeth I, there was decidedly and undercurrent of intellectual unrest and emotional tension; there were touches of skepticism, cynicism, a view of the world and of life as theatre, resignation as well as defiance. All these are the various reactions to the political, religious and spiritual situation and reality prevailing at the time. Let me take two examples of direct expression of this mood. The most complete single statement of the theme of world-stage is Raleigh's epigram:

> What is our life? A play of passión,
> Our mirth the music of división,
> Our mother's wombs the tiring houses be,
> Where we are dress'd for this short comedy,
> Heaven the judicious sharp spectator is,
> That sits and marks still who doth act amiss,
> Our graves that hide us from the searching sun,
> Are like drawn curtains when the play is done,
> Thus march we playing to our latest rest,
> Only we die in earnest, that's no jest.

---

[1] Introduction to *The Poetical Works of Edmund Spenser* OUP. 1912, p.38.

For Donne as for Hamlet, the world is "out of Joint":

> Then, as mankind, so is the world's whole frame
>
> Quite out of joint, almost created lame:
>
> For, before God had made up all the rest,
>
> Corruption entered and depraved the rest.
>
> And, Oh, it can no more be questionéd,
>
> That beauty's best, proportion, is dead,
>
> Since even grief itself, which now alone
>
> Is left us, is without proportión.

That the anniversary of the death of a girl of 14 should call up in Donne the image of the world as a corpse (an "anatomy") is in itself symptomatic. In this lopsided world, love itself hardly offers any solace or security:

> And now good-morrow to our waking souls,
>
> Which watch not one another out of fear.

Let others go out and face danger, but let us hold on securely to each other:

> Let sea discoverers to new worlds have gone,
>
> Let maps to other, worlds on worlds have shown,
>
> Let us possess one world; each hath one and is one.
>
> Where can we find two better hemispheres
>
> Without sharp North, without declining West?

Another reaction takes the form of defiance:

Death, be not proud, though some have call'd thee
Mighty and dreadful, for thou art not so;
For those whom thou think'st thou dost overthrow
Die not, poor Death, nor yet canst thou kill me.

There are contemporary attempts at explaining the spiritual crisis. Burton in his pseudoscientific way, attributes the cause of illusory vision to imagination. "As it (imagination) is eminent in all, so most especially it rageth in melancholy persons, in keeping the species (i. e. sight) of objects so long, mistaking, amplifying them by continual and strong meditation, until at length it produceth in some parties real effects, causeth this, and many other maladies. And although this phantasy of ours be a subordinate faculty to reason, and should be ruled by it, yet in many men, through inward or outward distemperatures, defect of organs, which are unapt, or otherwise contaminated, it is likewise unapt, or hindered, and hurt."[1] Again: "Imagination is the medium deferens (means of carrying of course) of passions, by whose means they work and produce many times prodigious effects."[2] The whole notion is that Man's mind is diseased and imagination acts as a catalyst to effect his illusory vision of the world. And he gives some instances of these "prodigious effects". "That some are turned to wolves, from men to women, and women again to men (which is constantly believed) to the same imagination; or from men to asses, dogs, or any other shapes. Wierus ascribes all those famous

[1] *The Anatomy of Melancholy*, ed. A. R. Shilleto, London, 1903. Vol. Vo I. I. p.291.
[2] Ibid., p. 297.

transformations to imagination."[1] If Shakespeare turns Bottom the Weaver into an ass, it is by a feat of imagination, and Titania falling in love with it indicates an imagination gone wrong, literally drugged. One may however argue that Shakespeare here is merely playing with fancy. But in a tragic situation, things become very different. The sleep-walking Lady Macbeth, her doctor says, "is troubled with thick-coming fancies / That keep her from her rest." And Macbeth calls hers "a mind diseased", with "rooted sorrow", suffering from "troubles of the brain", from "perilous stuff / Which weighs upon her heart."

After the laughing Democritus came the trained physician Thomas Browne, a staunch royalist living almost all his life in a Puritan town, with morbid interest in the dead, the bizarre, the remote, the mysterious and legendary. His theory about "vulgar errors" is that they are due to "an inborn tendency (in man) to see things and to remember things as they are not, an erroneous inclination of the mind."[2] It is in human nature to err. "Men that look upon my outside, perusing only my condition and fortunes, do err in my altitude; for I am above Atlas his shoulders."[3] (Certum est quia impossibile est.) He calls the age he lived in "This ill-judging age" (*Garden of Cyrus*). When one is unable to explain things, one leaves them to Chance. The very first sentence of the Dedicatory Epistle of the *Hydriotaphia* reads: "When the funeral pyre was out, and the last valediction over, men took a lasting adieu of their interred friends, little expecting the curiosity of future ages should comment on their ashes, and having no old experience of the duration of their Reliques, held no opinion of such after-considerations." Death is the end-all. Everything

---

[1] Ibid.
[2] Edmund Gosse, "Sire Thomas Browne", London, 1905, p.95.
[3] *Religio Medici*, part II, para, ii.

depends on Chance.

But neither Burton nor Browne offers the real explanation of this abnormal psychology. T. S. Eliot's essay on *Shakespeare and the Stoicism of Seneca*, which I quoted at the beginning of this paper, notices a certain "attitude" in some of the great tragedies. He calls it "the attitude of self-dramatization" which is "assumed by some of Shakespeare's heroes at moments of tragic intensity." It is also conspicuous in Chapman and Marston. Eliot takes the last great speech of Othello's as an example of "cheering himself up". "He is endeavouring to escape reality."

Escape can take various forms. Feigned madness is a common form. There are many famous examples in Chinese literature. Liu Ling (3rd century poet) for instance is reported to have taken to drinking and behaved as though he were mad in order to escape political involvement and court intrigue. He would sit in his house stark-naked. When seen and laughed at by visitors, he replied: "I take Heaven and Earth to be my house, and my house my pants. Why do you gentlemen intrude into my pants?" Self-dramatization is another form of escape. Walter Raleigh is a supreme example. While he was imprisoned in the Tower, he stabbed himself apparently attempting suicide. And in a letter he wrote: "For myself I am left of all men, that have done good to many. All my good turns forgotten, all my errors revived, and expounded to all extremities of ill."[1] Compare it with Othello's "Soft you; a word or two before you go. / I have done the state some service, and they know it; / No more of that." How similar even in wording, except that Othello follows up with a self-analysis and Raleigh continues with desperate indignation.

---

[1] Stephen Greenblatt, Sir Walter Raleigh: *The Renaissance Man and His Roles*, Yale Univ. Press, 1973, p.115.

Escape is not only a form of self-preservation from external pressure but also a sign of internal and spiritual disturbance.

Eliot thinks that self-dramatization is a *modern* attitude, which culminates in the attitude of Nietzsche. He will not say it is Shakespeare's "philosophy", "yet many people lived by it." And Shakespeare by his "instinctive recognition" sees it to be "something of theatrical utility." It is important to note that Eliot implies that self-dramatization as an attitude was epidemic in the early 20th century. It may also be said to be epidemic in Shakespeare's time. It was one of the symptoms of a pervading, prevalent disease of the mind. It is not merely that Shakespeare was cognizant of its existence; he was part of it. He obeys "the weight of this sad time" (*Lear*, V. iii 322) and breathes in the "foul and pestilent congregation of vapours" (*Hamlet*, II. ii. 322).

A recent critic, Anne Righter, commenting on Elizabethan view of the world and of life as stage, has this to say: "Comparison between the world and the stage were so common as to become, in many instances, almost automatic, an unconscious trick of speech...The play metaphor was for Elizabethans an inescapable expression, a means of fixing the essential quality of the age."[1]

This brings us to the question of creative process. As in all human activities, so in literary creation, both the conscious and the unconscious are at work. Can we not perhaps attribute the "automatic", "instinctive", "unconscious", native and inexplicable dramatic devices as well as "tricks of speech" to the workings of the unconscious "the deep well of unconscious cerebration" (Henry James)? The unconscious aspect of the creative process was adumbrated long ago by the third-century

---

[1] Ibid., p. 182.

Chinese critic Lu Ji who in his rhymed *Essay on literature* (the *Wen Fu*), while admitting that literary creation is motivated by the external world, by "Nature's seasonal changes", dwells at some length on what may be equivalent to inspiration, "which, when it comes, cannot be stopped, and when it goes cannot be retained".[1] And he goes on: "Though the thing (i.e. literary creation) is on me, (or stems from me, or is within me,) it is not done by any effort on my part. I pat my empty bosom with surprise, for I do not know by what means it (i.e. my heart) opens and closes".[2] Again, a Tang (9th-century) statesman and man of letters Li Deyu expresses a similar view: "Literary creation is a thing due to natural inspiration. It comes as in a trance, and without thinking it arrives".[3] The 5th-century poet Xie Lingyun in reply to a question on a celebrated line of his says "this line was written with the help of the gods; it is not mine." Professor Qian Zhongshu in his *opus magnum* the *Guan Zhui Pian* (pp.1205-6) quotes the 18th-century German physicist Lichtenberg as saying: "Man soll nich sagen 'Ich denke', sondern 'Es denkt'" and Rimbaud in a letter to Georges Izambard as saying "C'est faux de dire: Je pense. On devrait dire: On me pense. Je est un autre."

It looks as though in creative writing there is an "I" and a "not-I". the "not-I" is the buried consciousness. This can be individual as well as collective. It is the collective unconscious of an age.

Herein perhaps lies a clue to the apparent incongruities in Shakespeare's plays. Shakespeare could not have been so naïve as to really believe that a person in disguise will not be detected. Even considered as a dramatic convention at an early stage of dramatic development, accepted by both

---

[1] 来不可遏，去不可止。
[2] 虽兹物之在我，非余力之所戮，故时抚空怀而自惋，吾未识夫开塞之所由也。
[3] 文之为物，自然灵气，恍惚而来，不思而至。

the playwright and the audience, that convention must have a psychological basis. To build a play on a violent emotion without sufficiently convincing motivation is to ask the audience to accept unconditionally a coercive premise, which to say the least is unfair. The sudden change of heart is equally abrupt. Again why mix the comic with the terribly tragic, as the neoclassicists objected?

I believe the answer must be sought in the universal mood of the time which Shakespeare shared with his sensitive intelligent contemporaries.

The supreme example of a diseased mind in literature is of course Don Quixote. He is the diseased mind externalized. There is in the make-up of Shakespeare, as in that of any other thinker of the age, a Don Quixote. It is the Don Quixote, the diseased mind, the unconscious in him that is accountable for the discrepancies in his plays.

Milton's "Canie Waggons Light": A Note on Cross-cultural Impact

In Book II of *Paradise Lost* (1665), Satan, hearing that another world was created, decided to search out the truth of the matter. In Book III, he flew to the earth, described by the poet as like a vulture that files from the Himalayas in an attempt to get its prey in India:

> But in his way lights on the barren Plaines
> Of *Sericana*, where Chinese drive
> With Sails and Wind thir canie Waggons light:
> (Book III, 437-39)

Sericana is an area in what is probably now the Xinjiang Uygur Autonomous Region, or vaguely China as a whole. It is not uncommon that references to Chinese culture have appeared in the works of Western writers since Marco Polo, and it is not surprising that in the works of Milton and other 17th century writers things Chinese are frequently mentioned. The present paper is an attempt to show some of the history of the specific object of the "sailing waggon", or the wind-driven land-cart, which underwent an interesting evolution in the West.

In his *opus magnum Science and Civilization in China*, Joseph Needham traces in great detail the history of how the sailing waggon was described, spread and imitated in the West. The earliest written record of the sailing waggon in Europe, according to Needham, is in the *Historia de las Cosas mas notables, Ritos y Costumbres del Gran Reyno de la China* (1585) by Gonzales de Mendoza. Three years after its publication, Robert Parke, commissioned by Hakluyt, translated the book into English. One passage in the book reads:

> (The Chinese) are great inventors of things, and that they have amongst them many coaches and waggons that goe with sailes, and made with such industrie and policie that they do governe them with great ease; this is crediblie informed by many that have seen it; besides that, there be many in the Indies, and in Portugall, that have seene them painted upon clothes, and on their earthen vessell that is brought from thence to be solde: so that it is signe that painting hath some foundation.

A dozen years later, in 1596, the Dutch voyager Jan Huyghen van Linschoten (1563-1611) wrote his *Itinerario, Voyage ofte Schipvaert van J. H. van Linschoten near oost ofte Portugaels Indien* (1579-1592) (English translation 1598), in which he also mentioned that:

> The men of China are great and cunning workmen, as many well bee seene by the Workmanship that commeth from thence. They make and use waggons or cartes with sayles (like Boates) and with wheeles so subtilly made, that being in the Fielde they goe and are driven forwards by the Winde as if they were in the Water.

Needham also quotes a report by an Englishman R. Cocks, submitted in 1614 to the East India Company. In this report, Cocks states that "in the country of Korea...great waggons have been invented to go upon broad flag wheels under sail as ship do, in which they transport their goods." The report further says that the Japanese emperor once intended to use this waggon as transport vehicle to invade China, but was dissuaded by a certain Korean aristocrat. The Italian philosopher Campanella in his *Civitas Solis* attributed this sailing waggon to Ceylon, and added something from his own imagination about the waggon. His Ceylonese Utopians used "waggons fitted with sails, which are borne along by the wind even when it is contrary, by the marvelous contrivance of wheels within wheels."

The above evidences suffice to show that, like other alien things, the sailing waggon caught the imagination of the Europeans at the turn of the century. Their interest can well be traced back to the Middle Ages, lasting through Milton's age well into the 19th century.

Apart from these reports, the cartographers in 16th and 17th-century Europe would indicate China by showing a sailing waggon on the map. In the *Theatrum Orbis Terrarum*[1] (1570) by the Dutch-born German cartographer Ortelius and in Mercator's Atlas (1613), and also in *The Kingdom of China* by the Englishman John Speed published in 1626, for instance, there are illustrations of the waggon.[2]

The European interest in the sailing waggon, however, is far from being confined to writings and map-making. People actually made the waggons by imitation. The most well-known example before Milton's time was that of Simon Stevin, a Flemish mathematician and engineer, whose experiment was fully recorded by Needham (IV. i. 227-28; IV. II, 279-80).

---

[1] When Matteo Ricci came to China (in 1583), he brought Ortelius' atlas and reprinted it with Chinese transliterations and annotations. See *Baike Zhishi* 12, 1980.

[2] Prof. Fan Cunzhong pointed out in a letter to me that Swift also mentioned the waggon in his works. Cf. Prose Works, ed. Temple Scott. 1970. I. p.87.

Around the year 1600, financed by price Maurice of Orange, he, made two sailing waggons, one small and the other large, and travelled from Scheveningen to Petten, a distance of 54miles. It took less than two hours, as compared with fourteen hours on foot. Needham comments: "When one remembers the excitement caused by modest speeds in the first days of railways, one is not inclined to underestimate the impact on European culture of what was really the first essay at rapid transportation. The Chinese stimulus, if it was no better, cannot be ignored, and the results were overwhelming." Stevin's "land ship" was repeatedly imitated by Europeans, and its popularity lasted at least 200 years[1].

Illustration: John Wilkins: Mathematical Magick, 1648

Illustration: Lin Qing（麟庆）(1791—1846):"Hong Xue Yin Yuan Tu Ji" 鸿雪因缘图记

The sailing waggon, therefore, was if not universally at least widely known in Europe. The speed with which it spread was amazing, and Milton was by no means the first poet to appropriate the waggon in his creative work. Needham is writing about 17th century European admiration for the Chinese inventions when he makes mention of Milton's use of the sailing waggon, which, as a matter of fact, had already appeared in Ben Jonson's *News from the New World Discovered in the Moon* (1620), a masque that satirizes contemporary mores as well as the rising news

---

[1] Wang Zheng（王徵 1571—1644), an important inventor of the Ming Dynasty, inspired by records in the *Di Wang Shi Ji* 帝王世纪 made at almost the same time as Stevin's "flying carts" driven by wind. John Wilkins (1614-72) had "many ideas, original or borrowed, which include...a chariot for flying to the moon". See Douglas Bush: *English Literature in the Early Seventeenth Century 1600-1660*, O. U. P. p.271.

medium. One of the "Heralds" in the masque is saying that on the moon, there are ladies, and knights and squires and servants and coaches just as is the case on earth. It bears evidence that at the beginning of the 17th century, the sailing waggon was already fairly familiar to English readers.

I Herald: But the coaches are much o' the nature of the ladies, for they go only with the wind.

Chronicler: Pretty, like China waggon.

Perhaps more interesting still is that Stevin's experiment is also alluded to in another of Jonson's works. In his comedy *The New Inn*, (produced in 1629) during a conversation between the Host, Sir Glorious Tipto and the parasite Fly, about fencing, the Host is saying that both Euclid and Archimedes are fencing masters who were engaged in a fencing contest only a week ago in the Elysium. When questioned, he answers that he got it from "A post that came from thence, / Three days ago, here, left it with the tapster." And Fly confirms:

Fly: Yes, and he told us,
Of one that was the Prince of Orange's fencer.
Tipto: Sir, the same had challenged Euclid
At thirty weapons more than Archimedes
E'er saw, and engines: most of his own invention.

Stevin was Jonson's senior contemporary, and he once served in the court of Prince of Orange. During this office, he designed a sluice as part of a military defense system. It is most likely that this invention had by then became more or less legendary.

The earliest Chinese record of this kind of waggon can be found in *A Record of All Things* (*Bo Wu Zhi* 博物志) and *Record of Emperors and Kings* (*Di Wang Shi Ji* 帝王世纪), Guo Pu's (郭璞) annotation of the *Shan Hai Jing* (山海经) was mostly probably based on *Bo Wu Zhi*, which records: "The people of Qigong were skilled in making flying waggons which travelled far with wind. At the time when Tang was emperor, they came with the wind which blew their waggons as far as Yuzhou. Emperor Tang demolished the waggons lest his subjects should see them. Ten years later when an east wind arose, Tang had new waggons made for them and sent them home. The country of Qigong was 40,000 *li* from Yumen Guan. Though this is but a legend, it caught the imagination of the Chinese men of letters of that time and of later times. According to Needham, after the Jin Dynasty, in Shen Yue's (沈约) annotations to the *Zhushu Jinian* (竹书纪年 *Bamboo Chronicles*), in Xiao Yi's (萧绎) *Jin Lou Zi* (金楼子), and in Ren Fang's (任昉) *Shu Yi Ji* (述异记 *Strange Stories Retold*) there are descriptions of the flying waggon. Evidently it was well-known before the Song Dynasty. But these flying waggons were purely imaginary and did not actually exist. Such an imagined cart was first illustrated in the record of the *Yiyu Tuzhi* (异域图志 *An Illustrated Chronicle of Foreign Lands*, 1489), and later Wang Chongqing (王崇庆 1597), Wu Renchen (吴任臣 1786), Hao Yixing (郝懿行 1809), Wang Fu (汪绂 1895) all illustrated the cart for the *Shan Hai Jing*. There is very little documentation about it as an actual object and its origin is not traceable. Needham identifies Lin Qing's (麟庆) *Hong Xue Yin Yuan Tu Ji* (鸿雪因缘图记 1849 selected English translation by T. C. Lai, entitled *A Wild Swan's Trail*, Hong Kong Book Centre, 1978) as the earliest book with a picture of an authentic waggon, to be followed by Liu Xianzhou's (刘仙洲) *A History of Chinese Mechanical Engineering* (中国机械工程史料 1935). These pictures are what Needham identifies as modern illustrations of sailing waggons that "can still be seen in today's Shandong and Henan provinces". We are not certain whether there was anything of the kind during Marco Polo's stay in China because he didn't mention it in his *Travels*. But this can hardly be used as a proof of its non-existence, for neither did Marco Polo mention such an obvious thing as the Great Wall. It is most likely, however, that the waggon existed at least by the Ming Dynasty, for according to Needham, Stevin's experiment on the waggon was inspired by the Ming prince, Zhu Zaiyu (朱载堉 1536—1611). That was a time when Western traders, sea adventurers and missionaries came streaming to the East and, because their contact with Chinese society and its scholars, Chinese culture was directly or indirectly introduced to Europe. Thus it would not be inconceivable that Milton knew about the sailing waggon of China, but it is difficult to prove from which book or atlas he learned about it. The American scholar E. N. S. Thompson might have made the attempt in his *Milton's Knowledge of Geography* published in 1919. I am inclined to believe that Milton became informed about the waggon from the then widely-read *Microcosmus*; *or A Little Description of the Great world* (1621) by Peter Heylyn[1] (1599-1662), which was later enlarged and entitled *Cosmographie* (1652). In it there is this reference to China: "the country is so plain and level, that they have carts and coaches driven with sails". Milton spelt many of the geographical names in the same way as Heylyn did. Of course, Milton might have also read other popular atlases of his time.

It is clear that with the growth of capitalism in Europe in 16th and 17th centuries, accompanied by a zest for seeking adventure abroad, unheard

---

[1] See also Walton, *The Compleat Angler*, chap. XIX.

news about the outside world was brought home, rousing infinite curiosity. On the other hand, dissatisfaction with feudal reality led people to a thirsty quest for a commonwealth in the past or in remote regions. Almost every writer had his blue-print for the ideal state: from *Utopia*, *Civitas Solis*, Bacon's *New Atlantis*, Sidney's *Arcadia*, Shakespeare's *The Tempest* to Burton's *Anatomy of Melancholy*. This thirst for knowledge about today as well as yesterday, about the West as well as the East, reflects an urgent need of the time, and writers sought knowledge in order to solve the problems they were most concerned about. The sailing waggon is but one tiny item in the vast amount of knowledge assiduously acquired by the men of the Renaissance.

Of course, the knowledge acquired was a mixed bag. They often tended to idealize strange cultures. Mistaken ideas were taken for granted. The great scholar Scaliger (1540-1609) for example, believed that Chinese porcelain could counteract poison and spark off fire, though Sir Thomas Browne in his *Vulgar Errors* was doubtful about this widely current belief. Andrew Marvell still held on to this mistaken idea in his *Last Instruction to a Painter*. In spite of this, knowledge about the East increased, and more elements of Chinese culture appeared in literary works, such as Chinese medicine, wine, porcelain, geese, oranges etc., not to mention silk.[1]

It is out of such a great zest for knowledge that a great number of learned men emerged, some of them quite outstanding in literary history. Robert Burton is in a sense typical of the trend. He describes himself as one who has a great desire "to be *aliquis in ominibus, nullus in singulis*" and likens himself to "ranging spaniel that barks at every bird he sees". There are in the *Anatomy of Melancholy* some 30 allusions to China, mostly from

---

[1] Cf. Shakespeare, *Measure for Measure* (II, I, 90).

Marco Polo's *Travels* and Matteo Ricci's *Expeditione apud Sinas*, covering such topics as religion, superstition, idolatry, sorcery, shamanism, political institutions, economy, law, official examinations, city planning, geography, hygiene, food, medicine, and various aspects of the reportedly Chinese mentality. The spirit that runs through this great work is humanism. He praises the perfectly planned cities, including Xanadu, the industriousness of the Chinese people and the general prosperity of the country.

We might also take a look at his knowledge of geography. As stated before, expansionism led the West Europeans to the discovery of new lands, which aroused great curiosity and interest. The works of the early and mid-17th century demonstrate an extensive knowledge of geography. Books of geography and travels sold extremely well. Considering the printing facilities then prevailing, the speedy appearance of translations is also amazing. Some of the pamphlet writers had travel experiences, but the majority depended on second-hand information, for even those who had travelled, like Milton, who had been only to Italy, were limited in their personal experiences. We can perhaps gauge the scope Milton's knowledge of geography from Burton's reading of geographic books.

Unlike the great Chinese traveler, Xu Xiake (徐霞客 1586—1641), Burton never travelled, but confined himself to his study where his thought travelled far and wide. "I never travelled but in map or card, in which my unconfined thought have freely expatiated, as having ever been especially delighted with the study of cosmography[1] ." And again: "Methinks it would well please any man to look upon a geographical map, *suavi animum delectatione allicere, ob incredibilem rerum varietatemet jucunditatem, et ad pleniorem sui cognitionem excitare* (to entice

---

[1] *Anatomy of Melancholy*, ed A. R. Shilleto (1903) I. p.14.

the mind with sweet delight on account of the incredible variety and pleasantness of the subject, and would exult excitement to further steps in knowledge), chorographical, topographical, delineations, to behold, as it were, all the remote provinces, towns, cities of the world, and never go to forth of the limits of his study, to measure by the scale and compass their extent, distance, examine their site[1] ." As support for his argument he immediately invokes the authority of no less a personage than Charlemagne himself: "Charles the Great, as Platina writes, had three fair silver tables, in one of which superficies was a large map of Constantinople, in the second Rome neatly engraved, in the third an exquisite description of the whole world, and much delight he took in them."

Burton's story provides us with a vivid picture of how zealous people were in their pursuit of knowledge and how much satisfaction they got from it. And it may be of interest to look at the maps and books of travel he read. They include Ortelius, Mercator, Hundius, and travel accounts of Marco Polo, Camden, Haklyt, Linschonten, and books about Columbus' and Vespucci's discoveries, amounting to the number of 20-30. It may safely be surmised that these same source-books provided Milton with his knowledge of geography.

An impressive number of learned men emerged in England at the beginning of the 17th century, historians, antiquarians, philosophers, ecclesiastics, physicians and poets, such as Camden, Hooker, Andrews, Bacon, Selden, Hobbes, Browne, Taylor, Donne, Jonson and Milton. The common characteristic of these writers, scholars and poets is their erudition and versatility, their knowledge ranging from literature, history,

---

[1] Ibid, II, 102-3. Latin quotation from Hondius, *Prae fat Mercatoris*.

philosophy, religious literature, to foreign cultures and modern sciences. Their writings and poetry are likewise characterized by extensive allusions and references, and a unique school the Baroque came into existence with their peculiar style and poetic expression. The Baroque represents a mental state of restlessness and tension and puzzlement, accompanied with an exuberance and paradoxicality and theatricality of expression. It signals a decline of the rationalism and the optimistic belief in the order of nature of the Renaissance. And it was not until the end of the 17th and the beginning of the 18th century that reason and confidence recovered. These Baroque writers were fond of exhibiting their erudition which was, on the surface, pretentious and often ornamental, but fundamentally functional, satisfying the spiritual, ideological and emotional needs of the writers.

Taylor is a good example. As a preacher and prose writer, he was almost completely forgotten in the 18th century, but "re-discovered" by 19th century Romantic critics. Like his contemporaries, he was concerned with the most important and fundamental problems of the age: the contradictions between the God and man, Heaven and hell, good and evil, bright and dark, the healthy and the sick, life and death, Christianity and Pagan culture. These reflect the distresses and dilemmas common to all living in a turbulent age in history. It was Taylor's intention to reconcile religion and reason, hoping that this could solve all other contradictions. His reading was so extensive that Coleridge calls it "oceanic". Religious writings, ancient literature, history and philosophy, and geographical works were the materials that contributed to the formation of his ideas. All literary works are the product of the social life as reflected in the mind of the writers, therefore, the study of the component of a writer's ideology should be an important part of literary criticism. What is inside the mind?

And how does the mind work? These are questions that deserve our study. This reminds us of Eliot's comment on the Metaphysical poets:

> When a poet's mind is perfectly equipped for its work, it is constantly amalgamating disparate experience; the ordinary man's experience is chaotic, irregular, and fragmentary. The latter falls in love, or reads Spinoza, and these two experiences have nothing to do with each other, or with the noise of the typewriter or the smell of cooking; in the mind of the poet these experiences are always forming new wholes.

These remarks seem to give us a clue and an explanation to the process of literary creation, a process generally held to be mysterious, involving inspiration and genius. Only when we have entered the mind of the writer, just like the Monkey King entering the abdomen of the Princess of the Iron Fan, can our criticism be really revealing.

Though Taylor's knowledge of geography is perhaps less extensive than that of Burton and Milton, acquaintance with geography and astronomy provided him with a wide temporal and spatial vision. This is needed for the presentation of his idea, which demanded a high comprehensiveness and universality, a quality Milton also possesses. He wanted to propagate religion, which he held to be the key to the solution of the fundamental and universal issues that mankind was faced with. His vision, for that matter, is wide and far-reaching. He describes God's mercy in *Holy Dying* in true Baroque fashion:

> And as the Sun passing to its Southern Tropic looks with an open eye upon his sun-burn Ethiopians, but at the same time sends light

from its posterns and collateral influences from the backside of his beams, and sees the corners of the East, when his face tends towards the West, because he is a round body of fire, and hath some little images and resemblances of the infinite; so is God's mercy.

Critics have pointed out the similarities of his style to that of Browne, Milton and even Shakespeare (he was dubbed in the 18th century as the "Shakespeare of the divines") but this is not a mere matter of style, for style cannot be separated from thought and emotion, just as Wang Guowei (王国维)remarks that "when people in the past discussed *shi* (诗)and *ci* (词), they distinguished different kinds of poetic discourses, one relating to the scene *jing yu* (景语), and the other to emotion *qing yu* (情语), quite ignorant of the fact that discourse about scenes is also discourse about emotions".

Among those writer of the early 17th century, Milton was of course the most outstanding, being an active revolutionary on the one hand and a learned scholar on the other. His interest extended from classic literature to religion, music, history and geography. In addition to his political tracts, he wrote a *History of Britain* (1646-1670), as he felt dissatisfied with the discursiveness and credulity of previous histories of England as compared with the more dignified Greek and Roman historians. His *Brief History of Moscovia* published in 1650, was written after the English Revolution when the revolutionary government was very much concerned about Russia's attitude. Russia had expelled the English merchants, and the English Parliament had protested against it. Milton drew for his book from Hakluyt's *Voyages and Discoveries* and Samuel Purchas' (1575-1626) *Purchas, his Pilgrimage or Relations of the World and the Religions Observed in All Ages and Places Discovered from the Creation Unto This Present* and *Hakluytus Posthumus or, Purchas his Pilgrimes, Contayning a History of the World in Sea Voyages and Land Travells by Englishmen and others.* Milton also rewrote some of the travels by Renaissance voyagers, crossing out the superstitious and fantastic, improving on the over-euphemistic or over-prosaic language, to be published in 1682 after his death. This body of knowledge finds expression in his poetic works such as *Paradise Lost.* Besides, Milton once made some efforts in studying languages. Ben Jonson wrote a grammar of the English language, Milton one of Latin. He started compiling a Latin dictionary, but left it unfinished.

In the 800 lines in Book I of *Paradise Lost,* there are 34 names of places taken from the Bible, 16 from the classics, three from romances, 30 real geographical names, and one (Pandemonium) coined by himself. These places range from Norway (in the Books, the range extends as far as the North Pole) to Africa (in later Books farther south to the Cape of Good Hope), from India (and China in later Books) to the farthest west region of Spain, Gibraltar and Ireland (later to the Atlantic and America). Milton's vision extends not only to the whole world, but the whole universe.

The reason why Milton needs such a great spatial area is determined by the nature of his epic. The "literary epic," or "secondary epic," as it is sometimes called, is different from the Homeric epic or the "primary epic". After Homer, the European epic underwent a fundamental change. The Homeric epic celebrating heroism is the culmination of a long oral tradition. Virgil's epic, or the "secondary epic" though still with the heroic theme, and a formal imitation of Homer, is thin in plot on the one hand and mainly expresses his political and philosophical ideas. The style is grave and solemn, with somber and elegiac touches every now and then.

So by Milton's *Paradise Lost*, epic had lost through modifications by various writers, much of its heroism typical of Homer's epic except a few stylistic features, and none of the characters can be called an "epic hero". Milton himself called his *Paradise Lost* "a poem in 12 Books", which bears thematic affinity to Virgil's *Aeneid* and Dante's *Divine Comedy*. In a certain sense, they are all political and allegorical poems, concerning the fate either of an empire, or of mankind. They have a universal significance and are similar in style. Matthew Arnold having, in his *On Translating Homer*, compared the styles of Milton and Homer, pointed out that the differences in their styles have to do with differences of thought: "Homer's movement...is a flowing, a rapid movement; Milton's on the other hand, is a laboured, a self-retarding movement. In each case, the metrical cast corresponds with the mode of evolution of thought, with the syntactical cast, and is indeed determined by it. Milton charges himself so full with thought, imagination, knowledge, that his style will hardly contain them... and all this fullness, this pressure, this condensation, this self-constraint, enters into his movement, and makes it what it is, noble but difficult and austere." *Paradise Lost* is in a sense Milton's reflection on the English Revolution. For him the English Revolution was not only to be the liberation of one nation from tyranny, but concerned the fate of all mankind, thus assuming universal significance. Such being his intention, the selection of motif and composition (organization) were all aimed at meeting it. Since the theme is about the whole mankind, the space demanded by the story is naturally the whole universe, which accounts for the fact that when we read the *Paradise Lost*, we are struck by the immensity of space.

One passage in Book XI is highly representative of the effect, though at one time it caused controversy. It tells how God dispatched Michael to expel Adam and Eve from Eden. Michael led Adam to a high hill and showed him a vision of the future of the human race to the time of the Flood.

So both ascend
In the Visions of God: It was a Hill
Of Paradise the highest, from whose top
The Hemisphere of Earth in clearest Ken
Stretch out to amplest reach of prospect lay.
Not higher that Hill nor wider looking round,
Whereon for different cause the Tempter set,
Our second Adam in the Wilderness,
To shew him all Earth's Kingdomes and thir Glory.
His Eye might there command wherever stood,
City of old or modern Fame, the Seat
Of mightiest Empire, from the destind Walls,
Of *Cambalu*, seat of *Cathaian Can*,
And *Samarchand* by *Oxus*, *Temirs* Throne,
To *Paquin* of *Sinaean* Kings, and thence
To *Agra* and *Lahor* of great *Mogul*
Down to the golden *Chersonese*, or where
The *Persian* in *Ecbatan* sate, or since
In *Hispahan*, or where the *Russian Ksar*
In *Mosco*, or the Sultan in *Bizance*,
Turchestan-born; nor could his eye not ken
Th' Empire of *Negus* to his utmost Port
Ercoco and the less *Martine* Kings
Mombaza, and *Quiloa*, and *Melind*,

And Sofala thought *Ophir*, to the Realme

Of *Congo*, and *Angola* fardest South;

Or thence from *Niger* flood to *Atlas* Mount

The Kindoms of *Almansor*, Fez and *Sus*,

Morocco and *Algers*, and *Tremisen*;

On *Europe* thence, and where *Rome* was to sway

The World: in Spirit perhaps he also saw

Rich *Mexico* the seat of *Motezume*,

And *Cusco* in *Peru*, the richer seat

Of *Atabalipa*, and yet unspoil'd

Guiana, whose great Citie *Geryons* Sons

Call *El Dorado*: but to nobler sights

Micheal from *Adam*'s eyes the Filme remov'd...(377-412)

This muster-roll of geographical names cannot arouse the interest of the modern reader, and might even be regarded as Faulty. It is certainly the despair of a Chinese translator when he comes to it.[1] But no critic has ever considered such description redundant or unnecessary. This is not only a generic requirement of the epic, but is closely related to the main theme of the poem, which I will leave for the moment in order to look at T. S. Eliot's comment on this passage.

T. S. Eliot likes Milton the least of all major poets. He complains about the lack of visual imagery, the lack of spatial and temporal specificity, in Milton's poetry, and, concerning the passage quoted above, he feels that "this is not serious poetry...but rather a solemn game", though he

---

[1] A worse case is probably the Gerusalemme Liberata. But Bentley's interesting comment on this page: "Very useful, if he was explaining to a young boy a sheet map of the World". See Empson: *Some versions of Pastoral*, 1935. p. 152.

concedes that "for the single effect of grandeur of sound, there is nothing finer in poetry."[1] What he dislikes at first about Milton is his unspecific description and unclear imagery. But later he modifies his view and says: "To me it seems that Milton is at his best in imagery suggestive of vast size, limitless space, abysmal depth, and light and darkness."[2] But E. M. Forester's view in *Aspects of the Novel* might serve as an earlier defense of spatial magnitude in narratives, when he says "Many novelists have the feeling for place—*Five Towns*, Auld Reekie, and so on. Very few have the sense of space, and the possession of it ranks high in Tolstoy's divine equipment. Space is the lord of *War and Peace*, not time." Immediately preceding this, Forster writes:

> After one has read *War and Peace* for a bit, great chords begin to sound, and we cannot say exactly what struck them. They do not arise from the story, though Tolstoy is quite as interested in what comes next as Scott, and quite as sincere as Bennett. They do not come from the episodes nor yet from the characters. They come from the immense area of Russia, over which episodes and characters have been scattered, from the sum total of bridges and frozen rivers, forests, roads, gardens, fields which accumulate grandeur and sonority after we have passed them.

These remarks can be appropriately applied to *Paradise Lost*. In addition to its grandeur and sonority, the poem also gives the reader a

---

[1] "A Note on the Verse of John Milton", in *Essays and Studies by Members of the English Association.* X XI, 1935.

[2] *Milton* (Annual Lecture on a Master Mind, *Proceedings of the British Academy*), XXXIII, 1947.

strong feeling of boundless space as well as a strong feeling of history and time. The creation of this environment does not depend on realistic details, but details of another kind which is constituted by time and space. Milton's knowledge of geography, and of history plays a decisive role in it. This knowledge, further more, is not "technical trivialities" that come from outside, but a part of his vision of the universe and human life, and a part of his view of human history.

Two viewpoints deserve consideration here. Once view regards details as trimmings which are superimposed into what the Chinese critic, Lin Shu (林纾 1852—1924) calls *jushi qimai* (局势气脉 overall structure and general movement).

The *jushi qimai* concerns the major divisions of a literary work; decorative passages and sentences are insignificant technicalities (小技 *xiaoji*). But though they are unimportant, they nevertheless deserve our knowing. Since efforts have been made about the main body, small details should also be attended to.[1]

Technical details are organically integrated with the world-outlook of the writer, and their choice is determined by it.

Another viewpoint holds that a writer can bring out a sense of vastness is due to his ability of distancing himself. Laurence Binyon says of Milton: "In *Paradise Lost*, what is presented to the mind's eye is almost always

---

[1] *Weilu Lunwen* (畏庐论文). Lin Shu is discussing "word-combination" in prose writing and advises writers "so to combine everyday words they produce unexpected effects. 'Bee' and 'butterfly' are common words, so are 'sad' and 'sorrowful'. But in juxtaposition—a sorrowful butterfly and a sad bee—they produce a strange effect." This reminds one of the *Discordia concors* of the Metaphysical poets and Wordsworth's use of language "really used by men" to represent ordinary things "in an unusual aspect."

viewed from a certain distance."[1] Wang Guowei (1877-1927) says almost the same thing in his *Renjian Cihua* (人间词话 *Remarks on Lyrics in the World of Men*). In an often-quoted passage, he writes: "A poet must be at once within the cosmos and life and outside them. To be within them, he can give life to his work, and by being outside them, he can achieve sublimity (高致 *gaozhi*)." It is easy to understand the meaning of "being within", but what does "being outside or beyond them" mean? Does it mean to keep a certain distance? And how to contemplate? Is it the same as Wordsworth's "recollection in tranquility"? In Milton's *Paradise Lost*, the overall structure and general movement (*jushi qimai*) as well as sublimity (*gaozhi*) are the manifestation of his Weltanschauung. The same reality of fact might find different expressions in the works of different writers, some sublime, some prosaic, because their minds or outlooks differ. Owing to his sublime world outlooks, and profound mind, Milton tried to capture the most fundamental. Maybe this is what is called "being outside" or beyond.

Now let's go back to the passage in *Paradise Lost* under discussion. It has caused conflicting interpretations. Critics who defend Milton are keenly aware of the poet's intention. Disagreeing with T. S. Eliot, Tillyard, for example, says "Milton's immediate business is to give the reader the impression of great space of the earth and great epochs of history— to do so succinctly is quite necessary to the scheme of the poem." And he goes on:

> Yet for all the brevity every name or place mentioned is strictly associated, and should be associated, with a great event in history or

---

[1] J. Dover Wilson (ed.): *Seventeenth Century Studies presented to Sir Herbert Grierson*, CUP. 1938.

some place made famous by the accounts of travellers. And they all have to be perpended to the full. Mr. Eliot writes as if Marco Polo and Camoens had never existed or aroused men's interests.[1]

Tillyard mentions only men's interests but I think it is more than mere interest. However, he is careful to notice that geographical names in Milton's work are closely related with important historical events, though he does not elaborate. We know that Milton was very serious about life and ambitious. This listing of geographical and historical names in his work manifests that over the years he had accumulated a vast amount of knowledge not without a purpose. The knowledge accumulated, in turn, influenced the formation of his outlook on the cosmos and human life, which accounts for the sublimity of his poetry. Knowledge, just as "trivial technicality" is not merely ornamental, but is the raw material that informs his outlook and is closely bound with the most fundamental.

The story of the passage in question is fairly simple, telling how Michael led Adam to a hill in Eden to show him the future. When Milton wrote the passage, he already had in mind another scene which he was to represent in *Paradise Regained* (III. 251ff.). Here once again a geographical muster-roll plays a very prominent part. When he purposely juxtaposes the two scenes, it is justifiable to assume that he meant to establish a certain relationship between the themes conveyed in them, i. e. the temptation of imperial power and worldly glory and the final redemption of mankind toil and trails. What faces Jesus and Adam alike is trial. Milton's accumulated knowledge comes to his assistance to represent it.

The accumulation of knowledge is one of the sources of the influence a

---

[1] E. M. W. Tillyard: *The Miltonic Setting: Past and Present*, 1947, p.98.

writer receives. The question of influence is a complicated one. Essentially when a writer is said to be "influenced" in his creation by an "emitter", the latter must assuredly meet the immediate need of the writer. In the matter of influence the ultimate determinant factor is the writer. In the accumulation of experience, including reading, a writer inevitably eliminates some by the simple process of forgetting, but retains what interests him. And the things that interest him are invariably those which he agrees with, sympathizes with, admires, respects, or even worships. (Of course he can also be influenced adversely, that is, by things that cause strong aversion, but that is rather the exception than the rule.) A case at hand is Burton when he designs his utopia, using what he read about Mexico and China:

> It is almost incredible to speak what some write of *Mexico* and the cities adjoining to it, no place in the world at their first discovery more populous, and what *Mat. Riccius*, the Jesuit, and some others[1] , relate of the industry of the *Chinese*, most populous countries, not a beggar or an idle person to be seen, and how by that means they prosper and flourish. We have the same means, able bodies, pliant wits, matter of all sorts, wool, flax, iron, tin, wood, etc, many excellent subjects to work upon, only industry is wanting. We send our best commodities beyond the sea, which they make good use of to their necessities, set themselves a work about, and severally improve, sending the same to us back at dear rates, or else make toys and baubles of the tails of them, which they sell to us again, at as great a reckoning as they bought the whole.

---

[1] A. R. Rhilleto, ed. *Anatomy of Melancholy*, I., p.102.

It is quite obvious that Burton is idealizing Mexico and China for the sake of contrast.

It is quite often that a writer is content with vague notions so long as they satisfy his needs. In the passage quoted above of Milton's poem for example, Cambalu (or Cambaluc) is identical with Paquin (Peking). China is called by such names as Sericana, Cathay,[1] Sina. This is obviously the result of confusing names from different sources, but it is also possible that Milton was aware they were different names of the same nation. As his purpose was to build up a magnificent atmosphere and a grand tone, it doesn't matter even if he was not very exact. It would be interesting to study influences derived from misinformation, misunderstanding and even distortion on purpose. But accuracy of information does not necessarily guarantee the excellence of a literary work. Flaubert and George Eliot made exhaustive study of historical facts when the former wrote *Salamo* and the latter *Ronola*, but neither work is a success. Of particular interest is the fact that the two works were published in 1862 and 1863 respectively, and might have been written under the influence of positivism which lays so much emphasis on fact that the boundary between literature and history is blurred.[2]

When we talk about expanding the range of knowledge and receiving influence, we usually refer to the reception of superior cultural heritage

---

[1] Until Matteo Ricci, Cathay and Sina had been understood to be two different places.

[2] Yuan Mei (袁枚) in his *Sui-yuan Shi-hua* (随园诗话) Vol. V, has this entry: "Yan Youyi of the Song dynasty defames Su Dongpo for the latter's mistaking the onion for the chive, and Changsang Jun for Cang Gong...But in the 700 years that followed, people knew of Su Dongpo and none had heard of Yan Youyi" – a good instance showing that precise factual information does not make a great poet. Another case of inaccuracy is Douglas Bush's mildly satirical remark on modern translations of the Bible: "Whatever the shortcomings of the old version, it may be doubted if modern accuracy has led more souls to heaven." (*English Literature in the Early 17th Century*)

according to our subjective need.

Another aspect of influence involves the contact of one mind with another, which leads to further reflections, thus turning what is merely passive reception to active "exploration". Social practice and life experience however involved and rich, cannot produce great works. Great works need an exalted perspective ("lowering height"), depth of vision and sublimity of expression, Mathew Arnold's view in this regard is worth recalling. Though it is somewhat conservative, he is quite right in saying that criticism can do real service not only to the critic's own mind and spirit, but to the minds and spirits of others. In Arnold's own words, criticism can make the best ideas prevail. "Presently these new ideas reach society, the touch of truth is the touch of life, and there is a stir and growth everywhere; out of this stir and growth come the creative epochs of literature." (*The Function of Criticism at the Present Times.*) Inactivity of the mind and stagnant spiritual life cannot produce great works. This is true of a society as well as of an individual writer. If a poet's mind does not have contact with other minds, whereby he can form comparison and modify or improve his own, it would be difficult for him to achieve depth and sublimity. The creation of a great work needs not only deep involvement and commitment, but also depth of perception. Milton was indeed deeply involved in revolutionary activities, but if he had not been so well read, it would be unimaginable that he could have accomplished such a great poem as *Paradise Lost*.

In his *Second Defense*, he states how from his youth he devoted himself to the study of law, both ecclesiastical and civil, placing it above all else, because he considered that, whether he would be of use or not, he should be prepared for service to his country, to his church and to those who preached the gospel at the risk of their lives. He tells how he devoted his leisure at Horton to the perusal of the classics with occasional visits to London "either for the sake of purchasing books, or of learning something new in mathematics or in music." In Italy, he "was a constant attendant at their literary parties, a practice which...tends so much to the diffusion of knowledge and the preservation of knowledge." Coming back, he "put on board a ship the books I had collected in Italy". Back home, he gladly ceased reading and study to devote himself to the tasks entrusted to him by the people and by God. In the ten years of the bourgeois revolution, he actively plunged himself into political struggle, to which he made great contribution by writing a series of powerful pamphlets, and making good use of his profound knowledge. After the failure of the revolution, he felt sad and set about to express his strong feelings by means of poetry, and again his great knowledge played an important role in three immortal poems.

From the example of Milton and a number of other 17th century writers, we can see that the pursuit of knowledge was not merely aimed at satisfying their own needs and also the needs of the age. Knowledge exercised certain influences on them. But knowledge alone cannot make a great writer, for there are cases where the writer, filling his work with book knowledge, failed to make it superior. On the other hand, however, it would be hardly imaginable that Milton could produce his three masterpieces and other works without his profound knowledge. Milton's knowledge is shown in his "loftiness" as well as in its specific applications in his works. The sailing waggon is only one minor component in the vast expanse of Milton's oceanic learning.

(Translated by Han Jining from *Gong Yu Ji* (攻玉集)Reprinted from *Cowrie: A Chinese Journal of Comparative Literature* No. 3, 1986.)

Dao-wang Shi(悼亡诗), or Poetry Lamenting the Deceased Wife[1]

It is odd that a very distinct Chinese lyric kind—the *dao-wang shi*, or poetry lamenting the deceased wife—should have escaped the special attention of Chinese literary critics. It occurs in the history of Chinese lyric poetry in an almost unbroken chain that one may claim for it to have become a tradition. It developed its own convention and system of imagery, distinct from other lyric kinds. On the other hand, such kind of lyric poetry is extremely rare in Western literature.

In this paper I propose to offer a description of it along with a comparison with a few rare specimens in English literature, to try to find an explanation as to why it flourished in Chinese literature and cast some light on the disparity between Chinese and Western concepts of love, and finally to assess the contribution it makes to the concept of lyric in world literature.

One can trace the origin of the *dao-wang* poetry as far back as to the very fountain-head of Chinese poetry, the *Book of Odes* (诗经), though the designation was unknown until much later. In it we find such poems as *Lü-yi* (绿衣), "Green is the Jacket" and *Ge-sheng* (葛生), "The *Ge* Creepers Grow", which it is generally agreed are commemorative verses. The first reads partly:

---

[1] Lecture delivered at the International Comparative Literature Symposium, Tokyo University, June 16, 1987.

Green is the jacket,	绿兮衣兮
A green jacket with yellow lining.	绿衣黄里
The grief of the heart,	心之忧矣
How will it end?	曷维其已
......	
Green is the silk,	绿兮丝兮
It was worked by you	女所治兮
I think of my old mate,	我思古人
May I not be reproached!	俾无訧兮

And the second reads partly:

The *ge* creepers grow and cover the thorns,	葛生蒙楚
The *lian* creepers spread to the wilds,	蔹蔓于野
My fair one has gone from here,	予美亡此
Who will be with me—alone I dwell.	谁与独处
......	
The horn pillow is painted,	角枕粲兮
The brocade coverlet is bright.	锦衾烂兮
My fair one has gone from here,	予美亡此
Who will be with me—alone I watch the dawn.	谁与独旦

After days of summer,	夏之日
After nights of winter,	冬之夜
After a hundred years,	百岁之后
I shall join him in his abode.	归于其居
......	

The second poem is ambiguous. The person mourned for here is apparently the husband but it can also be understood to be the husband mourning the loss of his wife.

One will have noticed that the dominant images in those verses are personal belongings and objects closely connected with home life. The sentiment is genuine though simply expressed as befits unsophisticated early poetry. The second poem describes a progress: namely, a visit to the grave, coming back from the visit to the house where the poet sees objects that remind him of his married life. Finally it expresses a wish to reunite with his partner. It is a narrative in miniature. These early anonymous poems become the crude paradigm for later *dao-wang* poetry.

When we come to later times we find such poetry to be often set in the frame of a dream. Take the *three Dreams at Chiang-ling*[1] （江陵三梦） by the Tang poet Yuan Zhen （元稹 779—831) for example. They record three dreams the poet had on three successive nights when he had newly arrived at his official post in the provinces. In the first dream, which is the longest, the wife appeared much worried about their only daughter whom Yuan had left behind in the capital. Quoting his wife the poet writes:

You said: "We have only this daughter,	嘱云唯此女
And regrettably we have no son.	自叹总无儿
I remember her then so naughty and cute,	尚念娇且骏
I can't bear to think of her hungry or cold."	未禁寒与饥

Apart from the dream motif, there are three things worth noticing: first

---

[1] See *Sunflower Splendor: Three Thousand Years of Chinese Poetry*, Co-ed, by Wu-chi Liu and Irving Yucheng Lo. Anchor Press, N. Y. 1975, pp.216-18.

unlike the anonymous early poetry, we now know the occasion on which the poems were written—it was when the poet-official was demoted to a remote post which meant virtual exile; secondly, it continues the tradition of introducing into the poems elements of nature more sophisticated and more closely corresponding to the poet's feelings than in the *Book of Odes*. At the end of the first poem, we read:

I sit here watching the sky out to light,	坐见天欲曙
The river wind humming in the trees.	江风吟树枝

Or, at the end of the second poem:

Startled awake by the moon flooding in my bed,	惊觉满床月
Wind and waves are heard from the river.	风波江上声

And at the end of the third poem:

As I sit watching the morning sun come up,	坐看朝日出
A flock of birds by two's return.	众鸟双徘徊

Thirdly, a sense of despair ("My heart has turned to ashes"我心长似灰) at the finality of separation is much more heightened. Chiang-ling (Jiang-ling) to which Yuan was banished is a city on the Yangtze River. Referring to it, he writes:

I can't even cross a single river,	一水不可越
And the Styx, it has no shores.	黄泉况无涯

Yuan wrote his poems probably on the third anniversary of his wife's death. When we come to a very touching *ci*（词）by the Song（宋）poet Su Shi（苏轼 1037—1101）commemorating the death of his wife ten years earlier（十年生死两茫茫，不思量，自难忘）, we find a convincing testimony of enduring conjugal love. In the poem he tells briefly how he dreamed that he had on a sudden returned to his home town in Sichuan（四川）province in southwest China while he was serving as magistrate of Mizhou（密州）in Shan-dong（山东）province on the eastern tip of China's coast. He saw in his dream that his wife was combing her hair and adorning herself in front of the little window as of old, and they looked at each other speechless. "Only the tears streamed down in endless strings".（夜来幽梦忽还乡，小轩窗，正梳妆。相顾无言，惟有泪千行。）Earlier on, there is an interesting conceit. The poet has been saying that since his wife's lone grave is thousands of miles away, nowhere can he alleviate his sad loneliness（千里孤坟，无处话凄凉）. And then he goes on:

> Even should we meet, you would not recognize me, 纵使相逢应不识
> My face all covered with dust,　　　　　　　　　　 尘满面
> My hair on the temples like hoar-frost.　　　　　　 鬓如霜

It can be a literal translation of Ovid in one of his *Epistulae ex Ponto* (I. iv):

> Nec, si me subito videas, agnoscere possis,
> Aetatis facta est tanta ruina meae.
> (On a sudden shouldst thou see me, thou couldst not recognize me,
> Such havoc hath been wrought with my life.)

We shall return to the similarity between Ovid and Chinese poets in exile in a moment.

As an outstanding and special example, I would like to mention a rather obscure disappointed poet-scholar of the latter half of the 17th century, Li Biheng (李必恒). Two of his poems (or his two poems)[1] lamenting his wife are included in the anthology by his later contemporary Shen Deqian (沈德潜, 1672—1769), the *Guochao Shi Biecai Ji* (国朝诗别裁集). Of these poems, each consisting of twenty-four lines, the first describes how his wife knowing that she was going to die, rose up in the morning, washed herself, bade farewell to her father-and mother-in-law and entrusted the care of her young son to her sister-in-law and bade her to alter some of her own simple wedding-clothes for him against the advent of autumn. The remarkable thing about this first poem is that certain supernatural elements are introduced creating an ominous atmosphere which foreboded death. It begins:

The whole room is full of twitterings—	一室何啾啾
Human speech mixed with ghostly sobs.	人语杂鬼哭
……	
A white-necked bird alights	飞来白项鸟
On the roof of my house, croaking.	哑哑上我屋

The second poem describes the derelict room after his wife's death and a brief vision succeeded by a dream:

The emptied room is shadowy even in broad daylight, 空房起昼阴

---

[1] Shen Deqian regards that Li's poems had never been collected.

Out of pillows and mattresses arises a gust of icy air; 冷气出枕席

Many cobwebs are spun by spiders on the window, 窗多蛛结网

The table dotted full with prints of rat's paws. 案尽鼠行迹

In the basket some hemp is left 亦有筐中麻

Which she used to spin under lamplight; 灯火手自绩

The mirror also still stands, 亦有所对镜

The jeweled flowers lie pell-mell. 花钿恣狼藉

Loitering I recall her words and smiles, 徘徊思言笑

Her face appears vividly before me. 仿佛面如觌

She turns her head as of about to speak, 回头谒欲语

Rubbing her bosom in sad despair. 抚心一摽擗（抚心悲痛）

Then the poet recounts a dream he had:

Last night I dreamed of her, 前夜梦见之

Her face horridly pale, her frame emaciated. 色惨体更瘠

Vaguely we conversed, 恍惚絮语间

She asking after her son's diet. 问儿何所食

It was a brief encounter of the *hun* and *po*.[1] 暂时魂魄聚

Waking I found we were separated by the Yellow Spring. 觉后泉壤隔

Not being, alas, the Great Sage emotion free, 忘情愧太上

How can bear to beat the musical urn like Zhuangzi? 庄缶犹可击

The editor of the anthology, Shen Deqian, introduces the poet as a poor scholar and a good poet. Among the 15 young man highly praised for their

---

[1] *Hun* （魂） or spiritual soul and *po* （魄） or animal soul. The *hun* not only continues to exist after death, but can also wander about and meets the *po* in dreams. See Gloss to Year seven of Zhao-kung in the *Zuo Zhuan* 《左传》.

poetic talent by the Great Minister Song Luo (宋荦), he was the only one who never achieved officialdom and died a poor scholar of the lowest rank (秀才). "Furthermore he was deaf and suffered from many ailments. He died in his middle age. What ill fate. But his poetry is of the most exalted kind and his poetic talent is of the greatest. His poetry unlike that of many other poets will certainly last."[1] Commenting on his two *dao-wang* poems, Shen remarks: "Wang Shizhen's (王士祺)commemorative verses are too elegant and ostentatious of his wealth and rank, while Li's celebrate what Yuan Zhen calls 'shared poverty and sad experiences of husband and wife'. The more trivial and humdrum the details, the more genuine the feeling. Even strangers to the poet reading them will be touched and feel sad."[2]

This is one of the rare *loci critici* where one finds something like a criterion for the dao-wang poetry, namely, details of home-life are essential to the effectiveness of such poetry. It also implies that a better knowledge of the poet's life is conducive to better appreciation.

In the latter respect, Li Zhi (李贽 1527—1602) provides us with an excellent example. He may not be as good a poet as Li Biheng, but he had left us a pretty full account of the ups and downs of his life as scholar and minor official, of the deaths in the family, his conversion to Buddhism, his involvement in a minor offence which caused him to be imprisoned and his suicide in prison. In his writings, correspondences, autobiographical sketch and his will, we learn how his wife shared with him his hardships, how they respected each other, how on hearing of her death in their home-town he dreamed of her every night, how he wished that her spiritual soul

---

[1] 且耳聋多病，年止中寿，何其厄也。然诗格之高，才力之大，可只者应让此人。
[2] 渔洋悼亡诗，风雅之中，纯乎富贵气象。此则元相所云，"贫贱夫妻百事哀"也。越琐屑，越见真至，即他人读之，亦为感伤。（按二诗均用仄韵。）

would wait for him to join her. He also recounts their conversations, their arguments, and their separation. He instructs in his will among other things, how he should be shrouded. His obsession with death reminds one immediately of John Donne as told by Izaak Walton.

In his verses mourning his wife, he writes:

| Never did you and I quarrel, | 反目未曾有 |
| For forty years there was harmony. | 齐眉四十年 |

I hope I have shown by the above account the basic features of the Chinese *dao-wang* poetry. To sum up then, this kind of lyric is often occasioned by setbacks in the poet's career. It echoes the feeling of disappointment and depression the poet is experiencing. By recalling the memory of shared companionship through poverty and adverse circumstances, and the harmonious family relationship the deceased succeeded in maintaining, the poet is meeting a psychological need of compensation for the loss. Considering the occasion of such poetry written during demotion or self-exile, it can be called poetry of exile, often with the sense of the finality of separation, a separation beyond recall. A familiar case in Western literature is Ovid. Though Ovid hoped against hope that he might be recalled to Rome, and exiles unlike bereaved husbands often do rejoin their families, he finally realized that there was no hope for pardon and he drew his own epitaph. In the position of an exile, the poet would consider his wife as a spiritual support, the loss of which would be acutely felt. Ovid expresses this sentiment in the line: "te mea supposita ueluti trabe fulta ruina est" (upon thee as upon a supporting pillar rest my ruins) (*Tristia* I. vi.), a feeling which is shared by

Chinese poets.

To compensate for the irreparable loss, to absorb the shock occasioned by the death of the beloved wife, the poet has to resort to some sort of philosophy, hoping to rise above life and death, above mortal love, like the philosopher Zhuangzi (庄子) or resort to religion such as Buddhism.

Such poetry necessarily involves memory. So it is natural for it to assume a narrative form recalling events in the shared life with the deceased. The poet remembers it not only during his waking hours but, since the memory is so deep, it is often transformed into a dream.[1] Hence the dream motif. That is a dream the living may meet the dead is based on the theory that the dead have a soul, called *hun* or spiritual soul, and the soul of the living called *po* is an animal soul[2]; the communication of the living and the dead is brought about by the meeting of the two souls in a dream. The dream motif lends the poetry a supernatural quality and an eerie air which makes this kind of poetry most effective. At the same time Nature is called in as a foil to the emotional state of the poet.

The most prominent imagery in this genre or sub-genre of lyric derives from home-life; clothing, bedding, female ornaments, the spinning wheel, clothes-mending, entertainment of guests, the caring of children, of parents or other members of the family. These objects and activities fall into three groups: one denoting conjugal love, the second denoting personal adornment, and the last denoting wifely duty. When the Chinese poets wrote extra-material love-lyrics, they wrote them to or for courtesans, often not in a serious mood. They seldom or never wrote

---

[1] As instances that intense feelings about certain things during waking hours often continue into dreams, one may cite Su Shi (苏轼) in his *Dongpo Zhilin* (东坡志林), in which he records about a dozen of his dreams, many of them about composing verses, the dominant passion of his waking hours.

[2] See note45.

them for the intended bride or the affianced, whom they very likely never met until the wedding. Pre-marital love did not exist except in fiction or romances. Love, if any, grew out of post-marital companionship, mutual understanding, help and sympathy. And also the expression of love must be within the bounds of etiquette, and the death of a partner was a proper occasion when the bereaved could express his natural feelings freely. (Verse-epistles to the wife were also in order.)

Now let us turn to some of the rare specimens of such lyric in Western literature. I shall confine myself to specimens in English literature. The one that strikes me as closest to the Chinese *dao-wang shi* is Milton's sonnet:

> Methought I saw my late espoused Saint
> Brought to me like Alcestis from the grave.
> Whom Jove's great Son to her glad Husband gave,
> Rescu'd from death by force, though pale and faint.
> Mine as whom washt from spot of child-bed taint,
> Purification in the old Law did save,
> And such, as yet once more I trust to have
> Full sight of her in Heaven without restraint,
> Came vested all in white, pure as her mind:
> Her face was veil'd, yet to my fancied sight,
> Love, sweetness, goodness, in her person shin'd
> So clear, as in no face with more delight.
> But O! as to embrace me she enclin'd
> I wak'd, she fled, and day brought back my night.

This is a deeply moving poem, even pathetic, considering that when

Milton marries the second time he had already gone blind. The sonnet is set in the frame of a dream with a beginning and an ending, a narrative in miniature, like some of the Chinese *dao-wang shi*. With the blurred contour of the image, it conveys vagueness and a sense of mystery. With the waking of the poet one is given the impression of the finality of the separation and left only with the hope of their reunion in heaven. As to the occasion of the poem, we are pretty certain that Milton wrote it shortly after the death of Catherine Woodcock in 1658 on the 3rd of February, followed by the death of the infant daughter in March and before he wrote his last pamphlet *On the Ruptures of Commonwealth* in October 1659. In September of the previous year Cromwell had died and was succeeded by his son Charles. The new Republic was facing imminent danger. It was at this juncture of deep depression that Milton, like the Chinese poets, wrote his sonnet. But here the similarity ends. What strikes one most about the poem is its deeply religious quality. He calls her saint, not only physically purified but spiritually pure, the personification of love, sweetness and goodness. She is likened to Alcestis, symbol of self-denial and self-sacrifice, the pagan equivalent almost of Jesus, though on a limit scale. This concept of womanhood may have some relation with the medieval Germanic concept of *Frauendienst* minus the sense of humility but retaining the element of religious worship. This attitude is most explicitly stated by Erasmus in his *Enchiridion Militis Christiani*, or the *Handbook of the Militant Christian* (I. 7),[1] where he says: "You say you love your wife simply because she is your spouse. There is really no merit in this. Even the Pagans do this, and the love can be based upon physical pleasure alone. But, on the other hand, if you love her because

---

[1] Eng. Tr. by John P. Dolan, in *The Essential Erasmus*, New American Library, 1987, p.51.

in her you see the image of Christ, because you perceive in her His reverence, modesty and purity, then you do not love her in herself but in Christ. You love Christ in her. This is what we mean by spiritual love."

Also conjugal love is often conceived as a bridge between oneself and God. In John Donne's 19 *Holy Sonnets*, all written after the death of Ann More, one, the 17th, can be considered as a *dao-wang shi*:

> Since...her Soul early into heaven ravished,
> Wholly on heavenly things my mind is sett.
> Here the admyring her my mind did whett
> To seeke thee God; so streames do shew their head.

To Browning, conjugal relationship is one of spirit and flesh. In *Balaustion's Adventure*, he puts his sentiment in the mouth of Admetos addressing Alkestis who chooses to die in his stead:

> Since death divides the pair,
> 'Tis well that I depart and thou remain
> Who was to me as spirit is to flesh.

The closest to the Chinese *dao-wang shi* are perhaps a series of short poems written by Thomas Hardy between 1912 and 1913, when he was well over 70, to the memory of his wife. In these he recalls mostly the mundane side of their long companionship for nearly forty years, their journeys together, picnics, entertainments, and the room she lived in. In *The Walk* he describes his visit to a familiar hill:

> I walked up there today

Just in the former way;

Surveyed around

The familiar ground

By myself again;

What difference, then?

Only that underlying sense

Of the look of a room on returning thence.

How Chinese in the simplicity of expression and the domesticity of sentiment. Perhaps this is because Hardy, like the Chinese, is pagan at heart with a calm detachment and concern for what is cosmic.

How does one account for the repeated occurrence of this particular kind of lyric in the history of Chinese poetry? The answer may be found in the life-pattern of the poet-scholar. Chinese who received an education follow Confucius' maxim of seeking public employment, and failing that, living in retirement（用之则行，舍之则藏）. Public employment might lead to success but more often it was full of pitfalls and danger. Against life's many perils, Chinese intellectuals of old, in office or out, found a haven and consolation in family, in friendship, in Nature, and they would often look nostalgically at their home-country from whence they issued forth into the world, hanker after a retired country life or cast a homesick look back at the Past. These themes form the staple of Chinese lyric poetry. The ideal family life is often pictured quite realistically, e. g. by Bai Juyi (Bo Chu-i 白居易）in a poem written shortly before his death celebrating the life of his old age, to be shown to family members（自咏老身示诸家属）:

I have lived to 75,　　　　　　　　　　寿及七十五

My salary was 50,000;	俸沾五十千
My wife as old as myself,	夫妻偕老日
My nephews live with us.	甥侄聚居年
I eat tasty gruel of fresh rice.	粥美尝新米
I wear a gown padded with new cotton;	袍温换故绵
My house may be bare of furniture,	家居虽濩落
But I rejoice to have my family around me.	眷属幸团圆
A couch is placed below a plain screen,	置榻素屏下
A stove set before my dark-blue curtain;	移炉青帐前
I am read to by my grandson,	书听孙子读
And I watch the servant boy boil herbs.	汤看侍儿煎
I rush my brush to write verse I promised,	走笔还诗债
I pawn my clothes to buy medicine;	抽衣当药钱
All these trivial businesses dispatched,	支分闲事了
I sprawl with my back to the sun and fall asleep.	爬背向阳眠

A peaceful though not plentiful life was their ideal. The wife occupied a very important place. It was she who looked after the whole household. Conjugal love was often enhanced because of the sharing of a needy life. Separation, however, always posed a threat to this harmonious life. It may be due to the mother's displeasure for the wife, or the husband's disloyalty, and on some very rare occasion, the wife's disappointment at the poverty which she was unwilling to bear. The commonest occasion of separation was the husband's departure to take up a post or for a military expedition, or sometimes imprisonment, and finally the death of one spouse.

Looked at in this context, i. e., in view of the life pattern, the kind of life-ideal and the vicissitudes of life, it is understandable that the death of the wife would not be passed over lightly without any expression of deep grief. Further, the Chinese concept of one of the functions of poetry is that it is a vehicle for the expression of disappointment or grievance (诗可以怨), a shock-absorbing device. What greater shock or grief could there be than the loss of a life-companion to a Chinese scholar of old?

The concept of love in the West is almost diagonally opposed to that of the East. For one thing, woman is idealized. For another, man ever since the Renaissance has been liberated from being merely a "member of a race, people, party, family or corporation."[1] He is free to love as an individual. Even earlier on, the cult of chivalric love had already appeared as the precursor of this emancipation. Premarital love was the natural thing. As the late Professor Chen Shih-hsiang (陈世骧) of Berkeley says, "Love in eastern literature is present not as the pursuit of an eternal but as a thing of the past, a matter for reflection, never for speculation."[2]

The Chinese *dao-wang* poetry by celebrating post-marital love modifies the concept of the love-lyric as a universal genre, highlighting the mundane and domestic aspect of love. Love is conceived as arising from mutual understanding and mutual help, especially under adverse circumstances, thus assuming a moral quality. That secular love not of the hedonistic kind can be exalted to something approaching the sublime without resorting to religious sentiment is an attribute peculiar to the *dao-wang* poetry. The hoped-for reunion in the grave (not heaven) or the Yellow Springs, bears little connotation with religion. In the Zuo Zhuan (左传) year one of the reign of Duke Yin (隐公), the duke Zhuang of Zheng (郑庄公) curses

---

[1] Jakob Burckhardt, *The Civilization of the Renaissance in Italy*, Eng. Tr., Phaedon Press, Oxford and London, 1945, p.81.

[2] *The Cultural Essence of Chinese literature*, in *Interrelation of Cultures: Their contribution to International Understanding*, Unesco, Paris, 1953, p.64, quoted by Peter H. Lee, *Celebration in Continuity*, Harvard, 1979, p. 95.

his mother who hates him: "Not until I reach the Yellow Springs may we meet again." An ironic case is Li Zhi (李贽) who abandoned his family to espouse Buddhism, but on hearing the death of his wife, hastened to write a number of elegies, in one of which he regrets having parted from her for the life of a Buddhist recluse (缘余贪佛去，别汝在天涯). A true Buddhist would foreswear all emotional life. Religion in the true sense of the word, if there is any in *dao-wang* poetry, is engrafted rather than ingrained. The indigenous belief in the *hun* or spiritual soul and the *po* or the animal soul, whose union causes the dream, may be the vestige of an early religion, but it is not inherent and hardly affects the secular nature of such poetry. On the literary level, most importantly, the blending of household imagery with natural phenomena and supernatural (superstitions not religious) elements to arouse deep sympathy with astonishing effect is perhaps unique in the lyric tradition in world literature.

The Mirror and the Jigsaw: A Major Difference between Current Chinese and Western Critical Attitudes

This paper is an attempt at contrasting, in very broad outline, two widely different kinds of critical approach or temperament that currently prevail in China and the West. One of them I venture to denote by the emblem of the mirror, and the other by that of the jigsaw.

The basic assumptions underlying all present-day Chinese literary criticism are that literature reflects or should reflect social life, that it cannot be divorced from social life and that it is politically orientated with a didactic purpose. Writers are repeatedly called upon to involve themselves deeply in life, especially the life of the working masses. Consequently, the literary critic mainly concerns himself with the writer's involvement and the success or ill success of the process of reflection. So critical terms such as "world-view," "tendency," "progressiveness," "eulogy or exposure," "essence," "conflict and contradiction," "informational value" (in speaking of foreign works and Chinese classics) are in constant use when the critic is focusing on the author's attitude to life and on the thought, content, while other terms like "realism," "characterisation," "type," "epitome," "life-likeness," "detail," "romanticism and idealisation," are used in dealing with the aesthetic aspect of the work under consideration.[1]

Alongside of this we find in modern Western literary criticism an entirely different set of critical terms. Admittedly, Western literary criticism is far from being homogeneous and uniform, but, as it happens, various critical schools have a tendency to spread into each other's domain, thus sharing some common characteristics, chiefly among which is a concentration on the formal aspects of a literary work. Words like "texture," "pattern," "dimension," "plane," "structure," "construction" have become the *sine qua non*. They betray the critic's attitude toward the work he is examining, which is rather like that of a surgeon, scalpel in hand, ready to cut the anatomy to pieces to find out the parts it is composed of, or that of a person puzzling over a set of jigsaw pieces.

The difference between the two sets of critical terms shows that the Chinese critic's gaze is fixed steadily on the life as it is reflected in the work, while the Western critic looks at the work itself without bothering much about "extraneous matters." The one corresponds approximately to the extrinsic, and the other to the intrinsic approach in professor Wellek's classification. Why it is so may be due to a variety of causes. Perhaps a glance at history may not be out of place here.

---

[1] The theoretical basis of this view is in Mao Tse-tung's *Yenan Forum* which postulates that the chief source of literature and art is social life, while literary classics are tributaries or secondary inspiration; that in judging a literary work, political criterion comes first, and artistic second; that a work's historical progressiveness and the author's attitude to the people are measures by which to judge a work's relative value; as well as in Marxist-Leninist "theory of reflection" and Engels' definition of realism which "implies, besides truth of detail, the truth of typical characters under typical circumstances." (Engels is speaking of the novel or what he calls the "*Tendenzroman*," and incidentally current Chinese literary criticism has, in most cases, to do with that genre. In fact, the obsession with realism has also found expression in the reinterpretation of classical Chinese literary criticism: The *Wen Xin Diao Long or The Literary Mind and the Carved Dragon* has been said to be a treatise on realism. Critics forget that Chinese Literature, in its proper sense, before Liu Xie and long since, was mainly lyrical.)

The Confucian concept of literature is formulated in the phrase *shi yan zhi* (诗言志) which may be rendered into "Poetry is the expression of ideas or emotions." *Shi* refers to the body of poems, most of which were collected in the *Shi-jing* (《诗经》). In the light of this collection, *shi* already means more than personal feelings or simple lyricism; it is both social and political, for poetry here serves as an admonition or corrective (*ci* 刺) for social or political iniquities, or as a means of laudation (*mei* 美). Confucius further widens the function of poetry in the following dictum: "Poetry serves to inspire, serves as a mirror, serves to facilitate communion or intercourse, and to give vent to grievances". (*xing* 兴 , *guan* 观 , *qun* 群 , *yuan* 怨). The last three functions have caused little dispute among scholars, whereas the first, from being a technical term meaning inspiration simulated by external objects,[1] assumes gradually a moral and political significance, directing the inspiration to matters moral and political. At all events, poetry as a source of information (*guan*), as a tool of diplomatic dialogue (*qun*), as social criticism (*yuan*), as a means of moral teaching[2] (*xing*) is well established. This concept is further reinforced in the "Great Preface" to the *Shi-jing*: "The ancient kings used poetry to affirm the relationship between husband and wife, to establish the principle of filial duty and reverence for one's superiors, to strengthen the ethical code among men, to promote fine education and culture, and to change social customs." Here we have all the germinal ideas about literature as a vehicle for the ethical, social and political doctrines to be epitomized finally by Zhou Dun-yi (周敦颐 1017—1075) in the slogan

---

[1] D. C. Lau translates "to stimulate the imagination" in Confucius (《论语》). *The Analects* (Penguin Classics, London, 1979).

[2] 郑众：《周礼·大司乐》注 "兴者以善物喻善事"。郑玄：《周礼·大师》注 "兴见今之美，嫌于媚谀，取善事以喻劝之"。

wen yi zai dao(文以载道 "literature is the vehicle of *dao* or *tao*"), thus giving the function of literature a theoretical and philosophical basis.

The effect of Taoism on literary theory and criticism was not felt until the third century A. D. and subsequently it became the dominant trend for at least three hundred years. It was entirely free from traditional ethical and social preoccupations and brought out many newkey notions about literature. This change of conception occurred simultaneously with the propagation of Buddhism.[1] Some notions were evidently taken over from Confucian vocabulary and given a curious twist.

The term *qi* (气), for instance, made its appearance as early as in Cao Pi (曹丕 187—226 A.D.), when he comments on the special quality of the poetry of Xu Gan (徐幹), contending that "his poetry often conveys the spirit of the State of Qi" (徐幹时有齐气). The application of the principle of *qi* to literary criticism is an important shift in that it diverts the critic's attention from social to purely aesthetic considerations. The term may have been taken over from Mencius (我善养吾浩然之气) who meant by it a moral self-cultivation, but the usage Cao Pi gives it implies rather the poet's temperament as revealed in his style. Incidentally, it is also interesting to note that Cao Pi seems to be aware, like Taine, that a poet's temperament may be shaped by the locality from which he hails. The same term is used by Cao in his appreciation of other contemporary poets.

Another new departure from ethical-social preoccupations in classical Chinese literary criticism is the re-interpretation of *xing*. Lu Ji (陆机 261—303 A. D.) in his *Rhymed Essay on Literary Composition* (文赋) gives

---

[1] Critics are generally agreed that Buddhism, especially its later variety, Zen, is really Taoism or "metaphysics" under a kasaya cloak.

prominence to compositions inspired by nature,[1] and gives a graphic description of how inspiration operates: "It cannot be stopped when it comes, and cannot be detained when it goes away. It vanishes like a shadow and moves like a rising sound."[2]

Like the Confucians, the Taoist critics are also keenly aware of the supreme difficulty of expression—the discrepancy between meaning and the uttered or written word. The Confucian school did not offer any solution.[3] Creditably, critics with Taoist leanings, notably Lu Ji, deriving inspiration from Zhuang-zi, attempt to offer a solution by bringing forward, for the first time in the history of Chinese literaty criticism, a theory of imagination.[4] Lu not only describes the power of imagination as a capacity to break the bonds of space and time, but also describes, in metaphorical language, the actual process of how imagination develops into expression.[5] The theory of imagination is reiterated and further

---

[1] 遵四时以叹逝，瞻万物而思纷；悲落叶于劲秋，喜柔条于芳春。
    "The passage of the four seasons causes regret. Contemplation of the myriad objects (of nature) sets one's mind astir. Fallen leaves in harsh autumn arouse sadness. Supple twigs of sweet spring give joy."

[2] 若夫应感之会，通塞之纪，来不可遏，去不可止，藏若景灭，行犹响起。

[3] 《论语》：辞达而已矣。孟子《万章上》：故说诗者，不以文害辞，不以辞害意；以意逆志，是为得之。
    The Analects of Confucius: "The function of the word is to put one's idea across and no more."Mencius, Wan Zhang pt. I: "A (good) commentator of the *Shi-jing* concentrates less on its rhetoric than on the plain word, less on the plain word than the idea behind it. Look for the idea and you will be a competent interpreter of the *Shi-jing*."

[4] 《文赋》：精骛八极，心游万仞……观古今于须臾，抚四海于一瞬。
    "The spirit roams to the eight limits of the universe; the mind travels thousands of leagues...Past and present can be grasped at a moment's glance; one glimpse is enough to embrace all four seas."

[5] 《文赋》：选义按部，考辞就班，……磬澄心以凝思，眇众虑而为言，笼天地于形内，挫万物于笔端。
    "Choose your meaning from a category, and deliberate on the proper classification of works...Purge the heart so that you may concentrate your mind; dispel all irrelevant thought before you compose. Enclose both heaven and earth in a proper form as in a cage so that with the tip of your pen you will be able to pick up the myriad objects."

elaborated by Liu Xie (刘勰? 465—? 520) on the basis of Zhuang-zi (庄子) and the *Yi-jing* (易经). In addition to the unbounded capacity of the imaginative power, Liu Xie analyses the operation of the faculty in the following terms:

> The wonderful operation of the mind lies in the communion of the spirit with the external world. The spirit which is house in the bosom has a temperamental inclination for its mainspring. And the perception of the external world through the senses hinges on language. If the hinge is smooth, the image of the external world will be manifest: but if it is blocked, then the spirit tends to run away.[1]

Liu Xie's statement about imagination and expression is couched in terms liable to widely different interpretations; the subject has remained unclarified.[2] But this attempt as a solution for expression has left an interesting and fruitful residual effect on Chinese literary criticism. It becomes a credo with the Taoist critics that the deepest and subtlest things are beyond expression, taking the clue probably from the very first sentence of the *Dao-de-jing*(《道德经》): "The *dao* (or *tao*) that can be put in words is not the constant or immanent *dao*." This has exercised a profound influence on Chinese literary criticism. It is the highest aspiration of every poet to achieve an effect beyond the written word and the highest criterion by which to judge poetry. The principle is put in a

---

[1] 《文心雕龙·神思》：故思理为妙，神与物游。神居胸臆，而志气统其关键；物沿耳目，而辞令管其机枢。机枢方通，则物无隐貌；关键将塞，则神有遁心。

[2] Shao Yao-cheng: "Liu Xie's Dual-strata Theory of Literary Creation," in *Studies in Classical Literary Theory*, vol. v (Shanghai, 1981).

brief phrase: "the idea lies outside the spoken word."[1] This exaltation of suggestiveness, of innuendo, has become the hallmark of classical Chinese poetry. It is reinforced by the Buddhist or Zen tenets of "sudden perception" and freedom from speech or the written word.[2]

Granted that an awareness existed that literature could be studied from psychological and semantic viewpoints, it would be interesting to speculate whether Chinese literary criticism, if it had been pursued on the Taoist-Buddhist line, might not have converged on the path which Western literary criticism has followed. But the fact is that Confucian frame of mind with its sober common sense, unfailing consciousness of reality and deep regard for man's moral wellbeing, has all along been the dominant influence. At the turn of the twentieth century, first Liang Qi-chao（梁启超）and then Wang Guo-wei（王国维）brought in from the West the term "realism," thus giving the finishing touch to the long tradition. The present-day attitude may be said, in a sense, to be continuation of that tradition.

In the West, literary criticism follows a different line of development. Reaction against Matthew Arnold has been continuous with perhaps a few short-lived skirmishes from the Arnoldian camp (Babbitt, More, Forester) and the Leftists of the 1930s. The critical scene on the whole, however,

---

[1] 意在言外。It is interesting to note that Zhong Rong（钟嵘）identifies this principle with *xing* 文已尽而意有余，兴也。The same principle is applied to painting and calligraphy. Sun Qian-li（孙虔礼）in *Shu-pu*（书谱）writes: "Those who write (i. e. on ancient masters of calligraphic art) can write only about their dross" 著作者假其糟粕，i. e. the subtlest and finest qualities cannot be conveyed by words. The late Ko Mo-jo in his *English Poetry in Translation*（英诗译稿，Yi Wen She Publishers, Shanghai, 1981) having made an excellent translation of *The Daffodils* by Wordsworth, comments: "Not a good poem; the first one or two stanzas are enough. The last two stanzas (especially the very last stanza) are superfluous. Pulling a long face and preaching is always tiresome. A taste for suggestiveness and a distaste for plain statement in poetry are of long standing."

[2] 顿悟。离言说相，离文字相。

is dominated by "formalism" (in the broadest sense of the word), which prefers to leave out of account the social function of literature and declines to pass moral judgments. It is a strong current against realism and didacticism. For convenience's sake, I shall offer examples from modern Shakespearean criticism alone, as Shakespeare has had the good fortune to be subjected to the scrutiny of nearly all modern critical schools.[1] And I would like to single out the word "pattern" as symptomatic of modern Western critical mentality, a word incidentally difficult to translate into one corresponding Chinese word owing to its multiple applications:

Pattern inherent in the actual word.

Intensity followed by weak ending—a pattern occurring in many other poems

The plot follows the regular wish-fulfillment pattern.

New Comedy exhibits the general pattern of Aristotelian causation.

The characters who impede the progress of the comedy towards the hero's victory... the miser, the hypochondriac, the hypocrite, the pedant, the snob... who are slaves to a predictable self-imposed pattern of behaviour.

Shakespeare's comedies follow a profound pattern of the ritual of death and renewal.

Whether it is the rhythmic recurrence of motifs or symbols or even words in a work, or the habitual or abnormal variations of human behaviour, or the way a society or the world is organized, they are all

---

[1] References are all taken from *Modern Shakespearean Criticism*, ed. Alvin B. Kernan (New York, 1970).

conceived as a body made up of parts that fit together and can be pulled apart.

An excellent and well-argued essay by Professor Maynard Mack[1] will bear out my point. Professor Mack rightly criticizes Bradley's analysis of the construction of Shakespearean tragedy into "the management of exposition, conflict, crisis, catastrophe; the contrasts of pace and scene; overall patterns of rise-and-fall, variously modulated" which remains "the best account of the outward shape of Shakespearean tragedy," but which "can apply as well to potboilers." Professor Mack attempts with single success to explore the "inward structure," "Shakespeare's capacity...to point, evoke, imply," and thus "by indirection to find directions out." As an example, he picks out the Fool's part in *Lear* and contends that the Fool is a sort of "dramatic shorthand for the going-on in the King's brain," for "he does not enter the play as a speaking character till after the King has behaved like a fool, and leaves it before he is cured." Thus the example of the Fool "introduces us to devices of play construction and ways of recording the progress of inward 'action,' which, though the traditional categories say nothing about them, are a basic resource of Shakespeare's play-writing."

Professor Mack, unlike Bradley, is attempting to find out "the authentic tragic Muse" in Shakespearean tragedy, but like Bradley he also resorts to the method of structural analysis, not in terms of exposition, etc., but in terms of "recapitulations of motifs," "mirror scenes," "cycle of psychic change."

Meanwhile the historical school persists, of course, but its concept of history is rather different from the Marxist concept. Among other things,

---

[1] "The Jacobean Shakespeare: Some Observations on the Construction of the Tragedies."

historical critics consider history, as reflected in literature, to consist of actual events and personages, of social and even political institutions, while Marxist critics consider historical events to be merely manifestations of the "laws of social development." Hence their emphasis on "essence" when discussing the reflection of reality in a literary work—and essence is embodied in "type." Further, the Marxist concept of reality as a process of conflicts and their resolution is contrasted with the static or evolutionary view of the historical school. Still further, the historical school, like the formalist school avoids moral judgement and aims at "objectivity," while the Marxist implicitly or explicitly stresses edification.

It should be added that the current Chinese critical temperament results from many causes, among which is the Soviet school of Marxist literary theory of the 1950s. It was seeded on a soil favorable to its growth, a literary critical tradition dominated by Confucianism with its political-didactic orientation, its emphasis on life, its realistic utilitarianism. The soundness of this critical temperament lies in its insistence that literature is a social phenomenon, that a work of art cannot be divorced from social life and exist in a vacuum. In this way it helps readers to understand a work of art in its social context. But in interpreting the relationship between life and art, it tends to be simplistic precisely because it considers art from a single, though essential, viewpoint, that of realism. The complex process of reaction, the author's cultural up-bringing, the cultural tradition and climate, the psychology of author and reader, and especially the structuring of a work of art and its linguistic aspect, are often neglected. Chinese literary criticism has thus arrived at a crossroad where, if it is to proceed, it has to recognize the complexity of creative work. L. C. Knights, when criticizing the Bradleyan school, has this to say: "The most fruitful of irrelevancies is the assumption that Shakespeare was preeminently a great 'creator of characters'... He was able to present them 'real as life' before us... Poetry is an added grace." This applies aptly to current Chinese criticism. There are, however, signs that Chinese critics are beginning to be aware of the importance of the intrinsic approach.

Similarly, Western criticism, it seems, has also come to a crossroad. It has helped deepen the reader's appreciation and understanding, especially New Criticism. But somehow it is unsatisfactory in that it is limited and reluctant to go beyond the formal aspect of a literary work. Another eminent Shakespearean critic, Wolfgang Clemen, says in his *Development of Shakespeare's Imagery*:

> We believe that our perceptive faculties have reached their goal when we have divided and subdivided phenomena of poetry and history into a system of pigeon-holes and have pasted a label on to everything. That is a curious error. Often enough such a rigid schematic system of classification destroys a living feeling both for the unity and for the many hued iridescent richness of the poetical work.

This is an apt description of Western criticism, though what he means by "unity" and "richness" may be argued. Unity, it seems to me, should be the unity of the literary work with life itself, and richness the richness also of life itself. Much, for instance, has been written about *Ulysses*, about its structure, but little has been said about what social forces were at work at its creation. Unless this has been elucidated, criticism is incomplete, because such elucidation will help toward a fuller understanding of the work. It makes a vast deal of difference whether the critic is socially conscious, or not, because his outlook affects his artistic analysis.

It will have been clear, I hope, that a comparative study of the larger issues involved in literary criticism is as much needed as the comparative study of specific critical concepts, or rather the comparative study of specific critical concepts should lead to that of larger issues—the attitude or philosophy underlying criticism. Neither the mirror-approach nor the jigsaw-approach is in itself adequate. What literary criticism needs is a synthesis, not mutual exclusiveness, eclecticism, not bias.

Fictionality in Historical Narrative—Different Interpretations

By historical narrative I mean the re-telling of historical events. The excuse for bringing in historiography in a discussion of literary narrative is that there is close affinity between the two. Admittedly history is not literature. History deals professedly with events that actually took place while literary narrative generally deals with events that may happen. The difference is one of content. Even in the matter of content, both historical narrative and literary narrative are mimesis of the objective world, though the latter is the one removed from it. And further the content of neither is verifiable. In both there is room for fictionalization. Thus in the mode of presentation also there is close affinity.

In fact, traditional Chinese scholarship considers historiography and literary creation to have stemmed from the same source,[1] and history is considered the kind of writing where literariness exceeds substance.[2] At all events, in historical writing literariness is held in equal esteem as substance.[3] The same view is held by Western scholarship.[4]

It may not be amiss here to note that fictionalization has two implications. In the first place, it implies its opposite historical truth.

---

[1] 文史同源，刘知几：《史通》："文之将史，其流一也。"

[2] 《论语·雍也》："文胜质则史。"

[3] 《论语·颜渊》："文犹质也，质犹文也。"

[4] Cf. Alastair Fowler: *Kinds of Literature: An Introduction to the Theory of Genres and Modes.* Harvard UP 1982, p.120: "The novel has ramifying roots in earlier fiction and non-fiction". Andrew H. Plaks: *Towards a Critical Theory of Chinese Narrative, in Chinese Narrative,* ed. Plaks, Princeton UP, p.312 where speaking in general terms Plaks remarks: "Both history and fiction are engaged in the mimesis of action."

Historical truth, unlike scientific truth, cannot be verified or repeated. As factual truth we have to take it as given, as it were, on trust. All that one can do is to check whether an account is logically, inferentially or conceptually true. It is an approximation rather than absolute truth. Any discussion of fictionality in history has to proceed from this premise.

The second implication is that fictionalization is a mode of presentation and concerns methodology. And methodology is determined by the way the historian looks at a set of given events, which in its turn is determined by personal limitations or bias and external circumstances. The last is of great importance.

In this paper I shall try to present some interpretations, direct or implied, of fictionalization as offered by noted authorities, both Western and Chinese and make a comparison with the hope of arriving at some generalization on the subject.

Toynbee distinguishes three different methods of viewing and presenting "the objects of our thought and, among them, the phenomena of human life"[1] the ascertainment and recording of "fact," which is the technique of history; the elucidation, through a comparative study of the facts ascertained, of general "laws," which is the technique of science; and artistic recreation of the facts in the form of "fiction", which is the technique of the drama and the novel. The distribution is not "watertight". History, besides recording facts, also has recourse to fiction, and makes use of laws. In respect of the affinity between history and fiction, history, in order to be "great" and not to be "dryasdust," cannot entirely dispense with the fictional element. It has to be, like the drama or novel,

---

[1] Arnold J. Toynbee: *A Study of History*. Abridgement by D. C. Somervell. Vols. I-IV, Oxford U. P., 1947, Introduction.

a recreation of facts. The model for such a recreation is of necessity a certain literary form. The instance Toynbee gives is Thucydides, who is generally accounted the first and one of the greatest of severely factual historians, but, as shown by F. M. Cornford, his whole presentation of his subject is governed by the conventions of contemporary Greek tragedy.

The second point of resemblance lies in the process of the selection, arrangement and presentation of facts. The only difference is that the real facts in history are in the foreground while those of fiction are in the background, which are equally authentic.

A third point which is very interesting is the quantitative theory Toynbee advances. When the data, e. g., human relations, are too numerous, the infinite must be expressed in finite forms and forms fiction. On the other hand, history is possible only when the data are of manageable quantity. The infinite human relations in history must be reduced to institutional relations before history can be written. This distinction is all very good. The interesting point is that Toynbee calls these institutions—"England," "France," "the Conservative Party," "the Church," "the Press"— "fictitious personifications," thus implying that his concept of history—the history of civilized societies—is basically a drama or a novel, i. e., a literary recreation with institutions rather than individuals as *dramatis personae.*

From Toynbee we can gather that fictionality in historical narrative may derive from the selection of source material which is likely to be a mixed bag, and the arrangement and presentation depend entirely on the judgement of the historian. Secondly, fictionality stems from imposing a literary form on the material.

With Collingwood[1] , history is not a mere scissors-and-paste business,

---

[1] R. G. Collingwood: *The Idea of History*, Oxford U. P. , 1951.

but is concerned with the "mind" behind the events. Without it, any event or series of events is unintelligible. To make history intelligible, to make it "a plausible story," the historian has to exercise what Collingwood calls "constructive imagination," that is, an imagination that is not merely decorative as in the case of Macaulay who in his *Essay on History* asserts that "A perfect historian must possess an imagination sufficiently powerful to make his narrative affecting and picturesque." To Collingwood, imagination concerns the basic interpretations of history. A historian's job is not merely to record the fact that Caesar crossed the Rubicon but to reveal the "thought" or "mind" behind the act. History to Collingwood as a Kantian is the history of the Mind. In order to discover the mind behind phenomena, the historian must excise his imagination, or "reenact" the thought, to find out by deduction or inference the motive and purpose. In this sense, the historian plays the same role to historical events as an actor to the dramatic text. History becomes highly subjective as it reflects the mind of the historian through the reconstruction of historical events. But the historian's mind is necessarily different, spatially and temporally, from that of the historical personage. Any inference or deduction the historian makes is liable to falsification or fictionalization. Thus Collingwood's theory touches on a basic cause of fictionality in historical narrative.

Hayden White, in connection with his discussion of Collingwood, asserts that the "fiction-making operation" is made possible by what he calls the "pregeneric plot structure," which the historian has in his mind before he puts pen to paper. "How a given historical situation is to be configured depends on the historian's subtlety in matching up a specific plot structure with the set of historical events that he wishes to endow with a meaning of a particular kind,"[1] i. e., a tragedy or comedy or romance or satire. This brings us to the archetypal theory of literature of Northrop Frye.

Though Frye excludes history and biography from his four types of *mythoi* as noncreative, he yet concedes that "When a historian's scheme gets to a certain point of comprehensiveness, it becomes mythical in shape, and so approaches the poetic in its structure."[2] This is tantamount to say that history like fiction or literature has what Hayden White calls "pregeneric plot structure", even though the historian works inductively "towards" a "unifying form," not, as the poet does, "form" it.

Hayden White's own initial concern is the affinity between history and literary narrative lies in the fact that both are different from science. Historical narrative being the representation of processes long past, is "therefore not subject to either experimental or observational control."[3] Historical narratives are "verbal fictions, the contents of which are as much *invented* as *found* and the forms of which have more common with their counterparts in literature than they have with those in the sciences,"[4] though he acknowledges that fiction-making does not "detract from the status of historical narratives as providing a kind of knowledge."[5]

For history to be a plausible story, to make sense, it is necessary that the thematic content corresponds with certain *mythoi* or "pregeneric plot structures," to fall within one of the four categories formulated by Frye.

---

[1] Hayden White: *Topics of Discourse: Essays in Cultural Criticism*, Johns Hopkins UP, 1986, p.85.
[2] Northrop Frye: *New Directions from Old* pp.53-54. See Hayden White Ibid. 57.
[3] White Ibid. p.82.
[4] White Ibid. p.82.
[5] Ibid. p.85

The events then become comprehensible because they are "encoded as a story of a particular kind," with which the reader is familiar "as part of his cultural endowment";[1] they are "likened" to some such form as tragedy "with which we have already become familiar in our literary culture."[2]

The second point White proposes (following Levi-Strauss) is that to make a coherent comprehensible story out of a congeries of facts it is necessary to "tailor" the facts. The historian, in White's phrase, "mediates" between the facts. And "it is this mediative function that permits us to speak of a historical narrative as an extended metaphor," to fall into one of the Viconian categories of trope. "The historical narrative does not *reproduce* the events it describes; it tells us in what direction to think about the events and charges out thought about the events with different emotional valences."[3]

We may gather from the above account that historical narrative involves first of all the selection and arrangement of data; secondly the imposition on them (i. e., selection and arrangement specified) of a certain culturally determined literary pattern (which may or may not conform to "general laws"); thirdly, *an a priori* inference to the mind or motive behind the events in order to make "a plausible story"; and lastly, the emplotment being directional or tropical, in the sense that historical narrative, like literary narrative, should evoke certain reflections and emotional responses. The likening of historical narrative to literary narrative implies that the former by the very nature of its being is fictional.

Before going on to the Chinese accounts of historical narrative it should be noted that no parallel was drawn between it and continuous literary

---

[1] Ibid. p.86.
[2] Ibid. p.91.
[3] White Ibid. p.91.

narrative for the simple reason that literary narrative did not achieve its full stature until Yuan. Early narrative like the *Zuo Zhuan* is episodic in the nature of an isolated tale much like the fables in the Warring-States philosophers. The *chuan-chi* of Tang and later times are also tales. Tale-like pieces can even be found in the *gu-wen* (archaic style) essays of Tang and Song periods. If there is any narrative model to speak of, it is within the scope of an episode and concerns local matters rather than overall structure or generic type. An interesting case of this kind of criticism is the "Eight Principles of Writing" by Lin Shu[1] (which deserves special study), which he applies to essayistic as well as historical compositions. Further the drama did not come into its own until Yuan, thus no analogy could be drawn between history and drama. But this does not mean that Chinese historical narrative is devoid of tragic, comic, romantic or satiric content. Such "directions" are implicit rather than emplotted.

The second point to be noted is that along with the fact that there was no fictional model for historical, narrative history all along aimed at truthfulness and held it as its ideal. Sima Qian says: "What I mean by retelling past events is to put in order the records of the past; I do not mean to recreate."[2] Commenting on the *ji* (纪 chronicle) and the *zhuan* (传 biography), Liu Xie (刘勰, c.465—522) in the *Wenxin Diaolong (The Literary Mind and the Carving of Dragons)* asserts that they should not consist of wayward commentary but factual records,[3] or again he advises: "When in doubt, let the lacunae stand, because we set value on history's reliability".[4] The great historiologist Liu Zhiji (刘知几, 661—

---

[1] 林纾：《畏庐论文·用笔八法》。
[2] 司马迁：《太史公自序》："余所谓述故事，整齐其世传，非所谓作也。"
[3] "文非泛论，按实而书。"
[4] "文疑则阙，贵信史也。"

721) devotes the greater part of his book *Shi Tong* (史通) to combating errors. So had the Han philosopher Wang Chong (王充，AD29—79) done in his *Lun Heng* (论衡). Even in the discussion of the historical novel of much later times, emphasis is laid on factual truth. But it must be acknowledged that Chinese historians in practice never or seldom followed this precept to the letter. Still this basic stance provides a stimulus to historical criticism to keep the eye wide open for errors, falsifications and fictionalizations.

The great rationalist philosopher Wang Chong, the Chinese Voltaire, holds up reason as the criterion by which to judge all writings including history. He is interested in such concepts as *xu* (empty) as opposed to *shi* (solid, factual), and *zeng* (the additional, the extraneous, plethora). Any account that does not tally with fact or common-sense, that is patently superstitious, that is superimposed by Confucian bias is fiction. In addition, fiction may arise from the misuse, or abuse of language, particularly from hyperbolic language or exaggeration of expression. The famous examples are the descriptions of the physical appearances of the emperors Yao and Shun, the one looking like dehydrated meat and the other like dehydrated fowl owing to over-solicitude over the welfare of their people.[1] Fiction may also arise from misinterpretation of the language in the source material, in the literal interpretation of metaphorical language.

The great literary theorist Liu Xie almost despairs of truthfulness in historical narrative. The reasons are: that ancient records are often of doubtful authenticity; that it is difficult to put into chronological order the accumulated mass of material through the ages (Few countries in the world have left such a mass of written records as China); that man hanker

---

[1] 王充：《论衡·论增》："尧若腊，舜若腒。"

after the strange and extraordinary and disregard solid commonsense; lastly and most importantly men easily succumb to external pressure especially in recording contemporary events. By external pressure he means "the way of the world which causes the consideration of profit and harm"[1] on the part of the historian.

To Liu Xie, a historical narrative should be "directional," not merely pointing to the reader's emotional response, but rather to moral judgement. It should embody advice and warning and show approval or disapproval.[2]

The greatest theorist of historiography in ancient China is undoubtedly Liu Zhiji. One of his central theses concerns historical truthfulness and literariness. To him a good history depends first of all on the narration of events and the ideal narration is to strike a balance between literariness and factuality. "A history should have literariness without being ornate, and factuality or truthfulness without being crude".[3] Untruthfulness arises from preponderance of literariness. Thus to report contemporary speech anachronistically in the mould of archaic speech-style in order to achieve literariness or to report the speeches of the Barbarians in "civilized" Chinese is to upset the balance to the detriment of truthfulness.

Secondly, slavish imitation of old models will lead falsehood. In a chapter entitled *Imitation*, Liu Zhiji grants that "It has always been the case that historians imitate each other." Apparently he takes this as a general ruler. But he is against what he calls "imitation of the appearance" or formal resemblance, and advocates "imitation of the spirit," much like

---

[1] "世情利害。"
[2] "劝戒予夺。"
[3] "文而不丽"，"质而非野"。

the theory of imitation in Chinese painting and calligraphy.[1] To him, disregard or ignorance concerning the spirit or intention of the model and eagerness to follow slavishly the outward trappings just to be different will result in the distortion of the present account. "Times change and events change with them; when events are different, all else are different," he quotes the philosopher Han Fei.[2]

Thirdly, Liu, like his namesake Liu Xie, thinks that political and ethical scruples are among the causes of historical distortion. But he is different from the elder Liu in allowing for distortion due to respect to the sovereign and the parents in the interest of ethical code, but not for distortion due to personal love or hate or due to having received bribes.

A comparison of the two sets of observations on historical narrative brings about some issues of general interest.

Both modern Western and classical Chinese scholarships agree that fictionality or literariness in history is inevitable, even desirable. As to the question what makes a historical narrative fictional in the sense that it is "literary", Western scholarship offers an answer, namely it conforms to a literary genre or *mythos*. But Chinese scholarship is almost silent on this point for reasons already stated, except when Liu Zhiji criticizes those historians who impose earlier historical models on to the material in hand without understanding properly the intention of the earlier historians. But this emplotment is not literary but historical. Further it does not concern the structure of the narrative but concerns only phraseology of local importance.

As to fiction in the sense that it is "untrue", Chinese scholarship

---

[1] "貌同心异","貌异心同"。
[2] 韩非:《五蠹》:"世异则事异,事异则备变。"

abounds in proposed causes: hankering after the strange, distortions through Confucian bias, through linguistic and rhetorical "additions", political and personal considerations. Causes offered by Western scholarship can only be inferred, i. e. mistakes or untruthfulness can possibly arise out of the application of "constructive imagination", which can produce a variety of versions of the same story, e. g., the different accounts of 18 Brumaire by Victor Hugo, Proudhon and Marx. It may also be noted that among the causes offered by Chinese critics some are subjective and others objective, while those offered by Western historians—deduction, inference, imagination—are purely subjective, though as an afterthought it is said to be constrained by culture.

According to Hayden White, emplotment is "directional"; it causes the reader 1) to reflect and 2) to react emotionally. He is not specific about what to reflect on. On this point the Chinese historians are always very explicit—to give advice and warning, approval or disapproval. At one place Liu Zhiji advises the historian to look for the *dao* behind history which reminds one of Collingwood's "mind", but *dao* and mind are quite different, the former mainly concerning Confucian ethics while the latter being the motive behind a particular action.

It is interesting to observe that Thucydides can hardly be said to be ambiguous about his political and moral sympathy (e. g., Pericles' funeral oration, the Melian dialogue), Gibbon is conspicuously anti-Christian and Macaulay patently Whiggish, to name but a few examples. But modern Western historical criticism tends to pass over this point. But it seems to me that historian's political stance is perhaps equally important if not more so than the cultural environment in which he works, in the formation of his "mind" which gives direction to his interpretation and determines his method, out of which arises fictionality.

·Paper presented at the Second Sino-American Comparative Literature Symposium, Princeton University and Indiana University, Bloomington, 1987. A fuller Chinese version is found in *Tang Tai*, No. 29, Taipei, 1988, and in *Zhongguo Bijiao Wenxue* (*Comparative Literature in China*), Shanghai, 1989.

Disjecta Membra: Supplementary Remarks

It is impossible for any historical narrative to tally perfectly with historical reality even if it be a narrative of a single historical event or movement. For one thing, historical events cannot be repeated exactly, or verified like scientific experiments, and for another, the sheer mass of events big and small that actually happened is forbidding, or again the scarcity of available data, or misreport, makes it impossible. As Bolingbroke remarks, "There are few histories without lies, and none without some mistakes." But still history can achieve a verisimilitude or near-truth or partial truth, and it would be folly, in Bolingbroke's words, "to establish universal Pyrrhonism in matters of History" (Letter IV, *Letters on the Study and Use of History*).

Fiction in historical narrative means two things: literary structuring (fictio) and misrepresentation. They share the common quality of untruth or partial truth, but are different in mode of presentation and in motivation.

Literary fictionalisation consists of historical events, e. g., Livy's account of the Sack of Rome by the Gauls with its dramatic suspenses, or Tacitus' account of the Fire of Rome under Nero, or Macaulay's account of the Massacre of Glencoe. These accounts are not far different from e. g., the Sack of Troy in the *Aeneid*, or a scene in a Scott novel.

Literary fictionalisation is brought about by concentration on characterisation, e. g., Herodotus' characterisation of Xerxes. Sometimes historians go into the workings of a historical personage's mind, e. g., Livy's account of what passed, or what he imagined had passed through the mind of the Roman general Marcellus when he was about to destroy Syracuse during the First Punic War, with deep human touches.

When a historian inserts a lot of anecdotes or elaborates on incidental but not unimportant details, he can be said to be fictionalising history, e. g., Sallust in his *Bellum Catilinae*, when he describes the bravery of Catiline's soldiers, writes that they were slain "but all fell with wounds in front" (sed omnes tamen advorsis volneribus conciderant).

More importantly, literary fictionalization stems not from technical considerations but rather from a larger concept of history in literary terms. E. g., Herodotus conceives of history as a fairy tale with all its accessories (repetition of action, moral ending, etc.), like his account of Solon's visit to Croesus, last king of Lydia. Thucydides conceives of history as tragedy, notably, for instance, in his narrative of the Athenian defeat at Syracuse in the third Peloponnesian War, as due to their hubris. So is Gibbon's concept a tragic one. The splendour that was Rome was suddenly brought to a down fall. Its cause flashed past his mind at the sight of the barefooted friars singing vespers among the ruins of the Forum.

James Anthony Froude (1818-94) even thinks that Shakespeare's history plays are "the most perfect English history".

Fictionalisation of history is part of cultural tradition. Gibbon greatly admires Robertson's *History of Scotland* (1795) and says in his *Autobiography*, "The perfect composition, the nervous [sinewy] language, the well-turned periods of Dr. Robertson inflamed me to the ambitious hope that I might one day tread in his footsteps...[They] often forced me to close the volume with a mixed sensation of delight and despair".

Macaulay in his essay, *History*, expressly says that "By judicious selection, rejection and arrangement" of materials, the perfect historian "gives to truth those attractions which have been usurped by fiction," highlighting "small and vivid incidents and circumstances."

Again in his *Autobiography*, Gibbon likens history to something like general reading, for he says, "History is the most popular species of writing since it can adapt itself to the highest or the lowest capacity," implying evidently that history is more akin to literature than any branch of learning or science. It provides delight as well as instruction.

To incorporate superstitions into historical accounts is apparently part of antique culture in the West, as in China, e. g., Herodotus inset of portents in his account of Xerxes' march to Hellas (an eclipse of the sun, a mare giving birth to a hare, a mule to a mule).

All history tells partial truth, not the whole truth. Fictionalisation in historical narrative is a matter of degree or scope. It may be due to the following causes:

Technical causes. Lack of data. The remoter the age, the fewer will be the data, or more faulty and less reliable. In the case of an abundance of data, selection may lead to the distortion of the whole truth. Even in the case of the historian as a participant of the events he narrates—and there is no lack of such cases, (all the three Greek historians, Polybius, Caesar, Sallust, Tacitus or Clarendon), it is impossible for him to tell the whole truth. Thucydides has this to say about the speeches he reports: "It has been difficult to recall with strict accuracy the words actually spoken, both for me as regards that which I myself heard, or for those who from various other sources have brought me reports. Therefore the speeches are given in the language in which, as it seemed to me the several speakers would express." Qian Zhongshu (I. p.165) comments on the dialogues in the *Zuo Zhuan*, "Zuo imagines himself in the position of the speaker, and relying on his own understanding of the character and status of the speaker, lends him his own tongue. It's all a matter of 'I think so'."

The historian's philosophy of history gives his narrative a general colouring to or reads certain kind of meaning into what actually happened, which may not be the right representation. Herodotus believes that "human prosperity never continues in one stay." Does history really evolve cyclically, or is it just a continuous flow? Gibbon thinks that the accumulation of social momentum brings about the sudden collapse of the Roman Empire, which may very well be the case. But his prejudice against Christianity induces him to denigrate Christianity, and gives us a partial if not incorrect picture of the role Christianity played.

The historian's personal bias is, it seems to me, ultimately due to social and political causes. Gibbon's prejudice is part of the battle between Enlightenment and superstition. We shall notice that the publication of Vol. I of the *Decline and Fall* in 1776 coincide with Adam Smith's *The Wealth of Nations*, the *Declaration of Independence* and Bentham's *Fragment on Government*, which embodies the political and ethical theory: "It is the greatest happiness of the greatest number that is the measure of right and wrong." The violent contrast, as has been just mentioned, of Rome's ruins with the bare-footed friars singing vespers triggered the *Decline and Fall*. Why did Gibbon not choose Raleigh as his subject? "I shrink with terror from modern history of England," says Gibbon, "where every character is a problem, and every reader a friend or an enemy." "I must embrace a safer and more extensive time." Even this theme meets with attacks. Hume writes to Gibbon on Vol. I, "It was impossible to treat the subject so as not to vive grounds of suspicion against you, and you may expect that a clamour will arise." And a clamour, to be sure, did arise. Gibbon had to write *My Vindication*. He who follows truth too closely at the heels may get a kick in the face.

Partisan spirit or political bias exists in the source itself. Thucydides has this to say: "Those who were eyewitnesses of the several events did not give the same reports about the same things, but reports varying according to their companionship of one side or the other." Clarendon warns himself when recording the events of 1645 that impartiality will "call both his (i. e. the King's) wisdom and his courage in question...All which consideration might very well discourage and even terrify me from prosecuting this part of the work with (that) freedom and openness..." He would rather not "pry too strictly into the causes of those effects, which might seem rather to be the production of Providence, and the instances of divine pleasure, than to proceed from the weakness and inadvertency of any man."

Historical truth is always partial. What is truth, said the jesting Pilate, and would not stay for an answer.

In this sense, essentially, historical narrative is not different from fiction. The difference lies in form and mode of presentation.

Literary narrative may take either verse (epic, metrical romance) or prose as medium while history is as a rule in prose, though Naevius and Ennius wrote verse.

Literary narrative evolves around a central theme with actions and characters organised in such a way as to best bring out the theme. It has a beginning and an end. The author as a rule does not intrude.

Historical narrative is constrained by what actually happened. In this sense, a historian is less free than for instance a novelist. Of course historians always strive after literariness. But however much creative imagination he may exercise, he is bounded by what actually happened.

Regarding the cause of fictionality in history, Chinese and modern Western historical theories differ. Modern Western critics tend to attributes the cause to literary patterning. But the practice and theory of early Western historians bear out the fact that fictionalisation is due in most cases to political scruples. One of Herodotus' aims in writing his history of the Peloponnesian wars was to refute Persian versions of the same events. "The Persian learned men say that Phoenicians were the cause of the feud...For my own part, I will not say that this or that story is true, but I will name him whom I myself know to have done unprovoked wrong to the Greeks, and so go forward with my history, and speak of small and great cities alike." Thucydides' reported speeches for or against a particular course of action, with a large measure of literary imagination, are politically oriented. Polybius, though of Greek origin, voices in his *Histories* for the first time the greatness of Rome, as compared with all previous empires. Caesar's *Commentaries* are patently political.

Chinese historical criticism attributes the causes of fictionality to faults in the data, to literary and linguistic additions, but most of all, to political and moral considerations.

My modest aim is merely to point out a cardinal fact that historical fictionalisation is due ultimately to external pressure, a fact neglected but perhaps tacitly recognised by modern historical theory.

Can the same principle be applied to historical fiction? To all fiction? What is the difference between a historical novel and history? Is there any similarity between them in the choice of material and in the mode of presentation? Some of these questions may have already been answered. There may be other questions. But these will be beyond the scope of the present essay.

Gibbon: *Mémorire sur la monarchie des Mèdes* III 46: "[L'historien philosophe] choisira parmi les fai ts contestes, ceux qui s' accordent lemieux avec ses principes, et ses vues... Le désir de les émployer [sic] leur donera même un degré d'évidence qu'ils n'ont pas; et la logique du coeur ne l'emportera que trop souvent sur celle de h'ésprit." Quoted from W. B. Carnochan; *Gibbon's Solitude*, Stanford UP, 1987, p.199.

Chinese Theory of Literary Classification

The theory of literary genres has for a long time been a moot issue among Western literary theorists and comparatists. It will probably remain a moot issue for some time to come. It may perhaps never be resolved simply because literary genres themselves may evolve with time and new hypotheses may arise.

Against this background it may not be inappropriate to intrude upon the scene a set of generic concepts which in some ways are strange if not totally unacceptable to Western concepts.

What I mean by Chinese theory of literary classification is the theory which is not explicitly stated but rather underlines the classification of literature by Liu Xie (刘勰), the greatest and perhaps unique authority on the matter. Liu Xie was active in the early years of the 6th century (c.465-522). Scholars before him had made attempts at sorting out all existing writings and documents, including works of literature e. g. Liu Xiang (刘向? 77 B. C.—6A. D.), and Ban Gu (班固 32—92 A. D.), but they are strictly bibliographers. Later critics up to the modern period followed Liu Xie's model without any important improvement. In the 20th century, little work has been done in China on literary genre.[1] In the West, as far as I know, Cyril Birch edited a book on Chinese literary genres. The present

---

[1] Chu Binjie(褚斌杰): *Zhongguo Gudai Wenti Gailun* (《中国古代文体概论》 *A Survey of Classical Chinese Literary Genres*) Peking Univ. Press, 1984. Scattered articles in various scholarly journals.

paper aims merely at an interpretation of the theory inherent in Liu's work which I hope may contribute to an enlivening of discussion on the subject.

Liu Xie's treatise, the *Wen-xin Diao-long* (文心雕龙 *The Literary Mind and the Carving of Dragons*),[1] consists of three parts: theory of literary creation, an interpretation of literary history, and a critical survey of the various literary genres. It was completed about 501-2. Of the 50 chapters, 20 deal with the different genres.

Liu's treatise has happily a companion work in the *Wen-xuan* (文选, *Anthology of Literature*) compiled by Liu's young patron, the prince Zhao-ming (昭明, 501-531) of the Liang-dynasty, the first of its kind since the *Shijing* (诗经, *Book of Odes*). This anthology supplies concrete examples to the genres discussed in Liu's treatise.[2] Between the two, there is general agreement in classification with some difference. They are in general agreement in that both exclude the Confucian classics, Liu on the ground that the Confucian classics are the fountain-head of all subsequent literary genres, though they themselves do not bear any classification; the Prince on the ground that he, as editor of an anthology, dares not "cut" them out of their context. But the two men differ in that while Liu counts historical writings and the speculative writings of the philosophers on Zhu-zi (朱子) as literary genres, the Prince excludes them from his anthology because, he asserts, speculative writings are concerned with ideas without any claim to being literary; the writings of political tacticians (a breed of intellectuals who throve on, or lost their lives dismally by, giving advice to warring overlords, one-time lobbyists) are too "heterogeneous" and have already

---

[1] *The Literary Mind and the Carving of Dragons*, trans. By Vincent Yu-chung Shin, the Chinese Univ. Press, Hong Kong, 1983.

[2] See appended chart.

appeared in historical records and elsewhere; and historical writings themselves belong to the province of moral philosophy (it was history's business "to praise the right and condemn the wrong"). The Prince's conception of literature is that a literary work should be "pleasant to the ear and appealing to the [mind's] eye". In other words, his conception of literature is hedonistic, while Liu's is more orthodox and comprehensive. It is Liu's classification which was adopted by later critics.

It should be noted that the literature Liu knew naturally predates the 6th century, which means that there was no drama yet nor novel (long prose narrative, and epic never existed in Chinese literature). Thus the Chinese definition of literature as well as genres is different from the Western division of epic, drama and lyric.

That the various kinds of non-fictional prose should be considered as literature is because they all convey a message, and this fact tallies very well with the function given to poetry—*shi yan zhi* (诗言志), i. e., poetry is the expression of feelings or/and ideas. Thus prose, whether practical, philosophical, historical or whatever, belongs by right to the realm of literature. So basically and from the start, Chinese conception of literature is not mimetic but expressivist. Even when subsequently the scope of literature was enlarged to embrace tales, fiction and drama, these were still considered not as mirroring nature but as illustrations either of moral philosophy or as expression of personal feelings. [It would be interesting to compare Chinese portrait painting or figure painting of the Ming or early Qing (16th-17th centuries) literati with European paintings of the Renaissance. Take for instance Chen Hongshou's so-called "portrait" of the poet Qu Yuan (屈原, 343—278 B. C.), gaunt and towering, emphasising the poet's loneliness, melancholy and resentment, and expressive of the painter's own sentiments, called up through sympathy with the poet.]

Another point is that none of the literary works which men of the 6th century down perhaps to the 11th century knew is of any great length.

The *Wen-xin Diao-long* divides this body of literature into two major divisions: the *wen* (文 rhymed composition) and the *bi* (笔 *prose*). Under *wen*, Liu Xie lists 14 different kinds of rhymed composition. Under *bi*, he lists 17 different kinds. There are also 3 intermediary kinds where rhyme and non-rhyme are used indiscriminately. The amount in all is 34 genres.

The first feature to be noticed is that out of the 34 genres, 19 are connected with the Court, imperial or princely. They are noticeably politically oriented. The *Book of Odes* (诗经) itself and later the *Yue-Fu* (乐府 Musical Poetry) consist of works collected or composed by a special bureau at court, serving the function of monitoring public opinion like a Gallup poll. Among compositions in rhyme, the genre known as *meng* or Oath made at the signing of a treaty, the four different types of imperial edit or official proclamation, and among prose works the four different kinds of memorial submitted to the court, all have direct bearing on contemporary politics. The idea that literary genres are closely linked with princely courts or reigning dynasties is certainly alien to Western conceptualization, but perhaps not really peculiarly Chinese. One thinks of Hobbes's division of literature into the heroic, the scommatic and the pastoral which he matches with Court, Town and Country,[1] which are certainly unusual. While Western literary genres have never been so directly linked, at least not purely on typological basis, with a political institution, we have nevertheless the *Carmen Saeculare*, the *Astraea Redux* and other Establishment literature, though they have never been classified by literary historians and critics as genres. One also remembers the institution of the

---

[1] Wellek and Warren: *Theory of Literature*, Penguin, 1982, p.228.

Poet Laureate.

Several of Liu's genres are connected with rituals, such as the *zhu* (Sacrificial Oath), the *feng-shan* (封禅 compositions made on the occasion of offering sacrifices to Heaven and Earth), the *lei, ai* and *diao* (Obituaries and Elegies). The *zhu* and the *feng-shan* perhaps bear some resemblance to the hymn, while *lei, ai* and *diao* are elegiac in nature.

To moral teachings belong notably the *song* (颂), *zan*(赞), *ming* (铭), *zhen*(箴), *xie* (谢), and *yin* (应), all political institutions aiming at moral improvement. The *song* is an encomium glorifying the deeds of a ruler; the *zan* is usually a rhymed piece giving praise or censure to all ranks. The *ming* is an inscription carved on a vessel or on stone commemorating an event, and later developed into reminder about the rules of conduct. The *zhen* is a warning against wrong-doing as it was the duty of one of the court officials to compose the *zhen* regulating court decorum, cf. 女史箴 , painting in British Museum by Gukaizhi (4-5cent.). Most interesting are the *xie*. (Humour) and the *yin* (Riddle). The function of the *xie* was to correct the conduct usually of a ruler by cracking jokes or facetious remarks. An intimate court favourite usually did this, somewhat like a court fool. The *yin* is a type of writing using equivocal language or crafty simile or metaphor also for the purpose of correction, which later developed into pure riddles. In Liu Xie's eyes, these are inferior genres.

The next large category is non-official and may be termed assertive composition: the *zhu-zi* (Various Masters), which comprises speculative or philosophical writings. Then there are the *lun* or analytical expositions and the *shuo* or persuasions. All three genres share the common characteristic of functioning as vehicles for conveying ideas or presenting arguments. Their claim to being literary genres lies in the fact that they are not purely formal ratiocinations or bare logical statements but endowed with imaginative qualities.

History may also be counted among Establishment writings. The historiographer was a court official, much like the historiographer royal, and the purpose of history-writing was didactic, much like what Bolingbroke says of history that "history is philosophy teaching by examples." Technically it was the historiographer's business "to arrange historical facts in neat order", to institute a new schema of historical events, hence technically a re-grouping of source material. In practice, no historian can be absolutely objective. Liu Xie points out that the common vice of historians was rather "his love for the strange, contrary to the spirit of the Classics." The unreliability of historical accounts is due (apart from subjective inclination) according to Liu Xie, first to distance in time ("the farther back the past is, the more chances there will be that reports are unreliable"), next to the fact that "people in general love what is strange and pay no attention either to facts or to what ought to be," and lastly when treating contemporary events, to contemporary influences and pressures. The conclusion to be drawn from this is that no history is wholly reliable, thus blurring the boundary between fact and fiction.

It will be seen from Liu Xie's classification that *shi* (poetry, specifically the *Book of Odes*), the genre known as *sao* (骚 poetry from the state of Chu), the *yue-fu* (乐府 Musical Poetry) and the *fu* (赋 a rich ornate kind of verse-form) can be accepted without reservation as distinct literary genres. The rest are questionable in that they all serve practical purposes whether political, ritual, moral or occasional. It is a fact that the speculative writings of the philosophers are connected primarily with ideas, but these are not presented in the form of abstract logical reasoning. Rather they are presented topically, with parables, fables and illustrations. The most notable example is Zhuang-zi. It is fairer to call Zhuang-zi's writing poetry in prose than philosophy as understood in the West. And Lao-zi is written in verse. The *lun* (exposition or discussion) "as a genre, perform the function of establishing what is true and what is not. It goes over all available tangible evidence and pursues truth to the realm of the intangible. It was the Chinese habit of reasoning not in abstract terms but "with tangible evidence." This is probably what gives those prose works their "literariness" and justifies their classification as literary genres. Take the *lun* (论) on the "Fall of the Qin Empire" (过秦论 *Guo-Qin-Lun*) by Jia Yi (贾谊 201—169B. C.) for illustration. In an analysis of the causes of the fall of the great empire of Qin, the writer lays out a panoramic array of events, locations and dramatis personae, employs strong and exaggerated contrasts to build up a perilous balance, bringing the entire weight of the argument on to the last simple statement that the fall was due to failure in clemency and justice. It is not merely a matter of rhetoric or structure; it is a matter of presenting a philosophy of history in concrete terms. Concreteness becomes not only a source of eloquence but also of aesthetic enjoyment. Even the edicts proclamations and memorials on mundane immediate business are not without literary qualities. The occasions which called them into being may no longer interest later readers except perhaps the historians, but they are still delightful reading. It may be said that the "literariness" of "non-literary" genres grows with time, and the practical purposes for which they were designed are lost sight of to give place to aesthetic experience.

It will be seen that classical Chinese theory of genres always takes into simultaneous consideration both content and form, practical purpose and aesthetical quality. Noticeably absent is the criterion of pure aestheticism or formalism. Genres are differentiated by their different functions, moral, social, political, philosophical, but hardly ever by their structural or purely linguistic function. Genres are institutions or conventions. If genres are different modes of conveying messages, the messages themselves are naturally the chief concern. But to make them effective, the mode of presentation is of vital importance. The "literariness" of those prose-genres is not something super-imposed but stems from a mental habit of thinking in concrete terms, and is functional.

The different concepts of literature and the different systems of classification based on these concepts are worth some closer scrutiny. Professor Earl Miner in a paper read at the Sino-American Comparative Literature Symposium 1983 in Beijing,[1] following Lévi-Strauss, labels the undifferentiated concept of literature as "primitive". "Anthropologists have shown that in early societies or primitive societies in our time, the elements of literature, religion, economics, politics etc. do exist but in differentiated form." He calls it a "proto or Ur-conception of literature". Perhaps out of habit, he prefers to discuss literature and poetics in terms of distinct categories— lyric, drama or narrative. "Such thought [i. e., what he calls the Urconception of literature] differs from our own thinking and practice." This is precisely why it is worth while comparing. Is the taxonomy of literature an advancement, the reduction of the humanities to a literary science and advancement?

To lift "literature" out of "its setting, its environment, its external causes"[2] has been the result of a critical trend beginning with Russian Formalism and New Criticism. It is time now, I think, to reassess the validity of the independent existence of "literariness". Do images, symbols, metaphors exist for their own sake? Does a genre merely denote

---

[1] Comparative Poetics: Some Theoretical and Methodological Topics for Comparative Literature.

[2] Wellek and Warren: *Theory of Literature*, Penguin, 1982, p.73.

a separate grouping of literary works of the same form? It is interesting to note that Professor Warren distinguishes between outer form (specific metre or structure) and inner form (attitude, tone, purpose). The inner form is a tell-tale designation. One is entitled to ask to what is the attitude or tone directed, and what the purpose may be. Liu Xie's classification provides an answer. The Prince Zhao-ming, much like Horace, frankly advocates hedonism. The Chinese veteran aesthetician, the late Professor Zhu Guangqian, in anessay on "Exposition"[1] *lun-shuo-wen*（论说文）objects to the opposition of "aesthetic or artistic composition" to "practical utilitarian composition". Such antithesis, according to him, is a narrow view of literature. Practicalness and art are not mutually exclusive but supplementary. And he cites the *Zhao-ming Wen-xuan*（昭明文选）and other Chinese literary anthologies and Plato, Demosthenes, Plutarch, Montaigne and Bacon as evidences. He further argues that if a practical composition possesses affective quality, it should decidedly be considered as literature.

I would like to conclude my talk with a few words on Liu Xie's method of presentation. Invariably he begins each genre with a definition by tracing the etymology (sometimes contrived) and then gives a detailed account of its evolution in the hands of writers of successive ages. From the panoramic description of a genre, one gathers its various manifestations and characteristics. And the crisp epithets and remarks concerning each writer in this genre shows Liu's penetrating critical acumen, with a precision and accuracy unsurpassed by later critics. The purpose of this detailed historical description is evidently to gather momentum for the final *zan* (summing-up) which neatly prescribes the norm, which tells the reader what to expect from that particular genre.

---

[1] Zhu Guangqian: *Zhu Guangqian Mei-xue wen-ji*（《朱光潜美学文集》）Vol. III, p. 407-12, 1982.

In Liu Xie's own word "I have classified [all writings] into separate genres and traced each genre back to its source in order to make clear its development, and I have defined a number of literary terms in order to clarify their meaning. I have selected several literary works for treatment under each specific topic, and have advanced arguments to demonstrate the criterion [of the genre]".[1] Liu's method shows that it is at least difficult to separate the prescriptive approach from the descriptive.

From the brief account above, the difference between classical Chinese genology and Western generic theory can be said to lie (1) in the radical difference of the concept of literature. The Chinese concept is wider than the Western as it includes all non-fictional prose. The question may be raised: should assertive writing, documentary and didactic prose not be considered as literary genres, if they possess functional organic literary qualities? (2) The second difference is that Chinese theory of literary classification is based not solely of form, but on the simultaneous consideration of form and content, and the content is always socially often politically orientated. Even lyrics of a strictly personal character would contain some moral reflection or would reflect the social events that cause the emotions—sympathy, grief, remorse, etc. This practical,

---

[1] Trans. By Shih, p.9 with minor alterations.

"La tragédie n'est pas seulement une forme d'art; elle est une institution sociale, que,par al fondation des concours tragiques, la citémet en place à coté de ses organes politiques et judiciaires. En instaurant sous l'autorité de l'archonte epouyme, dans la même espace urbain et suivant les mêmes normes institutionelles que les assemblées ou les tribunaux populaires, un spectacle ouvert à dous les citoyens, dirigé, joué, jugé par les representants qualifiés des divers tribus, la cité se fait théâtre ; elle se prend en quelque sorte comme objet de représentation te se joue elle-même devant le public. Mais si latragédie apparaît ainsi, plus qu'aucun autre genre litteraire, enracinée dans la réalité sociale, cela ne signifie pas qu'elle en soit le reflect. Elle ne reflète pas cette réalité,elle la met en question. En la présentant déchirée, divisée, contre ellemê me, elle la rend tout entière problématique. "—Jean-Pierre Vernant, Mythe et Tragédie en Grec ancienne, Paris, 1979, pp.24-25.

non-formalistic attitude towards literature in general and generic theory in particular is, I think, highly salutary and perhaps not unhelpful towards clarifying the present state of confusion in genology and making it less confounded.

《文心雕龙》	《文选》
骚	骚、辞
诗	诗（包括乐府）
乐府	（并入诗类）
赋	赋
颂赞	颂、赞、史述赞
祝盟	祭文
铭箴	箴、铭
诔碑	诔、碑文、墓志
哀吊	哀、吊文
杂文（包括对问、七、连珠、典、诰、誓、问、览、略、谣、咏、曲、操、弄、引）	七、对问、设论、连珠
史传	（无）
诸子	（无）
论说	序、史论、论
诏策（包括命、制、敕、戒）	诏、册、令、教、文（策文）
檄移	檄
封禅	符命
章表	表
奏启	上书、启、弹事
议对	（无）
书记（包括奏、记、谱、籍、录、方、术、占、式、律、令、法、制、符、契、券、疏、关、刺、解、牒、状、列、辞、谚）	奏记、书、行状

Paper read at Indiana University and

Duke University, 1986.

Eurocentrism

The present paper was begun with the modest intention of discussing the viability of identifying late T'ang poetry with European baroque. It soon became evident that this process of identification means in fact a form of Eurocentrism, an imposition of a European category on to Chinese poetry. This led me to cast some thoughts on the topic of Eurocentrism and it further led me to a more general question of cultural interaction. It will be found, therefore, that this essay consists of three parts, the first two dealing with the specific matter of baroque and the last dealing with the more general question. The whole, however, has Eurocentrism as its core.

I. Eurocentrism in the Study of Chinese Literature

Eurocentrism is a way of looking at what Said has called "the Other" (*Orientalism*, 1978) from the European perspective. (It is used here synonymously with Western perspective.) A European cannot but look at the Other from a European perspective. Such is of course the case of European scholars when they study Chinese literature. There are cases where Chinese scholars in interpreting Chinese literature to Western readership adopt a European perspective. Such cases may perhaps be called surrogate-Eurocentrism, one remove from "true" Eurocentrism; still they are essentially Europe-centred.

In dealing with Chinese literature, Eurocentrism as an attitude is seldom motivated by any ulterior objective and generally to be descriptive and non-evaluative as in anthropology, sociology and related disciplines. Nevertheless it is a process of imposing Western categories onto Chinese data. Thus it is a highly selective process. A European canon of classical Chinese poetry will very likely consist of the lyrical, romantic, sentimental, and bizarre, neglecting for instance poetry of a realistic bent, e. g., poetry of social criticism and poetry on historical themes, with the result that such a canon is hardly totally representative of characteristic of Chinese poetry. It is a mode of accommodation, adapting Chinese poetry to European taste and categories. The drawing back of such an approach is the obscuring or attenuating of the uniqueness of Chinese literature, the obscuring of the fact that Chinese literature is *sui generis*.

A typical case of such imposition is perhaps the transformation of late T'ang poetry into baroque and the labelling of that period as baroque period in the history of Chinese poetry.

II. Baroque and Chinese Poetry

Studies of baroque as an art and literary category have been going on in the West for exactly a century. But the association of baroque with Chinese poetry is of recent date. The issue was first brought up, as far as I am aware, in the late 60s and early 70s by a small number of scholars of Chinese literature in the West. They find in the works of a group of Chinese poets of the late eighth and ninth centuries certain traits that coincide with European baroque.

The late professor James J. Y. Liu in his *The Poetry of Li Shangyin: Ninth-Century Baroque Chinese Poet*, 1969, points out that in Li

Shangyin's poetry one finds "conflict rather than serenity, tension between sensuality and spirituality, pursuit of the extraordinary or even bizarre, striving after heightened effect, tendency towards ornateness and elaboration, that would probably have been called 'baroque' had he been a Western poet." Liu further suggests that the ninth century may be termed the baroque period of Chinese literary history.

J. D. Frodsham in his *New Perspectives in Chinese Literature*, 1970, remarks that ninth- century Chinese poetry marks "a deviation from the mainstream of Chinese poetry," because Chinese poets of this period "wilfully distort the universe through their sensibility. They are concerned above all with the mutability of things, with Time as a creator and destroyer. The sensory world at once attracts them by its multifariousness and repels them as a shifting, restless simulacrum." He suspects that this attitude ultimately stems from Buddhist metaphysics. And it may account for the tension in Han Yü's poetry. With other poets like Lu T'ung and Meng Chiao, "the tropes and catachreses, metaphors and similes, hyperboles and oxymorons may not arise from an attempt to resolve a psychic tension but simply be 'the decorative over-elaborations of a highly conscious, sceptical craftsman, the pilings-up of calculated surprises and effects.'"

Russell Edward McLeod in his doctoral dissertation *The Poetry of Meng Chiao in the Chinese Baroque Tradition*, 1973,[1] also labels the century between 750 and 850 the baroque period of Chinese literary history. In this period two significantly new and related styles appeared in the Chinese poetic tradition: one marked by a king of sensuous phantasmagoria,

---

[1] The first part was published under the title *The Baroque as a Period Concept in Chinese Literature* in the *Tamkang Review* VII. 2 (Oct.1976), pp. 185-211.

similar to "High Baroque" in seventeenth-century Europe; the other marked by explicit logical order, similar to the "Metaphysicals".[1]

It is interesting to note that only a few years earlier, there appeared an anthology of Poems of Late T'ang, 1965, by A. C. Graham; Graham selects an identical group of poets who are later to be labelled baroque. Graham, agreeing with most Chinese opinion, describes this group as an aberration from the mainstream, forming a "tradition momentarily straying in the direction of our own."

Why did this happen? James Liu's explanation is: "The ninth century in China, like the seventeenth in Europe, was an age of intellectual uncertainty," when "the final synthesis among Confucianism, Taoism and Buddhism known as Neo-Confucianism had not yet taken place, and the intellectuals might have experienced unresolved mental conflicts." Liu's tone is tentative yet confident.

We may deduce from these statements that the so-called Chinese baroque poetry, like its European counterpart, is expressive of some sort of inner tension with a stylistic tendency toward ornateness and over-elaboration, toward the extraordinary or even bizarre. It is a poetry that reflects the intellectual uncertainty of the age.

Before discussing these statements, let us compare two sets of poems by two so-called Chinese baroque poets and two English baroque poets.

The Ornamented zither   Li Shang-yin (李商隐 812-858)

The ornamented zither, for no reason, has fifty strings.

---

[1] Qian Zhongshu: *Tan Yi Lu* (《谈艺录》Zhonghua, Beijing, 1984) p.22. compares Han Yü, Meng Jiao, Jia Dao, Lu Tong and Li Shang-yin to the Metaphysical Poets on account of their use of conceit.

Each string, each bridge, recalls a youthful year.

Master Chuang was confused by his morning dream of the butterfly:

Emperor Wang's amorous heart in spring is entrusted to the cuckoo.

In the vast sea, under the bright moon, pearls have tears;

On the Indigo Mountain, in the warm sun, jade engenders smoke.

This feeling might have become a thing to be remembered.

Only, at the time you were already bewildered and lost.

(Tr. James J. Y. Liu)

Hymn to St. Teresa (selection) Richard Crashaw

How kindly will thy gentle heart

Kiss the sweetly-killing dart!

And close in thine embrace keep

Those delicious wounds that weep

Balsam to heal themselves with. Thus

When these thy deaths so numerous,

Shall all at last die into one,

And melt thy soul's sweet mansion,

Like a soft lump of incense, hasted

By too hot a fire, and wasted

Into perfuming clouds, so fast

Shalt thou exhale to heaven at last

In a resolving sigh, and then—

O what! Ask not the tongues of men.

(How kindly will thy gentle heart

Kisse the sweetly-killing dart!

And close in his embraces keep

Those delicious wounds, that weep

Balsom to heal themselves with: thus

When these thy deaths, so numerous

Shall all at last dy into one,

And melt thy soul's sweet mansion;

Like a soft lump of incense, hasted

By too hott a fire, and wasted

Into perfuming clouds, so fast

Shalt thou exhale to Heaun at last

In a resoluing sigh, and then

O what? Ask not the tongues of men;)

The Ornamented zither is one of the most controversial poems in all Chinese literature and it has been variously interpreted. Disagreeing with all previous interpretation, Liu chooses to interpret it "in more general terms" and asserts that the theme of the poem is "Life is a dream." "When one recalls the past, who can not tell what is real and what is unreal?"

Liu further elaborates on the theme thus: "The world that emerges from the poem is one that transcends the limits of space and time. Things that cannot co-exist are brought together here: Moonlight and sunshine, sea and land, present sensation and emotion and past experiences, what actually happened and what is imagined."

Liu divides the poem into four layers of appeal: sensual, emotional, imaginative and intellectual. On the emotion level, the poem expresses "the poet's feelings of sadness, regret, disappointment and bewilderment." "Intellectually, it makes us wonder about the meaning of life and the nature of reality."

With these characteristics, Liu implies that the poem is baroque.

"Life is a dream" is indeed a common theme of European baroque literature. But is *The Ornamented Zither* telling us that life is a dream? What is the theme of the poem?

In reading Chinese poetry, one of the customary interpretative procedures is to pick out the so-called "non-substantive words" which give the poem its life. In this poem the "non-substantive words"—"for no reason" are of primary importance. They suggest the inexplicable "why so?" and set the keynote of the poem. This notion is reenforced by other "non-substantive words", i. e., "confused" and "bewildered" and by the imagery. "Non-substantive words" of equal importance in the poem are "may wait" (translated as "might have become", which seems to me to miss the point) and "at the time". The two lines may be rendered thus: "This feeling can be recalled now or in the future, though at the time I was (not "you were") already bewildered." If the feeling as it was experienced in the past was already very vague, then it cannot be otherwise when it is recalled now or in the future. In a word, it is a feeling that is ineffable because it is vague. It is not that the poet cannot express it fully, but that he leaves it open-ended on purpose, a mode of expression aspired to by all Chinese poets. The feeling is only suggested by the four middle lines.

We will notice that Master Chuang's dream occurs at dawn or daybreak, though in the original text of *Chuang Tzu* the philosopher does not specify the time of his dream. May we not take this insertion of "dawn" to mean that early in life (echoing "youthful year") the poet is already perplexed. Perplexed by what? The answer is found in the next line: frustrated or unfulfilled love ("spring heart"). There were moments of sadness ("tears") and also moments of warmth and joy ("warm sun" and "jade"). So all in all, I take the poem to be a statement of frustrated youthful love. To enlarge the theme to include a reflection on life as a whole is reading too much into the poem.[1] In terms of theme it is a love-lyric. It is emotionally effective through imagery, allusiveness and a touch of colloquialism, but the tension can hardly be said to be one between sensuality and spirituality.

Now the juxtaposition of contraries is indeed characteristic of baroque poetry. This kind of parallel structure or antithetical arrangement of words and phrases is a long-established convention in the so-called "regulated verse" in classical Chinese poetry, which may ultimately derive from the binary mode of thinking—the principle of "polar duality" traceable to the *Book of Changes* (*I Ching*). But the two terms that form the antithesis are set quite apart; they do not merge as they do in baroque poetry, e. g., Crashaw's "sweetly killing," "delicious wounds", etc.

Liu's division of the poem into four levels of appeal lacks inner cohesion. Let us take the emotional and intellectual levels. Here Liu confuses the different agents of the two activities: on the emotional level, as he says, it is the poet who is expressing his feelings, while on the intellectual level it is the reader who is reading a rational meaning into the poem. There is nothing both emotional and argumentative in the poem, such as we find in the poetry of John Donne.

On the imaginative level there are images which may look decorative and even bizarre, especially in translation: the butterfly in the philosopher's dream, the cuckoo as the re-incarnated love-lorn emperor, the tearful pearl and the smoking jade. The first two images lose some of their freshness to a Chinese reader because they form parts of the stock in trade with Chinese poets. Even the tearful pearl is not really startling. The smoking

---

[1] A danger I. A. Richards has warned against. See *Mencius on the Mind.*

jade may appear strange but it is hardly bizarre; it does not suggest anything violently out of the ordinary as a strange image normally do in baroque poetry. It rather suggests peace, calm, warmth.

Can this poem, typical of Li Shang-yin be called baroque then? The answer is no, as demonstrated above. A comparison with Crashaw will further bear this out. Li Shang-yin's poem, as we have shown, is poem expressive of feelings resulting from lost youthful love— disappointment, regret, puzzlement—feelings so involved that they are ineffable. The passage from Crashaw's *Hymn to St. Teresa* is also an attempt at describing a feeling that is ineffable by listing a series of feelings leading to or suggestive of the final ineffable. There are certain superficial similarities between two poems: The weeping wounds and tearful pearl; incense and perfuming clouds and smoking jade: the hot fire and the warm sun. But in Crashaw's poem there is the merging of very strong contraries which is lack in *The Ornamented Zither*. Joy and pain in Crashaw's poem are so intertwined that they are indistinguishable. In short, Crashaw is trying to convey the ineffable ecstasy, a mystic experience quite alien to Li Shang-yin, and for that matter, to Chinese experience.

Now let us turn to the second pair of poems.

Sadness of the Gorges   Meng Chiao (孟郊 751-814)

(Third of ten)
Above the gorges, one thread of sky:
Cascades in the gorges twine a thousand cords.
High up, the slant of splintered sunlight, moonlight:
Beneath, curbs to the wild heave of the waves.
The shock of a gleam, and then another,

In depth of shadow frozen centuries:

The rays between the gorges do not halt at noon:

Where the straits are perilous, more hungry spittle.

Trees lock their roots in rotted coffins

And the twisted skeletons hang titled upright:

Branches weep as the frost perches

Mournful cadences, remote and clear.

A spurned exile's shrivelled guts

Scald and seethe in the water and fire he walks through.

A lifetime's like a fine spun thread,

The road goes up by the rope at the edge.

When he pours his libation of tears to the ghosts in the stream

The ghosts gather, a shimmer on the waves.

(Tr. A. C. Graham)

The Storm (selection)　　John Donne

But when I wakt, I saw, that I saw not;

I, and the Sunne, which should teach mee' had forgot

East, West, Day, Night, and I could onely say,

If' the world had lasted, now it had beene day.

Thousands our noyses were, yet wee'mongst all

Could none by his right name, but thunder call:

Lightning was all our light, and it rain'd more

Then if the Sunne had drunke the sea before.

Some coffin'd in their cabbins lye, 'equally

Griev'd that they are not dead, and yet must dye;

And as sin-burd'ned soules from graves will creepe,

At the last day, some forth their cabbins peepe:
And tremblingly' aske what newes, and doe heare so,
Like jealous husbands, what they would not know.
Some sitting on the hatches, would seeme there,
With hideous gazing to feare away feare.
Then note they the ships sicknesses, the Mast
Shak'd with this ague, and the Hold and Wast
With a salt dropsie clog'd, and all our tacklings
Snapping, like too-high-stretched treble strings.
And from our totterd sailes, ragges drop downe so,
As from one hang'd in chaines, a year agoe.
Even our Ordinance plac'd for our defence,
Strive to breake loose, and scape away from thence.
Pumping hath tir'd our men, and what's the gaine?
Seas into seas throwne, we suck in againe;
Hearing hath deaf'd our saylers; and if they
Knew how to heare, there's none knowes what to say.
Compar'd to these stormes, death is but a qualme,
Hell somewhat lightsome, and the' Bermuda calme.
Darknesse, lights elder brother, his birth-right
Claims o'r this world, and to heaven hath chas'd light.
All things are one, and that one none can be,
Since all formes, uniforme deformity
Doth cover, so that wee, except God say
Another *Fiat*, shall have no more day.
So violent, yet long these furies bee,
That though thine absence sterve me,' I wish not thee.

There is something uncanny and even grotesque about Meng Chiao's poem, which is I think why it was chosen out of a series of ten poems on the same subject. The desolation of the scene is further enhanced by over-reading in the translation, e. g., "skeletons" for "a lone bone" in the original, "coffins" for a single coffin, and "shrivelled guts" for the simple feeling of forlornness, and "ghosts" for something more ethereal and sympathetic.

However if we compare this poem with Donne's *The Storm*, we will notice that both poets describe a journey, one along a river and the other on sea. Both poets describe darkness and glimmers of light; both introduce into their poems funereal images—the one introducing coffin, skeleton, ghost (read spirit) and the other coffin, grave and a hanged man. Both stress the auditory aspect of their experience. Generally speaking, both poets are trying to create an awesome, fearful atmosphere.

A closer look however will reveal some very fundamental differences. In Donne's poem the predominant mood is that of imminent doom as if the whole universe were on the verge of total breakdown—uniform deformity covered all forms. The noise which seems to accompany the world's collapse is astounding. In the midst of the horrendous din, one loses all sense of direction and of time. The turbulent world is immersed in total darkness. Man and the elements are engaged in a life and death struggle. The poem presents a picture of chaos and turmoil on a cosmic scale. The image of the sailors coming out of their cabins as if from coffins suggests further, symbolically, the life-in-death and death-in-life involution. If we take the ship allegorically and read it as representing the world, then the world is sick and men are "sin-burdened souls." The storm may thus be interpreted as evoked by God as a punishment, which gives the poem a religious undertone. All man's efforts seem unavailing. That God should say another *Fiat* is utterly impossible. I think this is a true reflection of the mentality of the men of late Renaissance. The whole poem is dynamic and the dynamism is enhanced by a theatricality of description.

Yet Donne's baroqueness lies even deeper than in what he appears to be saying. It lies in the way he says it. The poem is addressed to his friend Christopher Brooke. It belongs to the genre of epistolary verse. It reads like a Horatian epistle, chatty, jocular ("like jealous husband") and dramatic ("What news"?). In retrospection the poet could afford to look lightly upon a frightful and perilous experience. This is precisely the way a baroque poet would react. Fear was the prevalent mood. Montaigne says: "The thing I fear most is fear", and Donne offers a remedy: "to fear away fear" by joking about it. Like the masque which produces an illusion in order to hide the truth, the jocular attitude is also a mask hiding fear, just as Burton, worried by anxiety and melancholy, would wear the mask of Democritus.

On the other hand, Meng Chiao's poem seems to me to be an exile's statement of forlornness. "Life is fragile like a fine-spun thread—a figure repeated in another poem in the series. The overall mood is one of sadness and excruciating pain. The shimmering light in the gorges—not total darkness—is atmospheric. The coffin and the bone which may very well have been a realistic description of what the poet saw on the river-cliff, add to the sombre and gruesome atmosphere of the scene. The hungry spittle, which is a favourite figure with Meng Chiao, suggests both fear and disgust. The whole poem is set in a low key with tree-branches faintly whining and sobbing and with silent tears of libation. But even though life appears to be precarious and perilous, there is faint hope— the gorges are not completely enwrapped in darkness. Besides there is the rope along life's way to provide some safety and guidance. The spirits of the river who will respond to the poet's libation as they did to another exile. The poet Ch'ü Yüan, shows sympathy which is consolation of a sort.

Meng Chiao's poem is typical of the sentiment of an ancient Chinese scholar who for the moment failed in his official career. (We know very little about Meng's life except that he passed the *chin-shih* examination at the age of fifty, and a brief official career died on being appointed to serve in Hsing-hua.) He is said about his status as an exile and projects his feelings into Nature, as though the gorges share his feelings. As he travels along, the sadness of Nature increases his own sadness to an intolerable degree, as though his "forlorn heart were scalded in hot water and fire." But he does not end in total despair.

To sum up, the two English poems of course by no means exhaust the characteristics of baroque poetry, but I hope are sufficient to indicate some basic differences between baroque poetry and ninth-century Chinese poetry.

Now in Li Shang-yin's poem the regret for the loss of youthful years and youthful love and the vague bewilderment are a part of a larger frame of mentality. So is Meng Chiao's feeling of desolation and forlornness. Both, I think, stem from a sense of *non desideratus*, a sense of being unwanted, and with Meng Chiao there is also a *nil desperandum*. Here we need to compare the over-all mentality of the ancient Chinese literati and the seventeenth-century European consciousness.

If we look at the historical scene in Europe between the last quarter of the sixteenth century and the first half of the seventeenth century, we shall find that what dominated it were the Reformation and the Counter-Reformation. This struggle is marked both by its intensity and by its scope. The two camps are, to borrow a phrase from Sir Thomas Browne, "antipathies between two extremes," and a reconciliation was as impossible as "a union in the poles of heaven." When Gustav Adolph of Sweden landed in Peenemunde, he told the ambassador of the Elector of Brandenburg who came to dissuade him that "Neutrality is nothing but rubbish which the wind raises and carries away. What is neutrality and way?" (Quoted in the *New Cambridge Modern History*, Vol. IV, p.330) Everyone had to take sides.

John Donne was born and bred in a persecuted religion. Conversion for him was painful. He had to make "a constant study of some points of controversies between the English and Roman Church, and especially those of supremacy and allegiance." To him it was a matter of life and death. "I have ever been kept awake in a meditation of martyrdom, by being derived from such a stock and race as I believe no family... hath endured and suffered more in their persons and fortunes, for obeying the teachers of the Roman doctrine than it hath done."

The pervasiveness of this struggle during this great transitional period in the history of Europe is also noteworthy. It affected whole populations in various ways, including their way of thinking and artistic taste. In a recent study of Shakespeare and his audience (Ralph Berry: *Shakespeare and the Awareness of the Audience*, 1985), the author postulates "a single collective mind for (Shakespeare) to influence, however disparate individuals who compose the mind." By resorting to Jungian psychology, he explores the "social and tribal consciousness" of the audience and matches Shakespeare's plays to the different facets of the social and tribal consciousness—the "dark and primitive" energies of *Richard the Third*, the "archetypal experiences of wandering, loss and recovery" in the *Comedy of Errors*, the social consciousness of "unease, disturbance, insecurity, perhaps guilt, revulsion, repugnance, in a word and to simplify, discomfort" in *The Merchant of Venice*, a "theatre of blood sport" in the

Twelfth Night, and in *Julius Caesar* the "communal identity."

This broad sharing and community of feeling seems to me to be bound. Berry has already indicated the nature of this communal feeling, or mentality or consciousness. It can be further borne out by the audience-response to the drama of the day. The receipts of the various performances of two companies in Henslowe's *Diary* for 1592-97 (Alfred Harbage: *Shakespeare's Audience*, Appendix B IV) give us a convincing proof of the popular taste or mentality of the time. The most popular plays are those by Kyd and Marlowe and Shakespeare's *Henry VI*, Part I. There are other popular plays which either provide mirth, sentiment or romance (e. g., Chapman's *Humorous Day's Mirth*, Greene's *Friar Bacon and Friar Bungay*), or instruction (Greene's *Looking Glass for London and England*) or subjects of topical interest and adventure (Peele's *Battle of Alcazar, Captain Thomas Stukeley*), or pictures of low life (*Knack to Know a Knave*). They indicate the variety of popular taste but judging by the volume of box-office receipts, they are by no means a match to Kyd and Marlowe in meeting the public need which was for the horrible, the macabre, the grotesque and melo-dramatic.

The taste of the time can also be gauged by the reception of a play in successive ages. According to the editor of the *Yale Shakespeare* (1926), *Titus Andronicus* was one of the most popular of all the plays attributed to Shakespeare for a quarter of a century since its composition, but for the subsequent three hundred years it was the least played of all Shakespeare's play. Between 1717 and 1721 it was played intermittently with an "altered" version of 1678 (with added horror); the next staging of the play was 130 years later in 1852. What is particularly noteworthy is the fact that on both occasions it was felt necessary to follow the performance with a farce as if to tone down the distaste, an evidence of the shift in the taste of the audience.

From this it is easy to understand why in the literature of the seventeenth century there is the propensity towards pathos, morbidity, hallucination, the blurring of reality and illusion, excesses and indulgence in horror and frenzy, mysticism of all kinds. It makes us see Shakespeare's sonnets in a wider perspective. If we compare them for instance with Sir Philip Sidney's, we shall at once find a marked difference, a shift from the aristocratic Petrarchan vein to something very despondent. There is a definite pattern: the first three quatrains dealing with themes such as devouring Time rushing youth to old age and decay, Death, Fear, Distrust, passive Suffering, Fragility of Beauty, Fatigue, Feeling of Decline, Sickness, Betrayal, Disgust, Shame and Questionings, and the couplet is usually a reversal with affirmation. It is significant that Shakespeare should adopt this modified form of the sonnet perhaps with the intention to construct a precipitous and steep imbalance between the negative and the positive terms with the negative greatly outweighing the positive, in perfect accord with the prevailing mood of the time.

Now let us turn to the Chinese scene of the late eighth and the ninth centuries. According to James J. Y. Liu, "The ninth century in China, like the seventeenth in Europe, was an age of intellectual uncertainty." The term "intellectual uncertainty" implies an ideological dilemma. Says Liu: "In the ninth century the final synthesis among Confucianism, Taoism and Buddhism known as Neo-Confucianism had not yet taken place, and intellectuals might well have experienced unresolved mental conflicts." So in the poetry of Li Shang-yin, we find "a conflict between Confucian puritanism and Buddhist asceticism on the one hand and sybaritic hedonism associated with popular Taoist search for physical immortality on the other."

Granted that there is a conflict between Confucianism and Buddhism on the one hand and Taoism on the other, it is hardly comparable with the conflict between Reformation and Counter-Reformation in intensity and scope. Further these three sects (if we may so call them) were, as Liu indicates, on the way to a synthesis, which proves that they are not fundamentally antithetical. Taoism as a philosophy of life had long been adopted by Confucians, while Chinese absorption of Buddhism was highly selective. The impact of Buddhism as philosophy on the Chinese mind was slight. As an alien metaphysics it was rejected. Take the concept of *karma* for instance. The *Webster Third International* gives two definitions: 1. "The force generated by a person's action that is held in Hinduism and Buddhism to be the motive power for the round of rebirths and deaths endured by him until he has achieved spiritual liberation and free himself from the effects of such force." 2. "the sum total of the ethical consequences of a person's good or bad actions comprising thoughts, words, and deeds that is held in Hinduism and Buddhism to determine his specific destiny in his next existence." It is by the second definition that the Chinese understand the concept. It is easily and naturally absorbed into the Confucian ethical system.

But Liu is quite right when he says that the tension is "between the Confucian ideal of public service, mingled with personal ambitions for worldly fame, and the wish to withdraw from society prompted by both Taoism and Buddhism."

We may now draw a picture of the mentality of Chinese literati of old. Our premise is that they were, with hardly any exception, imbued with Confucian philosophy. They recognized unquestioningly the legitimacy and authority of the reigning dynasty under which they were born. In this they were different from the men of the Renaissance who, newly awakened, doubted the old established orders. As social conscience, the Chinese literati hoped for peaceful rule under the existing regime, never doubting the justice of its existence. They considered their function to be that of assistants, advisors, administrators, servants of the state. There were officials at court whose duty it was, just as it was laid down by Calvin in his *Institutes*, to regulate the behaviour of the ruler like the Spartan ephors, but they never dreamed of leading the people in rebellion against a tyrant as Calvin would allow. When in disfavour, they accepted exile as a matter of course and remained loyal.

In the event of factional strife, as was the case in the ninth century, they had three choices: active involvement with concomitant risks; withdrawal from the conflict; or non-involvement. The inner tension of a Chinese scholar-official is primarily one between service and withdrawal from service. While in service, it is between loyalty and disloyalty; when out of service, it is between life of obscurity and inactivity or sense of waste. To compensate for this sense of loss, some like Liu Tsung-yüan, would devote themselves to writing for the benefit of posterity. He says: "A man of wisdom unable to fulfill his ambition in the present should win esteem from later ages." They never experienced any conflict between "sensuality and spirituality" as has been suggested by James Liu, or between religious belief and disbelief. They might be dejected but were seldom obsessed by the idea of death. They were none of them mystics and were always in their senses. Their conflicts were always of a moral character. The inveterate habit of looking at everything realistically made it impossible for them to lapse into psychological aberrations or abnormality such as hallucination, vision, ecstasy or irremediable melancholy or hypochondria. Some of them feign madness but that was merely as a gesture of defiance or a way of avoiding danger.[1]

What is the political tension in ninth century China or the late T'ang dynasty? That era is dominated by two main issues: rampant warlordism in the provinces and unchecked usurpation of power by the eunuchs in the central government. The provincial warlords assumed a kind of semi-independence but posed only intermittent and remote threats to the central government. The more fierce struggles were waged at the court. The eunuchs who formed the "inner court" dominated over the "outer court". The situation is further complicated by factional struggles. The struggles at the court were often very bloody with assassinations and public executions no less cruel than the religious wars and persecutions. But compared with the history of seventeenth century Europe, Chinese history of late T'ang dynasty is different in two important aspects: 1. the scope of conflicts was limited, and 2. dynasty authority remained unshaken. (Admittedly the rebellion of An Lu-shan in the early years of the eighth century did threaten the downfall of T'ang but it was put down. And in the next century T'ang was over-thrown by a warlord. But for our period, the threat from the provinces was not imminent.) At all events, what is most important is that the political tension in ninth century China did not change the course of Chinese history (and for

---

[1] The intensity of the unresolved conflict of the Baroque poet may be gauged by statement of William Empson, himself an avowed follower of the Metaphysical poets. He says: "The objects of the style, in my mind and I believe in Donne's mind, is to convey a mental state of great tension, in which conflicting impulses have no longer any barriers between them and therefore the strangeness of the world is felt very acutely." In an interview with Christopher Ricks, he enlarges on the idea: "He thought the poem ought to be about conflict which is raging in the mind of the writer but hasn't been solved. He should write about the things that really worry him, in fact worry him to the point of madness. The poem is a kind of clinical object, done to prevent him from going mad." (John Haffenden's *Introduction* to Empson's *The Royal Beasts and Other Works*, Iowa U. P., 1986, p.16)

that matter nor did the dynastic changes), while the seventeenth century is a watershed in European history, a change from the old to the new. If baroque is the peculiar product of seventeenth century Europe, how could ninth century China, which is so dissimilar to seventeenth century Europe, produce baroque? Li Shang-yin and a few of his contemporaries are indeed an aberration from the mainstream, but the deviation is only partial and has, I think, been over-emphasized. There is much in Li Shang-yin's whole corpus that is a continuation of Chinese poetic tradition in its social concern as well as mode of expression.

With the historical scenario and the mentality of the Chinese literati in mind we can better understand the nature of Li Shang-yin's puzzlement and Meng Chiao's forlornness. Both express their feelings with consummate art, but they are not baroque.

The concept of baroque has undergone a process of change and extention from being merely a concept of style to being a designation of a special culture. Style can be repeated but the nature of one culture is invariably different from that of another. If we take baroque as a culture with definite historical and geographical boundaries, then it cannot be repeated. Stylistic similarities may just be coincidence. Of course they may also be due to influence. Even if stylistic similarities are due to influence, I would concur with José Antonin Maravall (*Culture of Baroque: Analysis of a Historical Structure*, 1975, Eng. tr, 1986) who asserts: "A culture always has borrowings and legacies from previous and distant cultures. But these antecedents and influences do not define a culture. They tell us, at most, that a culture of a given period is open to exotic currents that are geographically mobile." But it is absolutely impossible for ninth century Chinese poetry to have been influenced by seventeenth century European baroque. Even if it had been, it would still remain Chinese.

The question may be raised that if Romanticism or Symbolism has been in practice applied to works of certain Chinese poets such as Chü Yüan and Li Po, why not baroque? These two Chinese poets have been so labelled I think mainly because their poetry is highly imaginative. Imagination with Chü Yüan means the faculty to create a colourful, supernatural world, and with Li Po a world of strong Taoist colouring. Imagination with a Western Romantic poet such as a Wordsworth or a Shelley or a Keats in English literature is exercised in search for the transcendental, for pantheism, or truth, or liberty, or beauty. When the term Romanticism is applied to Chinese poets of the May Fourth Movement of 1919 and since, e. g., Kuo Mo-jo, there is some good reason as the new Chinese literature has become, so to speak, a part of world literature. Still, from Maravall's viewpoint, it will always remain in essence Chinese. The similarity is partial and confined to such aspects of Romanticism as sentimentalism and rebelliousness. Such application is pragmatic and convenient rather than strictly scientific.

A similar case is tragedy. In the strict Aristotelian sense, China's Yüan dramas are not tragedies at all.[1] They are moving but not cathartic.

It is interesting to note that James Liu himself a few years before the publication of *The Poetry of Li Shang-yin*, objected to applying Western terminology to schools of Chinese literary criticism (*The Art of Chinese Poetry*, 1962). It may be worth quoting in full:

It may be remarked here, in passing, that while discussing the various schools of Chinese critics I have resisted the temptation to

---

[1] See Ch'ien Chung-shu (Qian Zhong-shu), *Tragedy in Old Chinese Drama*, *T'ien Hsia Monthly*, Vol. I, No.1 August 1935.

draw facile analogies with European critics and to label the Chinese critics with names of Western origin. It would have been easy to dub the four schools (Moralist, Individualist, Technician and Intuitionalist) I discussed as "Classicists," "Romanticists," "Formalists" and "Symbolists" respectively, but to have done so would have been misleading. In the first place, some of these terms are vague enough in popular usage, carrying different implications and associations, flattering or derogatory according to the writer. However, when confined to their historical context, they can still be forced to mean something definite, whereas if we applied them to Chinese critics, they would lose all their terms of reference. Secondly, though the Chinese critics I discussed show some affinity with certain Western critics, there are many differences too. For example, the Individualists resemble the European Romanticists in their emphasis on self-expression, but they do not exhibit the kind of political and moral idealism often professed by the latter. Again, the Intuitionalists have some affinities with the Symbolists in their attempt to break down the barrier between the external world and the internal world, but the latter's preoccupation with verbal details and auditory effects bring them closer to the Chinese Technicians. It is therefore safer not to use any Western terms but to be content with such ad hoc labels as "Moralists," "Individualists," "Technicians" and "Intuitionalists" awkward and unwieldy as some of these may be.

It cannot be ascertained why he change his mind.

Again, there is an argument that to label a Chinese poet with a Western critical designation will make it easier for the Western reader to appreciate his works. But if the designation itself is a misnomer, it can only lead to imperfect understanding or even misunderstanding.

Frodsham in his attempt to justify the pinning of Western labels on Chinese literature nevertheless concedes that "to impose Western literary categories on non-Western material... may seem presumptuous." Apparently he is conscious that something is wrong there. It is, I think, Eurocentrism. Luckily many comparatists since Étiemble and Wellek have already awakened to the fact.

I have all along stressed difference and uniqueness, but I am by no means being blind to similarity, i. e., overlapping areas between different literatures and cultures. But I believe that contrast rather than similarity can better promote mutual understanding.

The study of Chinese literature from a European perspective can of course yield positive results by discovering aspects which traditional Chinese approach cannot. To give two outstanding examples. Wen Yiduo (闻一多) applies Western anthropological methodology to his study of the *Book of Odes* and successfully explains *ji* (hunger) as hunger for sex and fish as a sex symbol, thus rescuing the ancient text from distorted exegesis and restoring it to what it really is. The monumental analogizing by Qian Zhong-shu of Chinese classics and literature with Western philosophy and literature, his application of Western literary theory to elucidate Chinese literature, his synthetic approach to Eastern and Western cultures contribute greatly to mutual illumination.

But if it is the uniqueness of a given literature that interests us most, we may note that every culture also has its own unique way of interpreting its literature. In other words, there exists a literary critical tradition in a culture which is peculiarly suited to the interpretation of its literature. It has been pointed out (Arthure Waley, *Ballads and Stories from Tun-huang*, quoted in *Chinese: Classical, Modern and Humane*, Inaugural

Lecture, Oxford, 1961, by David Hawkes, Chinese University of Hong Kong, 1989) that Chinese studies, unlike those of the Near and Middle East "whose native tradition and native scholars simply do not exist," have a long indigenous exegetic tradition, which a Western scholar will do well "to depend on." This situation makes Eurocentrism lopsided for there has existed a gap in Western scholarship between the study of Chinese literary theory and the study of Chinese literature; there lacks a coordination between the two. It would be of profit to Western readership to interpret Chinese literature from the Chinese perspective so that the reader may have an idea not only of what Chinese literature is but of how a Chinese understands and appreciates his own literature, and have a holistic picture of a cultural activity.

III. Periodization

In the periodization of the history of Chinese poetry several tentative efforts have been made, notably by James J. Y. Liu who designates the ninth century as the baroque period, and by Frodsham who in his succinct survey of Chinese poetry marks out a lengthy Romantic period with two subsidiary divisions of Baroque and Symbolism in the late T'ang.

Liu approaches the question of periodization from two different angles. From the intellectual or ideological angles, the ninth century in Chinese history, according to Liu, is, like the seventeenth in Europe, an age of "intellectual uncertainty." This conclusion is arrived at partly from comparing the ninth century with other periods of Chinese intellectual history. The ninth century is, first, different from the "age of philosophers" (fifth to third centuries B. C.), "when various original schools of thought emerged"; it is different from the fifth and sixth century A. D., a period marked by Buddhist influence and strong religious faith. It is again different from the seventeenth and eighteenth centuries which were dominated by Neo-Confucianism.

From the purely literary angle, Liu offers two sets of comparison to validate the designation of baroque to ninth century Chinese poetry. First within the T'ang dynasty, the stages of development may be tabulated as follows:

T'ang poetry:	Formative phase (c. 618-710) experimentation, relative naivety	Full maturity (c.710-770) great creative vitality,	Sophistication (c.770-900) tendencies towards the exuberant or the grotesque
		technical perfection	

English poetry:	Sixteenth century Wyatt & Surrey	Elizabethan	Seventeenth century Metaphysical or baroque

Italian poetry:	Quatrocento	Cinquecento	Baroque

Secondly, extending further to Sung, Liu offers the following schema:

1. Age of expansion and creativity, i. e., seventh to eighth century, corresponding to European Renaissance;

2. Ninth century baroque, corresponding to seventeenth century European baroque;

3. Sung (960-1279), age of "neo-classicism", with "its conservatism, emphasis on reason rather than emotion in poetry and art, and its

advocacy of imitation of ancient poets rather than spontaneous expression"— a statement that describes European neoclassicism with extraordinary precision.

Premising that Chinese literature is not a closed system, Frodsham suggests: "The first step towards... bring Chinese poetry into the mainstream of world literature must obviously lie in the establishment of broad areas of periodization. If Chinese writers could be classified into well-established categories now accepted by all European critics— Classical, Neo-Classical, Romantic, Realist, Symbolist, Baroque and so on—this would surely constitute the essential preliminary to write a modern history of Chinese poetry—a history which will be quite distinct from either the history of individual poets and writers or from judgment of individual poems."

So with Frodsham the first task towards periodization is to set up a number of "key terms" analogues and parallel to European categories. This process may seem "presumptuous" but, on the authority of Etiemble, there do exist parallel developments in the literatures of Europe and China. Further, Frodsham argues, if such Western labels as "feudal" and "capitalist" have been pinned on the histories of non-Western societies, why can one not apply Western literary categories to the history of Chinese poetry?

According to Frodsham, the Romantic trend begins with the *Ch'u Tz'u* (楚辞) and reaches its height in Li Po (699-762), lasting for seven centuries (?) characterized by a "new feeling for wild nature and the cult of sorrow" which formed two of the main themes of Chinese Romantic poetry, accompanied by a "hypertrophy of the imagination and sensibility."

After the An Lu-shan (安禄山) rebellion (755-63), the history of Chinese poetry takes a turn in that sorrow becomes the dominant theme which can be traced back to the *Ch'u Tz'u* and post-Han poetry. Li Ho (李贺 791-817) is probably the last of the Romantics taking refuge in aestheticism, following a line of development similar to the decline from Wordsworth to the early Yeats.

Li Ho is followed by Li Shang-yin (李商隐 812-58), a "Symbolist" poet. Much as in European literature, the Chinese Romantic poets, disappointed in the "search for a millenary world," "turned their backs on reality and created a self-sustaining world of language."

At the same time as Romanticism modulated into Symbolism, or a little earlier, there appeared on the Chinese scene a school which Frodsham labels Baroque—"a deviation from the mainstream," headed by Han Yü (768-824), Meng Chiao (751-814) and Lu T'ung (d.835). They are an isolated group, out to shock. "They had no immediate successors though certain Sung poets come very close to them in style."

What does this account of the evolution of Chinese poetry amount to? It appears that from the time of Ch'ü Yüan to the ninth century, Romanticism was the dominating trend which reached its height with Li Po, followed in the next hundred years by Symbolism and Baroque—two subsidiaries of Romanticism.

Frodsham takes it as a general rule of literary evolution that Romanticism is necessarily followed by Classicism. As in Europe, so it was in China. The essence of Chinese Neo-Classicism is conformity of the individual to the social whole. This is the period of Sung and it was initiated by Mei Yao-ch'en (1002-60) and lasted for 250 years. The Romantic tradition now carried on in the *tz'u*, was "relegated to second place."

However, in the matter of periodization, Frodsham warns against the notion of dramatic change in literary history and against "clearly delineated epochs" (p.15). But this warning by no means invalidates what he believes to be the general soundness of his periodization.

Implicit in A. C. Graham's anthology *Poems of the Late T'ang* (1965) is the conception that Chinese poetry from the later Tu Fu ("after his arrival in K'uei-chou in 766") to Li Shang-yin (812-58) forms a distinct period characterized by increasing "metaphorical complexity," thus creating a "new Style of verse."

McLeod while following mainly the line of argument of James Liu and A. C. Graham and assigning the period "from around 750 when the poetry of Tu Fu begins to reveal a radically innovative style and tone, until the middle of the next century and the death of Li Shang-yin" as the Baroque period of Chinese poetry, introduces the new notion of "transitional modern." Basing his analysis on twentieth century Western and Japanese historical scholarship, he proposes that "the modern period in China properly begins in the Sung dynasty, that is, by the tenth or eleventh centuries (sic) A. D. In such an analysis it is usually recognized that the decades after the middle of eighth century are of a markedly transitional character." In terms of literary history, the same periodization is applicable, e. g., in the *Chung-kuo Shih-shih* (History of Chinese Poetry) by Lu K'an-ju and Feng Yüan-chün (1930) which adopted the periods Ancient (1401 B. C. - A. D. 220), Medieval and Modern (907-1911), indicating that "Modern Chinese poetry begins at the end of T'ang."

From these proposed schemes of periodization, there seems to be general agreement in setting apart the period from the late eighth to the ninth century as distinct from all other periods in the evolution of Chinese poetry. But the rationale each critic offers is different from all others.

In his periodization, James Liu adopts two criteria, the intellectual and the artistic, but fails to establish a correspondence between them. Granted that the late T'ang is a period of "intellectual uncertainty" and its artistic expression baroque, it leaves the intellectual situation of the "formative phase" and "full maturity" of T'ang poetry unaccounted for. Again the intellectual history stretches far backwards to the fifth century B. C. and reaches forward to the eighteenth century, covering the whole range of pre-Modern Chinese history, while the different stages of poetic development extend only from the seventh to the thirteenth century. Such analogy is, to say the least, unsatisfactory.

The practice of the triple division of a literary period is neither very convincing because it is almost universally applicable. Every living thing undergoes the stages of emergence, maturity and decline. One can equally well compare the three stages of T'ang poetry to Greek literature or Roman literature. "Nietzsche recognizes a baroque stage in art after the Renaissance, which he, however, conceives also as a recurrent phenomenon in history, occurring always at the decadence of great art as a decline into rhetoric and theatricality" (Rene Wellek: *Concepts of Criticism*, p.116)

Among the above critics there seems to be some confusion about critical category. While James Liu quite definitely assigns the label "baroque" to the late eighth and ninth centuries, Frodsham would rather consider the history of Chinese poetry as undergoing a very long period of Romanticism from Chü Yüan to Li Ho, and the late eighth and early ninth centuries as the decline of Romanticism. Thus Li Ho would be the last of the Romantics taking refuge in Aestheticism, often breaking through into Symbolism, and verging on the Baroque. According to Frodsham, Li Shang-yin is a Symbolist poet par excellence, and Han Yü, Meng Chiao and Lu T'ung are Baroque poets properly so-called. The inappropriateness of calling Li Ho even an occasional Aesthete like the early Yeats is evident because we find nothing of the joy in pure melodiousness of the early Yeats in Li Ho. To call Li Shang-yin a Symbolist because "like the European Symbolists, he is interested not in life but in art and dreams," and to say that his poetry displays "that cabalistic faith in the word which we associate with Mallarmé and Rimbaud," is also inappropriate, because Li Shang-yin was deeply involved in contemporary politics, in family life, in friendship, and as a skillful wielder of words he is entirely different from the French Symbolists for we do not find in his poetry anything remotely resembling Rimbaud's sonnet *Voyelles* or the bizarre typography of Mallarmé's *Un coup de dés jamais n'abolira le hasard.*

Looking forward to the Sung, which both Liu and Frodsham call the Neo-Classical period, McLeod calls it the "modern period" of Chinese literature and the century that precedes it is "transitional modern" apparently with emphasis on a tendency in Chinese literature towards modernity. McLeod does not elaborate on what is meant by "modern" in literary terms except by pointing out that "the literature which the Chinese people themselves mainly notice after the T'ang dynasty is almost entirely a vernacular literature: short stories, novels, plays, and new verse forms, employing the colloquial language." It is apparently that the periodization of Liu and Frodsham concerns poetry alone while that of McLeod in his description of the "modern" period brings in other genres than poetry.

The very title of A. C. Graham's anthology suggests that he is following wisely the practice of traditional Chinese literary historians of dividing T'ang poetry into "early," "high," "middle" and "late" periods consciously refraining from giving it a Western critical label. Indeed he is careful not to confuse or equate certain characteristics of a Chinese poet with a Western "counterpart." For instance, in his introductory note to Li Ho's poems, he remarks: "Li Ho reminds many readers of Baudelaire. The affinity is not altogether an illusion, but in one respect it can mislead. When we read that Li Ho was called a *kuei ts'ai*, a ghostly or daemonic genius, and notice his apparently familiar constellation of pessimism, voluptuousness, aestheticism, and an imagination haunted by dark forces, it is tempting to read him as a nineteenth century Satanist. But the Western sense of evil of course assumes a Christian background, and the *kuei* of Li Ho's poems are generally not devils but ghosts, sad rather than malevolent beings. Nor are there overtones of the flesh and the devil in Li Ho's sensuality, which may be disreputable for a strict Confucian, but hardly sinful. His pessimism also has none of the ambivalence which one expects in a Western artist obsessed by original sin, who is at least half on the side of the destructive element because he finds it at the bottom of his own heart." This insightful observation avoids the peril of misnaming by pointing out the basic difference in moral and religious outlooks between China and the West.

However, McLeod in counting A. C. Graham's concept of the late T'ang as a distinct period, notices the inadequacy of such a procedure "in the omission of one of the towering figures in late T'ang poetry, Po Chü-i (772-846), who is explained as a conscious reactionary against the late T'ang manner" (p.186). And Frodsham, as noted earlier on, also warns against "clearly delineated epochs" (p.15).

These observations pose a question of general interest—the dilemma of periodization. Discussing the European Baroque period, J. Rousset remarks: "En histoire de l'art comme en histoire literaire, c'est la diversité des tendance qui frappe autant que les similitudes, et les resistances au Baroque presque autant que les consentements." (Quoted in Claudio Guillén : *Second Thoughts on Literary Periods, Literature as System*, 1971, p.428)And Guillén continues: "There is no simple equivalence between the Baroque and the seventeenth century: Si le pricipe baroque est peut-être le plus actif, occupant dans l'époque une position centrale, il y a toutes sortes de currants parallèles ou latéraux, toutes sortes de solutions individuelles possibles ; et les grands artistes sont Présisément ceux qui réussissent des solutions singulières (Ibid. 428-9). In Guillén's words, no period is monolithic and there is "multiplicity of time" (p.443). "Men apparently live in more than one 'period' at once" (p.464). In any period there would be a main current and also undercurrents and cross-currents, as suggested by Guillén. There would be a majority of writers working in a similar style and isolated mavericks who may be greater giants. If this principle is followed to the letter, period-labelling would be wellnigh impossible.

The solution Guillén offers is as follows: "My hypothesis is that a section of historical time—that is, of the concept of period—should not be monistically understood as an undivided entity, a bloc, a unit, but as a plural number or a cluster of temporal processes, 'currents,' 'durations,' rhythms or sequences—flowing, like the Arve and the Rhone so vividly portrayed by Georg Brandes, simultaneously and side by side. If we conceive of the diachronic object of periodization as being multiple in the first place, it is then not so difficult to accept the idea of multiple periodization, either in terms of dynamic, dialectical periods or of separate 'durations,' 'currents,' processes, and other terms comparably diachronic in character."

"Thus we took notice of the fact that the seventeenth century has already been studied most convincingly not as a baroque period but as a blending of Baroque, Classical and Mannerist 'currents'." (p.464)

But the question remains whether we are to give equal emphasis to all the currents, if there are more than one, of a certain period, or to highlight the mainstream only. In the former case, the question is of non-inclusiveness. Unlike literary criticism and literary theory, literary history lacks its own system of terminology, a lack which Guillén feels acutely. Such terminology, according to him, should "show above all the ability to elaborate principles of construction in accordance with the particular nature of literary historical experience" (p.467). Failing that, we can only make do with "an interpretative chronology (in Italy, Trecento, Quattrocento, etc.)." (p.469)

With this in mind we may assume that the alternative to a Baroque period in Chinese poetry would be simply "the late T'ang," which, instead of being a political designation, is merely chronological. (The implication of chronological designations will be discussed later.)

Some critics would prefer periodization in terms of simple chronology from a slightly different angle. John H. Mueller in his *Baroque—Is It Datum, Hypothesis, or Tautology?* (JAAC XII. ii, 1954) argues that the data upon which the terminology of Baroque is based are selective and are centered around the so-called Baroque Zeitgeist, but that there is not only one spirit of the age, there are many.

Other critics such as Alden Buker (*The Baroque Storm: A Study in the Limits of the Culture-Epoch Theory*, JAAC XXII iii, 1964) argues that the so-called Baroque characteristics merely "represent artificially contrived generalities based at the same time upon some degree of historical evidence" (p.305) He proceeds to show that all these characteristics, in the arts as in literature, while they did prevail, had all their direct opposites. For instance, "To envisage the *Generalgeist* of the Baroque Era as one of histrionic emotionalism would be to ignore completely the prevailing spirit of intellectualism which characterized much of the activity of the seventeenth century" (p.307). "Hence for every thesis concerning Baroque, there is an antithesis" (p. 311). Buker offers a non-committal solution by advising literary and art historians to adopt "a positive middle-of-the-road attitude" (p.311).

Another drawback of rigid monolithic periodization of literary history is that it overlooks literary history as a continuum. Each stage of development, while qualitatively different from an earlier stage or stages, takes some residue of the earlier stage or stages along with it, and instead of abruptly breaking off shades into the next stage. The difference between these two approaches in one of philosophy of history. The Marxist view of history, as Guillén has rightly pointed out, lays "dialectical stress on history as ceaseless change through negation." Thus one historical period must be the total negation of the previous one and is to be negated by a succeeding one. So the late T'ang is the negation of "High T'ang" and "Middle T'ang," and is itself negated by Sung Neo-Classicism. Such conception of periodization has been found by critics not to tally with literary historical experience. In the Hegelian dialectics, "contradictions are seem to merge themselves in a higher truth that comprehend them" (OED). In this sense, any periodization is necessarily a misnomer because no terminology can comprehend opposites. It will seem evident that the Hegelian dialectics of history explains precisely the dialectics of literary history. Is there then a need, as Guillén suggests, a philosophy of literary history?

To stress the "literariness" of literature, to stress its uniqueness and independent status, ever since the rise of New Criticism, is, I think, fallacious. Nor is the view that literature is the passive reflection of social tensions a sufficient corrective. A holistic view of literature would seem to take literature along with other cultural activities against the background of general history. Literature not merely illuminates social history or history of civilization (Guillén, p.420). Like the arts, religion, social customs, popular beliefs and superstitions, the family institution, etc., it is an integral part of the cultural activities of a given society. And the cultural activities are intricately interwoven with political and economic activities. Purely aesthetic consideration, in the abstract, will inevitably lead to confusion, e. g., the so-called "Baroque" style characterized by ornateness and elaboration may equally be applied to the late T'ang poetry and to the *fu* of Han dynasty.

Ideally the labelling of a literary period will therefore be based on a holistic view of literary history. But this is wellnigh impossible, at all events at present. The same problem, I would imagine, also faces the histories of philosophy, religion, culture, the arts, economics, jurisprudence, and the sciences. In default of an adequate terminology, we are constrained to adopt the strategy of "simple" chronology. The customary procedure of the periodization of Chinese literary history is to follow the dynastic divisions. It may look like an imposition of the periodization of general history on that of literary history. And it certainly is. But in this "simple" or "pure" chronology, there are axiological implications through groupings of periods and through highlighting dominant genres and schools. "Sometimes pure chronology," remarks Guillén, "becomes colored with significance, as, in Italy, where a derogatory meaning was long attached to seicento and secentismo." (p.469n.) Similarly in English literature purely dynastic labels such as Elizabethan and Jacobean have long been associated not only with political, religious and social events but also with literary style.

IV. Some Thoughts on Eurocentrism and Cultural Interaction

Eurocentrism implies a multiplicity of perspectives or a whole spectrum of attitudes, from the disinterested, non-evaluative, purely descriptive to the axiological, emotional, laudatory, derogatory and hostile, the latter attitudes all activated by ulterior motives. None of the above attitudes can be entirely objective. Even with the purely descriptive approach, no absolute objectivity can be achieved, mainly because the knowledge and experience, whether gathered from direct contact with the Other or by indirect means, have limitations imposed by one's scope of experience, by the inevitable element of chance, and above all by one's own equipment and propensities, by one's culture and by historical time.

For the most part Eurocentrism is highly motivated by religious, intellectual and political consideration. From the very beginning Europe itself has been not merely a geographical entity but an emotional and political one. The Greeks of the fifth century B. C. already set in antithesis the continents of Europe and Asia in favour of the former (Denys Hay, *Europe, the Emergence of an Idea*, 1966, p.3). Strabo (*Geography*, II. V.26) describes Europe as blessed by nature. But the emergence of Europe as a distinct religious and political category dates from the early Middle Ages when Europe became Christianized. Europe as such has ever since been a notion firmly established in the consciousness of the Europeans.

We may turn to the various manifestations of Eurocentrism in Europe's contact with China throughout the ages.

There existed in pre-Christian times trade relations between China and the Mediterranean world. But the latter's knowledge of China, called *Seres*, was at best extremely vague and meagre. Silk was thought, like cotton, to grow on trees and the *Seres* people had a lifespan of more than

130 up to 200 years (Strabo, *Geography*, X V. i. 20; X V. i. i. 34, 37). China was a mythical land on the far border of the known world, like the *ultima Thule*.

During the early part of the Middle Ages, Europe's knowledge of China was still derived indirectly from Syrian traders and the Jews, and it was not until the end of the thirteenth and the beginning of the fourteenth century that there began to be direct contacts between Europe and China. John of Montecorvino arrived in Peking in 1294 and was soon welcomed by the Mongol emperor Ch'eng Tsung. He became the first Catholic archbishop of Peking until 1328. He died in 1330 at the age of 82. (*Cambridge Medieval History*, VI. 753; *New Catholic Encyclopedia*). But it was Marco Polo (c.1254-1324)'s *Travels* that brought China vividly before Europe's wondering eyes, China with its fabulous wealth, its large populous and well-planned cities and sea-ports and various institutions, which set afire Europe's imagination.

From then on information about China increased in volume. Apart from descriptions of great riches, large cities, customs and manners including religious rituals and inventions, the chief interest lay in China's political institutions and secular philosophy. The Chinese emperor was able, through the state examinations, to recruit the best men for the government of the empire, which was seen as what ensured stability, peace and prosperity in China. Chinese philosophy was laudable because it was founded on nature and reason, and it was even found to agree with Christian doctrine.

Such was the discovery of the early missionaries. The Franciscan and Dominican missionaries and later the Jesuits came to China convert the Chinese to Christian faith. But their success was superficial. "A great multitude of the idolaters are baptised, though many of the baptised walk not rightly in the way of Christianity," writes Andrew of Perugia, Bishop of Zaitûn in 1326 (*Cambridge Medieval History*, VI, 754). But they showed various degrees of acquiescence and with the Jesuits even a good amount of admiration for things Chinese.[1] In order to facilitate their work, the Jesuits adopted Chinese ways of life, learned the Chinese language, wore Chinese costumes and adopted Chinese hairstyle, with the result that, ironically, the Jesuits, the converters, were half converted to Chinese cultural ethos, leaving the Chinese to continue in their indigenous belief with only a Christian veneer. The Jesuit missionary Jean-Francois Foucquet (b. 1665) wrote in 1722 that after twenty-three years' study of Chinese philosophy: "The more I advanced, the more I discovered there true marvels, and at last I became convinced that these written relics are like a sanctuary of the most venerable antiquity, yet one unknown in Europe until this present time" (quoted in Jonathan Spence, *The Question of Hu*, 1988. P.45). Foucquet studied Chinese philosophy from a European perspective and with profound respect drew a parallel between Confucianism and Christianity, which is probably the highest estimate a European missionary could bestow on Chinese culture. In the name of helping Chinese to understand Christianity, the Jesuits translated Christian notions into a Chinese matrix and allowed themselves to be reconciled, if not entirely sinicized, ideologically.

China's attraction for seventeenth century European philosophers lies in the fact that Chinese philosophy, that is, Confucianism, did away with superstitions and regulated the conduct of man. "The Chinese

---

[1] The Jesuit fathers' efforts to bring China close to Europe by presenting her as a country ruled by reason and learning, the Chinese as a people whose native concept of a supreme deity was akin to the Christian God were motivated by a desire to justify their missionary practices against the attacks by rival orders. (See David Hawkes, *Chinese Influence in European Drama, in Classical, Modern and Humane*, p.103)

philosopher," as Paul Hazard asserts, "delights those who are calling for and hastening the coming of a new order" (Le philosphe chinois enchante ceux qui appellent and qui hâtent la venue d'un order nouveau. *La Crise de la conscience europénne*, 1935, Vol. I, pp.31-32)

The image of China in the eighteenth century however is a mixed one. In England we are told that while the love for Chinese art increased, enthusiasm for Chinese culture generally witnessed a gradual decline among the intelligentsia and men of letters (Ch'ien Chung-shu, *China in the English Literature of the Eighteenth Century* I, in *Quarterly Bulletin of Chinese Bibliography*, II, Nos, I-II, pp.7-8). "Confucianism was criticised as mere shallowness in metaphysics and theology" (*China in the English Literature of the Seventeenth Century*, Q. B. C. B. I, No. 4, 1941, p. 384).

Take the attitude of the English men of letters of the eighteenth century towards China for instance. It ranges from condescension to contempt. Defoe, for instance, priding himself on England's trade expansion, derides China's backwardness: "Our city of London has more trade than all their mighty empire" (Ch'ien I, p.12). China was not really so wonderful as people had claimed it to be; the Chinese were singular only because the surrounding countries were rude and ignorant (Ch'ien I, p.12). The same view is shared by Samuel Johnson: "I consider them [the Chinese] as great, or wise, only in comparison with the nations that surround them" (I. p.25). The well-regulated administration of the state now became absolute tyranny, the easiest way of ruling the world (I. p.12) The grave and serious character of the Chinese now turned into "timorousness, dissimulation and deceit" (I. p.44). Goldsmith (*Citizen of the World, Letter* LXIII) complains of China's xenophobia. "There was a time when China was a receptacle of strangers... now the empire is shut up from every foreign improvement" (II, Nos. III IV, pp.119-120). Bishop Percy mentions the "servile submission and the dread of novelty" of the Chinese mind (II. p.138)

Basing his judgment on information supplied by du Halde, the Jesuit father Parrenin and others, Montesquieu praises certain aspects of Chinese politics. He thinks highly of the wisdom of the Tartars (the Manchus) in their government of a conquered nation by appointing an equal number of Chinese and Tartars to every military corps, to every court of judicature, as a check to one another. "The want of so wise an institution as this has been the ruin of almost all the conquerors that ever existed" (*The Spirit of Laws*, tr. Thomas Nugent, X, XV). He also extols "the excellent decrees" of the Chinese emperors prohibiting luxury (VII, 6). But on the whole he looks on the government of China as despotism "whose principle is fear" (VIII. X XI). China, according to him, was neither a democracy, nor an aristocracy, nor a monarchy. A republic and an aristocracy need and encourage virtue, a monarchy honour, a despotic government fear. The last "requires the most passive obedience... Man is a creature that blindly submits to the absolute rule of the sovereign" (III, 9, 10). "Excessive obedience supposes ignorance in the person that obeys: the same it supposes in him that commands, for he has no occasion to deliberate, to doubt, to reason; he has only to will" (IV, iii).

But there is the other side. Following also the information supplied by the Jesuits, eighteenth century Europeans showed considerable enthusiasm for China. They were drawn to her for her freedom from religious bigotry and conflicts, for her respect for men of letters, who were acknowledged the only nobility, and "it was on this account that Voltaire paid tribute to them as intellectuals in every sense of the word" (Henri Baudet, *Paradise on Earth*, p.44).

Voltaire (1694-1778), in refuting superstition, links its existence with political system. It is hard, he says, to find a people free from all superstitious prejudices. But "It is said that there is no superstition in the magistrature of China." "Less superstition, less fanaticism; and less fanaticism, less misery" (*Philosophical Dictionary, Superstition*). In extolling the necessity of books in civilized countries, he mentions China as "ruled by the moral books of Confucius" which deserve as much praise as the Alcoran, the Gospel, the book of the Veidam and Zarathustra (Ibid. Book). (Voltaire's interest in India is also well known.) At the same time, as indicated earlier, admiration for things Chinese "found its fullest expression at the aesthetic level—in interior decorating and gardening, in fashion, decoration and other elements of style. For after all, the Chinese style was by definition synonymous with perfect beauty" (Baudet, p.44). Undoubtedly there were wicked and inferior Oriental that the eighteenth century European admired.

Although Rousseau is less interested in China than either Montesquieu or Voltaire, he nevertheless cites China as example on three occasions in his *Discours sur l'Économie politique*, his source being also Du Halde. The emperor as the chief magistrate of the nation always sides with his people whenever there arise disputes between them and the local officials. "A la Chine, le prince a pour maxime constante de donner le tort à ses officiers dans toutes les altercations qui s'élevent entr'eux et le peuple. Le pain est-il cher dans une province ? l'intendant est mis en prison : se fait-il dans une autre une émerte ? le gouverneur est cassé, et chaque mandarin répond sur sa téte de tout le mal qui arrive dans son département. Ce n' est pas qu'on examine ensuite l'affaire dans un procès régulier : mais une longue expérience en a fait prévenir ainsi le jugement. L'on a rarement en cela quelque injustice à reparer ; et l'empereur, persuadé que la clameur publique ne s'éleve jamais sans sujet, démêle toûjours autravers des cris séditieux qu'il punit, de justes griefs qu'il redresse" (*Oeuvres completes*, Pleiade, 1964, p.250). And in matters of taxation, it falls on the shoulders of the well-to-do. (Ibid. p.276)

From the nineteenth century on, the general tendency of Europe's attitude to China is a shift, as Ch'ien strongly puts it, from "contempt and jibe of the eighteenth century" to "bitter hatred and abuse." Even Marx (1818-1883), writing in mid-nineteenth century, shares the same European view of China, though sympathetic with China's lot and critical of "the English cannon forcing upon China that soporific drug called opium" (*Revolution in China and Europe*, 1853, in *Surveys from Exile*, N. Y., 1974, p.326). In this essay on the cause of the T'ai-P'ing Uprising (1851-56) and its effect on Europe, Marx, following the Hegelian law of the contact extremes, sees the East and the West as two extremes, each being the other's Other. While Europe was civilized, China being "the very opposite of Europe" was not (p.326). As a result of the Opium War, "the barbarous and hermetic isolation from the civilized world was infringed." Marx also spots the timorousness, unpredictableness and cunning of the Orientals, though they may be universal weaknesses. When the price of tea was going to rise, "the Chinese, ready though they may be, as are all people in periods of revolutionary convulsion, to sell off to the foreigner all the bulky commodities they have on hand, will as the Orientals are used to do in apprehension of great changes, set to hoarding, not taking much in return for their tea and silk, except hard money" (pp.329-330).

Marx's knowledge of India is decidedly deeper than that of China. In his mid-career and as a humanist, he sees the degradation of the Indians leading an "undignified, stagnatory and vegetative life," a "passive sort of existence" (*The British Rule in India*, 1853, in *Surveys from Exiles*, p.306), and as a materialist he lays the blame on the economic structure of India. "Idyllic village-communities... had always been the solid foundation of Oriental despotism." "They restrained the human mind within the smallest possible compass, making it the unresisting tool of superstition, enslaving it beneath traditional rules, depriving it of all grandeur and historical energies" (p.306). India itself is a "strange combination of Italy and Ireland, of a world of voluptuousness and a world of woe," which is "anticipated in the ancient traditions of the religion of Hindustan. That religion is at once a religion of sensualist exuberance, and a religion of self-torturing asceticism; a religion of the Lingam and of the Juggernaut; the religion of the monk, and of the bayadere" (p.301). As historian, Marx sees that India needed a revolution. Since the people were passive and abject, the revolution could, ironically, only be brought about through British domination, through Britain "was activated by the vilest interest."

On the whole Marx's view of China and India is not vastly different from Sir Evelyn Baring, Lord Cromer (1841-1917)'s view of Egypt and the Egyptians. Cromer was resident and consul general (1883-1907) and virtual ruler of Egypt. His concept of Egypt and the Egyptians is derived from direct observation supplemented by accounts of that country and its people by authoritative Orientalists. To him, the Egyptians are a people devoid of energy and initiative, given to fulsome flattery, intrigue, cunning, lying and unkindness to animals. More importantly, their mode of thinking is illogical and slipshod. In short, they are racially, morally and intellectually degenerated and so culturally inferior. To quote Cromer, "the Oriental generally acts, speaks, and thinks in a manner exactly opposite to the European" (quoted in Said, ibid, pp.38-39).

Perhaps the most insightful assessment of China is made by John

Stuart Mill (1806-1873), believer in progress, and zealous reformer. In his *On Liberty* (1859), Mill on the one hand idealizes China for having had "the good fortune" to be "provided at an early period with a particularly good set of customs" which were impressed "upon every mind in the community," and in China it was "those who have appropriated most of it [the good set of customs] shall occupy the posts of honour and power," but on the other hand he used China as a warning to Europeans for, as he puts it ironically, the Chinese "have succeeded beyond all hope... in making a people all alike, all governing their thoughts and conduct by the same maxims and rules" (Everyman edn. P.129). The Chinese social and political system encourages what Mill calls "collective mediocrity" (Ibid. p.124). Europe may turn into another China if individuality is killed by "the modern regime of public opinion." As to the Chinese, if they "are ever to be farther improved, it must be by foreigners." (How like Marx on India!) Because the Chinese social and political system encouraged conformity, so there was never, as Mill points out in earlier writings (*Essays on Bentham*, 1838; and *Coleridge*, 1840), any "organized opposition to the ruling power." A fact which accounts for the state of eternal stand-still that prevailed in China.

China's image in the West sank to its nadir in the latter part of the nineteenth century and the first few decades of the twentieth century when the bugbear of Yellow Peril was invented by those who feared vengeance from the down-trodden Chinese and other Eastern Asians. (The first recorded use of the term in English in the OED is dated 1900). But a radical change soon took place after World War I when Europe lost its self-confidence together with its sense of superiority and turned to the culture of the East, of China, for remedy.[1] Thanks to the re-interpretation of Chinese culture by scholars such as Richard Wilhelm (1873-1930), Europeans found once again among other things the idea of charitableness and pacifism in the teachings of Confucius and Lao-tzu. Poets and artists drew inspiration from the East. A notable example is T. S. Eliot. Perhaps because the Sermon on the Mount no longer proved effective to cure the rampant vice of lust, he had to resort to the Buddhist Fire Sermon and advocate the Hindu and Buddhist watchwords of charity, compassion and self-control in order to achieve peace (*The Waste Land*). This situation continued into the post-World War II period. Even critics were influenced by Oriental thought. William Empson's interest in comparative anthropology, a comparison of Hebrew, Mediterranean, Buddhist and Confucian rituals caused him to refute the Christian concept of Godhead as a person in contrast to the Buddhists and Confucian concept of Godhead as an Abstract, and to criticize the crucifixion as a "Neolithic craving for the human sacrifice" (*Milton's God*, 1981, p.241).

For millennia from pre-Christian times to the beginning of the twentieth century China changed little but remained a sort of constant, and the spectrum of Europe's changing attitudes reflects only the changes that took place in Europe itself. The various stages of Europe's concept of China—nebulous, marvelling, laudatory and derogatory and abusive and finally laudatory again—reflect not, or not merely, increasing knowledge through contact, but the gradual political and technological ascendency of Europe over the rest of the world. And it also reflects Europe's needs at the various stages of its development. In the age of geographical

---

[1] It is interesting to note that towards the end of the nineteenth century and particularly after the May 4 Movement of 1919, there was an enormous vogue in China of learning from the West.

discoveries, it is to meet the need of economic development. In the seventeenth century and the age of Enlightenment, it is the intellectual need with a strong political orientation. In the age of colonial expansion, it is the need to establish a *raison d'être* for exploitation. The Other now becomes a foil to European superiority. But at the same time when the European colonialist exploited and terminated the Other, he also saw the Other as an image of Europe's lost values and idealized the Savage and imagined the Other's land as Utopia to satisfy psychological urge, because the European man had been burdened since the Fall with a sense of sin and had been attempting self-renovation. The Other thus became a model that caused self-doubt and self-criticism (Heri Baudet, *Paradise on Earth*, 1959, Eng. tr., 1965). The apologists of European superiority also consider it a burden "most painful to abandon or adjust". Even "the spirit of detachment" and "the easy sympathy and regard" in relation to the Orient are "a product of superiority and of the conviction that there was nothing to fear" (R. W. Southern, *Western Views of Islam in the Middle Ages*, 1962, pp.2-4).

Whatever the need may have been, in the later stages of East-West contact, when Europe enjoyed world political supremacy, how did it affect the cultural life of the areas under its domination? Contact no doubt always result in mutual influence. The politically strong may totally reject the culture of the Other, but that is only another way of saying that it is negatively influenced, or that the Other reaffirms the values the politically strong holds. The reverse of the rejection of the Other by the politically strong is the xenophobia on the part of the politically weak, the fear of the intrusion of the foreigner bringing with him an alien culture. But cultural xenophobia, like cultural rejection, has always proved ineffectual. The shock is either shrugged off or simply absorbed. Cultures have a way of mutual adaptation. In the case of conquest, the conqueror may enjoy absolute hegemony, imposing a political structure and enforcing an alien culture and even language on the conquered, as in the case of British rule in India, and the conquered may accept a certain degree of influence from the conquering nation, but it is impossible for the latter to suppress and supplant the indigenous culture. In the case of Mongol and Manchu conquests of China, the cultural balance was in China's favour. The Japanese occupation of China before and during World War II left China culturally unshaken. On the other hand, China never subjugated Japan politically but exerted indelible cultural influence on Japan. The Islamic conquests of North Africa and Southern Europe yielded different results culturally. In Africa, Islam was strong both politically and culturally with the result that North Africa turned Islamic, overwhelming native primitive religions and Christianity. The Arab conquerors of Spain and Sicily, as carriers of superior culture, brought about a cultural efflorescence in a medieval Europe engulfed in ignorance. They were not merely the catalyst for the later Renaissance but left indelible marks on Spanish as well as European culture. It has ever been thought a vagary of history that the Arabs should have been halted by the Franks at Tours. But Arab influence ceased with the final success of the Reconquista. Political hegemony is not equivalent to cultural hegemony. Compare to politics, culture is far more stable and resilient.

Cultural interaction whether on a politically equal or unequal basis is a process of mutual accommodation. The activities of the Jesuits in seventeenth century China is a typical case. The Jesuits were out to convert the idolaters and succeeded in so far as a good number of Chinese, including abandoned and dying infants, were baptized and thus had their souls saved. It was also relatively easy to win the favour of the emperor by offering their service as astronomers, mathematicians and carriers of mechanical technology. But the hardest thing was to get across to the educated the true meaning of Christianity. Hazard's account is worth quoting (*La Crise de la conscience européenne* [1680-1715] 1935, pp.27-28):

"The Jesuits knew the importance of China in the world of ideas (dans la géographie des idées). As they entertained great ambition and hoped to win this enormous mass of Asians over the Christian faith by attenuating the differences and letting oppositions slip by, these courageous and learned Jesuits who had won the esteem of the Emperor in Peking, now tried to demonstrate that Chinese philosophy was so close to Catholicism that the one might assimilated with the other with a little good will (*avec un peu de bonne volonté*). Consequently according to them, Confucius who had fashioned the soul of his country, professed a doctrine in which one sensed instantly a divine breath. Confucius believed that human nature was derived from Heaven, very pure, very perfect, but it was subsequently perverted and so now it was time to restore it to its original beauty. Consequently the Chinese as the disciples of Confucius would obey God and conform to His will and love their neighbor like themselves. In reading the teachings of Confucius, the Jesuits thought to find a teacher of the new faith rather than an eminent man in the corrupt state of nature, a St Paul before his time, a Chinese St Paul. It is without doubt that the Chinese had caught the principle of truth in their source. The children of Noah (i. e., the offspring of Shem) who populated East Asia had brought with them the seeds which Confucius merely cultivated. Born 478 years before the Christ, he often said in prophecy: there is a true saint in the West. Sixty-five years after the birth of Christ, the emperor Ming-ti, on the strength of the Sage's saying and instigated by a dream, sent ambassadors to the West with the order to go on until they should have encountered the saint."

Apart from being syncretists by reconciling Chinese philosophy and Christian doctrine, the Jesuits also tried to explain away certain Chinese rites such as ancestor worship which the Church condemned as superstition, as only a civil and political cult. (Spence, *The Question of Hu*, p. 75). Other strategies employed include the use of Chinese language, the vernacular in liturgy, and the use of Chinese terms for the divinity, the connivance in the ancient practices honouring ancestors—all this in order to reach a compromise and make Christianity more palatable.

On the other hand the Chinese, notably Chinese scholars of the late sixteenth and early seventeenth century, were ready to adopt Christianity because they thought it could supply the deficiency of Confucian teachings and replace Buddhism. But even though they were formally Christianized, they remained Confucians at heart. Christianity was useful as supplement by introducing into the Confucian canon concepts unknown to it, at any rate not incompatible with it but enriching it, e. g., the ideas of the salvation of the soul, of confession, of God Himself; it was useful as a substitute of Buddhism which had degenerated into superstition, and it must be remembered that these scholars were all interested in science like their seventeenth century European counterparts and fought against superstition. (See article in Chinese entitled *From Confucian to Christian—the Changes of Li Zhizao*, by Yuansheng Liang, in *Chinese Cultural Quarterly*, or *Jiuzhou Xuekan* Vol. 3, No. 1, Winter 1988, Hong

Kong.)

The various stages of Eurocentrism, whether manifested as admiration for China or denigration, reveal two different strategies of representation, namely, exaggeration and analogizing. To describe China as a land of fabulous wealth and perfect government is as much exaggeration as to describe her as barbarous and ruled by cruel tyranny. To draw a parallel between Chinese cultural elements with European ones, as the Jesuits did, is to ignore the uniqueness of either.

I have been trying to show the various manifestations of Eurocentrism in relation to China and the East as determined by historical development of Europe itself, and the strategies Europe adopted in treating the culture of China. I have also tried to argue that political supremacy has little or negligible influence on the culture of the subjugated nation. The question remains why in cultural interaction one culture often exerts greater influence on the other rather than the other way round.

One has to admit that within a certain historical context cultures, like civilizations, differ in stage of development and in kind. Take the Sino-Japanese cultural interaction for example. It was largely a one-way flow. Japan adopted Chinese town-planning, architecture, script, Buddhism and poetry. It is a question of borrowing on the part of the Japanese, not an imposition on the part of China. Borrowing is selective and voluntary. It has been pointed out that certain favourite images in T'ang poetry such as the monkey's cry, the moth's-feelers-like eyebrows, the severed intestine were rejected while the willow, the chrysanthemum, the moon, the bamboo were loved by the Japanese poets.[1] The selectiveness is evident in Japanese adaptation of Chinese Buddhism. In terms of the

---

[1] 松浦友久：《诗歌语言研究——唐诗札记》。

outward trappings of culture, one may say there is a hierarchy of cultures. But in terms of mode of thinking, no such evaluative distinction can be made. The analytical and logical mode of thinking in Western tradition is not necessarily superior to the intuitive and imaginative mode of thinking of the Chinese though it was condemned as "illogical and slipshod." Both possess high potentialities and both have limitations. I. A. Richards long ago (*Mencius on the Mind*, 1932) warned against what he called Western "provincialism." "The danger to be guarded against is our tendency to force a structure... upon modes of thinking which may very well not have such structure at all—and which may not be capable of being analysed by means of this kind of logical machinery" (p.92). He likewise warned the Chinese: "Chinese thought is now taking over and absorbing the whole developed Western logical technique; and it will do so more perfectly and in a more balanced way and make fewer avoidable mistakes, if it does not turn its back upon ancient Chinese thinking—relegating it to a position of historical interest" (p. xiii). In the field of Chinese literary studies there has also emerged an awareness of the inadequacy of imposing European categories on Chinese literature, calling for "decentralization" and a need for mutual complementation (David Hawkes, in *Legacy of China* 1964, pp.84-87).

文
景

Horizon

社 科 新 知　文 艺 新 潮

攻玉集 · 镜子和七巧板 · The Mirror and the Jigsaw

杨周翰 著

出 品 人：姚映然
责任编辑：朱悠然
装帧设计：蔡立国

出　　品：北京世纪文景文化传播有限责任公司
　　　　　（北京朝阳区东土城路8号林达大厦A座4A　100013）
出版发行：上海人民出版社
印　　刷：山东临沂新华印刷物流集团有限责任公司
制　　版：北京大观世纪文化传媒有限公司

开 本：890mm×1240mm　1/32
印 张：16.5　字 数：364,000　插页：2
2016年4月第1版　2020年1月第2次印刷
定 价：69.00元
ISBN：978-7-208-13613-7 / I · 1490

图书在版编目（CIP）数据

攻玉集：镜子和七巧板 / 杨周翰著. —上海：上
海人民出版社，2016
（杨周翰作品集）
ISBN 978-7-208-13613-7

I.① 攻… II.① 杨… III.① 比较文学-文学研究-
文集 IV.① I0-03

中国版本图书馆CIP数据核字（2016）第029882号

本书如有印装错误，请致电本社更换　010-52187586